intent on raiding our camp; after he had released the equipment of the fire department, he stole also the divine weapons." Only then did the old demon realize what had happened. "There is no one else!" he said. "It has to be that thief, Sun Wu-k'ung! No wonder I had such a hard time when I tried to sleep just now! That larcenous ape must have gotten in here by means of transformation and gave my shoulder a couple of bites. Undoubtedly he wanted to steal my treasure, but when he saw how tightly it was attached to my body, he could not do it. That was the reason he stole the other weapons instead and let loose the fire dragons. How vicious of him! He wanted to burn me to death! O, thievish ape! You've made vain use of your trickery! When I have this treasure on me, I can't be drowned even when I plunge into the ocean, nor can I be burned if I leap into a pool of fire. But when I catch you, thief, this time, I'm going to skin and cut you up alive. Only then will I be satisfied."

He spoke sullenly in this manner for a long time, and soon there-after it was dawn. On the tall summit, the prince, holding his six weapons that had just been recovered, said to Pilgrim, "Great Sage, it's getting bright. Let's not wait any further. We should make use of this opportunity when that demon's will to fight has been blunted by you. With the help of the fire department, let us go again to do battle with him. Most probably he'll be captured this time." "You are right," said Pilgrim, chuckling, "let us unite and go to have some fun!"

In high spirits and eager to fight, each of them went up to the cave entrance. "Lawless demon, come out!" bellowed Pilgrim. "Come and fight with old Monkey!" The two stone doors of the cave, you see, had been reduced to ashes the night before by the intense heat. At the moment, several little fiends by the entrance were just in the process of gathering up the ashes and sweeping the ground. When they saw the various sages approach, they were so terrified that they aband-oned their brooms and ash forks and dashed inside to repor̶t̶ Wu-k'ung has led many gods to provoke battle ⌐⁻⁻ astounded was he by this report that th̶ teeth and rolled his ringlike eyes. He p treasure, and no sooner had he emerge began to castigate his adversary, saying camp-raider and arsonist! What skills do ̶ ̶ ̶ ̶ ̶ ̶ ̶ ̶ ̶at you dare treat me so contemptuously?" Smiling broa̶d̶ly, Pilgrim said, "You brazen fiend! If you want to know my skills, come up here and listen to my recital.

My skills were great since the time of my birth,
As was my name throughout the universe.
Enlightened, I practiced then th'immortal way;
In days past came the means to eternal youth.
I willed to bow at the place of the Heart,
To see with reverence the home of a sage.
I learned transformation, magic with no bounds—
My playground, the space of the whole cosmos.
At leisure I tamed tigers on the mount;
When bored I subdued dragons in the sea.
I claimed a throne at native Flower-Fruit
And flaunted my strength in Water-Curtain Cave.
A few times I lusted for Heaven's realm;
Ignorant, I robbed the Region Above.
The Most High named me Great Sage, Equal to Heav'n;
I was called also Handsome Monkey King.
When the Feast of Peaches was underway,
I took offense for no invitation came.
In secret I stole jade juice at Jasper Pool
And drank it covertly in the treasure tower.
A hundred delicacies I stole and ate.
Millennial peaches I freely enjoyed,
My food, the drugs and pills of ten thousand years.
Strange things of Heav'n I took piece by piece,
And rare treasures from sage mansions bit by bit.
When the Jade Emperor learned that I had skills,
He sent soldiers divine to the battlefield.
Violent Nine Luminaries I did banish;
Vicious Stars of Five Quarters I did wound.
All Heaven's warriors were no match of mine;
A hundred thousand troops dared not me oppose.
Hard pressed, the Jade Emperor gave a decree:
Libation Stream's Little Sage then raised his sword.
Seventy-two transformations we struggled through,
Each flaunting his power, each showing his might.
Kuan-yin of South Sea came, too, at length
To lend them her help with willow and vase.

Lao Tzu then made use of his diamond snare
To have me captured and brought up there
To see, bound firmly, the Great Emperor Jade,
As judge and tribunal charged me with guilt.
They told God Powerful to cut me dead,
But sparks flew up when knives fell on my head.
Since no means was found to put me to death,
They sent me in custody to Lao Tzu's hall:
A brazier, watched by the Six Gods of Light,
Refined me till my body was hard as steel.
With vessel opened on day forty-ninth,
I leaped out to work violence once again.
When gods hid themselves and none withstood me,
The sages agreed that Buddha be called.
Tathāgata's power was mighty indeed!
His wisdom, truly vast and limitless!
A somersault contest waged upon his hand,
He pinned me with a mountain, my strength all gone.
Now the Emperor gave the Feast for Peace in Heav'n;
The West regained its name of Ultimate Bliss.
Old Monkey, imprisoned for five hundred years,
Did not once taste a bit of tea or rice.
But, when the Elder Gold Cicada came to earth,
The East sent him to go to Buddha's home
And bring back scriptures for a noble state,
So that the Great T'ang ruler might save the dead.
Kuan-yin told me to submit to Good
And let faith, held firmly, my wildness check.
Free of my woe beneath that mountain root,
To seek the scriptures I'm now going West.
Lawless demon, cease your foxlike cunning!
Return my T'ang monk, bow to the dharma king!"

When he heard these words, he pointed at Pilgrim and cried, "So,
you were the big thief who robbed Heaven! Don't run away! Swallow
my lance!" The Great Sage met him with the rod and the two of
them began to fight. On this side Prince Naṭa became angry and the
Star of Fiery Virtue grew vicious: they hurled those six divine weapons together with the fire equipment at the demon. The Great Sage
Sun fought even more fiercely as the thunder squires took up their

thunderbolts and the devarāja his scimitar to rush at their enemy. Smiling scornfully, the demon calmly took out from his sleeve his treasure and tossed it in the air, crying, "Hit!" With a loud whoosh, the six divine weapons, the fire equipment, the thunderbolts, the scimitar of the devarāja, and the rod of Pilgrim were all snatched away. Once again, the deities and the Great Sage Sun were empty-handed. After the demon returned in triumph to his cave, he gave this order: "Little ones, gather rocks and boulders to rebuild our doors, and tidy up our rooms and hallways. When we finish our work, we shall slaughter the T'ang monk and his companions to thank the Earth. Then all of us can disperse the blessing and enjoy." The little fiends all obeyed, and we shall leave them for the moment.

We tell you now about the Devarāja Li, who led the rest of the gods back to the tall summit. Fiery Virtue then began to rail at Naṭa for being too impulsive, while the thunder squires blamed the devarāja for acting too recklessly. Water Lord, however, stood to one side and sulked. When Pilgrim saw how distraught they looked, he had little alternative but to appear cheerful and said to them, forcing a smile, "Please don't be so distressed, all of you. After all, the ancient proverb says, 'Victory or defeat is a common thing for the soldier.' If we want to consider the demon's fighting skill, it's no more than so-so. The reason he can cause so great harm is that fillet in his possession, which has again sucked away all our weapons. Nonetheless, try to relax. Let old Monkey go and see if he can find out something more about his pedigree." "When you first presented your memorial to the Jade Emperor," said the prince, "there was a thorough search made throughout the celestial realm, but not a trace of this monster could be found. Now where are you going to make further investigation?" Pilgrim replied, "Come to think of it, the dharma power of Buddha is boundless. I shall go now to the Western Heaven to question our Buddha Tathāgata; I shall ask him to scan with his eye of wisdom the four great continents of Earth and see where this fiend was born and raised. I want to learn what sort of treasure his fillet is, and no matter what, I'm determined to have him arrested. Only then will all of you be avenged and have a happy trip back to Heaven." "If that's your intention," said the gods, "don't delay. Go quickly! Go quickly!"

Dear Pilgrim! He said he would go, and at once he mounted his cloud-somersault. Instantly he arrived at the Spirit Mountain.

Lowering his auspicious luminosity, he looked everywhere. Marvelous place!

The noble Mount Spirit,
Fine, pure cloud-layers;
A divine peak whose head touches the blue sky.
A great town seen in Western Heaven;
A shape surpassing even China.
The primal breath flows freely 'twixt the wide Heav'n and Earth;
Flowers descend augustly to coat the terrace.
Often long notes of bells and stones are heard,
And clear, loud scripture recitations.
You see, too, lay-sisters lecturing beneath green pines
And arhats walking among jadelike cedars.
The white cranes, affectionate, come to Vulture Peak;
Blue phoenixes take care to stand by quiet arbors.
Black apes in pairs hold up immortal fruits;
Aged deer in twos present purple blossoms.
The rare birds' frequent calls seem like someone speaking,
And flowers too strange and pretty to have names.
The ranges turn and circle, fold upon fold;
The old path meanders, though it's level.
It is a spiritual place of pure void;
Solemn, enlightened—that's the Buddha's form.

As Pilgrim enjoyed the sight of the mountain scenery, he heard someone calling him: "Sun Wu-k'ung, where did you come from? Where are you going?" He turned quickly and found that it was the Honored One Bhikṣuṇi.[1] The Great Sage greeted her and said, "I have a matter that requires an audience with Tathāgata." "You rascal!" said Bhikṣuṇi, "if you want to see Tathāgata, why don't you ascend the treasure temple? Why stay here to look at the mountain?" "This is the first time I have been to this noble region," replied Pilgrim, "and that's why I am acting boldly." "Follow me quickly," said Bhikṣuṇi, and Pilgrim ran after her up to the gate of the Thunderclap Monastery, where their way was barred by the heroic figures of the Eight Great Diamond Guardians.[2] "Wu-k'ung," said Bhikṣuṇi, "wait here for a moment and let me announce your arrival." Pilgrim had no choice but to wait outside the gate. Going before the Buddha, Bhikṣuṇi pressed her palms before her and said, "Sun Wu-k'ung needs to have an audience with Tathāgata." Whereupon Tathāgata commanded him to enter, and only then did the diamond guardians allow him to pass.

After Pilgrim touched his head to the ground, Tathāgata asked, "Wu-k'ung, I heard previously that after the Honored One Kuan-yin had freed you, you made submission to Buddhism and agreed to accompany the T'ang monk to seek scriptures here. Why have you come all by yourself? What is the matter?" Again touching his head to the ground, Pilgrim said, "Let me report this to our Buddha. Since your disciple embraced the faith, he has followed the master from the T'ang court in his journey west. We reached the Golden Helmet Cave of the Golden Helmet Mountain, where we ran into an evil demon, who had the name of Bovine Great King. He had such vast magic powers that he abducted my master and brothers into his cave. Your disciple demanded their return, but he had no good will at all and we fought it out. My iron rod was snatched away by a ghostly white fillet of his. As I suspected that he might be some celestial warrior who longed for the world, I went to the Region Above to investigate. The Jade Emperor was kind enough to lend me the assistance of the father-and-son team of Devarāja Li, only to have him rob the prince of his six weapons. Then I asked the Star of Fiery Virtue to burn him with fire, but he took the fire equipment also. Next we asked the Star of Watery Virtue to drown him with water, but we couldn't even touch a single hair of his. After your disciple spent enormous energy to steal back the iron rod and other things, we went again to provoke battle. Once again his fillet sucked away all our weapons, and we are powerless to subdue him. That's why I have this special request for our Buddha, in his great compassion, to survey the world and find out what is the true origin of this creature. I shall then be able to capture his kin or neighbor so that it will facilitate the arrest of the demon and the rescue of my master. All of us then will be able to bow, with palms pressed together and with utter sincerity, to seek the right fruit."

After Tathāgata heard this, he trained his eyes of wisdom to peer into the distance and immediately he had knowledge of the whole affair. "Though I've learned the identity of that fiendish creature," he said to Pilgrim, "I can't reveal it to you because you have such a loose, apish tongue. If somehow you pass on the fact that it was I who disclosed his identity, he would not fight with you but he would start a quarrel up here in Spirit Mountain. That would cause me a lot of trouble. Let me give you the assistance of my dharma power instead to help you capture him." Bowing deeply again, Pilgrim thanked him and said, "What sort of dharma power will you bestow on me?" Tathāgata immediately ordered the Eighteen Arhats to open the treasury and take out eighteen grains of golden cinnabar sand to assist Wu-k'ung. "What will this golden cinnabar sand do?" asked Pilgrim. "Go before the cave," said Tathāgata, "and ask the demon for a contest. Entice him to come out and the arhats will at once release the sand, which will entrap him. Since he won't be able to move his body or raise his feet, you can beat him up at will." "Wonderful! Wonderful!" cried Pilgrim, laughing. "Bring them out quickly!"

Not daring to delay, the arhats at once took out the golden cinnabar sand and walked out of the gate. After Pilgrim thanked Tathāgata again, he ran after the crowd and found there were only sixteen arhats. "What sort of a place is this," yelled Pilgrim, "that you are taking bribes and releasing prisoners?" "Who is taking bribes and releasing prisoners?" asked the arhats, and Pilgrim said, "Originally eighteen of you were sent. Why is it that there are only sixteen now?" Hardly had he finished speaking when Dragon Subduer and Tiger Tamer, the two Honored Ones, walked out from inside. "Wu-k'ung," they said, "how could you be so mischievous? The two of us remained behind because Tathāgata had further instructions for us." "Much too clever! Much too clever!" said Pilgrim. "If I waited even a moment in hollering, you probably would not come out." Laughing uproariously, the arhats mounted the auspicious clouds.

In a moment, they arrived at the Golden Helmet Mountain, where they were met by Devarāja Li leading the rest of the deities. "No need to go into the details," said one of the arhats. "Go quickly and ask him to come out." Holding his fists high, our Great Sage went before the cave entrance and shouted, "Blubbery fiend! Come out quickly and try your hands with your Grandpa Sun." Again those little fiends dashed inside to make the report. Infuriated, the demon king said, "This thievish ape! I wonder whom he has invited to come make a nuisance here!" "There's no other warrior," said the little fiends, "he's all by himself." "I've already taken away his rod," said the demon king. "How is it that he shows up all by himself again? Could it be that he wants to box some more?" Picking up his treasure and his lance, he ordered the little fiends to move away the boulders and

leaped out of the cave. "Larcenous ape!" he scolded. "For several
times you haven't been able to gain the upper hand, and that should
make you stay away. Why are you here again making noises?"
Pilgrim said, "This brazen demon doesn't know good or evil! If you
don't want your Grandpa to show up at your door, you make submission, apologize, and send out my master and brothers. Then I'll
spare you." "Those three monks of yours," said the fiend, "have been
scrubbed clean. Soon, they will be slaughtered. And you are still
making a fuss? Go away!"

When Pilgrim heard the word "Slaughter," fire leaped up to his
cheeks. Unable to suppress the anger of his heart, he wielded his fists
and attacked the demon with hooks and jabs. Spreading out his long
lance, the fiend turned to meet him. Pilgrim jumped this way and that
to deceive the monster. Not knowing it was a trick, the demon left
the entrance of the cave and gave chase toward the south. At once
Pilgrim shouted for the arhats to pour the golden cinnabar sand down
on the demon. Marvelous sand! Truly,

Like fog, like mist, it spreads out at first;
In great profusion it drops from afar.
One mass of white
Blinding eyes everywhere.
A dark expanse
Flying to block the way.
The working woodsman has lost his partner;
The fairy youth picking herbs can't see his home.
It drifts and soars like fine wheat-flour;
Some grains are coarse like sesame.
The world seems opaque as the summits darken;
The sun's hidden and the sky disappears.
It's not quite the noise and dust at a horse's heels,
Nor the light fluffiness chasing a scented car.
This sand is by nature a ruthless thing
Which can blot out the world to seize the fiend.
Because a demon the right way assails,
The arhats by Law release their power.
In one's hands a bright pearl will soon appear;
In no time it will your eyesight obscure.

When the demon saw that the flying sand was clouding up his vision,
he lowered his head and discovered that his feet were already standing

in three feet of the stuff. He was so horrified that he tried to jump upward; before he could even stand up properly the sand grew another foot. In desperation, the fiend tried to pull up his legs while taking out his fillet. Throwing it up into the air, he cried, "Hit!" With a loud whoosh, the eighteen grains of golden cinnabar sand were sucked away. The demon then strode back to the cave.

All of those arhats with bare hands stopped their clouds, while Pilgrim drew near and asked, "Why are you not pouring down the sand?" "There was a sound just now," one of them said, "and instantly our golden cinnabar sand vanished." "That little something has sucked them away again!" sighed Pilgrim with a laugh. "If he's so hard to catch," said Devarāja Li to the rest, "how could we ever arrest him? When will we be able to return to Heaven? How could we face the Emperor?" On one side, Dragon Subduer and Tiger Tamer, the two arhats, said, "Wu-k'ung, did you know why we delayed in coming out of the door just now?" "Old Monkey only feared that you were trying to find some pretense not to come," said Pilgrim, "I don't know any other explanation." One of the two arhats replied, "Tathāgata told us two that the demon had vast magic powers. If we lost the golden cinnabar sand, he said, we should ask Sun Wu-k'ung to search for his origin at the place of Lao Tzu, the Tushita Palace of the Griefless Heaven. The demon would be caught with one stroke." When Pilgrim heard this, he said, "That's detestable! That's detestable! Even Tathāgata is trying to hornswoggle old Monkey! He should have told me right then and there, and there would have been no need for all of you to travel." "If Tathāgata made such a clear revelation," said Devarāja Li, "let the Great Sage go up there quickly."

Dear Pilgrim! "I'm off!" he said, and at once he mounted the cloud-somersault to enter the South Heavenly Gate. There he was met by the four grand marshals, who raised their folded hands to their chins to salute him, asking, "How's the affair of arresting that monster?" Answering them as he walked along, Pilgrim said, "It's unfinished! It's unfinished! But I'm on his trail now!" The four grand marshals dared not detain him and permitted him to walk inside the Heavenly Gate. Going neither to the Hall of Divine Mists nor to the Dipper Palace, he went instead straight up to the Tushita Palace of the Griefless Heaven, which was beyond the thirty-third Heaven. Two immortal youths were standing outside the palace. Without an-

nouncing who he was, however, Pilgrim walked right inside the
door, so startling the youths that they tugged at him, crying, "Who
are you? Where are you going?" Only then did Pilgrim say, "I'm the
Great Sage, Equal to Heaven. I wish to see Lao Tzu, Mr. Li." "Why
are you so rude?" said one of the youths. "Stand here and let us
announce you." But Pilgrim would have none of that. With a shout,
he dashed inside and ran smack into Lao Tzu, who was just coming
out. Bowing low hurriedly, Pilgrim said, "Venerable Sir, haven't seen
you for a while." "Why is this ape not going to seek scriptures?" said
Lao Tzu, chuckling. "What's he doing here?" Pilgrim replied,

That scripture-seeking
Is toil unending.
Since my way was blocked,
I came here shuffling.

"If the road to the Western Heaven is blocked," said Lao Tzu, "what
has that got to do with me?" Again Pilgrim said,

Ah, Heaven West!
That name's a jest!
I find my trail:
Then I'll protest.

"This place of mine," said Lao Tzu, 'is an unsurpassed immortal
palace. What sort of trail can you find?"

Eyes unblinking, Pilgrim went inside and looked left and right. He
walked past several corridors and all at once he discovered a boy
sound asleep by the corral. The green buffalo, however, was not
inside. "Venerable Sir," said Pilgrim, "your buffalo has escaped!
Your buffalo has escaped!" "When did this cursed beast escape?"
said Lao Tzu, highly astonished. All that clamor woke up the boy, who
immediately went to his knees and said, "Father, your disciple fell
asleep. I don't know when he escaped." "How could you fall asleep,
you rogue?" scolded Lao Tzu, and the boy kowtowed several times
before he answered, "Your disciple picked up one pellet of elixir in
the elixir chamber. As soon as I ate it, I fell asleep." "It must be the
Elixir of Seven Returns to the Fire that we made the other day. One
pellet fell out, and this rogue picked it up and ate it. Well, anyone who
eats one of those pellets will sleep for seven days. Because you fell
asleep, no one looked after that cursed beast, and he took the opportunity to go to the Region Below. Today is the seventh day." Immediately Lao Tzu wanted to make an investigation to see if any treasure

was stolen, but Pilgrim said, "He doesn't have any treasure except a fillet, and it is quite formidable."

Lao Tzu made a quick inventory; everything was there except the diamond snare. "This cursed beast stole my diamond snare!" said Lao Tzu. "So, that's the treasure!" said Pilgrim. "It was the same snare that hit me that time!³ Now it's going wild down below, sucking away who knows how many things." "Where's the cursed beast now?" asked Lao Tzu, and Pilgrim replied: "At the Golden Helmet Cave of the Golden Helmet Mountain. He caught my T'ang monk first and robbed me of my golden-hooped rod. When I asked the celestial soldiers to come help me, he also took away the divine weapons of the prince. When the Star of Fiery Virtue arrived, his equipment was also taken. Only Water Lord did not lose anything to him, but his water could not drown the demon either. Finally, I asked Tathāgata to order the arhats to use sand, but even that golden cinnabar sand was snatched away. When someone like you, Venerable Sir, lets loose a fiendish creature to rob and harm people, with what kind of crime should we charge him?" Lao Tzu said, "That diamond snare of mine is a treasure perfected since the time of my youth, and it was also an instrument with which I converted the barbarians when I passed through the Han-ku Pass. Whatever weapons you may have, including fire and water, you can't touch it. If the demon had stolen my plantain-leaf fan also, then even I would not be able to do anything to him."

Thereafter, Lao Tzu took up his plantain-leaf fan and mounted the auspicious cloud, followed by a happy Great Sage. They left the celestial palace, went through the South Heavenly Gate, and lowered their clouds on the Golden Helmet Mountain. There they were met by the eighteen arhats, the thunder squires, Water Lord, Fiery Virtue, and Devarāja Li and his son to whom they gave a thorough account of what had taken place. "Sun Wu-k'ung," said Lao Tzu, "may go again to entice him to come out; I'll put him away then."

Jumping down from the summit, Pilgrim again shouted, "You cursed blubbery beast! Come out quickly and submit to death!" Once more the little fiends went inside to report, and the old demon said, "This larcenous ape has asked someone to come again." Quickly he took up his lance and treasure and walked out of the door. "You brazen demon!" scolded Pilgrim. "This time you will die for sure! Don't run away. Have a taste of my palm!" He leaped right onto the chest of the demon and gave him a terrific whack on the ear before turning to flee. Wielding his lance, the demon gave chase, only to hear someone calling on the tall summit: "If that little buffalo doesn't come home now, what's he waiting for?" When the demon raised his head and saw that it was Lao Tzu, his heart shook and his gall quivered. "This thievish ape," he said, "is truly a devil of the Earth! How did he manage to find my master?"

Reciting a spell, Lao Tzu fanned the air once with his fan. The fiend threw the fillet at Lao Tzu, who caught it immediately and gave him another fan. All at once the fiend's strength fled him and his tendons turned numb; he changed back into his original form, which was that of a green buffalo. Blowing a mouthful of divine breath on the diamond snare, Lao Tzu then used it to pierce the nostrils of the fiend. Next, he took off the sash around his waist and fastened one end of it to the snare while his hand held the other. Thus the custom of leading the buffalo with a ring in its nose was established, a custom in use even now. This is also what we call, *pin-lang*.[4] After he took leave of the various deities, Lao Tzu climbed onto the back of his green buffalo.

Having mounted colored clouds,
He went back to Tushita Palace;
Having bound the fiend,
He ascended to the Griefless Heaven.

Then the Great Sage Sun fought his way with the other deities into the cave and slaughtered all the remaining little fiends, some one hundred of them. Each of the gods recovered his weapons, after which the father-and-son team of Devarāja Li went back to Heaven; the thunder squires to their mansions; Fiery Virtue to his palace; Water Lord to his rivers; and the arhats to the West. Pilgrim then took back his iron rod and untied the T'ang monk, Pa-chieh, and Sha Monk, who also gave thanks to him. After they got the horse and the luggage ready, master and disciples left the cave and found the main road to journey once more.

As they proceeded, they heard someone by the road calling, "Holy T'ang Monk, eat the food first before you go." The elder was terribly frightened. We do not know who it was that called them, and you must listen to the explanation in the next chapter.

The Zen Master, taking food, is demonically conceived;
Yellow Hag brings water to dissolve the perverse pregnancy.

Virtuous acts you must perform eight hundred;
Secret merits you must amass three thousand.
Let thing and self, kin and foe, be treated equally—
Only that suits the primal vow[1] of Western Heaven.
Weapons can't threaten the bull demonic;
In vain faultless water and fire have toiled.
Lao Tzu brings submission, it faces Heaven.
Laughing, he the green buffalo turns and leads.

We were telling you that someone by the road was calling the pilgrims.
"Who could it be?" you ask. They were actually the mountain god
and the local spirit of the Golden Helmet Mountain. Holding up the
almsbowl of purple gold, they cried, "O Holy Monk! This bowl of rice
was one which the Great Sage Sun succeeded in begging from a good
place. Because all of you did not listen to sound advice, you fell by
mistake into the hands of a demon. The Great Sage had to toil and
struggle most pitifully before he managed to rescue you today. Come
and eat the rice first before you journey. Don't abuse the filial reverence of the Great Sage." "Disciple," said Tripitaka, "I'm deeply
indebted to you, and I can't thank you enough. If I had known it
before, I would have never left that circle of yours and there would
have been no such mortal danger." "To tell you the truth, Master,"
said Pilgrim, "because you did not believe in my circle, you had to be
placed in someone else's circle. What suffering you had to bear! It's
lamentable!" "What do you mean by someone else's circle?" asked
Pa-chieh, and Pilgrim said, "Coolie, it was the doing of your cursed
mouth and cursed tongue that landed this great ordeal on Master.
What old Monkey dug up in Heaven and on Earth—the fire, the water,
the celestial soldiers, and the cinnabar sand of the Buddha—they
were all sucked away by a ghostly white fillet of his. Through two
arhats, however, Tathāgata secretly revealed to old Monkey the origin

35

of that fiend, and only then could we ask Lao Tzu to come here to subdue him. It was his green buffalo that was causing all the trouble." When Tripitaka heard this, he thanked him profusely, saying, "Worthy disciple, after this experience, I will certainly listen to you next time." Whereupon the four of them divided up the rice to eat, rice which was still steaming hot. "This rice has been here for a long time," said Pilgrim, "why is it still hot?" Kneeling down, the local spirit said, "Since this humble deity has learned that the Great Sage has achieved his merit, he heated up the rice first before serving it." In a moment, they finished the rice and put away the almsbowl.

Having taken leave of the mountain god and the local spirit, the master mounted his horse to pass the tall mountain. Thus it was that

With mind purged of care, they to wisdom[2] conform;

They dine on wind and rest on water to journey West.

After traveling for a long time, it was again early spring and they heard

Purple swallows murmuring

And orioles warbling.

Purple swallows murmur, tiring their scented beaks;

Orioles warble, their artful notes persist.

The ground full of fallen petals like brocade spread out;

The whole mountain sprouting colors like cushion-piles.

On the peak green plums are budding;

By the cliff old cedars detain the clouds.

Faint, misty lights o'er the meadows;

Sandbars warmed by bright sunshine.

In several gardens flowers begin to bloom;

The sun comes back to Earth, willow sprouts anew.

As they walked along, they came upon a small river of cool, limpid currents. The elder T'ang reined in his horse to look around and saw in the distance several thatched huts beneath willows hanging jadelike. Pointing in that direction, Pilgrim said, "There must be someone running a ferryboat in those houses." "It's likely," said Tripitaka, "but since I haven't seen a boat, I don't dare open my mouth." Dropping down the luggage, Pa-chieh screamed: "Hey, ferryman! Punt your boat over here." He yelled several times and indeed, from beneath the shade of willows a boat emerged, creaking as it was punted. In a little while, it approached the shore while master and disciples stared at it. Truly,

As a paddle parts the foam,
A light boat floats on the waves,
With olive cabins brightly painted
And a deck made of flat, level boards.
On the bow, iron cords encircle;
At the stern, a shining rudder stem.
Though it may be a reed of a boat,
It will sail the lakes and the seas;
Though without fancy cables and tall masts,
It has, in fact, oars of cedar and pine.
It's unlike the divine ship of great distance,
But it can traverse a river's width.
It comes and goes only between two banks;
It moves only in and out of ancient fords.

In a moment, the boat touched the bank, and the person punting called out: "If you want to cross the river, come over here." Tripitaka urged his horse forward to take a look at the boatman and saw that the person had

On the head a woolen wrap
And on the feet, two black silk shoes.
The body wore cotton coat and pants patched a hundred times;
A thousand-stitched, dirty cloth-skirt hugged the waist.
Though the wrists had coarse skin and the tendons, strength,
The eyes were dim, the brows knitted, and the features aged.
The voice was soft and coy like an oriole's,
But a closer look disclosed a woman old.

Walking to the side of the boat, Pilgrim said, "You are the one ferrying the boat?" "Yes," said the woman. "Why is the ferryman not here?" asked Pilgrim. "Why is the ferrywoman punting the boat?" The woman smiled and did not reply; she pulled out the gangplank instead and set it up. Sha Monk then poled the luggage into the boat, followed by the master holding onto Pilgrim. Then they moved the boat sideways so that Pa-chieh could lead the horse to step into it. After the gangplank was put away, the woman punted the boat away from shore and, in a moment, rowed it across the river.

After they reached the western shore, the elder asked Sha Monk to untie one of the wraps and take out a few pennies for the woman. Without disputing the price, the woman tied the boat to a wooden pillar by the water and walked into one of the village huts nearby, giggling loudly all the time. When Tripitaka saw how clear the water was, he felt thirsty and told Pa-chieh: "Get the almsbowl and fetch some water for me to drink." "I was just about to drink some myself," said Idiot, who took out the almsbowl and bailed out a full bowl of water to hand over to the master. The master drank less than half of the water, and when Idiot took the bowl back, he drank the rest of it in one gulp before he helped his master to mount the horse once more.

After master and disciples found their way to the West they had hardly traveled half an hour when the elder began to groan as he rode. "Stomach-ache!" he said, and Pa-chieh behind him also said, "I have a stomach-ache, too." Sha Monk said, "It must be the cold water you drank." But before he even finished speaking, the elder cried out: "The pain's awful!" Pa-chieh also screamed: "The pain's awful!" As the two of them struggled with this unbearable pain, their bellies began to swell in size steadily. Inside their abdomens, there seemed to be a clot of blood or a lump of flesh, which could be felt clearly by the hand, kicking and jumping wildly about. Tripitaka was in great discomfort when they came upon a small village by the road; two bundles of hay were tied to some branches on a tall tree nearby. "Master, that's good!" said Pilgrim. "The house over there must be an inn. Let me go over there to beg some hot liquid for you. I'll ask them also whether there is an apothecary around, so that I can get some ointment for your stomach-ache."

Delighted by what he heard, Tripitaka whipped his white horse and soon arrived at the village. As he dismounted, he saw an old woman sitting on a grass mound outside the village gate and knitting hemp. Pilgrim went forward and bowed to her with palms pressed together saying, "*P'o-p'o*,[3] this poor monk has come from the Great T'ang in the Land of the East. My master is the royal brother of the T'ang court. Because he drank some water from the river back there after we crossed it, he is having a stomach-ache." Breaking into loud guffaws, the woman said, "You people drank some water from the river?" "Yes," replied Pilgrim, "we drank some of the clean river water east of here." Giggling loudly, the old woman said, "What fun! What fun! Come in, all of you. I'll tell you something."

Pilgrim went to take hold of T'ang monk while Sha Monk held up Pa-chieh; moaning with every step the two sick men walked into the thatched hut to take a seat, their stomachs protruding and their faces turning yellow from the pain. "*P'o-p'o*," Pilgrim kept saying,

"please make some hot liquid for my master. We'll thank you."
Instead of boiling water, however, the old woman dashed inside,
laughing and yelling, "Come and look, all of you!"

With loud clip-clops, several middle-aged women ran out from
within to stare at the T'ang monk, grinning stupidly all the time.
Enraged, Pilgrim gave a yell and ground his teeth together, so frightening the whole crowd of them that they turned to flee, stumbling all
over. Pilgrim darted forward and caught hold of the old woman,
crying, "Boil some water quick and I'll spare you!" "O Father!" said
the old woman, shaking violently, "boiling water is useless, because
it won't cure their stomach-aches. Let me go, and I'll tell you."
Pilgrim released her, and she said, "This is the Nation of Women of
Western Liang.[4] There are only women in our country, and not even a
single male can be found here. That's why we were amused when we
saw you. That water your master drank is not the best, for the river is
called Child-and-Mother River. Outside our capital we also have a
Male Reception Post-house, by the side of which there is also a Pregnancy Reflection Stream. Only after reaching her twentieth year
would someone from this region dare go and drink that river's water,
for she would feel the pain of conception soon after she took a drink.
After three days, she would go to the Male Reception Post-house and
look at her reflection in the stream. If a double reflection appears, it
means that she will give birth to a child. Since your master drank
some water from the Child-and-Mother River, he, too, has become
pregnant and will give birth to a child. How could hot water cure
him?"

When Tripitaka heard this, he paled with fright. "O disciple," he
cried, "what shall we do?" "O father!" groaned Pa-chieh as he
twisted to spread his legs further apart, "we are men, and we have to
give birth to babies? Where can we find a birth canal? How could the
fetus come out?" With a chuckle Pilgrim said, "According to the
ancients, 'A ripe melon will fall by itself.' When the time comes, you
may have a gaping hole at your armpit and the baby will crawl out."

When Pa-chieh heard this, he shook with fright, and that made the
pain all the more unbearable. "Finished! Finished!" he cried. "I'm
dead! I'm dead!" "Second Elder Brother," said Sha Monk, laughing,
"stop writhing! Stop writhing! You may hurt the umbilical cord and
end up with some sort of prenatal sickness." Our Idiot became more
alarmed than ever. Tears welling up in his eyes, he tugged at Pilgrim

and said, "Elder Brother, please ask the *P'o-p'o* to see if they have some midwives here who are not too heavy-handed. Let's find a few right away. The movement inside is becoming more frequent now. It must be labor pain. It's coming! It's coming!" Again Sha Monk said chuckling, "Second Elder Brother, if it's labor pain, you'd better sit still. I fear you may puncture the water bag."

"O *P'o-p'o*," said Tripitaka with a moan, "do you have a physician here? I'll ask my disciple to go there and ask for a prescription. We'll take the drug and have an abortion." "Even drugs are useless," said the old woman, "but due south of here there is a Male-Undoing Mountain. In it there is a Child Destruction Cave, and inside the cave there is an Abortion Stream. You must drink a mouthful of water from the stream before the pregnancy can be terminated. But nowadays, it's not easy to get that water. Last year, a Taoist by the name of True Immortal Compliant came on the scene and he changed the name of the Child Destruction Cave to the Shrine of Immortal Assembly. Claiming the water from the Abortion Stream as his possession, he refused to give it out freely. Anyone who wants the water must present monetary offerings together with meats, wines, and fruit baskets. After bowing to him in complete reverence, you will receive a tiny bowl of the water. But all of you are mendicants. Where could you find the kind of money you need to spend for something like this? You might as well suffer here and wait for the births." When Pilgrim heard this, he was filled with delight. "*P'o-p'o*," he said, "how far is it from here to the Male-Undoing Mountain?" "About three thousand miles," replied the old woman. "Excellent! Excellent!" said Pilgrim. "Relax, Master! Let old Monkey go and fetch some of that water for you to drink."

Dear Great Sage! He gave this instruction to Sha Monk: "Take good care of Master. If this family ill behaves and tries to hurt him, bring out your old thuggery and scare them a little. Let me go fetch the water." Sha Monk obeyed. The old woman then took out a large porcelain bowl to hand over to Pilgrim, saying, "Take this bowl and try to get as much water as possible. We can save some for an emergency." Indeed Pilgrim took over the bowl, left that thatched hut, and mounted the cloud to leave. Only then did the old woman fall to her knees, bowing to the air, and cried, "O father! This monk knows how to ride the clouds!" She went inside and told the other women to come out to kowtow to the T'ang monk, all addressing him as arhat or bodhisattva. Then they began to boil water and prepare rice to present to the pilgrims, and we shall leave them for the moment.

We tell you now about the Great Sage Sun on his cloud-somersault; in a little while, he saw the peak of a mountain blocking his path. Dropping down from his cloudy luminosity, he opened wide his eyes to look around. Marvelous mountain! He saw

Rare flowers spreading brocade;
Wild grass unrolling blue;
Plunging streams—one after another;
Brooks and clouds, both leisurely.
Canyons, packed together, rank with creepers and vines;
Ranges, stretching afar, dense with forests and trees.
Birds call, and wild geese glide by;
Deer drink, and monkeys clamber.
A mountain green like a jade screen;
A ridge blue like locks of hair.
Difficult indeed to reach from this world of dust!
Rocks and water splashing, a sight that never tires!
One often sees immortal lads leave, picking herbs.
One often meets woodsmen come, bearing loads.
Truly it's almost the scenery of T'ien-t'ai,
Surpassing perhaps the three peaks of Mount Hua.

As the Great Sage stared at the scenery, he discovered also a building with its back on the dark side of the mountain and from where the sound of a dog barking could be heard. Going down the mountain, the Great Sage went toward the building, which was a rather nice place, too. Look at the

Stream piercing a small bridge;
Thatched huts nestling a green hill.
A dog barks near the lonely fence;
The recluse comes and goes at will.

In a moment he came up to the gate, where he found an old Taoist sitting cross-legged on the green lawn. When the Great Sage put down his porcelain bowl to bow to him, the Taoist rose slightly to return his greeting, saying, "Where did you come from? For what purpose have you come to this humble shrine?" Pilgrim replied, "This poor monk is a scripture pilgrim sent by imperial commission of the Great T'ang in the Land of the East. Because my master mistakenly drank water from the Child-and-Mother River, he is suffering from a swollen belly and unbearable pain. We asked the natives there and learned that the pregnancy thus formed has no cure. We are told, however, that there is an Abortion Stream in the Child Destruction Cave of the Male-Undoing Mountain, and its water can eliminate the conception. This is why I have come especially to see the True Immortal Compliant, in order to beg from him some water to save my master. May I trouble the old Taoist to lead me to him." "This used to be the Child Destruction Cave," said the Taoist, chuckling, "but it's now changed to the Shrine of Immortal Assembly. I am none other than the eldest disciple of the venerable father, True Immortal Compliant. What's your name? Tell me so I can announce you." "I am the eldest disciple of Tripitaka T'ang, master of the Law," said Pilgrim, "and my vulgar name is Sun Wu-k'ung." "Where are your monetary gifts," asked the Taoist, "your offerings of wine?" Pilgrim said, "We are mendicants on a journey, and we haven't prepared them."

"You are quite mad!" said the Taoist, chuckling again. "My old master is now the protector of this mountain stream, and he has never given its water free to anyone. You go back and bring some gifts, and I'll announce you. Otherwise, please leave. Don't think about the water!" Pilgrim said, "Good will can be more powerful than an imperial edict. If you go and announce the name of old Monkey, I am sure that he will express his good will. Perhaps he will turn over the entire well of water to me."

This statement of Pilgrim gave the Taoist little alternative but to go inside to make the announcement. As the True Immortal was just playing the lute, the Taoist had to wait until he finished playing before saying, "Master, there is a Buddhist monk outside, who claims to be Sun Wu-k'ung, the eldest disciple of Tripitaka T'ang. He wants some water from the Abortion Stream to save his master." It would have been better if the True Immortal had not heard the name, for the moment he came upon those words, Wu-k'ung,

Anger flared in his heart,

Wrath sprouted from his gall.

Jumping down quickly from his lute couch, he took off his casual garment and put on his Taoist robe. He picked up a compliant hook and leaped out of the door of the shrine. "Where is Sun Wu-k'ung?" he shouted. Pilgrim turned his head to see how that True Immortal was dressed.

A star cap of bright colors crowned his head;
He wore a red magic robe with golden threads.
His cloud shoes were topped by patterned brocade;
An elegant treasure belt wrapped around his waist.
A pair of stockings of embroidered silk;
Half visible, a patterned woolen kilt.
His hands held a compliant golden hook:
The blade, sharp; the handle, long and dragonlike.
Phoenix eyes glowed with brows going straight up;
Sharp, steely teeth within a blood-red mouth.
A beard soared like bright flames beneath his chin;
Like rushes flared his temple's scarlet hair.
His form seemed as violent as Marshal Wên's,[5]
Although their clothing was not the same.

When Pilgrim saw him, he pressed his palms together before him and bowed, saying, "This poor monk is Sun Wu-k'ung." "Are you the real Sun Wu-k'ung," said the master with a laugh, "or are you merely assuming his name and surname?" "Look at the way the master speaks!" said Pilgrim. "As the proverb says, 'A gentleman changes neither his name when he stands, nor his surname when he sits.' What would be the reason for me to assume someone else's name?" The master asked, "Do you recognize me?" "Since I made repentance in the Buddhist gate and embraced with all sincerity the teaching of the monks," said Pilgrim, "I have only been climbing mountains and fording waters. I have lost contact with all the friends of my youth. Because I have never been able to visit you, I have never beheld your honorable countenance before. When we asked for our way in a village household west of the Child-and-Mother River, they told me that the master is called the True Immortal Compliant. That's how I know your name." The master said, "You are walking on your way, and I'm cultivating my realized immortality. Why did you come to visit me?" "Because my master drank by mistake the water of the Child-and-Mother River," replied Pilgrim, "and his stomach-ache turned into a pregnancy. I came especially to your immortal mansion to beg you for a bowl of water from the Abortion Stream, in order that my master might be freed from this ordeal."

"Is your master Tripitaka T'ang?" asked the master, his eyes glowering. "Yes, indeed!" answered Pilgrim. Grinding his teeth together, the master said spitefully, "Have you run into a Great King

Holy Child?" "That's the nickname of the fiend, Red Boy," said Pilgrim, "who lived in the Fiery Cloud Cave by the Dried Pine Stream, in the Roaring Mountain. Why does the True Immortal ask after him?" "He happens to be my nephew," replied the master, "and the Bull Demon King is my brother. Some time ago my elder brother told me in a letter that Sun Wu-k'ung, the eldest disciple of Tripitaka T'ang, was such a rascal that he brought his son great harm. I didn't know where to find you for vengeance, but you came instead to seek me out. And you're asking me for water?" Trying to placate him with a smile, Pilgrim said, "You are wrong, Sir. Your elder brother used to be my friend, for both of us belonged to a league of seven bond brothers when we were young. I just didn't know about you, and so I did not come to pay my respect in your mansion. Your nephew is very well off, for he is now the attendant of the Bodhisattva Kuan-yin. He has become the Boy of Goodly Wealth, with whom even we cannot compare. Why do you blame me instead?"

"You brazen monkey!" shouted the master. "Still waxing your tongue! Is my nephew better off being a king by himself, or being a slave to someone? Stop this insolence and have a taste of my hook!" Using the iron rod to parry the blow, the Great Sage said, "Please don't use the language of war, Sir. Give me some water and I'll leave." "Brazen monkey!" scolded the master. "You don't know any better! If you can withstand me for three rounds, I'll give you the water. If not, I'll chop you up as meat sauce to avenge my nephew." "You damned fool!" scolded Pilgrim. "You don't know what's good for you! If you want to fight, get up here and watch my rod!" The master at once countered with his compliant hook, and the two of them had quite a fight before the Shrine of Immortal Assembly.

The sage monk drinks from this procreant stream,
And Pilgrim must th'Immortal Compliant seek.
Who knows the True Immortal is a fiend,
Who safeguards by force the Abortion Stream?
When these two meet, they speak as enemies
Feuding, and resolved not to give one whit.
The words thus traded engender distress;
Rancor and malice so bent on revenge.
This one, whose master's life is threatened, comes seeking water;
That one for losing his nephew refuses to yield.
Fierce as a scorpion's the compliant hook;

Wild like a dragon's the golden-hooped rod.
Madly it stabs the chest, what savagery!
Aslant, it hooks the legs, what subtlety!
The rod aiming down there[6] inflicts grave wounds;
The hook, passing shoulders, will whip the head.
The rod slaps the waist—a hawk holds a bird.
The hook swipes the head—a mantis hits its prey.
They move here and there, both striving to win;
They turn and close in again and again.
The hook hooks, the rod strikes, without letup—
Victory cannot be seen on either side.

The master fought the Great Sage for over ten rounds and then he began to weaken. The Great Sage, however, grew more fierce, the blows of his rod descended on his opponent's head like a meteor shower. His strength all gone, the master fled toward the mountain with his compliant hook trailing behind him.

Instead of chasing after him, the Great Sage wanted to go into the shrine to look for the water, but the Taoist had long had the door tightly shut. Holding the porcelain bowl, the Great Sage dashed up to the door and kicked it down with all his might. He rushed inside and saw the Taoist leaning on the well, covering its mouth with his body. The Great Sage lifted high his rod and shouted that he was about to strike, causing the Taoist to flee to the rear. Then he found a bucket, and just as he tried to bail some water, the master dashed out from the rear and caught hold of one of his legs with the compliant hook. One hard tug sent the Great Sage tumbling beak-first to the ground. Clambering up, the Great Sage at once attacked with his iron rod, but the master only retreated to one side. With hook in hand, he cried, "See if you could take away my water!" "Come up here! Come up here!" yelled the Great Sage. "I'll beat you to death!" But the master refused to go forward to fight; he just stood there and refused to permit the Great Sage to bail out the water. When the Great Sage saw that his enemy was motionless, he wielded his iron rod with his left hand while his right hand tried to let the rope down the well. Before the pulley had made several turns, however, the master again struck with his hook. As the Great Sage could hardly protect himself with only one hand, the hook once more caught hold of one of his legs, causing him to stumble and the rope to fall into the well, bucket and all. "This fellow is quite rude!" said the Great Sage, who clambered up and, holding the iron rod now with both hands, showered his opponent's body and head with blows. Not daring to face him and fight, the master fled away as before. Again the Great Sage wanted to get the water, but this time he had no bucket, and moreover, he was afraid that the master would return to attack him. He thought to himself: "I must go and find a helper."

Dear Great Sage! He mounted the clouds and went straight back to the village hut, crying, "Sha Monk." Inside Tripitaka was moaning to endure the pain, while the groans of Pa-chieh were continuous. Delighted by the call, they said, "Sha Monk, Wu-k'ung's back." Sha Monk hurried out the door to ask, "Big Brother, have you brought water?" The Great Sage entered and gave a thorough account to the T'ang monk. Shedding tears, Tripitaka said, "O disciple! How is this going to end?" "I came back," said the Great Sage, "to ask Brother Sha to go with me. When we reach the shrine, old Monkey will fight with that fellow and Sha Monk can use the opportunity to get that water to save you." Tripitaka said, "Both of you who are healthy will be gone, leaving behind the two of us who are sick. Who will look after us?" The old woman waiting on them said, "Relax, old arhat. You don't need your disciples. We will serve you and take care of you. When you first arrived, we were already fond of you. Then we saw how this bodhisattva traveled by cloud and fog, and we knew that you had to be an arhat or bodhisattva. We'll never dare to harm you again."

"You are all women here," snapped Pilgrim. "Whom do you dare to harm?" "O dear father!" said the old woman, giggling. "You're lucky to have come to my house. If you had gone to another one, none of you would have remained whole." "What do you mean," said Pa-chieh, still groaning, "by not remaining whole?" The old woman replied: "The four or five of us in this family are all getting on in years. We have given up the activities of love. If you go to another family, there may be more youthful members than old ones. You think the young ones will let you go? They will want to have intercourse with you, and if you refuse, they will take your lives. Then they will cut you up to use your flesh to make fragrant bags." "In that case," said Pa-chieh, "I won't be hurt. They all smell nice, and they'll be good for fragrant bags. I'm a stinking hog, and even when I'm cut up, I still stink. That's why I can't be hurt." "Don't be so talkative!" said Pilgrim, chuckling. "Save your strength, so you can give birth." The old woman said, "No need for delay. Go quickly to get the water." "Do you have a bucket in your house?" asked Pilgrim. "Please lend us one." The old woman went to the back to take out a bucket and rope to hand over to Sha Monk, who said, "Let's bring two ropes. We may need them if the well is deep."

After Sha Monk received the bucket and the ropes, he followed the Great Sage out of the village hut and they left together, mounting the clouds. In less than half an hour, they arrived at the Male-Undoing Mountain. As they lowered their clouds to go before the shrine, the Great Sage gave Sha Monk this instruction: "Take the bucket with the ropes and hide yourself. Old Monkey will go and provoke battle. When we are in the thick of fighting, you can use the opportunity to go inside, get the water, and leave." Sha Monk obeyed.

Wielding his iron rod, the Great Sage Sun approached the door and shouted: "Open the door! Open the door!" The Taoist who stood guard at the door hurried inside to report: "Master, that Sun Wu-k'ung is here again." Greatly angered, the master said, "This brazen ape is insolent indeed! I have always heard that he has considerable abilities, and today I know it's true. That rod of his is quite difficult to withstand." "Master," said the Taoist, "his abilities may be great, but yours are not inferior. You are, in fact, exactly his match." "But twice before," said the master, "I lost to him." "Only in a contest of sheer violence," said the Taoist. "Later, when he tried to bail water, your hook made him fall twice. Haven't you equalized the situation? He had little alternative but to leave at first, and now he's back. It must be that Tripitaka's pregnancy is so advanced and his body so heavy that his complaints have driven this monkey to return, against his better judgment. He must feel rather contemptuous toward his master, and I'm sure that you will win."

When the True Immortal heard these words, he became
Delighted and filled with elation;
Full of smiles and brimming with power.
Holding straight his compliant hook, he walked out of the door and shouted, "Brazen simian! Why are you here again?" "Only to fetch water," answered the Great Sage. "That water," said the True Immortal, "happens to be in my well. Even if you are a king or a prime minister, you must come begging with offerings of meat and wines, and then I will only give you a little. You are my enemy no less, and you dare to ask for it with empty hands?" "You really refuse

to give it to me?" asked the Great Sage, and the True Immortal replied,
"Yes! Yes!" "You damned fool!" scolded the Great Sage. "If you don't
give me the water, watch my rod!" He opened up at once and rushed
at the True Immortal, bringing down the rod hard on his head.
Stepping aside quickly to dodge the blow, the True Immortal met him
with the hook and fought back. This time, it was even more ferocious
a battle than last time. What a fight!

Golden-hooped rod,
Compliant hook,
Two angry men so full of enmity.
The cosmos darkens as sand and rocks fly up;
Sun and moon sadden as dirt and dust soar high.
The Great Sage seeks water to save his master,
Denied by the fiend for his nephew's sake.
The two exert their strength
To wage a contest there.
Teeth are ground together
To strive for a victory.
More and more alert,
They arouse themselves.
They belch cloud and fog to sadden ghosts and gods.
Bing-bing and bang-bang clash both hook and rod,
Their cries, their shouts shake up the mountain range.
The fierce wind, howling, ravages the woods;
The violent airs surge past the dipper stars.
The Great Sage grows happier as he strives;
The True Immortal's gladder as he fights.
They do this battle with their whole hearts and minds;
They will not give up until someone dies.

The two of them began their fighting outside the shrine, and as they
struggled and danced together, they gradually moved to the mountain slope below. We shall leave this bitter contest for a moment.

We tell you instead about our Sha Monk, who crashed inside the
door, holding the bucket. He was met by the Taoist, who barred the
way at the well and said, "Who are you that you dare come to get our
water?" Dropping the bucket, Sha Monk took out his fiend-routing
treasure staff and, without a word, brought it down on the Taoist's
head. The Taoist was unable to dodge fast enough, and his left arm
and shoulder were broken by this one blow. Falling to the ground, he

lay there struggling for his life. "I wanted to slaughter you, cursed beast," scolded Sha Monk, "but you are, after all, a human being. I still have some pity for you, and I'll spare you. Let me bail out the water." Crying for Heaven and Earth to help him, the Taoist crawled slowly to the rear, while Sha Monk lowered the bucket into the well and filled it to the brim. He then walked out of the shrine and mounted the cloud and fog before he shouted to Pilgrim, "Big Brother, I have gotten the water and I'm leaving. Spare him! Spare him!"

When the Great Sage heard this, he stopped the hook with his iron rod and said, "I was about to exterminate you, but you have not committed a crime. Moreover, I still have regard for the feelings of your brother, the Bull Demon King. When I first came here, I was hooked by you twice and I didn't get my water. When I returned, I came with the trick of enticing the tiger to leave the mountain and deceived you into fighting me, so that my brother could go inside to get the water. If old Monkey is willing to use his real abilities to fight with you, don't say there is only one of you so-called True Immortal Compliant; even if there are several of you, I would beat you all to death. But to kill is not as good as to let live, and so I'm going to spare you and permit you to have a few more years. From now on if anyone wishes to obtain the water,·you must not blackmail the person."

Not knowing anything better, that bogus immortal brandished his hook and once more attempted to catch Pilgrim's legs. The Great Sage evaded the blade of his hook and then rushed forward, crying, "Don't run!" The bogus immortal was caught unprepared and he was pushed head over heels to the ground, unable to get up. Grabbing the compliant hook the Great Sage snapped it in two; then he bundled the pieces together and, with another bend, broke them into four segments. Throwing them on the ground, he said, "Brazen, cursed beast! Still dare to be unruly?" Trembling all over, the bogus immortal took the insult and dared not utter a word. Our Great Sage, in peals of laughter, mounted the cloud to rise into the air, and we have a testimonial poem.

The poem says:
For smelting true lead you need water true;
True water mixes well with mercury dried.
True mercury and lead have no maternal breath;
Divine drugs and cinnabar are elixir.
In vain there is the form of child conceived;

Earth Mother with ease has merit achieved.
Heresy pushed down, right faith held up,
The lord of the mind, all smiles, now returns.

Mounting the auspicious luminosity, the Great Sage caught up with
Sha Monk. Having acquired the true water, they were filled with
delight as they returned to where they belonged. After they lowered
the clouds and went up to the village hut, they found Chu Pa-chieh
leaning on the door post and groaning, his belly huge and protruding.
Walking quietly up to him, Pilgrim said, "Idiot, when did you enter
the delivery room?" Horrified, Idiot said, "Elder Brother, don't make
fun of me. Did you bring the water?" Pilgrim was about to tease him
some more when Sha Monk followed him in, laughing as he said,
"Water's coming! Water's coming!" Enduring the pain, Tripitaka
rose slightly and said, "O disciples, I've caused you a lot of trouble."
That old woman, too, was most delighted, and all of her relatives
came out to kowtow, crying, "O bodhisattva! This is our luck! This
is our luck!" She took a goblet of flowered porcelain, filled it half full,
and handed it to Tripitaka, saying, "Old master, drink it slowly. All you
need is a mouthful and the pregnancy will dissolve." "I don't need
any goblet," said Pa-chieh, "I'll just finish the bucket." "O venerable
father, don't scare people to death!" said the old woman. "If you drink
this bucket of water, your stomach and your intestines will all be dissolved." Idiot was so taken aback that he dared not misbehave; he
drank only half a goblet.

In less than the time of a meal, the two of them experienced sharp
pain and cramps in their bellies, and then their intestines growled
four or five times. After that, Idiot could no longer contain himself:
both waste and urine poured out of him. The T'ang monk, too, felt
the urge to relieve himself and wanted to go to a quiet place. "Master,"
said Pilgrim, "you mustn't go out to a place where there is a draft. If
you are exposed to the wind, I fear that you may catch some postnatal
illness." At once the old woman brought to them two night pots so
that the two of them could find relief. After several bowel movements,
the pain stopped and the swelling of their bellies gradually subsided
as the lump of blood and flesh dissolved. The relatives of the old
woman also boiled some white rice congee and presented it to them to
strengthen their postnatal weakness. "P'o-p'o," said Pa-chieh, "I
have a healthy constitution, and I have no need to strengthen any
postnatal weakness. You go and boil me some water, so that I can

take a bath before I eat the congee." "Second Elder Brother," said Sha Monk, "you can't take a bath. If water gets inside someone within a month after birth, the person will be sick." Pa-chieh said, "But I have not given proper birth to anything; at most, I only have had a miscarriage. What's there to be afraid of? I must wash and clean up." Indeed, the old woman prepared some hot water for them to clean their hands and feet. The T'ang monk then ate about two bowls of congee, but Pa-chieh consumed over fifteen bowls and he still wanted more. "Coolie," chuckled Pilgrim, "don't eat so much. If you get a sand-bag belly, you'll look quite awful." "Don't worry, don't worry," replied Pa-chieh. "I'm no female hog. So, what's there to be afraid of?" The family members indeed went to prepare some more rice.

The old woman then said to the T'ang monk, "Old master, please bestow this water on me." Pilgrim said, "Idiot, you are not drinking the water anymore?" "My stomach-ache is gone," said Pa-chieh, "and the pregnancy, I suppose, must be dissolved. I'm quite fine now. Why should I drink any more water?" "Since the two of them have recovered," said Pilgrim, "we'll give this water to your family." After thanking Pilgrim, the old woman poured what was left of the water into a porcelain jar, which she buried in the rear garden. She said to the rest of the family, "This jar of water will take care of my funeral expenses." Everyone in that family, young and old, was delighted. A vegetarian meal was prepared and tables were set out to serve to the T'ang monk. He and his disciples had a leisurely dinner and then rested.

At dawn the next day, they thanked the old woman and her family before leaving the village. Tripitaka T'ang mounted up, Sha Monk toted the luggage, Chu Pa-chieh held the reins, and the Great Sage Sun led the way in front. So, this is how it should be:

The mouth washed of its sins, the self is clean;

Worldly conception dissolved, the body's fit.

We don't know what sort of affairs they must attend to when they reach the capital, and you must listen to the explanation in the next chapter.

Fifty-four

Dharma-nature, going West, reaches the Women Nation;
The Mind Monkey devises a plan to flee the fair sex.

We tell you now about Tripitaka and his disciples, who left the household at the village and followed the road westward. In less than forty miles, they came upon the boundary of Western Liang. Pointing ahead as he rode along, the T'ang monk said, "Wu-k'ung, we are approaching a city, and from the noise and hubbub coming from the markets, I suppose it must be the Nation of Women. All of you must take care to behave properly. Keep your desires under control and don't let them violate the teachings of our gate of Law." When the three disciples heard this, they obeyed the strict admonition.

Soon they reached the head of the street that opened to the eastern gate. The people there, with long skirts and short blouses, powdered faces and oily heads, were all women regardless of whether they were young or old. Many of them were doing business on the streets, and when they saw the four of them walking by, they all clapped their hands in acclaim and laughed aloud, crying happily, "Human seeds are coming! Human seeds are coming!" Tripitaka was so startled that he reined in his horse; all at once the street was blocked, completely filled with women, and all you could hear were laughter and chatter. Pa-chieh began to holler wildly: "I'm a pig for sale! I'm a pig for sale!" "Idiot," said Pilgrim, "stop this nonsense. Bring out your old features, that's all!" Indeed, Pa-chieh shook his head a couple of times and stuck up his two rush-leaf fan ears; then he wriggled his lips like two hanging lotus roots and gave a yell, so frightening those women that they all fell and stumbled. We have a testimonial poem, and the poem says:

The sage monk, seeking Buddha, reached Western Liang,
A land full of females but without one male.
Farmers, scholars, workers, and those in trade,
The fishers and plowers were women all.
Maidens lined the streets, crying "Human seeds!"

Young girls filled the roads to greet the comely men.
If Wu-nêng did not show his ugly face,
The siege by the fair sex would be pain indeed.

In this way, the people became frightened and none dared go forward; everyone was rubbing her hands and squatting down. They shook their heads, bit their fingers, and crowded both sides of the street, trembling all over but still eager to stare at the T'ang monk. The Great Sage Sun had to display his hideous face in order to open up the road, while Sha Monk, too, played monster to keep order. Leading the horse, Pa-chieh stuck out his snout and waved his ears. As the whole entourage proceeded, the pilgrims discovered that the houses in the city were built in orderly rows while the shops had lavish displays. There were merchants selling rice and salt; there were wine and tea houses. There were

Bell and drum towers with goods piled high;
Bannered pavilions with screens hung low.

As master and disciples followed the street through its several turns, they came upon a woman official standing in the street and crying, "Visitors from afar should not enter the city gate without permission. Please go to the post-house and enter your names on the register. Allow this humble official to announce you to the Throne. After your rescript is certified, you will be permitted to pass through." Hearing this, Tripitaka dismounted; then he saw a horizontal plaque hung over the gate of an official mansion nearby, and on the plaque were the three words, Male Reception Post-house. "Wu-k'ung," said the elder, "what that family in the village said is true. There is indeed a Male Reception Post-house." "Second Elder Brother," said Sha Monk, laughing, "go and show yourself at the Pregnancy Reflection Stream and see if there's a double reflection." Pa-chieh replied, "Don't play with me! Since I drank that cup of water from the Abortion Stream, the pregnancy has been dissolved. Why should I show myself?" Turning around, Tripitaka said to him, "Wu-nêng, be careful with your words." He then went forward to greet the woman official, who led them inside the post-house.

After they took their seats in the main hall, the official asked for tea to be served. All the servants working here combed their hair into three braids, and their garments were worn in two sections. Look at them! Even those serving tea were giggling. In a moment, they finished tea, and the official rose and asked, "Where did the visitors come from?" Pilgrim replied, "We are people from the Land of the East, sent by imperial commission of the Great T'ang emperor to worship Buddha in the Western Heaven and to seek scriptures. My master, the royal brother of the T'ang emperor, bears the title of Tripitaka T'ang. I'm Sun Wu-k'ung, his eldest disciple, and these two—Chu Wu-nêng and Sha Wu-ching—are my brothers. There are five of us altogether, including the horse. We have with us a travel rescript, and we beg you to certify it so that we may pass through." After the woman official wrote this in the register with a brush, she came forward to kowtow, saying, "Venerable fathers, please pardon me. This humble official is the clerk at the Male Reception Post-house. I did not know that such dignitaries from a noble nation were on their way, and therefore I did not go to a distance to meet you." After she kowtowed, she rose and immediately gave an order to the housekeeper to prepare food and drink. "Let the venerable fathers sit here for a while," she said, "and this humble official will enter the capital to present a memorial to our ruler. We will certify your rescript and use our seals, so that you can be sent on your way to the West." Delighted, Tripitaka sat down and we shall leave him for the moment.

We tell you now about that clerk of the post-house, who, after she had put on the proper attire, went to the Five Phoenix Tower inside the capital and said to the Custodian of the Yellow Gate: "I'm the clerk of the Male Reception Post-house, and I must have an audience with the Throne." The Yellow Gate at once presented the memorial, and the clerk was summoned up to the main palace hall. The queen asked: "Why does the Clerk of the post-house wish to see us?" "Your humble subject" said the clerk, "has just received in the post-house Tripitaka T'ang, the royal brother of the Great T'ang emperor in the Land of the East. He has three disciples by the names of Sun Wu-k'ung, Chu Wu-nêng, and Sha Wu-ching; there are altogether five of them, including a horse. They are on their way to seek scriptures from the Buddha in the Western Heaven. I have come especially to report this to my queen and to ask whether they may have their travel rescript certified and the permission to pass through." When the queen heard this report, she was filled with delight. "Last night," she said to the civil and military officials, "we dreamt that

Luminous hues grew from the screens of gold,

Refulgent rays spread from the mirrors of jade.

That had to be a good omen for today." "Mistress," said the women officials in unison as they prostrated themselves before the vermilion steps, "how could you tell that it was a good omen?" The queen said, "This man from the Land of the East is a royal brother of the T'ang court. In our country, the rulers of various generations since the time when chaos divided had never seen a man come here. Now the royal brother of the T'ang emperor has arrived, and he must be a gift from Heaven. We will use the wealth of an entire nation to ask this royal brother to be king; we are willing to be his queen. Such a sexual union will produce children and grandchildren, and the perpetuity of our kingdom will be assured. When you consider this, is not our dream a good omen?" The women officials all kowtowed to express their delight and acclaim.

Then the clerk of the post-house said, "What our mistress has proposed is good for extending the familial line to ten thousand generations. But those three disciples of the royal brother are savage men; their appearances are most unsightly." "According to what you have seen, worthy subject, how does that royal brother look?" asked the queen. "And how do his disciples look?" "The royal brother," said the clerk, "has features most dignified and handsome, truly befitting a man who belongs to the heavenly court of a noble nation, the China of South Jambūdvīpa. His three disciples, however, have such savage looks that they appear to be spirits." "In that case," said the queen, "let us provide his disciples with some supplies and certify the travel rescript for them. We shall send them off to the Western Heaven, and only the royal brother will remain here. Anything wrong with that?" Again the officials bowed to say, "The words of our mistress are most appropriate, and your subjects obey your instruction. The affair of marriage, however, requires a matchmaker, for as the ancients have declared,

The marriage contract depends on red leaves;[1]
A couple's joined by the moon-man's scarlet threads."[2]

"We shall follow the counsel of our subjects," replied the queen. "Let the present Grand Preceptor serve as our marriage go-between, and the clerk of the Male Reception Post-house as the one who officiates the ceremony. Let them go first to the post-house to propose to the royal brother. If he consents, we shall take our carriage out of the capital to receive him." The Grand Preceptor and the clerk accepted this decree and left the court.

We now tell you about Tripitaka and his disciples, who were just

enjoying their vegetarian meal at the hall of the post-house when
someone came in to report: "The Grand Preceptor and our own
governess have arrived." Tripitaka said, "Why does the Grand Preceptor come here?" "Perhaps the queen wants to give us an invitation," said Pa-chieh. "If not that," said Pilgrim, "then to offer a
proposal of marriage." "Wu-k'ung," said Tripitaka, "if they hold us
and want to force us to marry them, what shall we do?" "Master,"
replied Pilgrim, "just say Yes to them. Old Monkey will take care of
the matter."

They had hardly finished speaking when the two women officials
arrived and bowed deeply to the elder, who returned their salutations
one by one, saying, "This humble cleric is someone who has left the
family. What virtue or talent do I have that I dare let you bow to me?"
When the Grand Preceptor saw how impressive the elder looked, she
was delighted and thought to herself: "Our nation is truly quite
lucky! Such a man is most worthy to be the husband of our ruler."
After the officials made their greetings, they stood on either side of
the T'ang monk and said, "Father royal brother, we wish you ten
thousand happinesses!" "I'm someone who has left the family," replied
Tripitaka. "Where do those happinesses come from?" Again bending
low, the Grand Preceptor said, "This is the Nation of Women in the
Western Liang, and since time immemorial, there is not a single male
in our country. We are lucky at this time to have the arrival of father
royal brother. Your subject, by the decree of my ruler, has come
especially to offer a proposal of marriage." "My goodness! My goodness!" said Tripitaka. "This poor monk has arrived at your esteemed
region all by himself, without the attendance of either son or daughter.
I have with me only three mischievous disciples, and I wonder to
which of us is offered this marriage proposal." The post-house clerk
said, "Your lowly official just now went into court to present my
report, and my ruler, in great delight, told us of an auspicious dream
she had last night. She dreamt that

Luminous hues grew from the screens of gold,

Refulgent rays spread from the mirrors of jade.

When she learned that the royal brother is a man from the noble
nation of China, she was willing to use the wealth of her entire nation
to ask you to be her live-in husband.[3] You would take the royal seat
facing south to be called the man set apart from others,[4] and our
ruler would be the queen. That was why she gave the decree for the

Grand Preceptor to serve as the marriage go-between and this lowly official to officiate at the wedding. We came especially to offer you this proposal." When Tripitaka heard these words, he bowed his head and fell into complete silence. "When a man finds the time propitious," said the Grand Preceptor, "he should not pass up such an opportunity. Though there is, to be sure, such a thing in the world as asking a husband to live in the wife's family, the dowry of a nation's wealth is rare indeed. May we ask the royal brother to give his quick consent, so that we may report to our ruler." The elder, however, became more dumb and deaf than ever.

Sticking out his pestlelike snout, Pa-chieh shouted, "Grand Preceptor, go back and tell your ruler that my master happens to be an arhat who has attained the Way after a long process of cultivation. He will never fall in love with the dowry of a nation's wealth, nor will he be enamored with even beauty that can topple an empire. You may as well certify the travel rescript quickly and send them off to the West. Let me stay here to be the live-in husband. How's that?" When the Grand Preceptor heard this, her heart quivered and her gall shook, unable to answer at all. The clerk of the post-house said, "Though you may be a male, your looks are hideous. Our ruler will not find you attractive." "You are much too inflexible," said Pa-chieh, laughing. "As the proverb says,

The thick willow's a basket, the thin, a barrel—

Who in the world will take a man as an ugly fellow?"

Pilgrim said, "Idiot, stop this foolish talk. Let Master make up his mind: if he wants to leave, let him leave, and if he wants to stay, let him stay. Let's not waste the time of the marriage go-between."

"Wu-k'ung," said Tripitaka, "What do you think I ought to do?" "In old Monkey's opinion," replied Pilgrim, "perhaps it's good that you stay here. As the ancients said, 'One thread can tie up a distant marriage.' Where will you ever find such a marvelous opportunity?" Tripitaka said, "Disciple, if we remain here to dote on riches and glory, who will go to acquire scriptures in the Western Heaven? Won't the waiting kill my emperor of the Great T'ang?" The Grand Preceptor said, "In the presence of the royal brother, your humble official dares not hide the truth. The wish of our ruler is only to offer you the proposal of marriage. After your disciples have attended the wedding banquet, provisions will be given them and the travel rescript will be certified, so that they may proceed to the Western Heaven to acquire

the scriptures." "What the Grand Preceptor said is most reasonable,"
said Pilgrim, "and we need not be difficult about this. We are willing
to let our master remain here to become the husband of your mistress.
Certify our rescript quickly and send us off to the West. When we have
acquired the scriptures, we will return here to visit father and mother
and ask for travel expenses so that we may go back to the Great
T'ang." Both the Grand Preceptor and the clerk of the post-house
bowed to Pilgrim as they said, "We thank this teacher for his kind
assistance in concluding this marriage." Pa-chieh said, "Grand
Preceptor, don't use only your mouth to set the table! Since we have
given our consent, tell your mistress to prepare us a banquet first. Let
us have an engagement drink. How about it?" "Of course! Of course!"
said the Grand Preceptor. "We'll send you a feast at once." In great
delight, the Grand Preceptor left with the clerk of the post-house.

We tell you now about our elder T'ang, who caught hold of Pilgrim
immediately and berated him, crying, "Monkey head! Your tricks are
killing me! How could you say such things and ask me to get married
here while you people go to the Western Heaven to see Buddha?
Even if I were to die, I would not dare do this." "Relax, Master," said
Pilgrim, "old Monkey's not ignorant of how you feel. But since we
have reached this place and met this kind of people, we have no
alternative but to meet plot with plot." "What do you mean by that?"
asked Tripitaka.

Pilgrim said, "If you persist in refusing them, they will not certify
our travel rescript nor will they permit us to pass through. If they
grow vicious and order many people to cut you up and use your flesh
to make those so-called fragrant bags, do you think that we will treat
them with kindness? We will, of course, bring out our abilities which
are meant to subdue demons and dispel fiends. Our hands and feet are
quite heavy, you know, and our weapons, ferocious. Once we lift our
hands, the people of this entire nation will be wiped out. But you
must think of this, however. Although they are now blocking our
path, they are no fiendish creatures or monster-spirits; all of them in
this country are humans. And you have always been a man committed to kindness and compassion, refusing to hurt even one sentient
being on our way. If we slaughter all these common folk here, can
you bear it? That would be true wickedness."

When Tripitaka heard this, he said, "Wu-k'ung, what you have
just said is most virtuous. But I fear that if the queen asks me to enter

the palace, she will want me to perform the conjugal rite with her. How could I consent to lose my original yang and destroy the virtue of Buddhism, to leak my true sperm and fall from the humanity of our faith?" "Once we have agreed to the marriage," said Pilgrim, "she will no doubt follow royal etiquette and send her carriage out of the capital to receive you. Don't refuse her. Take a ride in her phoenix carriage and dragon chariot to go up to the treasure hall, and then sit down on the throne facing south. Ask the queen to take out her imperial seal and summon us brothers to go into court. After you have stamped the seal on the rescript, tell the queen to sign the document also and give it back to us. Meanwhile, you can also tell them to prepare a huge banquet; call it a wedding feast as well as a farewell party for us. After the banquet, ask for the chariot once more on the excuse that you want to see us off outside the capital before you return to consummate the marriage with the queen. In this way, both ruler and subjects will be duped into false happiness; they will no longer try to block our way, nor will they have any cause to become vicious. Once we reach the outskirts of the capital, you will come down from the dragon chariot and Sha Monk will help you to mount the white horse immediately. Old Monkey will then use his magic of immobility to make all of them, ruler and subjects, unable to move. We can then follow the main road to the West. After one day and one night, I will recite a spell to recall the magic and release all of them, so that they can wake up and return to the city. For one thing, their lives will be preserved, and for another, your primal soul will not be hurt. This is a plot called Fleeing the Net by a False Marriage. Isn't it a doubly advantageous act?" When Tripitaka heard these words, he seemed as if he were snapping out of a stupor or waking up from a dream. So delighted was he that he forgot all his worries and thanked Pilgrim profusely, saying, "I'm deeply grateful for my worthy disciple's lofty intelligence." And so, the four of them were united in their decision, and we shall leave them for the moment.

We tell you now about that Grand Preceptor and the clerk of the post-house, who dashed inside the gate of the court without even waiting for summons and went before the white-jade steps. "The auspicious dream of our mistress is most accurate," they cried, "and nuptial bliss will soon be yours." When the queen heard this report, she had the pearly screen rolled up; descending from the dragon couch, she opened her cherry lips to reveal her silvery teeth and asked, full of smiles and in a most seductive voice, "What did the royal brother say after our worthy subjects saw him?" "After your subjects reached the post-house," said the Grand Preceptor, "and bowed to the royal brother, we immediately presented to him our proposal of marriage. The royal brother still expressed some reluctance, but it was fortunate that his eldest disciple gave his consent for them without hesitation. He was willing to let his master become the husband of our ruler and call himself king, facing south. All he wanted was to have their travel rescript certified so that the three of them could leave for the West. On their way back after acquiring the scriptures, they will come here to bow to father and mother and ask for travel expenses to go back to the Great T'ang." "Did the royal brother say anything more?" asked the queen, smiling. The Grand Preceptor said, "the royal brother did not say anything more, but he seemed to be willing to marry our mistress. His second disciple, however, wanted to drink to their consent first."

When the queen heard this, she at once ordered the Court of Imperial Entertainments to prepare a banquet. She also requested that her imperial cortège be readied so that she might go out of the capital to receive her husband. The various women officials, in obedience to the queen's command, began to sweep and clean the palaces and to prepare the banquet with the utmost haste. Look at them! Though this Nation of Western Liang is a country of women, the carriage and chariot are not less opulent than those of China. You see

Six dragons belching colors—
Two phoenixes bringing luck—
Six dragons, belching colors, support the chariot;
Two phoenixes, bringing luck, lift up the carriage.
Strange fragrance in endless waves;
Auspicious airs continuously rise.
Fish-pendants of gold or jade by many officials worn;
Rows and rows of lovely locks and bejeweled hair.
A royal carriage shielded by mandarin-duck fans;
Through pearly screens glisten the phoenix hairpins.
Melodic pipes,
Harmonious strings.
What great sense of joy reaching to the sky!
What boundless bliss leaving the Estrade Numina.[5]
Three-layered canopies wave above the royal house;

Five-colored banners light up the imperial steps.
This land has ne'er seen the nuptial cup exchanged;
Today the queen marries a gifted man.

In a moment, the imperial cortège left the capital and arrived at the Male Reception Post-house. Someone went inside to announce to Tripitaka and his disciples: "The imperial cortège has arrived." On hearing this, Tripitaka straightened out his clothes and left the main hall with the three disciples to meet the carriage. As the queen rolled up the screen to descend from the carriage, she asked, "Which is the royal brother of the T'ang court?" Pointing with her finger, the Grand Preceptor said, "The one in a clerical robe standing behind the incense table outside the post-house gate." Lifting her moth-brows and opening wide her phoenix-eyes, the queen stared at him and found that this was an uncommon figure indeed. Look at him!

What handsome features!
What dignified looks!
Teeth white like silver bricks,
Ruddy lips and a square mouth.
His head's flat-topped, his forehead, wide and full;
Lovely eyes, neat eyebrows, and a chin that's long.
Two well-rounded ears betoken someone brave.
He is all elegance, a gifted man.
What a youthful and comely son of love,
So worthy to wed the pretty girl of Western Liang!

Utterly ravished by what she saw, the queen was swept away by amorous passion. Opening her tiny, cherrylike mouth, she cried out: "Royal brother of the Great T'ang, aren't you coming to take and ride the phoenix?" When Tripitaka heard these words, his ears turned red and his face, scarlet; filled with embarrassment, he dared not lift his head at all.

On one side, however, Chu Pa-chieh stuck up his snout and stared with glassy eyes at the queen, who was quite beguiling herself. Truly she had

Brows like kingfisher hair,
And flesh like mutton jade.
Peach petals bedeck her face;
Her bun piles gold-phoenix hair.
Her eyes' cool, liquid gaze—such seductive charm.
Her hands' young, tender shoots—such dainty form.

Colors flutter from a red sash hung aslant;
Bright gleams flash forth from jade and pearl pinned high.
Don't speak of the beauty of Chao-chün,[6]
She indeed surpasses even Hsi Shih.[7]
The willow waist bends slightly to gold-pendant sounds;
The light, lotus steps move the jadelike limbs.
The lunar goddess cannot come up to her,
Nor can the maids of Heaven compare with her.
This fair, palatial style's no common kind;
She's like Queen Mother who comes from Jasper Pool.

As our Idiot gazed at this pleasing figure, he could not restrain the saliva from drooling out of his mouth and the deer pounding at his heart. All at once, he grew weak and numb and simply melted away like a snow lion faced with fire!

The queen went forward and caught hold of Tripitaka. In a most seductive voice, she said, "Royal brother darling, please ascend the dragon chariot so that we may go to the Treasure Hall of Golden Chimes and become husband and wife." Shaking so hard that he could barely stand up, our elder behaved as if he were drunk or mesmerized. Pilgrim on one side whispered to him, "Master, don't be too modest. Please get in the carriage with our mistress. Go and have our rescript certified quickly so that we may proceed to fetch the scriptures." The elder did not dare reply; he tugged at Pilgrim a couple of times and he could no longer stop the tears from falling down. "Master, you must not be distressed," said Pilgrim. "Look at all these riches! If you don't enjoy them now, when are you going to do it?" Tripitaka had little alternative but to acquiesce. Wiping away his tears, he forced himself to appear happy and joined the queen, as they,

Holding hands together,
Rode the dragon carriage.
In great delight the queen wanted to get married;
In great fear the elder wished only to worship Buddha.
One desired amorous play in the bridal chamber;
One sought to see the World-Honored One at Mount Spirit.
The queen was sincere;
The monk pretended,
The queen was sincere,
Hoping to reach old age in harmony.
The monk pretended,

Guarding his feelings to nourish his soul.
One was so glad to see a man
That she would couple with him in broad daylight.
One dreaded to meet a woman
And thought only to flee and go to Thunderclap.
The two mounted together the chariot.
Who knew the T'ang monk had something else in mind!

When those civil and military officials saw that their ruler and the T'ang monk had ascended the phoenix carriage and sat side by side together, every one of them beamed with pleasure. The entire entourage turned around and went back into the capital.

Meanwhile, the Great Sage Sun told Sha Monk to pole the luggage and lead the white horse to follow the imperial cortège. Chu Pa-chieh, however, scurried ahead and ran madly up to the Tower of Five Phoenixes first, shouting all the while, "What comfort! What an opportunity! But this can't be done until we have drunk the wedding wine and presented ourselves to the kinfolk first." Those officials who were attending the cortège were so terrified that they went to the chariot and said, "My Lady, that monk who has a long snout and huge ears is shouting in front of the Five Phoenix Towers for wedding wine to drink." When the queen heard this, she leaned her fragrant shoulder over to the elder and put her peachlike cheeks up to his face. Opening her scented mouth, she said softly, "Royal brother darling, which disciple of yours is that one with a long snout and huge ears?" "He's my second disciple," said Tripitaka, "and he has a huge appetite. In fact, he loves to indulge his mouth throughout his life. He must be given some food and drink first before we can proceed with our business." The queen asked hurriedly, "Has the Court of Imperial Entertainments finished preparing the banquet?" "It has," reported one of the officials, "There are both meat and vegetarian dishes set up in the East Hall."[8] "Why both?" asked the queen again. "We fear that the royal brother of the T'ang court," said the official, "and his disciples are accustomed to keeping a vegetarian diet. That is why we have both meat and vegetarian dishes." Full of smiles, the queen again snuggled close to the elder and said, "Royal brother darling, do you eat meat, or are you keeping a vegetarian diet?" Tripitaka said, "This humble priest observes a vegetarian diet, but my disciples have not abstained from wine. My second disciple would like very much to have a few cups of dietary wine."

They had not finished speaking when the Grand Preceptor approached them and said, "Please go to the East Hall to attend the banquet. Today is an auspicious day, and Your Majesty can marry the venerable royal brother. Tomorrow Heaven will reveal the Yellow Road,[9] and we shall invite the venerable royal brother to ascend the treasure hall and face south. He can then designate the name of his reign and assume the throne." Highly pleased, the queen held hands with the elder to descend from the dragon chariot and enter the main palace gate. They were met by

Music divine, wind-wafted from the towers,
As the jade throne moved through the palace gates.
Phoenix doors flung wide to bright flares of light;
The palace now opened with rows of brocade.
The unicorn hall was draped o'er by incense smoke;
Bright corridors wound around the peacock screens.
Towers rose rugged like the noble state's,
With jade halls and gold horses more wondrous still.
When they reached the East Hall,
They heard a choir of melodious strings and pipes;
They saw two rows of winsome, graceful maids.

Two kinds of sumptuous repast were set up in the central hall: on the head table to the left was the vegetarian spread, whereas meat dishes were placed on the right. Two rows of single tables were also set up toward the front of the hall. Rolling up her sleeves to reveal her dainty, pointed fingers, the queen immediately picked up a jade cup to toast her guests. Pilgrim went forward to say: "We are all keeping a vegetarian diet. Let our master be seated at the head table on the left. Then we three brothers may take the single tables on both sides of him." "Yes! Yes!" said the Grand Preceptor in delight. "Master and disciples are just like father and sons. They should not sit side by side." The various officials hurriedly set up the tables in proper order, after which the queen toasted each of them as he took his seat. Thereafter, Pilgrim gave the T'ang monk a look, indicating to his master to return the salutation. Tripitaka, therefore, left his seat and, holding the jade goblet, also toasted the queen. The other civil and military officials all knelt to thank the imperial favor before they took the other seats on both sides according to their ranks. The music stopped and they began to drink and eat.

As Pa-chieh was bent on satisfying his stomach, he had little regard for consequence. It did not matter that the food before him was corn, steamed breads, sweet pastries, button mushrooms, black mushrooms, tender bamboo shoots, wood-ears, Chinese cabbage, seaweed, laver, green turnips, taros, white turnips, yams, or yellow sperms—in big gulps, he finished them all, washing down the food with seven or eight cups of wine. "Bring us more food!" he hollered. "Bring some big steins! After we drink a few more steins, each of us will attend to our business." "Such a fine feast and you don't want to enjoy some more?" asked Sha Monk. "What sort of business do you want to attend to?" With a laugh, our Idiot said, "As the ancients said,

Let the bow-maker make his bow,
The arrow-maker his arrow.

At this time, those of us who want to take a wife may take a wife, and those of us who want to marry a husband may marry a husband. Those who want to acquire scriptures need to be on their way to acquire scriptures. We can't let the coveted cup delay our affairs. Let's have our rescript certified quickly. As the saying goes,

If the general does not dismount,
Every man will go his own way."

When the queen heard this, she asked for big cups, and the attendants quickly took out several parrot cups, cormorant-shaped ladles, gold beakers, silver chalices, glass goblets, crystal basins, P'êng-lai bowls, and amber steins. They filled these with the mellowest of wines and all of the disciples drank a round.

Tripitaka then rose from the table and bowed to the queen with hands folded, saying, "Your Majesty, thank you for this lavish feast. We have drunk quite enough. Please ascend the treasure hall and certify our rescript. While there is still light, let us send the three of them on their way." The queen agreed. After the banquet had been dismissed, she led the elder by the hand up to the Hall of Golden Chimes and immediately wanted the elder to take the throne. "No! No!" said Tripitaka. "Just now the Grand Preceptor said that tomorrow would be the proper auspicious day, and only then would this poor monk dare assume the throne and call myself the man set apart. Today you should use your seal on the rescript so that they may be sent away." Again the queen agreed and sat down on the dragon couch. A golden high-backed chair was placed on the left of the couch for the T'ang monk to sit on. Then the disciples were asked to bring forth the travel rescript. After Sha Monk untied the wrap and took it out, the Great Sage presented the rescript with both hands to the queen. When she examined it, she found on the document the marks of nine treasure seals of the Great T'ang emperor, together with the seals of the Precious Image Kingdom, the Black Rooster Kingdom, and the Cart Slow Kingdom. After the queen had looked at the document, she said again, smiling seductively, "So royal brother darling also bears the name of Ch'ên?" "That is the surname of my secular family," said Tripitaka, "and my religious name is Hsüan-tsang. Because the T'ang emperor in his imperial kindness took me as his brother, he bestowed on me the name of T'ang." "Why is it," asked the queen, "that the rescript does not contain the names of your disciples?" "My three mischievous disciples," replied Tripitaka, "are not people from the T'ang court." "If they are not," asked the queen once more, "how is it that they are willing to follow you on your journey?"

"My eldest disciple," answered Tripitaka, "comes from the Ao-lai Kingdom in the East Pūrvavideha Continent; the second disciple, from a village in Tibet in the West Aparagodānīya Continent; and the third, from the River of Flowing Sand. All three of them had transgressed the decrees of Heaven. The Bodhisattva Kuan-shih-yin, however, liberated them from their sufferings, as a result of which they were willing to make submission and hold fast the good. So that their merits might atone for their sins, they resolved to accompany me and protect me on my journey to the Western Heaven to acquire scriptures. Since they became my disciples when I was already on my way, their names therefore had not been recorded on the rescript." "Let me add them on for you, all right?" asked the queen, and Tripitaka said, "Your Majesty may do as you please." The queen asked at once for brush and ink; after the ink had been rubbed out and the brush nicely soaked in it, she wrote at the end of the rescript declaration the names of Sun Wu-k'ung, Chu Wu-nêng, and Sha Wu-ching. Then she took out her imperial seal with which she neatly stamped the rescript before she signed her own name. The document was passed down again to the Great Sage Sun, who gave it to Sha Monk to put into the wrap.

Picking up a tray of small pieces of gold and silver, the queen left the dragon couch to hand it to Pilgrim, saying, "Take this, the three of you, as travel money, and may you reach the Western Heaven at an early date. When you return after you have acquired the scriptures, we shall have greater rewards for you." Pilgrim said, "We are those who have left the family, and we cannot accept gold or silver. There will be places on our way where we may beg for our living." When the queen saw that he refused, she took out ten bales of silk brocade and said to Pilgrim, "Since you are rushing away, there's no time for measurement or sewing. Take this and have some clothes made on the way to protect you from the cold." "Those who have left the family," said Pilgrim, "are not permitted to wear silk brocade. We have cloth garments to cover our bodies." When the queen saw that he refused again, she gave this order: "Take three pints of imperial rice, and you can use it for a meal on the road." When Pa-chieh heard the word, meal, he at once accepted it and put the rice in the wrap. "Brother," said Pilgrim, "the luggage is getting heavier. You have the strength to pole it?" "You wouldn't know," chuckled Pa-chieh, "but what's good about rice is that it's a product for daily consumption. One meal will finish it off." They all pressed their palms together to thank the queen.

Tripitaka said, "Let Your Majesty take the trouble to accompany this poor monk, who will send them off outside the capital. Let me give them a few instructions so that they may leave for the West. I will return and then I can enjoy forever with Your Majesty riches and glory. Only without such burdens or cares can we enter into conjugal bliss." The queen, of course, did not know that this was a trick, and she asked at once for the imperial cortège. Leaning her fragrant shoulder on Tripitaka, she ascended the phoenix carriage with him and proceeded to the west of the capital. At that time, all the people in the capital lined the streets with containers filled with clean water and urns with the finest incense. Wishing to see the cortège of the queen and the male form of the royal brother were all powdered faces and cloudlike hair; old and young, they crowded into the streets. In a moment, the imperial cortège went out of the capital and stopped before the western gate.

After putting everything in order, Pilgrim, Pa-chieh, and Sha Monk faced the imperial carriage and cried out in unison, "The queen need not go any further. We shall take our leave now." Descending slowly from the dragon chariot, the elder raised his hands toward the queen and said, "Please go back, Your Majesty, and let this poor monk go to acquire scriptures." When the queen heard this, she paled with fright and tugged at the T'ang monk. "Royal brother darling," she cried, "I'm willing to use the wealth of my entire nation to ask you to be my husband. Tomorrow you shall ascend the tall treasure throne to call yourself king, and I am to be your queen. You have even eaten the wedding feast. Why are you changing your mind now?" When Pa-chieh heard what she said, he became slightly mad. Pouting his snout and flapping his ears wildly, he rushed at the carriage, shouting, "How could we monks marry a powdered skeleton like you? Let my master go on his journey!" When the queen saw that hideous face and ugly behaviour, she was scared out of her wits and fell back into the carriage. Sha Monk pulled Tripitaka out of the crowd and was just helping him to mount the horse when another girl dashed out from somewhere and shouted, "Royal brother T'ang, where are you going? Let's you and I make some love!" "You stupid hussie!" cried Sha Monk and, whipping out his treasure staff, brought it down hard on the head of the girl. Suddenly calling up a cyclone, the girl carried away the T'ang monk with a loud whoosh and both of them vanished without a trace. Alas! Thus it was that,

Having just left the fair sex net,
Then the demon of love he met.

We do not know whether that girl is a human or a fiend, or whether the old master will die or live, and you must listen to the explanation in the next chapter.

Fifty-five

Perverse form makes lascivious play of Tripitaka T'ang;
Rectified mind safeguards the indestructible body.

We were just telling you of the Great Sage Sun and Chu Pa-chieh, who were about to use magic to render those women immobile when they heard the shouts of Sha Monk and the howl of the wind. They turned quickly to look, only to discover that the T'ang monk had vanished. "Who is it that has abducted Master?" asked Pilgrim, and Sha Monk said, "It's a girl. She called up a cyclone and took away Master." When Pilgrim heard this, he leaped straight up to the edge of the clouds; using his hand to shade his eyes, he peered all around and found a rolling mass of wind and dust heading toward the northwest. "Brothers," he shouted to them down below, "mount the clouds quickly to pursue Master with me." Pa-chieh and Sha Monk tied the luggage to the horse, and with a crack they all shot up to midair and left.

Those women of the State of Western Liang, ruler and subjects, were so terrified that they knelt on the ground, all crying, "So these are arhats who can ascend to Heaven in broad daylight!" Then the officials said to the queen, "Let not our ruler be frightened or vexed any more. The royal brother of T'ang has to be a Buddhist monk who has attained the Way. Since none of us possesses true discernment, we could not recognize these Chinese men for what they are and all our schemings have been wasted. Let our mistress ascend the carriage to go back to court." The queen herself became quite embarrassed, and as she went back to the capital with all her officials, we shall leave them for the moment.

We tell you instead about the Great Sage Sun with his two brothers, who trod on air and fog to give chase to that cyclone. In a little while, they came upon a tall mountain, where they saw the dust had died down and the wind subsided. Not knowing where the fiend had gone to, the three brothers lowered their clouds and began to search for the way. It was then that they saw on the side of the mountain a huge slab of stone, all shiny and green, that looked like a screen. The three of them led the horse to the back of the screen and discovered two stone doors, on which there was in large letters the following inscription: Toxic Foe Mountain, Cave of the Lute. As he had always been rather stupid, Pa-chieh immediately wanted to break down the doors with his rake, but he was quickly stopped by Pilgrim. "Don't be so hasty, Brother," he said. "After we followed the cyclone here, we had to search for a while before we found these doors. We don't even know the long and short of the matter. Suppose this is the wrong door. Won't your action offend the owner? I think the two of you should look after the horse and wait in front of that stone screen. Let old Monkey go inside to do some detection before we start anything." Greatly pleased by what he heard, Sha Monk said, "Very good! This is what I call caution in recklessness, composure in urgency." So, the two of them led the horse away.

The Great Sage Sun, meanwhile, displayed his magic power: making the magic sign with his fingers, he recited a spell and with one shake of his body changed into a bee—truly agile and light. Look at him!

His thin wings go soft with wind;
His waist in sunlight is trim.
A mouth once sweetened by flowers;
A tail that stripe-toads has tamed.
What merit in honey-making!
How modest his home-returning!
A smart plan he now conceives
To soar past both doors and eaves.

Crawling inside through a crack in the door, Pilgrim flew past the second level door and came upon a flower arbor in the middle of which sat a female fiend. Attending her on both sides were several young girls dressed in colored silk and with parted bangs on their foreheads. All of them appeared to be in a most pleasant mood, talking with great animation about something. Ever so lightly our Pilgrim flew up there and alighted on the trellis of the arbor. As he cocked his ear to listen, he saw two other girls with disheveled hair walking up to the arbor, each holding a plate of steaming hot pastries. "Madam," they said, "on this plate are buns stuffed with human flesh, and on the other buns stuffed with red bean paste." "Little ones," said the female fiend with a giggle, "help the royal brother of T'ang to come out." The girls dressed in colored silk went to one of the rear chambers and led the T'ang monk out by his hands. The master's face, however, had turned yellow and his lips, white; his eyes were red and brimming with tears. "Master has been poisoned!" sighed Pilgrim to himself.

The fiend walked out of the arbor and extended her dainty, spring-onion-like fingers to catch hold of the elder, saying, "Relax, royal brother! Though our place here is not like the palace of the Nation of Women of Western Liang and cannot compare with their wealth and luxury, it is actually less hectic and more comfortable. You will find it perfect for chanting the name of Buddha and reading scriptures. I'll be your companion on the Way, and we'll enjoy a harmonious union until old age." Tripitaka would not utter a word. "Don't be distressed," said the fiend again. "I know that you didn't eat much when you attended the banquet in the Nation of Women. Here are two kinds of flour goods, meat and vegetarian, and you may take whatever you want, just to calm your fear."

Tripitaka thought to himself: "I can remain silent and refuse to eat anything, but this fiend is not like the queen. The queen, after all, is a human being whose action is governed by propriety. This fiend is a monster-spirit most capable of hurting me. What shall I do? I wonder if my three disciples know that I am held in custody here. If she does harm me because of my stubborness, wouldn't I have thrown away my life?" As he questioned his mind with mind like that, he had no alternative but to force himself to open his mouth. "What's the meat made of and what's the vegetarian made of?" he asked. The fiend said, "The meat bun has human flesh stuffing, while the vegetarian has red bean paste stuffing." "This poor monk," said Tripitaka, "keeps a vegetarian diet." "Girls," said the female fiend, giggling, "bring us some hot tea so that the elder of your household can eat the vegetarian buns."

One of the girls indeed brought out a cup of fragrant tea and placed it in front of the elder. Picking up a vegetarian bun, the fiend broke it in half and handed the pieces to Tripitaka, who in turn took a meat bun and presented it whole to the fiend. "Royal brother," asked the fiend, laughing, "why didn't you break it first before you handed it to me?" Tripitaka pressed his palms together before he replied: "As someone who has left the family, I dare not break meat." "If you as someone who has left the family dare not break meat," said the fiend, "how is it that you were willing to eat water pudding[1] the other day

at the Child-and-Mother Stream? Having done that, do you still
insist on eating red bean paste stuffing today?" Tripitaka replied:

At high tide a boat leaves quickly;
In sand traps a horse trots slowly.

Pilgrim on the trellis heard everything; fearing that such banter
might confound the real nature of his master, he could no longer
contain himself. He revealed his true form at once and whipped out
his iron rod. "Cursed beast!" he shouted. "You're unruly!" When
the female fiend saw him, she at once blew out from her mouth a ray
of misty light to cover up the entire arbor. "Little ones," she cried,
"take away the royal brother!" Picking up a steel trident, she leaped
out of the arbor and yelled, "Lawless simian rascal! How dare you
sneak into my house and peep at me in secret? Don't run away! Have
a taste of your mamma's trident!" Using the iron rod to parry her
blows, the Great Sage fought back as he retreated.

The two of them fought their way out of the cave. Pa-chieh and
Sha Monk were waiting in front of the stone screen; when they saw
the combatants emerging, Pa-chieh hurriedly pulled the white horse
out of the way, saying, "Sha Monk, you guard the horse and the
luggage. Let old Hog go and help with the fight." Dear Idiot! Lifting
high the rake with both his hands, he rushed forward and shouted,
"Elder Brother, stay back! Let me beat up this bitch!" When the fiend
saw Pa-chieh approaching, she summoned some more of her abilities.
With one snort fire spurted out from her nostrils as smoke licked out
from her mouth. She shook her body once and there were now three
tridents dancing and thrusting in the air, wielded by who knows how
many hands. As she charged like a cyclone into the fray, she was met
by Pilgrim and Pa-chieh on both sides. "Sun Wu-k'ung," cried the
fiend, "you really have no judgment! I recognize you, but you can't
recognize me. But even your Buddha Tathāgata at the Thunderclap
Monastery is afraid of me. And two clumsy oafs like you, you think
you'll get anywhere! Come on up, both of you, and I'll give each of
you a beating!" How was this battle, you ask.

The female fiend's power expanded;
The Monkey King's vigor increased.
The Heavenly Reeds Marshal, striving for merit,
Wielded wildly his rake to show his vim.
That one with many hands and fast tridents the misty light
    encircled;

From these two—impulsive, with strong weapons—foggy air
  rose up.
The fiend wished only to seek a mate;
The monk refused to leak his primal sperm.
Yin and yang at odds now clashed together,
Each flaunting its might in this bitter strife.
Quiet yin, to nourish being, quickened in lust;
Tranquil yang purged desires to guard its health.
To these two parties thus came discord;
A contest was waged by trident, rake, and rod.
This one's rod was strong,
The rake, more potent—
But the fiend's trident met them blow for blow.
Three unyielding persons before Mount Toxic Foe;
Two ruthless factions outside the Cave of the Lute.
That one was pleased to seize the T'ang monk as her spouse;
These two resolved to seek with the elder scriptures true.
To do battle they stirred up Heaven and Earth
And fought till sun and moon darkened and planets moved.

The three of them fought for a long time and no decision was reached. Leaping suddenly into the air, the female fiend resorted to the Horse-Felling Poisoned Stake and gave the Great Sage a terrific stab on his head. "Oh, misery!" cried Pilgrim and at once fled in severe pain. When Pa-chieh saw that the tide was turning, he, too, retreated with the rake trailing behind him. The fiend thus retrieved her tridents and returned in triumph.

Gripping his head, with brows contracted and face woe-laden, Pilgrim kept crying, "Horror! Horror!" Pa-chieh went up to him and asked: "Elder Brother, how is it that, when you were just enjoying the fight, you suddenly ran away, whining up a storm?" Pilgrim gripped his head and could only say, "It hurts! It hurts!" "It must be your migraine," said Sha Monk.

"No! No!" cried Pilgrim, jumping up and down. "Elder Brother," said Pa-chieh, "I didn't see that you were wounded. But now your head hurts. Why?" "Lord, it's terrible!" said Pilgrim with a groan. "I was just fighting with her. When she saw that I was breaking through her defense with the trident, she suddenly leaped into the air. I don't know what kind of weapon it was that gave my head a stab, but the pain is unbearable. That was why I ran away."

"You have always bragged about that head of yours when things were quiet," said Pa-chieh with a laugh, "saying that it has gone through such a long process of cultivation. How is it now that it can't even take a stab?"

"Indeed," replied Pilgrim. "Since I achieved the art of realized immortality, and since I stole and ate the immortal peaches, celestial wine, and the golden elixir of Lao Tzu, this head of mine cannot be harmed. When I caused great disturbance in Heaven, the Jade Emperor sent the Demon King Powerful and the Twenty-Eight Constellations to take me outside the Dipper Star Palace and have me executed. What those divine warriors used on me were swords, axes, scimitars, bludgeons, thunderbolts, and fire. Thereafter Lao Tzu placed me within his brazier of eight trigrams and smelted me for forty-nine days. But there wasn't even a scratch on my head. I don't know what sort of weapon this woman used today, but she certainly wounded old Monkey!"

"Take away your hands," said Sha Monk, "and let me see if the skin has been torn." "No, it hasn't," replied Pilgrim.

"I'll go to the State of Western Liang and ask for some ointment to tape on you," said Pa-chieh. Pilgrim said, "There's no swelling, and it's not an open wound. Why should you want to tape ointment on it?"

"Brother," said Pa-chieh, chuckling, "I didn't come down with any pre- or postnatal illness, but you are getting a brain tumor." "Stop joking, Second Elder Brother," said Sha Monk. "It's getting late! Big Brother's head has been hurt and we don't know whether Master is dead or alive. What shall we do?"

"Master's all right," said Pilgrim with a groan. "I changed into a bee to fly inside, and I found that woman sitting inside a flower arbor. In a little while, two maids brought out two plates of buns: one had human flesh for stuffing and the other, red bean paste. Then she asked two other maids to help Master out to eat, just to calm his fear. She also said something about her desire to be Master's companion on the Way. At first, Master did not say anything to the woman, nor did he eat the buns. Later, perhaps it was because of all her sweet talk or some other odd reason, he began to speak with her and told her that he kept a vegetarian diet. The woman broke one of those vegetarian buns into halves to hand to Master, and he presented her with a meat one whole. 'Why didn't you break it?' the woman asked, and Master said, 'Those who have left the family dare not break meat.' 'In that case,' asked the woman, 'how was it that you were willing to eat water pudding the other day? And you still insist on eating stuffing made of red bean paste?' Master didn't quite understand her puns, and he replied:

At high tide a boat leaves quickly;
In sand traps a horse trots slowly.

I heard everything on the trellis, and I was afraid that Master's nature might be confounded. That was when I revealed my true form and attacked her with my iron rod. She, too, used her magic power; blowing out some mist or fog to cover the arbor, she shouted for the girls to take away the 'royal brother' before she picked up her steel trident and fought her way out of the cave with old Monkey." When Sha Monk heard this, he bit his finger and said, "We've been picked up and followed by this bitch from who knows where, but she certainly has knowledge of what has happened to us recently."

"If you put it that way," said Pa-chieh, "it looks as if we wouldn't be able to rest, doesn't it? Let's not worry if it's dusk or midnight. Let's go up to her door and provoke battle. At least our hubbub will prevent them from sleeping, so that she can't pull a fast one on our master." "My head hurts," said Pilgrim. "I can't go!" Sha Monk said, "No need to provoke battle. In the first place, Elder Brother has a headache, and in the second, our master is a true monk. He won't allow either form or emptiness to confound his nature. Let us sit here for the night beneath the mountain slope where there's no draft and regain our energy. Then we can decide what to do by morning." And so, the three brothers, after having tied up the white horse firmly, rested beneath the mountain slope, guarding the luggage.

We now tell you about that female fiend, who banished violence from her mind and once again took on a pleasant appearance. "Little ones," she said, "shut the front and back doors tightly." Two little fiends were instructed to stand watch against the intrusion of Pilgrim. If there were any sound at all at the door, they were told to report at once. Then she gave this order also: "Maids, fix up the bedroom nicely. After you have lit the candles and the incense, go and invite royal brother T'ang to come here. I want to make love with him." They therefore brought out the elder from the rear. Putting on her most seductive charms, she caught hold of the T'ang monk and said, "As the proverb says,

Though gold may have its price,
Our pleasure's more worthwhile.
Let's you and I play husband and wife and have some fun!"

Gritting his teeth, our elder would not permit even a sound to escape from his mouth. He was about to refuse her invitation, but he was afraid that she might decide to take his life. He had no alternative but to follow her into the fragrant room, trembling all the while. Completely in a stupor, he raised neither his eyes nor his head; he did not see what sort of coverlets or bedding there was in the room, nor was he eager to find out what kinds of furniture or dresser were placed therein. As for all the amorous declaration and sultry speech of the female fiend, he did not hear a word. Marvelous monk! Truly

His eyes saw no evil form;
His ears heard no lustful sound;
He regarded as dirt and dung this coy, silken face,
This pear-like beauty as ashes and dust.
His one love in life was to practice Zen,
Unwilling to step once beyond Buddha-land.
How could he show affection and pity
When all he knew was religion and truth?
That fiend, all vibrant
With boundless passion;
Our elder, most deadpan
And filled with zeal Buddhist.
One was like soft jade and warm perfume;
One seemed like cold ashes or dried wood.
That person undid her collar,
Her passion overflowing;
This person tied up his robe,
His resolve unswerving.
That one wanted to mate, breast to breast with thighs entwined;
This one wished to face the wall and seek Bodhidharma in the
    mount.
The fiend loosened her clothes
To display her fine, scented flesh;
The T'ang monk bundled up his cloak
To hide his coarse and thick skin.

The fiend said, "My sheets and pillows are ready, why don't
    you sleep!"
The T'ang monk said, "How could my bald head and strange
    attire join you there!"
That one said, "I'm willing to be the former period's
    Liu Ts'ui-ts'ui."[2]
This one said, "This humble monk is not a lovesick priest!"
The fiend said, "I'm pretty as Hsi Shih and e'en more lissome."
The T'ang monk said, "Like King Yüeh I have long been
    mortified!"
The fiend said, "Royal brother, remember
He who dies beneath the flowers,
His ghost's a happy lover."
The T'ang monk said, "My true yang is treasure most precious.
    How could I give it to a powdered cadaver?"

The two of them prattled on like that deep into the night, but the
elder T'ang showed no sign whatever that he had been aroused.
Though the female fiend tugged and pulled at him and refused to let
go, our master doggedly rejected her advances. By midnight, all this
hassle made the fiend mad, and she shouted, "Little ones, bring me a
rope!" Alas! The dearly beloved was at once trussed up until he
looked like a shaggy ape! After telling her subordinates to drag the
monk back to the corridor, she blew out the lamps and all of them
retired.

Soon the cock crowed three times, and beneath the mountain
slope our Great Sage Sun rose up, saying, "I had a headache for quite
a while, but now my head feels neither painful nor numb. In fact, I
have a little itch." "If you have an itch," chuckled Pa-chieh, "how
about asking her to give you another stab?" Pilgrim spat at him and
said, "Go! Go! Go!" Pa-chieh laughed again and replied, "Go! Go!
Go! But it was Master last night who went wild! Wild! Wild!" "Stop
gabbing, the two of you," said Sha Monk. "It's light. Go quickly to
catch the monster." "Brother," said Pilgrim, "stay here to guard the
horse and don't move. Chu Pa-chieh will go with me."

Arousing himself, our Idiot straightened out his black-silk shirt and
followed Pilgrim; they took their weapons and leaped up to the
mountain ledge to go before the stone screen. "Stand here," said
Pilgrim to Pa-chieh, "for I fear that the fiend might have harmed
Master during the night. Let me go inside to snoop around a bit. If

Master truly had lost his primal yang and his virtue because of her deception, then all of us could scatter. If he has not been confounded and if his Zen mind has remained unmoved, then we could in all diligence fight to the end, slaughter the monster-spirit, and rescue Master to go to the West." "You are quite numbskulled!" said Pa-chieh. "As the proverb says, 'Could dried fish be used for a cat's pillows?' Like it or not, it would receive a few scratches!" Pilgrim said, "Stop babbling! I'll go and see."

Dear Great Sage! He left Pa-chieh in front of the stone screen and shook his body again to change into a bee. After he flew inside, he found two maids sleeping, their heads resting on the watch-rattles. He went up to the flower arbor to look around. The monster-spirit, you see, had struggled for half the night; she and her attendants were all very tired. Everyone was still fast asleep, not knowing that it was dawn already. Flying to the rear, Pilgrim began to hear the faint moans of the T'ang monk, and then he saw that the priest was left, hogtied, in the corridor. Pilgrim gently alighted on his head and whispered, "Master." Recognizing the voice, the T'ang monk said, "Have you come, Wu-k'ung? Save my life, quick!" "How were the night's activities?" asked Pilgrim. Tripitaka, clenching his teeth, replied: "I would rather die than do anything of that sort!" "I thought," said Pilgrim, "I saw her showing you a good deal of tenderness yesterday. How is it that she is putting you through such torment today?"

"She pestered me for half the night," answered Tripitaka, "but I did not even loosen my clothes or touch her bed. When she saw that I refused to yield to her, she had me tied up like this. Please rescue me, so that I can go acquire the scriptures." As master and disciples spoke to each other like that, they woke up the monster-spirit. Though she was furious at the T'ang monk, she was still very fond of him. When she stirred and heard something about going to acquire scriptures, she rolled off the bed at once and shouted: "You mean to tell me that you don't want to get married and still want to go and seek scriptures?"

Pilgrim was so startled that he abandoned his master, spread his wings, and flew out of the cave. "Pa-chieh!" he cried, and our Idiot came around the stone screen, saying, "Has that thing been concluded?" "Not yet! Not yet!" said Pilgrim, laughing. "She worked on the old master for quite some time, but he refused. She got mad and had him hogtied. He was just telling me all this when the fiend woke up, and I became so startled that I came back out here." Pa-chieh said, "What did Master actually say?" "He said," replied Pilgrim, "that he did not even loosen his clothes nor did he touch her bed." "Good! Very good!" chuckled Pa-chieh. "He's still a true monk! Let's go rescue him!"

As he had always been a roughneck, our Idiot did not wait for further discussion. Lifting high his muckrake, he brought it down on the stone doors with all his might, and with a loud crash they broke into many pieces. The two maids sleeping on the watch-rattles were so terrified that they ran back to the second-level door and screamed: "Open up! Those two ugly men of yesterday have come again and smashed our doors!" The female fiend was just leaving her room. "Little ones," she cried, "bring some hot water for me to wash my face. Carry the royal brother, all tied up like that, and hide him in the rear room. I'm going out to fight them."

Dear monster-spirit! She ran out with her trident uplifted and shouted: "Brazen ape! Wild boar! You don't know when to stop, do you? How dare you break my doors?" "You filthy bitch!" scolded Pa-chieh. "You have our master imprisoned, and you still dare to talk with such insolence? Our master was only your kidnapped husband! Send him out quickly, and I'll spare you. If you dare but utter half a No, the blows of old Hog's rake will level even your mountain."

The monster-spirit, of course, did not permit such words to intimidate her. With enormous energy and using magic as before, she attacked with her steel trident while her nose and mouth belched fire and smoke. Pa-chieh leaped aside to dodge her blow before striking back with his rake, helped by the Great Sage Sun and his iron rod on the other side. The power of that fiend was tremendous indeed! All at once she seemed to have acquired who knows how many hands, waving and parrying left and right. After they fought for several rounds, she again used some kind of weapon and gave the lip of Pa-chieh a stab. His rake trailing behind him and his lips pouting, our Idiot fled in pain for his life. Pilgrim also became somewhat envious of him; making one false blow with the rod, he, too, fled in defeat. After the fiend returned in triumph, she told her little ones to place rock piles in front of the door.

We now tell you about Sha Monk, who was grazing the horse before the mountain slope when he heard some hog-grunting. As he raised his head, he saw Pa-chieh dashing back, lips pouted and grunting as he ran. "What in the world?..." said Sha Monk, and our Idiot blurted out: "It's awful! It's awful! This pain! This pain!" Hardly had he finished speaking when Pilgrim also arrived. "Dear Idiot!" he chuckled. "Yesterday you said I had a brain tumor, but now you are suffering from the plague of the swollen lip!" "I can't bear it!" cried Pa-chieh. "The pain's acute! It's terrible! It's terrible!"

Thus the three of them were in sad straits when they saw an old woman approaching from the south on the mountain road, her left hand carrying a little bamboo basket with vegetables in it. "Big Brother," said Sha Monk, "look at that old lady approaching. Let me find out from her what sort of a monster-spirit this is and what kind of weapon she has that can inflict a wound like this." "You stay where you are," said Pilgrim, "and let old Monkey question her." When Pilgrim stared at the old woman carefully, he saw that there were auspicious clouds covering her head and fragrant mists encircling her body. Recognizing all at once who she was, Pilgrim shouted, "Brothers, kowtow quickly! The lady is Bodhisattva!" Ignoring his pain, Pa-chieh hurriedly went to his knees while Sha Monk bent low, still holding the reins of the horse. The Great Sage Sun, too, pressed his palms together and knelt down, all crying, "We submit to the great and compassionate, the efficacious savior, Bodhisattva Kuan-Shih-yin."

When the Bodhisattva saw that they recognized her primal light, she at once trod on the auspicious clouds and rose to midair to reveal her true form, the one which carried the fish basket. Pilgrim rushed up there also to say to her, bowing, "Bodhisattva, pardon us for not receiving you properly. We were desperately trying to rescue our master and we had no idea that the Bodhisattva was descending to earth. Our present demonic ordeal is hard to overcome indeed, and we beg the Bodhisattva to help us." "This monster-spirit," said the Bodhisattva, "is most formidable. Those tridents of hers happen to be two front claws, and what gave you such a painful stab is actually a stinger on her tail. It's called the Horse-Felling Poison, for she herself is a scorpion spirit. Once upon a time she happened to be listening to a lecture in the Thunderclap Monastery. When Tathāgata saw her, he wanted to push her away with his hand, but she turned around and gave the left thumb of the Buddha a stab. Even Tathāgata found the pain unbearable! When he ordered the arhats to seize her, she fled here. If you want to rescue the T'ang monk, you must find a special friend of mine, for even I cannot go near her." Bowing again, Pilgrim said, "I beg the Bodhisattva to reveal to whom it is that your disciple should go to ask for assistance." "Go to the East Heavenly Gate," replied the Bodhisattva, "and ask for help from the Star Lord Orionis[3] in the Luminescent Palace. He is the one to subdue this monster-spirit." When she finished speaking, she changed into a beam of golden light to return to South Sea.

Dropping down from the clouds, the Great Sage Sun said to Pa-chieh and Sha Monk, "Relax, Brothers, we've found someone to rescue Master." "From where?" asked Sha Monk, and Pilgrim replied, "Just now the Bodhisattva told me to seek the assistance of the Star Lord Orionis. Old Monkey will go immediately." With pouting lips, Pa-chieh grunted: "Elder Brother, please ask the god for some medicine for the pain." "No need for medicine," said Pilgrim with a laugh. "After one night, the pain will go away like mine." "Stop talking," said Sha Monk. "Go quickly!"

Dear Pilgrim! Mounting his cloud-somersault, he arrived instantly at the East Heavenly Gate, where he was met by the Devarāja Virūḍhaka. "Great Sage," said the devarāja, bowing, "where are you going?" "On our way to acquire scriptures in the West," replied Pilgrim, "the T'ang monk ran into another demonic obstacle. I must go to the Luminescent Palace to find the Star God of the Rising Sun." As he spoke, T'ao, Chang, Hsin, and Têng, the four Grand Marshals, also approached him to ask where he was going. "I have to find the Star Lord Orionis," said Pilgrim, "and ask him to rescue my master from a monster-spirit." One of the grand marshals said, "By the decree of the Jade Emperor this morning, the god went to patrol the Star-Gazing Terrace." "Is that true?" asked Pilgrim. "All of us humble warriors," replied Grand Marshal Hsin, "left the Dipper Palace with him at the same time. Would we dare speak falsehood?" "It has been a long time," said Grand Marshal T'ao, "and he might be back already. The Great Sage should go to the Luminescent Palace first, and if he's not there, then you can go to the Star-Gazing Terrace."

Delighted, the Great Sage took leave of them and arrived at the gate of the Luminescent Palace. Indeed, there was no one in sight, and as he turned to leave, he saw a troop of soldiers approaching, followed by the god who still had on his court regalia made of golden threads. Look at

His cap of five folds ablaze with gold;
His court tablet of most lustrous jade.
A seven-star sword, cloud patterned, hung from his robe;
An eight-treasure belt, lucent, wrapped around his waist.
His pendant jangled as if striking a tune;
It rang like a bell in a strong gust of wind.
Kingfisher fans parted and Orionis came
As celestial fragrance the courtyard filled.

Those soldiers walking in front saw Pilgrim standing outside the Luminescent Palace, and they turned quickly to report: "My lord, the Great Sage Sun is here." Stopping his cloud and straightening his court attire, the god ordered the soldiers to stand on both sides in two rows while he went forward to salute his visitor, saying, "Why has the Great Sage come here?" "I have come here," replied Pilgrim, "especially to ask you to save my master from an ordeal." "Which ordeal," asked the god, "and where?" "In the Cave of the Lute at the Toxic Foe Mountain," Pilgrim answered, "which is located in the State of Western Liang." "What sort of monster is there in the cave," asked the god again, "that has made it necessary for you to call on this humble deity?"

Pilgrim said, "Just now the Bodhisattva Kuan-yin, in her epiphany, revealed to us that it was a scorpion spirit. She told us further that only you, sir, could overcome it. That is why I have come to call on you." "I should first go back and report to the Jade Emperor," said the god, "but the Great Sage is already here, and you have, moreover, the Bodhisattva's recommendation. Since I don't want to cause you delay, I dare not ask you for tea. I shall go with you to subdue the monster-spirit first before I report to the Throne."

When the Great Sage heard this, he at once went out of the East Heavenly Gate with the god and sped to the State of Western Liang. Seeing the mountain ahead, Pilgrim pointed at it and said, "This is it." The god lowered his cloud and walked with Pilgrim up to the stone screen beneath the mountain slope. When Sha Monk saw them, he said, "Second Elder Brother, please rise. Big Brother has brought back the star god." His lips still pouting, Idiot said, "Pardon! Pardon! I'm ill, and I cannot salute you." "You are a man who practices self-cultivation," said the star god. "What kind of sickness do you have?" "Earlier in the morning," replied Pa-chieh, "we fought with the monster-spirit, who gave me a stab on my lip. It still hurts." The star god said, "Come up here, and I'll cure it for you." Taking his hand away from his snout, Idiot said, "I beg you to cure it, and I'll thank you most heartily." The star god used his hand to give Pa-chieh's lip a stroke before blowing a mouthful of breath on it. At once, the pain ceased. In great delight, our Idiot went to his knees, crying, "Marvelous! Marvelous!" "May I trouble the star god to touch the top of my head also?" said Pilgrim with a grin. "You weren't poisoned," said the star god. "Why should I touch you?" Pilgrim replied, "Yesterday, I was poisoned, but after one night the pain is gone. The spot, however, still feels somewhat numb and itchy, and I fear that it may act up when the weather changes. Please cure it for me." The star god indeed touched the top of his head and blew a mouthful of breath on it. The remaining poison was thus eliminated, and Pilgrim no longer felt the numbness or the itch. "Elder Brother," said Pa-chieh, growing ferocious, "let's go and beat up that bitch!" "Exactly!" said the star god. "You provoke her to come out, the two of you, and I'll subdue her."

Leaping up the mountain slope, Pilgrim and Pa-chieh again went behind the stone screen. With his mouth spewing abuses and his hands working like a pair of fuel-gatherer hooks, our Idiot used his rake to remove the rocks piled up in front of the cave in no time at all. He then dashed up to the second-level door, and one blow of his rake reduced that to powder. The little fiends inside were so terrified that they fled to report: "Madam, those two ugly men have destroyed even our second-level door!" The fiend was just about to untie the T'ang monk so that he could be fed some tea and rice. When she heard that the door had been broken down, she jumped out of the flower arbor and stabbed Pa-chieh with the trident. Pa-chieh met her with the rake, while Pilgrim assisted him with his iron rod. Rushing at her opponents, the fiend wanted to use her poisonous trick again, but Pilgrim and Pa-chieh perceived her intentions and fled immediately.

The fiend chased them beyond the stone screen, and Pilgrim shouted: "Orionis, where are you?" Standing erect on the mountain slope, the star god revealed his true form. He was, you see, actually a huge, double-combed rooster, about seven feet tall when he held up his head. He faced the fiend and crowed once: immediately the fiend revealed her true form, which was that of a scorpion about the size of a lute. The star god crowed again, and the fiend, whose whole body became paralyzed, died before the slope. We have a testimonial poem for you, and the poem says:

Like tasseled balls his embroidered neck and comb,
With long, hard claws and angry, bulging eyes,
He perfects the Five Virtues forcefully,
His three crows are done heroically.
No common, clucking fowl about the hut,
He's Heaven's star showing his holy name.
In vain the scorpion seeks the human ways;
She now her true, original form displays.

Pa-chieh went forward and placed one foot on the back of the creature, saying, "Cursed beast! You can't use your Horse-Felling Poison this time!" Unable to make even a twitch, the fiend was pounded into a paste by the rake of the Idiot. Gathering up again his golden beams, the star god mounted the clouds and left, while Pilgrim led Pa-chieh and Sha Monk to bow to the sky, saying, "Sorry for all your inconvenience! In another day, we shall go to your palace to thank you in person."

After the three of them gave thanks, they took the luggage and the horse into the cave, where they were met by those maids, who knelt on both sides to receive them. "Fathers," they cried, "we are not fiends. We are all women from the State of Western Liang who have been kidnapped by this monster-spirit some time ago. Right now your master is weeping in a scented room in the rear." On hearing this, Pilgrim stared at them and saw that there was indeed no demonic aura about them. He therefore went to the rear, crying, "Master!" When the T'ang monk saw them, he was very pleased. "Worthy disciples," he said, "I have caused you a lot of trouble. What happened to that woman?" "She was a huge female scorpion," replied Pa-chieh. "We are fortunate to have received the revelation from the Bodhisattva Kuan-yin, whereupon Big Brother went to Heaven to acquire the assistance of the Star Lord Orionis. He came here and subdued her, and she has been reduced to mud by old Hog. Only then did we dare walk in here to see your face." The T'ang monk could not end his thanks to them. Then they found some rice and noodles with which they prepared a meal, after which they showed the way home to those girls who had been taken captive. Lighting up a fire, they burned out the entire cave-dwelling before they found the main road to the West once more. Thus it was that

They cut worldly ties to leave beauty and form;

The golden sea they drained to enter the mind of Zen.

We do not know how many more years they still need in order to perfect the art of realized immortality, and you must listen to the explanation in the next chapter.

Fifty-six

Spirit, in a frenzy, slays the bandits;
The Way, in confusion, expels Mind Monkey.

The poem says:
    That mind is pure when it nothing holds;
    It stays serene without a single thought.
    Firmly restrain both the ape and the horse.
    Take care to govern both spirit and sperm.
    Extirpate the Six Robbers;[1]
    Awake to the Three Vehicles;[2]
    Enlightenment comes when all nidānas cease.
    Depraved forms destroyed, to the true realm you rise
    E'er to enjoy the West's eternal bliss.

We were telling you about our Tripitaka T'ang, who, with such grim determination that he would have bitten through an iron nail, had managed to preserve his body from ruin. Moreover, he was fortunate enough to have had Pilgrim and his other assistants slaughter the scorpion spirit and rescue him from the Cave of the Lute. As they set out on their journey, it was the season of clear, clement weather again, when

    Warm breezes often waft the wild-orchid scent;
    Young bamboos cool off as the cleansing rain stops.
    None picks the moxa leaves all o'er the hills;
    Rush flowers fill the streams to display their hues.
    Bright pomegranates please the wandering bees.
    Yellow birds bustle in the brook's willow-shade.
    Rice-cakes[3] are not wrapped on such a long journey
    Though dragon boats now mourn at Mi-lo Stream.

As master and disciples enjoyed this scenery of the Double Fifth Festival season when the sun was high in the sky, they found once more a tall mountain blocking their path. Reining in his horse, the elder turned his head to address his disciples: "Wu-k'ung, there's a mountain ahead of us. I fear that it may breed fiends. Please be careful."

"Please don't worry, Master," replied Pilgrim. "We make submission to the faith in complete obedience. Why worry about fiends?"
Delighted by what he heard, the elder urged his horse forward, and in
a little while they arrived at a tall ledge on the mountain. This was
what they saw as they looked around:

The peak's pines and cedars join the clouds in blue;
Wild creepers hang on the cliff's briars and thorns.
Ten thousand feet, lofty—
A thousand tiers, sheer hanging—
Ten thousand feet of lofty, rugged peak;
A thousand tiers of sheer, hanging buff.
Jade-green moss and lichen on dark rocks spread;
Large forests formed by tall junipers and elms.
Deep in the forest,
Listen to the birds,
Their skillful voices making melodious songs.
The brooklet's water flows like splashing jade;
The roadside's petals rest as mounds of gold.
This treacherous mount
So hard to scale!
Walk ten steps and not even one is flat!
Foxes and deer in pairs the traveler meets;
He faces in twos black apes and white fawns.
All at once there's a fearsome tiger-roar,
Or the crane-cry that reaches Heaven's court.
Yellow plums, red apricots most worthy for food,
And nameless grass and flowers that bloom in the wilds.

The four of them entered the mountain and journeyed slowly for a
long time. After they passed the summit, they went down the west
slope until they came to a piece of level ground. Attempting to show
off his energy, Chu Pa-chieh asked Sha Monk to pole the luggage
while he raised high his muckrake with both his hands and went
forward to drive the horse. The horse, however, was not at all afraid
of him; though Pa-chieh whooped and hollered, he kept on trotting
slowly. "Brother," said Pilgrim, "why are you driving him? Let him
walk slowly." "It's getting late," answered Pa-chieh, "and we've been
walking for a whole day since we ascended this mountain. I'm getting
hungry. Let's hurry and see if we can find a house where we can beg
some food." When Pilgrim heard this, he said, "In that case, let me

make him run." He waved the golden-hooped rod once and gave a shout: immediately, the horse shot away like an arrow on the level road. For what reason, you say, is the horse afraid of Pilgrim and not of Pa-chieh? Pilgrim, you see, was appointed an official, the title being pi-ma-wên, at the Imperial stable in Heaven by the Jade Emperor five hundred years ago. Ever since that time, horses have been afraid of apes. Unable to hang on to the reins, our elder at this moment could only cling to the saddle and allow the horse to go in a gallop some twenty miles before it slowed again as it came upon some open fields.

At that moment, a sudden clang of gongs brought out from both sides of the road some thirty men, all armed with spears, scimitars, staffs, and rods. They barred the way and cried, "Monk! Where are you off to?" The T'ang monk was so terrified and shaking so violently that he fell down from the horse. Crouching in the bushes by the road, he could only say: "Great kings, spare me! Please spare me!" Two burly men at the head of the band said, "We won't hit you, but you must leave us your travel money." Only then did the elder realize that these were bandits. As he got up slowly, he stole a glance at them and saw that

One had a green face with fangs beating Jupiter's;
One had round and bulging eyes like Death himself.
Their temples' red hair seemed like soaring flames;
Like pins stuck to their chins were their yellow beards.
The two had striped tiger-skin caps on their heads
And sable battle kilts around their waists.
One held in his hands a wolf-teeth club,
And on one's shoulder rested a knotty staff.
Indeed, this one was no less than a hill-pawing tiger!
Truly, that one looked like a dragon darting out of water!

When he saw how ferocious they were, Tripitaka had no choice but to get up, and pressing his palms together before him, he said, "Great kings, this humble priest is someone sent by the T'ang emperor in the Land of the East to go to the Western Heaven to acquire scriptures. Since I left our capital, Ch'ang-an, it has been many years; even if I had any travel money, I have long spent it. Those of us who have left the family live by begging. Where do I have cash? I beg the great kings to be kind and let this humble priest pass through." The two bandit chiefs drew near and said, "We have resolved to stand guard by this main road like a tiger with the sole intention of picking up some cash or money. What do you mean by kindness? If you don't have any money, take off your clothes quickly and leave us the white horse, too. We'll let you pass then." "Amitabha!" replied Tripitaka. "The robe on this poor priest has been made from cloth begged from one family and needles from another. It is a garment, in fact, that has come from patch-work begging! Wouldn't it be just like killing me if you stripped me of it? You might be valiant men in this life, but you might become beasts in the next."

Angered by what he heard, one of the bandits wielded a big rod and wanted to hit the elder, who did not say a word but thought to himself, "Alas! Now you boast of your rod, but you have little idea of my disciple's rod!"

The bandit, of course, did not permit any further discussion; lifting his rod, he started to shower the elder with blows. Now, our elder had never lied in his life before, but faced with such a dilemma, he had no choice but to mouth falsehood. "Please do not raise your hands, great kings, both of you," he said. "I have a young disciple, who should arrive any moment. He has on him several ounces of silver, which I'll be glad to give to you." "This monk," said the bandit, "can't take any pain. Let's tie him up." His followers acted at once and bound their victim with a rope, after which, he was hung high on a tree.

We tell you now about those three mischievous spirits, who were chasing the horse from behind. Laughing uproariously, Pa-chieh said, "Master has gone off so quickly! I wonder where he's waiting for us." Then he caught sight of the elder hanging on a tree in the distance, and he said, "Look at master! He should have just waited for us. But no, he's so spirited that he has to climb a tree for fun, swinging back and forth on a vine!" When Pilgrim saw that, he said, "Idiot, don't babble! Isn't master being hung up there? The two of you stay back, and let me go take a look." Dear Great Sage! He jumped up to a knoll nearby, and when he stared in front of him, he recognized at once that there was a band of bandits. Secretly pleased, he thought to himself: "Lucky! Lucky! Business is at the door!" Walking down from the knoll, he changed with one shake of his body into a young priest wearing a clerical robe. He was only about sixteen years old, and he had a blue cloth-wrap on his shoulder. In big strides, he came up to where his master was, crying, "Master, what do you have to say for yourself? Who are these bad men?" "O disciple," replied Tripitaka, "aren't you going to rescue me? Why all these questions?"

"What sort of business are they engaged in?" asked Pilgrim, and Tripitaka said, "They are highwaymen; they barred my way and asked for toll money. As I had nothing on me, they tied me up and hung me here. They are waiting for you to show up to finish the discussion with them. If nothing works, we may have to give them this horse of ours."

On hearing this, Pilgrim chuckled and said, "Master, you are so weak! There are many monks in the world, but few are as thin-skinned as you. The T'ang emperor, T'ai-tsung, sent you to see Buddha in the Western Heaven. But who told you to give away this dragon horse?" "O disciple!" said Tripitaka. "They've already tied me up like this. If they want to beat me for fun, what shall I do?" "What did you say to them anyway?" asked Pilgrim. "They threatened me with beatings," said Tripitaka, "until I had no choice but to make a confession about you."

"Master," said Pilgrim, "you are such a lark! What kind of confession did you make about me?" Tripitaka replied: "I said that you had on you some travel money, just to make them stop hitting me. It was something to get me out of a jam." "Fine! Fine! Fine!" said Pilgrim. "Thanks for doing me this favor! That's exactly the sort of confession about me I want! If you can make it seventy or eighty times a month, old Monkey will have lots of business."

When those bandits saw him chatting with his master like that, they spread out and had them entirely surrounded. "Little monk," one of them said. "Your master told us that you had some travel money on you. Take it out quickly and your lives will be spared. If you but utter half a No, both of you will die on the spot!" Putting down his cloth wrap, Pilgrim said, "Officers, don't make a clamor! There is some travel money, not much, in this wrap: about twenty shoes of gold and perhaps thirty ingots of polished silver. I haven't made a count of the small change. If you want it, take the wrap, too, but please don't hit my master. As an ancient book says:

Virtue is fundamental;

Riches are accidental.

What you want is really the most peripheral thing. We are those who have left the family, and there will be other places for us to beg. When we run into some aged person who wishes to feed and supply the monks, we will have allowances and we will have clothing. How much can we use or spend? I just hope that you will release my master, and I'll offer you everything." When those bandits heard these words, they were most pleased, all saying, "That old monk is so stingy, but this young one is quite generous." One of the chiefs gave this command: "Release him!" When that elder got his life again, he leaped on the horse; without another thought for Pilgrim, he took whip in hand and headed straight back on the road from which he came.

"You are going the wrong way!" shouted Pilgrim hurriedly. Picking up his wrap, he gave chase at once, only to be barred by the bandits. "Where do you think you are going?" said the bandit leader. "Put your money down, before I start the torture!" "As I was saying," chuckled Pilgrim, "the travel money ought to be divided into three portions." "This young priest," said a bandit chief, "is pretty cagey! Now he wants to keep a little for himself after his master's gone. All right! Take it out first and let's have a look. If there's enough, we'll let you have a tiny bit—so that you can buy some goodies to eat when you are by yourself." "Oh, dear elder brother," said Pilgrim, "that's not what I meant. You think I really have travel money? What I meant was, that gold and silver you robbed from other people you must divide with me." When the thief heard this, he became enraged. "This monk doesn't know what's good for him!" he hollered. "You are not willing to give me anything, and you ask me instead for something? Bah! Watch the beating!" He raised up his knotty staff and gave the bald head of Pilgrim seven or eight blows, but Pilgrim behaved as if nothing whatever had happened. "Dear elder brother," he said, full of smiles, "if that's how you hit people, you can hit me until next spring and I won't consider you doing it for real." Horrified, the bandit said, "This monk has quite a hard head!" "Hardly! Hardly!" said Pilgrim, chuckling. "You praise me too much! It's just passable!" Without permitting further discussion, two more of the bandits joined their leader and started to shower blows on Pilgrim. "Please calm your anger, all of you," said Pilgrim. "Let me take out something."

Dear Great Sage! He gave his ear a rub and brought out a tiny embroidery needle. "Sirs," he said, "I'm someone who has left the family, and I haven't any travel money with me. I have only this needle, which I'll be glad to give to you." "What rotten luck!" said the bandit. "We released a wealthy priest and we have caught instead this poor, bald ass! You must be quite good at tailoring, I suppose. What do I need a needle for?"

When Pilgrim heard that he did not want the needle, he waved it once in his hand and it changed immediately into a rod with the thickness of a rice bowl. Growing fearful, the bandit said, "Though this monk appears to be young, he knows magic." Sticking the rod into the ground, Pilgrim said to them, "If any of you can pick it up, it's yours." The two bandit chiefs at once went forward to try to grab it, but alas, it was as if dragonflies were attempting to shake a stone pillar. They could not even budge it half a whit! This rod, you see, happened to be the compliant golden-hooped rod, which tipped the scale in Heaven at thirteen thousand, five hundred pounds. How could those bandits have knowledge of this? The Great Sage walked forward and picked up the rod with no effort at all. Assuming the style of the Python Rearing its Body, he pointed at the bandits and said, "Your luck's running out, for you have met old Monkey!" One of the bandit chiefs approached him and gave him another fifty or sixty blows. "Your hands must be getting tired!" chuckled Pilgrim. "Let old Monkey give you one stroke of the rod. I won't do it for real either!" Look at him! One wave of the rod and it grew to about seventy feet, its circumference almost as big as a well. He banged it on the bandit, and he at once fell to the ground: his lips hugging the earth, he could not make another sound.

The other bandit chiefs shouted, "This baldy is so audacious! He has no travel money, but he has killed one of us instead!" "Don't fret! Don't fret!" said Pilgrim, laughing, "I'll hit everyone of you, just to make sure that all of you will be wiped out!" With another bang he beat to death the other bandit chief. Those small thieves were so terrified that they abandoned their weapons and fled for their lives in all directions.

We tell you now about that T'ang monk, who rode toward the east and was caught by Pa-chieh and Sha Monk. "Master," they said, "where are you going? You are heading in the wrong direction." The elder pulled in his reins, saying, "Oh, disciples, go quickly and tell your elder brother to be merciful with his rod. Tell him not to kill all those bandits." "Master, stay here," said Pa-chieh, "and let me go." Idiot ran all the way back to the spot, shouting, "Elder Brother, Master tells you not to hit people." "Brother," said Pilgrim, "since when have I hit any people?"

"Where did those bandits go?" asked Pa-chieh, and Pilgrim replied: "All of them have scattered, but there are two of them sleeping here." "Plague on you two!" said Pa-chieh, with a laugh. "You must have been up all night, if you can take hardship like this! Why not go elsewhere? Of all places, you have to sleep here!" Idiot walked up to them and took a closer look. "They are just like me," he said, "sleeping soundly with their mouths open, they are drooling just a little." "One stroke of old Monkey's rod," said Pilgrim, "has brought out their bean curd!" "How could there be bean curd in people's heads?" said Pa-chieh. Pilgrim said, "I beat their brains out!"

On hearing this, Pa-chieh ran back hurriedly to say to the T'ang monk, "They have disbanded!" "My goodness! My goodness!" said Tripitaka. "Which road did they take?" Pa-chieh said, "They have been beaten until their legs are stiff and straight. You think they can walk somewhere?" "Why, then, did you say that they have disbanded?" asked Tripitaka.

"They have been beaten to death!" said Pa-chieh. "Isn't that disbanding?" "How do they look now?" asked Tripitaka again, and Pa-chieh said, "Two gaping holes in their heads." "Untie the wrap," said Tripitaka, "and take out a few pennies. Go somewhere quickly and see if you can buy two tapes with ointment to tape them up." "You aren't serious," said Pa-chieh, laughing. "Ointment can be taped on living people for their sores or boils. How could you cure the gaping holes of dead men?" "Are they really beaten to death?" asked Tripitaka, and he became terribly upset, so much so that he began to berate Pilgrim under his breath, calling him wretched ape and miserable simian as he turned around the horse. Soon, he and his two disciples arrived at the spot where they found two bloody corpses lying beneath the mountain slope.

Unable to bear the sight, the elder at once commanded Pa-chieh: "Use your muckrake quickly and dig a hole to bury them. I'll recite for them a scroll of scripture for the dead." "You've asked the wrong man, Master," said Pa-chieh. "It was Pilgrim who killed these people, and he should be asked to bury them. Why do you make old Hog the grave-digger?" Pilgrim, however, was irritated by his master's castigations, and therefore he shouted at Pa-chieh, "You lazy coolie! Bury them quickly! A little tardiness and you, too, will get the rod!" Horri-

fied, Idiot began digging at once beneath the slope. After the hole had
reached a depth of about three feet, rocks and boulders in the ground
resisted the rake. Abandoning his tool, our Idiot resorted to his snout
to remove the rocks. When he hit the soft element again, one shove of
his snout took away about two and a half feet of dirt and two shoves
created a hole of about five feet. Thus the two bandits were buried and
a mound was raised. "Wu-k'ung," Tripitaka called out, "bring me
some incense and candles, so that I may say a prayer and recite the
scriptures." "What silliness!" said Pilgrim, pouting. "Halfway up
this mountain, when there is no village in front and no store behind
us, where can I ask for incense and candles? There's no place for us
to buy some even if we have the money." "Move aside, ape head!"
said Tripitaka spitefully. "Let me pinch some dirt to use as incense and
then I'll pray." And so,

> Tripitaka left the saddle to mourn at a rustic grave;
> The sage monk in kindness prayed to a lonely mound.

This was his supplication:

> I bow to you noble ones,
> Hear the cause of my plea:
> I am a disciple,
> A T'ang man of the East.
> By the emperor T'ai-tsung's decree.
> I'm going to the West to seek scriptures.
> I came to this place
> And met many of you,
> Natives of some region, prefecture, or district,
> Who have assembled on this mountain.
> With good words and kind
> I earnestly begged you,
> But you failed to listen
> And instead grew angry.
> By the rod of Pilgrim
> You two lost your own lives.
> I pity your corpses exposed;
> I cover you with moundfuls of dirt.
> I break bamboo for candles;
> Though lightless,
> They mean well,
> I take stones for off'rings;

Though tasteless,
They're sincere.
If you should protest at the Hall of Darkness
And dig up the past,
Remember that his name is Sun
And my name is Ch'ên.
A wrong has its wrongdoer,
And a debt its creditor.
Please don't accuse *this* scripture seeker!

"Master," said Pa-chieh, chuckling, "you have neatly passed the buck! But when he hit these people, we weren't around either."

Tripitaka indeed scattered another pinch of dirt and prayed: "Noble ones, when you file suit, file it against Pilgrim only. Pa-chieh and Sha Monk have nothing to do with this." When the Great Sage heard these words, he could no longer refrain from snickering. "Master," he said, "there's not much kindness in you, is there? Because of your enterprise of seeking scriptures, I don't know how much energy or exertion I've spent. Now I've slaughtered these two crummy thieves, and you tell them instead to go file suit against old Monkey. Though it was I who raised my hands to kill them, I did it only for you. If you hadn't resolved to go to acquire scriptures in the Western Heaven, and if I hadn't become your disciple, how could I end up killing people at this place? Now that you have said all those things, I might as well give them a little benediction!" He lifted up his iron rod and pounded it three times on the grave mound, saying, "You plague-ridden bandits! Listen to me! You gave me seven whacks here and eight whacks there with your rods, beating me until I was sorely annoyed because your blows caused me neither itch nor pain. So, I made the mistake of beating you to death. You may go anywhere you like to file suit against me, but old Monkey is not afraid.

The Jade Emperor knows me;
The devarājas follow me;
The Twenty-Eight Constellations fear me;
The Nine Luminaries are afraid of me;
The prefectural, district, and municipal deities kneel before me;
Equal to Heaven, the guardian of Mount T'ai dreads me;
The Ten Kings of Hell once served me as my attendants;
The Five Grand Deities[4] have been my houseboys;
Whether they be the Ministers of the Five Phases,[5]

Or the Sundry Gods of the Ten Quarters,[6]
They regard me as an intimate friend.
You may go anywhere you like to lodge your complaint!"

When Tripitaka heard him using such strong language, he was quite shocked. "Oh, disciple," he said, "my prayer was meant to make you appreciate the reverence for life and become a virtuous person. Why are you taking it so hard?" "Master," replied Pilgrim, "what you've said is no joke! Anyway, let's go find shelter for the night." Still nursing his anger, the elder forced himself to mount the horse.

Thus the Great Sage Sun harbored feelings of hostility, while Pa-chieh and Sha Monk, too, were swayed by enmity. In fact, master and disciples, as they followed the main road westward, only appeared to be cordial. Presently a village north of the road came into sight, and, pointing with his whip, Tripitaka said, "Let's go over there to ask for shelter." "Very good," replied Pa-chieh.

They went up to the village where the T'ang monk dismounted. As they looked about, they found that it was a rather nice place after all. You see

The path filled with wild flowers;
The door by varied trees shrouded.
By distant banks the mountain stream flows;
On level fields mallow and wheat grow.
Sedge and reed dew-moistened, a small gull rests.
The willow in gentle breeze, a tired bird sleeps.
Fresh cedars, pine-studded: they rival in green.
The bright hues of red smartweeds with rushes compete.
The village dogs bark;
The evening cocks crow;
When cattle are well fed, the cowherds go home.
As smoke condenses, yellow millet is cooked.
This, for a mountain home, is the time of dusk.

As the elder walked forward, he saw an old man emerging from one of the village huts. The elder immediately greeted him, and the old man asked: "Where does the priest come from?" "This humble cleric," replied Tripitaka, "is someone sent by imperial commission to seek scriptures in the Western Heaven. It is getting late as I pass through your honored region, and that is why I have come to ask for a night's lodging." With a chuckle, the old man said, "It is an enormous journey from your place to mine. How is it that you have scaled the mountains and forded the waters all by yourself?" "This humble cleric," said Tripitaka, "also has three disciples in his company."

"Where are your honored disciples?" asked the old man, and Tripitaka pointed with his hand to reply: "Those three standing near the main road." Lifting his head, the old man discovered how hideous they looked and he immediately turned to try to flee inside. He was caught by Tripitaka, however, who said, "Old patron, I beg you to be merciful. Please grant us shelter for one night." Trembling all over, the old man could hardly speak. He waved his head and his hand, saying, "No! No! No! These can't be human beings! They must be monster-spirits!"

Attempting to placate him with a smile, Tripitaka said, "Please don't be afraid, patron. My disciples are born like that. They are not monster-spirits." "Oh, my father!" cried the old man. "One is a yakṣa, one is a horse-face, and one is a thunder squire." On hearing this, Pilgrim shouted back: "The thunder squire is my grandson, the yakṣa is my great grandson, and the horse-face is my great, great grandson." When the old man heard this, his spirit left him and his soul fled; his face drained of all color, he only wanted to go inside. Tripitaka took hold of him and entered the thatched hall. Smiling again, he said, "Old Patron, don't be afraid of them. All of them are quite rude, and they don't know how to speak properly."

As he was thus trying to pacify the old man, an old woman leading a child about five or six years old walked out from the rear. "Papa," she said, "why are you fretting like that?" Only then did the old man say, "Mama, bring us some tea." The old woman indeed left the child behind to go inside and brought out two cups of tea. After he drank it, Tripitaka turned to bow to the old woman, saying, "This humble cleric is someone sent by the Great T'ang of the Land of the East to go acquire scriptures in the Western Heaven. I just arrived in your region and wanted to beg from you a night's lodging. Because my three disciples are rather ugly in their appearances, the elder of your family has been struck with false alarm." "If you are so intimidated by ugly appearances," said the old woman, "what would happen if you faced tigers or wolves?" "Oh, Mama," replied the old man, "it's all right if they look ugly, but they are more scary once they open their mouths. I made the remark that they looked like a yakṣa, a horse-face, and a thunder squire, and one of them shouted back, saying that the thunder squire was his grandson, the yakṣa his great grandson, and the horse-face his great, great grandson. I was quite terrified by what I heard."

"No! No!" said the T'ang monk. "The one who looks like a thunder squire happens to be my eldest disciple, Sun Wu-k'ung; the one with the horse-face is my second disciple, Chu Wu-nêng, and the one who looks like a yakṣa is my third disciple, Sha Wu-ching. Though they may be ugly, they have embraced the faith of utter poverty and made submission to the virtuous fruit. They are no vicious demons or ferocious fiends. Why fear them?"

Greatly relieved by what they heard, the old couple said, "Please come in, please come in." The elder walked out of the door to instruct his disciples, saying, "Just now the old man found you three most repulsive. When you go in now to meet him and his family, don't offend them. All of you should behave more courteously." "I'm both handsome and civilized," said Pa-chieh, "and I'm not sassy like elder brother." "Indeed!" chuckled Pilgrim. "You're a fine man, if it weren't for that long snout, those big ears, and that hideous face!" "Stop wrangling," said Sha Monk. "This isn't the place for you to be smart-alecks. Let's go in! Let's go in!"

Thereupon they brought the luggage and the horse inside, and after they reached the thatched hall, they made a bow before taking their seats. As she was both good and kind, the old woman took the little boy inside and then asked for rice to be cooked and a vegetarian meal to be prepared for master and disciples. After they ate, it grew dark and lamps were brought into the thatched hall so that the pilgrims could sit and chat. "Patron," asked the elder, "what is your noble surname?" and the elder said, "My surname is Yang." When asked about his age, the old man replied that he was seventy-four. "How many sons do you have?" asked Tripitaka again, and the old man said, "Only one. Just now, the one following Mama is our little grandson."

"I would like to greet your son," said the elder, "if he's willing to meet us." "That fellow," replied the elder, "is not worthy of your bow. Life is rather cruel to this old moron, because I can't seem to be able to rear him. He's no longer staying with us." "Where is he then," said Tripitaka, "and what sort of profession does he have?" "Pity! Pity!" sighed the old man, shaking his head. "If he had a profession somewhere, that would be lucky for me. Unfortunately he is wicked in thought and has no regard for his origin. All he cares for is to plunder and rob, to kill and burn. His friends are all rascals and ruffians. He went out about five days ago, and he hasn't been back since."

When Tripitaka heard this, he dared not reply, thinking to himself, "Perhaps he's one of those beaten to death by Wu-k'ung . . ." As he grew more anxious, the elder rose from his seat and exclaimed, "My goodness! My goodness! How could such fine parents give birth to such a rebellious son!" Approaching them, Pilgrim said, "Venerable Sir, such a vile and pernicious offspring can only implicate his parents in dire troubles. Why keep him? Let me go find him and slay him for you!" "I would like to send him away, too," said the old man, "but I have no other heir. Though he lacks talents, I must still leave him behind to dig my grave." Smiling, both Pa-chieh and Sha Monk said, "Elder Brother, you should mind your own business. You and I are not officials. If his family is unwilling, this affair should no longer concern us. Let us ask the patron for a bundle of hay instead so that we may make our bedding somewhere. By morning, we should be on our way." The old man got up and took Sha Monk to the rear to pick up two bundles of hay. Then they were told to rest in a barn in the rear garden. After Pilgrim led the horse and Pa-chieh poled the luggage to the barn, they retired, and we shall leave them for the moment.

We tell you now about the son of the old man Yang, who was indeed one of those bandits. After Pilgrim had beaten to death the two chiefs on the mountain slope, the thieves scattered and fled for their lives. By about the time of the fourth watch, however, they had assembled again and came to knock on the door of the Yang house. When he heard the noise, the old man put on his clothes at once and said, "Mama, he's back." "If he's here," said the old woman, "go open the door and let him in." No sooner had he opened the door when those thieves swarmed inside, all crying, "We're hungry! We're hungry!" The son of old Yang hurried inside to wake up his wife, so that she could cook some rice. As there was no more firewood in the kitchen, he had to bring back some from the rear garden. Then he asked his wife in the kitchen, "Whose white horse is that in the rear garden?" "It belongs to some monks from the Land of the East," said the wife, "who are on their way to seek scriptures. They came to ask for lodging last night, and Papa and Mama fed them dinner before they were sent to sleep in the barn back there."

When the fellow heard this, he ran out to the thatched hall in front, laughing and clapping his hands. "Brothers," he said, "we're very lucky! Our foes are in the house!" "Which foes?" asked the thieves, and the fellow replied, "The monks who killed our chiefs came to our house to ask for shelter. They are sleeping in the haystacks in our barn." "How marvelous!" said the bandits. "Let's catch these bald asses, and we'll chop each of them into minced meat. For one thing, we'll get the luggage and the horse; for another, we'll avenge our leaders." "Don't be hasty," said the fellow. "All of you should sharpen your knives right now. Wait until the rice is cooked; after we have a full meal, we can attack them together." The thieves indeed went to sharpen their knives and spears.

When the old man heard them talking like that, however, he went quietly to the rear garden and woke up the T'ang monk and his three disciples. "That fellow has led a band of his friends here," he said, "and when they discovered that you were here, they planned to harm you. Mindful of the fact that you have traveled a great distance to reach our place, this old moron can't bear the thought of your getting hurt. Pack your bags quickly, and I'll let you out the back door." When Tripitaka heard this, he shook all over as he kowtowed to thank the old man. Then he called Pa-chieh to lead the horse, Sha Monk to pole the luggage, and Pilgrim to pick up the nine-ringed priestly staff. After the old man let them out of the back door, he returned to the front and quietly went to bed once more.

We tell you now about the fellow and his companions. When they had sharpened their knives and spears and eaten their fill, it was already about the time of the fifth watch. They rushed together into the rear garden, but no one was to be seen. Quickly lighting torches and lamps, they searched all around for a long time, but not a trace could be detected. Then they found that the back door was open, and they all said, "They've escaped from the back door!" With a shout, they gave chase immediately.

Every bandit was darting forward like an arrow, and by sunrise, they caught sight of the T'ang monk. When the elder heard shouts behind him, he turned to look and discovered a band of some thirty men rushing toward him, all armed with knives and spears. "Oh, disciples," he cried, "the brigand troops are catching up with us. What shall we do?" "Relax, relax!" said Pilgrim. "Old Monkey will go finish them off!" "Wu-k'ung," said Tripitaka as he stopped his horse, "you must not hurt these people. Just frighten them away." Unwilling, of course, to listen to his master, Pilgrim turned quickly to face his pursuers, saying, "Where are you going, sirs?" "You nasty baldie!" cried the thieves. "Give us back the lives of our great kings!"

As they encircled Pilgrim, the bandits lifted their spears and knives to stab and hack away madly. The Great Sage gave one wave of his rod and it had the thickness of a bowl; with it, he fought until those bandits dropped like stars and dispersed like clouds. Those he bumped into died at once; those he caught hold of perished immediately; those he tapped had their bones broken; and those he brushed against had their skins torn. The few smart ones managed to escape, but the rest of the dumb ones all went to see King Yama!

When Tripitaka saw that many men had fallen, he was so aghast that he turned and galloped toward the West, with Chu Pa-chieh and Sha Monk hard on the horse's heels. Pilgrim pulled over one of the wounded bandits and asked: "Which is the son of old Yang?" "Father," groaned the thief, "the one in yellow." Pilgrim went forward to pick up a knife and beheaded the one in yellow. Holding the bloody head in his hand, he retrieved his iron rod and, in great strides, caught up with the T'ang monk. As he arrived before the horse, he raised the head and said, "Master, this is the rebellious son of old Yang, and he's been beheaded by old Monkey." Paling with fright, Tripitaka fell down from the horse, crying, "Wretched ape! You've scared me to death! Take it away! Take it away!" Pa-chieh went forward and kicked the head to the side of the road, where he used the muckrake to bury it.

Sha Monk, meanwhile, put down the luggage and took hold of the T'ang monk, saying, "Master, please get up." After he regained composure, the T'ang monk stood on the ground and began to recite the Tight-Fillet Spell. The head of Pilgrim was clamped so painfully tight that his entire face turned scarlet, his eyes bulged, and dizziness overtook him. Rolling on the ground, all he could mutter was: "Stop that recital! Stop that recital!" The elder, however, went on for more than ten times, and still he would not stop. Pilgrim was doing somersaults and handstands, for the pain was truly unbearable. "Master, please forgive my sins!" he cried. "If you have something to say, say it. Just stop that recital!" Only then did Tripitaka halt his recitation and say, "I have nothing to say to you. I don't want you as my follower. Go back." Kowtowing despite his pain, Pilgrim said, "Master, how is it that you are chasing me away?" "Brazen ape," said Tripitaka, "you're just too vicious! You are no scripture pilgrim. When you slaughtered those two bandit chiefs below the mountain slope yesterday, I took offense already at your want of human kindness. When we reached that old man's house last night, he was good enough to give us lodging and food, and moreover, it was *he* who opened his back door to let us escape with our lives. Though his son is no good, he has not done anything to us to deserve this kind of execution. As if that's not enough, you have taken so many lives that you have practically destroyed the sentiment of peace in this world. I have tried to admonish you so many times, but there's not a single thought of kindness in you. Why should I keep you? Be gone, quickly! Or I will start reciting the magic words once more!" "Stop it! Stop it!" cried a horrified Pilgrim. "I'm going!" He said he would go, and immediately he vanished without a trace by his cloud-somersault. Alas, thus it is that

When mind is violent, elixir will not be cooked;

When spirit's unstable, it's hard to perfect the Way.

We don't know where the Great Sage headed, and you must listen to the explanation in the next chapter.

Fifty-seven

The true Pilgrim lays bare his woes at Mount Potalaka;
The false Monkey King transcribes documents at
   Water-Curtain Cave.

We were telling you about a heavy-hearted Great Sage Sun, who rose into midair. He was about to return to the Water-Curtain Cave of the Flower-Fruit Mountain, but he was afraid that those little fiends might laugh at him, for how could he be a true hero if he could betray his own word. He thought of seeking shelter in the celestial palace, but he feared that he would not be given permission to stay there long. He next thought of the islands in the sea, but then he was ashamed to face the resident immortals. Finally, he considered the dragon palace, but he could not stomach the idea of approaching the dragon kings as a suppliant. Truly, he had absolutely no place to go, and he thought sadly to himself: "All right! All right! All right! I'll go to see my master again, for only that is the right fruit."

He dropped down from the clouds and went before the horse of Tripitaka, saying, "Master, please forgive this disciple one more time! I'll never dare work violence again. I promise I'll accept all your admonitions, and I beg you to let me accompany you to the Western Heaven." When the T'ang monk saw him, however, he even refused to reply. As soon as he reined in the horse, he recited the Tight-Fillet Spell. Over and over again, he recited it for more than twenty times until the Great Sage fell prostrate to the ground, the fillet cutting an inch into his flesh. Only then did the elder stop and say, "Why don't you leave? Why have you come to bother me again?"

Pilgrim could only reply: "Don't recite anymore! Don't recite anymore! I can spend my days somewhere, but without me I fear that you can't reach the Western Heaven." Growing angry, Tripitaka said, "You are a murderous ape! Heaven knows how many times you've brought troubles on me! I absolutely don't want you anymore. Whether I can reach there or not, it's no concern of yours. Leave quickly! If you don't, I'll start the magic word again, and this time, I won't stop—not until your brains are squeezed out!" When the Great

Sage saw that his master refused to change his mind, and as the pain
was truly unbearable, he had no alternative but to mount his cloud-
somersault once more and rise into the air. Then he was struck by the
thought: "If this monk is so ungrateful to me, I'll go to the Bodhisattva
Kuan-yin at Mount Potalaka and tell on him."

Dear Great Sage! He turned his somersault around and in less than
an hour reached the Great Southern Ocean. Lowering his auspicious
luminosity, he descended on the Potalaka Mountain and sped at once
into the purple bamboo grove. There he was met by the disciple,
Mokṣa, who greeted him, saying, "Where is the Great Sage going?"
"I must see the Bodhisattva," replied Pilgrim. Mokṣa led him to the
entrance of the Tidal Sound Cave, where the Boy of Goodly Wealth
also greeted him, saying, "Why has the Great Sage come here?" "To
bring the Bodhisattva an accusation," Pilgrim said.

When he heard the word, accusation, Goodly Wealth laughed and
said, "What a smart-mouthed ape! You think you can oppress people
just like the time I caught the T'ang monk.[1] Our Bodhisattva is a holy
and righteous goddess, one who is of great compassion, great promise,
and great conveyance, one who with boundless power saves us from
our sufferings. What has she done that you want to bring an accusation on her?" Pilgrim was already deeply depressed; what he heard
only aroused him to anger and he gave such a snarl that the Boy
of Goodly Wealth backed off at once. "You wicked, ungrateful little
beast!" he shouted. "You are so dim-witted! You were once a fiend, a
spirit, but it was I who asked the Bodhisattva to take you in. Since
you have made your submission to the Right, you have been enjoying
true liberty and long life—an age as everlasting, in fact, as Heaven's.
Instead of thanking me, how dare you be so insulting? I said that I
was going to bring an accusation to the attention of the Bodhisattva.
How dare you say that I'm smart-mouthed?" Trying to placate him
with a smile, Goodly Wealth said, "You're still an impulsive ape! I was
just teasing you. Why do you change color so suddenly?"

As they were thus conversing, a white cockatoo came into view,
flying back and forth before them for a couple of times, and they knew
that this was the summons of the Bodhisattva. Whereupon Mokṣa
and Goodly Wealth led the way to the treasure lotus platform. As
Pilgrim went to his knees to bow to the Bodhisattva, he could no
longer restrain the tears from gushing forth and he wailed loudly.
Asking Moksa to lift him up, the Bodhisattva said, "Wu-k'ung, tell me

plainly what's causing you such great sorrow. Stop crying! I'll bring
relief to your suffering and dispel your woe."

Pilgrim, still weeping, bowed again before he said, "In previous
years, when has your disciple ever consented to be snubbed by anyone? When, however, I was liberated by the Bodhisattva from my
Heaven-sent calamity, and when I took the vow of complete poverty
to accompany the T'ang monk on his way to see Buddha for scriptures
in the Western Heaven, I was willing to risk my very life. To rescue
him from his demonic obstacles was like

Snatching a tender bone from the tiger's mouth,
Scraping off one scale, live, from a dragon's back.

My only hope was to be able to return to the Real and attain the right
fruit, to cleanse myself of sins and destroy the deviates. How could I
know that this elder could be so ungrateful! He cannot recognize *any*
virtuous cause, nor can he distinguish between black and white."
"Tell me," said the Bodhisattva, "a little about the black and white."
Whereupon Pilgrim gave a thorough account of how he had beaten
to death the brigands, which provoked the misgivings of the T'ang
monk; how without distinguishing black and white, the T'ang monk
had used the Tight-Fillet Spell to banish him several times; and how
he had to come to lay bare his woes to the Bodhisattva because there
was no place on Earth or in Heaven where he could find shelter. Then
the Bodhisattva said to him: "When Tripitaka T'ang received the
imperial decree to journey to the West, his sole intention was to be a
virtuous monk, and therefore he most certainly would not lightly
take away a human life. With your limitless magic power, why should
you beat to death these many bandits? The bandits are no good, to be
sure, but they are, after all, human beings and they don't deserve
such punishment. They are not like those fiendish fowl or monstrous
beasts, those demons or griffins. If you kill or slaughter those things,
it's your merit, but when you take human lives, then it's your wickedness. Just frighten them away, and you would still be able to protect
your master. In my opinion, therefore, you have not acted in a
virtuous manner."

Still tearful, Pilgrim kowtowed and said, "Though I may not have
acted in a virtuous manner, I should have been given a chance to use
my merit to atone for my sins. I don't deserve to be banished like this.
I beg now the Bodhisattva to have compassion on me and recite the
Loose-Fillet Spell. Let me be released from the golden fillet and I'll give

it back to you. Let me go back to the Water-Curtain Cave with my life." Smiling at him, the Bodhisattva replied: "The Tight-Fillet Spell was imparted to me originally by Tathāgata, who sent me in that year to go find a scripture pilgrim in the Land of the East. He gave me three kinds of treasure: the brocade cassock, the nine-ringed priestly staff, and three fillets named the golden, the tight, and the prohibitive. I was also taught in secret three different spells, but there was no such thing as the Loose-Fillet Spell."

"In that case," said Pilgrim, "let me take leave of the Bodhisattva." The Bodhisattva asked, "Where are you going?" "To the Western Heaven," replied Pilgrim, "where I'll beg Tathāgata to recite the Loose-Fillet Spell." "Wait a moment," said the Bodhisattva, "and let me scan the fortune for you." "No need for that," said Pilgrim. "This sort of misfortune is all I can take!" "I'm not scanning yours," said the Bodhisattva, "but the T'ang monk's."

Dear Bodhisattva! As she sat solemnly on the lotus platform, her mind penetrated the three realms and her eyes of wisdom surveyed from a distance the entire universe. In a moment, she opened her mouth and said, "Wu-k'ung, your master will soon encounter a fatal ordeal. Before long, he will be looking for you, and I will tell him then to take you back so that both of you can acquire the scriptures to attain the right fruit." The Great Sage Sun had no choice but to obey; not daring to misbehave, he stood at attention beneath the lotus platform where we shall leave him for the moment.

We tell you now about the elder T'ang, who, after he had banished Pilgrim, told Pa-chieh to lead the horse and Sha Monk to pole the luggage. All four of them headed toward the West. When they had traveled some fifty miles, Tripitaka stopped the horse and said, "Disciples, we left the village at the early hour of the fifth watch, and then that pi-ma-wên made me terribly upset. After this half a day, I'm quite hungry and thirsty. Which of you will go beg me some food?" "Please dismount, Master," said Pa-chieh, "and let me see if there's a village nearby for me to do so." On hearing this, Tripitaka climbed down from the horse, while Idiot rose on the clouds. As he stared all around, he found mountains everywhere, but there was not a single house in sight. Dropping down, Pa-chieh said to Tripitaka, "There's no place to beg food. I couldn't see a village anywhere." "If there's no place to beg food," said Tripitaka, "let's get some water for my thirst." Pa-chieh said, "I'll go fetch some water from the brooklet south of the mountain." Sha Monk therefore handed the almsbowl over to him, and supporting it with his palm, Pa-chieh left on the clouds and fog. The elder sat by the road to wait for him, but after a long while, he still did not return. The bitter thirst, alas, was becoming quite unbearable, for which we have a testimonial poem. The poem says:

To nourish breath and spirit's the essential thing:
Feelings and nature are formally the same.
Ailments arise from spirit and mind distraught;
The Way's o'erturned when form and sperm decline.
When the Three Flowers fail,[2] your labor is vain;
When the Four Greats[3] decay, you strive for naught.
Earth and wood sterile, metal and water decease.
True body's sluggish, when will it perfection reach?

When Sha Monk saw how greatly Tripitaka was suffering from his hunger and thirst, and Pa-chieh still had not returned with the water, he had no alternative but to put down the wraps and tie up the white horse. Then he said, "Master, please sit here for a moment; let me go and see if I can hurry him back with the water." Tears welling up in his eyes, the elder could only nod his head to give his reply. Quickly mounting the cloudy luminosity, Sha Monk also headed for the south of the mountain.

As he sat there all by himself enduring his agonies, the elder suddenly heard a loud noise near him. He was so startled that he jumped up, and then he saw that Pilgrim Sun was kneeling on one side of the road, his two hands holding high a porcelain cup. "Master," he said, "without old Monkey, you don't even have water. This is a cup of nice, cool water. Drink it to relieve your thirst, and let me then go beg some food for you." "I won't drink *your* water!" replied the elder. "If I die of thirst on the spot, I'll consider this my martyrdom! I don't want you anymore! Leave me!" "Without me," said Pilgrim, "you can't go to the Western Heaven." "Whether I can or not," said Tripitaka, "is no business of yours! Lawless ape! Why are you bothering me again?" Changing his color all at once, that Pilgrim became incensed and shouted at the elder, "You cruel bonze! How you humiliate me!" He threw away the porcelain cup and slammed the iron rod on the back of the elder, who fainted immediately on the ground. Picking up the two blue woolen wraps, the monkey mounted his cloud somersault and went off to some place.

We now tell you about Pa-chieh, who went to the south slope of the mountain with his almsbowl. As he passed the fold of the mountain, a thatched hut, the sight of which had been blocked previously by the mountain, came into view. He walked up to it and discovered that this was some sort of human residence. Idiot thought to himself: "I have such an ugly face. They will no doubt be afraid of me and refuse to give me any food. I must use transformation . . ."

Dear Idiot! Making the magic sign with his fingers, he recited a spell and shook his body seven or eight times. At last he changed into a yellowish, consumptive monk, still rather stoutish. Moaning and groaning, he staggered up to the door and called out: "Patron,

If your kitchen has surplus rice,

Let it starved wayfarers suffice.

This humble cleric is from the Land of the East, on his way to seek scriptures in the Western Heaven. My master, now sitting by the road, is hungry and thirsty. If you have any cold rice or burnt crusts, I beg you to give us some."

Now, the men of the household, you see, had all gone to plant the fields, and only two women remained behind. They had just finished cooking lunch and filled two large bowls with rice to be sent to the fields, while some rice and crusts were still in the pot. When they saw his sickly appearance, and when they heard all that muttering about going to the Western Heaven from the Land of the East, they thought that he was babbling because of his illness. Afraid, moreover, that he might fall dead right before their door, the women hurriedly packed the almsbowl with the leftovers, crust and all, which Idiot gladly received. After he left on the road from which he came, he changed back into his original form.

As he proceeded, he heard someone calling, "Pa-chieh!" Raising his head, he found that it was Sha Monk, standing on a cliff and shouting, "Come this way! Come this way!" Then he leaped down from the cliff and approached Pa-chieh, saying, "There's lovely, clean water here in the brook. Why didn't you bail some? Where did you run off to?" "When I reached here," said Pa-chieh, chuckling, "I saw a house in the fold of the mountain. I went there and succeeded in begging from them this bowl of dried rice." "We can use that," said Sha Monk, "but Master is terribly thirsty. How can we bring back some water?" "That's easy," replied Pa-chieh. "Fold up the hem of your robe, and we'll use that to hold the rice. I'll take the almsbowl to bail some water."

In great spirits, the two of them went back to the spot by the road, where they saw Tripitaka lying down with his face hugging the earth. The reins were loosened, and the white horse was rearing up and neighing repeatedly by the road. The pole with the luggage, however, was nowhere to be seen. Pa-chieh was so shaken that he stamped his feet and beat his breast, shouting, "This has to be it! This has to be it! The cohorts of those bandits whom Pilgrim Sun beat to death must have returned to kill Master and take the luggage." "Let's tie up the horse first," said Sha Monk, and then he, too, began to shout: "What shall we do? What shall we do? This is truly the failure that comes in midway!" As he turned to call but once, "Master," tears streamed down his face and he wept bitterly. "Brother," said Pa-chieh, "stop crying. When we have reached this stage of affairs, let's not talk about that scripture business. You watch over Master's corpse, and let me ride to some village store in whatever county or district nearby and see if I can buy a coffin. Let's bury Master and then we can disperse."

Unwilling, however, to give up on his master, Sha Monk turned the T'ang monk over on his back and put his own face up to the corpse's face. "My poor master!" he wailed, and presently, the elder's mouth and nose began to belch hot air as a little warmth could also be felt on his chest. "Pa-chieh," cried Sha Monk hurriedly, "come over here. Master's not dead!" Our Idiot approached them and lifted up the elder, who woke up slowly, groaning all the time. "You lawless ape!" he exclaimed. "You've just about struck me dead!" "Which ape is this?" asked both Sha Monk and Pa-chieh, and the elder could do nothing more than to sigh. Only after he drank several gulps of water did he say, "Disciples, soon after both of you left, that Wu-k'ung came to bother me again. Because I adamantly refused to take him back, he gave me a blow with his rod and took away our blue woolen wraps."

When Pa-chieh heard this, he clenched his teeth as fire leaped up from his heart. "This brazen ape!" he said. "How could he be so insolent? Sha Monk, you look after Master and let me go to his home to demand the wraps." "Stop being so angry," said Sha Monk. "We should take Master to that house in the fold of the mountain and beg for some hot liquids to warm up the rice we managed to get just now. Let's take care of Master first before you go look for him."

Pa-chieh agreed; after having helped their master to mount up, they held the almsbowl and carried the cold rice up to the house's door, where they found only an old woman inside. Seeing them, she quickly wanted to hide. Sha Monk pressed his palms together and said, "Old Mama, we are those from the Land of the East sent by the T'ang court to go to the Western Heaven. Our master is somewhat indisposed, and that is why we have come here especially to your house to beg some hot tea or water, so that he may eat some rice." "Just now," said the old woman, "there was a consumptive monk who claimed to have been sent from the Land of the East. We have already given him some food. How is it that you are also from the Land of the East? There's no one in the house. Please go to some place else." On hearing this, the elder held onto Pa-chieh and dismounted. Then he bent low and said, "Old P'o-p'o, I had originally three disciples, who were united in their efforts to accompany me to see Buddha for scriptures at the Great Thunderclap Monastery in India. My eldest disciple, whose name is Sun Wu-k'ung, has unfortunately practiced violence all his life and refused to follow the virtuous path. For this reason, I banished him. Little did I expect him to return in secret and give my back a blow with his rod. He even took our luggage and our clothing. I must now send a disciple to go find him and ask for our things, but the open road is no place to sit. Hence we have come to ask your permission to use your house as a temporary resting place. As soon as we get back our luggage, we'll leave, for we dare not linger."

"But there *was* a yellowish, consumptive monk just now," said the old woman, "who received our food. He also claimed to be part of a pilgrimage going to the Western Heaven from the Land of the East. How could there be so many of you?" Unable to restrain his giggles, Pa-chieh said, "That was I. Because I have this long snout and huge ears, I was afraid that your family might be frightened and refuse me food. That was why I changed into the form of that monk. If you don't believe me, just take a look at what my brother's carrying in the fold of his robe. Isn't that your rice, crust and all?"

When the old woman saw that it was indeed the rice that she had given him, she no longer refused them and asked them to go inside and take a seat. She then prepared a pot of hot tea, which she gave to Sha Monk for him to mix with the rice. After the master had eaten several mouthfuls, he felt more calm and said, "Which of you will go ask for the luggage?" "In that year when Master sent him back there," said Pa-chieh, "I went to look for him. So I know the way to his Flower-Fruit Mountain and the Water-Curtain Cave. Let me go! Let me go!" "You can't go!" replied the elder. "That monkey has never been quite friendly with you, and you are so rough with your words. A tiny slip when you talk to him and he may want to hit you. Let Wu-ching go."

"I'll go! I'll go!" said Sha Monk agreeably, whereupon the elder gave him this further instruction: "You must size up the situation as soon as you get there. If he's willing to give you our wraps, just pretend to thank him and take them. If he's unwilling, be sure not to argue or fight with him. Go directly to the Bodhisattva's place at the South Sea and tell her everything. Ask the Bodhisattva to demand the luggage from him." After he had listened most attentively, Sha Monk said to Pa-chieh, "When I'm gone, you must not be slack in your care of Master. And don't cause any mischief in this family, for I fear that they would not serve you rice then. I'll be back soon." "I know," said Pa-chieh, nodding. "But you must come back quickly, whether you succeed or not in getting our things back. I don't want something like 'Hauling firewood with a pointed pole: you lose both ends!' to happen!" And so, Sha Monk made the magic sign and mounted the cloudy luminosity to head for the East Pūrvavideha Continent. Truly,

Though body's present, spirit has left its home;
The brazier's fireless, how forge th'elixir?
Yellow Hag leaves her lord to seek Metal Squire;
Wood Mother engages her teacher though he appears ill.
We know not when he'll return once he leaves,
Nor can we surmise his hour of return.
The Five Phases' mutual growth or conquest is not smooth;
They wait for Mind Monkey to enter again the pass.[4]

Only after he had traveled in the air for three nights and days did Sha Monk finally reach the Great Eastern Ocean. As the sound of waves reached his ears, he lowered his head and saw that,

With black fog swelling skyward, the dark air's dense;
The brine holds the sun, e'en the light of dawn is cold.

He was, of course, too preoccupied to enjoy the scenery. Passing the immortal island of Ying-chou, he hurried toward the Flower-Fruit Mountain, riding on the oceanic wind and tide.

After a long while, he saw towering peaks jutting up like rows of halberds and sheer cliffs like hanging screens. He dropped down on the highest summit and began to search for his way to the Water-Curtain Cave. As he drew near his destination, he began to hear a noisy din made by countless monkey spirits living in the mountain. Sha Monk walked closer and found a Pilgrim Sun sitting high on a rock terrace, his two hands holding up a piece of paper from which he was reading aloud the following statement:

Li, the Emperor of the Great T'ang in the Land of the East, now commands the sage monk, Ch'ên Hsüan-tsang, royal brother before the Throne and master of the Law, to go to India in the West, and ask for scriptures in all sincerity from the Buddhist Patriarch, Tathāgata, in the Great Thunderclap Monastery on the Spirit Mountain.

Because of grave illness invading our body,[5] our soul departed for the region of Hades. It was our good fortune to have our life span unexpectedly lengthened, and the Kings of Darkness kindly returned us to life. Whereupon we convened a vast and goodly assembly to erect a plot of truth for the redemption of the dead. We were indebted to the salvific and woe-dispelling Bodhisattva Kuan-shih-yin, who appeared to us in her golden form and revealed that there were both Buddha and scriptures in the West, which could deliver and redeem the lost souls of the dead. We have, therefore, commissioned Hsüan-tsang, master of the Law, to traverse a thousand mountains in order to acquire such scriptures. When he reaches the various states of the Western region, we hope that they will not destroy such goodly affinity and allow him to pass through on the basis of this rescript.

This is an imperial document promulgated on an auspicious day in the autumn of the thirteenth year in the Chên-kuan reign period of the Great T'ang.

Since leaving my[6] noble nation, I have passed through several countries, and in midjourney, I have made three disciples: the eldest being Pilgrim Sun Wu-k'ung, the second being Chu Wu-nêng Pa-chieh, and the third being Sha Wu-ching Monk.

After he read it aloud once, he started again from the beginning. When Sha Monk realized that it was the travel rescript, he could no longer contain himself. Drawing near, he shouted: "Elder Brother, this is Master's rescript. Why are you reading it like that?" When that

Pilgrim heard this, he raised his head but could not recognize Sha Monk. "Seize him! Seize him!" he yelled. The other monkeys immediately had Sha Monk surrounded; pulling and tugging at him, they hauled him before that Pilgrim, who bellowed: "Who are you, that you dare approach our immortal cave without permission?"

When Sha Monk saw how he had changed color and refused to recognize his own, he had little choice but to bow low and say, "Let me inform you, Elder Brother. Our master previously was rather impetuous and wrongly put the blame on you. He even cast the spell on you several times and banished you home. Your brothers did not really try to pacify Master for one thing, and for another, we soon had to look for water and beg for food because of Master's hunger and thirst. We didn't expect you to come back with all your good intentions. When you took offense at Master's adamant refusal to take you in again, you struck him down, left him fainted on the ground, and took the luggage. After we rescued him, I was sent to plead with you. If you no longer hate Master, and if you can recall his previous kindness in giving you freedom, please give us back the luggage and return with me to see Master. We can go to the Western Heaven together and accomplish the right fruit. But if your animosity is deep and you are unwilling to leave with me, please give me back the wraps at least. You can enjoy your old age in this mountain, and you will have done at the same time all of us a very good turn."

When he heard these words, that Pilgrim laughed scornfully and said, "Worthy Brother, what you said makes little sense to me. I struck the T'ang monk and I took the luggage not because I didn't want to go to the West, nor because I loved to live in this place. I'm studying the rescript at the moment precisely because I want to go to the West all by myself to ask Buddha for the scriptures. When I deliver them to the Land of the East, it will be my success and no one else's. Those people of the South Jambūdvīpa Continent will honor me then as their patriarch and my fame will last for all posterity."

"You have spoken amiss, Elder Brother," said Sha Monk, smiling, "Why, we have never heard anyone speaking of 'Pilgrim Sun seeking scriptures'! When our Buddha Tathāgata created the three canons of true scriptures, he also told the Bodhisattva Kuan-yin to find a scripture pilgrim in the Land of the East. Then she wanted us to traverse a thousand hills and go through many nations as protectors of that pilgrim. The Bodhisattva once told us that the scripture pilgrim

was originally Tathāgata's disciple, whose religious designation was
the Elder Gold Cicada. Because he failed to listen attentively to the
lectures of the Buddhist Patriarch, he was banished from the Spirit
Mountain to be reborn in the Land of the East. He was then instructed
to bear the right fruit in the West by cultivating once more the great
Way. Since it was preordained that he should encounter many
demonic obstacles in his journey, we three were liberated so that we
might become his guardians. If Elder Brother does not wish to accompany the T'ang monk in his quest, which Buddhist Patriarch would
be willing to impart to you the scriptures? Haven't you dreamt up all
this in vain?"

"Worthy Brother," said that Pilgrim, "you've always been rather
blockish! You know one thing, but you fail to perceive another. You
claim that you have a T'ang monk, who needs both of our protection.
Do you really think that I don't have a T'ang monk? I have already
selected here a truly enlightened monk, who will go acquire the
scriptures and old Monkey will only help *him*. Is there anything wrong
with that? We have, in fact, decided that we'll begin the journey
tomorrow. If you don't believe me, let me show you." He then cried:
"Little ones, ask the old master to come out quickly please." The little
fiends indeed ran inside and led out a white horse, followed by a
Tripitaka T'ang, a Pa-chieh poling the luggage, and a Sha Monk
carrying the priestly staff.

Enraged by the sight, Sha Monk cried, "Old Sand here changes
neither his name when he walks, nor his surname when he sits. How
could there be another Sha Monk? Don't be impudent! Have a taste
of my staff!"

Dear Sha Monk! Lifting high his fiend-routing staff with both his
hands, he killed the specious Sha Monk with one blow on the head. He
was actually a monkey spirit. That Pilgrim, too, grew angry; wielding
his golden-hooped rod, he led the other monkeys and had Sha Monk
completely surrounded. Charging left and right, Sha Monk managed
to fight his way out of the encirclement. As he fled for his life by
mounting the cloud and fog, he said to himself: "This brazen ape is
such a rogue! I'm going to see the Bodhisattva to tell on him!" When
that Pilgrim saw that the Sha Monk had been forced to flee, he did not
give chase. He went back to his cave instead and told his little ones to
have the dead monkey skinned. Then his meat was taken to be fried
and served as food along with coconut and grape wines. After they

had their meal, that Pilgrim selected another monkey monster who knew transformation to change into a Sha Monk. He again gave them instructions on how to go to the West, and we shall leave them for the moment.

Once Sha Monk had left the Eastern Ocean by mounting the clouds, he reached the South Sea after journeying for a day and night. As he sped forward, he saw the Potalaka Mountain approaching, and he stopped his cloud to look around. Marvelous place it was! Truly

This secret spot of Heaven,
This hidden depth of Earth,
Where a hundred springs join to bathe both sun and stars,
Where the wind blows and the moon beams her rippling light.
When the tide rises, the big fishes change;[7]
When the waves churn, the huge scorpaenids swim.
Here water joins the northwest sea,
Its billows the Eastern Ocean fuse.
Here the four seas are linked by the same pulse of Earth,
Though each isle immortal has its own fairy homes.
Speak not of P'êng-lai's everywhere.
Let's look at Cave Potalaka.
What great scenery!
The peak's bright colors show prime essence strong.
Auspicious breeze wafts moonlight beneath the ridge.
Through groves of purple bamboo the peacocks fly;
On willow-branch a sentient parrot speaks.
Jade grass and flowers are every year fair;
Gold lotus, jewelled trees grow annually.
White cranes fly up to the peak several times;
The phoenix to the mount arbor often comes.
E'en fishes will seek th'immortal arts:
To listen to scriptures they o'erleap the waves.

Descending slowly from the Potalaka Mountain as he admired the scenery, he was met by the disciple, Mokṣa, who said to him, "Sha Wu-ching, why aren't you accompanying the T'ang monk to procure scriptures? Why are you here?"

After Sha Monk returned his bow, he said, "I have a matter that requires my having an audience with the Bodhisattva. Please take the trouble to announce me." Mokṣa already knew that it had to do with his search for Pilgrim, but he did not mention it. He went instead inside first and said to the Bodhisattva, "The youngest disciple of the T'ang monk, Sha Wu-ching, is outside seeking an audience." When Pilgrim Sun heard that beneath the platform, he chuckled and said, "This has to be that the T'ang monk has met some kind of ordeal, and Sha Monk is here to seek the assistance of the Bodhisattva."

The Bodhisattva at once asked Mokṣa to call him in, and Sha Monk went to his knees to kowtow. After his bow, he raised his head and was about to tell the Bodhisattva what had happened, when all of a sudden he saw Pilgrim Sun standing on one side. Without even a word, Sha Monk whipped out his fiend-routing staff and aimed it at Pilgrim's face. Pilgrim, however, did not fight back; he only stepped aside to dodge the blow. "You brazen ape!" screamed Sha Monk. "You rebellious simian guilty of ten evil deeds! So, you are even here to hoodwink the Bodhisattva!" "Wu-ching!" shouted the Bodhisattva. "Don't raise your hands! If you have a complaint, tell it to me first."

Putting away his treasure staff, Sha Monk knelt down before the platform, and, still huffing, said to the Bodhisattva, "This monkey has performed countless violent acts along the way. The day before, he beat two highwaymen to death beneath the mountain slope, and Master already found fault with him. Little did we expect that that very night we had to live right in the bandit camp, and he slaughtered a whole band of them. As if that weren't enough, he took a bloody head back to show to Master, who was so aghast that he fell down from his horse. It was then that Master gave him a reprimand and banished him. After we separated, Master found the hunger and thirst unbearable at one place and told Pa-chieh to go find water. When he didn't return after a long while, I was told to go find him. When Pilgrim Sun saw that we both had left, he sneaked back and gave Master a blow with his iron rod, after which he took away our two blue woolen wraps. When we finally returned, we managed to revive Master, and then I had to make a special trip to his Water-Curtain Cave to demand from him the wraps. How could I know that he would change his face and refuse to recognize me? Instead, he was reciting back and forth the travel rescript of Master. When I asked him why, he said that he was no longer willing to accompany the T'ang monk. He wanted to go procure sciptures in the Western Heaven and take them all by himself to the Land of the East. That, he said, would be his sole merit, and the people would honor him as their patriarch while his fame would be everlasting. I told him: 'Without the T'ang monk, who would be willing to give you scriptures?' He said then that he had already selected a true, enlightened monk, and he brought out a T'ang monk, all right, including a white horse, followed by a Pa-chieh and a Sha Monk for me to see. '*I'm* the Sha Monk,' I said, 'so how could there be another Sha Monk?' I rushed up to this imposter and gave him a blow with my treasure staff; it turned out to be a monkey spirit. Then this ape led his followers to try to capture me, and that was when I fled and decided to come here to inform the Bodhisattva. He must have used his cloud-somersault and arrived first, and I don't know what sort of balderdash he has mouthed to dupe the Bodhisattva."

"Wu-ching," said the Bodhisattva, "don't blame another person wrongly. Wu-k'ung has been here for four days, and I haven't let him go anywhere. How could he have gone to find another T'ang monk to go fetch scriptures by themselves?" "But," said Sha Monk, "I *saw* a Pilgrim Sun in the Water-Curtain Cave. You think I'm lying?" "In that case," said the Bodhisattva, "don't get upset. I'll tell Wu-k'ung to go with you to take a look at the Flower-Fruit Mountain. Truth is indestructible, but falsehood can easily be eliminated. When you get there, you'll find out." On hearing this, our Great Sage and Sha Monk took leave at once of the Bodhisattva and left. And so, the result of their journey will be that

Before Mount Flower-Fruit black and white will be made distinct;

By the Water-Curtain Cave the true and perverse will be seen.

We don't know, however, how that will be accomplished, and you must listen to the explanation in the next chapter.

Fifty-eight

Two Minds cause disturbance in the great universe;
It's hard for one substance to make perfect rest.

After our Pilgrim and Sha Monk kowtowed to take leave of the Bodhisattva, they rose on two beams of auspicious light and departed from the South Sea. Now, the cloud-somersault of Pilgrim, you see, was much faster than the mere cloud-soaring of Sha Monk. He, therefore, wanted to speed ahead, but Sha Monk pulled him back, saying, "Elder Brother, you need not try to cover up or hide your tracks by getting there first. Let me travel right beside you." The Great Sage, of course, was full of good intentions, whereas Sha Monk at that moment was filled with suspicion.

So, the two of them rode the clouds together and in a little while, they spotted the Flower-Fruit Mountain. As they lowered their clouds to glance around, they found indeed outside the cave another Pilgrim, sitting high on a stone ledge and drinking merrily with a flock of monkeys. His looks were exactly the same as those of the Great Sage: he, too, had a gold fillet clamped to his brownish hair, a pair of fiery eyes with diamond pupils, a silk shirt on his body, a tiger kilt tied around his waist, a golden-hooped iron rod in one of his hands, and a pair of deerskin boots on his feet. He, too, had

A hairy face, a thunder god beak,
An empty jowl unlike Saturn's;
Two forked ears on a big, broad head,
And huge fangs that have outward grown.

His ire aroused, our Great Sage abandoned Sha Monk and rushed forward, wielding his iron rod and crying, "What sort of a fiend are you that you dare change into my appearance, take my descendants captive, occupy my immortal cave, and assume such airs?" When that Pilgrim saw him, he did not utter a word of reply; all he did was meet his opponent with the iron rod. The two Pilgrims closed in, and you could not distinguish the true one from the false. What a fight!

Two iron rods,
Two monkey sprites,
This fight of theirs is truly no light thing!
They both want to guard the royal brother of T'ang,
Each seeking merit to acquire great fame.
The true ape accepts the poverty faith;
The specious fiend utters false Buddhist claims.
Their magic gives them transformations vast:
They're exact equals, that's the honest truth!
One is the Equal to Heaven Sage of the unified breath of
    Composite Prime;[1]
One is a long-cultivated sentient spirit, able to shorten the
    ground.
This one is the compliant, golden-hooped rod;
That one is the acquiescent staff of iron.
They block and parry and fight to a draw;
They buck and resist and neither can win.
They join hands at first outside the cave;
Soon they rise to do battle in midair.

Treading on the cloudy luminosity, the two of them rose into the sky
to fight. On the side, Sha Monk did not have the courage to join the
battle, for he found it truly difficult to distinguish between the two of
them. He wanted very much to lend his assistance, but he feared
that he might inadvertently inflict harm on the real Pilgrim. After
waiting patiently for a long while, he leaped down from the mountain
cliff and wielded his fiend-routing staff to disperse the various fiends
outside the Water-Curtain Cave. He then overturned the stone
benches and smashed to pieces all those eating and drinking utensils
before searching for his two blue woolen wraps. They were, however,
nowhere to be seen. The cave, you see, was located actually behind a
huge waterfall, which had the entrance neatly hidden as if it were
behind a white curtain. That was the reason for the name, Water-
Curtain Cave. Sha Monk, of course, had no idea of its history or its
layout, and it was therefore difficult for him to make his search.

Unable to recover his wraps, Sha Monk again mounted the clouds
to rush up to midair. He held high his treasure staff, but he simply
dared not strike at either of the combatants. "Sha Monk," said the
Great Sage, "if you can't help me, go back to Master and tell him
about our situation. Let old Monkey do battle with this fiend all the

way to the Potalaka Mountain of South Sea so that the Bodhisattva can distinguish the true from the false." When he finished speaking, the other Pilgrim also said the same thing. Since both of them had exactly the same appearance and there was not even the slightest difference even in their voices, Sha Monk could not distinguish one from the other. He had no choice but to change the direction of his cloud and go back to report to the T'ang monk. We shall now leave him for the moment.

Look at those two Pilgrims instead! They fought as they journeyed; soon they arrived at the Potalaka Mountain in the South Sea, trading blows and insults all the time. All the continuous uproar quickly alerted the various guardian deities, who rushed inside the Tidal Sound Cave to say, "Bodhisattva, there are indeed two Sun Wu-k'ungs who have arrived, fighting!" The Bodhisattva immediately descended from her lotus platform to go out of the cave with her disciples Mokṣa, the Boy of Goodly Wealth, and the Dragon Girl. "Cursed beasts," she cried, "where do you two think you are going?" Still entangled together, one of them said, "Bodhisattva, this fellow indeed resembles your disciple. We started our battle from the Water-Curtain Cave, but we have not yet reached a decision even after such a long bout. The fleshy eyes of Sha Wu-ching were too dim and dull to tell us apart, and thus he couldn't help us even if he had the strength. Your disciple told him to go back to the road to the West and report to my master. I have fought with this fellow up to your treasure mountain because I want you to lend us your eyes of wisdom. Please help your disciple to distinguish the true from the false, the real from the perverse." When he finished speaking, the other Pilgrim also repeated the same words. The various deities and the Bodhisattva stared at the two for a long time, but none could tell them apart. "Stop fighting," said the Bodhisattva, "and stand apart. Let me look at both of you once more." They indeed let go of each other and stood on opposite sides. "I'm the real one," said one side. "He's a fake!" said the other.

Asking Mokṣa and Goodly Wealth to approach her, the Bodhisattva whispered to them this instruction: "Each of you take hold of one of them firmly, and let me start reciting in secret the Tight-Fillet Spell. The one whose head hurts is the real monkey ; the one who has no pain is specious." Indeed, the two disciples took hold of the two Pilgrims as the Bodhisattva recited in silence the magic words. At once the two of them gripped their heads and rolled on the ground, both screaming, "Don't recite! Don't recite!" The Bodhisattva stopped her recital, and the two of them again became entangled together, fighting and shouting as before. Unable to think of anything else, the Bodhisattva asked the various deities and Mokṣa to go forward to help, but the gods were afraid that they might hurt the real person and they, therefore, dared not raise their hands. "Sun Wu-k'ung," called the Bodhisattva, and the two of them answered in unison. "When you were appointed pi-ma-wên," she said, "and when you brought chaos to Heaven, all those celestial warriors could certainly recognize you. You go up to the Region Above now and they should be able to distinguish between the two of you." This Great Sage thanked her and the other Pilgrim also thanked her.

Tugging and pulling at each other, screaming and hollering at each other, the two of them went before the South Heavenly Gate. The Devarāja Virūpākṣa was so startled that he led Ma, Chao, Wên, and Kuan, the four great celestial warriors, and the rest of the divine gate attendants to bar the way with their weapons. "Where are you two going?" they cried. "Is this a place for fighting?"

The Great Sage said, "I was accompanying the T'ang monk on his way to acquire scriptures in the Western Heaven. Because I slaughtered some thieves on the way, that Tripitaka banished me, and I went to tell my troubles to the Bodhisattva Kuan-yin at the Potalaka Mountain. I have no idea when this monster-spirit assumed my form, struck down my master, and robbed us of our wraps. Sha Monk went to look for our things at the Flower-Fruit Mountain and discovered that this monster-spirit had taken over my lair. Thereafter, he went to seek the assistance of the Bodhisattva, and when he saw me standing at attention beneath the platform, he falsely accused me of using my cloud-somersault in order to cover up my faults. The Bodhisattva, fortunately, was righteous and perceptive; she didn't listen to Sha Monk and told me to go with him instead to examine the evidence at the Flower-Fruit Mountain. I discovered there that this monster-spirit indeed resembled old Monkey. We fought just now from the Water-Curtain Cave to the place of the Bodhisattva, but even she found it difficult to tell us apart. That's why we came here. Let all of you deities take the trouble of using your perception and make distinction between the two of us." When he finished speaking, that Pilgrim also gave exactly the same account. Though the various gods stared at them for a long time, they could not tell the difference. "If all of you can't recognize us," the two of them shouted, "stand aside and let us go see the Jade Emperor!"

Unable to resist them, the various deities had to let them through the Heavenly Gate, and they went straight up to the Treasure Hall of Divine Mists. Marshal Ma dashed inside with Chang, Ko, Hsü, and Ch'iu, the Four Heavenly Preceptors, to memorialize, saying, "There are two Sun Wu-k'ungs from the Region Below who have fought their way into the Heavenly Gate. They claim they want to see the Emperor." Hardly had they finished speaking when the two monkeys brawled their way in. The Jade Emperor was so taken aback that he stood up and came down the treasure hall to ask, "For what reason did the two of you enter the celestial palace without permission? Are you seeking death with your brawling before us?"

"Your Majesty! Your Majesty!" cried our Great Sage. "Your subject has already made submission and embraced the vow of poverty. I would never dare be so audacious as to mock your authority again. But because this monster-spirit has changed into the form of your subject, . . ." whereupon he gave a thorough account of what had taken place, ending with the words, "I beg you to do this for your subject and distinguish between the two of us." That Pilgrim also gave exactly the same account.

Issuing a decree at once to summon Devarāja Li, the Pagoda-Bearer, the Jade Emperor commanded: "Let us look at those two fellows through the imp-reflecting mirror, so that the false may perish and the true endure." The devarāja took out the mirror immediately and asked the Jade Emperor to watch with the various celestial deities. What appeared in the mirror were two reflections of Sun Wu-k'ung: there was not the slightest difference between their golden fillets, their clothing, and even their hair. Since the Jade Emperor found it impossible to distinguish them, he ordered them chased out of the hall.

Our Great Sage was laughing scornfully, while that Pilgrim also guffawed jovially as they grabbed each other's head and neck once more to fight their way out of the Heavenly Gate. Dropping down to the road to the West, they shouted at each other: "I'll go see Master with you! I'll go see Master with you!"

We now tell you about that Sha Monk, who since leaving them

at the Flower-Fruit Mountain, traveled again for three nights and days before he arrived at the mountain hut. After he told the T'ang monk all that had taken place, the elder was filled with regret, saying, "I thought at that time that it was Sun Wu-k'ung who gave me a blow with his rod and who robbed us of our wraps. How could I know that it was a monster-spirit who had assumed the form of Pilgrim?" "Not only did that fiend do that," said Sha Monk, "but he had some-one change into an elder, and another into Pa-chieh poling our wraps. In addition to a white horse also, there was still another fiend who changed into the likeness of me. I couldn't restrain my anger and killed him with one blow of my staff. He was actually a monkey spirit. I left in a hurry to go to inform the Bodhisattva, who then asked Elder Brother to go with me to see for ourselves back at the Water-Curtain Cave. When we arrived, we discovered that that fiend was indeed an exact copy of Elder Brother. I couldn't tell them apart and it was difficult, therefore, for me to lend any assistance. That's why I came back first to report to you." On hearing this, Tripitaka paled with fright, but Pa-chieh laughed uproariously, saying, "Fine! Fine! Fine! The P'o-p'o of our patron's house has spoken true! She said that there had to be several groups of pilgrims going to procure scriptures. Isn't this another group?"

The members of that family, old and young, all came to ask Sha Monk: "Where have you been these last few days? Did you go off to seek travel money?" "I went to the place of my Big Brother," said Sha Monk with a laugh, "at the Flower-Fruit Mountain of the East Pūrvavideha Continent to look for our luggage. Next I went to have an audience with the Bodhisattva Kuan-yin at the Potalaka Mountain of South Sea. Then I had to go back to the Flower-Fruit Mountain again before I came back here."

"What was the distance that you had to travel?" asked an old man again. "Back and forth," replied Sha Monk, "it had to be about two hundred thousand miles." "Oh, Sire," said the old man, "you mean to tell me that you have covered all that distance in these few days? You must have soared on the clouds, or you would never have made it." "If he didn't soar on the clouds," said Pa-chieh, "how could he cross the sea?" "We haven't covered any distance," said Sha Monk. "If it were my Big Brother, it would take only a couple of days for him to get there and return." When those family members heard what he said, they all claimed that their visitors had to be immortals. "We are not immortals," said Pa-chieh, "but the immortals are really our juniors!"

As they were speaking, they suddenly heard a great uproar in the middle of the sky. They were so startled that they came out to look, and they found two Pilgrims locked in battle as they drew near. On seeing them, Pa-chieh's hands began to itch, and he said, "Let me see if I can tell them apart."

Dear Idiot! He leaped into the air and cried, "Elder Brother, don't fret! Old Hog's here!" The two Pilgrims cried out at the same time, "Brother, come and beat up this monster-spirit!" The old man was so astonished by the sight that he said to himself: "So we have in our house several arhats who can ride the clouds and mount the fog! Even if I had made a vow to feed the monks, I might not have been able to find this kind of noble people." Without bothering to think of the cost, he wanted at once to bring out more tea and rice to present to his visitors. Then he muttered to himself: "But I fear that no good can come out of these two Pilgrims, fighting like that. They will overturn Heaven and Earth and cause terrible calamity who knows where!"

When Tripitaka saw that the old man was openly pleased, though he was, at the same time, full of secret anxiety, he said to him, "Please do not worry, old Patron, and don't start any lamentation. When this humble cleric succeeds in subduing his disciple and in inducing the wicked to return to virtue, he will most certainly thank you." "Please don't mention it! Please don't mention it!" said the old man repeatedly. "Please don't say anything more, Patron," said Sha Monk. "Master, you sit here while I go up there with Second Elder Brother. Each of us will pull before you one of them, and you can start reciting that little something. We'll be able to tell, for whoever has pain will be the real Pilgrim." "You are absolutely right," said Tripitaka.

Sha Monk indeed rose to midair and said, "Stop fighting, the two of you, and we'll go with you to Master and let him distinguish the true from the false." Our Great Sage desisted, and that Pilgrim also dropped his hands. Sha Monk took hold of one of them and said, "Second Elder Brother, you take the other one." They dropped down from the clouds and went before the thatched hut. As soon as he saw them, Tripitaka began reciting the Tight-Fillet Spell, and the two of them immediately screamed, "We've been fighting so bitterly already.

How could you still cast that spell on us? Stop it! Stop it!" As his disposition had always been kind, the elder at once stopped his recitation, but he could not tell them apart at all. Shrugging off the hold of Sha Monk and Pa-chieh, the two of them were again locked in battle. "Brothers," said our Great Sage, "take care of Master, and let me go before King Yama with him to see if there could be any discrimination." That Pilgrim also spoke to them in the same manner. Tugging and pulling at each other, the two of them soon vanished from sight.

"Sha Monk," said Pa-chieh meanwhile, "when you saw the false Pa-chieh poling the luggage in the Water-Curtain Cave, why didn't you take it away?" Sha Monk said, "When that monster-spirit saw me slaying his false Sha Monk with my treasure staff, he and his followers surrounded me and wanted to seize me. I had to flee for my life, you know. After I told the Bodhisattva and went back to the entrance of the cave with Pilgrim, the two of them fought in midair while I went to overturn their stone benches and scattered the little fiends. All I saw then was a huge cascade flowing into a stream, but I could not find the cave entrance anywhere nor could I locate the luggage. That's why I came back to Master empty-handed." "You really couldn't have known this," said Pa-chieh. "When I went to ask him to return that year,[2] I met him first outside the cave. After I succeeded in persuading him to come, he said he wanted to go inside to change clothes. That was when I saw him diving right through the water, for the cascade is actually the cave entrance. That fiend, I suppose, must have hidden our wraps in there." "If you know where the entrance is," said Tripitaka, "you should go there now while he is absent and take out our wraps. Then we can go to the Western Heaven by ourselves. Even if he should want to join us again, I won't use him." "I'll go," answered Pa-chieh.

"Second Elder Brother," said Sha Monk, "there are over a thousand little monkeys in that cave of his. You may not be able to handle them all by yourself." "No fear, no fear," said Pa-chieh, laughing. He dashed out of the door, mounted the cloud and fog, and headed straight for the Flower-Fruit Mountain to search for the luggage.

We tell you now instead about those two Pilgrims, who brawled all the way to the rear of the Mountain of Perpetual Shade. All those spirits on the mountain were so terrified that they, shaking and quaking, tried desperately to hide themselves. A few managed to escape first and they rushed inside the fortified pass of the nether region and reported in the Treasure Hall of Darkness: "Great Kings, there are two Great Sages, Equal to Heaven, who are fighting their way down from the Mountain of Perpetual Shade." King Ch'in-kuang[3] of the First Chamber was so terrified that he at once passed the word to King of the Beginning River in the Second Chamber, King of the Sung Emperor in the Third Chamber, King of Complete Change in the Fourth Chamber, King Yama in the Fifth Chamber, King of Equal Ranks in the Sixth Chamber, King of T'ai Mountain in the Seventh Chamber, King of City Markets in the Eighth Chamber, King of Avenging Ministers in the Ninth Chamber, and King of the Turning Wheel in the Tenth Chamber. Soon after the word had passed through each chamber, the ten kings assembled together and they also sent an urgent message to King Kṣitigarbha to meet them at the Hall of Darkness. At the same time, they called up all the soldiers of darkness to prepare to capture both the true and the false. In a moment, they felt a gush of strong wind and then they saw dense, dark fog rolling in, in the midst of which were two Pilgrims tumbling and fighting together.

The Rulers of Darkness went forth to stop them, saying, "For what purpose are the Great Sages causing trouble in our nether region?" "I had to pass through the State of Western Liang," replied our Great Sage, "because I was accompanying the T'ang monk on his way to procure scriptures in the Western Heaven. We reached a mountain shortly thereafter, where brigands attempted to rob my master. Old Monkey slaughtered a few of them, but my master took offense and banished me. I went instead to the Bodhisattva at South Sea to make known my difficulties. I have no idea how this monster-spirit got wind of it, but somehow he changed into my likeness, struck down my master in midjourney, and robbed him of his luggage. My younger brother, Sha Monk, went to my native mountain to demand the wraps, but this fiend falsely claimed that he wished to go to seek scriptures in the Western Heaven in the name of Master. Fleeing to South Sea, Sha Monk informed the Bodhisattva when I was standing right there. The Bodhisattva then told me to go with him to look for myself at the Flower-Fruit Mountain, and I discovered that indeed my old lair was occupied by this fellow. I strove with him until we reached the place of the Bodhisattva, but in truth his appearance, his speech and the like are exactly like mine. Even the Bodhisattva found it hard to distinguish us. Then we fought our way up to Heaven, and the gods couldn't tell us apart. We next went to see my master, and when he recited the Tight-Fillet Spell to test us, this fellow's head hurt just like mine. That's why we brawl down to the nether region, in hopes that you Rulers of Darkness will examine for me the Book of Life and Death and determine what is the origin of the specious Pilgrim. Snatch away his soul at once, so that there will not be the confusion of two Minds." After he finished speaking, the fiend also repeated what he said in exactly the same manner.

On hearing this, the Rulers of Darkness summoned the judge in charge of the book to examine it from the beginning, but there was, of course, nothing written down that had the name, specious Pilgrim. He then studied the volume on hairy creatures, but the one hundred and thirty some entries under the name, monkey, you see, had already been crossed out by the Great Sage Sun with one stroke of the brush,[4] in that year when he caused great havoc in the region of darkness after he had attained the Way. Ever since that time, the name of any species of monkey was not recorded in the book. After he finished examining the volume, he went back to the hall to make his report. Picking up their court tablets to show their solemn intentions, the Rulers of Darkness said to both of the Pilgrims, "Great Sages, there is nowhere in the nether region for you to look up the imposter's name. You must seek discrimination in the world of light."

Hardly had they finished speaking when the Bodhisattva Kṣitigarbha said, "Wait a moment! Wait a moment! Let me ask Investigative Hearing to listen for you." That Investigative Hearing, you see, happened to be a beast which usually lay beneath the desk of Kṣitigarbha. When he crouched on the ground, he could in an instant perceive the true and the false, the virtuous and the wicked among all short-haired creatures, scaly creatures, hairy creatures, winged creatures, and crawling creatures, and among all the celestial immortals, the earthly immortals, the divine immortals, the human immortals, and the spirit immortals resident in all the cave heavens and blessed lands in the various shrines, rivers, and mountains of the Four Great Continents. In obedience, therefore, to the command of Kṣitigarbha, the beast prostrated himself in the courtyard of the Hall of Darkness, and in a little while, he raised his head to say to his master, "I have the name of the fiend, but I cannot announce it in his presence. Nor can we give assistance in capturing him." "What would happen," asked Kṣitigarbha, "if you were to announce his name?"

"I fear then," replied Investigative Hearing, "that the monster-spirit might unleash his violence to disturb our treasure hall and ruin the peace of the office of darkness."

"But why," asked his master again, "can't we give assistance in capturing him?" Investigative Hearing said, "The magic power of that monster-spirit is no different from the Great Sage Sun's. How much power do the gods of the nether region possess? That's why we cannot capture him." "How, then, shall we do away with him?" said Kṣitigarbha, and Investigative Hearing answered: "The power of Buddha is limitless." Waking up all at once, Kṣitigarbha said to the two Pilgrims, "Your forms are like a single person, and your powers are exactly the same. If you want clear distinction between the two of you, you must go to the Thunderclap Monastery, the abode of Śākyamuni." "You are right! You are right!" shouted both of them in unison. "We'll go to have this thing settled before the Buddhist Patriarch in the Western Heaven." The Rulers of Darkness of all Ten Chambers accompanied them out of the hall before they thanked Kṣitigarbha, who returned to the Jade Cloud Palace. The ghost attendants were then told to close up the fortified passes of the nether region, and we shall leave them for the moment.

Look at those two Pilgrims! Soaring on cloud and fog, they fought their way up to the Western Heaven, and we have a testimonial poem. The poem says:

If one has two minds, disasters he'll breed;
He'll guess and conjecture both far and near.
He seeks a good horse or the Three Dukes'[5] office,
Or the seat of first rank there in Golden Chimes.
He'll war unceasing in the north and south;
He'll not keep still assailing both east and west.
You must learn of no mind in the gate of Zen,
And let the holy babe[6] be formed thus quietly.

Tugging and pulling at each other, the two of them brawled in midair as they proceeded, and finally, they reached the Thunderclap Treasure Monastery on the Spirit Vulture Mountain in the great Western Heaven.

At that time the Four Great Bodhisattvas, the Eight Great Diamond Kings, the five hundred arhats, the three thousand guardians of the faith, the mendicant nuns and the mendicant monks, the upāsakas and the upāsikās—all this holy multitude was gathered beneath the lotus seat of seven jewels to listen to a lecture by Tathāgata. His discourse had just reached the point on

The existent in the nonexistent;
The nonexistent in the non-nonexistent;
The form in the formlessness;
The emptiness in the nonemptiness.
For the nonexistent is the existent,
And the non-nonexistent is the nonexistent.
Formlessness is verily form;
Nonemptiness is verily emptiness.
Emptiness is indeed emptiness;
Form is indeed form.
Form has no fixed form;
Thus form is emptiness.
Emptiness has no fixed emptiness;
Thus emptiness is form.
The knowledge of emptiness is not emptiness;
The knowledge of form is not form.
When names and action mutually illuminate,
Then one has reached the wondrous sound.

As the multitude bowed their heads in submission and chanted in unison these words of the Buddha, Tathāgata caused celestial flowers to descend upon them in profusion. Then he said to the congregation: "You are all of one mind, but take a look at two Minds in conflict arriving here."

When the congregation looked up, there were indeed two Pilgrims locked in a clamorous battle as they approached the noble region of Thunderclap. The Eight Great Diamond Kings were so aghast that they went forward to bar the way, crying, "Where do you two think you are going?"

"A monster-spirit," replied our Great Sage, "has assumed my appearance. I want to go below the treasure lotus platform and ask Tathāgata to make distinction between us." The Diamond Kings could not restrain them, and the two monkeys brawled up to the platform. "Your disciple," said our Great Sage as he knelt before the Buddhist Patriarch, "was accompanying the T'ang monk to journey to your treasure mountain and to beg you for true scriptures. I have exerted I don't know how much energy on our way in order to smelt demons and bind fiends. Some time ago, we ran into some bandits

trying to rob us, and in truth, your disciple on two occasions did take
a few lives. Master took offense and banished me, refusing to allow
me to bow with him to the golden form of Tathāgata. I had no choice
but to flee to South Sea and tell Kuan-yin of my woes. Little did I
anticipate that this monster-spirit would falsely assume my voice and
my appearance and then strike down Master, taking away even our
luggage. My younger brother, Wu-ching, followed him to my native
mountain, only to be told by the crafty words of this fiend that he had
another true monk ready to be the scripture pilgrim. Wu-ching managed to escape to South Sea to inform Kuan-yin of everything. Whereupon the Bodhisattva told your disciple to return with Wu-ching to
my mountain, as a result of which the two of us fought our way to
South Sea and then to the celestial palace. We went also to see the
T'ang monk as well as the Rulers of Darkness, but no one could tell
us apart. For this reason I make bold to come here, and I beg you in
your great compassion to fling wide the great gate of means. Grant
unto your disciple your discernment of the right and the perverse, so
that I may again accompany the T'ang monk to bow to your golden
form in person, acquire the scriptures to bring back to the Land of
the East, and forever exalt the great faith."

What the congregation heard was one statement made by two
mouths in exactly the same voice, and none of them could distinguish
between the two Pilgrims. Tathāgata, however, was the only one who
had the perception; he was about to make his revelation when a
pinkish cloud floating up from the south brought to them Kuan-yin,
who bowed to the Buddha.

Pressing his palms together, our Buddha said, "Kuan-yin, the
Honored One, can you tell which is the true Pilgrim and which is the
false one?" "They came to your disciple's humble region the other
day," replied the Bodhisattva, "but I truly could not distinguish between them. They then went to both the Palace of Heaven and the
Office of Earth, but even there they could not be recognized. I have
come, therefore, especially to beg Tathāgata to do this on the true
Pilgrim's behalf."

Smiling, Tathāgata said, "Though all of you possess vast dharma
power and are able to observe the events of the whole universe, you
cannot know all the things therein, nor do you have the knowledge of
all the species." When the Bodhisattva asked for further revelation,
Tathāgata said, "There are five kinds of immortals in the universe,

and they are: the celestial, the earthly, the divine, the human, and the spirit. There are also five kinds of creatures, and they are: the short-haired, the scaly, the hairy, the winged, and the crawling. This fellow belongs to none of these. But there are, however, four kinds of monkeys which also do not belong to any of these ten species." "May I inquire," said the Bodhisattva, "which four kinds they are?"

"The first," said Tathāgata, "is the intelligent stone monkey, who
Knows transformations,
Recognizes the seasons,
Discerns the advantages of earth,
And is able to alter the course of planets and stars.
The second is the red-buttocked baboon, who
Has knowledge of yin and yang,
Understands human affairs,
Is adept in its daily life
And able to avoid death and lengthen its life.
The third is the bare-armed gibbon, who can
Seize the sun and the moon,
Shorten a thousand mountains,
Distinguish the auspicious from the inauspicious,
And manipulate the cosmos.
The fourth is the six-eared macaque,[7] who has
A sensitive ear,
Discernment of fundamental principles,
Knowledge of past and future,
And comprehension of all things.
These four kinds of monkeys are not classified in the ten species, nor are they contained in the names between Heaven and Earth. As I see the matter, that specious Wu-k'ung must be a six-eared macaque, for even if this monkey stands in one place, he can possess the knowledge of events a thousand miles away and whatever a man may say in that distance. That is why I describe him as a creature who has
A sensitive ear,
Discernment of fundamental principles,
Knowledge of past and future,
And comprehension of all things.
The one who has the same appearance and the same voice as the true Wu-k'ung *is* a six-eared macaque."

When the macaque heard how Tathāgata had announced his

original form, he shook with fear; leaping up quickly, he tried to flee. Tathāgata, however, at once ordered the Four Bodhisattvas, the Eight Diamond Kings, the five hundred arhats, the three thousand guardians of the faith, the mendicant monks, the mendicant nuns, the upāsakas, the upāsikās, Kuan-yin, and Mokṣa to have him completely encircled. The Great Sage Sun also wanted to rush forward, but Tathāgata said, "Wu-k'ung, don't move. Let me capture him for you." The macaque's hair stood on end, for he supposed that he would not be able to escape. Shaking his body quickly, he changed at once into a bee, flying straight up. Tathāgata threw up into the air a golden almsbowl, which caught the bee and brought it down. Not perceiving that, the congregation thought the macaque had escaped. With a smile, Tathāgata said, "Be silent, all of you. The monster-spirit hasn't escaped. He's underneath this almsbowl of mine." The congregation surged forward and lifted up the almsbowl; a six-eared macaque in his original form indeed appeared. Unable to contain himself anymore, the Great Sage Sun raised his iron rod and killed it with one blow on the head. To this day this species of monkey has remained extinct.

Moved to pity by the sight, Tathāgata exclaimed: "My goodness! My goodness!" "You should not have compassion on him, Tathāgata," said our Great Sage. "He wounded my master and robbed us of our wraps. Even according to the law, he was guilty of assault and robbery in broad daylight. He should have been executed." Tathāgata said, "Now *you* go back quickly to accompany the T'ang monk here to seek the scriptures."

As he kowtowed to thank the Buddha, the Great Sage said, "Let me inform Tathāgata, that it is certain that my master will not want me back. If I go to him now and he rejects me, it's simply a waste of effort. I beg you to recite the Loose-Fillet Spell instead so that I can give back your golden fillet. Let me return to secular life." "Stop such foolish thought," said Tathāgata, "and don't be mischievous! If I ask Kuan-yin to take you back to your master, you should have no fear that he will reject you. Take care to protect him on his journey, and in due time

When merit's done and nirvāṇa's home,
You, too, will sit on a lotus throne."

When she heard that, Kuan-yin pressed together her palms to thank the sage's grace, after which she led Wu-k'ung away by mounting the clouds. They were followed at once by her disciple, Mokṣa, and the white cockatoo. Soon, they arrived at the thatched hut, and when Sha Monk saw them, he quickly asked his master to bow at the door to receive them. "T'ang monk," said the Bodhisattva, "the one who struck you the other day was a specious Pilgrim, a six-eared macaque. It was our good fortune that Tathāgata recognized him, and subsequently he was slain by Wu-k'ung. You must now take him back, for the demonic barriers on your journey are by no means entirely overcome, and only with his protection can you reach the Spirit Mountain and see the Buddha for scriptures. Don't be angry with him anymore." Kowtowing, Tripitaka replied, "I obey your instruction."

At that moment, they heard a violent gust of wind blowing in from the east: it was Chu Pa-chieh, who returned riding the wind with two wraps on his back. When Idiot saw the Bodhisattva, he fell on his knees to bow to her, saying, "Your disciple took leave of my master the other day and went to the Water-Curtain Cave of the Flower-Fruit Mountain to look for our luggage. I saw indeed a specious T'ang monk and another specious Pa-chieh, both of whom I struck dead. They were two monkeys. Then I went inside and found the wraps, and examination revealed that nothing was missing. I mounted the wind to return here. What, may I ask, has happened to the two Pilgrims?" The Bodhisattva thereupon gave him a complete account of how Tathāgata had revealed the origin of the fiend, and Idiot was thoroughly delighted. Master and disciples all bowed to give thanks. As the Bodhisattva went back to South Sea, the pilgrims were again united in their hearts and minds, their animosity and anger all dissolved. After they also thanked the village household, they put in order their luggage and the horse to find their way to the West once more. Thus it is that

Parting in midway disturbs the Five Phases;
The fiend's defeat fuses the primal light.
Spirit returns home and Zen can be still.
The six senses subdued, elixir's made.
We do not know when Tripitaka will be able to face the Buddha and ask for the scriptures, and you must listen to the explanation in the next chapter.

Fifty-nine

Tripitaka T'ang's path is blocked at the Mountain of Flames;
Pilgrim Sun seeks for the first time the palm-leaf fan.

Of the same source are many natures and kinds.
Boundless, the sea-space.
In sum, ten thousand thoughts and cares are vain;
Each form, each kind—they're all united.
One day when work and merit are done,
The perfect dharma-nature's exalted.
Don't err and let it[1] slip away to east or west;
Tighten your hold;
Take it and place within th'elixir oven
To refine until it's red as the sun,
Bright, glowing, and brilliant:
You may then ride the dragon where'er you please.

We were telling you about Tripitaka, who obeyed the instruction of the Bodhisattva and took back Pilgrim. Along with Pa-chieh and Sha Monk, he cut asunder the two Minds and tightly shackled the ape and the horse. United in mind and effort, they pressed on toward the Western Heaven. We cannot begin to describe how time flies like an arrow, how the seasons pass like the weaver's shuttle. After the torrid summer, the frosty scenery of late autumn again appeared. You see

Thin broken clouds in a brisk west wind;
Distant cranes cry, woods frosted like brocade.
This melancholy scene
Of endless hills and streams.
The geese to north borders fly;
To south lanes black birds return.
Lonely's the wayfarer's road;
Quickly the monk's robe turns cold.

As, however, master and disciples, the four of them, proceeded, they gradually felt a stifling heat. Reining in his horse, Tripitaka said, "It's now autumn. How is it that the heat is so intense?" "You may not know of this," said Pa-chieh, "but there is, on the journey to the West, a Sūrya Kingdom.[2] It is the place where the sun sets, and that's why its popular name is 'The End of Heaven.' During the time of late afternoon each day, the king will send people up to the battlements to beat the drums and blow the bugles, in order to dilute and weaken the sound of the sea boiling. For the sun, you see, is the true fire of grand yang, and when it drops into the Western Sea, it's like flames plunging into water and creating a deafening sizzle. If there were no drums or bugles to lessen the impact, the children in the city would all be killed. With this stifling heat here, this place must be where the sun sets."

When the Great Sage heard this, he could not hold back his laughter, saying, "Idiot, don't talk nonsense. If it's the Sūrya Kingdom you're thinking of, it's much too early. When you consider the sort of delays the Master has had to face night and day, it may take him several life times—from youth to old age and back again—and even then he may not get there." "Elder Brother," said Pa-chieh, "if you say that this is not the place where the sun sets, then why is it so hot?" "There must be something wrong with the climate," said Sha Monk, "so that you have summer weather in autumn." As the three of them debated like that, they came upon several buildings by the road, all having red tiles on the roof, red bricks on the wall, red painted doors, and red lacquered-wood benches. Everything, in fact, was red. As Tripitaka dismounted he said, "Wu-k'ung, go and ask in that house and see if you can uncover the reason for the heat."

Putting away his golden-hooped rod, the Great Sage straightened out his clothes and affected a civil manner as he left the main road to walk up to the house. Just then an old man emerged from the main door,

Who wore a not quite yellow
And not quite red robe of grass cloth;
His head had on a not quite blue
And not quite black hat of bamboo-splint;
His hands held a not quite crooked
And not quite straight staff of knotted bamboo;
His feet trod on a pair of not quite new
And not quite old calf-length leather boots.
His face was like red bronze;
His beard seemed like white chains.

Two aged eyebrows topped his lustrous eyes;
One grinning mouth revealed some teeth of gold.
When he caught sight of Pilgrim all of a sudden, the old man was somewhat startled. Leaning on his bamboo staff, he shouted, "What sort of a weird creature are you, and where are you from? What are you doing here before my door?" Bowing deeply, Pilgrim said, "Old Patron, please don't be afraid of me. I'm no weird creature. This poor monk has been sent by imperial commission of the Great T'ang in the Land of the East to go seek scriptures in the West. There are altogether four of us, master and disciples. We have just arrived in your noble region, and when we feel how hot the weather is, we want very much to know what the reason is for it and what is the name of the land here. I have come especially to seek your instruction." Greatly relieved, the old man smiled and said, "Elder, please don't be offended. This old man was somewhat dim-sighted just now, and I couldn't quite recognize you." "Not at all," replied Pilgrim. Then the old man asked him again, "Where is your master?" "Over there," said Pilgrim, "the one standing on the main road south of us." "Please ask him to come! Please ask him to come here!" said the old man. Delighted, Pilgrim waved at Tripitaka, who immediately approached with Pa-chieh and Sha Monk, leading the white horse and poling the luggage. They all bowed to the old man.

When the old man saw how distinguished Tripitaka appeared and how strange Pa-chieh and Sha Monk looked, he was both startled and delighted. He had no choice, however, but to invite them inside to be seated before he asked his houseboys to serve tea and to prepare a meal. When Tripitaka heard him, he rose to thank him, saying, "May I ask the *Kung-kung*[3] why it is that such intense heat returns to the autumn of your noble region?" "Our humble region," replied the old man, "is named the Mountain of Flames. There's neither spring nor autumn here; all four seasons are hot." "Where is this mountain?" asked Tripitaka. "Is it on the way to the West?" "You can't go to the West," replied the old man, "for that mountain, about sixty miles from here, sits squarely on the main road. It's covered with flames for over eight hundred miles, and all around not even a single blade of grass can grow. If you walk on this mountain, you will turn to liquid even if you have a bronze skull and an iron body." Paling with horror, Tripitaka dared not ask another question.

Just then, a young man passed by the front door, pushing a red cart and calling, "Rice-puddings!" Pulling off one piece of hair which he changed into a copper penny, the Great Sage went out to the young man to buy his puddings. After taking the money, and without dickering over the price, the man at once untied the wrap on his cart and took out a piece of steaming hot rice-pudding to hand over to Pilgrim. When it touched the palm of his hands, Pilgrim felt as if he had received a piece of lit charcoal or glowing nail taken from the blacksmith's stove. Look at him! He switched the pudding from the left hand to the right hand and back again to the left, and all he could say was "Hot! Hot! Hot! I can't eat this!" "If you're afraid of heat," said the man, chuckling, "don't come here. It's this hot around this place." "Look, fella," said Pilgrim, "you're not quite reasonable. The proverb says,

Without heat or cold,

Five grains will not grow.

But the heat of this place is intense! Where do you get your flour for the pudding?" The man said,

If you rice-pudding flour desire,

Immortal Iron-Fan inquire.

"What has Immortal Iron-Fan got to do with it?" asked Pilgrim. The man said, "That Immortal Iron-Fan happens to have a palm-leaf fan. If he lets you have it, one wave of the fan will extinguish the fire; the second will produce a breeze, and the third will start the rain. Only then can we sow and reap in due seasons, and that is how we produce the five grains. Without the immortal and the fan, not a blade of grass will grow in this region."

On hearing this, Pilgrim dashed inside and handed the piece of rice-pudding to Tripitaka, saying, "Relax, Master! Don't get anxious before you have to. Eat the pudding first, and I'll tell you something." Holding the pudding in his hand, the elder said to the old man of the house, "*Kung-kung,* please take some pudding." "I haven't even served you tea or rice," answered the old man. "Would I dare eat your pudding?" Smiling, Pilgrim said, "Dear Sir, you need not bestow on us any tea or rice. But let me ask you instead, where does the Immortal Iron-Fan live?" "Why do you ask?" said the old man.

Pilgrim said, "Just now the pudding peddler said that this immortal has in his possession a palm-leaf fan. If he lets us have it, one wave of the fan will extinguish the fire, the second will bring on a breeze, and the third will start the rain. Then the people of your region can sow and reap the five grains for your livelihood. I would like to find him and ask for the fan to extinguish the Mountain of Flames. We'll be able to pass then, and you people may also find a more stable existence by being able to plant and harvest according to the seasons."

"Yes," replied the old man, "what the peddler said was correct. But you people don't have any gifts, and I fear that the sage will be unwilling to come here." "What sort of gifts does he want?" asked Tripitaka, and the old man said, "The families of the region will seek an audience with the immortal once every ten years, with four hogs and four sheep, cash wrapped in red envelopes, rare flowers and fine fruits in season, chickens, geese, and mellow wine. After cleansing themselves in ritual baths, they will go up in all sincerity to his immortal mountain to beg him to come here to exercise his power."

"Where is that mountain located," asked Pilgrim, "and what's its name? How many miles away? I'll go ask him for the fan." "The mountain," replied the old man, "is southwest of here, and it bears the name of Jade Cloud Mountain. In the mountain there is a cave by the name of the Palm-Leaf Cave. When the believers from our region go to worship on that mountain, the round trip takes approximately a month, for the distance is slightly over one thousand four hundred and fifty miles." "That doesn't matter," said Pilgrim with a laugh, "I'll be back in no time." "Wait a moment," said the old man, "take some food first, and let us prepare you some dried goods. You will need two other companions, for there's no human habitation on that road, but there are plenty of tigers and wolves. You can't reach there in one day. It's not fun, you know." "No, no! I don't need any of that," said Pilgrim, laughing. "I'm going now!" Hardly had he finished speaking when he immediately disappeared. "Oh, Sire!" said the old man, greatly alarmed. "So you are a divine man who can soar on cloud and fog!"

We'll not continue to tell you how that family doubled its effort to be hospitable to the T'ang monk. We tell you instead about our Pilgrim, who arrived at the Jade Cloud Mountain instantly. He stopped his auspicious luminosity, and as he searched for the entrance of the cave, he heard the sound of a woodcutter chopping in the forest. When Pilgrim drew near, he heard the man chanting:

By yonder clouds my dear, old forest I'll know,
Though wild grass, rough boulders hide the path below.

When morning rain I see in western hills,
The south brook, as I return, will overflow.
Pilgrim went forward to salute him, saying, "Brother Woodsman,
please accept my bow." The woodcutter dropped his ax to return the
greeting, saying, "Where are you going, Elder?" "May I inquire,"
said Pilgrim, "whether this is the Jade Cloud Mountain?" The woodcutter replied, "It is." "There is, I understand, a Palm-Leaf Cave which
belongs to the Immortal Iron-Fan," said Pilgrim. "Where is it?"

Smiling, the woodcutter said, "We have a Palm-Leaf Cave, all
right, but there is no Immortal Iron-Fan. There is only a Princess
Iron-Fan, who also bears the name of Rākṣasī."[4] "People claim that
this immortal has a palm-leaf fan," said Pilgrim, "which can extinguish the Mountain of Flames. Is she the one?" "Exactly, exactly!"
replied the woodcutter. "Because the sage has in her possession this
treasure which can extinguish the fire and protect the families of
other regions, she is commonly called the Immortal Iron-Fan. But the
families of *our* region have no use for her; we only know her as
Rākṣasī, who also happens to be the wife of the Mighty Bull Demon
King."

When Pilgrim heard these words, he was so startled that he paled
visibly. He thought to himself: "I'm up against another fated enemy!
In a previous year, we brought to submission that Red Boy,[5] who
was said to have been reared by this woman. When I ran into his
uncle at the Child Destruction Cave of the Male-Undoing Mountain,[6]
he already was filled with desire for vengeance and absolutely refused
to give me the needed water. Now it is his parents that I have to face!
How could I possibly succeed in borrowing the fan?"

When the woodcutter saw that Pilgrim had become lost in his
deliberations, sighing to himself repeatedly, he said with a smile,
"Elder, you're someone who has left the family, and you should have
no anxious thoughts. Just follow this path eastward and you'll find
the Palm-Leaf Cave in less than five miles. Don't worry." "To tell you
the truth, Brother Woodsman," said Pilgrim, "I'm the eldest disciple
of the T'ang monk, a scripture pilgrim sent by the T'ang court in the
Land of the East to go to the Western Heaven. Some years back I had
a small feud with Red Boy, the son of Rākṣasī, at the Fiery Cloud Cave.
I feared that her hostility might cause her to refuse me the fan, and
that was the reason for my anxiety." "A man," replied the wood-

cutter, "must determine another's appearance by examining his color. You should go now with the sole purpose of borrowing the fan and not be bothered by any old grudge. I'm sure you'll succeed." On hearing this, Pilgrim bowed deeply and said, "I thank Brother Woodsman for this instruction. I'll go."

He thus took leave of the woodcutter and went up to the entrance of the Palm-Leaf Cave, where he found both of its doors tightly shut but lovely scenery outside. Marvelous place! Truly

This mountain uses rocks for bones,
And rocks form the essence of earth.
The mist keeps moisture overnight;
Lichen and moss then add fresh green.
The rugged shape soars to top Isle P'êng,
Its secluded blooms as fragrant as Ying-chou's.
Beneath a few knotty pines the wild cranes rest;
On some sad willows the orioles speak.
It's indeed an ancient spot of a thousand years,
An immortal site of ten thousand years.
The phoenix sings in the green wu-trees;
And living streams hide old dragons.
The path winds as beans and vines dangle;
The stone steps ascend with the creepers.
Apes of the peak wail, saddened by the moon rising;
Birds sing on tall trees, gladdened by the bright sky.
Two forests of bamboo, their shade cool as rain;
One path of dense flowers, thick little brocade.
From distant hills will white clouds often show;
Formless, they drift where gentle breezes blow.

Walking forward, Pilgrim cried out: "Big Brother Bull, open the door! Open the door!" With a creak, the doors opened and out walked a young girl who had in her hands a flower basket and on her shoulder a little rake. Truly

She had no adornment but only rags on herself;
Her spirit was full, for she had the mind of Tao.

Pilgrim approached her with palms pressed together and said, "Little girl, please take the trouble of announcing me to your princess. I'm actually a monk journeying to acquire scriptures. It's hard for me to cross the Mountain of Flames on this road to the West, and I've come especially to borrow your palm-leaf fan." The little girl said, "To which monastery are you attached and what is your name? Tell me and I'll announce you." "I'm a priest from the Land of the East," replied Pilgrim, "and my name is Sun Wu-k'ung."

The young girl turned around and went inside to kneel before Rākṣasī, saying, "Madam, there is a priest outside our cave by the name of Sun Wu-k'ung, who has come from the Land of the East. He wants to see you and ask to borrow the palm-leaf fan, so that he may cross the Mountain of Flames." When that Rākṣasī heard Sun Wu-k'ung, those three words, it was as if salt was added to a fire and oil was poured on flames.

Billowlike, redness swelled in her cheeks;
Savagely anger flared in her heart.

"This wretched ape!" she cried. "So, he's here today! Maids, bring out my armor and my weapons." She put on her armor at once, and holding two treasure swords of blue blade, she walked out of the cave. Pilgrim stepped aside to steal a glance at her and saw that she had on

Her head a flower-patterned scarf;
She wore a brocade priestly robe.
A belt of double tiger tendons bound her waist,
Her silk skirt slightly hitched up.
Phoenix-bill shoes, just three inches;
And trousers with knee-fringes of gold.
Her hands held treasure swords, she yelled angrily—
More fierce she seemed than the moon goddess.

As she walked out of the door, Rākṣasī shouted, "Where's Sun Wu-k'ung?" Pilgrim went forward to meet her, bowing, and said, "Sister-in-law, old Monkey's here to greet you." "Who's your sister-in-law?" hissed Rākṣasī, "and who wants your greeting?"

"The Bull Demon King of your household," replied Pilgrim, "and old Monkey once formed a fraternal alliance; there were, in fact, seven of us bond-brothers.[7] I understand that you, princess, are the consort proper of Big Brother Bull. Would I dare not address you as sister-in-law?" "Wretched ape!" said Rākṣasī. "If you have any regard for fraternal relations, then why did you ensnare my son?" Pretending not to know, Pilgrim asked: "Who's your son?" "He's the Red Boy," answered Rākṣasī, "The Great King Holy Child of the Fiery Cloud Cave by the Dried Pine Stream at the Roaring Mountain, who was brought down by you. I was just wondering where I could go to find you for vengeance, and you delivered yourself at the door. You think I would spare you?"

Smiling as broadly as he could to try to placate her, Pilgrim said, "Sister-in-law, you haven't quite probed to the depth of the matter, and you've wrongly blamed old Monkey. Your boy took my master captive and even wanted to steam or boil him. It was fortunate that the Bodhisattva Kuan-yin subdued him and rescued my master. Now he has become the Boy of Goodly Wealth at the Bodhisattva's place; having received from her the right fruit, he now undergoes neither birth nor death and he experiences neither filth nor cleanliness. He shares the same age as Heaven and Earth, the same longevity as the sun and the moon. Instead of thanking old Monkey for the kindness of preserving your son's life, you blame me. Is that fair?"

"You smart-mouthed ape!" said Rākṣasī. "Though my son was not killed, how could I ever get him back so that I could see him again?" Smiling, Pilgrim said, "If you want to see your boy, that's easy. Lend me your fan so that I can extinguish the fire. After I accompany my master across the mountain, I'll go at once to the Bodhisattva of South Sea and bring him back for you to see, and I'll return your fan at the same time. Is there anything wrong with that? At that time, you can examine him thoroughly to see if there's any harm done to him. If there is, then you can rightfully blame me. But if you find him even more handsome than ever, then you should thank me indeed."

"Monkey devil!" cried Rākṣasī. "Stop wagging your tongue. Stretch out your head and let me hack you a few times with my sword. If you can endure the pain, I'll lend you the fan. If you can't, I'll send you to see King Yama right away." Folding his hands before him, Pilgrim walked forward and said, laughing, "Sister-in-law, no need for further talk. Old Monkey will stretch out his bald head right now and you may hack me as many times as you please. You may stop when your strength runs out. But you must lend me your fan then."

Without permitting further discussion, Rākṣasī raised her hands and chopped at Pilgrim's head some ten or fifteen times. Our Pilgrim thought that it was all a game. Growing fearful, Rākṣasī turned around and wanted to flee. "Sister-in-law," said Pilgrim, "where are you going? Lend it to me quickly." "My treasure," said Rākṣasī, "is not to be lent lightly." "In that case," said Pilgrim, "have a taste of your brother-in-law's rod!"

Dear Monkey King! With one hand he caught hold of her, and with the other he took out from his ear the rod, which with one shake grew to the thickness of a bowl. That Rākṣasī, however, managed somehow to struggle free and turned to meet him with upraised swords. Pilgrim, of course, followed up at once and struck her with the rod. Before the Jade Cloud Mountain, the two of them discarded any fraternal sentiments; they were driven only by animosity. It was some battle!

The lady's a fiend deft in magic arts,
Who hates the monkey because of her son.
Though Pilgrim's anger has been aroused,
He still, for his master's sake, defers to her,
Saying at first he wants the palm-leaf fan
And not using his might on the gentle one.
Rākṣasī, foolishly, slashes with her sword,
But Monkey King wants to claim relation first.
(How could a woman battle with a man?
A man, after all, will a woman overtake.)
How fierce is this one's golden-hooped iron rod!
How thick and fast are that one's blue and frosty blades!
A blow on the face—
A slash on the head—
They bitterly fight and refuse to quit.
Left and right they parry with martial skill;
Back and front they cover most craftily.
They in their fighting are so wholly rapt
That they hardly notice the sun has set.
Swiftly Rākṣasī takes out her true fan
And one wave brings the gods and ghosts distress.

Rākṣasī fought with Pilgrim until dark; when she saw how heavy the rod of Pilgrim was and what great skills he had as a fighter, she knew that she could not prevail against him. She took out her palm-leaf fan and fanned Pilgrim once: a strong gust of cold wind at once blew him completely out of sight while she returned to her cave in triumph.

Drifting and soaring in the air, our Great Sage could not stop at all: he sank to the left but he was unable to touch ground; he dropped to

the right but he could not remain still. The wind bore him away like
  A cyclone dispatching fallen leaves,
  A stream sweeping some withered flowers.
On he tumbled for a whole night, and only by morning did he finally
drop down on a mountain. Hugging a rock on the summit with both
his hands, he rested for a long while before he looked around. Then
he recognized that this was the Little Sumeru Mountain. Heaving a
lengthy sigh, our Great Sage said, "What a formidable woman!
How in the world did she manage to send old Monkey back to this
place? I remember I once asked for the assistance of the Bodhisattva
Ling-chi here some years past to subdue the fiend Yellow Wind in
order to rescue my master.[8] The Yellow Wind Ridge is about three
thousand miles due north of here. Since I'm blown back here from
the road to the West, I must have traveled in a southeasterly direction for who knows how many tens of thousands of miles. I think I'd
better go down there to talk to the Bodhisattva Ling-chi and see if I
can find my way back."

As he thought to himself like that, he heard loud chiming bells.
He hurried down the slope to reach the temple, where he was recognized by the worker at the front gate, who immediately went inside to
announce: "The hairy-faced Great Sage who came some years back
to ask the Bodhisattva to go subdue the fiend Yellow Wind is here
again." Knowing it was Wu-k'ung, the Bodhisattva quickly left his
treasure throne to meet his visitor and to greet him, saying, "Congratulations! Have you acquired the scriptures already?" "Not quite, not
quite!" replied Wu-k'ung. "It's still too early." "If you have not yet
reached Thunderclap," said Ling-chi, "why is it that you have
returned to this humble mountain?"

Pilgrim said, "Since that year when you were kind enough to help
us subdue the fiend Yellow Wind, we have gone through countless
ordeals on our journey. We have now arrived at the Mountain of
Flames, but we can't proceed. When we asked the natives there, they
said that the palm-leaf fan belonging to an Immortal Iron-Fan could
extinguish the fire. Old Monkey went to visit her and discovered that
that immortal was in fact the wife of the Bull Demon King, the mother
of Red Boy. Because she claimed that she could no longer see her son
frequently since I had sent him to be the youth attendant of the
Bodhisattva Kuan-yin, she regarded me as her worst enemy, refused
to lend me the fan, and fought with me. When she saw how heavy

my rod was, she fanned me once with her fan and I drifted all the way back here before I dropped down. That's why I have intruded upon your abode to ask you for the way back. How many miles are there from here to the Mountain of Flames?"

Laughing, Ling-chi replied, "That woman is named Rākṣasī, and she's also called Princess Iron-Fan. Her palm-leaf fan happens to be a spiritual treasure begotten of Heaven and Earth at the back of Mount K'un-lun at the time when chaos divided. It is a finest leaf of the supreme yin, and that is why it can extinguish all fires. If a man is fanned by it, he will drift for eighty-four thousand miles before the cold wind subsides. There are only some fifty thousand miles between my place here and the Mountain of Flames. It is only because the Great Sage has the ability to halt the clouds that he is able to stop. No mortal person can possibly stand still after such a short distance!"

"Formidable! Formidable!" exclaimed Pilgrim. "How could my master overcome this hurdle?" "Relax, Great Sage," said Ling-chi. "It is actually the affinity of the T'ang monk that you have landed here. This will ensure your success." "How so?" asked Pilgrim, and Ling-chi said, "In years past when I received the instructions from Tathāgata, I was given a Flying-Dragon Staff and a Wind-Arresting Elixir. The staff was used to subdue the wind demon, but the elixir has never been used. I'll give it to you now, and you can be certain that that fan will not be able to move you. You can take the fan, extinguish the fire, and achieve your merit then." Pilgrim bowed deeply at once to thank him, whereupon the Bodhisattva took out from his sleeve a tiny silk bag in which there was the Wind-Arresting Elixir. The pellet was firmly sewn onto the underside of Pilgrim's collar with needle and thread. Then the Bodhisattva saw Pilgrim out the door, saying, "There's not time for me to entertain you. Go toward the northwest and you'll find the mountain home of Rākṣasī."

Taking leave of Ling-chi, Pilgrim mounted the cloud-somersault and went back to the Jade Cloud Mountain. In a moment he arrived and, beating the door with his iron rod, shouted: "Open the door! Open the door! Old Monkey wants to borrow the fan!"

The maid inside the door hurriedly went to report: "Madam, the person who wants to borrow the fan is here again." On hearing this, Rākṣasī became fearful, saying, "This wretched ape's truly able! When I fan someone with my treasure, he'll have to drift eighty-four thousand miles before he can stop. This ape was blown away not long ago.

How could he return so soon? This time, I'm going to fan him three or four times so that he won't be able to come back at all." She got up quickly, and after putting on her armor properly, she picked up both of her swords and walked out of the door, saying, "Pilgrim Sun, aren't you afraid of me? Are you here seeking death once more?" "Don't be so stingy, Sister-in-law," said Pilgrim, chuckling, "please lend me your fan. I'm a gentleman with an excess of honesty, not a small man who doesn't return what he borrows."

"You brazen baboon!" scolded Rākṣasī. "You're so impudent, so empty-skulled! I have yet to avenge the wrong of having my son taken. How could I possibly grant you the wish of borrowing the fan? Don't run away! Have a taste of this old lady's swords!" Our Great Sage, of course, was not to be intimidated; he wielded the iron rod to meet her. The two of them charged each other and closed in some six or seven times, when Rākṣasī's arms began to weaken while Pilgrim Sun grew stronger than ever. When she saw that the tide was turning against her, she took out the fan and fanned Pilgrim once. He, however, stood there without moving at all. Putting away his iron rod, he said to her, full of smiles, "This time is not the same as last time! You can fan all you want. If old Monkey budges a teeny bit, he's not a man!" Rākṣasī indeed gave him a couple more, but he remained unmoved. Horrified, Rākṣasī put away her treasure and dashed inside the cave, tightly shutting the doors behind her.

When Pilgrim saw her shutting the doors, he resorted to his other abilities. Tearing open his collar, he took out the Wind-Arresting Elixir and placed it in his mouth instead. With one shake of his body, he changed into a tiny mole-cricket and crawled inside through a crack in the door. There he found Rākṣasī crying, "I'm terribly thirsty! Bring me some tea." The maid attending her took up a pot of fragrant tea and filled the cup so hurriedly that bubbles welled up. Delighted by what he saw, Pilgrim spread his wings and dived right into the bubbles.

As she was extremely thirsty, Rākṣasī grabbed the tea and finished it in two gulps. Pilgrim by then already reached her stomach; changing back into his true form, he shouted: "Sister-in-law, lend me your fan!" Turning white, Rākṣasī cried, "Little ones, have you shut the front door?" "We have," they all replied. "If you have shut the door," she said, "then how is it that Pilgrim Sun is making noises in our house?" "He's making noises in your body," said one of the maids.

"Pilgrim Sun," said Rākṣasī, "where are you playing your tricks?"

"Old Monkey in all his life hasn't known how to play tricks," said Pilgrim. "What I rely on are all real competences, genuine abilities. I'm now having a little fun in my esteemed Sister-in-law's stomach! I am, as the saying goes, seeing right through you! I know how thirsty you must be, so let me send you a 'sitting bowl' to relieve your thirst." Suddenly he shoved his foot down hard and unbearable pain shot through Rākṣasī's lower abdomen, sending her tumbling to the floor and moaning. "Please don't refuse me, Sister-in-law," said Pilgrim, "I'm presenting you with an added snack[9] for your hunger." He jerked his head upward, and unbearable pain coursed through Rākṣasī's heart. She began to roll all over the ground, the pain turning her face yellow and her lips white. All she could do was to cry out: "Brother-in-law Sun, please spare my life!"

Only then did Pilgrim stop his movements, saying, "Do you now recognize me as your brother-in-law? I'll spare you for the sake of Big Brother Bull. Bring out the fan quickly for me to use." Rākṣasī said, "Brother-in-law, I have the fan. You come out and take it." "Bring it out and let me see it first," said Pilgrim.

Rākṣasī told one of her maids to hold up a palm-leaf fan and stand on one side. When Pilgrim crawled up to her throat and saw it, he said, "Since I'm going to spare you, Sister-in-law, I'll not scratch a hole in your rib-cage to come out. I'll leave through your mouth. Open it three times." That Rākṣasī did as she was told, and Pilgrim at once flew out as a mole-cricket, which then alighted on the palm-leaf fan. Rākṣasī did not even see him; she opened her mouth three times and kept saying, "Brother-in-law, please come out." Changing at once into his original form, Pilgrim took the fan in his hand and said, "I'm right here. Thanks for lending it to me." He started to walk out of the cave in big strides; the little ones hurriedly opened the door to let him out of the cave.

Mounting the clouds, our Great Sage headed back toward the east and, in a moment, arrived at his destination, dropping down beside the red-brick wall. Pa-chieh was delighted when he saw him. "Master," he shouted, "Elder Brother has returned!" Tripitaka came out of the house with the old man and Sha Monk to greet Pilgrim, and they all went back inside. Pilgrim stood the fan to one side and said, "Sir, is this the fan?" "It is, it is," said the old man.

Highly pleased, the T'ang monk said, "Worthy disciple, you have made a great merit, but you must have worked very hard to acquire this treasure." "No need to talk about the hard work," replied Pilgrim, "but who do you think is that Immortal Iron-Fan? It's actually the wife of the Bull Demon King, the mother of Red Boy, whose name is also Rākṣasī. She is also called the Princess Iron-Fan. I went to her cave to try to borrow the fan, but she wanted to settle the old score with me, hacking me a few times with her swords. I used the rod to frighten her, and that was when she brought out this thing and gave me a fan. I drifted all the way back to the Little Sumeru Mountain, where I was fortunate enough to see the Bodhisattva Ling-chi. He gave me a Wind-Arresting Elixir and pointed out to me the way back to the Jade Cloud Mountain. I saw Rākṣasī again, and when she couldn't drive me away with her fan this time, she retreated back into her cave. Old Monkey then changed into a mole-cricket to fly inside. She was just asking for tea, so I dived inside the tea bubbles and managed to get inside her stomach. When I waved my hands and feet, she had such unbearable pain that she couldn't stop calling me brother-in-law and asking me to spare her. When she was finally willing to lend me her fan, I did spare her and brought back this fan. After we have crossed the Mountain of Flames, I'll take it back to her." On hearing this, Tripitaka thanked him repeatedly. Then master and disciples took leave of the old man.

They proceeded westward for some forty miles, and they began to feel the heat growing more intense and more oppressive. "My feet are on fire!" Sha Monk could only cry. "They are killing me!" said Pa-chieh. Even the horse was trotting more rapidly than usual, but because the ground was becoming hotter all the time, they found it exceedingly difficult to go forward. "Master," Pilgrim said at length, "please dismount. And don't move, Brothers. Let me use the fan to extinguish the fire. Allow the wind and rain to cool off the earth first before we try to cross this mountain." Lifting high the fan, Pilgrim dashed up to the flames and fanned at them with all his might. On that mountain the blaze grew brighter than ever. He waved the fan a second time and the fire became more intense a hundredfold. He tried for a third time and the fire leaped ten thousand feet tall, roaring toward him. Pilgrim dashed away but already the hair on both his thighs were completely burnt off. He ran back to the T'ang monk, shouting, "Go back! Go back! The fire's coming!"

Climbing on the horse, our elder galloped toward the east, followed by Pa-chieh and Sha Monk. They retreated for some twenty miles before they rested. "Wu-k'ung," said the elder, "what happened?" "It's a mess!" replied Pilgrim, throwing the fan away. "She has tricked me!" On hearing this, Tripitaka became utterly dejected. Tears streaming down his face, he could only say: "What shall we do?" "Elder Brother," said Pa-chieh, "why did you yell for us to go back so hurriedly?" "I fanned at the mountain once," said Pilgrim, "and the blaze grew brighter. I did it a second time and the fire became even more intense. A third wave of the fan made the flames leap up ten thousand feet tall. If I hadn't run fast enough, all my hair would have been burned away." With a chuckle, Pa-chieh said, "You have often made the claim that you can be hurt neither by thunder nor by fire. How is it that you are afraid of fire now?" "Oh, Idiot!" said Pilgrim. "You just don't know anything! On those occasions, I was always prepared, and therefore I could not be hurt. Today I was only trying to extinguish the fire with the fan, and I did not even make the fire-repellant sign, nor did I use magic to protect my body. So, the hair on both my thighs is burned up."

"If the fire's so intense," said Sha Monk, "and there's no way to get to the West, what's to be done?" "Let's head for the direction where there's no fire," said Pa-chieh. "Which direction?" asked Tripitaka. Pa-chieh said, "There's no fire in the east, the south, and the north." "But which direction has scriptures?" Tripitaka asked again, and Pa-chieh said, "The West." "I only want to go where the scriptures are," said Tripitaka. Sha Monk said

Where there are scriptures, there's fire.

Where there's no fire, there are no scriptures.

We are in some dilemma!"

As master and disciples were chatting like that, they heard someone calling: "Great Sage, please do not be distressed. Take some food first before you think of what you want to do." The four of them turned to look and they saw an old man,

Who wore a wind-wafted cape

And a cap of half-moon shape;

Who held a dragon-head cane

And trod on iron-gaitered boots.

He was followed by a demon with a hawk beak and a fish jowl. The demon's head was supporting a copper pan in which were placed some steamed cakes, puddings, and rice of yellow millet. The old man stood by the road and bowed, saying, "I'm the local spirit of the Mountain of Flames. When I learned that the Great Sage and the holy monk could not proceed, I came to present you a meal." "Food is of small concern to us at the monent," said Pilgrim. "How can we extinguish this fire so that my master can cross over the mountain?" "If you want to extinguish the fire," said the local spirit, "you must ask the Rākṣasī for the palm-leaf fan." Picking up the fan from the side of the road, Pilgrim said, "Isn't this the fan? But the blaze grew bigger than ever when I fanned at it. Why?" When the local spirit saw it, he laughed and said, "This is not the real fan. You've been tricked." "How can I get the real one?" asked Pilgrim. Again bowing and smiling gently, the local spirit said,

If you want the real palm-leaf fan,

Then King Powerful you must find.

We do not know for what reason they must seek the Mighty King, and you must listen to the explanation in the next chapter.

Sixty

The Bull Demon King stops fighting to attend a lavish feast;
Pilgrim Sun seeks for the second time the palm-leaf fan.

The local spirit said, "King Powerful is, in fact, the Bull Demon King."
"So, this fire of the mountain was set by the Bull Demon King," said
Pilgrim, "and it was erroneously named the Mountain of Flames,
right?" "No, no," replied the local spirit, "but I dare not speak plainly
unless the Great Sage is willing to pardon this humble deity." "What
offense is there?" said Pilgrim. "Go ahead and tell us."

The local spirit said, "This fire originally was set by the Great
Sage." "Where could I have been at the time?" said Pilgrim, his anger
growing. "How could you babble like that? Am I an arsonist?" "You
can't possibly recognize me now," said the local spirit. "There was no
such mountain in this place originally. Five hundred years ago, when
the Great Sage caused great disturbance in the Celestial Palace, you
were caught by Illustrious Sagacity[1] and taken in custody to Lao Tzu.
He placed you inside the brazier of eight trigrams, and after the process of refinement, the reactionary vessel was opened. You jumped
out, kicking over the elixir oven in the process, and a few bricks still
on fire dropped down to this spot. They were transformed into the
Mountain of Flames. I was then the Taoist worker attending the
brazier in the Tushita Palace. Since Lao Tzu blamed me for carelessness, I was banished to become the mountain's local spirit." "No
wonder you are dressed like this!" said Pa-chieh, somewhat annoyed.
"You were actually a Taoist!"

Only half-believing what he heard, Pilgrim said, "Tell me further,
why did you say that I had to fight King Powerful?" "King Powerful,"
said the local spirit, "happens to be the husband of Rākṣasī, but he
left her some time ago and is currently residing at the Cloud-Touching
Cave of the Hoard-Thunder Mountain. A fox king of ten thousand
years used to be the cave-master there, but he passed away, leaving
behind a daughter by the name of Princess Jade Countenance and a
vast fortune with no one to care for it. Two years ago, when she

learned that the Bull Demon King had enormous magic powers, she
was willing to give up all her wealth as dowry and take him in as her
consort. The Bull King thus abandoned Rākṣasī and hasn't paid her a
visit since. Only if the Great Sage succeeds in finding him can you
acquire the real fan. If he is willing to lend it to you, you will be able
to do three good deeds: one, enable your master to proceed on his
journey; two, eliminate the blight of fire for the people of this region;
and three, obtain a pardon for me so that I may return to Lao Tzu in
Heaven." "Where is this Hoard-Thunder Mountain," asked Pilgrim,
"and how far away is it?" "Due south of here," said the local spirit,
"about three thousand miles." On hearing this, Pilgrim told Pa-chieh
and Sha Monk to protect their master with care, and he gave instruction as well to the local spirit to remain and keep them company.
With a loud whoosh, he at once disappeared.

In less than half an hour he came upon a tall mountain. He lowered
his cloud and stood on the peak to look all around. It was indeed a fine
mountain:

Though not too tall,
Its top touches the blue sky;
Though not too deep,
Its roots reach the yellow spring.
Before the mountain the sun's warm;
Behind the mountain the wind's cold;
Before the mountain the sun's warm,
Though the winter plants have no knowledge of it;
Behind the mountain the wind's cold:
Thus ice, e'en in late summer, stays unmelted.
The dragon lagoon's joined by an overflowing brook;
Flowers bloom early by the cliff's tiger lair.
Water flows like countless strands of flying jade,
And flowers bloom like bunches of brocade.
Sinuous trees twist round the sinuous peak;
Craggy pines grow beyond the craggy rocks.
Truly we have
The mountain that's tall,
The cliff that's sheer,
The stream that's deep,
The flower that's fragrant,
The fruit that's pretty,

The wisteria that's red,
The pine that's blue,
The willow that's jade-green—
Their features in all climes remain the same;
Their colours stay vibrant in ten thousand years.

After he looked at this scenery for a long time, our Great Sage walked down from the pointed summit to search for the way. He did not, in truth, know quite where to turn when a lissome young woman emerged from a shady pine forest, her hand holding a twig of fragrant orchid. Hiding himself behind some boulders, the Great Sage stared at her. How did she look, you ask.

A coy, empire-toppling beauty,
In slow, sedate steps she walks.
With a face like Wang Ch'iang's,[2]
With features like a girl of Ch'u,
She seems like a flower able to speak;
She resembles a fragrant figure of jade.
Her jet black hair-bun smartly rises high;
Her eyes, mascara-greened, shine like autumn's pools.
Beneath her silk skirt tiny shoes half-appear;
From sleeves, just upturned, extend long, white wrists.
How shall we speak of such seductive airs?
Truly she has pearl-like teeth, ruddy lips,
And moth-brows soft and smooth like the River Chin;
She surpasses even Wên-chün[3] and Hsüeh T'ao.[4]

Gradually, the girl drew near to the boulders. Bowing low to salute her, the Great Sage said slowly, "Lady Bodhisattva, where are you going?" As the girl did not notice him at first, she raised her head only when she heard his voice, and all at once she discovered how ugly the appearance of the Great Sage was. Terrified, she could neither retreat nor advance, and, trembling all over, she forced herself to reply: "Where have you come from? To whom are you addressing your question?"

The Great Sage thought to himself: "If I mention the business of seeking scriptures, I fear that she may be related to the Bull King. I'd better say something like I am some sort of a relative who has come here to ask for the return of the Demon King." When the girl, however, saw that he did not reply, her color changed and she said with anger in her voice, "Who are you and how dare you question me?"

Bowing again and smiling, the Great Sage said, "I have come from the Jade Cloud Mountain. As this is my first visit to your noble region, I don't know my way. May I ask the Lady Bodhisattva whether this is the Hoard-Thunder Mountain?" "Yes," said the girl. "There is a Cloud-Touching Cave," said the Great Sage. "Where is it located?" "Why do you want to find the cave?" asked the girl. The Great Sage said, "I have been sent here by the Princess Iron-Fan of the Palm-Leaf Cave at Jade Cloud Mountain to fetch the Bull Demon King."

Enraged by this one statement, the girl grew red from ear to ear and began to scream: "That filthy slut! She's a real numskull! It hasn't been two years since the Bull King arrived in my house, and during that time, he has sent back to her God knows how many pieces of jewels and precious stones, how many bolts of silk and satin. He provides her with firewood by the year and with rice by the month so that she can enjoy her life to her heart's content. Doesn't she know shame at all? Why does she want you to fetch him now?" When the Great Sage heard these words, he knew that the girl had to be the Princess Jade Countenance. Deliberately pulling out his golden-hooped rod, he bellowed at her: "You bitch! You used your wealth to buy the Bull King. Indeed you got your man by throwing money away. Aren't *you* ashamed? And you dare castigate someone else?"

When that girl saw his savage appearance, she was so terrified that her spirit left her and her soul fled. Shaking all over, she turned and fled, while the Great Sage gave chase from behind, still shouting and hollering at her. After they went through the pine forest, the entrance of the Cloud-Touching Cave immediately came into view. The girl dashed inside and slammed the door shut. Only then did the Great Sage put away his golden-hooped rod and pause to glance about. Lovely place!

Luxuriant forest;
Precipitous cliffs;
The broken shades of wisteria;
The sweet, pure scent of orchids.
A flowing stream, gurgling jade, cuts through old bamboos;
Cunning rocks are enhanced by fallen blooms.
Mist enshrouds distant hills;
The sun and moon shine through cloud-screens.
Dragons chant and tigers roar;
Cranes cry and orioles sing.

A loveable spot of pure serenity
Where jade flowers and grass are ever bright—
No less divine than a T'ien-t'ai[5] cave,
It surpasses e'en P'êng-Ying[6] of the seas.

Let's not speak anymore of Pilgrim enjoying the scenery; we tell you instead about the girl, who ran until she perspired heavily and her heart pounded. She dashed into the library, where the Bull Demon King was quietly studying the books on elixir. Full of anguish, the girl fell onto his lap and began to wail, pinching her ears and scratching her cheeks. The Bull King smiled broadly and tried to placate her, saying, "Fair Lady, don't be distressed. What's the matter?"

"Wretched demon!" cried the girl, jumping up and down. "You've just about killed me!" "Why are you scolding me?" said the Bull King, laughing. "Because I lost my parents," said the girl, "I took you in so that I could have protection and care. You have the reputation in the world of being a hero, but you are actually a henpecked nitwit!" On hearing this, the Bull King embraced her and said, "Fair Lady, where have I done wrong? Tell me slowly, and I'll apologize."

"Just now," said the girl, "I was taking a leisurely stroll outside the cave beneath the flowers to pick my orchids. I was stunned by a hairy-faced monk with a thunder god beak who suddenly barred my way and bowed to me. When I regained my composure and asked for his identity, he claimed that he was someone sent here by that Princess Iron-Fan to fetch the Bull Demon King. I tried to tell him off, but he gave me a severe reprimand instead and even chased me with a rod. If I hadn't run away so fast, I would have been struck to death by him. Isn't this calamity brought on by you? You're killing me!" When the Bull King heard what she said, he apologized to her and treated her with great tenderness. Only after a long time was the girl pacified, but then the Demon King became annoyed and said, "Fair Lady, to tell you the truth, though that Palm-Leaf Cave is an out of the way place, it's an unsullied and comfortable spot. My wife, who has practiced self-cultivation since her youth, is also an immortal who has attained the Way. She presides, in fact, over a rather strict household, and there is not a single male within it at the moment, not even a baby boy. How could she have sent a man with a thunder god beak to make demands here? This has to be a fiend from somewhere who has falsely assumed her name to search for me. Let me go out and have a look."

Dear Demon King! He strode out of the library and went up to the main hall to put on his armor. After he was suited up properly, he picked up a cast-iron rod and went out of the door, crying, "Who is being so rowdy at my place?" When Pilgrim caught sight of him, the figure he saw was quite different from that of five hundred years ago. He saw that

His head had on a wrought-iron helmet, water polished and
   silver bright;
He wore a yellow gold cuirass lined with silk brocade;
His feet were shod in a pair of pointed-toe and powdered-sole
   buckskin boots;
His waist was tied with a lion-king belt[7] of triple-braided silk.
A pair of eyes that shone like bright mirrors;
Two thick eyebrows that glowed like red lightning.
His mouth seemed like a bloody bowl;
His teeth stood like slabs of bronze.
A roaring snort that made mountain gods cringe;
An imposing stride that vile spirits feared.
Famed in the four seas, he was named World-Wrecker,
The Powerful of the West called Demon King.

Straightening his clothes, our Great Sage walked forward and bowed deeply, saying, "Eldest Brother, do you still recognize me?" Returning his bow, the Bull King said, "Aren't you Sun Wu-k'ung, the Great Sage, Equal to Heaven?" "Indeed, I am," replied the Great Sage. "I have not had the privilege of bowing to you for a long time. Just now I had to ask a girl before I got to see you again. You look better than ever. Congratulations!"

"Stop this clever talk!" bellowed the Bull King. "I heard that as a result of your causing great disturbance in the Celestial Palace, you were pinned beneath the Mountain of Five Phases by the Buddhist Patriarch. Recently liberated from your Heaven-sent calamity, you were accompanying the T'ang monk to see Buddha for scriptures in the Western Heaven. But why did you bring harm to my son, Bull Holy Child, the master of Fiery Cloud Cave by the Dried Pine Brook on Roaring Mountain? I'm quite mad at you already. Why do you come here to look for me?"

Bowing again to him, the Great Sage said, "Don't wrongly blame me, Eldest Brother. At that time your son caught my master and wanted to eat his flesh. Your youngest brother was not able to get near him at all, and it was fortunate that the Bodhisattva Kuan-yin came to rescue my master. She persuaded your son to return to the right. Now he has become the Boy of Goodly Wealth, a rank higher even than yours, and he's enjoying the halls of ultimate bliss and the joys of everlasting life. Is there anything wrong with that? Why blame me instead?" "You smart-mouthed ape!" scolded the Bull King. "I'll let you talk yourself free of the charge of hurting my son. But why did you insult my beloved concubine and attack her right at my door?"

With a laugh, the Great Sage said, "Because I had a hard time trying to find you, I questioned that girl, but I had no idea that she was my second Sister-in-law. She scolded me a little, and I lost my head momentarily and treated her rather roughly. I beg Eldest Brother to pardon me, please!" "If you put it that way," said the Bull King, "I'll spare you for old time's sake. Leave!"

"I can't thank you enough," said the Great Sage, "for your great kindness. But I still have another matter that I must bring to you, and I beg you to be hospitable." "Monkey," scolded the Bull King, "you don't know your limits! I've spared you already. Instead of going away, you stay here to pester me. What's this business about being hospitable?" "To tell you the truth, Eldest Brother," said the Great Sage, "I was accompanying the T'ang monk on his westward journey, but our path was blocked by the Mountain of Flames and we couldn't proceed. When we asked the natives of that region, we learned that my esteemed Sister-in-law, Rākṣasī, had in her possession a palm-leaf fan. Since it could be used to extinguish the fire, we went to your house and begged her to lend it to us. She adamantly refused. That's why I now come to you and beg you to extend to us the compassion of Heaven and Earth. Go with me to the place of my big Sister-in-law and persuade her to lend us the fan. As soon as the T'ang monk has safely crossed the Mountain of Flames, we shall return it to you."

When he heard these words, the Bull King could not suppress the fire leaping up in his heart. He gritted his teeth and shouted, "You claimed you weren't rowdy, but you wanted the fan all along. You must have insulted my wife first, and when she refused, you came to find me. What's more, you even chased my beloved concubine around! As the proverb says,

Ye must not slight
A friend's wife of thine,
Nor must ye snub
A friend's concubine.

You have, in fact, insulted my wife and snubbed my concubine. How insolent can you be? Come up here and have a taste of my rod!" "If you mention fight," said the Great Sage, "you won't frighten me. But I have come to beg you for the fan in all earnestness. Please lend it to me!"

The Bull King said, "If you can withstand me for three rounds, I'll tell my wife to give it to you. If not, I'll kill you—just to relieve my wrath!" "You are right, Eldest Brother," replied the Great Sage. "I have been rather remiss in visiting you, and I don't know whether your martial skill is as good as previous years. Let us practice a little with our rods." Without permitting further talk, the Bull King wielded his cast-iron rod and brought it down hard on his visitor's head, and it was met by the golden-hooped rod of the Great Sage. The two of them thus began quite a battle:

The golden-hooped rod,
The cast-iron rod—
Their colors change and they are no more friends.
That one says, "I still blame you, Monkey, for hurting my son!"
This one says, "Your son has attained the Way, so don't get
    mad!"
That one says, "How dare you be so brash as to approach my
    door?"
This one says, "I have good reason to give you a request."
One wants the fan to protect the T'ang monk;
One is too stingy to lend the palm-leaf.
Words are exchanged, their old amity's gone;
Friendship destroyed, they have but anger left.
The Bull King's rod like a dragon rears up;
The Great Sage's rod comes, gods and ghosts take flight.
Before the mountain they battle at first;
Then they rise together on auspicious clouds
To show in midair their magic powers,
To flaunt their wonders in five-colored lights.
Two rods resound to shake the gates of Heav'n—
None's the stronger, they're evenly matched.

Our Great Sage and the Bull King fought for over one hundred rounds, but no decision could be reached.

In that moment when it was virtually impossible to separate the two of them, someone suddenly called out from the mountain peak:

"Sire Bull, my Great King sends you his earnest invitation. Please come early so that the banquet may begin." On hearing this, the Bull King stopped the golden-hooped rod with his cast-iron rod and said, "Monkey, you stop for a moment. I have to attend a banquet in a friend's house first." He dropped down at once from the clouds and went inside the cave to say to Princess Jade Countenance, "Fair Lady, that man just now with a thundergod beak happens to be the monkey, Sun Wu-k'ung, who has been driven away by the blows of my rod. He won't dare return. I am off to drink in a friend's house." He took off his armor and put on instead a duck-green silk jacket. Walking outside, he mounted a water-repellent golden-eyed beast, and, after giving instructions to the little ones to guard the door, departed midway between cloud and fog toward the northwest.

When the Great Sage, standing on the tall summit, saw him leave, he thought to himself: "I wonder what sort of friend that old Bull has, and where he is going to attend a banquet. Let old Monkey follow him." Dear Pilgrim! With one shake of his body he changed into a gust of wind to catch up with the Bull King and proceed with him. In a little while, they arrived at a mountain, and the Bull King soon disappeared. Collecting himself to change back into his true form, the Great Sage entered the mountain to look around, and he came upon a deep lagoon with lovely clear water. There was, beside the lagoon, a stone tablet, on which there was in large letters this inscription: Scattered-Rocks Mountain, Green Wave Lagoon. The Great Sage thought to himself: "That old Bull must have gone into the water, and an aquatic fiend has to be some kind of dragon spirit, fish spirit, or turtle spirit. Let old Monkey go in also to have a look."

Dear Great Sage! Making the magic sign with his fingers, he recited a spell and with one shake of his body changed into a crab; neither too big nor too small, it weighed about thirty-six pounds. He leaped into the water with a splash and sank quickly to the bottom of the lagoon. There he saw all at once a towered gateway with finely carved openwork. Beneath the arch there was tied the water-repellent golden-eyed beast, but it was waterless inside the gateway. Crawling through, the Great Sage stared all around and he heard the sound of music coming from buildings still further in. This is what he saw:

Scarlet halls and shelled arches
Not commonly found in this world;
Roof tiles made of yellow gold;

Door frames formed by milk-white jade;
Railings built from coral twigs;
Spread screens of tortoise-shell inlay.
Auspicious clouds hang o'er the lotus throne—
Above, the Three Lights,[8] below, the Milky Way.
Though it's not Heav'n or the sea's treasure chest,
This place quite rivals the island of P'êng.
Guests and hosts gather in a tall banquet hall;
Pearls stud the caps of officials great and small.
They beckon jade girls to serve their ivory trays;
They urge divine maids to make merry tunes.
Long whales squeal;
Huge crabs dance;
Scorpaenids play flutes;
Iguanas roll drums.
Rare, lustrous pearls light up the food and drink;
Nature's patterns are carved on kingfisher screens.
Shrimp-whiskered curtains hang o'er corridors.
Eight instruments[9] play in divine harmony,
Their glorious tones resound throughout the sky.
Green-headed perch-cocottes stroke the zithers,
And red-eyed young boys[10] blow the flutes of jade.
Female perches present venison strips;
Gold-phoenix hairpins crown the dragon girls.
What they have to eat:
The eight treasure dainties[11] of Heaven's kitchen;
What have they to drink:
The rich mellow brew from the purple mansion.[12]

Sitting above in the middle honored seat was the Bull Demon King, while several female dragon spirits sat on his immediate left and right. Facing him was an old dragon spirit, attended by scores of dragon sons, dragon grandsons, dragon grandmothers, and dragon daughters on both sides. They were toasting one another and drinking with abandon when the Great Sage Sun walked right in. The old dragon caught sight of him, and he at once gave the order: "Seize that wild crab!" The various dragon sons and grandsons surged forward and took hold of the Great Sage, who assumed human speech, crying, "Spare me! Spare me!" The old dragon said, "Where did you come

from wild crab? How dare you barge into our hall and hobble around
without permission? Confess quickly, and we'll spare your life!"
  Dear Great Sage! With specious words, he made this confession:
Since birth the lake's my livelihood,
I dwell in a cave by the ridge.
Of late time has exalted my station—
My rank, Private Sidewise-Motion.
Treading on grass and trailing mud,
I've ne'er learned to walk properly.
Untaught in law, I your kingly might offend;
I beg your Grace to pardon me.
When those spirits attending the banquet heard what he said, they
all rose to bow to the old dragon and to say, "This is the first time that
Private Crab has entered the royal palace, and he's unfamiliar with
the proper etiquette. We beg our lord to pardon him." The old dragon
expressed his consent, and one of the spirits gave this command:
"Release him. We'll stay the sentence of flogging. Let him go outside
and wait on us." The Great Sage dutifully gave his obedient reply
before fleeing outside. Once he reached the towered gateway, he
thought to himself: "This Bull King is so fond of his cup. How could I
wait for him to leave here? And even when he leaves, he won't lend
me the fan. Why don't I steal his golden-eyed beast, change into his
appearance, and go deceive that Rākṣasī? I can then wangle her fan
and help my master cross the mountain. That's a much better move."
  Dear Great Sage! Changing back into his original form all at once,
he untied the reins of the beast and mounted the carved saddle. He
rode it out of the lagoon's bottom and went up to the surface of the
water. He then changed himself into the form of the Bull King;
whipping the beast and mounting the clouds, he reached the entrance
of the Palm-Leaf Cave on the Jade Cloud Mountain in no time. "Open
the door!" he cried, and two maids inside immediately opened the
door when they heard his call. When they saw, moreover, that it was
the Bull King, they rushed inside to report: "Madam, our sire has
come home."
  On hearing this, Rākṣasī quickly straightened her hairdo and
walked out of her room to receive him. Our Great Sage thus
    Dismounted
    To lead in the golden-eyed beast;

In boldness
He would deceive the fair lady.
As Rākṣasī had only eyes of flesh, she could not recognize him. They entered the cave hand in hand, and she told the maids to present tea. When the whole family saw that the master had returned, each member treated him with great respect.

In no time at all, the couple were exchanging greetings. "Madam," said the specious Bull King, "it's been a long time!" "I wish the Great King ten thousand blessings," replied Rākṣasī, and then she said, "the Great King is so partial toward his newlywed that he has forsaken this humble maid. Which gust of wind today has blown you back here?"

Smiling at her, our Great Sage said, "I dare not forsake you. Since I was invited to join Princess Jade Countenance, however, I was plagued by all kinds of domestic concerns as well as by the affairs of my friends. That's why I have stayed away for so long, as I had to take care of another household. Anyway, I heard recently that the fellow Wu-k'ung, in the company of the T'ang monk, is about to arrive at the Mountain of Flames. I fear that he may want to ask you for the fan. I hate him, and we have yet to avenge our son's wrongs. When he comes, send someone to report to me at once so that I can seize him and have him chopped to pieces. Only that can bring us satisfaction."

On hearing this Rākṣasī fell to weeping and said, "Great King, the proverb says:

A man without wife, his wealth has no boss;
A woman without a husband herself has no boss.

My life was nearly taken by this monkey!" When he heard that, the Great Sage pretended to be outraged. "When did this wretched ape pass through here?" he cried. "He hasn't yet," replied Rākṣasī. "But he came here yesterday to borrow our fan. Because he brought harm to our son, I put on my armor and went outside to hack at him with my swords. Enduring the pain, he addressed me even as sister-in-law, saying that he was once your bond-brother." "There were indeed seven of us," said the Great Sage, "who entered into a fraternal alliance some five hundred years ago."

"He didn't dare answer me at first," said Rākṣasī, "even when I scolded him, nor did he dare raise his hands when I hacked him with the swords. Afterwards, I fanned him once and sent him away. But he found some sort of wind-arresting magic somewhere and came to our door again this morning to make noises. I used the fan on him once more, but this time I couldn't budge him at all. When I attacked him then with the swords, he wasn't so kind anymore. I was intimidated by the weight of his rod and ran inside the cave, tightly shutting the door. I didn't know where or how he got through, but he managed to crawl into my stomach and almost took my life. I had to address him several times as brother-in-law and give him the fan."

Again feigning dismay the Great Sage pounded his chest and said, "What a pity! What a pity! You have made a mistake, Madam! How could you give our treasure to that monkey? I'm so upset I could die!" Laughing, Rākṣasī said, "Please don't get mad, Great King, I gave him a fake fan, just to get him away." "Where did you put the real one?" asked the Great Sage. "Relax! Relax!" replied Rākṣasī. "It's in my possession." After she ordered the maids to prepare wine to welcome him, she took up the cup herself and presented it, saying, "Great King, you may have your new-found joy, but don't ever forget your proper wedded wife. Please have a cup of home brew." The Great Sage did not dare refuse it; he had no choice, in fact, but to raise the cup and say to her, full of smiles, "Madam, please drink first. Because I had to look after external property, I was away from you for a long time. You have been good enough to watch over our home day and night. Please accept my thanks." Rākṣasī took the cup and filled it some more before handing it to the Great King again, saying, "As the ancients put it, a wife is one who manages, but the husband is like a father who provides support. What is there to thank me for?" Thus the two of them conversed with great courtesy before they sat down to drink and eat in earnest. Not daring to break his vegetarian diet, the Great Sage took only a few fruits to keep the conversation going.

After drinking a few rounds, Rākṣasī felt somewhat tipsy and her passion was gradually aroused. She began to move closer to the Great Sage Sun, rubbing against him and leaning on him.

Holding hands with him,
She murmured affection;
Shoulder to shoulder,
She whispered endearment.

She took a mouthful of wine, and then he took also a mouthful of

wine from the same cup. They also traded fruits with their mouths.
The Great Sage, of course, was feigning tenderness in all this, although he had no choice but to laugh and dally with her. Truly

The muse's hook—
The sorrow's broom—[13]
To banish all cares nothing's better than wine!
The man resolves to act with less restraint;
The girl has slackened and begins to laugh.
Her face reddens like a ripe peach;
Her body sways like young willow.
They mumble and murmur, thus the prattle grows;
They pinch and they fondle with flirtatious glee.
Often she strokes her hair
And wields her dainty hands.
Her tiny feet she'd wiggle frequently
And shake her sleeves a few times purposely.
She'd lower her creamy neck;
She'd twist her slender waist.
Amorous words have never left her lips;
Gold buttons are loosened, her bosom's half-revealed.
Her reason truly totters for she's drunk.
Rubbing her glazed eyes, she's almost disgraced.

When the Great Sage saw that she was acting with such abandon, he
took care to bait her with the words: "Madam, where have you put
the real fan? You must be careful constantly, for I fear that Pilgrim
Sun with his many ways of transformation will sneak in somehow
and wangle it." Giggling, Rākṣasī spat out a tiny fan no bigger than
an almond leaf. Handing it over to the Great Sage, she said, "Isn't this
the treasure?"

When he held it in his hand, the Great Sage could not believe what
he saw, and he thought to himself: "This little thing! How could it
extinguish the flames? Could this be another false one?" When
Rākṣasī saw him staring at the treasure in complete silence, she
could not refrain from putting her powdered face up to Pilgrim's and
calling out: "Dearest, put away the treasure and drink. What are you
thinking of, anyway?" Immediately the Great Sage took this opportunity to follow up with the question: "A tiny thing like this, how
could it extinguish eight hundred miles of flames?"

Since the wine had virtually overwhelmed her true nature, Rākṣasī felt no constraint whatever and she at once revealed the truth, saying, "Great King, in these two years of separation, you must have given yourself over to pleasures night and day, allowing that Princess Jade Countenance to dissipate even your intelligence! How could you possibly forget how your own treasure works? Use your left thumb to press the seventh red thread attached to the fan's handle and utter the magic words, *Hui-hsü-ho-hsi-hsi-ch'ui-hu*,[14] and it will grow to twelve feet long. This treasure can change in boundless ways. You may have eighty thousand miles of flames, but one wave of the fan will extinguish them all."

Tucking these words firmly in his memory, the Great Sage put the fan inside his mouth before giving his own face a wipe to change back to his original form. "Rākṣasī," he shouted, "take a good look at me to see if I'm your dear husband! How you've pestered me with all your shameful doings! Aren't you embarrassed?" So astonished was that woman by the sight of Pilgrim that she fell to the ground, kicking over the tables and chairs. She was smitten with such terrible shame that she could only cry: "I'm so mad I could die! I'm so mad I could die!"

Our Great Sage, of course, had no regard for her whether she was dead or alive. Struggling free, he left the Palm-Leaf Cave in big strides; truly

With no desire for such beauty,

He triumphed in gaiety.

Leaping up, he mounted the auspicious cloud to rise to the tall summit, where he spat out the fan at once to test its magic. Using his left thumb to press on the seventh red thread attached to the fan's handle, he recited: *"Hui-hsü-ho-hsi-hsi-ch'ui-hu."* Immediately it grew to twelve feet long. When he examined it carefully in his hand, he found that it was indeed quite different from the one before. The whole fan was shrouded by auspicious light and hallowed airs, and it was covered by thirty-six strands of red threads, plaited warp and weft. Pilgrim, however, had only acquired the magic of enlarging it, and he had not thought of asking Rākṣasī for the oral formula to make it small again. After fussing with the fan for some time without being able to alter its size at all, he had no choice but to carry it on his shoulder and find his way back. We shall leave him for the moment.

We tell you instead about that Bull Demon King, who finally ended the banquet with those various spirits at the bottom of the Green

Wave Lagoon. When he walked out of the door, he discovered that the water-repellent golden-eyed beast had disappeared. Calling the spirits together, the old dragon king asked, "Who stole the golden-eyed beast of Sire Bull?" The spirits all knelt down and said, "No one would dare steal the beast. After all, all of us were presenting wines and serving the trays before the banquet, while others sang and made music. There was no one out in front." "No member of this family," said the old dragon, "would ever dare do such a thing, I know. But did any stranger come in?" "Shortly after we took our seats," said one of the dragon sons, "there was a crab spirit who got in here. He was a stranger, all right."

On hearing this, the Bull King at once realized what had happened. "No need to talk anymore," he said. "At the time when the invitation of my worthy friend arrived, I was just doing battle with one Sun Wu-k'ung, who was accompanying the T'ang monk to seek scriptures. When they could not pass the Mountain of Flames, Sun came to ask me for the palm-leaf fan. I refused and we fought to a draw. Then I left him to attend your great banquet, but that ape has extraordinary intelligence and vast abilities. He must have taken the form of the crab spirit to spy on us, steal the beast, and then go off to my wife's place to try to wangle that palm-leaf fan."

When they heard this, all those spirits shook with fear. "Is this the Sun Wu-k'ung who caused great disturbance in the celestial palace?" they asked. The Bull King said, "The very same. All of you should take care to avoid offending him on the road to the West." "In that case," said the old dragon, "what will you do about your beast of burden, Great King?" "Don't worry," said the Bull King, laughing. "Please go away now. Let me chase him down."

He opened up a path in the water and leaped out of the lagoon. Mounting a yellow cloud, he soon arrived at the Palm-Leaf Cave in the Jade Cloud Mountain, where he heard Rākṣasī wailing loudly, beating her chest and stamping her feet. He pushed open the door and saw the water-repellent golden-eyed beast tied up inside. "Madam," shouted the Bull King, "where has Sun Wu-k'ung gone to?" When the maids saw the Bull Demon, they all went to their knees to say, "Sire, have you returned?" Catching hold of the Bull King, Rākṣasī began to ram him with her head as she screamed: "You wretched reprobate! How could you be so careless and allow that ape to steal your golden-eyed beast, change into your appeareance, and deceive me here?" Gritting his teeth, the Bull King said, "Where did that ape go?" Rākṣasī pounded her own chest some more and screamed again: "After he wangled our treasure, that miserable ape changed back into his original form and left. Oh, I'm so mad I could die!"

"Madam," said the Bull King, "please take care of yourself, and don't be distressed. Let me catch up with the ape and get back our treasure. I'll skin him, I'll break his bones, and I'll gouge out his heart —just to give you satisfaction!" Then he bellowed: "Bring me my weapon!" One of the maids said, "But your weapon isn't here." "Then bring me the weapons of your mistress," said the Bull King. The maids at once took out the two blue-bladed treasure swords. Taking off his duck-green silk jacket that he wore to the banquet, the Bull King tightened the belt around his undershirt before he took up the swords with both hands and walked out of the Palm-Leaf Cave to give chase toward the Mountain of Flames. So it was that

The ungrateful man
Had the silly wife deceived;
The fiery demon
Now approached the disciple.

We do not know whether good or ill will befall him after he leaves, and you must listen to the explanation in the next chapter.

Chu Pa-chieh assists in defeating the demon king;
Pilgrim Sun seeks for the third time the palm-leaf fan.

We tell you now about that Bull Demon King, who caught up with the
Great Sage Sun. When he saw that the Great Sage was carrying the
palm-leaf fan on his shoulder and walking merrily along, he was
greatly shaken. "So, this monkey," said the Demon King to himself,
"has succeeded in swindling even the method of operating the fan! If
I ask him for it face to face, he will certainly refuse me. Moreover, if he
fans at me once, he will send me one hundred and eight thousand
miles away. Wouldn't that be to his liking? I have heard that the
T'ang monk on his journey is also accompanied by a Hog spirit and a
Flowing-Sand spirit, both of whom I have met in previous years when
they were fiends. Let me change into the appearance of that Hog
spirit to deceive the monkey instead. I suppose he's so pleased with
his own success that he must have thrown caution to the winds."

Dear Demon King! He, too, was capable of undergoing seventy-two
types of transformation, and his martial skill was about the same as
that of the Great Sage, albeit his body was huskier, less agile, and not
as nimble. Putting away his treasure swords, he recited a spell and,
with one shake of his body, changed into the exact appearance of Pa-
chieh. He sneaked up to the road in front and then walked back
facing the Great Sage and calling out: "Elder Brother, I'm here."

Our Great Sage was indeed quite pleased with himself! As the
ancients said,

The cat triumphant exults like a tiger.

He was thinking only of his own power and hardly paid attention to
the design of this person drawing near. When he saw a figure resemb-
ling Pa-chieh, he at once spoke up: "Brother, where are you going?"
"When Master saw that you didn't return after such a long time,"
replied the Bull Demon King, working his ploy, "he was afraid that the
Bull Demon King was too powerful for you to overcome, and that it
would be difficult for you to get his treasure. He therefore asked me to

come to meet you." "Don't bother," said Pilgrim, chuckling, "I've made it." "How did you make it?" asked the Bull King.

Pilgrim said, "That old Bull tangled with me for over a hundred rounds and we fought to a draw. Then he left me to drink with a bunch of female dragons and dragon spirits at the bottom of the Green Wave Lagoon in the Scattered-Rocks Mountain. I followed him secretly by changing into the form of a crab: I stole the water-repellent golden-eyed beast on which he was riding and then changed into the form of the old Bull to go deceive that Rākṣasī in the Palm-Leaf Cave. That woman and old Monkey became a bogus couple for a while, during which time I managed to wangle the treasure from her." "You've been sorely taxed, Elder Brother," said the Bull King, "and you're working too hard. Let me carry the fan for you." As the Great Sage Sun had no concern to distinguish between the true and the false, he handed over the fan immediately.

That Bull King, of course, knew how to make the fan grow big or small. After he took it in his hands, he recited some kind of a spell and it at once became as tiny as an almond leaf. Changing back into his true form, he shouted: "Wretched ape! Can you recognize me?" On seeing him, Pilgrim sighed, "It's my fault this time!" Then he stamped his feet and bellowed: "Damn! I've been shooting wild geese for years, but now a little goose has pecked me blind!" He became so enraged that he whipped out his iron rod and slammed it down hard on the Bull King's head. Stepping aside, the Demon King at once used the fan on him. He did not know, however, that when the Great Sage changed previously into a tiny mole-cricket to enter the stomach of Rākṣasī, he still had in his mouth that Wind-Arresting Elixir, which he swallowed unwittingly. All his viscera had become firm; his skin and bones were wholly fortified. No matter how hard the Bull King fanned at him, he could not be moved. Horrified, the Bull King tossed the treasure into his own mouth so that he could wield the swords with both of his hands to slash at his opponent. It was some battle that the two of them waged in midair:

The Great Sage Sun, Equal to Heaven—
The world-wrecker, lawless Bull King—
Because of the palm-leaf fan,
They met, each flaunting his might.
The careless Great Sage had people deceived;
The audacious Bull King did swindle the fan.

For this one, the golden-hooped rod uplifted could no mercy
     show,
For that one, the double blue-blades had both power and skill.
The Great Sage exerting his vigor belched colored fog;
The Bull King letting loose violence spat out white rays.
A test of strength
By two dogged foes;
Gritting their teeth, they loudly huffed and puffed.
Spraying dirt and dust made dim Heav'n and Earth;
Flying rocks and sand awed both ghosts and gods.
This one said, "You dare be so foolish as to trick me back?"
That one said, "Would my wife permit you to play chess with
     her?"
Their words grew rough;
Their tempers flared.
That one said, "When you trick someone's wife, you deserve
     to die!
You'll be found guilty when I file my charge!"
The clever Equal to Heaven Sage—
The ferocious King Powerful—
They wished only to kill
And would not deliberate.
The rod struck, the swords came, both working hard.
A little slackness will make you see King Yama!

We shall leave this intense conflict between the two of them for the
moment and tell you instead about the T'ang monk who was sitting
by the road racked by heat, thirst, and anxiety. He said to the local
spirit of the Mountain of Flames, "May I inquire of the honorable
deity, how powerful is that Bull Demon King?" "That Bull King,"
replied the local spirit, "has vast, boundless magic powers. He is, in
fact, the real match of the Great Sage Sun." "Wu-k'ung is usually
quite able when it comes to traveling," said Tripitaka. "A couple of
thousand miles hardly requires very much time for him to be back.
How is it that he's gone for a whole day today? He must be fighting
with the Bull King." Then he called out: "Wu-nêng, Wu-ching, which
of you would like to go meet your elder brother? If you happen to see
him fighting our adversary, you can lend him assistance, so that all
of you can acquire the fan to relieve my distress. Once we get across
this mountain, we can be on our way again."

"It's getting late," said Pa-chieh. "I'd like to go meet him, but I don't know my way to the Hoard-Thunder Mountain." "This humble deity knows the way," said the local spirit. "Let's ask the Curtain-Raising Captain to keep your master company. I'll go with you." Highly pleased, Tripitaka said, "Thank you for taking the trouble. I'll express my gratitude once more when merit is achieved."

Rousing himself, Pa-chieh tightened his black silk shirt and put the rake on his shoulder before rising with the local spirit on cloud and fog to head for the east. As they proceeded, they suddenly heard terrific shouts and the howling of wind. When he stopped his cloud to look, Pa-chieh discovered that Pilgrim Sun was just doing battle with the Bull King. "Go forward, Heavenly Reeds," said the local spirit. "What are you waiting for?"

Firmly gripping his muckrake, our Idiot shouted, "Elder Brother, I'm here!" "Coolie," said Pilgrim spitefully, "how you've upset my great enterprise!" "Master told me to come meet you," said Pa-chieh, "but since I didn't know the way, I had to discuss the matter before the local spirit agreed to lead me here. I know I'm late, but what do you mean by upsetting your great enterprise?" "I'm not blaming you for your tardiness," said Pilgrim. "It's this wretched bull who is most audacious! I got hold of the fan from Rākṣasī, but this fellow changed into your appearance, saying that he came here to meet me. I was so pleased at that moment that I handed over the fan to him. He then changed back to his true form and strove with old Monkey at this place. That's what I meant by upsetting my great enterprise."

Infuriated by what he heard, our Idiot lifted high his muckrake and screamed, "You bloody plague! How dare you change into the form of your ancestor, deceive my elder brother, and cause enmity to rise among us brothers?" Look at him! He charged into the fray and showered blows madly on the Bull King with his rake. The Bull King, after all, had fought with Pilgrim for nearly one whole day; when he saw how savagely Pa-chieh was attacking him with his rake, he could no longer stand his ground and retreated in defeat. His way was barred, however, by the local spirit leading a host of ghost soldiers. "King Powerful," said the local spirit, "you'd better stop! There is no god who would not protect the T'ang monk on his journey to seek scriptures in the Western Heaven, no Heaven who would not grant him his blessing. This enterprise is known throughout the Three Regions; it has the support of all ten quarters. Quickly use your fan to extinguish the flames so that he may cross the mountain unharmed and unhindered. Otherwise, Heaven will find you guilty and you will certainly be executed."

"Local spirit," said the Bull King, "you're completely unreasonable! That wretched ape robbed me of my son, insulted my concubine, and deceived my wife. These were his misdeeds time and again. I hate him so much I wish I could swallow him whole and reduce him to dung to feed the dogs! How could I give him my treasure?"

Hardly had he finished speaking when Pa-chieh caught up with him, screaming, "You bezoardic bull! Take out the fan quickly, and I'll spare your life!" The Bull King had no choice but to turn and fight Pa-chieh again with the treasure swords, while the Great Sage Sun raised his rod to help his companion. This was again some battle!

A spirit-boar,
A fiend-bull,
And an ape who stole to Heav'n to gain the Way.
As always Zen nature knows refinement and strife,
For earth must be used to fuse the primal cause.
The rake's nine prongs are both pointed and sharp;
The treasure swords' double-blades are quick and smooth.
The iron rod in use is determination's staff;[1]
The earth god gives aid to form th'elixir.
The three of them together thus feud and strive,
Each showing his talents to try to win.
Seize the bull to plow the ground, and gold coins grow;
Call back the hog to the oven, and wood breath declines.
When mind is absent, how can one practice Tao?
To guard one's spirit is to tie up the ape.
They brawl and growl
In bitter strife:
Three kinds of weapon thus crackle and clang.
The rake rakes, the swords cut with wicked aim
And with good cause rises the golden-hooped rod.
They fight till stars lose their brightness and the moon its light,
Till the sky's full of cold fog both dense and dark.

Plunging into the battle with fresh courage, the Demon King fought as he moved along. They strove for a whole night but no decision could be reached. By morning, they had arrived at the entrance of the Cloud-Touching Cave of the Hoard-Thunder Mountain. The deafening din created by the three fighters, the local spirit, and the band of ghost soldiers soon alerted the Princess Jade Countenance, who asked the maids to see who was making all the racket. The little fiends came back to report: "It's the sire of our family fighting with the fellow who came here yesterday, the one who had a thunder-god beak. Joining the battle are also a monk with long snout and huge ears and the local spirit of the Mountain of Flames with his followers."

When she heard this, Princess Jade Countenance at once summoned the captains, young and old, of the external guards and ordered them to give armed assistance to her husband. The various soldiers, tall and short, that they managed to call up numbered over a hundred, all of them eager to show off their vigor. Gripping lances and waving rods, they swarmed out of the door, shouting, "Sire Great King, by the order of Madam, we have come to assist you." Highly pleased, the Bull King said, "Welcome! Welcome!" The fiends rushed forward to attack. Taken completely by surprise, Pa-chieh could not fend off so many opponents and he fled in defeat, his rake trailing behind him. The Great Sage too mounted his cloud-somersault to leap free of the encirclement, and the various ghost soldiers immediately scattered. Having thus achieved his victory, the old Bull gathered back the various fiends to return to the cave and to shut the door tightly, where we shall leave them for the moment.

We tell you now about Pilgrim, who, after getting away, said to Pa-chieh and the local spirit, "This fellow's very tough! Since about the hour of *shên*² yesterday, he fought with old Monkey until nightfall and we couldn't reach a decision. Then the two of you arrived to relieve me. But after we went through the bitter struggle of half a day and one whole night, he still didn't seem to tire very much. And the band of little fiends who came out just now also appeared to be quite tough. Now that he has shut his door tightly and refused to come out, what shall we do?"

"Elder Brother," said Pa-chieh, "you left Master yesterday in the morning. How was it that you didn't start fighting with him until some time in the afternoon? Where were you during those few hours in between?"

Pilgrim said, "Since I left you people, I was on this mountain in an instant. I ran into a young woman whom I saluted, and she turned out to be the Princess Jade Countenance, his beloved concubine. I gave her a scare with my iron rod, and she ran into the cave to bring

out the Bull King, who harangued old Monkey for some time before
we began to fight. After about two hours, someone came to invite
him to a banquet. I followed him to the Green Wave Lagoon at the
Scattered-Rocks Mountain, where I spied on him and his hosts by
changing into a crab. I then succeeded in stealing his water-repellent
golden-eyed beast and took on the appearance of the Bull King.
Returning to the Palm-Leaf Cave on the Jade Cloud Mountain, I
fooled Rākṣasī and wangled the fan from her. After leaving her door,
I tried to work the magic: the fan was enlarged all right, but I forgot
to ask her for the formula to make it small again. As I journeyed back
carrying the fan on my shoulder, the Bull King met me, having
assumed your features, and wangled the fan back. That's what
happened during all that time."

Pa-chieh said, "It's like what the proverb says,
A bean-curd boat's[3] capsized in the ocean—
In liquid they come,
In water they go!
If it's so difficult to get his fan, how can we help Master cross this
mountain? Let's go back, find another way, and scat!"

"Please don't be anxious, Great Sage," said the local spirit, "and
you shouldn't slacken, Heavenly Reeds. When you mention finding
another way, you are bound to fall into heterodoxy, and you are no
longer someone concerned with the proper method of cultivation.
As the ancients said, where can one walk but on the main road? How
can you possibly think of finding another way? Remember your
master, now sitting with bulging eyes by the road and waiting for
you to succeed!" Growing vehement, Pilgrim said, "Exactly! Exactly!
Don't talk nonsense, Idiot! What the local spirit said is quite right.
With that demon we are just about to

Wage a contest
And try our gifts.
Let me exploit my vast transforming powers.
Since coming West I've ne'er met a true foe,
For Bull King was in fact from Mind Monkey changed.[4]
Now's the best time for us to reach the source.
We must fight to borrow the treasure fan.
With the pure and cool
To put out the flames,
The stubborn void pierced, we'll see Buddha's face.

Merit fulfilled we'll rise to ultimate bliss;
We'll all then attend Buddha's Birthday Feast."
Greatly inspired by what he heard, Pa-chieh replied in earnest:
Yes! Yes! Yes!
Go! Go! Go!
Who cares if the Bull King says yes or no!
Wood's born at *hai*,[5] the hog's its proper mate,
Who'll lead back the Bull to return to earth.
Monkey's the one who is born under *shên*:
Harmless, docile, how harmonious it is!
When palm-leaf's used,
As water it's meant.
When flames are extinct, Completion's attained.[6]
In work we must persevere both night and day.
Merit done, we'll rush to Ullambana Feast.[7]

Leading the local spirit and the ghost soldiers, the two of them rushed forward and, with their muckrake and iron rod, smashed to pieces the front door of the Cloud-Touching Cave. The captain of the external guards was so terrified that he dashed inside to make his report, trembling all over: "Great King, Sun Wu-k'ung has led a crowd to break down our front door!"

The Bull King was just telling the Princess Jade Countenance all that had taken place and how deeply he hated Pilgrim. When he heard that his front door had been broken down, he became enraged. Putting on his armor hurriedly, he took up the iron rod and came out. "Wretched ape!" he expostulated as he emerged. "How big do you think you are, that you let loose such violence here and break down my door?" Pa-chieh rushed forward and roared, "You old carcass! What sort of a person are you that you dare measure someone else? Don't run away! Watch my rake!" "An overgorged coolie like you," shouted the Bull King, "isn't that impressive! Tell that monkey to come up here quickly!" "You stupid grass-eater!" said Pilgrim. "Yesterday, I was still talking to you as a bond-brother, but today you are my enemy. Take care to eat my rod!" Boldly the Bull King met the two of them, and the conflict this time was even more fierce than the last one. Three valiant persons, all tangled together. What a battle!

Muckrake and rod exert their godly might.
They lead ghost soldiers the old bull to fight,

Who displays alone his violent trait
And his magic powers vast as Heaven.
One uses his rake to rake;
One uses his rod to strike;
The heroic iron's more uncanny still.
Three kinds of weapon make clangorous sounds:
They block, they parry, they will yield to none.
He claims he's the first;
He claims he's on top.
Ghost soldiers, looking on, can't separate
Wood and earth feuding and darting up and down.
These two say, "Why don't you lend us the palm-leaf fan?"
That one says, "How dare you be so bold as to trick my wife?
I have yet to avenge my hunted mistress and my son,
When you alarm us some more by breaking our door."
This one says, "You just watch out for my compliant rod.
One tiny brush and it will break your skin!"
That one says, "Do try to dodge the rake's sharp teeth!
One wound will make nine bloody holes!"
Undaunted the Bull Demon lets loose his power;
His iron rod held high, he waits for his chance.
They churn up rain and cloud, going back and forth.
They belch out wind and fog and do as they please.
For this bitter struggle they risk their lives.
They, full of hate, with each other strive.
The stylized limbs
Go up and down;
They cover the front, the back without let up.
Two brothers together now strain and toil;
One man with one rod performs all alone.
From dawn till late morning they fight and fight;
At last the Bull Demon will leave with his hands tied.

With no thought for life or death, the three of them again fought for
over one hundred rounds, when Pa-chieh, his idiotic nature aroused
and strengthened by the magic power of Pilgrim, began to attack
madly with his rake. No longer able to ward off the blows, the Bull
King fled in defeat and headed straight for the cave's entrance. Leading the ghost soldiers to bar the way, the local spirit shouted, "King
Powerful, where are you fleeing to? We are here!" Unable to enter

the cave, the old Bull turned swiftly and saw Pa-chieh and Pilgrim rushing toward him. He became so flustered that he abandoned his armor and his iron rod; with one shake of his body, he changed into a swan and flew into the air.

When Pilgrim saw it, he chuckled and said, "Pa-chieh, the old Bull's gone!" That Idiot was completely ignorant of the matter, and the local spirit did not perceive either what had happened. All of them were staring this way and that, madly searching before and behind the Hoard-Thunder Mountain. "Isn't he up there flying in the air?" said Pilgrim as he pointed with his finger. "That's a swan," said Pa-chieh. "A transformation of the old Bull," said Pilgrim. "In that case," said the local spirit, "what shall we do?" "Fight your way in, the two of you," said Pilgrim, "and exterminate all those fiends. In short, we'll break up his lair and cut off his retreat. Let old Monkey go and wage a contest of transformation with him." Pa-chieh and the local spirit followed his instruction and we shall leave them for the moment.

Putting away his golden-hooped rod, the Great Sage shook his body and changed into a Manchurian vulture, which spread its wings and darted up to a hole in the clouds. It then hurtled down and dropped onto the swan, seeking to seize its neck and peck at the eyes. Knowing also that this was a transformation of Pilgrim Sun, the Bull King hurriedly flapped his wings and changed himself into a yellow eagle to attack the vulture. At once Pilgrim changed himself into a black phoenix, the special foe of the yellow eagle. Recognizing him, the Bull King changed next into a white crane which, after a long cry, flew toward the south.

Pilgrim stood still, and shaking his feathers, changed into a scarlet phoenix which uttered a resounding call. Since the phoenix was the ruler of all the birds and fowl, the white crane dared not touch him. Spreading wide his wings, he dived instead down the cliff and changed with one shake of the body into a musk deer, grazing rather timorously before the slope. Recognizing him, Pilgrim flew down also and changed into a hungry tiger which, with wagging tail and flying paws, went after the deer for food. Greatly flustered, the demon king then changed into a huge spotted leopard to attack the tiger. When Pilgrim saw him, he faced the wind and, with one shake of his head, changed into a golden-eyed Asian lion, with a voice like thunder and a head of bronze, which pounced on the huge leopard. Growing even more anxious, the Bull King changed into a large bear, which extended his paws to try to seize the lion. Rolling on the ground, Pilgrim at once turned himself into a scabby elephant, with a trunk like a python and tusks like bamboo shoots. Whipping up his trunk, he tried to catch hold of the bear.

With a loud giggle, the Bull King then revealed his original form— that of a gigantic white bull, with a head like a rugged mountain and eyes like bolts of lightning. The two horns were like two iron pagodas, and his teeth were like rows of sharp daggers. From head to toe, he measured more than ten thousand feet, while his height from hoof to neck was about eight hundred.

"Wretched ape!" he roared at Pilgrim. "What will you do with me now?" Pilgrim also changed back to his true form; yanking out his golden-hooped rod, he bent his back and then straightened out, cry-ing, "Grow!" At once he grew to a height of one hundred thousand feet, with a head like Mount T'ai, eyes like the sun and the moon, a mouth like a bloody pond, and teeth like doors. Lifting high his iron rod, he brought it down on the bull's head, and it was met by a pair of flinty horns. This battle truly rocked the ridges and the mountains, alarmed both Heaven and Earth. We have a testimonial poem, and the poem says:

Tao is one foot, though the demon's ten thousand feet,
Which clever Mind Monkey must toil to beat.
If one wants the mountain flameless to be,
The treasure fan must bring the coldness pure.
Yellow Hag's resolved the elder to uphold;
Wood Mother's kind to sweep clean the fiends.
Five Phases, peaceful, return to right fruit;
Cleansed of dirt and demon, they go to the West.

Releasing their vast magic powers, the two of them battled in mid-mountain, and it soon alerted all those deities inhabiting the empty void: the Golden-Headed Guardian, the Six Gods of Darkness and the Six Gods of Light, and the Eighteen Guardians of Monasteries all came to surround the Demon King, who was not the least daunted. Look at him!

He headed east,
He headed west,
With two erect
And gleaming iron horns
Charging back and forth;

He stampeded north,
He stampeded south,
His dark, hairy,
Hard tendonous tail
Whipping left and right.

The Great Sage Sun met him head-on, while the various deities attacked him from all sides. Exasperated, the Bull King rolled on the ground and changed back into his original form to flee to the Palm-Leaf Cave. Changing back to his normal size, Pilgrim gave chase from behind with the deities. Dashing inside the cave, the Demon King shut the door and refused to come out, while the gods had the Jade Cloud Mountain tightly surrounded.

As they were about to charge the door, they heard the noisy arrival of Pa-chieh, the local spirit, and his band of ghost soldiers. When Pilgrim saw them, he asked, "What happened at the Cloud-Touching Cave?" "The mistress of that old Bull," replied Pa-chieh, chuckling, "was killed by one blow of my rake. When I stripped her, she turned out to be a white-faced fox. The rest of the fiends were all donkeys, asses, cows, stallions, badgers, foxes, musk deer, goats, tigers, antelopes, and the like—they have all been wiped out. We set fire also to his cave-dwelling. The local spirit then told me that he has another household in this mountain, and that's why we've come back here to make a clean sweep of them."

"You have achieved great merit, Worthy Brother," said Pilgrim. "Congratulations! Old Monkey has waged in vain a contest of transformation with him, for I have not yet achieved a victory. He finally changed into the biggest possible white bull, and I therefore assumed the appearance that imitated Heaven and Earth. As I clashed with him, the various deities were kind enough to descend on us and have him completely surrounded. He then changed back into his original form and fled inside the cave." "Is this that Palm-Leaf Cave?" asked Pa-chieh. Pilgrim said, "Indeed it is. This is where Rākṣasī lives." "In that case," said Pa-chieh, growing more vehement, "why don't we fight our way in, attack him, and demand from him the fan? Why should we let him wait and get wiser, or let him enjoy the company of his wife?"

Dear Idiot! Rousing his strength, he lifted high his rake and brought it down on the door; with a loud crash, both the door and one side of the ledge collapsed. One of the maids fled into the cave to report,

"Sire! Someone has wrecked our front door!" The Bull King had just dashed inside; still panting, he was telling Rākṣasī about how he took the fan from Pilgrim and then waged the contest with him. When he heard the report, he became enraged. Spitting out the fan, he handed it over to Rākṣasī, who, when she received it, began to weep. "Great King," she said, "let's give that monkey the fan so that he'll withdraw his troops." "Oh Madam," said the Bull King, "the fan's a small thing, but my hatred is deep. You sit here, while I go to contend with them once more."

Putting on his armor again, the demon took up the two treasure swords and walked out. Pa-chieh was still using his rake on the door; when the old Bull saw him, he hacked away with his swords without another word. Pa-chieh retreated a few steps, protecting himself with the upraised rake. After they left the doorway, the Great Sage immediately joined them with his iron rod. Mounting a violent gust of wind, the Bull Demon leaped clear of the cave-dwelling, and they began a fresh skirmish above the Jade Cloud Mountain, encircled by the many gods, the local spirit, and the band of ghost soldiers. This was again some battle!

Clouds over the world;
Mist shrouds the cosmos;
Dark wind blows soughing, sand and rocks roll;
Angry breaths rise up and ocean waves churn.
Two swords are sharpened again;
The whole body's armed once more.
There's hatred deep as the sea,
As anger grows from enmity.
Watch the Great Sage, Equal to Heaven who, for merit's sake,
Rejects now a friend he has known for years.
Pa-chieh uses his power to seek the fan;
The gods hunt the Bull King to protect the Law.
The Bull King's two hands will not stop or pause:
With vigor they parry both left and right.
They fight till the birds fold their wings and cease to fly,
Till fishes stop leaping and submerge their scales,
Till ghosts and gods wail as Heav'n and Earth grow faint,
Till tigers and dragons cower as sunlight fades.
Abandoning any regard for his life or body, the Bull King fought them

for over fifty rounds before he weakened and was forced to retreat in defeat. As he fled toward the north, he was met at once by the Diamond Guardian Dharma Diffusion of vast magic powers and of the Cliff of Mysterious Demons in the Mountain of Five Platforms, who shouted at him, "Bull Demon, where are you going? I have been sent by the Buddhist Patriarch Śākyamuni to set up cosmic nets here to capture you."

Hardly had he finished speaking when the Great Sage, Pa-chieh, and the other deities came rushing toward them, so frightening the demon king that he turned and fled toward the south. He ran right into the Diamond Guardian Victorious Ultimate of immeasurable dharma-power and of the Pure-Cool Cave in the O-mei Mountain, who shouted at him, "I received the Buddha's decree to capture you."

His legs turning weak and his heart growing faint, the Bull King hurriedly tried to head toward the east, when he was met by the Diamond Guardian Great Strength, a Vaiśramaṇa ascetic from the Ear-Touching Ridge of the Sumeru Mountain, who shouted at him: "Where are you going, old Bull? By the secret command of Tathāgata, I am here to arrest you." Backing off in fear, the Bull King fled toward the west, but he was greeted by the Diamond Guardian Ever Abiding, the indestructible honored rāja of the Golden Beam Summit at the K'un-lun Mountain, who shouted at him: "Where is this fellow going? I am stationed here by the personal order of the aged Buddha in the Great Thunderclap Monastery of the Western Heaven. Who'll let you get away?"

In fear and trembling, the Bull King did not have time even for regret when he saw Buddhist warriors and celestial generals approaching from all sides with cosmic nets spread so wide that there was virtually no way to escape. In that abject moment, he heard Pilgrim and other pursuers closing in, and he had to mount the clouds to try to flee toward the sky.

Just then, Devarāja Li, the Pagoda-Bearer, and Prince Naṭa led Fish-Bellied Vajrayakṣa and Celestial General Mighty-Spirit to block his path in midair. "Slow down! Slow down!" they cried. "By the decree of the Jade Emperor, we are here to arrest you." In desperation, the Bull King shook his body as before and changed into a huge white bull, wielding his two ironlike horns to try to gore the devarāja, who met him with his scimitar.

Meanwhile, Pilgrim Sun arrived at the scene. "Great Sage," shouted Prince Naṭa, "we have our armor on, and we can't salute you properly. Yesterday we father and son saw Tathāgata, who asked us to present a memorial to the Jade Emperor and inform him that the journey of the T'ang monk has been blocked at the Mountain of Flames, and that it was difficult for the Great Sage Sun to bring the Bull Demon King to submission. The Jade Emperor therefore issued a decree for my father king to lead the troops here to lend you assistance." "But this fellow has considerable magic powers," said Pilgrim. "Now he has changed into such a body. What shall we do?" "Great Sage, don't worry!" said the prince with a laugh. "Watch me capture him!"

Shouting "Change!" the prince immediately changed into a figure having three heads and six arms. He leaped onto the bull's back and brought his monster-cleaving sword down on the bull's neck: the bull was beheaded at once. Putting away his scimitar, the devarāja was about to greet Pilgrim when another head emerged from the torso of the bull, his mouth belching black air and his eyes beaming golden rays. Naṭa lifted his sword once more and cut off the bull's head; as soon as it dropped to the ground, another head came out. It went on like this for more than ten times. At last, Naṭa took out his fiery wheel and hung it on the Bull's horn. The wheel at once started a great blaze of true immortal fire, which burned so fiercely that the bull began to growl and roar madly, shaking his head and wagging his tail. He would have liked to use transformation to escape, but the Devarāja Pagoda-Bearer trained his imp-reflecting mirror steadfastly on him so that he could not change out of his original form. As he had no way to flee, he could only cry: "Don't take my life! I'm willing to make submission to Buddhism." "If you do pity your own life," said Naṭa, "bring out the fan quickly." The Bull King said, "The fan is being kept by my wife."

On hearing this, Naṭa took out his monster-tying rope and draped it around the bull's neck. Then he threaded the rope through his nostrils so that the bull could be pulled with the hand. Pilgrim then collected together the Four Great Diamond Guardians, the Six Gods of Darkness and the Six Gods of Light, the Guardians of Monasteries, the Devarāja Pagoda-Bearer, the Celestial General Mighty-Spirit, Pa-chieh, the local spirit, and the ghost soldiers. Surging around the white bull, they all went back to the entrance of the Palm-Leaf Cave. "Madam," called the old bull, "please bring out the fan to save my life."

When Rākṣasī heard the call, she took off her jewels and her colored clothing. Tying up her hair like a Taoist priestess and putting on a plain colored robe like a Buddhist nun, she took up with both hands the twelve-foot long palm-leaf fan to walk out of the door. When she caught sight of the Diamond Guardians, the devarāja and his son, and the other sages, she hurriedly went to her knees to kowtow and say, "I beg the Bodhisattvas to spare our lives. We are willing to give this fan to Brother-in-law Sun so that he may achieve his merit." Pilgrim drew near and took up the fan; then all of them mounted the auspicious clouds to return toward the east.

We tell you now about Tripitaka and Sha Monk, who were alternately sitting and standing by the main road as they waited for Pilgrim. They were indeed full of anxiety because he did not return for such a long time. Then, all of a sudden, auspicious clouds filled the sky and hallowed lights flooded the earth, as the various divine officers drifted near. Turning quite apprehensive, the elder said, "Wu-ching, who are those divine warriors approaching us?" Recognizing the figures he saw, Sha Monk replied, "Master, those are the Four Great Diamond Guardians, the Golden-Headed Guardian, the Six Gods of Darkness and the Six Gods of Light, the Guardians of Monasteries, and other deities of the air. The one leading the bull is Third Prince Naṭa, and the one holding the mirror is Devarāja Li, the Pagoda-Bearer. Big Brother is carrying the palm-leaf fan, followed by Second Elder Brother and the local spirit. All the rest happen to be celestial guards." On hearing this, Tripitaka put on his Vairocana hat and changed into his cassock before he led Wu-ching to bow to the sages, saying, "What virtue does this disciple possess that he should cause all you honored sages to descend to the mortal world?" "You should be congratulated, sage monk," said one of the Four Great Diamond Guardians, "for your perfect merit is nearly achieved. We have come to assist you by the decree of Buddha. You must persist in your cultivation with all diligence, and you must not slacken at all." Tripitaka kowtowed repeatedly to receive this instruction.

Holding the fan, the Great Sage Sun walked near the mountain and waved the fan once with all his might. Immediately the flames

on the mountain subsided and there was only the faintest glow left. He fanned at it a second time and a cool, gentle breeze rustled through the region. He fanned at the mountain a third time, and as
  Hazy clouds filled the sky,
  A fine rain drizzled down.
We have a testimonial poem, and the poem says:
  Eight hundred miles long, this Mountain of Flames,
  The light of its fire has worldwide fame.
  Elixir can't ripen with five senses scorched;
  When three passes[8] are burned, the Tao's impure.
  Now and then the palm-leaf may bring dew and rain;
  It's luck that Heav'n's hosts lend their godly pow'r.
  Lead the bull to Buddha, let it sin no more:
  Nature's conquered when water's joined with fire.
At this time Tripitaka was liberated from heat and delivered from distress; his mind was purified and his will made quiescent. The four pilgrims renewed their submission and thanked the Diamond Guardians, who returned to their treasure mountains. The Six Gods of Darkness and the Six Gods of Light then rose into the air to provide continual protection, while the other deities all scattered. The devarāja and the prince led the bull to return to see Buddha. Only the local spirit remained to watch Rākṣasī, who was still standing at attention on one side.

"Rākṣasī," said Pilgrim, "how is it that you are not on your way? Why are you still standing here?" Going to her knees, Rākṣasī said, "I beg the Great Sage to be merciful and give me back my fan." "You bitch!" shouted Pa-chieh. "You don't know when to stop! Isn't it enough that we spare your life? You still want your fan? After we have taken it across the mountain, you think we won't trade it for a snack? We are not going to give it back to you after we have expended all this energy! Look how the rain drizzles! Why don't you go back!"

"The Great Sage," said Rākṣasī, bowing again, "said originally that he would return the fan to me once the fire was extinguished. I didn't listen to you at first, and now it's too late for regret after such a battle. Because of our recalcitrance, an army had to be sent here to toil and fight. I would, however, like to tell you that we have actually attained the way of humanity, though we have not returned to the right fruit. Now that I have witnessed the epiphany of the true body going back to the West, I shall never dare misbehave again. I beg you to give me back my fan, so that I may start a new life in self-cultivation."

"Great Sage," said the local spirit, "since this woman knows the means by which the flames can forever be extinguished, you should ask her for it before you return the fan to her. This humble deity will remain in this region to care for its populace and beg from them some offering for my livelihood. You will have done us all an act of grace." "When I spoke to the local people," said Pilgrim, "they told me that when the fan extinguished the fire on this mountain, they could only harvest the five grains for one year. Then the fire would start again. How could it be extinguished forever?" "If you want it extinguished forever," replied Rākṣasī, "you must fan at the mountain forty-nine times. It will never start again."

When he heard this, Pilgrim indeed took the fan and fanned with all his strength at the summit forty-nine times: a great torrential rain descended on the mountain. It was truly a treasure, for the rain came down on only the area where there was fire before; where there was no fire, the sky remained clear. Master and disciples thus stood on the spot where there was no fire and they did not get wet at all. After staying there for the night, they put in order the luggage and the horse the next morning and gave the fan back to Rākṣasī. Pilgrim said to her, "If old Monkey didn't do this, I fear that people might say that my words are not trustworthy. You go back to a mountain with your fan now and don't start any trouble. I spare you because you have already attained a human body." After she received the fan, Rākṣasī recited a spell, and it changed again back into an almond leaf which she placed in her mouth. She bowed to thank the pilgrims and went off somewhere to practice self-cultivation as a recluse. In the end she, too, attained the right fruit and a lasting reputation in the sūtras.

As Rākṣasī and the local spirit thanked them and walked to send them off, Pilgrim, Pa-chieh, and Sha Monk were again accompanying Tripitaka to move forward, truly with their bodies pure and cool and with moisture beneath their feet. This is what we mean by

K'an and Li after completion, true beginning's fused;
Water and fire in harmony, the great Tao is born.

We don't know in what year they will return to the Land of the East, and you must listen to the explanation in the next chapter.

Sixty-two

To wash off filth, to clean the mind, is to sweep a pagoda;
To bind demons and return to the lord is self-cultivation.

In all twelve hours[1] you must never forget
To reap the fruition of night and day.[2]
In five years or one hundred and eight thousand rounds,[3]
Let not the holy water dry up,
Nor let fire bring you distress.
When water and fire are blended and there's no lack,
The Five Phases are joined as if enchained.
With yin and yang harmonious you climb the cloudy tower:[4]
You ride the phoenix to go to Heaven;
You mount the crane to reach Ying-chou.

The melodic name of this *tz'u* poem is *Lin-chiang-hsien* [Immortal by the River], which we use to depict Tripitaka and his three disciples. Since they attained the condition wherein water and fire were in perfect equilibrium, their own natures became pure and cool. Successful in their endeavour to borrow the treasure fan of pure yin, they managed to extinguish the large mountain of torrid flames; and in less than a day, they traversed the distance of eight hundred miles. Leisurely and carefree, master and disciples proceeded toward the West. As it was the time of late autumn and early winter, this was what they saw:

Withered blooms of wild chrysanthemum drop,
And tender buds grow from new plums.
At each village they harvest the grains;
Everywhere they eat their fragrant fare.
The woods shed their leaves and distant hills are seen;
By the brook frost thickens, making pure the ravine.
Moved by the wintry breeze,
The insects their labor cease.
Pure yin now becomes yang,
The month's divine ruler being Yüan-ming;[5]
Water's its seasonal character,

Though a peaceful reign loves a bright, clear day.
The Earth's aura descends;
The Heavenly aura rises;
The rainbow leaves without a trace;
Ice slowly forms in pools and ponds.
Dangling by the ridges, wisteria flowers fade;
Absorbent of cold, pines and bamboos grow greener still.

After they traveled for quite a while, the four of them again found themselves approaching a moated city. Reining in his horse, the T'ang monk called out to his disciple: "Wu-k'ung, look at those tall, towering buildings over there. What kind of a place do you think it is?" Pilgrim raised his head to look and saw that it was indeed a moated city. Truly it has

The shape of a coiled dragon,
This crouched-tigerlike strong city.
On all sides bright canopies overhang it;
With many turns the royal plains level out.
Beasts of jade and stone form the bridges' railings;
Statues of worthies stand on golden mounts.
Truly it seems like a capital of China,
A metropolis of Heaven.
A secure domain of ten thousand miles;
A prosperous empire of a thousand years.
Barbarians yield to the ruler's far-reaching grace;
Mountains and seas pay tribute to the sages' court.
The royal steps are clean;
The royal path's serene;
The taverns bustle with songs;
Flowered towers are full of joy.
Evergreens outside the Wei-yang Palace[6]
Should let the phoenix sing to greet the dawn.

"Master," said Pilgrim, "that moated city has to be the domain of a ruler or king." "In this world," said Pa-chieh with a laugh, "there are cities that belong to a prefecture, and there are cities that belong to a district. How do you know that this is the domain of a ruler or a king?"

"Don't you know," said Pilgrim, "that the domain of a king or a ruler is quite different from a prefecture or a district? Just look at those gates on all four sides of the city: there must be over ten of them. The circumference around it has to be over a hundred miles. The buildings are so tall that there are clouds and fog hovering over them. If this is not a royal capital of some sort, how could it have so grand and noble an appearance?" "You have good eyes, Elder Brother," said Sha Monk, "and you may recognize that it's a royal city. Do you know it's name?" Pilgrim replied, "There are neither banners nor plaques. How could I know its name? We have to make inquiries inside the city, and then we'll know."

Urging his horse on, the elder soon arrived at the gate, where he dismounted to walk across the moat-bridge. As he looked around after he entered the gate, he discovered flourishing trades in all three markets and the six boulevards; and he saw, moreover, that in their elegant attire, the people looked most distinguished. As they walked along, they suddenly caught sight of a score of monks begging from door to door, everyone carrying the cangue and wearing a lock. They looked most destitute indeed!

"When the hare dies," sighed Tripitaka, "the fox will grieve, for a creature will mourn its kind." Then he called out:

"Wu-k'ung, go up there and question them. Why are they so condemned?" Obeying his master's words, Pilgrim said, "Hey, monks! Which monastery do you belong to? Why are you carrying the cangue and wearing the lock?"

Going to their knees, the monks said, "Father, we are monks of the Golden Light Monastery who have been grievously wronged." "Where is this Golden Light Monastery?" asked Pilgrim. "Just around the corner there," said one of the monks.

Pilgrim brought them before the T'ang monk before he asked them again: "What do you mean by grievously wronged? Tell me." "Father," said the monks, "we don't know where you came from, though you seem quite familiar to us. We dare not tell you here. Please come to our humble residence, and we will disclose our woes." "That *is* more appropriate," said the elder. "Let's go to their monastery, and we can then question them carefully." They went together up to the monastery gate, where they found in gold letters this horizontal inscription: Golden Light Monastery Built by Imperial Command. As master and disciples entered the gate, they saw

Cold scented lamps in aged halls;

Wind-swept leaves in vacant corridors.

Atop the clouds, a thousand-foot pagoda;

To nourish one's nature, a few pine trees.

The ground's flower-strewn, but no guests pass by;
The eaves are amply screened by spider webs.
Drums mounted in vain;
Bells hung up unused;
The walls are dust-covered, the murals blurred.
The lectern's so quiet for no monk is seen;
The Zen Hall's silent, only birds you'll meet.
Such lamentable plight!
Such endless, lonely pain!
Though incense urns are before the Buddhas placed,
The ashes cool, the petals wilt, and all are vain.

Grief-stricken, Tripitaka could not restrain the tears welling up in his eyes. Wearing the cangues and locks, the monks pushed open the door to the main hall and invited our elder to worship the Buddha. After he entered the hall, the elder could only offer the incense of his heart, though he touched his face to the ground three times. Then they went to the back, where they found another six or seven young priests chained to the pillar before the abbot's hall, an intolerable sight for Tripitaka. When they reached the abbot's hall, the monks leading the way, all came to kowtow, and one of them asked, "The features of our Venerable Fathers are not all the same. Do you happen to be those who have come from the Great T'ang in the Land of the East?"

"You monks must know the magic of foreknowledge without divination," said Pilgrim laughing. "We're indeed such persons. But how did you recognize us?" "Father," said the monk, "what sort of foreknowledge without divination do you think we really possess? It's just that we've been grievously wronged, and there's nowhere for us to turn for justice except to call on Heaven and Earth day in and day out. We must have disturbed the gods, I suppose, for each of us had a dream last night, when we were told that a holy monk arriving from the Great T'ang in the Land of the East would be able to save our lives. Our grievances, too, would be rectified. When we came upon the strange appearances of you Venerable Fathers today, we were thus able to recognize you."

Highly pleased by these words, Tripitaka said, "What is the name of your region here? What sort of grievances do you have?" The monks all knelt down again, and one of them said, "Holy Father, this city is called the Sacrifice Kingdom, and it is a major city in the Western Territories. In years past, barbaric tribes of all four quarters came to pay us tribute: to the south, the Yüeh-t'o Kingdom, to the north, the Qoco Kingdom;[7] to the east, the State of Western Liang; and to the west, the Pên-po Kingdom. They brought annually fine jade and lustrous pearls, beautiful girls and spirited horses. Without our use of arms or expeditionary forces, all of them would of their own accord venerate us as the superior state." "If they do that," said Tripitaka, "it must be because you have an upright king, worthy civil officers, and noble military officers."

"Holy Father," said the monk, "neither our civil officers are worthy, nor our military officers noble. And the king is not upright either. It has to do with this Golden Light Monastery of ours, which from the beginning had auspicious clouds covering our treasure pagoda and hallowed mists rising from our whole edifice. At night beams of light flashed from the building and people as far away as ten thousand miles had seen them; by day, colored airs sprouted and all four of our surrounding nations had witnessed them. This is why we have been regarded as the divine capital of a Heavenly prefecture, and why we have enjoyed the tributes of the four barbaric tribes. But three years ago, during the first day of the first month of winter, a rainstorm of blood descended upon us at the hour of midnight. By morning every household was fearful; every home was grief-stricken. The various ministers made haste to memorialize to the king, with all sorts of speculation on why such chastisement was sent by the Heavenly Lord. At the time, Taoists were summoned to say their mass and Buddhists their scriptures in order to pacify Heaven and Earth. Who would have suspected, however, that, since our treasure pagoda of gold had been defiled by that rainstorm, the foreign nations would stop coming to pay tribute these last two years? Our king wanted to send out expeditionary forces, but he was restrained by the ministers, who accused the monks of this monastery of stealing the treasure in the pagoda. That was the reason they gave for the disappearance of the auspicious clouds and hallowed mists and for the cessation of tribute on the part of the foreign nations. The dim-witted ruler never gave the matter another thought; at once those venal officials had us monks arrested and inflicted on us endless tortures and interrogations. There were altogether three generations of monks in this monastery; two of them, unable to withstand such terrible treatments, died. The rest of us are now locked up in cangues and locks, still accused of this crime. Think of it, Venerable Father, how could we dare be so bold as to steal the treasure in the pagoda? We beg you in your great compassion to have regard for the special affinity of our kind. Vouchsafe your great mercy and exercise your mighty dharma power to save our lives."

When Tripitaka heard this, he nodded his head and sighed, saying, "There are certainly hidden aspects to this matter that have not yet come to light. For one thing, the Court has been remiss in its rule, and for another, all of you may be faced with a fated calamity. But if it was the shower of blood sent by Heaven that had defiled the treasure pagoda, why didn't you people at the time prepare a memorial to present to your ruler, so that you would be spared such affliction?" "Holy Father," said the monk, "we are only common folks. How could we know the will of Heaven? Moreover, if our senior colleagues could not determine what to do, how would we be able to settle the matter?"

"Wu-k'ung," said Tripitaka, "what time is it now?" "About the hour of *shên*,"[8] replied Pilgrim. "I would like to have an audience with the ruler," said Tripitaka, "so that our travel rescript may be certified. But we have not yet fully understood what has happened to the monks here, and it's hard for me to speak to the ruler about this matter. After I left Ch'ang-an, I made a vow in the Temple of the Law Gate that on my journey to the West, I would burn incense in every temple, I would bow to Buddha in every monastery, and I would sweep a pagoda whenever I came across a pagoda.[9] Today we have met you monks who have been grievously wronged because of a treasure pagoda. Why don't you people fetch me a new broom? Let me bathe first, and then I'll go up there to sweep it clean. Let me see if I can discover exactly what has caused the defilement and the loss of the pagoda's brilliance. Once we determine that, we can memorialize to their ruler and deliver them from this affliction."

When they heard this, some of those monks carrying the cangues and locks dashed into the kitchen and picked up a kitchen knife to hand over to Pa-chieh, saying, "Father, please take the knife and see if you can sever the chains on the pillar over there, so that those young priests can be freed. They can then go to prepare a meal and a scented bath for the holy fathers here. We'll go to the streets to beg a new broom for him to use to sweep the pagoda." "It's so easy to open locks!" said Pa-chieh, chuckling. "There's no need for a knife or an ax. Ask that hairy-faced father. He's a seasoned lock-picker."

Pilgrim indeed went forward and, using the lock-opening magic, gave the shackles a wipe with his hand. Immediately, all the chains and locks fell to the ground. Those young priests ran into the kitchen to scrub the pots and pans and prepare a meal. After Tripitaka and his disciples ate, it was gradually turning dark when some of these monks still cangued and locked came in with two brooms. Tripitaka was very pleased.

As he was speaking with them, another young priest came in with a lamp to invite him to go take his bath. By then, the moon and the stars were shining brilliantly outside as the sound of bamboo drums started from the watchtowers. Truly

At four walls the cold wind rises;
In every house the lamps burn bright.
Shutters in all six lanes go up;
The doors of three markets are shut.
Fishing boats retire to the woods;
The ploughmen stop their short ropes.
The ax of the woodcutter rests,
And a student recites his book.

After he finished bathing, Tripitaka put on a short-sleeved undershirt, which he tied with a sash. He changed into a pair of soft-soled shoes and picked up a new broom. "You should all go to sleep," he said to the monks, "and let me go sweep the pagoda." "If the pagoda had been defiled by a bloody rainstorm," said Pilgrim, "and if it had grown dark for such a long time already, some vicious things might have been bred up there. If you go up all by yourself in this cold, windy night, you may run into something unexpected. How about letting old Monkey be your companion?" "Very good! Very good!" replied Tripitaka.

Each of them thus took up a broom. They went first to the main hall and lit the glass chalice and burned fresh incense. Tripitaka went to his knees before the Buddha image and prayed, saying, "Your disciple, Ch'ên Hsüan-tsang, by the decree of the Great T'ang in the Land of the East, was sent to worship our Buddha Tathāgata in the Spirit Mountain and to ask for scriptures. Arriving here at the Golden Light Monastery of the Sacrifice Kingdom, I was told by the monks of this monastery that the treasure pagoda had been defiled. The king suspected that the monks had stolen the treasure, and they were wrongly charged with a crime, the cause of which no one, in fact, had knowledge. In all earnestness, therefore, your disciple has decided to sweep this pagoda. I beg our Buddha to reveal quickly by his mighty spirit the true source of the pagoda's defilement, so that the innocence of these mortal men can be established." After his prayer, he and Pilgrim opened the door of the pagoda and began to sweep it, beginning with the lowest tier. Truly this pagoda

Leans ruggedly toward the sky
And rises, towering, in the air.
It's justly called a pagoda of five-colored glass,
A śārī-peak of a thousand gold;
Its stairs winding like a tunnel;
An open cage when its doors unfold.
Its treasure vase reflects the moon in the sky;
Its golden bells ring with the wind of the sea.
You can see the empty eave saluting the stars
And the lofty top detaining the clouds.
The empty eave saluting the stars
Creates a phoenix piercing strange rocks and flowers;
The lofty top detaining the clouds
Brings forth a pagoda-dragon fog-entwined.
Your gaze on top will reach a thousand miles;
Up there it'll feel like the Ninefold Heaven.
In glass lamp at the door of each tier,
There's dust but no fire;
On white-jade railings before every eave
Gather dirt and flying insects.
Inside the pagoda,
Above the votive tables,
Smoke and incense all extinguished;
Outside the windows,
Or before the images,
Cobwebs opaque and widespread.
There's more rat dung in the urns
Than there's oil in the chalice.
Because a treasure was in secret lost,
Priests have been killed, their lot made bitter and vain.
Since Tripitaka wills to sweep it clean,
The pagoda's old form will, of course, be seen.

The T'ang monk used his broom to sweep clean one tier before going up to another tier. By the time he reached the seventh tier, it was already the hour of the second watch, and the elder began to tire. "You're getting tired," said Pilgrim. "Sit down, and let old Monkey do the sweeping for you."

"How many tiers are there on this pagoda?" asked Tripitaka. Pilgrim said, "I'm afraid there are at least thirteen tiers." Attempting to endure his fatigue, the elder said, "I must finish sweeping it to fulfill my vow." He swept three more tiers, and his torso and legs ached so badly that he had to sit down on the tenth tier. "Wu-k'ung," he said, "you sweep clean the rest of the three tiers for me and then come back down."

Rousing his energy, Pilgrim went up to the eleventh tier, and in a moment, he ascended to the twelfth tier. As he swept the floor, he heard someone speaking on the top of the pagoda. "That's strange! That's strange!" said Pilgrim. "It has to be about the hour of the third watch now. How could there be anyone speaking on the pagoda top? This has to be some sort of deviate creature. Let me go and have a look."

Dear Monkey King! Stealthily he picked up the broom and put it under his arm; hitching up his clothes, he crawled out of the door and rose into the clouds to look around. There in the middle of the thirteenth tier of the pagoda were seated two monster-spirits, and before them were placed a basin of coarse rice, a bowl, and a wine pot. They were drinking and playing the finger-guessing game.[10] Using his magic, Pilgrim abandoned the broom and whipped out the golden-hooped rod. He stood at the doorway and shouted: "Dear fiends! So, _you_ stole the treasure on the pagoda!" Terrified, the two fiendish creatures quickly got up and pelted Pilgrim with the pot and the bowl, but he blocked the blows with his iron rod and said, "If I slay you, there'll be no one to make the confession." With the rod, he backed them against the wall until they could not move at all, and all they could say was, "Spare us! Spare us! It has nothing to do with us. Someone else took the treasure."

Using the magic of seizure, Pilgrim grabbed them with one hand and went back to the tenth tier. "Master," he announced, "I have caught the thieves who stole the treasure." Tripitaka was just dozing: when he heard this, he was both startled and pleased. "Where did you catch them?" he asked. Pilgrim pulled the two fiends forward and made them kneel down. "They were having fun on top of the pagoda," he said, "drinking and playing the finger-guessing game. When old Monkey heard all that noise, I mounted the cloud to leap up there and block their escape with no effort at all. But I feared that if I killed them with one blow of the rod, no one would make the confession. That's why I brought them here. Master, you can take their testimony and see where they come from and where they have stashed the treasure."

Trembling all over, the two fiends could only utter "Spare us!" Then one of them made this honest confession: "We have been sent here to patrol the pagoda by the All Saints Dragon King of the Green Wave Lagoon in the Scattered-Rock Mountain. He is called Busy Bubble, and I am called Bubble Busy. He's a sheatfish spirit, and I'm a black fish spirit. This all came about because our All Saints Old Dragon once gave birth to a daughter by the name of Princess All Saints, who was blessed with the loveliest features and the most extraordinary talents. She took in a husband by the name of Nine-Heads, who also had vast magic powers. Year before last, he came here with the dragon king and, exerting great divine strength, sent down a rainstorm of blood to have the treasure pagoda defiled. Then he stole the śarīra Buddhist treasure[11] from the building. Thereafter the princess also went up to the great Heaven where she stole the nine-leaved agaric which the Lady Queen Mother planted before the Hall of Divine Mists. The plant and the Buddhist treasure are both kept now at the bottom of the lagoon, lighting up the place with their golden beams and colored hues night and day. Recently we received the news that there was one Sun Wu-k'ung on his way to the Western Heaven to acquire scriptures. We are told not only that he has vast magic powers, but also that he loves to meddle with the faults of others. That's why we've been sent here frequently to patrol the area, so that we'll be prepared when that Sun Wu-k'ung arrives."

Laughing scornfully at what he heard, Pilgrim said, "How audacious are these cursed beasts! No wonder he sent for the Bull Demon King the other day to attend their banquet! So, he was in league with this bunch of brazen demons who specialize in evil deeds!"

Hardly had he finished speaking when Pa-chieh and a few young priests holding two lanterns walked up from below. "Master," he said, "why haven't you gone to bed after you finished sweeping the pagoda? Why are you still sitting here and talking?" "Brother," said Pilgrim, "it's a good thing you've come. The treasure on the pagoda was stolen by the All Saints Old Dragon. He was the one who sent

two little fiends to patrol the pagoda here and to spy on our movements, but they were caught by me just now." "What are their names,"
asked Pa-chieh, "and what sort of monster-spirits are they?"

"They just gave us a confession," said Pilgrim. "One of them is
called Busy Bubble, and the other is called Bubble Busy. One is a sheat
fish spirit, and the other is a black fish spirit." Whipping out his rake,
Pa-chieh wanted to strike at them, saying, "If they are monster-
spirits who have made their confession, why not beat them to death?
What are we waiting for?" Pilgrim said, "You haven't thought about
this. If we keep them alive, it'll be easier for us to go speak to the king
about this matter, and they can be used as informants too, for catching the thieves and recovering the treasure."

Dear Idiot! He indeed put away the rake; he and Pilgrim then each
picked up a fiend and pulled him down the pagoda. All the fiends
could say was "Spare us!" Pa-chieh said to them, "We were just
looking for some sheat fish and black fish like you, so that we could
make some soup for those wronged priests."

The several young priests, in great delight, held their lanterns high
to lead the elder down the pagoda. One of them ran ahead to report
to the other monks, crying, "It's great! It's great! We've finally seen
the day! The fiends who stole our treasure have been caught by the
fathers." Pilgrim gave this order: "Bring us some iron chains, pierce
their lute bones, and lock them up here. You people stand guard over
them and we'll go to sleep. We'll dispose of them tomorrow." Those
monks indeed watched over the fiends with great care while Tripitaka
and his disciples rested.

Soon it was dawn, and the elder said, "I'll go into the court with
Wu-k'ung to have our travel rescript certified." Whereupon he
changed into his brocaded cassock and put on his Vairocana hat. In
full clerical attire, he strode forward, accompanied by Pilgrim, who
also tightened his tiger-skin skirt and straightened out his silk shirt
after he took out the travel rescript. "Why aren't you bringing along
the two fiendish thieves?" asked Pa-chieh. "Let us inform the king
first," said Pilgrim, "and there will be royal summoners sent here to
fetch them."

They walked before the gate of the court, and there were endless
scenes of scarlet birds and yellow dragons, of divine capitals and
celestial arches. Approaching the East Flower Gate, Tripitaka saluted
the grand official of the gate and said, "I beg Your Honor to make

this announcement for us: this humble cleric has been sent by the Great T'ang in the Land of the East to go acquire scriptures in the Western Heaven. We seek an audience with your ruler in order to have our travel rescript certified." Willing, indeed, to grant this request, the Custodian of the Yellow Gate went before the steps to memorialize: "There are two monks of strange features and attire outside who claim to have been sent by the T'ang court in the Land of the East of the South Jambūdvīpa Continent to go seek scriptures from Buddha in the West. They wish to have an audience with our king in order to have their travel rescript certified."

On hearing this, the king gave the order to have the visitors summoned, and the elder thus led Pilgrim to walk into court. When the civil and military officials caught sight of Pilgrim, they all became frightened, some saying that this was a monkey priest while others observing that he was a monk with a thunder-god beak. All of them were so alarmed that they dared not stare at him for long. While the elder went through elaborate ritual before the steps to salute the Throne, Pilgrim stood with hands folded before him and remained unmoved. Then the elder spoke: "Your priestly subject has been sent as a scripture pilgrim by the Great T'ang nation in the Land of the East of the South Jambūdvīpa Continent to worship Buddha at the Great Thunderclap Monastery in the India of the West. Our journey takes us to your noble region, and we dare not pass through without permission. We have with us a travel rescript, which we beg you to certify before we leave."

Greatly pleased by what he heard, the king gave the order for the sage monk of the T'ang court to ascend the Hall of Golden Chimes. A cushion of embroidered silk was granted him as his seat. Going up the hall by himself, the elder first presented the rescript before he took the seat. After the king had read carefully the rescript from beginning to end, he was delighted. He said to Tripitaka, "Though the Great T'ang Emperor was indisposed, he was fortunate to have been able to select a noble priest who was willing to seek scriptures from Buddha without any fear of the lengthy distance. But the priests of our region are good only for stealing, for bringing ruin upon our nation and ruler." When he heard this, Tripitaka folded his hands before his chest and said, "In what way do they bring ruin upon your nation and ruler?"

"This kingdom of ours," said the king, "is a superior state of the Western Territories. In the past, the four barbaric tribes frequently

came to us to pay tribute, all on account of the Golden Light Monastery
within our kingdom. In that monastery was a treasure pagoda of
yellow gold, the luster and brilliance of which filled the sky. Recently,
however, the larcenous monks of the monastery secretly have stolen
the treasure, and for the last three years, there was no brilliance at all.
The foreign nations during this time also stopped their tributes, and
this matter has aroused our deepest hatred."

"Your Majesty," said Tripitaka with a smile, his hands still folded,

"To err by a hair's breadth

Is to miss by a thousand miles!

When this humble priest arrived at your Heavenly domain last
evening, I caught sight of some ten priests, all carrying cangues and
wearing locks, the moment I entered the city gate. I questioned them
on their crime, and they told me that they were innocent victims from
the Golden Light Monastery. An even more thorough investigation I
made after my arrival at their monastery disclosed that the priests
there had nothing to do with this, for when I swept the pagoda at
night, I caught the fiendish thieves who stole the treasure." "Where
are these fiendish thieves?" asked the king, highly pleased. Tripitaka
said, "They have been locked up by my humble disciple in the Golden
Light Monastery."

Hurriedly issuing a golden tablet, the king gave this decree: "Let the
Embroidered-Uniform Guard bring back the fiendish thieves from
the Golden Light Monastery. We ourselves will then interrogate
them." "Your Majesty," said Tripitaka, "though you may want to
send the Imperial Guard, it is better that my humble disciple accompany him." "Where is your noble disciple?" asked the king.

Pointing with his finger, Tripitaka said, "He's the one standing by
the jade steps." When the king saw Pilgrim, he was astounded, saying,
"The sage monk has such elegant features! How is it that your noble
disciple has that sort of appearance?" When the Great Sage Sun
heard this, he spoke up in a loud voice, "Your Majesty,

Do not judge a man by his face,

Nor measure the sea by a vase.

If you only cared for men of good appearance, how could you seize the
fiendish thieves?" These words of Pilgrim turned the king's astonishment to delight, and he said, "What the sage monk says is true indeed.
We shall not select talents according to their appearances. All we
want is to catch the thieves and return the treasure back to the

pagoda." He then gave the order for the court attendant to prepare a canopied carriage, and for the Imperial Guard to wait on the sage monk in all diligence when he went to fetch the fiendish thieves.

The court attendant at once sent for a huge carriage and a yellow umbrella. The Embroidered-Uniform Guard also summoned the guardsmen; Pilgrim was placed in the carriage which was borne by four people in front and four behind, while four outriders shouted to clear the way as they headed toward the Golden Light Monastery. This entourage soon disturbed the populace of the whole city, and not one failed to show up to try to see the sage monk and the fiendish thieves.

When Pa-chieh and Sha Monk heard the shouts for clearing the way, they thought that some official sent by the king had arrived, and they hurried out of the monastery to receive him. Pilgrim, they discovered, was the one sitting in the carriage. Facing him, our Idiot said, giggling, "Elder Brother, you've acquired your true form!" Pilgrim descended from the carriage and took hold of Pa-chieh, saying, "What do you mean?" Pa-chieh said, "You have a yellow umbrella above you, and your carriage is borne by eight carriers. Don't these betoken the office of Monkey King? That's why I said you've acquired your true form." "Don't make fun of me!" said Pilgrim.

He untied the two fiendish creatures so that they could be taken to see the king. "Elder Brother," said Sha Monk, "please take us along." "But you should stay here to guard the luggage and the horse," said Pilgrim. One of the priests who were still cangued and locked said, "Let the fathers go to enjoy imperial favor. We will remain here to watch your things." "In that case," said Pilgrim, "let us go report to the king first. Then we'll come to free you." Pa-chieh grabbed one of the fiendish thieves, while Sha Monk took hold of the other; the Great Sage Sun climbed into the carriage as before. The entire entourage returned to court with the fiendish thieves in custody.

In a moment, they arrived before the white jade steps to address the king: "We've brought the fiendish thieves here." Coming down from his dragon couch, the king led the T'ang monk and the various officials, both civil and military, to look at the fiends: one had pouchy jowls and black scales, a pointed mouth and sharp teeth, while the other had smooth skin and a huge belly, a large mouth and long whiskers. Though they had legs that could walk, they barely looked human. "Where are you from, monster-spirits," asked the king, "and in what year did you invade our domain to steal our treasure? How

many thieves are there altogether, and what are their names? Make
your confession, in truth and in detail."

The two fiends went to their knees before him (though their necks
were dripping with blood, they did not seem to mind the pain), and
made this confession:

Three years ago,
On the first of the seventh month,
There was one All Saints Dragon King,
Who led many of his kindred
To settle southeast of this state
From here miles some one hundred.
His lagoon's called Green Wave;
His mountain, Scattered-Rock.
To him was born a daughter
Most pretty and seductive,
Who took in a husband named Nine-Heads
Of magic powers matchless.
Learning of your pagoda's treasure,
He joined the Dragon King as bandits.
First they sent down a bloody rainstorm;
Then the pagoda's śāri they lifted.
Now it lights up the dragon palace,
Making bright days out of darkness.
As well the princess plotted
In deep and silent secret;
She stole the Queen Mother's agaric,
With which the lagoon's treasure she nourished.
We two are no bandit leaders:
The Dragon King sent only privates.
Tonight we've been captured;
Our confession's most honest.

"If you have made your confession," said the king, "why don't you
reveal your names?" One of the fiends said, "I'm called Busy Bubble,
and he's called Bubble Busy. I'm a sheat fish spirit, and he's a black
fish spirit." The king instructed the Embroidered-Uniform Guard
to jail them, after which he issued this decree: "The monks of the
Golden Light Monastery will be freed at once from their cangues and
locks. Let the Court of Imperial Entertainments prepare a banquet
quickly, and we will thank the sage monks in the Unicorn Hall for

capturing these thieves. We will also discuss the matter of asking the sage monks to arrest the bandit chief."

The Court of Imperial Entertainments at once prepared a banquet composed of both vegetarian and meat dishes. After the king invited the T'ang monk and his three disciples to take their seats in the Unicorn Hall, he asked, "Sage Monk, what is your honored style?" "The secular family of this humble cleric," replied the T'ang monk with folded hands, "goes by the name of Ch'ên, and my religious name is Hsüan-tsang. I also had bestowed on me the surname of T'ang by my emperor, and my humble style is Tripitaka." "And what are the honored styles of your noble disciples?" asked the king again.

"My disciples are without styles," said Tripitaka. "The first one is called Sun Wu-k'ung; the second, Chu Wu-nêng; and the third, Sha Wu-ching. These names were given by the Bodhisattva Kuan-shih-yin of the South Sea. Since they made submission to this humble cleric and addressed me as master, I have also named Wu-k'ung Pilgrim. Wu-nêng I have named Pa-chieh, and Wu-ching is now called Monk." When he finished speaking, the king asked Tripitaka to take the head table, Pilgrim Sun to take the side table to his left, and Chu Pa-chieh with Sha Monk to take the side table to his right. Spread upon the tables were all vegetarian foods, fruits, teas, and rice. Facing them, the king took the table that had on it meat dishes, while the rest of the civil and military officials occupied over a hundred tables down below, all with meat dishes. After the officials thanked the king and the disciples excused themselves to their master, they were all seated. The king lifted his cup, but Tripitaka dared not drink; only the three disciples accepted the seat-taking toast. From down below came the harmonious strains of pipes and strings provided by the Office of Music. Look at the appetite of Pa-chieh! It did not matter whether fruits or vegetables were set on the table; he wolfed them down and finished them all. A little while later, additional soup and rice were brought to him, and these he also cleaned up completely. When the wine stewards came by, he never once refused the cup. And so, this banquet lasted well past the hour of noon before it ended.

As Tripitaka gave thanks for this lavish banquet, the king tugged at him to say, "This is merely to thank you for capturing the fiends. Let's change the banquet quickly to Chien-chang Palace,[12] where we shall ask the sage monk for the plan to arrest the bandit chief and return the treasure to the pagoda." "If you want us to do that," said

Tripitaka, "there is no need for another banquet. All of us humble clerics will take leave of you, Your Majesty, and we shall go to capture the fiends."

The king, however, would have none of it, and he insisted that they proceed to the Chien-chang Palace, where they were fêted once more. Raising a cup of wine, the king said, "Which one of you sage monks will lead the troops to go arrest the fiends?" "We'll send Sun Wu-k'ung our eldest disciple," said Tripitaka, and the Great Sage saluted him with folded hands to signify his obedience. "If Elder Sun is willing to go," said the king, "how many men and horses do you need? When do you want to leave the city?"

No longer able to restrain himself, Pa-chieh said in a loud voice, "Who needs men and horses! Who cares what time it is! While we are still full of wine and rice, let me go with Elder Brother. We'll just stretch our hands and bring them back at once."

Highly pleased Tripitaka said, "You're quite diligent nowadays, Pa-chieh!" "In that case," said Pilgrim, "let Brother Sha Monk protect Master. We two will go." "If the two elders do not need men or horses," said the king, "do you want any weapons?" "The weapons that you have," said Pa-chieh, chuckling, "are of no use to us. We brothers have our own weapons that accompany us wherever we go." On hearing this, the king asked for a large goblet of wine with which he wanted to send them off. "We won't drink wine now," said the Great Sage Sun, "but ask the Embroidered-Uniform Guard to bring out the two little fiends. We'll take them along as informants." The king ordered them brought out at once; taking hold of the two fiends and mounting the wind, the two disciples employed the magic of traction to head for the southeast. Lo! When those

Ruler and subjects saw them mounting wind and fog,

They knew master and disciples to be sage monks.

We do not know how they will capture the other monsters, and you must listen to the explanation in the next chapter.

Sixty-three

Two monks, quelling fiends, disturb the dragon palace;
The sages, destroying deviates, acquire the treasures.

We were tellir_g you about the king of the Sacrifice Kingdom and the various officials, both great and small. When they saw how the Great Sage Sun and Pa-chieh mounted the wind and fog and glided away, each holding one of the little fiends, all those dukes and marquises bowed toward the sky, saying, "It's indeed the truth! Not until today did we realize that there *are* such immortals, such living Buddhas!" When the two disciples vanished from sight, the king then turned to thank Tripitaka and Sha Monk, saying, "This Solitary One is of fleshly eyes and mortal stock. We only thought that your worthy disciples had sufficient power to capture the fiendish thieves. Little did we realize that they are actually superior immortals who can ride the fog and mount the clouds!"

"This humble cleric," said Tripitaka, "has hardly any magic power, and he's dependent on these three lowly disciples throughout the journey." Sha Monk said, "To tell you the truth, Your Majesty, my Big Brother happens to be the converted Great Sage, Equal to Heaven. Once he caused great havoc in Heaven, using a golden-hooped rod, and among one hundred celestial warriors there was none who could withstand him. Even the Jade Emperor and Lao Tzu were intimidated by him. My Second Elder Brother is none other than the Marshal of Heavenly Reeds who has embraced the right fruit. He used to command a mighty force of eighty thousand marines of the Celestial River. Compared with them, this disciple has very little magic power, but I, too, happen to be the Curtain-Raising Captain who has received the commandments. We brothers may not be very good at doing other things, but if you want something like catching fiends and binding monsters, seizing thieves and arresting fugitives, taming tigers and subduing dragons, kicking down Heaven and pulling up wells—including even stirring up seas and overturning rivers—we know a little of these. As for activities such as mounting the cloud and riding the fog, calling up rain and summoning wind, moving the stars and changing the dipper, poling the mountains to chase after the moon, they are simple matters, hardly worth mentioning."

When the king heard this, he became even more respectful toward them; asking the T'ang monk to take the honored seat, he addressed him as "Venerable Buddha," while Sha Monk and his companions were given the title, "Bodhisattva." The civil and military officials of the entire court were all delighted, while the people of the whole kingdom paid them homage, and we shall leave them for the moment.

We now tell you about the Great Sage Sun and Pa-chieh who, astride the violent wind, brought the two young fiends to the Green Wave Lagoon at the Scattered-Rock Mountain. After they stopped their clouds, the Great Sage blew a mouthful of divine breath onto his golden-hooped rod, crying, "Change!" It changed at once into a ritual razor, with which he cut off the ears of the black fish spirit and the lower lip of the sheat fish spirit. After casting the fiends into the water, Pilgrim shouted to them: "Go quickly and make a report to that All Saints Dragon King. Tell him that his Venerable Father Sun the Great Sage, Equal to Heaven, has arrived. Tell him to bring out immediately the original treasure taken from the top of the Golden Light Monastery in the Sacrifice Kingdom, and the lives of his whole family will be spared. If he but utters half a 'No,' I'll clean out this lagoon, and everyone in his household, both old and young, will be executed!"

Those two little fiends were only too glad to have their lives back. Enduring their pain and dragging along their iron chains, they fled by darting into the water. The spirits of fishes, shrimps, crabs, sea turtles, iguanas and huge tortoises were so startled that they swarmed around them and asked, "Why are you two draped with ropes and chains?" One of the two, hands still hugging the sides of his head, kept wagging his tail and shaking his head; the other one, holding his mouth, stamped his feet and beat his breast. In a noisy throng, they went up to the palace of the dragon king and the two made this report: "Great King, disaster!"

The All Saints Dragon King was just drinking wine with Nine-Heads, his son-in-law. When he saw them dashing in, he put down his glass and inquired about the disaster. "We were on patrol last night," said one of the two fiends, "when we were caught by the T'ang monk and Pilgrim Sun, who happened to be sweeping the pagoda. We were, in fact, bound by iron chains. This morning we were taken to see the king, after which that Pilgrim and Chu Pa-chieh hauled the two of us back here; one of us had his ears cut off and the other, his lower lip. They then threw us into the water and told us to make this report. They are demanding from us the treasure taken from the pagoda top." When they gave a thorough account of what had happened, and when the old dragon heard the name Pilgrim Sun, the Great Sage, Equal to Heaven, he was so terrified that his spirit fled his body and his soul floated up to the ninefold Heaven. Shaking all over, he said to Nine-Heads, "Oh, worthy son-in-law! It may be all right if another person shows up, but if it's he, then we're in a bad situation!"

"Relax, great father-in-law!" said the son-in-law with a laugh. "Since his youth your foolish son-in-law has mastered the rudiments of the martial arts. Within the four seas he has, moreover, met quite a few stalwart warriors. Why fear *him*? Let me go out now and fight three rounds with him. I promise you that that fellow will bow his head in submission, not daring even to look up!"

Dear fiend! He leaped up at once and put on his armor, picking up a weapon which had the name of crescent-tooth spade.[1] Striding out of the palace, he opened a path in the water and rose to the surface, cying, "What sort of Great Sage, Equal to Heaven, is here? Come over quickly and yield your life!"

Standing on the shore, Pilgrim and Pa-chieh stared at the monster-spirit to see how he was attired.

He wore a bright silver helmet,
Its luster whiter than snow;
He had on a cuirass of steel
Luminous as autumn's frost,
Which topped a damask martial robe
Patterned like colored clouds enfolding jade.
His waist had a belt of rhinoceros grain,
Which seemed like a python spotted with gold.
His hands held the crescent-tooth spade
Flashing with beams of light;
His feet wore two pigskin boots
Which parted water and waves.
Seen from afar he had one head and one face;
Drawing near, he seemed human all around.
Eyes in front,

Eyes behind,
He could see all eight quarters.
A mouth on the left,
A mouth on the right,
Nine mouths talking at once!
One shout he gave and it shook the distant void,
As if a crane's cry had the planets pierced.

When the monster-spirit found no reply, he shouted once more: "Who is the Great Sage, Equal to Heaven?" Giving his golden fillet a pinch and his iron rod a bounce, Pilgrim replied, "Old Monkey's the person."

The fiend said, "Where do you live? Where did you come from originally? How did you get to the Sacrifice Kingdom to become the guard of the pagoda for that king? How dare you capture my captains and work further violence by provoking battle on my treasure mountain?"

"You thievish fiend!" scolded Pilgrim. "So, you don't recognize your Grandfather Sun! Come up here and listen to my recital.

Mount Flower-Fruit's where old Monkey once had lived,
At the great ocean's Water-Curtain Cave.
I've wrought a perfect body since my youth;
Emperor Jade made me Equal-to-Heav'n Sage.
When I caused great havoc in the Dipper Hall,
The gods in Heaven found me hard to beat.
The Buddha was asked to lend his wonderous might
And use his boundless wisdom transcendently.
In a somersault wager—a test of might—
His hand formed a mountain to have me pressed
Beneath it till now, a full five hundred years.
My life was spared when Kuan-yin intervened:
Great T'ang's Tripitaka would go to the West
To seek on Spirit Mountain the Buddhist verse.
To give him protection I found release
And did cultivation, purging imps and fiends.
At Sacrifice Kingdom of the West we met
Priests wrongly accused, three generations all.
In mercy we inquired about the cause
And learned the pagoda had lost its light.
My master swept it to get to the truth:
The night reached third watch when all sounds had ceased,

We caught two monsters who at once confessed.
You all, they claimed, had the treasure stolen;
The gang of thieves e'en had a dragon king,
To which a princess added her name, All Saints.
By raining blood on the pagoda's beams,
She took someone's treasure for her own use.
That true statement before the court obtained,
We sped to this place by the king's command
That we might find you and provoke a fight.
There's no need to ask for Father Sun's name.
Return the treasure quickly to the king
And we'll spare your kin's lives, both old and young.
If you're so foolish as to want to strive,
I'll drain your water, topple your mountain, and stamp you out!"
When the son-in-law heard these words, he smiled scornfully and said,
"So, you're a monk on your way to fetch scriptures. Don't you have
anything more important to do than to meddle in someone's affairs?
You're to seek your scriptures from Buddha, and I am the one who
steals treasures. What has that to do with you? Why must you come
here to fight with me?"

"This thievish fiend," said Pilgrim, "has very little understanding!
Of course, I'm not a recipient of the king's favor, nor do I feed on his
water or rice, and thus I'm not obliged to serve him. But you not only
stole his treasure and defiled his pagoda, you also brought suffering
to the priests of the Golden Light Monastery. They belong, after all,
to the same community as we. How could I not exert my strength on
their behalf and bring their injustice to light?" "In that case," said the
son-in-law, "you must want to do battle. As the proverb says, 'War is
an unkindly act.' When I raise my hands, I fear I'll not spare you. I
may take your life all of a sudden, and that may upset your scripture
enterprise!"

Enraged, Pilgrim shouted: "You brazen thievish fiend! What power
do you have that you dare mouth such big words? Come up here
and have a taste of your father's rod!" Not in the least intimidated,
the son-in-law parried the blow with his crescent-tooth spade; a
marvelous battle thus broke out on top of that Scattered-Rock
Mountain.

Its treasures stolen, the pagoda grew dark.
Pilgrim caught fiends and informed the king.

Into the water two little fiends fled;
The old dragon took counsel, all in dread.
His son-in-law, Nine-Heads, would flaunt his might;
He armed himself to go to show his power
And roused the Great Sage, Equal to Heaven's ire,
Whose iron rod, upraised, was hard and strong.
That fiend
Had on nine heads eighteen eyes
All ablaze both back and front;
This Pilgrim,
Whose steely arms could raise a thousand pounds,
Did spread auspicious rays around.
The spade looked like the moon at the first stroke of yang;[2]
The rod seemed like frost flying o'er ten thousand miles.
The rod met the spade as both strove to win,
But none had yet won on this battlefield.

Charging back and forth, the two of them fought for more than thirty rounds but no decision could be reached.

Chu Pa-chieh was standing all this time before the mountain slope; he waited until the battle had reached its sweetest moment before he lifted high his muckrake and brought it down hard on the back of the monster-spirit. The fiend, you see, possessed nine heads, and on each one of them he had eyes which could see clearly. When he saw Pa-chieh coming at him at the back, he immediately used the lower part of the spade to block the rake while the upper part parried the iron rod. They fought thus for another six or seven rounds when the monster could no longer withstand the double offensive, front and back. He somersaulted at once into the air and changed into his original form: it was a nine-headed insect, exceedingly ugly and ferocious. Look at his appearance! You'd be scared to death! He had

Feathers like brocade spread out,
A stoutish body with curly fleece.
His size, at least twelve feet in length;
A shape rather like the turtle's or iguana's.
His two feet were pointed and sharp like hooks;
Nine heads joined together to form a ring.
Spreading his wings he could fly so well
That e'en the roc was no match for his strength.
Crying out he could shake the edge of Heaven,

Able to call louder than a fairy crane.
With eyes flashing beams of golden light,
His proud looks differed from those of common birds.

Horrified by what he saw, Pa-chieh cried, "Elder Brother! I've never seen such a vicious thing in all my life! Which creature of blood and breath would bring forth a beast like this?" "It's rare! It's rare, all right!" replied Pilgrim. "Let me get up there to strike him."

Dear Great Sage! Quickly mounting the auspicious cloud, he leaped into the air and aimed a blow of his iron rod at the creature's heads. To display his abilities, that fiendish creature spread his wings and flew to one side. Rolling over, he suddenly darted down the side of the mountain as another head popped out from the middle of his torso. A huge, gaping mouth like a butcher bowl caught hold of Pa-chieh's bristles with one bite. Tugging and pulling his victim, he hauled him into the water of the Green Wave Lagoon. When he reached the dragon palace, he changed back into his previous form and threw Pa-chieh on the ground. "Little ones, where are you?" he cried. Those spirits of mackerels, culters, carps, and perches along with the turtle, iguana, and sea turtle fiends all surged forward, shouting, "We're here!" "Take this priest," said the son-in-law, "and tie him up over there. I want to avenge our soldiers who were sent on patrol." The raucous mob of spirits carried Pa-chieh inside as a delighted old dragon king came out saying, "Worthy son-in-law, you've made great merit! How did you manage to capture him?" After the son-in-law gave a thorough account of what took place, the old dragon immediately ordered a banquet to celebrate this victory, and we shall leave them for the moment.

We tell you now about Pilgrim Sun, who was quite dismayed when he saw how Pa-chieh had been captured by the monster-spirit. "This is a formidable fellow!" he thought to himself. "I would like to go back to see Master in the court, but I'm afraid the king would laugh at me. If I make noises to provoke battle again, I'll have to face them single-handed. Moreover, I'm not used to doing business in water. I'd better transform myself to go inside and see what that fiend is going to do to Idiot. If there's a chance, I'll smuggle him out again so that we may proceed with our business." Dear Great Sage! Making the magic sign with his fingers, he shook his body, changed into a crab to splash into the water, and went before the towered gateway. This was a familiar way to him, you see, for he had traveled it before when he spied on the Bull Demon King and stole his golden-eye beast. After he crawled sideways through the arch, Pilgrim saw inside the old dragon king drinking merrily with the nine-headed insect and other members of their family. Not daring to go near them, Pilgrim crawled over to the east corridor where there were several shrimp and crab spirits frolicking. After he had listened to their chatter for a while, Pilgrim imitated their manner of speech and asked: "That priest with a long snout caught by our venerable son-in-law, has he died?" "Not yet," the spirits replied. "The one tied up in the west corridor and moaning, isn't he the one?"

On hearing this, Pilgrim crawled silently over to the west corridor, and indeed he discovered our Idiot bound to a pillar and moaning. "Pa-chieh," whispered Pilgrim as he approached him, "you recognize me?" When Pa-chieh heard the voice, he knew it was Pilgrim and said, "Elder Brother, what shall we do? I've been caught by this fellow instead!" When Pilgrim glanced around and saw no one, he snapped the ropes with his claws and told Pa-chieh to leave. After he was freed, Idiot said, "Elder Brother, my weapon was taken by him. What are we to do?" "Do you know where he has put it?" asked Pilgrim, and Pa-chieh replied, "It must have been taken up to the main hall by that fiend."

Pilgrim said to him, "Go beneath the towered gateway and wait for me." Fleeing for his life, Pa-chieh slipped out quietly, while Pilgrim turned and crawled up to the main hall once more. A luminous object he saw on the left side was actually the rake of Pa-chieh. Using the magic of Body Concealment, he stole it and went to the towered gateway. "Pa-chieh, take your weapon," he said. After Idiot took the rake, he said, "Elder Brother, you leave first and let old Hog fight his way into the palace. If I win, I'll seize their entire family. If I'm defeated, I'll flee outside and you can come to my assistance by the edge of the lagoon." Highly pleased, Pilgrim told him to be careful, "No fear," said Pa-chieh, "for I do have some abilities in water." Pilgrim left him and swam back to the surface of the water.

Straightening out his black cotton shirt and gripping his rake with both hands, our Pa-chieh gave a shout and fought his way into the palace. Those aquatic relatives, both young and old, were so startled that they dashed up to the main hall, screaming, "It's terrible! That long-snout priest has broken out of the ropes and he's attacking us!" The old dragon, the nine-headed insect, and their family members were hardly prepared for this; jumping up, they scattered in every direction and tried to hide themselves. Our Idiot, however, had no regard for life or death; crashing into the main hall, he wielded his rake to fracture doors, demolish tables and chairs, and shatter all those drinking utensils. We have for him a testimonial poem, and the poem says:

Wood Mother was caught by a water fiend;
Mind Monkey, unyielding, searched hard for him
And used a clever trick to pick the lock.
They then displayed their power and deepest ire.
The son-in-law with his princess quickly hid;
The dragon king fell silent in fear and dread.
As palatial arches and windows broke up,
Dragon sons and grandsons all lost their wits.

This time the tortoise-shelled screens were pulverized by Pa-chieh and the coral plants were smashed to pieces. After he had safely hidden the princess inside, the nine-headed insect grabbed his crescent-tooth spade to rush back to the front palace, shouting, "Lawless swine! How dare you be so insolent as to frighten my kin?" "You thievish fiend!" scolded Pa-chieh. "How dare you capture me? It's not my fault now! It's *you* who have invited me to bust up your household. Return the treasures quickly so that I can go back to see the king. That'll be the end of it. Otherwise, I'll definitely not spare the lives of your entire family!"

The fiend, of course, was not about to yield. Clenching his teeth, he plunged into battle with Pa-chieh. Only then did the old dragon manage to collect himself sufficiently to lead his son and grandson, armed with scimitars and spears, to mount an attack also. When Pa-chieh saw that the tide was turning against him, he dealt a weak blow with his rake before turning to flee, followed by the old dragon and his companions. In a moment, they all darted out of the water, bobbing up and down on the surface of the lagoon.

We tell you now about Pilgrim Sun, who stood waiting on the shore. When all at once he saw Pa-chieh leaving the water, chased by his opponents, he quickly rose on cloud and fog and wielded his iron rod, crying, "Don't run away!" One blow and the old dragon's head was all smashed up. Alas!

As blood spilled in the lagoon, red water swelled.
The corpse floated on the waves with dying scales.

The dragon son and grandson were so terrified that they all fled for their lives. Only the son-in-law, Nine-Heads, retrieved the corpse and retreated to the palace.

Pilgrim and Pa-chieh, however, did not give chase immediately; they went back to the shore instead to talk about what had happened. "This fellow's will to fight has been blunted now," said Pa-chieh. "With my rake, I fought my way in and caused tremendous wreckage. They were frightened out of their wits. I was just fighting with that son-in-law when the old dragon chased me out. It was a good thing that you beat him to death. When they get back inside, they will undoubtedly prepare for mourning and the funeral, and they certainly will not come out again. It's getting late also. What shall we do?"

"Why worry about the time?" said Pilgrim. "You should make use of this opportunity and go down to attack them once more. We must recover the treasure before we can return to the court." Our Idiot, however, had turned slothful and indolent, refusing to go with all sorts of excuses. "Brother," urged Pilgrim, "there's no need for all your deliberations. Just entice them to come as before and I'll attack them."

As the two were conversing like that, they suddenly saw a vast expanse of dark fog moved by a churning, violent gale from the east toward the south. When Pilgrim took a more careful look, he found that it was Erh-lang of Illustrious Sagacity traveling with the Six Brothers of Plum Mountain.[3] Leading hawks and hounds, they were also poling foxes, hares, deer, and antelopes. Each of them had a curved bow dangling from his waist and a sharp blade in his hand as they sped forward astride the wind and fog. "Pa-chieh," said Pilgrim, "those seven sages happen to be my bond-brothers. We should detain them and ask them to help us do battle. If we succeed, it'll be a wonderful opportunity for us." "If they're your brothers," replied Pa-chieh, "we should indeed ask them to stay." "But they have in their midst Big Brother Illustrious Sagacity," said Pilgrim, "who once defeated me. I'm a little embarrassed about showing myself abruptly to him. Why don't you block the path of their clouds and say, 'Lord Immortal, please stop for a moment. The Great Sage, Equal to Heaven, is here to pay you respect.' When he hears that I'm here, he will certainly stop. When he settles down, it'll be easier for me to see him."

Our Idiot indeed mounted the clouds and rose quickly to the peak of the mountain. "Lord Immortal," he cried with a loud voice, "please slow your horses and chariots. The Great Sage, Equal to Heaven, wishes to see you." On hearing this, that holy father gave the order for the six brothers to stop. After they met Pa-chieh, he asked, "Where is the Great Sage, Equal to Heaven?" Pa-chieh said, "He awaits your summons below there in the mountain." "Brothers," said Erh-lang, "please invite him to come here." The six brothers, being K'ang, Chang, Yao, Li, Kuo, and Chih, all ran out of the camp and cried, "Elder Brother Sun Wu-k'ung, Big Brother requests your presence."

Pilgrim went forward and, after he greeted each of them, they went up the mountain together. He was met by the Holy Father Erh-lang, who extended his hands to him and said, "Great Sage, you were delivered from the great ordeal and received the commandments in the Buddhist order. The days may be counted when your merit will be achieved and you will ascend your lotus throne. You are to be congratulated!" "Hardly," said Pilgrim. "I received a great kindness from you in the past, and I have yet to repay you. Though I have been delivered from my ordeal and am now journeying toward the West, I have no idea what sort of merit I shall accomplish. We are passing through at this moment the Sacrifice Kingdom, and in order to rescue some priests from their calamity, we have come here to capture fiends and demand the return of a treasure. By accident we saw the noble entourage of Elder Brother, and we make bold to request your assistance. We have no knowledge as to where you have come from or whether you will be pleased to grant us our wish."

"Because I had nothing to do," said Erh-lang with a smile, "I went hunting with the brothers, from which we were just returning. The Great Sage is most kind in asking us to stop, which is ample proof of how greatly he cherishes an old friend. If you want me to help you defeat some fiends, dare I not obey you? But what fiendish thieves are occupying this region?"

"You must have quite forgotten, Big Brother," said one of the six sages. "This is the Scattered-Rock Mountain, and below it is the Green Wave Lagoon, the dragon palace of All Saints." Somewhat startled, Erh-lang said, "But the old dragon All Saints doesn't cause any trouble. How would he dare steal a pagoda treasure?" "He recently took in a son-in-law," said Pilgrim, "a nine-headed insect who had become a spirit. The two of them conspired together as thieves and brought down a rain shower of blood on the Sacrifice Kingdom, after which they took away the śarīra Buddhist treasure on top of the Golden Light Monastery. Not perceiving the truth of the matter, the king bitterly persecuted and tortured the priests of that monastery instead. My master in mercy was moved to sweep the pagoda during the night, during which I caught two small fiends on the top. They were sent there on patrol, and when we took them into court this morning, they made an honest confession. The king therefore asked our master to subdue the fiends, and that was how we were sent here. During our first encounter, Pa-chieh was hauled away by that nine-headed insect when an additional head popped out of his torso. I went into the water by means of transformation and managed to rescue Pa-chieh. We had another fierce battle when I slew the old dragon, whose corpse was taken away by that fellow and his cohorts. We were just in the midst of discussing how to provoke battle again when you and your noble companions arrived. Hence our imposition on you."

"If you did smite the old dragon," said Erh-lang, "this is the best time to attack them. They'll not be prepared, and we can exterminate the whole nest of them." "That may be so," said Pa-chieh, "but after all, it's getting late now." Erh-lang replied, "As the military theorist says, 'An army does not wait for the times.' Why worry about how late it is?"

K'ang, one of the brothers, spoke up: "There's no hurry, Big Brother. Since his family members live here, that fellow is not about to run away. Now, since Second Elder Brother Sun is our honored guest, and since Stiff Bristles Hog⁴ also has returned to the right fruit, we should have a party right now, especially when we have brought wine and food along to our camp. The little ones can start a fire and we can set it up right at this place. We may toast the two of them and enjoy a nice visit together this evening. By morning, we can then provoke battle, and there'll still be plenty of time." Exceedingly pleased, Erh-lang said, "Our worthy brother has spoken well!" and he gave the order at once for the little ones to prepare the banquet. "We dare not decline the noble sentiments of all of you," said Pilgrim, "but since becoming priests, we have been observing the dietary laws. I hope we'll not cause any inconvenience." "But we do have fruits and the like," replied Erh-lang, "and even our wines are vegetarian." And so, by the light of the moon and the stars, the brothers lifted their cups in friendship, using Heaven as their tent and Earth as their mat.

Truly the lonely watches are long, but a happy night is all too short. Soon, the east turned pale with light. A few goblets of wine had given Pa-chieh enormous inspiration, and rousing himself, he said, "It's about dawn. Let old Hog go into the water to provoke battle." "Do be careful, Marshal," said Erh-lang. "Just trick him into coming out and we brothers will do our part." "I know! I know!" said Pa-chieh, laughing. Look at him! Tightening his clothes and gripping the rake, he used the water-division magic and leaped down there. The moment he arrived before the towered gateway, he gave a shout and fought into the palace hall.

At the time, the dragon son, having draped himself with a mourning gown of hemp, was standing guard over his father's corpse, and weeping. The dragon grandson and that son-in-law were busily preparing a coffin in the back. Shouting abuses, our Pa-chieh rushed forward and his upraised hands delivered a heavy blow with his rake. Nine gaping holes at once appeared on the head of that dragon son. The dragon dame was so aghast that she ran madly inside, wailing, "That long-snout monk has killed my son also!" When he heard this, the son-in-law immediately took up his crescent-tooth spade and led the dragon grandson out to do battle. Lifting his rake to oppose them, our Pa-chieh fought as he retreated, and soon they arrived on the surface of the water. All at once, the Great Sage, Equal to Heaven and the seven brothers swarmed all over them, and in no time at all, the showering blows of swords and spears reduced the dragon grandson to a few meat patties.

When that son-in-law saw that things were going badly, he rolled on the ground immediately and changed back into his original form. Spreading his wings, he soared into the air. Erh-lang took out his golden bow, affixed a silver pellet, and sent it hurtling toward the insect. The fiend quickly flapped his wings and darted down, wanting to bite Erh-lang. Just when another head popped out from the middle of his torso, however, the small hound of Erh-lang leaped into the air with a terrific bark and bit it clean off. In great pain, the fiend fled toward the north sea. Pa-chieh was about to give chase, but he was stopped by Pilgrim, who said, "Let's not follow him. As the proverb has it, 'The desperate fugitive should not be chased.' One of his heads has been bitten off by the small hound, and it's unlikely that he'll survive. Let me change into his appearance instead, and you open up a path in the water. Chase me into his palace. After we find the princess, we can wangle back the treasure." Erh-lang said, "I suppose it's all right that we don't track him down. But if this kind of creature remains in the world, it will undoubtedly bring great harm to people in posterity." Thus we have even today the blood-dripping nine-headed fowl, which is, in fact, the descendant of that creature.[5]

Pa-chieh meanwhile agreed to what Pilgrim told him and opened up a path in the water. Pilgrim, having changed into the appearance of the fiend, ran ahead while Pa-chieh followed behind, shouting and hollering. As they drew near the dragon palace, they were met by the princess All Saints, who asked, "Son-in-law, why are you in such a panic?" "That Pa-chieh has defeated me," replied Pilgrim, "and is chasing me here. I don't think I can resist him anymore. You'd better hide the treasures quickly." In such a hurry the princess, of course, could not distinguish truth from falsehood. She immediately took out from the rear hall a golden box to hand over to Pilgrim, saying, "This is the Buddhist treasure." After that, she took out also a white jade box and gave it to Pilgrim, saying, "This is the nine-leaf divine agaric. You take these treasures and hide them. Let me battle Chu Pa-chieh for a few rounds just to slow him down. After you have put away the treasures, you can come out and fight with him again."

Having taken over the boxes, Pilgrim gave his face a wipe and changed back into his original form, saying, "Princess, take a good look and see if I'm the son-in-law!" Thoroughly shaken, the princess tried to make a grab for the boxes, but Pa-chieh rushed in and one blow of the rake on her shoulder sent her to the ground.

There was only an old dragon dame left; she turned and tried to flee, only to be caught hold of by Pa-chieh. He was about to hit her with the rake, too, but was stopped by Pilgrim, who said, "Wait a moment. Let's not kill her. We should take a live one back to the capital so that we may announce our merit." Pa-chieh, therefore, dragged her up to the surface of the water, followed by Pilgrim holding the two boxes. He said to Erh-lang, "We're indebted to the authority and power of Elder Brother. We have recovered the treasures and wiped out the fiendish thieves." Erh-lang said, "We owe this rather to the excellent luck of the king in the first place, and to the boundless magic power of you two worthy brothers in the second. What have I done?" His brothers also said, "Since Second Elder Brother Sun has accomplished his merit, we should leave at once." Pilgrim could not stop thanking them; he would have liked to get them to go see the king, but they steadfastly refused. The sages thus left and returned to the River of Libation.

Pilgrim took up the boxes while Pa-chieh dragged along the dragon dame; moving midway between cloud and fog, they reached the kingdom in an instant. Those priests who had been freed in the Golden Light Monastery, you see, were waiting outside the city. When they saw the two of them stopping their cloud and fog, they went forward, bowing, to receive them into the city. At that time, the king and the T'ang monk were conversing. Forcing himself to be bold, one of the monks ran ahead and went into the gate of the court to memorialize: "Your Majesty, the two venerable fathers, Sun and Chu, have returned, bringing with them the treasures and the thief." On hearing this, the king left the hall quickly with the T'ang monk and Sha Monk. As he met the two disciples and praised them repeatedly for their divine merit, he also gave the command that a thanksgiving banquet be prepared. "There's no need for you to bestow on us food and drink as yet," said Tripitaka. "Let my humble disciples restore the treasure to the pagoda first. Then we may drink and feast." He then turned to Pilgrim to ask: "You two left the kingdom yesterday. How was it that you did not return until today?" Whereupon Pilgrim gave a detailed account of how they fought with the son-in-law and the dragon king, how they met the lord immortal, how they defeated the monster-spirits, and how they finally wangled the treasures. Tripitaka, the king, and all his civil and military officials could not have been more pleased.

"Does the dragon dame know human speech?" asked the king also. Pa-chieh said, "She is the wife of the dragon king who has given birth to many sons and grandsons. How could she not know human speech?" "If she does," said the king, "let her give us a complete account of the robbery."

The dragon dame said, "I know nothing of stealing the Buddhist treasure. It was entirely the work of my deceased husband and our son-in-law, Nine-Heads. When they discovered that the radiance on top of your pagoda was emitted by a Buddhist relic, they brought down a rain shower of blood three years ago and therewith stole the treasure."

"How did you steal the divine agaric plant?" asked the king again, and the dragon dame said, "That was the work of my daughter,

Princess All Saints, who sneaked into Heaven and stole from before the Hall of Divine Mists the nine-leaf divine agaric planted by the Lady Queen Mother of the West. Nourished by the divine breath of this plant, the śarīra would remain indestructible for a thousand years and luminous in all ages. Even if you just wave it slightly on the ground or in the fields, it will emit myriad shafts of colored rays and a thousand strands of auspicious beams. Now you have seized these things, and moreover, you have slaughtered my husband and my sons, you have done away with my son-in-law and my daughter. I beg you to spare my life."

"We're not about to spare *you*, of all persons!" said Pa-chieh. Pilgrim said, "Guilt cannot be borne by an entire family. We'll spare you. But you are required to be the perpetual guardian of the pagoda for us." "Even a good death is not as good as a wretched existence!" replied the dragon dame. "If you spare my life, you can do whatever you please with me." Pilgrim at once asked for an iron chain. After the attendant before the throne brought it out, Pilgrim pierced the lute bone of the dragon dame with the chain before saying to Sha Monk, "Invite the king to witness how we secure the pagoda."

Hurriedly asking for his carriage, the king left the court hand in hand with Tripitaka. Accompanied by many civil and military officials, they went to the Golden Light Monastery and ascended the pagoda. The śarīra was placed carefully inside a treasure vase on the thirteenth floor of the pagoda, while the dragon dame was chained to a pillar in the center. Pilgrim recited the magic words to summon together the local spirit of the capital, the city deity, and the guardian spirits of that monastery. Food and drink were to be brought to the dragon dame once every three days, they were told, but if she ever dared misbehave, she would be executed at once. The various gods obeyed in silence. Then Pilgrim used the agaric plant as a broom and swept each of the thirteen layers of the pagoda clean before returning it to the vase to nourish the śarīra. Thus it was the old had become the new once more, with myriad shafts of colored beams and a thousand strands of auspicious air. Once more the eight quarters could witness the radiance, and the four surrounding nations could wonder at the treasure. After they walked out of the pagoda's door, the king said, "If the old Buddha and the three Bodhisattvas had not come this way, how could we ever get to the bottom of this affair?"

"Your Majesty," said Pilgrim, "the two words, Golden Light, are not the best, for neither of these is a thing of permanence. Gold, after all, is an unstable substance, and light is air that flickers. Since this humble priest has already exerted such efforts for you, he would suggest that you change the monastery's name to Dragon-Subduing Monastery. It will last forever, I assure you." At once the king ordered the name be changed, and a new plaque, bearing the words Dragon-Subduing Monastery Built by Imperial Command, was hung across the main gate in front. He asked for an imperial banquet also and for the painter to make portraits of the four pilgrims. Their names, too, were recorded in the Five-Phoenix Tower. Thereafter, the king took the pilgrims personally in his own carriage out of the city to see them off. When they were offered gold and jade as a reward, master and disciples refused to take even a penny. Truly it was that

Fiends extirpated, all realms are cleansed;

The pagoda light's restored, the great earth is bright.

Then they departed; we do not know what their journey ahead would be like, and you must listen to the explanation in the next chapter.

At the Bramble Ridge Wu-nêng makes a great effort;
At the Shrine of Sylvan Immortals Tripitaka discusses poetry.

We were telling you about the king of the Sacrifice Kingdom, who expressed his thanks to Tripitaka T'ang and his disciples for recovering the treasure and capturing the fiends by offerings of jade and gold to them, which they refused to accept. The king therefore ordered the attendant before the throne to have two suits of clothing made for each of the pilgrims, according to the style that they had been wearing. Two pairs of shoes and socks and two silk sashes were also made for each person. In addition to these, dried goods—both baked and roasted foods—were also prepared. After their travel rescript had been certified, the king called for the imperial cortege; many civil and military officials, the people of the entire capital, and the monks of the Dragon-Subduing Monastery followed him to send the four out of the city, accompanied by the sonorous sounds of pipes and drums. When they had gone for some twenty miles, they took leave of the king first, while the rest of the officials and people retired after another twenty miles. Those priests from the Dragon-Subduing Monastery, however, refused to turn back even after walking with the pilgrims for some fifty or sixty miles, a few insisting that they would travel with the pilgrims to the Western Heaven, and a few others saying that they would practice austerities while serving the pilgrims on their way. When Pilgrim saw that none of them was willing to turn back, he had to use his magic. Pulling off some thirty strands of his hair, he blew a mouthful of divine breath on them, crying, "Change!" They changed at once into a herd of ferocious striped tigers, prowling and growling, which had the main road completely blocked. Only then did these monks become frightened and dared not proceed, so that the Great Sage could tell his master to urge his horse forward. In a little while, they faded in the distance, and the monks burst into loud wailing, all crying, "Most gracious and kind fathers! You're unwilling to save us because we have no affinity!"

Leaving those monks behind, we tell you instead about the master and his three disciples who headed toward the West. Only after they had gone for quite a distance did Pilgrim retrieve his hairs. Truly the seasons were quick to change, and soon it was the end of winter and the beginning of spring. Neither too hot nor too cold, it was a pleasant time to travel. As they walked along, they came upon a long ridge over which the main road had to pass. When Tripitaka reined in his horse to look at the place, he saw that the ridge was covered with brambles and clogged with creepers and vines. Though there was a faint trace of the road, it was flanked by the prickly thorns of brambles crowding in from left and right. "Disciples," the T'ang monk called out, "how could we walk through this road?" "Why not?" asked Pilgrim.

"Oh, disciples!" said the T'ang monk. "Below's the faded path; above are the brambles. Only reptiles or insects creeping on the ground can get through. Even for you, it means walking while bending double. How could I possibly stay on horse back?" "Don't worry," said Pa-chieh. "Let me show you my ability to rake firewood and spread open the brambles for you. Don't speak of riding a horse. Even if you were to ride a carriage, you would be able to get through."

"Though you may have the strength," said Tripitaka, "you can't last over a long distance. I wonder how wide this ridge is. Where can we find the energy?" Pilgrim replied, "No need to discuss this anymore. Let me go and have a look." He leaped into the air and what he saw was an endless stretch. Truly

They cloak the earth and fade into the sky,
They gather mist and hold up rain —
These soft, dishevelled mats flanking the road,
These jade-green tops shading the mount.
Dense and luxuriant the newly sprouted leaves;
Rank and prolific they thrive and bloom.
They seem from a distance to have no end;
Close up they look like a vast green cloud.
Furry and lush,
In fresh dark green,
They rustle loudly in the wind
As the bright sun makes them glow.
In their midst are pines, cedars, and bamboos;
Many plums, willows, and mulberries even more.
Creepers wind around old trees

And wisteria, the drooping willows.
Laced together like a prop,
They seem like a matted cot.
There are flowers blooming like brocade,
And wild buds send fragrance far away.
Which man has not met some brambles during his life?
Who has e'er seen such vast thickets of the West?

After he had stared at the region for a long time, Pilgrim lowered his cloud and said, "Master, this ridge is enormous!" "How enormous is it?" asked Tripitaka. "I can't see the end of it," replied Pilgrim. "It seems to be at least a thousand miles long." Horrified, Tripitaka said, "What shall we do?"

"Please don't worry, Master," said Sha Monk with a laugh. "Let's follow the example of those who burn off the land and set fire to the brambles so that you may pass through." "Stop babbling!" said Pa-chieh. "To burn off the land, you must do it around the time of the tenth month when the vegetation has dried up and is readily ignitable. Right now it is growing luxuriantly. How could it be burned?" "Even if you could," added Pilgrim, "the flame would be quite terrifying." "How are we to get across then?" asked Tripitaka. "If you want to get across," said Pa-chieh with a laugh, "you'll have to do as I say!"

Dear Idiot! Making the magic sign with his fingers, he recited a spell and gave his torso a stretch, crying, "Grow!" At once he reached the height of some two hundred feet. Shaking his muckrake, he cried, "Change!" and the handle of the rake attained the length of some three hundred feet. In big strides, he walked forward and, his two hands wielding the rake, pushed away the brambles left and right. "Let Master follow me!" he said, and a highly pleased Tripitaka quickly urged his horse forward, followed by Sha Monk poling the luggage and Pilgrim also using his iron rod to clear up the path.

That whole day they did not rest at all and journeyed for some one hundred miles. By evening they arrived at a small clearing, where they came upon a stone monument. On top were inscribed in large letters the words, Bramble Ridge. Down below there were two rows of smaller characters, which read:

Eight hundred miles of brambles intertwined,
A road that few since days of old have trod.

When Pa-chieh saw the monument, he said, laughing, "Let old Hog add two more lines to the inscription:

But now Pa-chieh's able to clear a path
Straight to the West, which is level and broad."
Delighted, Tripitaka dismounted and said, "Oh, disciple! We've tired
you out! Let's spend the night here, and we'll journey again when it's
light tomorrow." "Don't stop now, Master," said Pa-chieh. "While the
sky is still fair and we're inspired, we should clear the path right
through the night and get on with it!" The elder had to comply.

Pa-chieh went forward and again made a great effort; with the
rider not resting his hands and the horse not stopping its trotting,
master and disciples journeyed for one whole night and another day.
Once more it was getting late, but what lay before them was a bosky
sight. They also heard the song of wind-whipped bamboos and the
sound of rustling pines as they came upon another stretch of clearing,
in the center of which was an old shrine. There, outside the door, were
pines and cedars arrested in green, peaches and plums vying to display
their beauty.

After he dismounted, Tripitaka and his three disciples looked
around. What they saw was

An old shrine atop a cool stream before the cliff,
And desolate grounds, mist-wrapped, met their eyes.
For clumps of sāla trees long years had passed;
A mossed-terrace stood there as seasons went by.
Like swaying jade the bamboos seemed to speak,
And grief was told by a bird's fading cry.
Scant traces of man, or of beast and fowl;
Just wild blooms and creepers on walls most high.

After he had surveyed the region, Pilgrim said, "This place portends
more evil than good. We shouldn't stay here long." "Elder Brother,
aren't you overly suspicious?" said Sha Monk. "There's not even a
trace of humans here, let alone of a weird beast or a fiendish bird.
What's there to be afraid of?" He had hardly finished speaking when
a gust of cold wind brought out from behind the shrine door an old
man. He had on his head a square turban, a simple robe on his body,
a cane in his hand, and a pair of straw sandals on his feet. He was
followed by a demon attendant who had a red beard and a scarlet
body, a green face with jutting tusks, and who had on his head a
platter of wheat cakes. Going to his knees, the old man said, "Great
Sage, this humble deity is the local spirit of the Bramble Ridge. Having
learned of your arrival, I have little to offer you except this platter of

specially prepared steamed cakes. I present this to all of you venerable masters and ask you to have a meal. Throughout this region of eight hundred miles, there is no human household. So, please take some cakes for the relief of your hunger."

Delighted, Pa-chieh walked forward with outstretched hands and was about to take one of the cakes. Pilgrim, however, who had had the old man under scrutiny for some time, shouted immediately, "Stop! This isn't a good fellow! Don't you dare be impudent! What sort of a local spirit are you that you dare come to deceive old Monkey? Watch my rod!"

When the old man saw him attacking, he spun around and at once changed into a gust of cold wind. With a loud whoosh, it swept the elder high into the air. Tumbling over and over, he soon vanished from sight. The Great Sage was so taken aback that he did not know how to begin to search for his master, while Pa-chieh and Sha Monk stared at each other, paling with consternation. Even the white horse neighed in fear. The four of them, three brothers and the horse, seemed to be in a trance; they looked far and near but there was not a trace of their master. We shall leave them there, busily searching.

We tell you now instead about that old man and his demon attendant, who hauled the elder before a mist-shrouded stone house and then lowered him gently. Taking the hand of the elder, the old man said, "Sage monk, please don't be afraid. We are not bad people. I'm actually the Squire Eight-and-Ten[1] of Bramble Ridge. Since ours happens to be a night of clear breeze and bright moonlight, I have brought you here especially to meet a few friends and to talk about poetry, just to spend a pleasant moment of leisure." Only then did the elder manage to collect himself. As he glanced about carefully, this was truly what he found:

A haunt of misty clouds obscure,
A house in scenes divinely pure,
Good for keeping the self pure in training,
For flower and bamboo planting.
Cranes on verdant cliffs will be seen;
Frogs croak from ponds lovely and green.
T'ien-t'ai's magic hearth it surpasses,
Brighter than Mount Hua's air masses.
Fishing and plowing need we mention?
Worthy is this place of reclusion.

Sit still and your thoughts turn serene.
As faint moonlight ascends the screen.
As Tripitaka enjoyed the scenery, he felt that the moon and the stars
grew even brighter. Then he heard voices, all saying, "Squire Eight-
and-Ten has succeeded in inviting the sage monk here." When the
elder raised his head, he saw three old men: the first bore frostlike
features, the second had flowing green hair and beard, and the third
was meek mannered and dark colored. They each had different looks
and different garments, and they all came to salute Tripitaka. Returning their bows, the elder said, "What merit or virtue does this disciple
possess that he should win such kind attention from these aged
immortals?"

"We have always heard," replied Squire Eight-and-Ten with a
smile, "that the sage monk is possessed of the Way. Having waited for
you for a long time, we are fortunate indeed to be able to meet you
now. If you are willing to share with us the pearl and jade of your
wisdom, we beg you to sit and chat with us, as we long to know the
true teachings, the mysteries of Zen."

Again bending low, Tripitaka said, "May I ask the honorable styles
of the aged immortals?" "The one with the frostlike features," replied
Squire Eight-and-Ten, "is called Squire Lonesome Rectitude. The
green-haired one has the name of Master Void-Surmounting, and the
humble one goes by the title of Cloud-Brushing Dean. This old moron
bears the name of Knotty Virtue." "And what is the honorable age of
the immortals?" asked Tripitaka.

Squire Lonesome Rectitude said,

My age has a thousand years attained:
Dense leaves, ever young, reach toward the sky.
Thick, fragrant boughs shaped like dragons and snakes;
Of luscious shade, a frame tried by frost and snow.
Hardy since childhood and not worn by time,
Upright e'en now, I love the magic arts.
Phoenixes, no common birds, find shelter here—
Lush and lofty, far from this world's dust.

Smiling, Master of Void-Surmounting said,

A thousand years old, I've braved wind and frost
With tall, spiritual stems by nature strong.
My sounds are like raindrops in a quiet night;
My shade spreads cloudlike in a fine autumn day.

My roots are coiled for longevity I've known;
I've been taught the way of eternal youth.
My guests are cranes and dragons, not worldly beings.
Vibrantly green, I live near the realm of gods.
Smiling, Cloud-Brushing Dean said,
A thousand cold autumns I, too, have passed:
Old but cheerful, my form's both pure and quaint.
Aloof, I shun mixing with worldly dust and noise.
Still romantic, though I've borne frost and snow.
The Seven Worthies[2] are my friends of the Way;
The Six Hermits[3] are partners all in verse.
Not ditties or jingles, we make noble rhymes.
I am by nature the immortal's friend.
Smiling, Knotty Virtue, Squire Eight-and-Ten said,
I, too, am over a thousand years old.
Still fair and true, I delight in my green.
Loveable's my strength born of dew and rain;
The world's creative mystery I have tapped.
Only I thrive in all canyons' wind and mist;
None's more reposeful than I in all four climes.
A jade canopy I spread to shade my guests,
When they speak on Tao or play the lute and chess.
Thanking them, Tripitaka said, "All four of you immortals are enjoy-
ing long life. Why, Master Knotty Virtue is more than a thousand
years old! Having attained the Way at such an advanced age, and
blessed with such extraordinary and refined features, could you be
the Four White-Haired Ones[4] of the Han?" "You praise us far too
much!" replied the four old men together. "We are not the Four
White-Haired Ones, but only the Four Principled Ones deep in the
mountain. May we ask in turn the sage monk for his age?"
    With hands folded before his chest and bowing, Tripitaka replied:
Forty years ago I left my mother's womb:
My life saw disaster e'en before my birth!
Fleeing for life, I tossed on wave and tide.
By luck I met Gold Mountain and cast my shell.
Myself I trained and sūtras read with zeal;
In true worship of Buddha I dared not slack.
Now my King sends me to go to the West.
I'm favored by you divines on my way.

The four old men all joined in praising him, and one of them said,
"From the moment he left his mother's womb, the sage monk has
followed the teachings of Buddha. He has indeed practiced austerities
from childhood, and thus he is in truth a superior monk who possesses
the Way. Now that we have this good fortune of receiving your honorable presence, we make bold to seek from you your great doctrine.
We beg you to instruct us on the rudiments of the law of Zen, and
that would gratify our lifelong desire."

When he heard these words, the elder was not in the least daunted.
He began to speak to the four of them, saying, "Zen is quiescence, and
the Law is salvation. But the salvation of quiescence will not be
accomplished without enlightenment. The cleansing of the mind and
the purgation of desires, the abandonment of the worldly and departure from the dust—that is enlightenment. Now, it's a rare opportunity
to attain a human body, to be born in middle land,[5] and to encounter
the correct doctrine of Buddha. There is no greater blessing than the
possession of these three things. The wondrous ways of ultimate
virtue, vast and boundless, can neither be seen nor heard. It can,
however, extinguish the six organs of sense and the six kinds of perception. Thus perfect wisdom has neither birth nor death, neither
want nor excess; it encompasses both form and emptiness, and it
reveals the non-reality of both sages and common people.

To seek the truth you must perceive the mallet and tongs of
    Primal Origin;[6]
To intuit the Real you must perceive the technique of Śākyamuni.
Make known the power of mindlessness;[7]
Tread and shatter Nirvāṇa.
By means of the awakening of awakening, you must
Comprehend the enlightenment of enlightenment.
One spark of spiritual light is the protector of all.
Let the fierce flame shine like a dancer's robe,
Dominating the dharma realm as the one object seen.
Pierce the dark and tenuous;
Fortify also the strong.
This mysterious pass, thus spoken of, who can go through?
Mine's the originally practiced Zen of great awakening,
Retained and known only by those having affinity and will."
The four elders showed boundless delight when they received this
instruction. With hands folded and bowing in submission, all of them

said, "The sage monk is indeed the very source of enlightenment in the principle of Zen!"

Then Cloud-Brushing Dean said, "Though Zen is quiescence and the Law, salvation, it is still required of us to be firm in our nature and sincere in our mind. Even if we became the true immortal of great awakening, it is, in the end the way of no life. The mystery we live by, you see, is greatly different from yours." "The Way is indeed extraordinary," said Tripitaka, "but while substance and function are one, how could there be any difference?" Smiling, Cloud-Brushing Dean said,

Since we were born hardy and strong,
Our substance and function differ from yours.
Indebted to Heaven and Earth for giving us a body,
We're beholden to rain and dew for our colors' nourishment.
Smiling, we disdain the wind and frost
And pass the days and months.
Not one leaf of ours would wither;
All our branches hold firm to virtue.
In this way, instead of consulting the Lieh Tzu,
You read your texts in sanskrit.
Now, the Tao[8]
Was originally established in China.
Instead, you seek its illumination in the West.
You're wasting your straw sandals!
I wonder what it is that you are after?
A stone lion must have gouged out your heart!
Your bones must have been pumped full of wild foxes' saliva!
You forget your origin to practice Zen,
Vainly seeking the Buddha's fruit.
Yours are like the prickly riddles of my Bramble Ridge,
Like its tangled enigmas.
This sort of superior man
How could he teach and lead?
With this kind of style
How could he pass on the essence of true doctrine?
You must examine the appearances before you,
For there's life by itself in quiescence.
The bottomless bamboo basket will draw water;
The rootless iron tree will bring forth flowers.

Plant your feet firmly on the Ling-pao summit;

On your return you'll attend the fine assembly of Maitreya.

When Tripitaka heard these words, he kowtowed to thank the speaker, but he was raised by Squire Eight-and-Ten. As Squire Lonesome Rectitude also came forward to pull him up, Master Void-Surmounting let out a loud guffaw and said, "The words of Cloud-Brushing are obviously shot full of holes. Please rise, sage monk, and don't believe all he says. In this moonlight we never intended at all to discuss the theories of self-cultivation. Let's indulge rather in the composing and chanting of poetry." "If you want to do that," said Cloud-Brushing with a smile, "Let's go inside our little shrine for a cup of tea. How about it?"

The elder leaned forward to stare at the stone house, which had on top of its entrance an inscription of four words written in large characters: Shrine of Sylvan Immortals. They walked together inside and took their proper seats. Then the scarlet-bodied demon attendant came to serve them with a platter of China Root pudding and five goblets of fragrant liquid. The four old men invited the T'ang monk to eat first, but he was so suspicious that he dared no t take it right away. Only after the four old men partook of the food did Tripitaka also eat two pieces of the pudding. Each of them then drained the fragrant liquid and the goblets were taken away.

As he glanced cautiously around, Tripitaka saw that it was so bright and luminous inside the shrine that they seemed to be sitting directly beneath the moon.

From rock edges water flowed out

And from flowers came forth fragrance.

Unsoiled by half a speck of dust,

This place of grace and elegance.

Gladdened and comforted by such heavenly scenery, the elder could not refrain from chanting the following line:

The mind of Zen seems like the dustless moon.

With a broad grin, the elder Knotty Virtue immediately followed the lead and chanted:

On us our muse shines as the cloudless noon.

Squire Lonesome Rectitude said,

Fine phrases are cut like rolled-out brocade;

Master Void-Surmounting said,

Like rare treasures good lines are fashioned and made.

Cloud-Brushing Dean said,

Six Periods[9] are purged of their vain conceits;

The *Book of Odes* a new compiler meets.[10]

"This disciple," said Tripitaka, "has in an unguarded moment blurted out a few words. It's like swinging the axe before the Carpenter God! When I heard just now the fresh and elegant lines of you immortals, I knew I had met poetic masters." The elder Knotty Virtue said, "No need for irrelevant talk, sage monk. Those who have left the family must finish the work they started. If you begin a poem, you can't avoid finishing it, can you? We hope you will complete it." "This disciple can hardly do that," replied Tripitaka. "May I trouble Squire Eight-and-Ten to find the concluding lines and render the poem whole. That'll be wonderful!" "How cruel you are!" said Knotty Virtue. "You had the first line, after all. How could you refuse the last two? To withhold your talents is hardly reasonable." Tripitaka had no choice but to finish the last two lines by reciting:

Ere the tea darkens as pine breezes sing,

This gay mood of songs fills my heart with spring.

"Bravo!" said Squire Eight-and-Ten. "What a magnificent line—'This gay mood of songs fills my heart with spring'!"

"Knotty Virtue," said Squire Lonesome Rectitude, "since you are verily addicted to poetry, you love to mull over every line. Why not start another poem?"

Without hesitation, Squire Eight-and-Ten said, "I'll begin in the manner of 'Pushing the Needle':[11]

Spring quickens me not, nor does winter dry;

For me they are nothing, though clouds float by.

Master Void-Surmounting said, "I'll follow you in that manner also.

By me, though windless, is formed a dancing shade.

One loves such blessing and long life displayed."

Then Cloud-Brushing Dean said,

Displayed like West Mountain's noble sire,

I'm pure as southland's empty-hearted squire.

Finally, Squire Lonesome Rectitude said,

Squired by slanting leaves and wood of highest grade,

I yield the crossbeams of the king's estrade.[12]

On hearing this, the elder was full of praise for them, saying, "This is truly the most sublime poetry, its nobility reaches up to Heaven! Though this disciple is without talents, he would make bold to begin another two lines." "Sage monk," said Squire Lonesome Rectitude, "you are someone accomplished in the Tao, someone who has received profound nurture. There's no need for you to do another linking verse. Please grant us an entire poem by yourself, and we shall make the utmost effort to reply in kind."[13] Tripitaka had no alternative but to compose, smiling, a poem in the style of the regulated verse:

A priest goes West to seek the dharma king:
To farthest shores some wondrous scripts he'd bring.
"Thrice-blooming plants the poet's luck augment;
Jewel-tree blossoms waft the Buddha scent."[14]
To reach beyond the highest heights he'll strive
And try in all the worlds his office to live.
When he the noble jade form captivates,
The plot of truth lies before Nirvāṇa's gates.

When the four old men heard this, they paid him the highest compliments.

Then Squire Eight-and-Ten said, "This old moron has no other abilities except audacity. I shall force myself to answer your poem with this one of mine:

Aloof's Knotty Virtue, I scorn the sylvan king.
My fame spreads wider than this long-lived thing![15]
Tall, serpentine shade o'er the mount is bent;
The stream drinks my millennial, amber scent.
I reach out to enhance the universe,
Though wind and rain will my act and aim reverse.
Declining I lack those immortal bones,
With naught but fungi as my own gravestones."

"This poem," said Squire Lonesome Rectitude, "begins with a heroic line, and the middle parallel couplets, too, show tremendous strength. But the concluding lines are far too modest. How admirable! How admirable! This old moron will also reply with this poem:

My frosty face oft pleases the avian kings.
My talents thrive by the Hall of Four Great Things.[16]
Pearl drops of dew adorn my jade-green tent;
A gentle breeze will spread my chilly scent.
My murmurs at night the long porches attend;
An old shrine in autumn my shadows befriend.
To spring I give birthday gifts on new year's day;
I'm the old master of the mountain way."

"Marvelous poem! Marvelous poem! said Master Void-Surmounting,
laughing. "Truly it's as if the moon is putting the center of Heaven
under duress. How could this old moron reply in kind? But I shouldn't
allow this opportunity to pass by, I suppose, and so, I'll have to throw
together a few lines:
> Of towering talents close to lords and king,
> My fame by Grand Pure Palace[17] once did spring.
> On kiosks are seen green ether's descent;
> By darkened walls passes my faint, crisp scent.
> Upright forever I retain my mirth,
> For these roots are formed deep within the earth.
> Above the clouds my dancing shadow soars,
> Beyond those vainglorious, floral corps."

"The poems of the three squires," said Cloud-Brushing Dean, "are
most noble and elegant; they show the finest purity and simplicity.
Truly they can be said to have come from a brocaded bag. My body
has little strength and my bowels have little talents, but the instruction I received from the three squires has opened up my mind. So, I,
too, will offer this doggerel. Please don't laugh at me!
> In Ch'i-Yü[18] gardens I delight sage kings;
> Through fields of Wei[19] I'm free to sway and swing.
> No Naiad's tears my jadelike skin had stained,
> But mottled sheaths had Han histories contained.[20]
> By frost my leaves their true beauty reveal.
> Could mist henceforth my stems' luster conceal?
> With Tzu-yu's[21] passing my true friends are few,
> Though scholars' praise my fame ever renews."[22]

"The poems of the various immortal elders," said Tripitaka, "truly
resemble pearls emitted by phoenixes. Not even Tzu-yu and Tzu-hsia,
those two disciples of Confucius, could surpass you. Moreover, I'm
extremely grateful for your kindness and hospitality. It is, however,
deep in the night, and I fear that my three humble disciples are waiting
for me somewhere. Your student, therefore, cannot remain here long.
By your boundless love, let me leave now and go find them. I beg you
to point out to me the way back." "Please don't worry, sage monk,"
said the four old men, laughing. "Ours is an opportunity that comes
but once in a thousand years. Though the night is deep, the sky is fair
and the moon is very bright. Please sit here for a while longer. By

morning we shall escort you across the ridge, and you'll without fail
meet up with your disciples."

As they were thus speaking, there walked in from outside the stone
house two blue-robed maidens, holding a pair of red-gauze lanterns
and followed by an immortal girl. She was twirling in her hand a
sprig of apricot blossoms, and smiling broadly, she walked in to greet
them. How did she look, you ask. She had

A young face kingfisher adorned,
And colors better than rouge;
Luminous starlike eyes;
Moth brows neat and refined.
Down below: a light pink skirt patterned with five-colored plums;
Up above; a maroon blouse without collar or sleeves.
Small slippers pointed like phoenix beaks,
And slender stockings of silk brocade.
Seductive and coy like a T'ien-t'ai girl,[23]
She seems to be the charming Ta-chi[24] of old.

"To what do we owe this visit, Apricot Immortal?" asked the four old
men as they rose to greet her. After the girl had bowed to all of them,
she said, "I learned that a charming guest is being entertained here
and I've come especially to make his acquaintance. May I meet him?"
"The charming guest is right here," said Squire Eight-and-Ten, pointing at the T'ang monk. "There's no need for you to *ask* to see him."
Bending low, Tripitaka dared not utter a word. "Bring us some tea,
quickly!" cried the girl, and two more yellow-robed maidens walked
in with a red-lacquered tray, on which there were six small porcelain
tea cups, several kinds of exotic fruits, and a spoon for stirring placed
in the middle. One of the maidens also carried a tea pot of white iron
set in yellow copper, from which arose the overpowering aroma of
fine tea. After tea had been poured, the girl revealed ever so slightly
her slender fingers and presented a cup of it to Tripitaka first. Then
she gave the drink to the four old men before taking one herself.

"Why doesn't the Apricot Immortal take a seat?" asked Master
Void-Surmounting, and only then did she take a seat. When they had
finished their tea, the girl bowed again and said, "You immortals are
reveling in great pleasures this evening. May I be instructed a little
by your excellent verses?" "Ours are all crude and vulgar utterances,"
said Cloud-Brushing Dean, "but the compositions of the Sage Monk

can truly be considered a product of the high T'ang. They're most admirable." "If it's not too great an imposition," said the girl, "I would like to hear them." Whereupon the four old men gave a thorough rehearsal of the elder's poems and his discourse on Zen.

Smiling broadly, the girl said to them, "I'm so untalented, and I really shouldn't air my incompetence. But since I've had the privilege of hearing such magnificent poetry, I shouldn't allow myself to go uninspired. I shall exert myself to the utmost to answer the second poem of the sage monk with a regulated verse of my own. How about that?" She thus chanted loudly:

My fame was made lasting by Han-wu King;[25]
To me his pupils did Confucius bring.[26]
Tung Hsien's[27] affection would my growth foment;
Sun Ch'u[28] once loved my Feast-of-Cold-Food scent.
How tender and coy is this rain-moistened bloom!
What fresh verdant hues half veiled in misty gloom!
Ripeness makes me a little tart, I know.
Banished each year to wheat fields, that's my woe.

When those four men heard this poem, they all congratulated her, saying, "It's most elegant and sublime! And the lines are so full of vernal longings. Such a marvelous line—'How tender and coy is this rain-moistened bloom!'"

Smiling in a coquettish manner, the girl said, "I'm in fear and trepidation! The composition of the sage monk just now was something that could be said to have come from a mind of silk and a mouth of brocade. Let me say to him: if you can be persuaded to show us your talent, how about granting me another of your poems?" The T'ang monk, however, dared not reply. As the girl gradually became amorous, she began to sidle closer to where he was seated. "What's the matter with you, charming guest?" she asked softly. "If you don't have some fun on such a beautiful night, what else are you waiting for? The span of a life time, how long could that be?"

"If the Apricot Immortal," said Squire Eight-and-Ten, "entertained such genial feelings, how could the sage monk not reciprocate by giving his consent? If he withholds his favors, then he doesn't know how lucky he is." "But the sage monk," said Squire Lonesome Rectitude, "is a gentleman of fame and accomplishment in the Tao, who certainly will not indulge in anything improper. If we insist on such activities, it is we who are guilty of impropriety: we would be soiling a man's fame and spoiling his virtue. That's hardly the proper thing to do! If Apricot Immortal is indeed so inclined, let Cloud-Brushing Dean and Squire Eight-and-Ten serve as go-betweens. Master Void-Surmounting and I can be the witnesses. They can then seal this marital contract. Wouldn't that be nice?"

On hearing this, Tripitaka turned red in anger. Leaping up all at once, he shouted: "You are all fiendish creatures! How you've tried to tempt me! At first, I allowed your platitudes to goad me into discussing the mysteries of Tao, and that was still all right. But how could you use this 'beauty trap' now to try to seduce me? What have you to say to this?" When the four elders saw how enraged Tripitaka had become, they became so startled that every one of them bit his fingers and fell completely silent. The scarlet-bodied demon attendant, however, grew very angry and bellowed: "Monk, you can't even tell when someone's trying to do you a favor! Is there anything bad about this dear sis of mine? Look at her refinement and talents, her lovely jadelike features. Let's not talk about her skills in the feminine arts. Just a single poem of hers has already demonstrated that she is a worthy match for you. Why do you so brusquely refuse her? You'd better not let this opportunity slip by. What Squire Lonesome Rectitude says is most appropriate. If you refuse to do anything improper, let me serve as your marriage official."

Tripitaka turned pale with fright, but he refused to give his assent no matter how urgently they pleaded with him. "You foolish priest!" said the demon attendant again. "We speak to you in a kindly manner, and you refuse us. If you arouse our wild and unruly passions and make us abduct you to another region, where you can neither pursue your priestly life nor take a wife, won't you have lived in vain?" With a mind like metal or stone, that elder adamantly refused to comply. He thought to himself: "I wonder where my disciples are looking for me. . . ." So speaking to himself, he could not restrain the tears from rolling down his cheeks. Trying to placate him with a smile, the girl sat down close to him and took out from her sleeve a honey-scented handkerchief to wipe away his tears. "Charming guest," she said, "don't be so upset! Let's you and I nestle in jade and perfume and have some fun!" Uttering a loud cry, the elder bounded up and tried to dash out of the door, only to be grabbed by all those people. They brawled and struggled like that until dawn.

Suddenly another cry could be heard: "Master, Master, where are you speaking?" The Great Sage Sun, you see, together with Pa-chieh and Sha Monk had been leading the horse and poling the luggage for a whole night without stopping. Going through brambles and thorns, searching this way and that, they managed to cover the entire eight hundred miles of the Bramble Ridge halfway between cloud and fog. By morning they reached the western edge of the ridge, and that was when they came upon the noises made by the T'ang monk. They responded with the cry, and the elder somehow managed to struggle out of the door, yelling, "Wu-k'ung, I'm here! Come and save me, quick!" In a flash, those four old men, the demon attendant, the girl, and her maidens all disappeared.

Soon Pa-chieh and Sha Monk arrived, saying, "Master, how did you get here?" Tugging at Pilgrim, Tripitaka said, "Oh, disciples! I've been a great burden on you. That old man we saw last night, who claimed to be the local spirit coming to offer us food, was the person who hauled me to this place when with a shout you were about to hit him. He led me inside the door by the hand and introduced me to three other old men, all addressing me as the sage monk. Every one of them was quite refined in speech and manner, and they were all able poets. We spent our time in the exchange of verses until about midnight, when a beautiful girl accompanied by lanterns also arrived to meet me. She, too, composed a poem and addressed me as the charming guest. Then because of my looks she wanted to marry me. I woke up to their scheme all at once and refused. They began to put pressure on me, one wanting to be the go-between, another the marriage official, and still another the witness. I swore I would not comply, arguing with them and desperately trying to struggle free. Out of the blue you people arrived. I suppose partly because it was getting light already, and partly because they seemed to be afraid of you, they all vanished suddenly, though they were still pulling and tugging at me just a moment ago."

"If you talked and discussed poetry with them," said Pilgrim, "did you not ask them for their names?" "I did ask them for their styles," replied Tripitaka. "The first old man called himself Squire Eight-and-Ten, and his style was Knotty Virtue. The second was styled Squire Lonesome Rectitude; the third, Master Void-Surmounting; and the fourth, Cloud-Brushing Dean. They addressed the girl as Apricot Immortal." "Where are these creatures located?" asked Pa-chieh.

"Where did they go?" Tripitaka said, "I don't know where they went, but the place where we discussed poetry was not far from here."

As the three disciples looked around with their master, they discovered a cliff nearby, and on the cliff was a plaque bearing the words, Shrine of Sylvan Immortals. "It was right here," said Tripitaka. When Pilgrim examined the place more carefully, he saw nearby a huge juniper tree, an old cypress tree, an old pine tree, and an old bamboo. Behind the bamboo was a scarlet maple tree. As he looked toward the far side of the cliff, he saw also an old apricot tree, flanked by two stalks of winter plum and two cassia plants.

"Have you people found the fiends?" said Pilgrim with a laugh. "Not yet," replied Pa-chieh. "Don't you know," said Pilgrim, "it is these several trees right here that have become spirits?" "Elder Brother," said Pa-chieh, "how do you know that?"

"Squire Eight-and-Ten," replied Pilgrim, "is the pine; Squire Lonesome Rectitude is the cypress; Master Void-Surmounting is the juniper; Cloud-Brushing Dean is the bamboo; the scarlet-bodied demon is the maple; Apricot Immortal is, of course, the apricot tree, while the maids are the cassia and the winter plum." When Pa-chieh heard this, he rushed forward without further ado: using his rake along with several shoves of his snout, he brought to the ground those winter plum, cassia, old apricot, and maple. From beneath the roots of these trees, fresh blood indeed spurted out. Tripitaka walked forward to pull at him, saying, "Wu-nêng, don't hurt them. Though they have reached the stage of becoming spirits, they have done me no harm. Let us find our way and leave."

"Master, you shouldn't pity them," said Pilgrim. "For I fear that they may become great fiends later, and then they will bring much harm to humans." Our Idiot thus decided to work his rake some more and toppled the pine, cypress, juniper, and bamboo as well. Only after that did they help their master to mount up and all proceeded along the main road to the West once more. We do not know what the future holds for them, and you must listen to the explanation in the next chapter.

Fiends in deception set up the Small Thunderclap;
The four pilgrims all meet a great ordeal.

This chapter's karmic import
Is to persuade man to do good
And to shun all evil works.
Even a single thought
Is known to all the gods,
Do whatever you will.
Folly or cleverness, how would you learn?
No-mind is still the cure for both of these.
While yet alive, the Way you should cultivate;
Don't drift or roam.
Recognize your source
And cast your shell.
To seek long life,
You must catch it.
Be ever enlightened;
Let ghee[1] annoint you
When the Three Passes[2] are pierced and the dark ocean's filled,
The virtuous will surely ride the phoenix and crane.
At that time compassion is with mercy joined
As you reach ultimate bliss.

We were telling you about Tripitaka T'ang, who was most single-minded in his piety and sincerity. We need not mention how he was protected by the gods above; even such spirits as those of grass and wood also came to keep him company. After one night of elegant conversation on the arts, he was delivered from the thorns and thistles, no longer encumbered by vines or creepers. As he and his three disciples journeyed westward, they traveled for a long time, and it was again the end of winter. This was, in truth, a day of spring:

All things thrive and flourish
As the Dipper's handle returns to *yin*.[3]

Young grasses cover the earth with green,
And verdant willows line the banks.
A ridge of peach blossoms red like brocade;
Half a stream of misty water like jade-green silk.
How rain and wind persist
To one's endless grief!
The sun enhances the flowers' grace;
The swallows fetch light mossy buds.
Like a Wang Wei's painting[4] the mountain's shaded dark and
    light;
And birds chatter like the sharp tongue of Chi-tzu.[5]
There's no one to enjoy such lovely embroidery
Except the dancing butterfly and the singing bee.

Master and his disciples proceeded with the slow trotting of the horse, enjoying themselves all the while by searching out the fragrant flowers and treading on the green meadows. As they walked along, they came upon a tall mountain which, from a distance, seemed to touch the sky. "Wu-k'ung," said Tripitaka, pointing with his whip, "I wonder how tall that mountain is. It seems that it is actually touching the blue sky, or it may have even punctured the azure heavens!" Pilgrim said, "I remember two lines of an ancient poem that say:

Only the sky remains high above;
No mountain can equal its height.

These two lines are trying to describe the extreme height of one particular mountain, such that no other mountain could be compared with it. But how could a mountain actually touch the sky?"

"If it did not," said Pa-chieh, "then why did people call Mount K'un-lun 'the pillar of Heaven'?" Pilgrim replied, "Don't you know the old adage,

Heaven was not filled in the northwest.

Now, Mount K'un-lun is located in the northwest, at the position of *ch'ien*, and that's why it is commonly thought to be a mountain that can hold up the sky by filling the void. Hence the name, pillar of Heaven." "Elder Brother," said Sha Monk, laughing, "don't give him all these nice explanations! When he hears them, he will try to out-smart someone else. Let's get moving. When we've climbed the mountain, then we'll know how tall it is."

Our Idiot tried to lunge at Sha Monk, and as the two of them

pranced along, the old master urged the horse into a gallop. In a
moment, they drew near to the mountain cliff. As they ascended the
mountain step by step, what they saw was this:
A forest where the wind was howling;
A brook where the water gurgled.
No crow or bird flew over this mountain;
Even immortals might say, "It's hard!"
Ten thousand cliffs and ravines,
A million twists and turns.
No man ever reached this place of churning dust;
No end the sight of strange, ghostly rocks.
Clouds at some spots seemed like shimmering pools;
Trees everywhere filled with raucous calls of birds.
Deer left, holding agaric;
Apes returned, bearing peaches.
Foxes and badgers jumped about the ledge;
Antelopes played on the mountain peak.
A sudden roar of the tiger made one cringe
As striped leopards and grey wolves barred the road.
The moment that Tripitaka saw all this, he was terrified, but Pilgrim
Sun displayed his vast magic powers. Look at him with his golden-
hooped rod! He gave one shout and all those wolves, tigers, and
leopards scattered. Opening up a path, he led his master straight up
the tall mountain. After they passed the summit, they descended
westward until they reached a plateau, where they suddenly came
upon rays of divine light and strands of colored mists. There was in
the distance a magnificent building, from which the faint, harmonious
sounds of bells and sonorous stones could be heard. "Disciples," said
Tripitaka, "take a look and see what kind of place that is."
    Shading his eyes with his hand, Pilgrim lifted his head to stare at
the building. It was a good place indeed! Truly
A bejewelled edifice,
A noble monastery.
An empty valley that heightens the music of earth;
A quiet place that diffuses nature's fragrance.
Verdant pines, rain soaked, shroud the tall towers;
Green bamboos, cloud-wrapped, guard the lecture hall.
Lights radiate from this distinctive dragon palace;
Colors flutter around this Buddhist domain.

Scarlet rails and jade portals;
Painted pillars and carved beams.
Sūtras explained, incense fills the seats.
Mysteries exposed, the moon lights up the screens.
Birds sing within the scarlet trees;
Cranes drink at the pebbled brook.
Flowers bloom everywhere in this Jetavana park;
On three sides Śrāvastī light spills through open doors.
Doors of rugged buildings face the mountain range.
Hollow bells and stones strike languidly and long.
The opened windows in a gentle breeze,
The rolled up screen in curls of smoke.
With monks here the life's ascetic,
A peace not marred by things profane.
Truly a place divine which the world can't touch:
A quiet monastery, a good plot of truth.

After Pilgrim had looked at the place, he turned to Tripitaka, saying,
"Master, that is a monastery over there. I don't know why, however,
within the aura of Zen and the auspicious lights there seems to be an
air of violence also. When I look at this scenery, it reminds me greatly
of Thunderclap, but the road just does not seem right. When we reach
the building, don't walk in immediately, for I fear that some sinister
hand may bring us harm."

"If this place reminds you of Thunderclap," said the T'ang monk,
"could it be verily the Spirit Mountain? You'd better not slight my
sincerity and delay the very purpose of my journey." "No! No!" said
Pilgrim. "I have traveled on the way to the Spirit Mountain several
times before. How could it be this one?" "Even if it is not," said Pa-
chieh, "there must be a good person staying here." Sha Monk said,
"We don't have to be so suspicious. This road has to take us right past
that door. Whether it is Thunderclap or not, one look will tell us."
"What Wu-ching says," said Pilgrim, "is quite reasonable."

Urging his horse with the whip, the elder soon arrived before the
monastery gate, on top of which he saw the three words, The Thunderclap Monastery. He was so astonished that he rolled off the horse and
fell to the ground. "You wretched ape!" he scolded. "You've just
about killed me! It is The Thunderclap Monastery, and you still want
to deceive me!" Attempting to placate him with a smile, Pilgrim said,
"Don't get upset, Master. Take another look. There are four words on

the gate of the monastery, and you have only seen three of them. And you still blame me?" Trembling all over, the elder scrambled up and took another look. There were indeed these four words: The Small Thunderclap Monastery.

"If it's only The Small Thunderclap Monastery," said Tripitaka, "there must be a Buddhist patriarch inside. The sūtras mentioned some three thousand Buddhas, but I suppose they can't be all in one place. Kuan-yin, after all, is in South Sea, Viśvabhadra is located at Mount O-mei, and Mañjuśri lives on the Mountain of Five Platforms. I wonder which Buddhist patriarch presides over this plot of truth. The ancients said,

With Buddhas there are scriptures;
Without temples there are no treasures.
We should go inside."

"You shouldn't," said Pilgrim. "This place portends more evil than good. If you run into calamity, don't blame me." "Even if there's no Buddha," said Tripitaka, "there must be his image. This disciple has made a vow that I shall bow to Buddha whenever I encounter him. How could I blame you?" Whereupon he ordered Pa-chieh to take out his cassock. After he changed into his clerical cap and tidied his clothing, Tripitaka strode forward.

As they walked inside the monastery gate, they heard a loud voice saying, "T'ang monk, you came all the way from the Land of the East to seek an audience with our Buddha. How dare you be so insolent now?" On hearing this, Tripitaka at once prostrated himself; Pa-chieh, too, kowtowed as Sha Monk went to his knees. Only the Great Sage, however, led the horse and remained behind, picking up the luggage. When they went inside the second door, they came upon the great hall of Tathāgata. Outside the great hall door and beneath the treasure throne stood in rows the five hundred arhats, the three thousand guardians of the faith, the Four Great Diamond Kings, the mendicant nuns, and the upāsakas, along with countless sage monks and workers. Truly, there were also glamorous fragrant flowers and auspicious rays in abundance. The elder, Pa-chieh, and Sha Monk were so overcome that they touched their heads to the ground with each step they took, inching their way toward the spirit platform. Only Pilgrim remained boldly erect.

Then they heard another loud voice coming from the top of the lotus throne, saying, "You, Sun Wu-k'ung! How dare you not bow down before Tathāgata?" Little did anyone expect that Pilgrim would look up and carefully scrutinize the one who spoke. When he recognized that it was a specious Buddha, he at once abandoned the horse and the luggage. Gripping the rod in his hands, he shouted, "You bunch of accursed beasts! You are audacious! How dare you take in vain the Buddha's name and soil the pure virtue of Tathāgata! Don't run away!" Wielding the rod with both his hands, he attacked at once.

With a loud clang there dropped from midair a pair of golden cymbals; they fell on Pilgrim and had him enclosed completely from head to foot. Chu Pa-chieh and Sha Monk were so aghast that they reached for their rake and staff, but they were overwhelmed at once by those arhats, guardians, sage monks, and workers who surged forward to surround the three pilgrims. Tripitaka, too, was thus caught, and all three of them were then firmly bound by ropes.

The one who appeared as the Buddhist patriarch sitting on the lotus throne, you see, was actually a monster-king, and those arhats were all little fiends. After they put away their Buddha appearances, they revealed again their fiendish forms and hauled the elder and his two disciples to the rear so that they could be locked up. Pilgrim was to remain sealed in the golden cymbals and never to be released. With the cymbals placed on the jewelled platform, he was expected to be reduced to pus and blood in the period of three days and nights. After that, then the other pilgrims were to be steamed in an iron cage and eaten. Truly

The green-eyed Monkey knew both false and real,
But Zen Spirit bowed, eyeing a golden form.
Yellow Hag in blindness paid homage, too:
Wood Mother also spoke up foolishly.
A fiend, growing strong, one's true self oppressed;
A wicked demon deceived the natural man.
Indeed the Tao is small and the demon, large.
A wrong turn to Side Door,[6] your work is vain!

At the time, the various fiends shut up the T'ang monk and his two disciples in the rear, and there they tied the horse also. After they placed his cassock and his clerical cap inside the luggage wrap, they hid these also in a guarded place. We shall leave them for the moment.

We tell you now about that Pilgrim, who had been enclosed within the golden cymbals. It was pitch black inside, and he became so exasperated that he perspired all over. He tried pushing left and shoving right, but he could not get out. Then he struck madly at the cymbals with his iron rod, but he could not dent them even one whit. With no further alternative, he wanted to break the cymbals by sheer brute force. Making a magic sign with his fingers, he at once grew to thousands of feet tall, but the cymbals also grew with him. There was not even the slightest crack to let in a ray of light. He made the magic sign again and at once his body diminished in size until he became as small as a mustard seed. The cymbals grew smaller, too, with his body, so that there was not the tiniest hole. Gripping the iron rod, Pilgrim blew on it a divine breath, crying "change!" It changed into a flag pole which he used to hold up the cymbals. Then he selected two of his longer hairs behind his head and pulled them off, crying, "Change!" They changed immediately into a plum-flowerlike, five-pointed drill; along the base of the rod, he drilled away for over a thousand times. There were loud scraping noises from the drill, but he could not puncture the cymbals at all.

In sheer desperation, Pilgrim made the magic sign again and recited the spell:

Let *Oṁ* and *Ram* purify the dharma realm.

Ch'ien: Origination, Penetration, Harmony, and Firmness.[7]

With this he summoned the Guardian of Five Quarters, the Six Gods of Light and the Six Gods of Darkness, the Eighteen Guardians of Monasteries, who gathered outside the golden cymbals, saying, "Great Sage, we were all giving protection to your master so that the demons could not harm him. Why did you summon us?"

"That master of mine," said Pilgrim, "refused to listen to me! It's no big loss even if he were put to death! But what I want you to do is think of some way quickly to pry open these cymbals and let me out. Then we can take care of other matters. Right now, there's not a bit of light inside, and I'm so hot that I'm about to suffocate." The various deities indeed tried to pry open the cymbals, but they were so tightly closed up that they seemed to have grown together. The gods could not even budge them. "Great Sage," said the Golden-Headed Guardian, "we don't know what sort of treasure this pair of cymbals is, but from top to bottom, they have become one whole piece now. Your humble deities are too weak to pry them loose." "I don't know how much magic power I've used inside," said Pilgrim, "but I can't budge them either."

On hearing this, the Guardian told the Six Gods of Light to protect the T'ang monk and the Six Gods of Darkness to watch over the golden cymbals. As the various other Guardians of Monasteries took up positions of patrol front and back, he mounted the auspicious luminosity and, in a moment, went straight through the South Heavenly Gate. Without waiting for further summons, he went up to the Hall of Divine Mists and prostrated himself before the Jade Emperor. "My lord," he said, "your subject is the Guardian of Five Quarters. I commend to you the Great Sage, Equal to Heaven, who is accompanying the T'ang monk to acquire scriptures. Passing through a mountain, they came upon The Small Thunderclap Monastery. By mistake the T'ang monk thought it was the Spirit Mountain and he entered the monastery to worship. It was actually an edifice set up by a fiendish monster to ensnare the master and his disciples. At this moment, the Great Sage is imprisoned within a pair of golden cymbals, from which he cannot be extracted at all. He is about to die, and that's why I've come here especially to memorialize to you." The Jade Emperor at once gave this decree: "Let the Twenty-Eight Constellations go quickly to subdue the fiends and bring deliverance to the pilgrims."

Not daring to linger, the Constellations followed the Guardian to leave the heavenly gate and arrived inside the monastery. It was about the time of the second watch at night; those monster-spirits, both great and small, having been rewarded by the old fiend for capturing the T'ang monk, had all gone to sleep. Without disturbing them, the Constellations gathered outside the cymbals and reported: "Great Sage, we are the Twenty-Eight Constellations sent here by the Jade Emperor to rescue you."

Exceedingly pleased by what he heard, Pilgrim said immediately, "Use your weapons and break the thing. Old Monkey will be out at once." "We dare not do so," replied the stars. "This thing is of metallic substance. If we strike at it, there'll be noises and the demon will be awakened. Then it'll be hard for us to rescue you. Let us use our weapons instead and see if we can puncture it. Wherever you detect even the faintest speck of light, you'll be able to escape." "Exactly," said Pilgrim.

Look at them! Wielding spears, swords, scimitars, and axes, they began to pry at the pair of cymbals and stab at them, hauling them back and forth. They did this until about the time of the third watch, but the cymbals could not be loosened at all. The pair seemed to be

like a won-ton that had been forged together. Pilgrim inside was
looking this way and that; he crawled over here and rolled to the
other side, but he could not detect even the faintest speck of light.

"Oh, Great Sage," said Gullet the Gold Dragon,[8] "please be more
patient. As I see it, this treasure must be a compliant thing which
knows transformation also. Try to feel with your hands inside along
the edges where the cymbals come together. I'm going to use the tip
of my horn and see if I can wedge it inside. Then you can use some
kind of transformation and escape through the spot where it comes
apart." Pilgrim agreed and started to use his hands to feel along the
edges. Meanwhile, this Constellation made his body smaller until his
horn became like a pointed needle. At the top of the cymbals where
they were joined, he tried to stick the horn through. Alas, he had to
use every ounce of his strength before he managed to reach inside.
Then he caused his body and his horn to take on the dharma form,
crying, "Grow! Grow! Grow!" The horn grew to the thickness of a
rice bowl. The edge of the cymbals, however, did not behave like any
metallic object at all; instead, they seemed to have been made of skin
and flesh, which had the horn of Gullet the Gold Dragon in a viselike
grip. There was not the slightest crack anywhere around the horn.
When Pilgrim felt the horn with his hands, he said, "It's no use!
There's no crack above or below! I have no choice. You must bear a
little pain and take me out." Marvelous Great Sage! He changed the
golden-hooped rod into a steel drill and drilled a hole on the tip of the
horn. Transforming his body into the size of a mustard seed, he stuck
himself inside the hole and yelled, "Pull the horn out! Pull the horn
out!" Again, the Constellation exerted who knows how much
strength before he yanked it out and fell exhausted to the ground.

As soon as Pilgrim crawled out from the hole he drilled in the tip of
the Constellation's horn and changed back into his true form, he
whipped out the iron rod and slammed it down with a crash on the
cymbals. It was as if a copper mountain had been toppled, a gold mine
blown open. What a pity! An instrument belonging to the Buddha
was instantly reduced to a thousand fragments of gold! The Twenty-
Eight Constellations were terrified and the Guardian of Five Quarters'
hair stood on end. All those various fiends, old and young, were
roused from their dreams, and even the old monster-king was startled
in his sleep. He scrambled up, and as he put on his clothes, he ordered
a roll of drums to assemble the rest of the fiends and arm them. It was

about dawn at this time when they rushed beneath the treasure throne. There they saw Pilgrim Sun and the various Constellations hovering over the pieces of the golden cymbals. Paling with fright, the monster-king gave this order: "Little ones! Shut the front door quickly and don't let anyone out."

On hearing this, Pilgrim led the star spirits to mount the clouds and rose into the air. After the monster-king had put away the gold fragments, he ordered his troops to line up in formation outside the monastery gate. Nursing his anger, the monster-king hurriedly put on his armor and picked up a short, pliant wolf-teeth club[9] to walk out of his camp, crying, "Pilgrim Sun, a brave man shouldn't run away! Step forward quickly and fight three rounds with me!" Unable to contain himself, Pilgrim led the star spirits to lower their clouds and to take a good look at that monster-spirit. They saw he had

Dishevelled hair,
Strapped down by a thin and flat gold band;
Glowering eyes,
Topped by thick, bushy yellow brows;
A gall-like nose
With nostrils flaring;
A four-square mouth
With sharp, pointed teeth.
He wore a cuirass of chain mail.
Tied with a sash spun with raw silk.
His feet were shod in calfskin boots;
His hands held up a wolf-teeth club.
His form was beastlike, though he was no beast;
With looks nonhuman, still he seemed like man.

Sticking out his iron rod, Pilgrim shouted: "What kind of fiendish creature are you, that you dare play the Buddhist patriarch, occupy this mountain, and falsely set up The Small Thunderclap Monastery?"

"So, the little monkey doesn't know my name!" replied the monster-king, "and that's why you've transgressed the territory of this divine mountain! This place is called the Little Western Heaven. By my self-cultivation I have attained the right fruit, and thus Heaven bestowed on me these treasure bowers and precious towers. My name is the Old Buddha of Yellow Brows, but the people of this region, ignorant of that, address me as the Great King Yellow Brows or Holy Father Yellow Brows. I have known all the while that you are on your way to the West, and that you have some abilities. That's why I displayed my powers and set up the image to lure your master to enter. I want to make a wager with you. If you can withstand me, I'll spare you all, master and disciples, so that you, too, can perfect the right fruit. If you can't, I'll slay all of you, and I'll go myself to see Tathāgata for the scriptures, so that *I* can attain the right fruit for China." "Monster-spirit," said Pilgrim with a laugh, "no need to brag! If you want this wager, come up quickly and receive the rod!" Very amiably the monster-king met him with the wolf-teeth club, and this was some battle!

The club and rod
Are not the same.
Come to speak of it, they have their own forms!
One is a short and pliant Buddhist arm;
One is a deep-sea treasure stiff and hard.
Both can transform according to one's wish;
They join this time and each strives to be strong.
The short, pliant wolf-teeth's jewel bedecked;
The sturdy golden-hooped is dragonlike.
They can turn thick or thin, how marvelous!
They can grow long or short with perfect ease.
Demon and ape
Together fight
A hot, furious battle—that's not a lie!
The ape tamed by faith Mind Monkey becomes;
The fiend mocks Heaven in his image false.
Raging and fuming, they both turn cruel;
Vicious and violent they both look the same.
This one aims at the head and refuses to quit;
That one stabs at the face with no let up.
Spat-out clouds darken the sun;
Belched-out fog cover the mount.
Rod and club, as they join, swing back and forth;
For Tripitaka they slight life or death.

Look at the two of them! They closed in for more than fifty times, but no decision could be reached. Before the gate of the monastery, those various monster-spirits began to shout their encouragements, beating their drums and gongs at the same time and waving their banners. On this side, the Twenty-Eight Constellations, the Guardian of Five

Quarters, and the other sages immediately uttered a cry and, each wielding his weapon, had the demon surrounded. The fiends before the monastery were so terrified that they could no longer beat the drums; trembling all over, they could hardly sound the gongs.

The old fiendish demon, however, was not in the least afraid. With one hand he used his wolf-teeth club to fence off all those weapons; with his other hand he untied from his waist a little wrap made of old white cloth. He flung the wrap skyward and, with a loud whoosh, the Great Sage Sun, the Twenty-Eight Constellations, and the Guardian of Five Quarters were all wrapped up inside it. Retrieving the wrap, the monster swung it on his shoulder and turned to stride back to his camp, while all those little fiends were elated by this sudden triumph.

Asking his little ones to fetch him several dozen ropes, the old fiend told them to untie the wrap: as each of the prisoners was fished out, he was immediately bound. All of the deities were weak and numb, and even their skin seemed to be wrinkled and their appearance emaciated. After they were bound, they were hauled to the rear of the monastery and thrown to the ground. Then the monster-king ordered a large banquet for himself and his subjects, and they drank until dusk before scattering to retire. We shall thus leave them for the moment.

We tell you now about the Great Sage Sun, who was tied up along with the other deities. By about midnight there suddenly came to them the sound of someone weeping. When the Great Sage listened closely, he discovered that it was the voice of Tripitaka, who wailed, "Oh, Wu-k'ung!

I loathe myself for not heeding you then,
Thus bringing this day such woe on my head!
Now you are hurt in the cymbals of gold.
Which person knows I'm bound here with ropes?
Fate, most bitter, caused what we four had met,
And merits, three thousand, are all o'erthrown.
What will free us from this painful restraint,
That we may reach the West smoothly and leave?"

On hearing this, Pilgrim was moved to compassion, saying to himself: "Though that master refused to believe my words and landed in this calamity, he nonetheless does think of old Monkey when he is in such straits. Since the night is quiet and the fiend is sleeping, I may as well make use of this unguarded moment and go free the rest of them."

Dear Great Sage! Using the Magic of Body-Vanishment, he caused his body to shrink and immediately became free of the ropes. He approached the T'ang monk and whispered, "Master!" Recognizing his voice, the elder said, "How did you get here?"

Softly Pilgrim gave him a thorough account of what had happened, and the elder was exceedingly pleased. "Disciple," he said, "please rescue me quickly! Whatever happens hereafter I'll listen to you. I won't ever overrule you again." Then Pilgrim raised his hands and freed his master, after which he untied Pa-chieh, Sha Monk, the Twenty-Eight Constellations, and the Guardian of Five Quarters. Dragging the horse over, he told them to hurry out the door. Just as they stepped outside, however, he remembered the luggage and wanted to go back inside to search for it.

"You really value things more than the person!" said Gullet the Gold Dragon. "Isn't it enough that you have saved your master? Why must you look anymore for luggage?" "The person's important, of course," said Pilgrim, "but the cassock and the bowl are even more important. In our wrap are the imperial travel rescript, the brocaded cassock, and the almsbowl of purple gold, all superior Buddhist treasures. How could we not want them?" "Elder Brother," said Pa-chieh, "you go look for them, and we will wait for you by the road."

Look at those star spirits who had the T'ang monk surrounded! Using the Magic of Displacement, they called up a gust of wind and had themselves taken clear out of the high walls. After they reached the main road, they headed straight down the mountain slope until they arrived at a level region. There they waited.

It was about the hour of the third watch that the Great Sage Sun walked slowly and stealthily inside. The doors at every level, you see, were tightly shut. When he climbed to the tallest tower to take a look, he found that even the windows and casements were completely closed. He wanted, of course, to go inside down below, but afraid that windows or the shutters might make a noise, he dared not push at them. Making the magic sign with his fingers, therefore, he shook his body once and changed into a divine mouse, commonly called the bat. How does he look, you ask?

A pointed head like a rat's,
Like it his eyes shine, too.
With wings he comes out at dusk;
Sightless he sleeps in the day.

SIXTY-FIVE   251

He hides in hollow tiles
To find mosquitoes for food.
He loves most the bright, fair moon
And knows when to fly and soar.
Through the space that was not sealed up between the rafters and the
roof tiles, he crawled inside. Passing through several doors, he
reached the very center of the building, where under the third-level
casement he came upon something glowing. It was not the light of
lamps or fireflies, neither the glow of twilight nor the blaze of lightning.
Half leaping and flying, he went near there to have another look and
found that it was the wrap of their luggage that was emitting the
glow. That monster-spirit, you see, had stripped the T'ang monk of his
cassock, and instead of folding it properly, he merely stuffed it inside
the wrap again. The cassock was, after all, a Buddhist treasure which
had on it compliant pearls, Maṇi pearls, red cornelian beads, purple
coral, relics, and the night-luminescent pearls. That was why it
glowed.

Exceedingly pleased by this discovery, Pilgrim changed back into
his own form and picked up the luggage. Without even bothering to
check whether the ropes were properly attached to the pole or not, he
threw the load on his shoulder and began to walk out. One end of the
luggage unexpectedly slipped off the pole and fell with a thud to the
floor. Alas! This was what had to happen! The old monster-spirit was
sleeping on the floor immediately down below, and he was wakened
by that loud thud. Jumping up, he screamed: "Someone's here!
Someone's here!" Those various fiends, old and young, all arose and
lit torches and lamps. In a noisy throng, they rushed about to inspect
the front and rear. One of them arrived to say, "The T'ang monk has
escaped!" Another came to report: "Pilgrim and the rest are gone,
too!" The old fiend immediately gave this order: "Guard all the doors!"
When he heard this, Pilgrim feared that he might fall into their net
again. Abandoning his load of luggage, he mounted the cloud-
somersault and leaped clear of the building through a window.

The monster-spirit led a thorough search for the T'ang monk in front
and in back of the monastery but they failed to turn up anyone. When
he saw that it was almost light, he took his club and led his troops to
give chase. Beneath the mountain slope, still shrouded by cloud and
fog, were the Twenty-Eight Constellations, the Guardian of Five
Quarters, and the other deities. "Where do you think you're going?"

shouted the monster-king. "Here I am!" "Brothers!" cried Horn the
Wood Dragon, "the fiendish creature's here!"

Whereupon Gullet the Gold Dragon, Woman the Earth Bat,
Chamber the Sun Hare, Heart the Moon Fox, Tail the Fire Tiger,
Winnower the Water Leopard, Dipper the Wood Unicorn, Ox the Gold
Bull, Base the Earth Badger, Barrens the Sun Rat, Roof the Moon
Swallow, House the Fire Hog, Wall the Water Porcupine, Straddler
the Wood Wolf, Harvester the Gold Hound, Stomach the Earth Hog,
Mane the Sun Rooster, Net the Moon Crow, Beak the Fire Monkey,
Triaster the Water Ape, Well the Wood Hound, Ghost the Gold Ram,
Willow the Earth Antelope, Star the Sun Horse, Spread the Moon
Deer, Wing the Fire Serpent, and Axeltree the Water Earthworm led
the Golden-Headed Guardian, the Silver-Headed Guardian, the Six
Gods of Light and Darkness, the Guardians of Monasteries, Pa-chieh,
and Sha Monk to meet their pursuers. Abandoning the Tripitaka
T'ang and forsaking the white dragon horse, they rushed into battle,
each with weapon in hand.

When this monster-king saw them, he laughed scornfully and gave
a loud whistle. Immediately some four or five thousand monster-
spirits, old and young, surged forward, all strong and sturdy, and
they began a terrific battle on the west mountain slope. Marvelous
fight!

The vile, vicious demon mocks the true Self.
The true Self's so gentle, what could it do?
A hundred plans used up, they can't escape their pain.
A thousand schemes cannot achieve their peace.
The gods lend their protection;
The sages help with their arms.
Wood Mother may still be kind,
But Yellow Hag has made up its mind.
Their brawl shakes Heaven and disturbs the Earth;
Their fight expands like a net spread out.
On this side, banners wave and soldiers shout;
On that side, they roll drums and beat gongs.
A mass of swords and spears coldly gleaming;
Thick rows of halberds veiled in deathly pall.
The fiendish troops are so fierce and brave,
What could those divine fighters do?

Wretched clouds hide both sun and moon;
Grievous fog shrouds mountains and streams.
They strain and struggle in a bitter row,
All for the T'ang monk who must to Buddha bow.

Growing more fierce all the time, the monster-spirit led his troops to charge again and again. Just at that moment when neither side proved to be the stronger, they heard the roar of Pilgrim: "Old Monkey's arrived!"

Pa-chieh met him and asked, "Where's the luggage?" "Old Monkey almost lost his life already," answered Pilgrim. "Don't mention any luggage!" Gripping his precious staff, Sha Monk said, "Stop talking now! We must go fight the monster-spirit!" The star spirits and those Gods of Darkness and Light by now were encircled completely by the various fiends, and the old fiend wielded his club to attack the three of them. Pilgrim, Pa-chieh, and Sha Monk opened up their rod, staff, and rake to meet him head-on. They fought till truly the Heaven grew dim and the Earth darkened, but they could not prevail against the demon. They fought some more until the sun sank down in the west and the moon arose in the east.

When the fiend saw that it was getting late, he signaled his subjects to be on guard by whistling loudly; then he took out his treasure. When Pilgrim saw clearly that the fiend had untied his wrap and held it in his hand, he cried, "Look out! Let's run!" Without further regard for Pa-chieh, Sha Monk, and the other dēvas, he somersaulted all the way up to the ninefold Heaven. The gods and his companions, however, were not quick enough to understand why he fled, and they were all captured once more inside the wrap after the monster-spirit had thrown it in the air. Only Pilgrim thus managed to escape.

After the monster-king and his troops returned to the monastery, he asked for ropes again and ordered the prisoners to be tied up as before. The T'ang monk, Pa-chieh, and Sha Monk were to be hung up high on the rafters, while the white horse was to be tied up in the back. After the deities had been trussed up, they were to be thrown into the cellar and the entrance would be covered and sealed. The little fiends obeyed each of his instructions, and we shall leave them for the moment.

We tell you now about Pilgrim, who had leaped up to the ninefold Heaven and succeeded in preserving his life. When he saw the withdrawal of the fiendish troops with banners lowered, he knew that his companions had been captured. Lowering his auspicious luminosity onto the eastern slope of the mountain,

He hated, teeth grinding, the fiend;
He thought of the monk, shedding tears.
Lifting his face to stare skyward,
He sighed sadly and voiced his fears.

"Oh, Master!" he cried. "In which previous incarnation did you incur such ordeals of bondage, that you must in this life face monster-spirits every step of the way! It's so hard now to rid you of your sufferings. What shall we do?" He lamented like that all by himself for a long time, and then he began to calm himself and think, allowing the mind to question the mind. "I wonder what sort of wrap this fiendish demon has," he thought to himself, "that can hold so many things. Now he has even hauled away all those celestial warriors! I would go seek the Jade Emperor for assistance, but I fear he might take offense. I recall, however, that there's a Chên-Wu of the North,[10] whose style is the Demon-Conquering Celestial-Honored One, and who lives in the Wu-tang Mountain[11] of the South Jambūdvīpa Continent. Let me go fetch him here to rescue Master from this ordeal. Truly it is that,

The immortal way undone, ape and horse disperse;
The Five Phases dry up when mind and spirit are lost.

We do not know what is the result of his journey, and you must listen to the explanation in the next chapter.

Sixty-six
Many gods meet injury;
Maitreya binds a fiend.

We were telling you about the Great Sage Sun, who had no alternative but to mount an auspicious cloud by means of his somersault to head directly for the Wu-tang Mountain on the South Jambūdvīpa Continent, where he hoped to solicit the help of the Demon-Conquering Celestial-Honored One to rescue Tripitaka, Pa-chieh, and Sha Monk, and the various celestial warriors from their ordeal. Without a moment's pause in midair, he soon caught sight of the patriarch's immortal realm. Gently lowering his cloud, he stared around. A marvelous place, it was!

Grandly it guards the south-east,
This towering divine mountain.
The soaring Hibiscus Peak:
The rugged Purple-Canopy Summit.
Nine Streams[1] flow from it to distant Ching and Yang.[2]
It joins the Yüeh mountains reaching the state of Ch'u.
On top are the treasure cave of Grand-Void,
The numinous estrades of Chu and Lu.[3]
Golden stones resound in thirty-six halls,
Where to offer incense ten thousand pilgrims come.
King Shun visits it and King Yü[4] prays at this place,
Adorned with jade tablets and letters of gold.
Blue birds fly about the towers;
Banners flap like scarlet skirts.
A land set on a mountain famed in all the world,
A Heav'n-born region touching the spacious void.
A few sprigs of plum trees just now in bloom;
A mountain of rare grasses spreading their verdure.
Dragons lie beneath the brooks;
Tigers crouch by the cliffs.
The birds sound as if they're talking;

By people tame deer are walking.
White cranes perch with the clouds on old junipers;
Facing the sun, blue and red phoenixes sing.
This has the looks of a true, immortal realm,
Where portals of gold and mercy rule the world.

The august patriarch was the offspring of King Pure Joy and Queen Triumphant Virtue, who was conceived with child after she dreamed that she had swallowed the sun. After carrying the child for fourteen months, she gave birth to him in the palace at noon on the first day of the third month, in the *chia-ch'ên* year which was the first year of the K'ai-huang reign period. This Holy Father was

Fierce and bold in his youth,
Astute and keen when he grew up.
Declining the throne of kingship,
He sought only austerities.
His parents could not stop him
From leaving the royal palace.
The mysteries and meditation
He embraced on this mountain.
Merit and work accomplished,
He rose in daylight to Heaven.
The Jade Emperor forthwith decreed
That he be titled Chên-wu.
Above, the dark void blessed him;
Below, the snake and turtle⁵ joined him.
The entire Heaven and Earth
Addressed him as All Efficacious,
From whom no secret was hidden,
For whom no act e'er met failure.
From start to end of each kalpa,
He routed the demon-spirits.

As he was enjoying the sight of this immortal scenery, the Great Sage Sun soon arrived before the Palace of Grand Harmony, having passed through the first, the second, and the third Heavenly gates. There in the midst of hallowed light and auspicious air he found a group of five hundred spirit-ministers, who met him and said, "Who are you?" "I'm Sun Wu-k'ung, the Great Sage, Equal to Heaven," replied the Great Sage, "and I'd like to have an audience with the patriarch."

After the spirit-ministers went inside to make their report, the patriarch left the main hall to escort his visitor into the Palace of Grand Harmony. Pilgrim saluted the patriarch and said, "I must trouble you with a matter." "What is it?" the patriarch asked.

"I was accompanying the T'ang monk on his way to the Western Heaven to acquire scriptures," said Pilgrim, "and our path has landed us in a dangerous ordeal. At the West Aparagodānīya Continent, there is a mountain by the name of the Little Western Heaven, in which a demonic fiend has set up a Little Thunderclap Monastery. When my master entered the monastery gate and laid eyes on rows of arhats, guardians, bikṣus, and sage monks, he thought that he had come upon the real Buddha. Just as he bent low to bow to them, he was seized and bound. I, too, was caught off guard and was clamped within a pair of gold cymbals which the fiend threw up into the air. Those cymbals had me completely sealed inside, and there was not even the slightest crack for me to escape. It was a good thing that the Golden-Headed Guardian went to memorialize to the Jade Emperor, who commanded the Twenty-Eight Constellations to descend to earth that very night. Even they, however, could not pry the cymbals open. Luckily, Gullet the Gold Dragon managed to pierce the cymbals with his horn and took me out with him. I smashed the cymbals afterwards and aroused the fiendish creature. When he gave chase and fought with us, he threw up a white cloth wrap which had all of us, including the Twenty-Eight Constellations, stored away. We were tied up with ropes once more, but that evening I managed to escape and free the Constellations and our T'ang monk. Thereafter, my search for our robe and almsbowl again disturbed the fiend, who chased us down once more to do battle with the celestial warriors. When that fiend took out his white cloth wrap and fiddled with it, I recognized his tune and fled at once. The rest of my companions were stored up by him as before. I had no other alternative but to come here to beg assistance from the patriarch."

The patriarch said, "In years past, I ruled over the north and that was the reason I had assumed the position of Chên-wu to extirpate the fiends and deviates of the world by the decree of the Jade Emperor. Thereafter, by the command of the Celestial-Honored One of Primal Origin I led, with loosened hair and naked feet and with the soaring serpent and divine turtle under my feet, the Five Thunder Deities, the huge-maned lion, and various ferocious beasts and poisonous dragons to subjugate the dark and fiendish miasmas of the northeast. Today I

am enjoying the peace of Wu-tang Mountain and the serenity of the
Palace of Grand Harmony, the calm seas and clear universe, only
because the fiendish demons and devious spirits have all been exterminated in our South Jambūdvīpa Continent and in our North Uttara-
kuru Continent. Now that the Great Sage has come to make this
request, it is difficult for me not to respond, but without the decree from
the Region Above, it is also difficult for me to respond in arms. If I
were to send forth the gods with my formal command, I fear that the
Jade Emperor would be offended. But if I refused the Great Sage, I would
go utterly against human sentiments. I suppose, however, that those
fiends on the road to the West could not be too terribly formidable. I'll
ask Turtle and Serpent, the two generals, and the Five Divine Dragons
to assist you. I'm certain they will capture the monster-spirit and
rescue your master from this ordeal."

After he bowed to thank the patriarch, Pilgrim went back to the
region of the West accompanied by Serpent, Turtle, and the dragon
deities, all wielding their powerful weapons. In less than a day, they
arrived at the Little Thunderclap Monastery, where they dropped
from the clouds and began to provoke battle before the monastery gate.

We tell you now about that Great King Yellow Brow, who gathered
the various fiends below his treasure tower and said, "These two days
Pilgrim Sun has not even shown up. I wonder where he has gone to
seek help." Hardly had he finished speaking when the little fiend
guarding the gate came in to report: "Pilgrim is leading several
persons with the looks of dragon, serpent, and turtle to provoke battle
outside our gate." "How did this little monkey," said the demon,
"manage to acquire people with looks like that? Where did such
people come from?"

He put on his armor immediately and walked out of the monastery
gate, crying, "What dragon deities are you that you dare transgress
our immortal territory?" With looks most rugged and spirited, the
five dragons and the two generals shouted: "You brazen fiend! We
are the Five Dragon Deities and Turtle and Serpent, the two generals,
before the Demon-Conquering Celestial-Honored One, who is the
Pontiff of Composite Prime in the Palace of Grand Harmony, located
on Wu-tang Mountain. By the invitation of the Great Sage, Equal to
Heaven, and the amulet summons of the Celestial-Honored One, we
came here to arrest you. You, monster-spirit, send out the T'ang
monk and the Constellations quickly and we shall spare your life. If

not, we will hew to pieces the fiends of this entire mountain, and we
will burn to ashes your several buildings!"

On hearing this, the fiend grew enraged, "You beasts!" he cried.
"What great magic power do you have that you dare mouth big
words like that? Don't run away! Have a taste of my club!" Whereupon these five dragons churned up cloud and rain, and those two
generals sprayed dust and dirt, as they rushed forward together to
attack with spears, scimitars, swords, and halberds. The Great Sage
Sun, too, followed them, wielding his iron rod. This was another
terrific battle:

The vicious demon used force—
Pilgrim sought armed assistance—
The vicious demon used force
As he took a precious tower to set up the Buddha's form;
Pilgrim sought armed assistance,
Going far to a treasure region for the dragon gods.
Turtle and Serpent started water and fire;
The fiend raised weapons and arms.
Five dragons were ordered to the Westward way,
Followed by Pilgrim for his master's sake.
Swords and halberds flashed like electric bolts;
Spears and knives glowed like lightning bright.
The wolf-teeth club of this one,
Strong but short and pliant;
The golden-hooped rod of that one,
Both yielding and compliant.
You hear loud bangs and booms like firecrackers,
And clanging chords like gold being struck.
Water and fire came to conquer the fiend;
Arms and weapons encircled a monster-spirit.
Their cries startled tigers and wolves;
Their brawl alarmed spirits and gods.
This raucus battle had just reached a draw,
When the demon seized the treasures once more.

Leading the five dragons and the two generals, Pilgrim battled the
demon for half an hour. Then the fiend untied his wrap and held it in
his hand. Alarmed by what he saw, Pilgrim shouted, "Be careful, all
of you!" Not realizing why they had to be careful, the dragon deities,
the turtle, and the serpent all lowered their weapons and stepped

forward to look. With a loud whoosh, the monster-spirit threw up the wrap again. Unable to care for the five dragons and the two generals any longer, the Great Sage Sun leaped up to the Ninefold Heaven with his somersault and fled. Those dragon deities along with the turtle and the serpent were stored up also in the wrap and taken captive. After the monster-spirit returned to the monastery in triumph, he had his prisoners bound with ropes and locked in the underground cellar, where we shall leave them for the moment.

Look at the Great Sage, who dropped down from the clouds! Reclining listlessly on the mountain slope, he said spitefully to himself, "This fiendish creature is most formidable!" Unwittingly, his eyes became shut and he looked as if he had fallen asleep. Suddenly, he heard someone crying, "Great Sage, don't sleep! Go get help quickly! Your master's life won't last very long!"

Opening wide his eyes and leaping up, Pilgrim saw that it was the Day Sentinel. "You clumsy deity!" shouted Pilgrim. "Where have you been all this time lusting after your bloody offerings? You haven't shown up to answer your roll call, and yet you dare come to disturb me today! Stick out your shanks, and let old Monkey give you a couple of strokes of my rod—just to relieve my boredom!"

Bowing hurriedly, the sentinel said, "Great Sage, you are the joyous immortal among men. How could *you* be bored? By the decree of the Bodhisattva, all of us are to give secret protection to the T'ang monk. We thus work with the local spirits and the like, not daring to leave him at all. That's why we have not come to see you. How could you blame us instead?" "If you're giving him protection," said Pilgrim, "tell me where has that monster-spirit imprisoned my master, the Constellations, the guardians, the protectors of monasteries, and the rest of them? What sort of suffering are they enduring now?"

"Your master and your brothers," replied the sentinel, "are all hanging in the corridor by the side of the treasure hall, while the Constellations have been herded into the underground cellar to suffer there. We haven't had any news from you for these two days. Only when we saw just now that the monster-spirit had captured some divine dragons, a turtle, and a snake, and sent these, too, into the cellar did we realize that they were warriors fetched here by the Great Sage. Your humble deity came especially to find you. The Great Sage must not grow weary. You must go again quickly to seek help."

When he heard these words, Pilgrim began to shed tears as he said to the sentinel, "At this moment,

I'm ashamed to go up to Heaven,
I'm embarrassed to go down to the seas.
I dread the Bodhisattva's questions;
I'm sad to see the Buddha's jade form.

Those who had been taken captive just now were Turtle, Snake, and the Five Dragon sages of Patriarch Chên-wu. I have no other place to go for help. What am I to do?"

Smiling, the sentinel said, "Please do not worry, Great Sage. Your humble deity can think of another powerful army which, if you succeed in bringing it here, will certainly subdue this monster. Just now, the Great Sage went to Wu-tang of the South Jambūdvīpa Continent. Well, this army is also stationed at the same continent, in the city of Pin-ch-êng on the Hsü-i Mountain, what is now called Ssŭ-chou. Located there is the National Preceptor-King Bodhisattva, who has vast magic powers. Under his tutelage is a disciple of his by the name of Prince Little Chang. He has in his service also four great divine warriors, who brought to submission in years past the Lady Water Mother. If you go there now in person and ask for his kind assistance, I am certain that the fiend will be captured and your master rescued." Delighted, Pilgrim said, "You go back to protect my master and don't let him be harmed. Let old Monkey go for help."

Mounting his cloud-somersault, Pilgrim left the fiend's place and headed straight for the Hsü-i Mountain. He arrived there in less than a day. As he stared at it carefully, it was a marvelous place indeed!

To the south it's near river fords;
To the north, it presses on the River Huai;
To the east it reaches the sea coast;
To the west it connects with Fêng-fou.
On the peak there are towering edifices;
In its fold there are surging streams.
Strange, craggy boulders;
Handsome, knotty pines;
A hundred kinds of fruits all in season and fresh;
A thousand sprigs of flowers blooming in the sun.
People, teeming like ants, go back and forth;
Like rows of wild geese the boats come and leave.

On top there are the Temple of Auspicious Cliff,
The Palace of Eastern Mountain,
The Shrine of Five Miracles,
And the Monastery of Turtle Mountain,
Where bell-tones and incense rise toward the sky.
There are also the Crystal Stream,
The Five Pagoda Valley,
The Immortals Terrace,
And the Apricot Garden—
All lighting up the city with their pastoral hues.
Languid white clouds stretch o'erhead;
Birds, though tired, serenely sing.
Why mention the charm of T'ai, Sung, Hêng, and Hua?[6]
Here's immortal beauty like P'êng and Ying!

The Great Sage could hardly make an end of enjoying this scenery. After he passed the River Huai, he went through the city of Pin-ch'êng and went up to the gate of the Great Sage Buddhist Monastery, where he found magnificent halls and elegant long corridors. There was, moreover, a towering pagoda, truly

A thousand cubits tall, jabbing clouds and sky,
A golden flask piercing the jade-green void.
Up and down its halo holds the universe;
Not one shade darkens its screens both east and west.
Treasure bells, wind blown, will make celestial chimes;
Shell-bark pines, sun drenched, face this Sanskrit hall.
Spirit birds, in flight or rest, speak frequently
When you gaze on the Huai's endless flow.

Enjoying the scenery as he walked along, Pilgrim went straight up to the second-level door. By then, the National Preceptor-King Bodhisattva had already learned of his arrival and he went out of the door with Prince Little Chang to meet his visitor. After they saluted each other, Pilgrim said, "I'm accompanying the T'ang monk to go to the Western Heaven for scriptures. On our way we ran into The Little Thunderclap Monastery, where a Yellow Brow Fiend disguised himself as the Buddhist patriarch. Unable to distinguish the true from the false, my master immediately bowed before him and was caught. The fiend then had me sealed inside a pair of cymbals, but fortunately I was rescued by the Constellations descending from Heaven. I smashed his cymbals and fought with him, but he used a cloth wrap and took captive all of the gods, the guardians, my master, and my brothers. I went just now to the Wu-tang Mountain to seek the help of the August One of the Mysterious Heaven, who ordered the Five Dragons, Turtle, and Serpent to capture the fiend. But they, too, were caught by his wrap. Your disciple now has neither refuge nor home, and that's why he has come especially to see the Bodhisattva. I beg you to exercise your mighty power—the magic which brought the Water Mother to submission and the wondrous potency that redeemed the multitudes—and go with your disciple to rescue his master from this ordeal. When we succeed in acquiring the scriptures so that they may be forever implanted in China, we shall proclaim the wisdom of our Buddha and his everlasting perfection."

"Your affair today," said the National Preceptor-King, "indeed concerns the prosperity of our Buddhist religion, and I should go with you in person. But this is early summer, a time when the River Huai threatens to overflow. It was only recently that I brought to submission the Great Sage Water Ape. That fellow, however, tends to grow restless whenever he comes into contact with water. I fear that my departure from this place will lure him into mischief, and there's no other god who can bring him under control. Let me ask my young disciple and four other warriors under his command to go with you. They'll assist you in capturing this demon." Pilgrim gave thanks before mounting the clouds with Prince Little Chang and the four warriors to return to The Little Thunderclap Monastery.

Prince Little Chang used a mulberry-white lance while the four warriors all wielded red-steel swords. When they went forward with the Great Sage Sun to provoke battle, the little fiends again went inside to report. Leading the rest of the monsters, the fiendish king came roaring out and cried, "Monkey! What other persons have you brought here this time?"

Ordering the four warriors forward, Prince Little Chang shouted, "You lawless monster-spirit! You have no flesh on your face and no pupils in your eyes, and that's why you can't recognize us."

"Where are you from, little warrior," said the fiendish king, "that you dare come here to give him assistance?" "I'm the disciple of the National Preceptor-King Bodhisattva," replied the prince, "the Great Sage of Ssŭ-chou. These are the four divine warriors under my command, who have been ordered here to arrest you."

With a laugh, the fiendish king said, "What sort of martial prowess

does a little boy like you possess that you dare to be so insulting?" "If
you want to know about my martial prowess," said the prince, "listen
to my recital:

The state, Flowing Sand, was my ancestral home.
My father was the ruler of that land.
Illness plagued me when I was in my youth,
A victim of a baleful natal star.
For long life I sought a teacher far away;
I was lucky to meet him and be giv'n a cure.
Half a pellet and my ailments dispelled,
I left my princeship to follow his way
And acquired the art of ne'er growing old.
My features are those of eternal youth!
I have attended Buddha's Birthday Feast.
I have trod the clouds to reach his great hall.
I've caught a water fiend with the wind and fog;
I've tamed a mountain's tigers and dragons.
The grateful race built me a pagoda tall,
And śarī light illumed the deep, calm sea.
My mulberry lance is quick to bind a fiend;
My cleric sleeve can a monster subdue.
In Pin-ch'êng now a peaceful life I lead,
Though Little Chang's famous throughout the earth."

When the fiendish king heard what was said, he smiled scornfully,
saying, "Prince, what method of longevity did you manage to cultivate, when you left your own country and followed that National
Preceptor-King Bodhisattva? Good enough, I suppose, to capture a
water fiend of the River Huai! How could you allow those false and
specious words of Pilgrim Sun to goad you across a thousand hills and
ten thousand waters and into surrendering your life here? You think
you still have longevity when you look me up!"

Enraged by what he heard, Little Chang picked up the lance and
stabbed at his opponent's face, while the four great warriors also
joined in the attack at once. The Great Sage Sun, too, struck with his
iron rod. Dear monster-spirit! Not the least daunted, he wielded his
short, pliant, wolf-teeth club and parried the blows left and right,
charging forward and sideways. This was another fierce battle!

The youthful prince,
His mulberry-white lance,
And four even stronger red-steel swords.

Wu-k'ung, too, used his golden-hooped rod
To encircle together the fiendish king,
Who, in truth, possessed vast magic powers.
Not daunted at all, he charged left and right.
The wolf-teeth club being a Buddhist prize
Could not be harmed by blows of spear and sword.
You could only hear the howl of violent gale;
You could only see the dark, baleful air.
That one in worldly lust would show his ability;
That one steadfastly sought Buddha for the holy writ.
They dashed about a few times;
They fought again and again.
The belched out cloud and fog
Had the Three Lights[7] hidden.
Their anger and wrath would do each other ill.
For the Three Vehicles'[8] most perfect law
A hundred arts engaged in bitter strife.

The multitude fought for a long time but no decision could be reached.
Once more the monster-spirit untied his wrap, and again Pilgrim
cried out: "Be careful, all of you!" The prince and the rest of the
warriors, however, did not comprehend what Pilgrim meant by "be
careful"! With a loud whoosh, the fiend wrapped up also the prince
and the four great warriors. Only the prescience of Pilgrim enabled
him to escape. Returning in triumph to the monastery, the fiendish
king again had his prisoners bound with ropes and sent to be locked
up in the underground cellar, where we shall leave them for the
moment.

Mounting his cloud-somersault, our Pilgrim rose to midair, and he
lowered his auspicious luminosity only after he saw the fiend had
withdrawn his troops and shut the gates. As he stood on the west
mountain slope, he wept dejectedly, saying, "Oh, Master!

Since I in faith entered the grove of Zen,
When Kuan-yin freed me from my great ordeal,
I squired you westward to seek the great Way,
To reach, by mutual help, the Thunderclap.
We hoped our twisted path would smooth out at last,
Not knowing such fiendish foes would us attack.
A thousand plans could hardly rescue you.
My pleas east and west were all made in vain."

As the Great Sage was thus grieving, he suddenly saw toward the southwest a colored cloud descending to earth as torrential rain fell on the mountain. "Wu-k'ung," someone called out, "do you recognize me?" Running forward to have a look, Pilgrim came upon a person with

Huge ears, jutting jaw, and a squarelike face;
Broad shoulders, large belly, and a stoutish frame.
His complexion was filled with joyous spring;
His eyes sparkled like two autumnal pools.
His wide sleeves flapped and fluttered with good luck;
In smart straw sandals he looked tough and strong.
First among those honored in paradise,
All hail to Maitreya, the laughing priest!

On seeing him, Pilgrim quickly kowtowed, saying, "Buddhist Patriarch of the Eastern Journey, where are you going? Your disciple has improperly barred your way! I'm guilty of ten thousand crimes!"

"I came," replied the Buddhist patriarch, "especially on account of the fiend in The Little Thunderclap." "I'm grateful for the profound grace and virtue of the holy father," said Pilgrim. "May I ask from what region did that fiend originate! What sort of treasure is that wrap of his? I beg the holy father to reveal it to me."

The patriarch said, "He happens to be a yellow-browed youth in charge of striking the sonorous stone before me. On the third day of the third month, I went to attend a festival of Primal Origin and left him to guard my palace. He stole several treasures of mine and, disguising himself as Buddha, became a spirit. That wrap is my fertility bag, its common name being 'The Bag of Human Seed.' That wolf-teeth club is the mallet for striking the sonorous stone."

On hearing this, Pilgrim shouted: "Dear laughing priest! You let this boy escape to give himself the false name of Buddhist patriarch and to ensnare old Monkey. Aren't you guilty of negligence in domestic governance?" "It is my negligence in the first place," said Maitreya, "but it is also because you and your master have yet to pass through all your *mara* hindrances. That is why a hundred deities must descend to earth to inflict upon you your fated ordeals. I've come now to bring to submission this fiend for you." "But the monster-spirit," said Pilgrim, "has vast magic powers. You don't even have a weapon. How could you bring him to submission?"

Laughing, Maitreya said, "I'll set up below this mountain slope a grass hut and a huge melon field. You go to provoke battle, but you are not permitted to win when you fight with him. Lure him to my melon field. All my melons, however, will be raw, but you yourself will change into a large, ripe melon. When he arrives, he will certainly want to eat some melon, and I'll present you for him to eat. When he swallows you into his stomach, you may do whatever you please with him. By then, I should be able to retrieve that wrap from him and take him back inside it."

"Although this is a marvelous plan," said Pilgrim, "I wonder how you would be able to recognize the ripe melon which will be my transformation. Moreover, how would he be willing to follow me here?" Laughing again, Maitreya replied, "I'm the Honored One who governs the world. How could my percipient eyes of wisdom not recognize you? You may change into whatever you like and I'll know about it. But if the fiend's not willing to follow you, I'll teach you some magic."

"What he most certainly wants to do," said Pilgrim, "is to catch me with that wrap of his. He won't follow me here! What sort of magic do you have that will make him come here?" Smiling, Maitreya said, "Stretch forth your hand."

Pilgrim stretched out his left palm; dipping his right index finger into his mouth, Maitreya wrote on his palm the word, restrain, with the divine saliva. Pilgrim was told to hold his left hand in a fist and open it only toward the face of the monster-spirit. Then the monster-spirit would certainly follow him.

Holding fast his fist and obeying amiably these instructions, Pilgrim wielded his iron rod with a single hand and went before the monastery gate. "Fiendish demon," he cried, "your Holy Father Sun's here again! Come out quickly so that we may decide who's the stronger!"

Those little fiends again dashed inside to make the report. "How many warriors has he brought with him this time?" asked the fiendish king. "There are no other warriors," replied one of the little fiends, "he's the only one." "That little monkey has used up all his plans and exhausted his strength," said the fiendish king, laughing. "He has nowhere to go to ask for help, and he has just come to give up his life for sure."

After he had put on his armor properly, the fiend took his treasure and held up his light and soft wolf-teeth club to walk out of the door. "Sun Wu-k'ung," he cried, "you can't struggle anymore this time!" "Brazen fiend!" scolded Pilgrim. "What do you mean that I can't struggle any more?" "I see that you have used up all your plans and exhausted your strength," said the fiendish king. "You have nowhere to go for help, and you've forced yourself here to do battle. There won't be any divine warriors to assist you this time, and that's why I say you can't struggle anymore."

Pilgrim said, "This fiend doesn't know what's good for him! Stop bragging! Have a taste of my rod!" When the fiendish king saw that he was wielding the rod with only one hand, he could not refrain from laughing. "This little ape!" he said. "Look how mischievous he is! Why are you fooling around with only one hand?" "My son," said Pilgrim, "you can't stand up to the attack of both my hands! If you don't use your wrap, even if there are three or five of you, you won't be able to overcome this one hand of old Monkey."

On hearing this, the fiendish king said, "All right, all right! I won't use my treasure. I'll fight in earnest with you this time, and we'll see who's the stronger." Thereupon he raised his wolf-teeth club to rush into battle. Aiming directly at his face, Pilgrim let loose his fist before gripping the iron rod with both his hands. The monster-spirit was immediately bound by the spell; with no thought at all for retreat or for using the wrap, he only had in mind using the club to attack his opponent. After delivering a weak blow with his rod, Pilgrim immediately retreated, and the monster-spirit chased him all the way to the west mountain slope.

When Pilgrim saw the melon field, he rolled right into it and changed at once into a huge melon, both ripe and sweet. The monster-spirit stood still and glanced everywhere, but he did not know where Pilgrim had gone to. When he ran up to the grass hut, he cried, "Who's the planter of these melons?" Having changed himself into a melon farmer, Maitreya walked out of the hut, saying, "Great King, I'm the one who has planted them." "You have any ripe ones?" asked the fiendish king. "Yes," replied Maitreya. "Pick a ripe one for me to relieve my thirst," cried the fiendish king.

Maitreya at once presented with both hands the melon into which Pilgrim had changed himself. Without even examining it, the fiendish king took it and began to bite at it. Using this opportunity, Pilgrim somersaulted at once down his throat, and without waiting for another moment, he began to flex his limbs. He grabbed the intestines and bent the stomach; he did handstands, cartwheels, and whatever he felt like doing at the time. The pain was so intense that the monster-spirit clenched his teeth and opened wide his mouth as big drops of tears welled up in his eyes. He rolled so hard on the ground that the patch of melon field was completely flattened like a plot of land for pounding grain. "Finished! Finished!" he could only mutter. "Who will save me?"

Changing into his original form, Maitreya giggled loudly and said, "Cursed beast! You recognize me?" When the fiend raised his head and saw the figure before him, he went hurriedly to his knees. Hugging his stomach with both hands and pounding his head on the ground, he cried, "My lord! Please spare my life! Please spare my life! I'll never dare do this again!" Maitreya strode forward and grabbed the fiend. After he had untied the bag of fertility and taken away the mallet for striking the sonorous stone, he cried, "Sun Wu-k'ung, for my sake, please spare him." Pilgrim, however, was so bitter that he started punching and kicking left and right, madly pounding and scratching inside. Unable to bear the terrible pain, the fiend slumped to the ground.

"Wu-k'ung," cried Maitreya again, "he has had enough! Spare him!" Only then did Pilgrim cry, "Open wide your mouth, and let old Monkey come out." Though that fiend had been racked by sharp pains in his stomach, his heart had not yet been hurt. As the proverb says,

Before the heart breaks a person can't die;

Flowers fade and leaves drop when roots are dried.

When he heard that he should open wide his mouth, he did so at once, trying desperately to endure the pain. Pilgrim leaped out, and, as he changed back into his original form, he wanted immediately to strike with his rod. The monster-spirit, however, had already been stuffed into the wrap by the Buddhist patriarch and fastened to his waist. Picking up the sonorous stone mallet, the patriarch said, "Cursed beast! Where are the stolen cymbals?"

Having only concern for his life, the fiend in the bag of fertility moaned: "The gold cymbals were smashed by Sun Wu-k'ung." "If they have been smashed," said the Buddhist patriarch, "return my gold." The fiend said, "The gold fragments are piled on the lotus throne in the hall."

Holding the bag and the mallet, the Buddhist patriarch said, giggling, "Wu-k'ung, I'll go look for my gold with you." When Pilgrim saw this kind of dharma power, he did not dare tarry another moment. He had no other alternative, in fact, than to lead the Buddha up the mountain to return to the monastery, where they found the gates tightly shut. The Buddhist patriarch pointed his mallet at them and at once the gates flew open. When they went inside, all the little fiends were just in the process of packing and fleeing, having learned already that the old fiend had been captured. When Pilgrim ran into them, he struck them down one by one, until some seven hundred of them were slain. As they revealed their original forms, they were all spirits of mountains and trees, the monsters of beasts and fowl. After the Buddhist patriarch had gathered the gold fragments together, he blew at them a mouthful of divine breath and recited a spell. Immediately they changed back into their original form of a pair of gold cymbals. He then took leave of Pilgrim and mounted the auspicious clouds to return to the world of ultimate bliss.

Thereafter our Great Sage untied the T'ang monk, Pa-chieh, and Sha Monk from the rafters. Having been hung for several days, our Idiot was so hungry that he did not even bother to thank the Great Sage. His torso bent low, he dashed into the kitchen to try to find rice to eat. The fiend, you see, was just preparing lunch, but he was interrupted when Pilgrim came to provoke battle. When Idiot saw the rice, he ate half a pot first before taking two large bowls to his master and brother. Then they thanked Pilgrim and asked about the defeat of the fiend. Pilgrim gave a thorough account of how he went first to solicit the help of the Taoist patriarch and his two warriors, turtle and serpent, how he went next to see the Great Sage and the prince, and finally how Maitreya brought the fiend to submission. When Tripitaka heard this, he could not make an end of his thanksgiving for all the devas. "Disciple," he said afterwards, "where are these gods and sages imprisoned?" "The Day Sentinel told me yesterday that they had all been sent to an underground cellar," replied Pilgrim. "Pa-chieh, you and I must go and free them."

After he had had some food, our Idiot had grown strong once more. Picking up his muckrake, he went to the rear with the Great Sage and broke open the cellar door to untie all the prisoners. When they came back out to the jewelled tower, Tripitaka put on his cassock to bow to each one of the deities to thank them. Thereafter the Great Sage sent the five dragons and two warriors back to Wu-tang, Prince Little Chang and the four warriors back to Pin-ch'êng, and finally the Twenty-Eight Constellations back to Heaven. The guardians and the protectors of monasteries, too, were released to return to their stations.

Master and disciples then rested for half a day at the monastery, where they also fed the white horse and tidied up the luggage before starting out again in the morning. As they left, they lit a fire and had all those jewelled towers, treasure thrones, tall turrets, and lecture halls reduced to ashes. So it was that,

Without care or hindrance, they escaped their ordeal;

Their calamity dispelled, they were free to leave.

We do not know how long it was before they reached the Great Thunderclap, and you must listen to the explanation in the next chapter.

Sixty-seven

Having rescued T'o-lo, the Nature of Zen is secure;
Having escaped defilement, the Mind of Tao is pure.

We were telling you about Tripitaka and his three disciples, who set out on the road once more, glad to have left the Little Western Heaven. They spent about a month traveling, and now it was the time of late spring when flowers blossomed. They saw the green fading at various gardens and groves, and a sudden squall of wind and rain brought the evening near. Reining in his horse, Tripitaka said, "O disciples, it's getting late! Which road shall we take to find lodging?"

"Master, relax!" said Pilgrim, laughing. "Even if there's no place for us to ask for lodging, the three of us at least have some abilities. You may ask Pa-chieh to chop some grass and Sha Monk to cut down a few pine trees. Old Monkey knows how to play carpenter. I can build for you right by the road a little thatched hut in which you can live for at least a year. Why are you so anxious?" "Oh, Elder Brother," said Pa-chieh, "a place like this is not fit to be lived in! The whole mountain is full of tigers and wolves, and there are spirits and goblins everywhere. Even in daylight it's difficult enough to get through. How could you dare rest here at night?"

"Idiot," said Pilgrim, "you're becoming more and more backward! Old Monkey isn't bragging, but this rod I hold in my hands can even hold up the sky—if it collapses!" As master and disciples were conversing like that, they suddenly caught sight of a mountain village not far away. "Marvelous!" said Pilgrim. "We've a place for the night." "Where?" asked the elder. Pointing with his finger, Pilgrim replied, "Isn't that a household over there beneath the trees? We can go over there to ask for one night's lodging. Tomorrow we'll leave."

Delighted, the elder urged on his horse and went up to the entrance of the village before he dismounted. As the wooden gates were tightly shut, the elder knocked on them, saying, "Open the door! Open the door!" From within a house an old man emerged: he had a staff in his hands, rush sandals on his feet, a black cloth wrap on his head, and a plain white robe on his body. As he opened the door, he asked immediately: "Who's making all these noises here?"

Folding his hands before his chest, Tripitaka bowed deeply and said, "Old patron, this humble priest is one sent from the Land of the East to seek scriptures in the Western Heaven. It was getting late when we arrived at your honored region. We have come, therefore, especially to ask you for one night's lodging. I beg you to grant us this boon."

"Monk," said the old man, "you may want to go to the West, but you can't get there. This is only the Little Western Heaven. If you want to go to the great Western Heaven, the distance is exceedingly great, not to mention all the difficulties ahead of you. Even this region here will be hard for you to pass through." "What do you mean by hard to pass through?" asked Tripitaka. Pointing with his hand, the old man said, "Approximately thirty miles west of our village there is a Pulpy Persimmon Alley, located in a mountain by the name of Seven Extremes." "Why do you call it Seven Extremes?" asked Tripitaka again.

The old man said, "The mountain is about eight hundred miles across, and the whole mountain is full of persimmon fruit. According to the ancients,[1] 'There are seven types of extremes characteristic of the persimmon tree. They are: long-lasting, shady, without birds' nests, wormless, lovely leaves when frosted, hardy fruits, and large, luxuriant branches.' Hence it is called the Mountain of Seven Extremes. Our humble region here, however, is large but sparsely inhabited, and since the time of antiquity, hardly anyone has ever journeyed deep into the mountain. Every year the persimmons, ripened and rotted, would fall on the ground and completely fill up the mountain path, which is shaped like an alley flanked by boulders on both sides. After the frost and snow of the winter and the heat of the summer, the road would become one of such horrid filth that the families of this region nicknamed it, Slimy Shit Alley. Whenever the west wind rises, a terrible stench would drift here, fouler than any privy you may want to clean. Right now it happens to be late spring and we have this brisk southeast wind. That's why you can't smell it yet." On hearing this, Tripitaka fell silent, utterly dejected.

Unable to contain himself, Pilgrim shouted: "Oldie, you're rather blockheaded! We've come from a great distance to ask you for lodging, and you have to tell us all these things to frighten us! If your house is so crowded that there's no room for us to sleep in, we can just squat here beneath the trees to spend the night. Why must you be so windy?"

Greatly startled by the hideous figure before him, the old man stopped talking for a moment. Then he gathered up enough courage to point his staff at Pilgrim and say in a loud voice, "You! Look at your skeleton face, flattened brow, collapsed nose, jutting jowl, and hairy eyes. A consumptive ghost, no doubt, and yet, without any manners at all, you dare use your pointed mouth to offend an elderly person like me!" Trying to placate him with a smile, Pilgrim said, "Venerable Sir, so you have eyes but no pupils, and thus you can't recognize the worth of this consumptive ghost! As the books on physiognomy would say, 'The features may be strange and bizarre, but it is a piece of fine jade hidden in the stone.' If you judge people only by their looks, you're completely wrong. I may be ugly, but I have some abilities!"

"Where are you from?" asked the old man. "What are your name and surname? What sort of abilities do you have?" With a smile, Pilgrim said

Pūrvavideha was my ancestral home,
I did cultivation on Mount Flower-Fruit.
I bowed to the Patriarch of Heart and Mind
And perfected with him the martial arts.
I can tame dragons, stirring up the seas;
I can tote mountains to chase down the sun.
In binding fiends and demons I'm the best;
Moving stars and planets, I scare ghosts and gods.
Stealing from Heav'n and Earth gives me great fame,
I'm the Handsome Stone Monkey of boundless change.

On hearing these words, the old man's displeasure turned to delight. He bowed, saying, "Please, please come inside to rest in our humble dwelling." The four pilgrims thus led the horse and toted their luggage inside, where they saw thorny bushes on both sides of the yard. The second-level door was flanked by stone walls, which were covered also by briars and thistles. Finally, they reached three tiled houses in the center. The old man at once pulled some chairs over for them to be seated and asked for tea to be served. He also gave an order for rice to be prepared. In a little while, some tables were brought out on which were placed dishes of fried wheat gluten, bean curds, tarro sprouts, white radishes, mustard greens, green turnips, fragrant rice, and mallow soup made with vinegar. Master and disciples thus enjoyed a full meal.

After they finished eating, Pa-chieh tugged at Pilgrim and whispered to him: "Elder Brother, this oldie at first didn't want to give us lodging. Now he gives us a sumptuous feast. Why?" "How much could a meal like this be worth?" replied Pilgrim. "Just wait till tomorrow. He's going to send us off with ten kinds of fruit and ten different dishes!"

"Don't you have any shame?" said Pa-chieh. "So, you managed to wangle a meal from him with those few big words of yours. Tomorrow you'll be leaving. Why should he entertain you some more?" "Don't worry," replied Pilgrim, "I'll take care of this."

In a little while, it was almost completely dark, and the old man asked for lamps to be brought out. "Kung-kung," said Pilgrim, bowing, "what is your noble surname?" "It is Li," replied the old man. "I suppose this must be Li Village then," said Pilgrim.

"No," replied the old man, "for this is called the T'o-lo Village. There are over five hundred families living here, with many other surnames. Only I go by the name of Li." "Patron Li," said Pilgrim, "what particular good intention has moved you and your family to bestow on us this rich vegetarian feast?" Rising from his seat, the old man said, "I heard you say just now that you are an expert in catching fiends. We have one here, and I'd like to ask you to catch him for us. You shall have a handsome reward."

Bowing immediately to him, Pilgrim said, "Thanks for giving me some business!" "Look how he causes trouble!" exclaimed Pa-chieh. "When someone asks him to catch fiends, that person is dearer to him than his maternal grandpa! Without further ado, he bows already." "Worthy Brother," said Pilgrim, "you don't know about this. My bow is actually like a down payment. He isn't going to ask anyone else."

On hearing this, Tripitaka said, "This little monkey is so egocentric in everything. Suppose that monster-spirit has such vast magic powers that you can't succeed in catching him. Wouldn't that make you, someone who has left the family, guilty of falsehood?" "Master, don't be offended," said Pilgrim, laughing, "Let me question him further?" "On what?" asked the old man.

Pilgrim said, "Your noble region here seems to be a clean and peaceful piece of land. There are, moreover, many families living together, hardly a remote area. What sort of monster-spirit is there who dares approach your high and noble gates?"

"To tell you the truth," said the old man, "our region has enjoyed peace and prosperity for a long time. But three years ago, a violent gust of wind arose during the time of the sixth month. At the time, all the people of our village were out in the fields busily planting rice or beating grain. Quite alarmed by the wind, they thought that the weather had changed. Little did they expect that after the wind a monster-spirit would descend on us and devour all the cattle and live-stock left grazing outside. He ate chickens and geese whole, and he swallowed men and women alive. Since that time, he has returned frequently during these past three years to harass us. O elder! If you indeed have the abilities to catch this fiend and cleanse our land, all of us will most surely give you a big reward. We won't treat you lightly!"

"This kind of monster," Pilgrim said, "is quite difficult to catch." "Difficult indeed!" exclaimed Pa-chieh. "We're only mendicants—we want a night's lodging from you, and tomorrow we'll leave. Why should we catch any monster-spirit?" "So, you're actually priests out to swindle a meal!" said the old man. "When we first met, you were boasting of how you could move planets and stars, how you could bind fiends and monsters. But when I tell you now about the matter, you pass it off as something very difficult."

"Oldie," said Pilgrim, "the monster-spirit is not hard to catch. It is hard *only* because the families in this region are not united in their efforts." "How did you reach this conclusion?" asked the old man.

"For three years," Pilgrim replied, "this monster-spirit has been a menace, taking the lives of countless creatures. If each family here were to donate an ounce of silver, I should think that five hundred families would yield at least five hundred ounces. With that amount of money, you could hire an exorcist anywhere who would be able to catch the fiend for you. Why did you permit him to torture you for these three years?"

"If you bring up the subject of spending money," said the old man, "I'm embarrassed to death! Which one of our families did not indeed disburse three or four ounces of silver? The year before last we found a monk from the south side of this mountain and invited him to come.

But he didn't succeed." "How did that monk go about catching the fiend?" asked Pilgrim.
The old man said,
That man of the *Saṅgha*,
He had on a *kasāya*.
He first quoted the *Peacock*;
He then chanted the *Lotus*.
In an urn he burned incense;
With his hand he grasped a bell.
As he thus sang and chanted,
He aroused the very fiend.
Astride the clouds and the wind,
He came to this village.
The monk engaged the fiend—
What a battle to relate!
One stroke delivered a punch,
One stroke delivered a scratch.
The monk tried to respond,[2]
A respondent without hair!
In a while the fiend triumphed
And went back to mist and smoke.
(It's like sunning a dried scab!)
We drew near to take a look:
The bald head was beaten like a rotten watermelon!
"When you put it like that," said Pilgrim, laughing, "he really lost out!" The old man said, "He only paid with his life; we were the true victims. We had to buy the coffin for his funeral, and we had to give some money to his disciple. That disciple, however, has yet to be satisfied, and wants to bring litigation against us even now. What a mess!"

"Did you try to find someone else to catch the monster?" asked Pilgrim again. The old man replied, "We found last year a Taoist." "How did that Taoist go about catching him?" asked Pilgrim. "That Taoist," said the old man,
Wore on his head a gold cap,
And on himself, a ritual robe.
He banged aloud his placard;
He waved his charms and water.
He sent for gods and spirits;

He brought on only the ogre.
A violent gale blew and churned,
And black fog dimmed everywhere.
The monster and the Taoist,
The two went forth to battle.
They fought till dusk had set in
When the fiend left with the clouds.
The cosmos was bright and fair,
And we were all assembled.
Going to search for the Taoist,
We found him drowned in a brook.
We fished him out for a better look:
He seemed like a chicken poached in soup!

"The way you put it," said Pilgrim, laughing, "he, too, lost out!" "He, too, only paid with his life," said the old man, "but we again had to spend all sorts of unnecessary money." "Don't worry! Don't worry!" said Pilgrim. "Let me catch him for you." "If you really have the ability to seize him," said the old man, "I will ask several elders of our village to sign a contract with you. If you win, you may ask whatever amount of money you wish, and we won't withhold from you even half a penny. But if you get hurt, don't accuse us of anything. Let all of us obey the will of Heaven." "This oldie is weary of being wrongly accused!" said Pilgrim, laughing. "I'm not that kind of person. Go and fetch the elders quickly."

Filled with delight, the old man immediately asked a few houseboys to go and invite eight or nine elders to his house—all neighbors, cousins, and in-laws of his. After they met the T'ang monk and had been told of the matter of catching the fiend, they were all very pleased. "Which noble disciple will go forth to catch him?" one elder asked.

With his hands folded before his chest to salute them, Pilgrim said, "This little priest will." Astonished, the elder said, "That won't do! That won't do! The monster-spirit has vast magic powers and a hulking body. A lean and tiny priest like you probably won't even fill the cracks of his teeth!"

"Venerable Sir," said Pilgrim, laughing, "you haven't guessed correctly about me! I may be tiny, but I'm quite hardy. 'Having drunk a few drops off the whetstone, I've been sharpened up!'" On hearing this, those elders had no alternative but to give their consent. "Elder," they said, "how much reward do you want after you've caught the monster-spirit?"

"Why mention reward?" replied Pilgrim. "As the saying goes,

Gold dazzles your eyes;

Silver is not shiny;

Copper pennies are stinky!

We're priests trying to accumulate merit, and we certainly do not desire cash rewards."

"The way you speak," said one of the elders, "indicates that you're all noble priests who take your commandments seriously. You may not want cash rewards, but we can't allow you to work for us free. Now, all of us either farm or fish for our livelihood. If you truly can rid us of this cursed fiend and purify our region, each family will donate two acres of the finest land—a thousand acres in all—which will be set aside at one place. All of you, master and disciples, can then build on the land a nice temple or monastery, in which you can meditate and practice Zen. That's much better than wandering with the clouds all over the world."

Laughing again, Pilgrim said, "That's even messier! If you give us land, we'll have to graze and groom horses, to find feed and make hay. At dusk, we can't go to bed, and by dawn, we still cannot rest. That sort of a life will kill us!" "If you don't want all these," said the elder, "just what do you want as your reward?" "We're people who have left the family," replied Pilgrim. "Give us some tea and rice, and that's sufficient reward."

The elders were very pleased. "That sort of reward is easy," said one of them, "but we'd like to know your plan to catch him?" "When he comes," said Pilgrim, "I'll do it." "But that fiend is huge," said another elder. "He touches Heaven above and Earth beneath. He comes with the wind and departs with the fog. How can you even get near him?" "If he's a monster-spirit able to summon the wind and ride the fog," said Pilgrim with a laugh, "I'll just treat him as my grandson. If he's big in size, I still can hit him."

As they chatted, they suddenly heard the howling of the wind, which so terrified those eight or nine elders that they all quaked and quivered. "This priest has such a bad luck mouth!" they cried. "He speaks of the monster-spirit, and at once the monster-spirit shows up!"

Flinging wide the side door, that Old Li herded the T'ang monk and his relatives inside, crying, "Come in! Come in! the fiend's here." Pa-chieh and Sha Monk were so intimidated that they, too, wanted to follow them into the house. Pilgrim, however, yanked them back with both hands, saying, "Have you lost your senses? Priests like you, how could you behave like that? Stand still! Stay with me in the courtyard so that we can find out what kind of a monster-spirit this is."

"Oh, Elder Brother!" cried Pa-chieh. "These are all savvy people! When the wind howls, it means the fiend's coming, and that's why they are in hiding. We are neither kinfolk nor acquaintances of theirs, neither bond relatives nor old friends. What's the point of looking at this monster?"

Pilgrim, however, was so strong that he was able to hold them down right there in the courtyard as the wind grew even more fierce. Marvelous wind!

It felled woods and trees, daunting tigers and wolves;
It stirred seas and rivers, alarming gods and ghosts;
It toppled rocks of Mount Hua's triple peaks;[3]
It upturned the world's four great continents.
Rustic homes and households all shut their doors;
The whole village's children all hid their heads.
Massive black clouds covered the starry sky.
Lamps and lights faded as the whole earth grew dark.

Pa-chieh was so terrified that he fell on the ground; digging a hole with his snout, he buried his head in it and lay prone as if he had been nailed to the Earth. Sha Monk, too, covered up his head and face, for he found it difficult even to open his eyes.

Only Pilgrim sniffed at the wind to try to determine what sort of fiend that was. In a little while the wind subsided and the faint glow of what seemed to be two lanterns appeared in midair. Lowering his head, Pilgrim said, "Brothers, the wind's gone! Get up and take a look!"

Pulling out his snout, our Idiot shook off the dirt and raised his head skyward. When he saw the two lights, he burst out laughing, crying, "What fun! What fun! So, this monster-spirit is someone who knows properly when to move or rest! We should befriend him." "In a dark night like this," said Sha Monk, "you haven't even seen his face yet. How could you know what sort of a person he is?"

Pa-chieh replied, "The ancients said,

To move by lights at night is best;
When there are no torches, we rest.[4]

Look at him now! He has a pair of lanterns leading the way. He must be a good man."

"You're wrong!" said Sha Monk. "Those aren't lanterns. They're the glimmering eyes of the monster-spirit!" Our Idiot was so appalled that he lost three inches of his height. "Holy Father!" he cried. "If those are his eyes, how big is his mouth?"

"Don't be afraid, Worthy Brothers," said Pilgrim. "Stay here and guard our master. Let old Monkey go up there and demand a confession. We'll see what kind of monster-spirit he is." "Elder Brother," said Pa-chieh, "don't confess that *we* are here."

Dear Pilgrim! He whistled loudly and leaped into the air. Gripping his iron rod, he cried out in a loud voice, "Slow down! Slow down! I'm here!" When the fiend saw Pilgrim, he stood erect and began to wave a long lance back and forth in the air. Holding high his rod to assume a position of combat, Pilgrim asked, "From what region a fiend are you? Of what place a spirit are you?" The fiend gave no reply whatever; all he did was to wave his lance. Pilgrim asked again, but still there was no reply from the fiend, who only persisted in waving the lance. Smiling to himself, Pilgrim said, "You've got to be both deaf and dumb! Don't run away! Watch my rod!"

The fiend, however, was not frightened in the least; brandishing his lance, he parried Pilgrim's blows, and the two of them charged back and forth, up and down, in midair. They fought till it was about the hour of the third watch and no decision was reached. Standing down below in the courtyard, Pa-chieh and Sha Monk saw everything clearly. The fiend, you see, only wielded the lance to parry the blows, but he did not attack his opponent at all. Pilgrim's rod, therefore, hardly ever left the head of the fiend. "Sha Monk," said Pa-chieh with a laugh, "you stand guard here, and let old Hog go and help with the fight. We can't allow that monkey to make this merit all by himself, or he'll be rewarded with the first goblet of wine."

Dear Idiot! He leaped up to the edge of the clouds and attacked at once with his rake, which was met by another lance of the fiendish creature. The two lances danced in the air like flying serpents and flashing thunderbolts. Praising him, Pa-chieh said, "This monster-spirit shows great technique with the lance! He's not using the style of the 'Mountain-Back Lance,' but it's more like the 'Winding-Silk Lance.' It's not the 'Ma-Family Lance,' but it probably has the name of the 'Flabby-Handle Lance.'"

"Stop babbling, Idiot!" said Pilgrim. "There's no such thing as the

'Flabby-Handle Lance!'" Pa-chieh said, "Just look at how he uses the pointed ends of the lances to parry our blows, but the handles of the lances are nowhere to be seen. Where has he hidden them, I wonder?"

"Maybe it *is* the 'Flabby-Handle Lance,'" said Pilgrim, "but what's important is that this fiendish creature does not know how to speak, because he has not yet attained the way of humans. He is still heavily under the influence of the yin aura. In the morning when the yang aura grows stronger, he will certainly want to flee. We must give chase and not let him get away." "Exactly! Exactly!" said Pa-chieh.

They fought for a long time and then the east paled with light. Not daring to linger, the fiend turned and fled, while Pa-chieh and Pilgrim gave chase together. As they sped along, they suddenly encountered an oppressively foul stench rising from the Pulpy Persimmon Alley of the Seven Extremes Mountain. "Which family is cleaning its privy?" cried Pa-chieh. "Wow! The smell's horrible!"

Clamping a hand over his nose, Pilgrim could only mutter, "Chase the monster-spirit! Chase the monster-spirit!" Darting past the mountain, the fiend at once changed back into his original form: a huge, red-scaled python. Look at him!

His eyes flashed forth the stars of dawn;
His nose belched the morning fog.
His teeth, like dense rows of steel swords;
His claws curved like golden hooks.[5]
From the brow rose a horn of flesh
That seemed to be formed by a thousand pieces of carnelian;
His whole body was draped in red scales
That resembled a million flakes of rouge.
Coiled up on earth, he could be confused with a brocade quilt;
Flying in the air, he could be mistaken for a rainbow.
Where he rested, putrid fumes rose to the sky;
When he moved, scarlet clouds covered his body.
Big or not,
People on his east end couldn't see the west.
Long or not,
He was like a mountain stretching from pole to pole.

"So, it's such a long snake!" said Pa-chieh. "If it wants to devour people, one meal will probably take five hundred persons, and it'll still not be filled." Pilgrim said, "That 'Flabby-Handle Lance' has to be his forked tongue. He has been weakened by our chase. Let's hit him from behind!" Bounding forward, our Pa-chieh brought his rake down hard on the fiendish creature, who darted swiftly into a hole. Only seven or eight feet of the tail remained outside when it was grabbed by Pa-chieh, abandoning his rake. "I've got him! I've got him!" he cried, as he used all his might to try to pull the fiend out of the hole, but he could not even budge him.

"Idiot," said Pilgrim, laughing, "leave him inside. I know what to do. Don't try to pull a snake backward like that!" Pa-chieh indeed let go and the fiend slithered inside the hole. "Before I let go just now," complained Pa-chieh, "half of him was already ours. Now he has slithered inside. How could we make him come out again? Isn't this what you call no more snake to play with?"

Pilgrim said, "This fellow has quite a hefty body. The hole is so small that he can never turn around inside. He has to move in a straightforward manner, and there has to be also a rear entrance. Go find it quickly and bar the hole. I'll attack him from the front entrance here."

Idiot dashed past the mountain, where he indeed discovered another hole. He paused, but had hardly stood still when Pilgrim at the front entrance sent a terrific jab with his rod into the hole. In great pain, the fiendish creature darted out of the rear entrance. Caught off guard, Pa-chieh was struck down by his tail and, unable to get up again, he lay on the ground to nurse his pain. When Pilgrim saw that the hole was empty, he picked up his rod and ran over to the rear, shouting for Pa-chieh to chase the fiend. On hearing Pilgrim's voice, Pa-chieh became so embarrassed that, regardless of his pain, he scrambled up and began to beat the ground madly with his rake. When he saw him, Pilgrim laughed and said, "The fiend's gone! What are you doing that for?" Pa-chieh said, "Old Hog's here 'Beating the Bush to Stir the Snake.'" "What a living Idiot!" said Pilgrim. "Let's chase him!"

The two of them ran past a brook, when they found the fiend had coiled himself into a mound on the ground. Rearing his head, he opened wide his huge mouth and wanted to devour Pa-chieh. Terrified, Pa-chieh turned and fled, but our Pilgrim went forward to meet him and was swallowed by the fiend in one gulp. Pounding his chest and stamping his feet, Pa-chieh screamed, "Alas, Elder Brother! You're dead!" Inside the stomach of the monster-spirit, Pilgrim held up his iron rod and said, "Don't worry, Pa-chieh. Let me ask him to build a bridge for you to see!"

He stuck his rod up a bit more, and the fiendish creature had to raise his torso until he resembled a bow-shaped bridge. "He looks like a bridge, all right," said Pa-chieh, "but no one would dare walk on it." "Let me ask him again to change into a boat for you to see," said Pilgrim. He plunged the iron rod downward; with the stomach hugging the ground and the head upraised, the fiendish creature looked like a sloop from the Kan River district.

"He may look like a boat," said Pa-chieh, "but there is no top mast for him to use the wind." "Get out of the way," said Pilgrim, "and I'll make him use the wind for you to see." Using all his strength, Pilgrim pushed his iron rod upward from the spine of the fiendish creature until it reached a height of some seventy feet and the shape of a mast. In desperate pain and struggling for his life, the fiend shot forward, faster than any wind-blown vessel, and made for the road on which he came. Some twenty miles down the mountain, he finally fell motionless to the dust and expired. Pa-chieh caught up with him from behind and attacked him madly once more with his rake. Meanwhile, Pilgrim ripped a big hole in the creature's body and crawled out, saying, "Idiot, he's dead already. Why use your rake on him?" "Oh, Elder Brother," said Pa-chieh, "don't you know that old Hog all his life has loved to strike at dead snakes?" They thus put away their weapons and dragged the creature back by his tail.

We tell you now about Old Li in the T'o-lo Village; he and the rest of the people said to the T'ang monk, "For a whole night your two disciples have not returned. They must have lost their lives." "I don't think it's that serious," said Tripitaka. "Let us go out to have a look first." Soon they caught sight of Pilgrim and Pa-chieh approaching, dragging a huge python behind them and shouting to clear the way. Only then did the people become delighted; the old and young, the men and women of the entire village all came to kowtow and say, "Holy Fathers, this is the very monster-spirit that has taken many lives here. We are fortunate to have you exercise your power today and extirpate the fiendish deviate, for now our lives are secure."

All the households were filled with gratitude, so much so that each one of them insisted on thanking the pilgrims with gifts and feasting. Master and disciples were detained for nearly a week, and only after much pleading on their part were they permitted to leave. When the people saw that the pilgrims refused to accept any kind of monetary rewards, they all prepared some dried goods and fruits. With laden horses and mules, colored banners and red ribbons, they came to say farewell. There were only five hundred families in the region, but those who came to send them off numbered more than seven hundred.

They journeyed amiably, and in a little while they arrived at the entrance of the Pulpy Persimmon Alley in the Mountain of Seven Extremes. When Tripitaka smelled the wretched odor and saw how clogged the road was, he said, "Wu-k'ung, how could we pass through?" Clamping his hand over his nose, Pilgrim said, "This is rather difficult!" When Tripitaka heard him say "difficult," tears dropped from his eyes. Old Li and others went forward and said, "Father, please do not be anxious. When we accompanied you here, we had already made up our minds. Since your noble disciples subdued the monster-spirit for us and delivered the entire village from such calamity, we are all determined to open up a road for you to pass through."

"Oldie," said Pilgrim, smiling, "your words aren't very reasonable! You told us earlier that the distance across this mountain is some eight hundred miles. You are no celestial engineers under the command of the Great Yü.[6] How could you blast open mountains and build roads? If you want my master to get across the ridge, it's up to us again to exert ourselves. None of you can do something like this."

As he dismounted, Tripitaka said, "Wu-k'ung, how are you going to exert yourself?" "If you want to cross this mountain in the twinkling of an eye," said Pilgrim, smiling, "that's difficult. If you want to build another road, that's difficult, too. We have to push through, using the old alley, but right now, I fear that no one will take care of our meals."

"Don't talk like that, Elder!" said Old Li. "No matter how long you four are delayed here, we can support you. How could you say that no one would take care of your meals!" "In that case," said Pilgrim, "go and prepare two piculs of dried rice, and make some steamed buns and breads also. Let that priest of ours with a long snout eat to his fill. He'll then change into a huge hog to shovel out the old road. Our master will ride the horse and we'll accompany him. We'll get across."

On hearing this, Pa-chieh said, "Elder Brother, all of you want to be clean. How could you ask old Hog alone to become stinky?" "Wu-nêng," said Tripitaka, "if you truly have the ability to shovel out the alley and lead me across the mountain, I'll have it recorded that you are ranked first in merit on this occasion." With a laugh, Pa-chieh said, "Master, you and the rest of our venerable patrons here should not tease me. I, old Hog, after all, am capable of thirty-six kinds of transformation. If you want me to change into something delicate, elegant, and agile, I simply can't do it. But if it's a mountain, a tree, a boulder, an earth mound, a scabby elephant, a graded hog, a water buffalo, or a camel, I can change into all these things. The only thing is that if I change into something big, my appetite is going to be even bigger. I must be satisfactorily fed before I can work."

"We have the stuff! We have the stuff!" cried the people. "We have all brought along dried goods, fruits, baked biscuits, and assorted pastries. We were planning to present them to you after you had crossed the mountain. We'll take them out now for you to enjoy. When you have assumed your transformation and begun your work, we'll send people back to the village to prepare more rice for you."

Filled with delight, Pa-chieh took off his black cloth shirt and dropped his nine-pronged rake. "Don't tease me!" he said to the people. "Watch old Hog achieve this stinky merit!" Dear Idiot! Making the magic sign with his fingers, he shook his body once and changed indeed into a huge hog. Truly he had

A long snout and short hair—all rather plump.
He'd fed on herbs of the mountain since his youth.
A black face with round eyes like the sun and moon;
A round head with huge ears like plantain leaves.
His bones were made lasting as Heaven's age;
Tougher than iron was his thick skin refined.
In deep nasal tones he made his oink-oink cry.
What gutteral grunts when he puffed and huffed!
Four white hoofs standing a thousand feet tall;
Swordlike bristles topped a hundred-yard frame.
Mankind had long seen fatted pigs and swine,
But never till today this old hog elf.
The T'ang monk and the people all gave praise;
At such high magic pow'r they were amazed.

When Pilgrim Sun saw this transformation of Pa-chieh, he ordered those people who accompanied them to put their dried goods into a huge pile so that Pa-chieh could enjoy the foodstuff. Without regard for whether it was cooked or raw, Pa-chieh went forward and gulped down all of it. Then he proceeded to shovel out a path. Pilgrim asked Sha Monk to take off his shoes and to pole the luggage with care. He told his master to sit firmly on the carved saddle, while he himself also took off his boots. Then he gave this instruction to the people: "If you are grateful, go and prepare some rice quickly for my brother's sustenance."

Over half of those seven hundred people who accompanied them to send them off came along with horses and mules; they, therefore, dashed back to the village like shooting stars to prepare the rice. The rest of the people, some three hundred of them, had come on foot, and these stood below the mountain and watched the pilgrims depart. The distance between the village and the mountain, you see, was some thirty miles. By the time the people went back to the village and returned with the rice, master and disciples were almost a hundred miles away. Not willing to let them go, however, the people urged their horses and mules into the alley and spent the night traveling. Only by morning did they succeed in catching up with the pilgrims. "Holy Fathers who are going to acquire scriptures," they cried, "please slow down! Please slow down! We are bringing you rice!"

On hearing these words, the elder was filled with gratitude. "Truly they are kind and faithful people!" he said. Then he asked Pa-chieh to stop so that he could take some rice for strength. Our Idiot had been shoveling for one whole day and night, and he was beginning to feel keenly his hunger. Though there were more than seven or eight piculs of rice brought by those people, he gulped it all down, regardless of whether it was rice or other types of grain. After a hearty meal, he proceeded again to shovel out the road. Tripitaka, Pilgrim, and Sha Monk thanked the people and took leave of them. So, it is that

The T'o-lo villagers return to their homes,
While Pa-chieh opens up a mountain path.
Devout Tripitaka godly strength upholds;
Wu-k'ung shows magic and the demon fails.
An aeon's Pulp Persimmons this day are cleansed;
Henceforth the Seven Extremes' Alley is unclogged.
Six forms of desires having all been purged.
In peace, unhindered, they'll bow to lotus seats.

We do not know how great a distance they still must travel or what sort of fiends they may encounter, and you must listen to the explanation in the next chapter.

Sixty-eight

In the Scarlet-Purple Kingdom the T'ang monk speaks of
   past epochs;
Pilgrim Sun performs as one who can heal an arm
   broken in three places.[1]

Virtue attained, all causations gone,
Your fame through four great continents will spread.
Wise and enlightened you ascend yonder shore.
The wind will sigh
As hazy cirrus climbs the distant sky.

Those Buddhas will receive you;
You'll live at Jade Terrace forever and e'er.
Break up the human dream of butterfly,
Let it all pass!
No grief befalls you when defilement's purged.
We were telling you about Tripitaka and his disciples who,
   Having cleaned out an alley of sullage,
   Now walked on the path of freedom.
Time went by swiftly and again it was torrid summer, when
   Pomegranates display ornate fruits,
   And lotus leaves spread like green pans.
   In two rows of willlow young swallows hide,
   As travelers wave silk fans to flee the heat.
As they proceeded, they suddenly saw a moated city looming up.
Reining in his horse, Tripitaka called out: "Disciples, take a look.
What kind of a place is that?" "Master," said Pilgrim, "so you are
actually illiterate! How could you have accepted the decree of the
T'ang emperor to leave the court?"

"I became a priest when I was still a child," replied Tripitaka. "I
have mastered thousands of sūtras. How could you say I'm illiterate?"
"If you are literate," said Pilgrim, "why couldn't you recognize those
three big words written plainly on the apricot-yellow banner? Why
did you have to ask what sort of a place this is?"

"Brazen ape!" bellowed the T'ang monk. "You're babbling! That
banner is whipped by the wind. There might be words on it, but I can't

see them clearly!" "Of all persons," said Pilgrim, "why is it that old Monkey's able to see them?" "Master," both Pa-chieh and Sha Monk said, "don't listen to Elder Brother's jabberings! From this distance, we can hardly see the moated city clearly. Who could see any words?" "Aren't those words, the Scarlet-Purple Kingdom?" asked Pilgrim. Tripitaka said, "The Scarlet-Purple Kingdom must be a state in the Western domain. That means we must have our rescript certified." "That goes without saying," said Pilgrim.

In a little while, they arrived before the gate of the city, where Tripitaka dismounted. As they strolled through the triple-layered gates, they found that it was a marvelous national capital indeed. What they saw were

Soaring towered gates,
Orderly parapets.
Around the city running water flowed freely;
North and south, it fronted on tall mountains.
Cargoes heaped up in its streets and markets;
Business flourished in every house and home.
Truly it was a meeting place of royalty,
A great capital, a Heavenly residence.
Towered boats came from distant shores.
Laden with foreign jades and gems.
Its noble form joined distant hills;
Its palaces reached the clear void.
Its three passes firmly secured,
Therein peace forever prospered.

As master and disciples walked through the main boulevards, they found the looks of the people distinguished and imposing, their attire orderly and neat, and their language clear and resonant. Truly it was no different from the world of the Great T'ang. Now, when those people on both sides busily engaged in buying and selling suddenly discovered the ugly visage of Pa-chieh, the dark face and tall frame of Sha Monk, and the hairy features of Pilgrim Sun, they all abandoned their businesses and crowded around the pilgrims to stare at them. Tripitaka felt compelled to call out: "Don't start any trouble! Lower your heads and walk on!"

Obeying his master, Pa-chieh stuffed his lotus-rootlike mouth inside his bosom, and Sha Monk dared not raise his head. Only Pilgrim kept staring left and right as he walked closely beside the T'ang monk.

After they had looked at the pilgrims for a while, those people who were more sensible went back to their own activities. The loiterers and the mischievous youths, however, all surged around Pa-chieh; laughing and clamoring, they threw tiles and bricks at Pa-chieh to tease him. The T'ang monk became so nervous that he was perspiring. All he could say was, "Don't start anything!" Our Idiot dared not lift his head.

In a moment, they turned the corner and came upon a large residence surrounded by an outer wall. On top of its entrance were the words, College of Interpreters.² "Disciples," said the T'ang monk, "let's go inside this official mansion." "What for?" asked Pilgrim. "The College of Interpreters," said the T'ang monk, "is a meeting place for people from all parts of the world. Even we can make use of it. Let us go in and rest ourselves. After I have seen the Throne and have had our rescript certified, we can then leave the city and be on our way once more."

On hearing this, Pa-chieh brought out his snout and frightened off several scores of those people following them. "What Master says is quite right," he said as he walked forward. "Let's hide inside so that we won't be bothered by the cacklings of these bird-brains!" They thus entered the college, and the people gradually dispersed.

We tell you now that there were two officials inside the college, a minister proper and a vice-minister. They were both taking the roll in the great hall and preparing to meet other officials arriving. Startled by the sight of the T'ang monk walking in, they both said, "Who are you? Who are you? Where do you think you are going?"

Folding his hands before his chest, Tripitaka said, "This humble cleric has been sent by the Throne of the Great T'ang in the Land of the East to go seek scriptures in the Western Heaven. We came upon your treasure region, and we dared not pass through without permission. We would like to have our travel rescript certified, and we would like to ask for temporary lodging in your noble mansion." When those two college ministers heard what he said, they asked their attendants on both sides to step back. Fixing up their caps and tightening their belts, the ministers left the main hall to greet the T'ang monk. At once they asked that guest rooms be cleaned out for the pilgrims to rest in, and they also ordered the preparation of vegetarian meals. After Tripitaka thanked them, the two officials departed with their staff, leaving only a few attendants to look after the priest. As

Tripitaka began to walk out, Pilgrim said spitefully, "These rogues! Why didn't they allow old Monkey to stay in the main suite?"

The T'ang monk said, "Their territory here is not governed by our Great T'ang, nor do we have any formal diplomatic relations. Moreover, the college is frequently visited by distinguished guests or high rank officials. That's probably why they find it difficult to entertain us here." "If you put it that way," said Pilgrim, "I would want them all the more to entertain us here."

As they were speaking, a steward came in with some supplies: a large bowl of white rice, a large bowl of wheat flour, two bunches of green vegetables, four cakes of bean curd, two fried wheat gluten, one dish of dried bamboo shoots, and one dish of wood-ears. Tripitaka told his disciples to accept these and thank the steward. The steward said, "In the west rooms there are clean pots and pans. The fires and stoves are ready. Please go there and cook the meal yourselves."

"Let me ask you this," said Tripitaka. "Is the king still in the main hall?" "His Majesty has not held court for a long time," replied the steward. "Today happens to be an auspicious day, and at this very moment he is discussing with many civil and military officials the publication of a special proclamation. If you want to have your travel rescript certified, you should hurry there for you may still catch him. By tomorrow, you will not be able to have an audience with him, and I don't know how long you'll have to wait for another opportunity."

"Wu-k'ung," said Tripitaka, "all of you stay here and prepare our meal. Let me hurry there to have our rescript certified. I'll then come back, eat, and we will leave." Quickly Pa-chieh took out the cassock and the travel rescript: after Tripitaka put on the proper attire, he told his disciples not to leave the college and cause trouble outside before he went into court.

In a moment, he arrived before the Five Phoenix Tower, and we cannot begin to tell you how magnificent were those palatial halls and buildings. He went before the front gate proper and requested the imperial messenger to make known to the Heavenly Court his desire to have the rescript certified. The Custodian of the Yellow Gate indeed went before the white jade steps to memorialize: "Outside the gate of the court, there is a priest from the Great T'ang in the Land of the East who, by imperial commission, is journeying to the Thunderclap Monastery in the Western Heaven to seek scriptures from Buddha. Desirous of having his travel rescript certified, he awaits our royal summons."

On hearing this, the king said in delight, "We have been ill for a long time and we have not ascended our throne. What a happy coincidence this is that the moment we appear in the main hall with the intent to find a good physician through the promulgation of a special proclamation, a noble priest immediately appears." He at once had the priest summoned to the hall, where Tripitaka prostrated himself to pay the king homage. The king then asked him to take a seat in the golden hall, after which the Court of Imperial Entertainments was asked to prepare a vegetarian banquet. Having thanked the king for his royal favors, Tripitaka presented the travel rescript.

After he read the document, the king was very pleased. "Master of the Law," he said, "through how many successions of rulers and how many generations of ministers has your Great T'ang passed? As for the T'ang emperor, how did he return to life from his illness, so that he could ask you to traverse mountains and rivers to seek scriptures?" Faced with these questions, the elder bowed with hands folded to make his reply, saying, "In the native land of your humble cleric,

Three Kings first governed our world;
Five August Ones set relations.
Yao and Shun defined kingship;
Yü and T'ang³ gave the people peace.
But descendants of Ch'êng and Chou⁴
All desired independence.
Using might to oppress the weak,
They laid claim to sundry kingdoms.
They totaled eighteen rulers,
Dividing land and frontiers.
They decreased to twelve later,
And the world became tranquil.
For want of chariots and horses,
They again devoured each other.
Seven powers strove together,
And six states all bowed to Ch'in.
But Heaven gave birth to P'ei of Lu,⁵
Each envious of the other.
The empire then became Han's,
Which fixed laws for all to obey.
Then Han succumbed to Ssŭ-ma,⁶
And Tsin, too, became unruly.

North and South twelve states in all—
Such as Sung, Ch'i, Liang, and Ch'ên—
Lasted in close succession
Till Great Sui became the true heir.
Then came a lecher and despot
Who made the people suffer.
Our king with Li as his surname
Took T'ang as his empire's title.
After emperor *Kao-tsu* departed,
Shih-min became our present ruler.
Our rivers are clean, our seas tranquil,
For great is his kindness and virtue.
Now, north of the capital Ch'ang-an,
There was a water sprite, a dragon god,
Who reduced an amount of rain
And thus deserved to perish.
Through a dream at night, however,
He begged our king for assistance.
The king promised him his pardon,
And summoned a worthy subject,
Who was kept within the palace
To play chess slowly with the king.
When the time reached the noon hour,
That worthy subject slew the dragon in a dream."

On hearing what Tripitaka said, the king suddenly groaned a few
times and said, "Master of the Law, from which country did that
subject come?"

"He was the prime minister before the throne of our emperor,"
replied Tripitaka. "His surname is Wei and his given name is Chêng.
He knows astronomy and geography, and he can distinguish between
yin and yang. He is truly a great minister and helper, one who knows
how to secure the empire and establish the state. Because he executed
the Dragon King of the Ching River in his dream, the dragon king filed
suit in the region of darkness, accusing our emperor of reneging on
his promise to spare his life. That was why our emperor became mort-
ally ill. Then Wei Chêng wrote a letter for our emperor to take to the
region of darkness and give to Ts'ui Chüeh, a judge in the Capital of
Death. When the T'ang emperor indeed expired after a little while, he
came back to life three days later all because of Wei Chêng, who

moved Judge Ts'ui to alter a document and add twenty more years to the emperor's age. Thereafter when the emperor gave a Grand Mass of Land and Water, he commissioned this humble cleric to traverse a great distance through many nations in order that I may seek from the Buddhist Patriarch the three baskets of Mahāyāna scriptures, which will help redeem the cursed and wretched souls to Heaven."

Groaning some more, the king sighed, "Truly yours is a nation and a Heavenly Court! Your ruler is righteous, and your ministers are upright! Look at us! We have been ill for a long time, but not one minister is able to assist us." When he heard this, the elder stole a glance at the king and saw that his face looked yellow and his body seemed emaciated. His whole appearance, in fact, was weary and spiritless. The elder was about to question him further when the official from the Court of Imperial Entertainments approached to invite the T'ang monk to dine. The king at once gave this command: "Set out our meal at the Hall of Unfurling Fragrance. We shall dine with the Master of the Law." Tripitaka thanked him, and we shall leave them dining together.

We tell you now about Pilgrim in the College of Interpreters, who asked Sha Monk to make tea and rice and to prepare some vegetarian dishes. Sha Monk said, "It's easy to make the tea and the rice, but it won't be easy to prepare the vegetarian dishes." "Why?" asked Pilgrim. "Oil, salt, soy sauce, and vinegar," replied Sha Monk, "none of these can be found here." Pilgrim said, "I have a few pennies small change. Tell Pa-chieh to go buy some on the streets."

At once turning lazy, our Idiot said, "I dare not go. My features aren't that nice looking, and I fear that Master will blame me if I cause any trouble." "We are doing business fair and square!" said Pilgrim. "We aren't begging, and we aren't robbing. How could you cause any trouble?"

"Haven't you seen what I could do just now?" said Pa-chieh. "I yanked out my snout before the door and scared off over ten persons. If I go to the bustling market, I don't know how many persons will be frightened to death." "All you know is the bustling market," said Pilgrim, "but have you seen what they are selling in this market?" "Master told me to walk with my head bowed," replied Pa-chieh, "so as not to cause any trouble. In truth I haven't seen anything."

Pilgrim said, "There are wine shops, rice dealers, mills, and fabric stores, which we need not mention in detail. There are truly fine tea houses, noodle shops, huge biscuits, and gigantic buns. Moreover, the restaurants display nice soups and rice, fine spices, and excellent vegetables. I saw also exotic puddings, steamed goods, pastries, rolls, fried goods, and honey cakes—in fact, countless goodies. I'll go buy some of these to treat you. How's that?"

When our Idiot heard this, saliva drooled from his mouth and his throat gurgled as he swallowed hard a few times. "Elder Brother," he said, leaping up. "I'll let you treat me this time. I'll save some money so that next time I can return your favor." Smiling to himself, Pilgrim said, "Sha Monk, be careful in cooking the rice. We'll go and buy some seasoning." Knowing that he was making fun of Idiot, Sha Monk played along and replied, "Go ahead, both of you. After you've fed yourself, bring back a lot of seasoning."

Picking up a container, our Idiot followed Pilgrim out the door. Two officials asked, "Where are the elders going?" "To buy seasoning," replied Pilgrim. "Go west on this street," said one of them, "and make a turn at the corner watchtower. You'll find a grocery owned by the Chêng family, where you can buy however much you like. Oil, salt, soy sauce, vinegar, ginger, pepper, and tea—they have them all."

The two of them, arm in arm, followed the street to the west. Pilgrim walked right past several teahouses and restaurants, refusing to buy what ought to be bought, to eat what ought to be eaten. "Elder Brother," Pa-chieh called out, "let's not be so choosy. Just buy something here and we'll enjoy it." Pilgrim, who had wanted to sport with him, refused, of course, to buy anything. "Worthy Brother," he said, "don't be such a spendthrift! Let's walk a bit further, and we'll buy something big to eat." As the two of them chatted, they again caused many people to follow them, staring. In a little while, they reached the watchtower, beneath which they found a large, noisy crowd blocking the street. On seeing them, Pa-chieh said, "Elder Brother, I'm not going over there. Look at the mob. I fear that they may want to arrest monks, especially those who are strangers. If they seize me, what'll happen to me?"

"Nonsense!" said Pilgrim. "Monks haven't broken the law. Why should they want to arrest us? Let's walk past them so that we can buy some seasoning from the Chêng family store." "All right! All right! All right!" said Pa-chieh. "I won't cause any trouble. I'll just squeeze into the crowd, flap my ears a couple of times, and frighten them into falling down. Let a few of them fall to their deaths, and I'll just pay with my life!"

"If you put it that way," said Pilgrim, "why don't you stand still here at the base of the wall. Let me go to the store and get the seasoning. Then I'll buy some vegetarian noodles and biscuits for you to eat." Handing the container over to Pilgrim, our Idiot faced the wall, stuck his snout against it, and stood absolutely still.

Pilgrim walked up to the tower, and it was crowded indeed. As he pushed his way through the throng, he learned that a special royal proclamation had been mounted beneath the tower, and that was why so many people fought to look at it. When he finally squeezed through to where the document was, Pilgrim opened wide his fiery eyes and diamond pupils to stare at it, and this was what he read:

> Since we, the king of the Scarlet-Purple Kingdom in the West
> Aparagodānīya Continent, assumed our throne, the four quarters
> have remained submissive and the populace have enjoyed
> leisure and peace. Recently, however, the affairs of state have
> turned inauspicious, for we have been gravely ill, and recovery
> has been most difficult even after a long time. The college of
> imperial medicine of our nation has administered repeatedly its
> excellent prescriptions, but these have not given us cure. There-
> fore, we publish now this proclamation for all the worthy
> scholars throughout the world, regardless of whether they
> are going to the North, coming from the East, or are even
> natives of China, the foreign state. If there is anyone skillful in
> medicine and the therapeutic arts, let him ascend the treasure hall
> and restore our health. We most solemnly pledge that the
> moment we are healed, we will divide the kingdom with him.
> For this reason we have mounted this necessary proclamation.

When he finished reading it, Pilgrim was filled with delight, saying to himself, "The ancients said, 'Moving about may bring us riches!' We certainly shouldn't have sat idly in the college, nor is there any need now to buy seasoning. Let's delay for one day this business of fetching scriptures and allow old Monkey to play physician for a bit."

Dear Great Sage! He stooped low and left the container on the ground; picking up a pinch of dirt, he flung it up into the air and recited a spell. Immediately, the Magic of Body-Concealment rendered him invisible, so that he could walk up to the proclamation and gently peel it off. Then he faced the ground toward the southwest and sucked in a deep breath before blowing the air out again. At once a strong whirlwind arose and scattered the multitude. He turned around and went back to where Pa-chieh was standing. There he found Pa-chieh leaning on the base of the wall with the support of his snout and appearing as if he had fallen asleep. Without disturbing him, Pilgrim folded up the proclamation and gently stuck it in Pa-chieh's bosom. In big strides he then went back first to the College of Interpreters, where we shall leave him.

We tell you now instead about those people beneath the watch-tower. When the wind arose, all of them covered their heads and shut their eyes. Little did they anticipate that after the wind had passed, the royal proclamation would be nowhere to be seen, and each one of them was terrified. Originally, you see, the proclamation was accompanied by twelve eunuchs and twelve palace guards as it left the court that morning. It had not been hung up for more than three hours when it was blown away by the wind. Trembling all over, those eunuchs and guards searched for it left and right, and that was when they suddenly caught sight of a slip of paper sticking out from the bosom of Chu Pa-chieh. "Did you peel off the proclamation?" shouted the officials as they ran up to him.

All at once that Idiot raised his head and stuck out his snout, so frightening those several palace guards that they stumbled backwards and fell down. He turned around and wanted to flee, but he was pulled back by several of the braver ones. "You took down the royal proclamation for the recruitment of physicians," they cried. "Where do you think you are going if you aren't going into court to heal His Majesty?"

More and more flustered, our Idiot said, "Your son is the one who took off the royal proclamation! Your grandson is the one who knows anything about healing!" One of the palace guards spoke up: "What's that you have in your bosom?" Only then did Idiot lower his head and find that there was indeed a piece of paper there. When he spread it open and took one look, he clenched his teeth and cried, "That wretched ape has killed me!" He became so furious that he would have ripped up the document if the people had not stopped him.

"You *are* dead!" they shouted. "This is a proclamation of our reigning monarch. Who dares to tear it up? If you have taken it down and stuffed it into your bosom, you must be a physician able to heal him. Go with us, quickly!"

"You have no idea," shouted Pa-chieh, "that I did not take down this proclamation. It was taken down by my elder brother, Sun Wu-k'ung. After he stuck it secretly in my bosom, he abandoned me and left. If you want to get to the bottom of this matter, I have to go find him for you." "What sort of wild talk is that?" said the people. "You think 'We'd forsake a ready-made bell to strike one about to be forged'? You took down the proclamation! And you tell us now to find someone else! Never you mind! We'll haul you back to see our lord!"

Without further investigation of the matter, that group of people began to push and shove Idiot. Our Idiot, however, stood perfectly still, and he seemed to have taken root in the earth. Not even a dozen people could budge him. "All of you don't know any better!" said Pa-chieh. "If you pull at me some more, you will pull out my idiotic ire! Don't blame me then!"

Soon the entire neighborhood was aroused by all that hubbub to come and have Pa-chieh surrounded. Among the people were two elderly eunuchs, who said to him, "Your looks are strange and your voice sounds unfamiliar. Where have you come from, and why are you so headstrong?"

"We are those from the Land of the East sent to seek scriptures in the Western Heaven," replied Pa-chieh. "My master is a Master of the Law and the bond-brother of the T'ang emperor. Just now he has gone into court to have his travel rescript certified. My elder brother and I came here to buy seasoning. When I saw the crowd beneath the watchtower, I dared not go forward, and my elder brother told me to wait for him here. When he saw the proclamation, he called up a whirlwind and had it taken off and stuck secretly in my bosom. Then he left me." "Just now," said one of the eunuchs, "I saw a stoutish priest with a white face heading straight for the gate of the court. He, I suppose, must be your master." "He is indeed," said Pa-chieh.

"Where has your elder brother gone to?" asked the eunuch. Pa-chieh said, "There are altogether four of us. Our master has gone to have our travel rescript certified, but the rest of us—three disciples, a horse, and our luggage—are all resting at the College of Interpreters. After my elder brother had played this trick on me, he must have returned to the college." "Palace guards," said the eunuch, "stop tugging at this man. Let us go with him to the college, and we'll know the whole truth of the matter." "These two mamas are far more sensible!" said Pa-chieh.

"This priest is truly uninformed!" said one of the palace guards. "How could you address the papas as mamas?" "Aren't you ashamed of yourself?" said Pa-chieh, laughing. "*You* are the one who's switching the sexes! These two old mamas should be addressed as *p'o-p'o*s or madams. And you want to call them papas?" "Stop your saucy tongue!" the people said. "Go find your elder brother quickly."

By that time the noisy crowd had grown to over five hundred people, all surging up to the entrance of the college. "Stop here, all of you," said Pa-chieh. "My elder brother is not like me, who allows you this spoofing. He is rather hot-tempered, and terribly serious. When you meet him, you must extend to him a grand salutation and address him as Venerable Father Sun. Then he'll do business with you. Otherwise, he may change his colors and you won't succeed with your enterprise." "If your elder brother truly has the ability to heal our king," said the eunuchs and the palace guards, "he will inherit half the kingdom. He certainly deserves our bow."

While the idlers milled about noisily before the college, Pa-chieh led the troop of eunuchs and palace guards inside, where they heard Pilgrim laughing and telling Sha Monk the trick he had played on Pa-chieh. Pa-chieh dashed forward and grabbed him, screaming, "Some person you are! You tricked me out there and promised to buy vegetarian noodles, biscuits, and buns for me to eat. They're all fibs! Then you brought on the whirlwind and took down this so-called royal proclamation to have it stuck secretly in my bosom. You are playing me for a fatso! Is that how you treat your brother?"

Laughing, Pilgrim said, "Idiot, you must have taken the wrong road and gone off to some place else! I passed the watchtower, bought the seasoning, and came back quickly to where you were, but I couldn't find you. So, I returned here first. Where did I peel off any royal proclamation?" "The officials guarding the proclamation are right here," said Pa-chieh.

Hardly had he finished speaking when those several eunuchs and palace guards went forward to bow deeply to Pilgrim. "Venerable Father Sun," they said, "today our king must be exceedingly fortunate, for Heaven has sent you to descend to us. We beseech you to exercise your great talents in healing and your profound knowledge in the therapeutic arts. If you succeed in curing our king, you will have claim to half the kingdom."

On hearing these words, Pilgrim became more sober. He took the proclamation and asked the people, "Are you the officials guarding the proclamation?" Kowtowing, the eunuchs said, "Your slaves are palace officials belonging to the Directorate of Ceremonials. These are the Embroidered-Uniform Guards." "This proclamation for recruitment of physicians," said Pilgrim, "was indeed taken down by me. I purposely arranged for my brother to lead you to see me. Your lord is indisposed, but as the proverb says,

Medicines are not lightly bought;
A doctor's not casually sought.

You go back and ask the king to come here in person to invite me. I guarantee that when I stretch forth my hand, his illness will at once disappear."

When they heard these words, all of the eunuchs were astonished. "A stupendous claim like this can be made only by someone in the know," said one of the palace guards. "Half of us will remain here to continue our silent entreaty. Half of us will return to memorialize to the Throne."

Whereupon four eunuchs and six palace guards, without waiting for any summons, went inside the court and memorialized before the steps, saying, "My lord, ten thousand happinesses have come upon you!" Having finished his meal, the king was just having a quiet chat with Tripitaka. When he heard this, he asked, "Where has this happiness come from?" One of the eunuchs said, "This morning your slaves took the royal proclamation for the recruitment of physicians to have it mounted beneath the watchtower. It was taken down by Elder Sun, a sage monk sent from the distant Land of the East to acquire scriptures. He is now residing in the College of Interpreters and desires the personal appearance of the king to invite him. He has promised us that when he stretches forth his hand, the illness will disappear. That is why we have come to memorialize to you."

On hearing this, the king was filled with delight. He turned to ask the T'ang monk: "Master of the Law, how many noble disciples do you have?" "This humble cleric," replied Tripitaka with hands folded before him, "has three mischievous disciples." "Which of them is conversant with the therapeutic arts?" asked the king.

"To tell you the truth, Your Majesty," said Tripitaka, "my mischievous disciples are all ordinary men of the wilds. Their knowledge is confined to pulling the horse and toting the luggage, to fording streams and leading your poor monk across the mountains. When we pass through the more dangerous regions, they may even be able to subjugate demons and fiends, to tame tigers and dragons. But that's all! None of them knows anything about the nature of medicine."

"Why must you be so modest, Master of the Law?" said the king. "It is truly a Heavenly affinity that you should arrive on this very day when we ascend the main hall. If your noble disciple were not an able physician, how would he be willing to take down our proclamation and demand our going there in person to invite him? He must have the ability to heal the highest ruler of the state." Then the king gave this order: "Let our civil and military subjects represent us, for our body is weakened and our strength depleted, and we dare not ride the imperial chariot. You must therefore proceed beyond the court to extend our most earnest invitation to Elder Sun to come and examine our illness. When you see him, you must be careful not to treat him discourteously. You must address him as Elder Sun, the divine monk, and you must greet him as if he were your ruler."

Having received this decree, the various officials went with the eunuchs and the palace guards to the College of Interpreters. Standing in rows according to their ranks, they paid homage to Pilgrim. Pa-chieh was so taken aback that he dashed inside a side room while Sha Monk ran out to stand beneath the wall. Look at our Great Sage! He sat firmly in the middle of the room and remained unmoved. "This wretched ape," grumbled Pa-chieh to himself, "is hanging himself alive with all these undeserved honors! How could he not return the bow of these many officials? Why, he won't even stand up!"

Soon the ceremony was over, and the officials separated into two files before they presented this memorial, saying, "Let us inform Elder Sun, the divine monk, that we are the subjects of the king of the Scarlet-Purple Kingdom. By royal decree, we come to honor the divine monk with due reverence and ceremony. We beseech you to enter the court and examine a patient." Only then did Pilgrim stand up and say to them, "Why didn't your king come here?"

"Because his body is weakened and his strength depleted," replied the officials, "our king dares not ride the chariot. He has commanded

us subjects to observe this ceremony on his behalf and invite you, the
divine monk."

"In that case," said Pilgrim, "please lead the way, all of you, and
I'll follow."

The various officials departed in groups, in accordance with their
ranks, while Pilgrim walked behind them after having tidied his
clothes. "Elder Brother," said Pa-chieh, "don't you put us up to anything now!" "I won't," said Pilgrim, "but I want you two to accept the
medicines for me." "What medicines?" asked Sha Monk. "There will
be some medicines sent to us," said Pilgrim. "Accept them in the quan-
tities that they are delivered. I'll make use of them when I return."
The two of them agreed, and we shall leave them for the moment.

Our Pilgrim soon arrived at court with the many officials, who
walked ahead to report to the king. As the pearly screen was rolled up,
the king opened his phoenix eyes and dragon pupils to look at his
visitor and his golden mouth to say, "Who is the divine monk, Elder
Sun?" Taking a big step forward, Pilgrim said in a loud voice, "Old
Monkey's the one!"

When the king heard this savage voice and encountered the bizarre
countenance, he shook so violently that he fell back onto the dragon
couch. Those harem girls and palace attendants hurriedly had him
borne inside the palace, and all the king could say was, "We are
scared to death!" All the officials began to chide Pilgrim, saying,
"How could this monk be so rude and impetuous? How could you be
so audacious as to take down the proclamation?"

When he heard them, Pilgrim smiled and said, "All of you have
wrongly taken umbrage at me! If that's how you treat people, the
illness of your king won't be cured for another thousand years!"
"How long can a man live," asked the officials, "that he should be ill
for a thousand years?"

Pilgrim said, "That man at the moment is a sick ruler. After he
dies, he'll be a sick ghost. Even in the next incarnation, he will still
be a sick man. Isn't it true then that he won't be cured for a thousand
years?" Growing angry, the officials said, "Monk, you have absolutely no manners! How dare you mouth such nonsense?"

"That's no nonsense!" replied Pilgrim with a laugh. "Listen to
what I have to say:

Most mysterious is the physician's art;
His mind must ever be alert and keen.

To look, listen, ask, and take—these four things—
If one is missing, his craft's not complete.
One, we look at the patient's complexion:
Is it moist, dry, fat, or thin in waking or sleep?
Two, we listen for clear or turbid voice
When he speaks lucid or frenetic words.
Three, we ask for the ailment's cause and length.
For how he eats and drinks and eliminates.
Four, we scan the conduits[7] by taking the pulse,
To learn how submerged or floating[8] in and out.[9]
If we do not look, listen, ask, and take,
In this life his ailment will ne'er him forsake!"

Amid those two rows of military and civil officials, there was the royal physician who, when he heard these words, spoke up with great approbation. "What this monk says," he said, "is most reasonable. Even an immortal examining a patient must look, listen, ask, and take—these very activities accord well with the efficacy of gods and sages." Persuaded by this statement, the officials asked a palace attendant to send in the message: "The elder would like to exercise the principles of looking, listening, asking, and taking, before he could diagnose the illness and prescribe the medicine.

Lying on his dragon bed, the king gasped out his answer: "Tell him to go away! We can't bear to see an unfamiliar face!" The attendant walked out of the palace and said, "Monk, our king decrees you to leave, for he can't bear to see an unfamiliar face." "If he can't do so," replied Pilgrim, "I know that art of 'Dangling a Thread to take the Pulse.'"

The various officials were secretly pleased, saying to themselves, "We have heard of this rare technique, but we have never seen it." They said to the attendant, "Go and memorialize once more." Again the attendant went inside the palace to say, "My lord, if that elder is not permitted to see your face, he can dangle a thread to take the pulse." The king thought to himself, "We have been sick for three years but we've never tried this." He therefore gave the reply, "Summon him in." Immediately the attendant transmitted the message: "Our lord has given him the permission to take the pulse by dangling a thread. Summon Elder Sun quickly into the palace."

Pilgrim at once started to ascend the treasure hall, only to be met by the scolding of T'ang monk. "Wretched ape!" he cried. "You've injured me!" Smiling, Pilgrim said, "Dear Master, I have put you in the limelight! How could you say that I've injured you?"

"Which person did you manage to cure," shouted Tripitaka, "during these few years you've been following me? You don't even know the nature of medicines, nor have you read any medical texts. How could you be so audacious as to rush into this big calamity?" Laughing, Pilgrim said, "Master, you didn't know about this. I know a few herbal prescriptions which can cure even grave illnesses. All they care is that I heal him. But even if I kill him, all I'll be guilty of is merely manslaughter because of medical incompetence. I won't be executed. Why are you so worried? Relax! Relax! Take a seat and see if I'm any good at taking the pulse."

The elder again said, "Have you ever seen what sort of sentences there are in the *Candid Questions*, *The Classic of Medical Problems*, the pharmacopoeias, and the *Formulas of the Pulse*?[10] Do you know their proper gloss and exegesis? How could you babble like this about some dangling the thread to take the pulse?" Laughing, Pilgrim said, "I carry with me some threads of gold which you have never seen."

He reached back with his hand and pulled off three strands of hair from his tail. Giving them a pinch, he cried, "Change!" They changed at once into three threads, each twenty-four feet long and thus corresponding to the Twenty-Four Solar Terms. Holding them in his hands, he said to the T'ang monk, "Aren't these my golden threads?" The attending eunuch spoke up from the side, "Let the elders refrain from further conversation. Please enter the palace to examine the patient." Taking leave of the T'ang monk, Pilgrim followed the attendant to walk inside the palace. Truly it was that

The mind's secret prescription can heal a state;

The wondrous inward formula assures long life.

After he had gone inside, we do not know what sort of illness he was able to discern or what kind of medicines he prescribed. If you want to know the result, you must listen to the explanation in the next chapter.

Sixty-nine

At night the Lord of the Mind prepares the medicines;
At the banquet the king speaks of the perverse fiend.

We were telling you about the Great Sage Sun, who went with the palace attendant to the interior division of the royal palace. He stood still only after he had reached the door of the royal bedchamber. Then he told the attendant to take the three golden threads inside along with the instruction: "Ask one of the palace ladies or eunuchs to tie these three threads to the inch,[1] the pass, and the foot sections of His Majesty's left hand where the radial pulses are felt. Then pass the other ends of the threads out to me through the window shutters."

The attendant followed his instruction. The king was asked to sit up on the dragon bed, while the three sections of his pulse were tied by the golden threads, and their other ends were then passed out to Pilgrim. Using the thumb and the index finger of his right hand to pick up one of the threads, Pilgrim first examined the pulse of the inch section; next, he used his middle finger and his thumb to pick up the second thread and examine the pulse of the pass section; finally, he used the thumb and his fourth finger to pick up the third thread and examine the pulse of the foot section.

Thereafter Pilgrim made his own breathing regular[2] and proceeded to determine which of the Four Heteropathic *Ch'is*,[3] the Five Stases,[4] the Seven External Images[5] of the Pulse, the Eight Internal Images of the Pulse, and the Nine Pulse Indications[6] were present. His pressure on the threads went from light to medium to heavy;[7] from heavy to medium to light, until he could clearly perceive whether the condition of the patient was repletion or depletion of energy and its cause. Then he made the request that the threads be untied from the king's left wrist and be attached as before to the positions on his right wrist. Using now the fingers on his left hand, he then examined the pulse on the right wrist section by section. When he had completed his examination, he shook his body once and retrieved his hairs.

"Your Majesty," he cried in a loud voice, "on your left wrist the pulse of your inch section feels strong and tense, the pulse of your pass section feels rough and languid, and the pulse of your foot section feels hollow and sunken. On your right wrist the pulse of your inch section feels floating and smooth, the pulse of your pass section feels retarded and hesistant, and the pulse of your foot section feels accelerated and firm. Now, when the pulse of your left inch section feels strong and tense, it indicates an internal energetic depletion with pain in the cardiac system of functions. When the pulse of your left pass section feels rough and languid, it indicates sweating that has led to numbness in the flesh. When the pulse of your left foot section feels hollow and sunken, it indicates a pink tinge to your urine and blood in your stool. When the pulse of the inch section on your right wrist feels floating and smooth, it indicates a congestion blocking the *ch'i* circulation and leading to cessation of menses.[8] When the pulse of your right pass section feels retarded and hesitant, it indicates a stasis of alimentary matter in the stomach system with retention of fluids. When the pulse of your right foot section feels accelerated and firm, it indicates discomfort caused by sensations of stuffiness and chills caused by energetic depletion. To sum up, your illness has been caused by fear and anxiety, and it may be the manifestation type of an illness called the 'Paired Birds Separated from Company.'"

On hearing these words, the king was so delighted that he roused himself to answer loudly: "Your fingers have brought out the truth! Your fingers have brought out the truth! This is indeed our illness. Please go outside and prescribe us some medicines."

Only then did the Great Sage walk slowly out of the palace, while the eunuchs who saw everything clearly from the side had already reported the result to the rest of the people. In a moment, Pilgrim walked out and he was questioned by the T'ang monk. "I have examined the pulse," said Pilgrim, "and now I have to prescribe some medicines for the illness." Approaching him, the officials said, "Just now the divine monk said that this might be the manifestation type of an illness called the 'Paired Birds Separated from Company.' What does that mean?"

Smiling, Pilgrim said, "There are two birds flying together, one male and one female. Suddenly they are separated by violent wind and rain, so that the female cannot see the male, nor can the male see the female. The female longs for the male and the male longs for the female. Is this not the 'Paired Birds Separated from Company?'"

On hearing this, all the officials cried in unison, "Bravo! Truly a divine monk! Truly a divine physician!" Then the imperial physician said, "You have already diagnosed the illness. What medicines would you use to cure it?" "No need to write a prescription," said Pilgrim. "I'll take all the medicines you can give me."

"But according to a classic," said the physician, "'There are eight hundred and eight flavors of medicine, and a human may have four hundred and four kinds of illness.' All of those illnesses cannot be found in a single person. How could all the medicines be used? Why do you want everything?"

Pilgrim replied, "The ancients said, 'Medicines are not confined to prescriptions; they are to be used as one sees fit.' That is why I must have all the medicines so that I can add or subtract as I see fit." Not daring to argue any further, the physician went out of the gate of the court and sent those on duty in his bureau to go to all the pharmaceutical stores of the city and purchase three pounds of each kind of medicine, both raw and cooked, for Pilgrim to use. Pilgrim said, "This is not the place to prepare the proper drug. Take the medicines and the necessary drug-making utensils and send them all to the College of Interpreters. Let my brothers receive them for me." The physician obeyed. Three pounds each of the eight hundred and eight flavors of medicine, along with grinders, rollers, drug mortars and pestles and the like, were sent to the college, where they were received item by item.

Pilgrim went back up the hall to ask his master to go with him to the college so that they might prepare the drug. As the elder rose from his seat, a decree was issued from the internal palace, requesting that the Master of the Law remain behind to spend the night at the Wên-hua Pavilion.[9] After the king had taken the drug in the morning and had been restored to health, all of them would be rewarded and the rescript would be certified to permit their departure. Greatly alarmed, Tripitaka said, "O disciple! This means that he wants me kept here as security. If he is cured, he'll send us off with delight. If he is not, my life will be finished. You'd better take extra caution and prepare a specially effective drug!" "No need to worry, Master," said Pilgrim, smiling. "Enjoy yourself here. Old Monkey has the ability to bring healing to the state."

Dear Great Sage! He took leave of Tripitaka and the various officials and went straight to the college. When Pa-chieh met him, he smiled and said, "Elder Brother, now I know you!" "What do you know about me?" asked Pilgrim. "You must have realized," said Pa-chieh, "that this scripture-seeking enterprise will not succeed, but you don't have any capital to start a business. When you see today how prosperous this region is, you are drawing up plans to open a pharmacy."

"Stop babbling!" snapped Pilgrim. "When we have cured the king, we'll be content to leave the court and journey once more. What are you talking about, opening up a pharmacy?" "If you are not," said Pa-chieh, "what do you want to do with all these medicines? There are eight hundred and eight different kinds, and you ordered three pounds for each variety. Altogether, there are two thousand four hundred and twenty-four pounds. How many pounds can you use just to cure one person? I wonder how many years it'll take him to finish your prescription!"

"You think I really need that much?" said Pilgrim. "But those imperial physicians are all stupid and blind. I asked for such a huge amount of medicines only to prevent them from ever guessing what are the exact flavors I have used. It'll be difficult for them to learn my mysterious prescription."

As they were speaking, the two college officials came in, knelt before them, and said, "We invite the Holy Fathers, the divine monks, to dinner." Pilgrim said, "You treated us rather casually in the morning. Now you kneel to inform us of a meal. Why?" Kowtowing again, the officials said, "When the Venerable Fathers arrived, these lowly officials had eyes but no pupils, and we did not recognize your esteemed countenances. Now we have heard that you are exercising your profound knowledge in the therapeutic arts to bring healing to the ruler of our state. If our lord is indeed cured, the Venerable Father will share in his empire, and we will all be your subjects. Proper etiquette, therefore, requires us to kneel to address you."

On hearing this, Pilgrim ascended the main hall in delight and took the middle seat, while Pa-chieh and Sha Monk sat on both sides of him. As they were served the vegetarian meal, Sha Monk asked, "Elder Brother, where is Master?" "He is being kept by the king as security," replied Pilgrim, laughing. "Only after the king has been cured will he be thanked and permitted to leave." "Does he get to enjoy anything?" asked Sha Monk again. Pilgrim said, "How could anyone in the company of the king be without enjoyment? When I left, Master already had three Senior Secretaries hovering about him as they proceeded toward the Wên-hua Pavilion." "Listening to what you've said," said Pa-chieh, "I think Master is certainly more exalted than we are. He has the company of three Senior Secretaries, while we are being served by only two college officials. But never mind, let old Hog enjoy a full meal!" The three brothers thus ate to their hearts' content.

It was getting late, and Pilgrim said to the officials, "Take away the bowls and dishes, and bring us plenty of oil and candles. We must wait until late at night before we can prepare the drug." The officials indeed brought in a great deal of oil and candles before they retired. By midnight, human traffic had ceased and the whole place was quiet. Pa-chieh said, "Elder Brother, what kind of drug do you want to prepare? Let's do it now, for I'm getting drowsy." "Bring me an ounce of *ta-huang*,"[10] said Pilgrim, "and grind that into powder."

Sha Monk spoke up: "*Ta-huang* is bitter in flavor; its disposition is cold and nonpoisonous. Its nature is sinking and not rising, and its function concerns movement and not fortification. It can take away various kinds of pent-up feelings and unclog congestion; it can conquer chaos and bring about peace. Hence its name is 'General,' for it is a laxative. I fear, however, that prolonged illness has weakened the person, and perhaps you should not use it."

Smiling, Pilgrim said, "Worthy Brother, you don't realize that this medicine will loosen phlegm and facilitate respiration; it will also sweep out the chill and heat congealed in one's stomach. Don't mind me. You go also and fetch me an ounce of *pa-tou*.[11] Shell it and strip away the membranes. Pound away also the oil, and then grind it to powder."

"The flavour of *pa-tou*," said Pa-chieh, "is slightly acrid; its nature is hot and poisonous. Able to pare down the hard and the accumulated, it will therefore sweep out the submerged chills of one's internal cavities. Able to bore through clottings and impediments, it will therefore facilitate the paths of water and grain. This is a warrior who can break down doors and passes, and it should be used lightly."

"Worthy Brother," said Pilgrim, "you, too, don't realize that this medicine can break up congestion and drain the intestines. It can also take care of swellings at the heart and dropsy in the abdomen. Prepare it quickly, for I still must use an auxiliary flavor to lend the medicines further assistance." After the two of them had ground the medicines into powder, they said, "Elder Brother, what other flavors will you use?" "None," replied Pilgrim.

Pa-chieh said, "There are eight hundred and eight flavors, each of which you have three pounds, but you use only these two ounces. You are truly playing tricks on someone!" Picking up a flowered porcelain flask, Pilgrim said, "Worthy Brother, don't talk so much. Take this flask and scrape me half a flask of soot from the bottom of the frying pan." "What do you want it for?" asked Pa-chieh. "For the drug," replied Pilgrim. "This little brother," said Sha Monk, "has never seen the use of soot for a drug."

Pilgrim said, "The proper name for this kind of soot is 'Hundred-Grass Frost,' and you have no idea that it can soothe a hundred ailments." Our Idiot indeed brought him half a flask of the soot, which was also ground into powder. Then Pilgrim gave him the flask once more and said, "Go and fetch me half a flask of urine from our horse." "What for?" asked Pa-chieh. "I want it to make some pills," replied Pilgrim.

Laughing, Sha Monk said, "Elder Brother, this is no joking matter! Horse urine is both pungent and stinky. How could you put that into the medicines? I have seen pills made from vinegar, aged rice soups, clarified honey, or pure water, but never from horse urine. That stuff is so foul and pungent, the moment a person with a weakened stomach smells it, he will vomit. If you feed him further with *pa-tou* and *ta-huang*, he'll be throwing up on top and purging down below. You think that's funny?"

"But you don't realize," said Pilgrim, "that our horse is no mortal horse of this world. Remember he was originally a dragon from the Western Ocean. If he is willing to urinate, it will cure any kind of disease a human may have when it is ingested. The only problem is that you can't get it in a hurry." On hearing this, Pa-chieh ran out to the stable, where he found the horse lying prone on the ground and asleep. A few swift kicks by our Idiot, however, roused him immediately, whereupon our Idiot positioned the flask below his abdomen and waited for a long time. When he saw that the horse did not urinate at all, he ran back and said to Pilgrim, "O Elder Brother, let's not try to heal the king. Go quickly to heal the horse first. That outcast has dried up! He hasn't even pissed a drop!" "I'll go with you," said Pilgrim, smiling, and Sha Monk said, "I, too, will go and take a look."

As the three of them approached the horse, he leapt up and assumed human speech, saying to them in a loud voice, "Elder Brother, don't you know? I was originally a flying dragon of the Western Ocean. The Bodhisattva Kuan-yin rescued me after I had disobeyed Heaven; she sawed off my horns, stripped off my scales, and changed me into a horse to carry Master to acquire scriptures in the Western Heaven. My merit thus accrued will atone for my sins. If I leave my urine while passing through water, the fishes who drink it will turn into dragons. If I leave my urine in the mountain, the grasses there will change into divine agaric, to be picked by immortal lads as their plants of longevity. How could I be willing to part with it so lightly in this world of dust?"

"Brother," said Pilgrim, "do be careful with what you say. This is a kingdom in the West, not just any worldly region. You are not parting with it lightly either. As the proverb says, 'Many pelts are needed for a coat.' We need your help to cure the king's illness. If he is healed, all of us will share the glory. Otherwise, I fear we may not be able to leave this place in peace." Only then did the horse reply, "Wait for it!"

Look at him! His front legs lunged forward while he squatted somewhat with his hind ones, and he clenched his teeth so hard that they ground together noisily. All he could squeeze out after all these efforts were a few drops before he stood straight up once more. "This wretch!" said Pa-chieh. "Even if it's potable gold, he can certainly piss a little bit more!" When Pilgrim saw that they had received slightly less than half a flask already, he said, "It's enough! It's enough. Take it away." Sha Monk was delighted.

The three of them went back into the hall, where they mixed the horse urine into the other medicines, They then kneaded the paste into three large pills. "Brothers," said Pilgrim, "they're too big." "No more than the size of a walnut," said Pa-chieh. "If I'm going to take them, they won't be enough for a mouthful!" They stored the pills in a small box before they all retired, still fully dressed.

In the morning, the king attended court once more in spite of his illness. After he had asked the T'ang monk to meet him in the hall, he immediately ordered the various officials to hurry over to the College of Interpreters so that they could bow to the divine monk, Elder Sun, and ask for the drug.

The officials arrived at the college and prostrated themselves before Pilgrim, saying, "Our king has commanded us to bow to receive your wondrous prescription." After Pilgrim asked Pa-chieh to take out the box, he took away the cover and handed the box over to the officials. "What is the name of this drug?" asked one of them. "We have to tell the king when we see His Majesty." Pilgrim said, "This is called the Elixir of Black Gold." Smiling, Pa-chieh and Sha Monk said to themselves, "There's soot mixed in it. It has to be black gold!"

"What sort of medical supplement[12] will be needed?" asked the official again. Pilgrim answered, "There are two kinds of supplement that can be used, but only one is easily obtainable. I need six items to be boiled in water, and the liquid will then be used for the king to take the pills." "Which six items?" asked the official. Pilgrim replied,

The fart of an old crow flying in the air;
The piss of a carp in swift flowing streams;
The face powder of the Lady Queen Mother;
The elixir ashes in Lao Tzu's brazier;
Three pieces of the Jade Emperor's torn head-wrap;
And five strands of whiskers from a tired dragon.
The drug taken with the liquid boiled with these six things
Will in no time banish the woe and ailment of your king.

On hearing this, the various officials said, "None of these things can be found in the world. May we ask what is the other supplement?" Pilgrim said, "Take the drug with sourceless water." Smiling, one of the officials said, "That's easy to get." "How do you know?" asked Pilgrim.

"According to the people of our region here," said the official, "this is the way to get sourceless water: take a container to a river or a well, fill it with water, and go straight back to the house without spilling a drop or looking back. When you return to the house, that will be considered sourceless water with which the person who is sick may take the medicine." "But the water in a well or a river," said Pilgrim, "both have sources. That's not what I mean by sourceless water. What I need is water that drops from the sky, and you drink it without letting it first touch ground. That's what I mean by sourceless water." "Well, even that is easy to get," said the official. "All we have to do is to wait until it rains before we take the medicine." They thanked Pilgrim and returned to present the medicine to the king.

Highly pleased, the king asked his attendant to bring the medicine up for him to look at. "What kind of pills are these?" he asked, and one of the officials replied, "The divine monk told us that this is the Elixir of Black Gold. You are to take it with sourceless water." At once the king asked some palace stewards to go fetch sourceless water, but the official said, "According to the divine monk, sourceless water is not to be found in either rivers or wells. Only that dropping from the sky and without having touched the ground may be considered the true sourceless water." The king immediately ordered the official before the throne to command the official in charge of magic to pray for rain. As the officials issued the decree, we shall leave them for the moment.

We tell you instead about Pilgrim, who remained at the hall of the College of Interpreters. He said to Chu Pa-chieh, "Just now I told them that the medicine could be taken only with water dropping from the sky. But how could we get rain water immediately? As I look at the king, I think he's undoubtedly a ruler of great worthiness and virtue. Let's you and I help him to get some rain. How about it?"

"How shall we help him?" asked Pa-chieh. "Stand on my left," said Pilgrim, "and be my assistant star. Sha Monk, you stand on my right, and be my supportive lodge. Let old Monkey help him get some sourceless water."

Dear Great Sage! He began to tread the stars and recite a spell. In no time at all, a dark cloud from the east drifted near until it was directly over their heads. "Great Sage," a voice came from midair, "Ao-kuang, the Dragon king of the Eastern Ocean is here to see you." "I wouldn't have bothered you for nothing," said Pilgrim, "for I have asked you to come here to lend us some sourceless water for the king to take his medicine."

The dragon king said, "When the Great Sage summoned me, he did not mention anything about water. This humble dragon came all by himself without bringing any rain gear. I do not have the assistance of wind, cloud, thunder, and lightning either. How could I make rain?" "There's no need for wind, cloud, thunder, and lightning at this time," said Pilgrim, "nor do we require much rain. All we need actually is a little water to act as medical supplement." "In that case," said the dragon king, "let me sneeze a couple of times and give him some of my saliva to take his medicine." Exceedingly pleased, Pilgrim said, "That's the best! That's the best! Don't wait any more! Please do it at once!"

From midair, the old dragon lowered his dark cloud gradually until it hovered above the royal palace. With his whole body hidden by the cloud, the dragon spat out a mouthful of saliva which changed into rain. The officials of the entire Court shouted "Bravo" in unison, crying, "Ten thousand happinesses to our lord! Heaven has sent down sweet rain to us!" At once the king gave this decree: "Set out vessels to store it. Let everyone, inside and outside the palace, of high rank or low, store up this divine water so that we may be saved."

Look at those many civil and military officials, those ladies of three palaces and six chambers, those three thousand colorful girls, and those eight hundred tender maidens! Every one of them held up a cup or flask, a bowl or pan, to receive this sweet rain. In midair above the royal palace the old dragon kept up this transformation of his saliva for nearly an hour before he took leave of the Great Sage to return to the ocean. When the officials brought back their containers, some managed to gather two or three drops, others acquired four or five drops, while there were those who did not receive even one drop. They poured the contents together and there were about three flasks of the rain to be presented to the royal table. Truly

Strange fragrance filled the Hall of Golden Chimes;
Goodly scent wafted through the royal court.

Taking leave of the Master of the Law, the king took the Elixir of Black Gold and the sweet rain back to his palace. He swallowed first one pill with one flask of the rain; then he took another with the second flask. He went through this for a third time, swallowing all three pills and drinking all three flasks of the rain. In a little while, his stomach began to make a loud, rumbling noise, and he had to sit on the night pot and move his bowels four or five times. Thereafter, he took a little rice soup before he reclined on the dragon bed. Two palace ladies went to examine the pot; the filth and phlegm were indescribable, in the midst of which there was also a lump of glutinous rice. The ladies approached the dragon bed to report: "The root of the illness has been purged."

Delighted by what he heard, the king took some more rice gruel, and after a little while, his chest and abdomen began to feel more at ease. As his configurative energies and his blood became harmonious once more, his spirit was fully aroused. Rising from his dragon couch, he put on the court attire and ascended the treasure hall. The moment he encountered the T'ang monk, he bowed low. The elder hurriedly returned his salute. After the bow, the king took hold of the elder's hand and gave this command to his attendants: "Prepare a formal invitation card at once, and write on it such words as 'We beseech you with head touching the ground.' Send some officials to invite with all reverence the three noble disciples of the Master of the Law. Open up the entire East Hall, and ask the Court of Imperial Entertainments to prepare a thanksgiving banquet." In obedience to the decree, many officials went to work on it at once: some prepared the invitation card, while others arranged the banquet. Truly a state has the strength of moving mountains, and in a moment everything was accomplished.

When Pa-chieh saw the officials arriving and bearing an invitation card, he could not be more pleased. "O Elder Brother," he cried, "it's marvelous medicine indeed! Now they've come to thank us, all because of your merit." Sha Monk said, "Second Elder Brother, that's no way to talk! As the proverb says,

One man's good fortune,
Will bless the whole commune.

Since we all participated here in mixing the medicines, we are all meritorious persons. Let's go enjoy ourselves and don't talk anymore!" Ah! Look at those three brothers! In great delight, they went into court.

The various officials met them and led them to the East Hall, where the king, the T'ang monk, and the Senior Secretaries of the Hall were already sitting at the banquet. Our Pilgrim, Pa-chieh, and Sha Monk bowed to their master, while the various officials followed in. There were four vegetarian tables laden with so many dishes of fine food that one could only eat a small amount and stare at the rest. A huge banquet table in front was also heaped with all kinds of delicacies. On both sides, several hundred small, single tables were set out, arranged in orderly rows.

As the ancients said,

"A hundred kinds of rare viand;
A thousand bowls of fine grain;
Jadelike fats and mellow wines;
Ornate slices and plump redness."
Bright, colorful decorations
And fruits rich in taste and fragrance.
Large candies shaped like lions and immortals;
Cakes and biscuits baked like phoenix pairs.
For meat, there were pork, lamb, chicken, goose, fish, duck, and
   every other kind.
For vegetables, there were greens, bamboo shoots, wood ears,
   and mushrooms.
A few kinds of dumplings;

Various candy brittles.
Yellow millet soft and smooth;
Rice gruel fresh and pure.
Noodle soups of all kinds, both fragrant and hot;
And many, many dishes so nice and sweet.
Ruler and subjects made their very first toast;
Then according to rank they passed the cup.

With his royal hands holding high the goblet, the king wanted to make the first "Settle the Banquet" toast to the T'ang monk. Tripitaka, however, said to him, "This humble cleric does not know how to drink wine." "It's made for those keeping a religious diet," said the king. "Let the Master of the Law drink just one goblet. How about it?" "But wine," replied Tripitaka, "is the first prohibition of a priest." Feeling rather badly about the matter, the king said, "If the Master of the Law is prohibited from drink, what shall we use to pay our respect?"

Tripitaka said, "Let my three mischievous disciples represent me in drinking." Delighted, the king took his gold goblet and handed it to Pilgrim. After he had bowed to the rest of the people, Pilgrim drained the goblet. When the king saw how readily he drank the wine, he presented him another goblet of it. Pilgrim did not refuse and drank that, too. Chuckling, the king said, "Please drink a Three Jewels round." Pilgrim did not refuse and drank that, too. Asking that the goblet be filled once more, the king said, "Please drink the Four Seasons round!"

Seated on one side and eyeing the wine which never seemed to come his way, Pa-chieh could hardly refrain from swallowing hard his own saliva. When he saw, moreover, that the king was intent on toasting only Pilgrim, he started to holler: "Your Majesty, you owe it to me, too, for the medicine you took. In that medicine, there's horse . . ."

On hearing this and fearing that Idiot might reveal everything, Pilgrim immediately handed the wine in his hand to Pa-chieh, who took it and drank without saying a further word. The king asked: "The divine monk said that there was horse in the medicine. What kind of horse is that?" Taking it upon himself quickly to answer the question, Pilgrim said, "That's the way my brother speaks all the time. Whenever he has a tried and true prescription, he would share it with everyone, The medicine which you took this morning, Your Majesty, did contain Horse-Saddle-Bell."[13]

"What kind of medicine is this Horse-Saddle-Bell," asked the king, "and what does it cure?" The imperial physician by his side said, "My lord, this Horse-Saddle-Bell

Tastes bitter, being cold and nonpoisonous;
Most potent to stop wheezing and remove phlegm.
It loosens breath and rids one of poisoned blood;
Quiets cough, fights exhaustion, and brings relief."

"Well used! Well used!" said the king, smiling. "Elder Chu should take another goblet." Without uttering a word, our Idiot also drank a Three Jewels round. Then the king handed the wine to Sha Monk, who also drank three goblets before everyone took his seat.

After they drank and feasted for some time, the king again took up a huge goblet to present to Pilgrim. "Your Majesty," said Pilgrim, "please be seated. Old Monkey will drink all the rounds. I'll never dare refuse you." "Your great kindness to me," said the king, "is as weighty as a mountain, and we can't begin to thank you enough. No matter what, please drink this huge goblet of wine first, and then we have something to tell you." "Please tell me first," said Pilgrim, "and old Monkey will be happy to drink this."

"Our illness of several years," replied the king, "was caused by great anxiety. The single formula of efficacious elixir prescribed by the divine monk, however, broke through the cause and that's how I recovered." With a chuckle, Pilgrim said, "When old Monkey examined Your Majesty yesterday, I knew already that the illness had been caused by anxiety. But I don't know what you were anxious about."

The king said, "According to the ancients, 'The disgrace of a family should never be spread without.' But the divine monk, on the other hand, is our benefactor. If you do not laugh at us, we shall tell you." "How could I dare laugh at you?" said Pilgrim. "You need not hesitate to tell me." "As you journeyed from the East," said the king, "how many states have you passed through?" "About five or six," replied Pilgrim. "How do they address the consorts of the king?" he asked again. Pilgrim said, "The ranking wife of a king would be called the Central Palace, and those two consorts next in rank would be called the East Palace and the West Palace, respectively."

"The titles here are slightly different," said the king. "Our Central Palace bears the name of the Golden Sage Palace; the East Palace is called the Jade Sage Palace, and the West Palace has the title of Silver Sage Palace. At the moment, we have only the Jade and Silver consorts with us." "Why is the Golden Sage Palace absent?" asked Pilgrim.

As tears fell from his eyes, the king said, "She hasn't been with us for three years." "Where has she gone to?" asked Pilgrim again. The king said, "Three years ago, during the time of the Double Fifth Festival,[14] our consorts and we were all gathered inside the Pomegranate Pavilion of our garden, cutting up rice cakes, affixing the artemisia plant to our garments, drinking wine made from the calamus and realgar,[15] and watching the dragon boat races. Suddenly a gust arose and a monster-spirit appeared in the air. Calling himself Jupiter's Rival, he claimed that he lived in the Cave of the Mythic Beast[16] at the Unicorn Mountain. Because he did not have a wife, he made investigation and learned of the great beauty of our Golden Sage Palace. He demanded that we turn her out, and if we did not after his asking us three times, he would first eat us alive and then proceed to devour the various officials and the people of the entire capital. Burdened, therefore, by the care of the state and the people at the time, we had no alternative but to push Golden Sage Palace out of the Pomegranate Pavilion, where she was immediately abducted by the fiend with a single sound. That incident, of course, gave us a great fright, and the glutinous rice cakes we ate thus remained undigested in our body. Moreover, we were ridden with anxious thoughts night and day, which led to three long years of bitter illness. Now that we have had the good fortune of taking the efficacious elixir of the divine monk, we have purged several times, and all that waste accumulated three years ago has been eliminated. That's why our frame has turned healthy and our body has lightened, and we feel as energetic as before. The life I regain today is entirely a gift of the divine monk. Even the weight of Mount T'ai cannot compare with the magnitude of your favor!"

When Pilgrim heard these words, he was filled with delight, so much so that he drank in two gulps that huge goblet of wine. Smiling broadly, he said to the king, "So, that was the cause of Your Majesty's fear and anxiety. Now you've met old Monkey, and you are lucky to be cured. But do you want the Golden Sage Palace returned to your kingdom?" Shedding tears again, the king replied, "There's not a day or a night that we do not yearn for her presence, but no one is able to arrest the monster-spirit for us. How could I not want her return?" "Let old Monkey go and bring that perverse fiend to submission," said Pilgrim. "How about it?" The king immediately went to his knees and said, "If you can rescue our queen, we are willing to lead all the residents of this palace and all my consorts out to the city to live as common people. We shall present our entire kingdom to you and let you be the ruler."

When Pa-chieh on the side saw the king speak and act in this manner, he could not refrain from laughing uproariously. "This king has lost his sense of propriety!" he cried. "How could he refuse his kingdom just for the sake of his wife and kneel to a monk?" Hurrying forward to raise the king, Pilgrim said, "Your Majesty, since he has abducted the Golden Sage Palace, has that monster-spirit ever returned?" "After he took away the Golden Sage Palace during the fifth month year before last," replied the king, "he returned during the tenth month to demand two palace maidens to serve our queen. We immediately gave him what he requested. Last year, in the third month, he came to ask for two more palace maidens; by the seventh, he took away two more; and in the second month of this year, he came again for still two more. We do not know when he will come to make his demand anew." "After he has come so many times," said Pilgrim, "aren't you afraid of him?"

The king said, "His many visits have frightened us indeed, and, moreover, we fear that he may even harm us further. In the fourth month of last year, we ordered the engineers to build us a Fiend Shelter. Whenever we hear the sound of the wind and know that he's coming, we will hide in the shelter with our two consorts and nine concubines."

"If your Majesty is willing," said Pilgrim, "please take old Monkey to have a look at the Fiend Shelter. How about it?" Using his left hand to take hold of Pilgrim, the king left the banquet as all the officials rose to their feet. "Elder Brother," said Chu Pa-chieh, "you are so unreasonable! All this imperial wine and you refuse to drink it. You have to break up the nice party! Why must you go look at this shelter?" On hearing this, the king realized that Pa-chieh's only interest was his mouth. He at once ordered the stewards to carry two tables of vegetarian food and wine to the shelter and wait there for them. Only then did Idiot stop his complaints and say to his master and Sha Monk, laughing, "Let's change to another banquet!"

Led by a row of civil and military officials, the king went with Pilgrim through the palace to the rear imperial garden, but there was

not a single building in sight. "Where's the Fiend Shelter?" asked
Pilgrim. Hardly had he finished speaking when two eunuchs, gripping
two red lacquered poles, pried loose from the ground a huge slab of
stone. The king said, "That is the shelter. It's more than twenty feet
deep down there, with nine dug-out chambers. Placed in there are
four huge cisterns filled with clear oil, which is used for keeping the
lamps lit night and day. When we hear the sound of the wind and go
in there to hide, people outside will close up the hole with the stone
slab." Pilgrim chuckled and said, "That monster-spirit obviously does
not wish to harm you. If he does, you think you can hide from him
down there?"

He had not quite finished his sentence when a powerful gust of
wind roared in from due south, spraying dirt and dust into the air.
Those officials became so frightened that they all protested in unison,
"This monk has such an ill-luck mouth! He speaks of the monster-
spirit, and at once the monster-spirit shows up!" Abandoning Pilgrim,
the terrified monarch at once crawled into the hole in the ground,
followed by the T'ang monk and all the other officials.

Pa-chieh and Sha Monk, too, wanted to hide, but they were pulled
back by Pilgrim's two hands. "Brothers," he said, "don't be afraid.
Let's you and I try to discover what kind of monster-spirit this is."
"You must be jesting!" said Pa-chieh. "Why do you want to make
such a discovery? The officials have hidden themselves, Master has
gone out of sight, and the king has stepped aside. Why don't we just
leave? Who cares about his pedigree!" Our Idiot twisted left and right,
but he could not struggle free of Pilgrim's firm grip. After some time,
there emerged in midair a monster-spirit. Look how he appeared!

A nine-foot long body, savage and fierce;
A pair of round eyes flashing like gold lamps.
Two large forked ears like protruding fans,
And four sharp teeth like steel nails sticking up.
Red hair flanked his head, his eyebrows sprouted flames.
A bottle-nose dangled with nostrils flaring.
A few strands of beard like thick scarlet threads;
His cheek bones were rugged, his face was green.
Two arms of red veins, two indigo hands,
And ten pointed claws holding high a lance.
A leopard-skin kilt wrapped around his waist:
A ghost with tousled hair and naked feet!

When he saw the monster, Pilgrim said, "Sha Monk, do you recognize him?" "I haven't made his acquaintance," replied Sha Monk. "How could I recognize him?" Pilgrim asked again, "Pa-chieh, do *you* recognize him?" "I have never had tea or wine with him," replied Pa-chieh, "nor am I a friend or neighbor of his. How could I recognize him?" Pilgrim said, "He rather looks like the demon gatekeeper with golden pupils and shrivelled face under the command of Equal to Heaven, the Eastern Mountain." "No! No!" said Pa-chieh. "How do you know that?" asked Pilgrim.

"A demon," said Pa-chieh, "is a spirit of darkness, and it will make its appearance only late in the day, say, between the hour of Monkey and that of the Boar.[17] Right now it's still noon. Which demon would dare come out? Even if he's a demon, he can't mount the clouds. And if he knows how to use the wind, he will only be able to summon a little whirlwind, not a violent wind like this. Perhaps he is the very Jupiter's Rival."

"Dear Idiot!" said Pilgrim, chuckling. "You have a point there! You two stand guard here, and let old Monkey go ask for his name. Then we can rescue the Golden Sage Palace for the king." "If you want to go, go," said Pa-chieh, "but don't reveal that we are here." Without further reply, Pilgrim mounted the auspicious luminosity to leap into the air. Ah! So it is that

To secure a state one must first cure the king's disease;

To safeguard the Way one must purge the evil-loving heart.

We do not know, as he rises into the air, whether he will win or lose, or how he manages to capture the fiend and rescue the Golden Sage Palace. You must listen to the explanation in the next chapter.

Seventy

The fiendish demon's treasures release smoke. sand. and fire;
Wu-k'ung uses a trick to steal the purple-gold bells.

We were telling you about that Pilgrim Sun, who, arousing his divine
might and gripping his iron rod, trod on the auspicious luminosity
to rise into the air. Facing the fiend, he shouted, "Where did you come
from, perverse demon? Where do you think you're going to perpetrate
your lawlessness?" The fiendish creature replied in a loud voice, "I
am none other than the vanguard under the command of the Great
King Jupiter's Rival, the master of the Cave of the Mythic Beast at Unicorn Mountain. By the order of the great king, I have come here to fetch
two palace maidens for the service of Lady Golden Sage. Who are you
that you dare question me?" "I'm Sun Wu-k'ung, the Great Sage,
Equal to Heaven," said Pilgrim. "I am passing through this kingdom
because I am giving protection to the T'ang monk from the Land of
the East, who is on his way to worship Buddha in the Western Heaven.
When I learned of how you bunch of perverse demons were making
mockery of the ruler here, I resolved to exercise my talents to heal
the state and drive out the bogies. I was just wondering where to look
for you when you arrived to give up your life."

Though he heard these words, that fiend did not know any better
than to pick up the lance to stab at Pilgrim. Pilgrim met him head on
with upraised iron rod, and a marvelous battle began in midair.

The rod's a dragon hall's sea-ruling treasure;
The lance is but iron refined by man.
How could mortal arms compare with one divine,
A tiny stroke of which would dispel your soul?
The Great Sage is first a Great Monad god;
The monster's only a demon accursed.
How could a ghost approach a righteous man?
Righteousness's one mite kills all things perverse.
That one uses wind and sprays dirt to scare the king;
This one treads the fog and clouds to hide the sun and moon.

They assume fighting postures to try to win.
Which weakling would dare claim a hero's name?
In the end the Great Sage's the stronger man:
P'ing-p'ang cracks the rod and the lance does snap.

As his lance was broken in two by one blow of Pilgrim's iron rod, the terrified monster-spirit changed the direction of his wind and fled for his life toward the west.

Deciding not to give chase for the moment, Pilgrim dropped from the clouds and went up to the Fiend Shelter. "Master," he cried, "please ask His Majesty to come out. The fiendish creature's gone." The T'ang monk used his hands to support the king as both of them climbed out of the hole. The entire sky had cleared up and there was not the slightest appearance of a fiend anywhere. The king walked up to one of the banquet tables, picked up the wine pot himself, and filled a golden goblet to present to Pilgrim, saying, "Divine monk, just a little thanks!" The Pilgrim took the goblet in his hand, but before he could make his reply, an official rushed in from outside the court to say, "There's a fire at the west gate of the capital!"

On hearing this, Pilgrim flung the wine-filled goblet into the air. When it fell with a clang to the ground, the startled king bowed quickly and said, "Divine monk, please forgive me! Please forgive me! It was indeed our fault! Proper etiquette requires that you ascend the main hall to receive our thanks. It was because the wine was placed conveniently here that I presented it to you. You threw the cup away. Are you offended?" "No! No!" replied Pilgrim, laughing. "You have got it all wrong!"

Just as they were speaking, another official came in to report: "What a marvelous rain! Just now a fire broke out at the west gate, but a great shower extinguished it. The streets are filled with water that smells like wine!" "Your Majesty," said Pilgrim, still laughing, "when you saw me throwing away the cup, you thought I was offended. But actually, I was not. That fiend fled toward the west in defeat; because I did not give chase, he started a fire. That goblet of wine was what I used to extinguish the fiendish fire and save the families located in the western part of the capital. That was all!"

More than ever filled with delight and respect, the king invited Tripitaka and his three disciples to return to the treasure hall, where he was ready to abdicate his throne and hand it over to the priests. "Your Majesty," said Pilgrim, smiling, "that monster-spirit just now

claimed that he was a vanguard in the command of Jupiter's Rival,
sent here to demand two more palace maidens. Since he was defeated,
he would certainly flee to his master to report, and his master would
certainly want to come strive with me. I fear that when he brings his
troops here, it will be difficult to prevent them from frightening the
populace and alarming Your Majesty. I'd like to meet him in midair
instead and capture him right there, but I don't know which is the
proper direction. What's the distance between here and his mountain
cave?"

The king said, "We did send some military scouts to go there once
to make investigation. The round trip took some fifty days, as the cave
was about three thousand miles due south of here." On hearing this,
Pilgrim said, "Pa-chieh, Sha Monk, stand guard here. Old Monkey
will make a trip there." Tugging at him, the king said, "Divine monk,
please wait for another day. Let us prepare some dried and baked
goods for you, give you some travel money, and select a speedy horse
for you. Then you may go." With a laugh, Pilgrim said, "What you
are referring to, Your Majesty, is the laborious way of scaling mountains and peaks by those who must stay on their feet. To tell you the
truth, old Monkey can traverse these three thousand miles and be
back here before the wine poured out turns cold in the goblet." "Divine
monk," said the king, "don't be offended by what we have to say, but
your estimable countenance resembles that of an ape. How could you
possess such magic power to move so quickly?" Pilgrim replied,

Though I'm numbered among the simian kind,
I've cut since my youth the bond of birth and death.
All tutors I've sought to teach me the Tao;
For countless days I've trained[1] before the mount.
With Heaven as top and Earth as brazier,
Two kinds of drug whirled round the hare and crow.[2]
I picked yin and yang, mating water and fire;
In time I broke through the mysterious pass.
I relied on the stars' transportive power,[3]
And on the Dipper for moving my steps.
Most punctual to boost or reduce the fire,
I watched to add quicksilver or pull out lead.
Five Phases conjoined, creation began.
Four images[4] balanced, the times were fixed.
With Two Breaths returned to the Yellow Way,[5]

Three Houses[6] joined on the Gold-Elixir Path.
These laws, all realized, now move my four limbs;
My somersault works as though I'm helped by gods.
One leap will bring me beyond Mount T'ai-hang;[7]
One turn sends me past Cloud-Transcending Stream.[8]
I fear not ten thousand folds of rugged peak,
Nor scores or hundreds of long, wide rivers.
No hurdle can my transformation block;
One turn, a hundred and eight thousand miles!

Both astonished and delighted by this recital of Pilgrim's, the king took a goblet of imperial wine and, smiling broadly, presented it to Pilgrim, saying, "Divine monk, you have to travel far. Take this to prepare for your journey." As our Great Sage was intent on leaving to subdue the fiend, how could he care about drinking wine any more? All he could say was, "Please put it down. Let me drink it after I return." Dear Pilgrim! He said he was leaving, and with a whistle, he vanished from sight. We shall leave those astonished ruler and subjects for the moment.

We tell you now about our Pilgrim, who leaped into the air and soon discovered a mountain rearing up at the edge of the fog. He lowered his cloud immediately and stood on the peak to survey the region. Marvelous mountain!

It rushes the sky and overruns the earth;
It blots out the sun and begets the clouds.
Where it rushes the sky,
Pointed peaks rise erect.
Where it overruns the earth,
Wide ranges spread unending.
What blots out the sun
Are fresh thick pines of the summit.
What begets the clouds
Are sharp, jagged rocks beneath the cliff.
Fresh thick pines
Remain ever green in all four seasons;
Sharp jagged rocks
Stay unchanged in ten thousand years.
You'll hear now and then apes wailing in the woods,
And often monstrous serpents passing through the brook;
Screeches of mountain fowl;

Grunts and growls of mountain beasts.
Mountain deer and antelope
Dash about here and there in pairs and twos;
Mountain crows and magpies
In flocks and tight formations soar and fly.
The endless sight of mountain flowers and grass;
The timely glow of mountain peaches and fruits.
Though it's too treacherous a passageway,
It's a bogus immortal's reclusive place.

Thoroughly delighted by this scenery, our Great Sage was just about to search for the entrance of the cave when all at once he saw a roaring fire leaping up from the fold of the mountain. In an instant the sky was filled with red flames, in the midst of which there arose also a nasty column of smoke, more vicious than even the fire.

Marvelous smoke! You saw

A flare shining like ten thousand gold lamps;
And fumes leaping like a thousand red rainbows.
The smoke was no oven's or stove's,
Nor that of grass and wood.
That smoke had five colors:
Green, red, white, black, and yellow.
It scorched the pillars of the South Heavenly Gate;
It seared the beams of the Divine Mists Hall.
It burned till the beasts in their lairs rotted with their skins,
And feathers on the forest fowl all dissolved.
When one saw such venomous smoke, how then
Could one enter the mount to tame the fiend king?

As the Great Sage stared at this in astonishment, a sandstorm also erupted from within the mountain.

Marvelous sand, truly hiding Heaven and blanketing Earth! Look at that

Great, whirling shower spreading through the sky;
The huge, blinding mass all over the earth;
The fine dust dimming one's sight everywhere;
Thick ashes rolling down hill like sesame.
The herb-picking lad has his partner lost;
The working woodsman cannot find his house.
Though your hands may hold a luminous pearl,
You will soon reel under this blowing sand.

Spellbound by what he saw, Pilgrim did not notice that some sand

and dust flew into his nose until the itch made him sneeze a couple of times. He turned and picked up from beneath the ledge two small pebbles, which he used to stop up his nostrils. Shaking his body once, he changed into a sparrowhawk able to penetrate fire. He flew right into the smoke and flame, but all of a sudden, the sand and dust vanished, and even the smoke and fire subsided. Quickly he changed back into his true form and dropped down from the air. As he looked about, there came to his ears the loud clanging of a brass gong. "I must have taken the wrong road!" he thought to himself. "This can't be where the monster-spirit lives. The gong sounds like one of those belonging to a postal soldier. This must be a state highway, and some postal soldier is on his way to deliver a document. Let old Monkey go and question him a bit."

As he walked along, he saw a little fiend with a yellow banner on his shoulder and an official document bag on his back. Banging aloud the gong, the fiend was running swiftly toward him. "So, this is the fellow who's beating the gong!" said Pilgrim, laughing. "I wonder what sort of document he's carrying. Let me eavesdrop on him."

Dear Great Sage! With a shake of his body he changed into a midge and gently alighted on the fiend's document bag. All he heard was the monster-spirit banging the gong and mumbling to himself: "Our great king is quite vicious! Three years ago he abducted the Golden Sage Queen from the Scarlet-Purple Kingdom, but he didn't have the affinity even to touch her. Only those palace maidens brought here as substitutes were the ones who suffered. Two of them came, and they were driven to death; then four arrived, and they, too, were driven to death. Year before last, he wanted the maidens; last year, he wanted more; this year, he wanted more; and even now, he still wants some more. But he has run into an adversary, for that vanguard sent to make demands for the palace maidens has been defeated by some Pilgrim Sun. Angered by this, our great king wanted to go into war with that kingdom and asked me to send them some declaration of war. Once I deliver this document, that king had better decide not to fight, for any war would only go against him. When our great king uses his smoke, fire, and flying sand, none of them, the king and his subjects, can ever hope to remain alive. We will certainly occupy their city; our great king will become emperor and we will become his officials. High or low, we will have some appointments or ranks, but I fear that our action would be intolerable to Heaven."

When Pilgrim heard this, he was secretly delighted. "Even a

monster-spirit," he thought to himself, "can have good intentions. Just listen to what he has said about how their 'action would be intolerable to Heaven.' Isn't he a good man? But concerning the Golden Sage Queen, I don't quite understand what he means by the fiend king not having affinity to touch her body. Let me question him a bit." With a buzz, he flew away from the monster-spirit and darted ahead for several miles. A shake of his body changed him into a little Taoist lad:

His head had two tufts of hair;
He wore a patched cleric robe.
Tapping a wooden-fish drum,
A Taoist hymn he hummed.

Rounding the mountain slope, he met the little fiend and saluted him with hand upraised, saying, "Officer, where are you going? What's the document you are delivering?" Behaving as if he knew his interrogator, the fiendish creature stopped his gong and, giggling loudly, returned the greeting. "Our great king," said he, "has sent me to deliver a declaration of war to the Scarlet-Purple Kingdom." "Has that someone from the Scarlet-Purple Kingdom," continued Pilgrim, "mated with the great king?"

"Almost immediately after she had been abducted," replied the little fiend, "an immortal presented to her as a present a five-colored divine robe. Once she had put it on, however, needlelike prickles sprouted all over her body. Our great king didn't even dare to give her the slightest touch, for the merest contact would inflict terrific pain on his hand. We don't know how those prickles grew, but that's the reason for his not claiming her body from the beginning until now. Earlier this morning, he sent his vanguard to demand two palace maidens for his service, but the vanguard was defeated by one so-called Pilgrim Sun. Our great king was angered, and that was why he sent me to deliver a declaration of war. He is going to do battle with him tomorrow." "Is the great king still angry?" said Pilgrim. "Indeed he is," replied the little fiend. "You should go cheer him up with a Taoist song or two."

Dear Pilgrim! After a bow with hands folded, he turned and walked away, while the fiend struck up his gong and journeyed as before. Unleashing his violence all at once, Pilgrim whipped out his rod, turned around again, and delivered a blow on the back of the little fiend's head. Alas! This one blow made

The head shatter, the blood flow, the brains burst out;
The skin rift, the neck split, and his life expire.

As he put away the rod, he was smitten with regret, saying to himself,
"I'm a little too impatient! I hadn't even asked his name. O, all right!"
He took down his declaration of war to put in his own sleeve; the
yellow banner and the brass gong were stuffed into the grass by the
road. As he picked up the fiend by the legs and was about to throw
him into the brook, a gold-plated name plate dropped down from his
waist with a clang. On the plate was the following inscription:

One trusted junior officer by the name of Going and Coming:
rather short, pimply face, beardless. To be worn at all times. The
person without this plate is an imposter.

"So this fellow has the name of Going and Coming," chuckled Pilgrim,
"but my rod has rendered him Going without Coming." He took down
the name plate and attached it to his waist. He was about to throw
away the corpse when the thought of the threat of smoke and fire
stopped him from searching further for the cave-dwelling. Raising his
rod instead, he punched it through the chest of the little fiend, toted
the corpse to rise to the air, and went back to the kingdom to annouce
his first merit. Look at him! Thinking and wondering to himself, he
soon arrived at the capital.

Before the Hall of Golden Chimes, our Pa-chieh was standing guard
over the king and his master, when all of a sudden he saw Pilgrim
approaching in midair and toting a monster-spirit. "Ah, this fribble
business!" he muttered to himself. "If I had known it earlier, old Hog
would have gone to arrest the fiend. That would have been counted
as my merit, wouldn't it?" Hardly had he finished speaking when
Pilgrim lowered his cloud and threw the monster-spirit before the
steps. Dashing up to the corpse, Pa-chieh gave him a blow with his
rake, crying, "This is the merit of old Hog!"

"What merit of yours is that?" asked Pilgrim. "Don't cheat me
out of it!" replied Pa-chieh. "I have evidence here. Aren't those nine
holes made by the rake?" "Take another look," said Pilgrim, "and
see if he has a head or not." "So, he's headless!" said Pa-chieh, chuckling. "I was wondering why he didn't move at all when I struck him
with my rake."

"Where's Master?" asked Pilgrim, and Pa-chieh said, "Talking
with the king in the hall." "Go and ask him to come out," said Pilgrim.

Pa-chieh ran up to the hall and nodded his head, whereupon Tripitaka rose and descended the hall to meet Pilgrim. Pilgrim took out the declaration of war and stuffed it into the sleeve of Tripitaka, saying, "Put it away, Master, and don't let the king see this."

As they were speaking, the king also came down the hall and met Pilgrim. "Divine monk, you've returned," he said. "How did the matter of arresting the fiend go?" Pointing with his finger, Pilgrim said, "Isn't that a monster-spirit who has been slain by old Monkey?" The king took one look and said, "It is the corpse of a fiend, but he's no Jupiter's Rival, whom we have seen twice with our own eyes. The archfiend is eighteen feet tall, and his shoulders are five times as wide as other men's. His face resembles a golden beam, and his voice is like thunder. He is no vulgar-looking midget like this one."

Smiling, Pilgrim said, "Your Majesty, you are perceptive, for this is indeed no Jupiter's Rival, but only a little fiend serving as a messenger, who ran into old Monkey. I slew him and toted him back to announce my merit." "Fine! Fine! Fine!" said the king, highly pleased. "This should be considered your first merit. We have often sent our people out there to gather intelligence, but we have never managed to turn up anything substantial. The moment the divine monk goes forth, he's able to bring back a captive. That's true magic power!" Then he called out: "Warm up the wine, so that we may congratulate the elder for his merit."

"Drinking wine is a trivial matter," said Pilgrim. "Let me ask your Majesty, did the Golden Sage Palace leave you any memento when she departed? If she did, give it to me." When the king heard him mention, the word, "memento," he felt as if a sword had run his heart through and he wept aloud, saying,

When we toasted brightness and warmth that year,
The vicious Jupiter uttered his cries.
He took by force our queen to be his wife;
We yielded her up for the people's sake.
There were no words of greeting or farewell,
No tender partings by the wayside stands.[9]
Mementos, scented purse—everything is gone,
Except myself, all bitter and forlorn.

"Your Majesty," said Pilgrim, "your pain is near its end. Why torture yourself like that? If our lady did not leave you any memento, are there objects in the palace that she is most fond of? Give me one of these." "Why do you want them?" asked the king.

Pilgrim said, "That fiend king does have magic powers. When I saw the smoke, the fire, and the sand he released, I knew it would be difficult to bring him to submission. Even if I were to succeed, I fear that our lady would refuse to accompany me, a stranger, to return to the kingdom. She will trust me only if she sees me entrusted with some object most dear to her when she was in the palace. That's why I must take such an object along with me."

"In the dressing alcove," said the king, "at the Palace of the Bright Sun, there is a pair of gold bracelets, originally worn by our Golden Sage Palace. Because that day was the festival when she had to tie five colored threads to her arms, she took off the bracelets. As these were some of her favorite things, they are still kept in a jewel box. Because of the way we were separated, however, we could not bear the sight of these bracelets, for they reminded us so much of her lovely face. The moment we see them, we would be sicker than ever." "Let's not talk about illness anymore," said Pilgrim. "Bring me the bracelets. If you can part with them, give them to me. If not, I'll just take one of them."

The king asked the Jade Sage Palace to take them out. When the king saw the bracelets, he cried several times "Dearest, dearest Lady" before handing them over to Pilgrim. After Pilgrim took them, he put them on his arm.

Dear Great Sage! He refused the wine of merit and mounted the cloud-somersault instead. With a whistle he arrived once more at the Unicorn Mountain. Too preoccupied to enjoy the scenery, he at once began searching for the cave. As he walked along, he heard the raucous noise of people speaking. When he stood still to look more carefully, he found soldiers posted at the entrance of the Cave of the Mythic Beast, some five hundred of them,

All tightly lined up,
And densely arrayed.
Tightly lined up, they held spears and swords
Which gleamed in the sun;
Densely arrayed, they unfurled the banners
Which fluttered in the wind.
Tiger generals, bear captains, all able to change;
Leopard warriors, striped-cat marshals, most spirited.
Grey wolves, how savage!
Brown elephants, still more potent!
Sly hare, clever deer, wielding halberds and swords;

Long snakes, huge serpents, hung with sabers and bows.
The chimpanzee who understands human speech
Leads the troops, secures the camp as one informed.

When Pilgrim saw them, he dared not proceed; instead, he turned and walked back out the way he came. Why did he turn back, you say. It was not because he was afraid of them. Actually, he returned to the spot where he had slain the little fiend and found again that brass gong and that yellow banner.

Facing the wind, he made the magic sign;
Thinking the image, he went into motion.

With one shake of his body, he changed himself into the form of that Going and Coming. Banging loud his gong, he stepped forward in great strides and marched right up to the Cave of the Mythic Beast. Just as he was looking over the cave, he heard the chimpanzee say, "Going and Coming, are you back?" Pilgrim had no alternative but to reply, "I'm back." "Get inside quickly!" said the chimpanzee. "The great king is waiting for your reply at the Skinning Pavilion." On hearing this, Pilgrim strode inside the front door, still beating his gong. Once inside, he saw hanging cliffs and precipitous walls, rock chambers and quiet rooms. There were exotic grasses and flowers on the left and right, and there were plenty of old cedars and aged pines front and back.

Soon he walked through the second-level door, where he saw an octagonal pavilion with eight translucent windows. In the middle of the pavilion was a gold inlaid armchair, on which was seated solemnly a demon king. Truly he had a savage appearance! You see

Colored nimbus soaring up from his head
And violent air bursting forth from his chest.
Pointed teeth protrude like rows of sharp swords;
His temple's tousled locks flare like red fume.
Whiskers like arrows stick onto his lips;
Hairs wrap his body like blanket layers.
Mocking Jupiter are two copper-bell eyes;
An iron club he holds looks tall as the sky.

Though Pilgrim saw him, he was bold enough to make light of the monster-spirit. Without in the least affecting good manners, Pilgrim turned his back on him and kept beating the gong. "Have you returned?" asked the fiend king, but Pilgrim did not answer him. "Going and Coming, have you returned?" he asked again, and still

Pilgrim did not answer him. The fiend king walked up to him and tugged at Pilgrim, saying, "Why are you still beating the gong after you have come home? I ask you a question, and you don't answer me. Why?"

Dashing the gong to the ground, Pilgrim cried, "What's this Why, Why, Why? I told you I didn't want to go, and you insisted that I should. When I got there, I saw countless men and horses already arrayed in battle formations. The moment they saw me, they cried, 'Seize the monster-spirit! Seize the monster-spirit!' Pushing and shoving, they hauled me bodily into the city to see the king, who at once ordered me executed. It was fortunate that counselors from both rows of ministers invoked the old maxim that 'When two states are at war, the envoys are never executed.' They spared me and took away the declaration of war. Then they sent me out of the city, where before the entire army they caned me thirty times on my legs. I was released to tell you that they would be here soon to do battle with you."

"As you have put the matter," said the fiend king, "you have lucked out! No wonder you didn't answer me when I questioned you." Pilgrim said, "I was silent not because of anything. It's just that I was nursing my pain, and that's why I didn't reply."

"How many horses and men do they have?" asked the fiend king again. Pilgrim said, "I was scared silly, and I was further intimidated by their beatings. You think I would be able to account for the number of their horses and men? All I saw in thick rows were

Bows, arrows, sabers, mail, and armor;
Lances, swords, halberds, and tasseled banners;
Poleaxes, crescent spades, and head-coverings;
Huge axes, round shields, and iron caltrops;
Long battle staffs;
Short, fat cudgels;
Steel tridents and petards and helmets, too.
To be worn are tall boots, head gear, and quilted vests.
Crops and whips, sleeve-pellets, and bronze mallets.

When the fiendish king heard this, he laughed and said, "That's nothing! That's nothing! A little fire and all such weapons will be wiped out. You should go now and tell our Lady Golden Sage not to worry. When she heard that I was growing angry and about to go into battle, she was already full of tears. Why don't you go now and tell her that the men and horses of her country are most fearsome and that they will certainly prevail against me. That ought to give her some relief for a while."

On hearing this, Pilgrim was very pleased, saying to himself, "Old Monkey can't ask for anything better!" Look at him! He seems to be especially familiar with the way! Rounding a small side door, he passed through halls and chambers. Deep inside the cave, you see, were all tall buildings and edifices, quite unlike what was in front. When he reached the rear palace where the Lady Golden Sage lived, he saw brilliantly colored doors. Walking through these to look around, he found two choirs of fiendish vixen and deer, all made up to appear as beautiful maidens standing on the left and right. In the middle was seated the lady, who held her chin in her hand as tears fell from her eyes. Indeed she had

Soft, youthful features,
Seductive good looks.
Too lazy to do her hair,
She left it piled up loosely;
Fearful of make-up,
She wore neither pins nor bracelets.
Her face had no powder,
She being scornful of rouge.
Her hair had no oil,
For she kept unkempt her tresses.
Her cherry lips pouted
As she clenched her silvery teeth;
Her moth brows knitted
As tears drenched her starlike eyes.
All her heart
Yearned for the Scarlet-Purple ruler;
All her thoughts
Dwelled on fleeing at once this snare and net.
Truly it had been thus:
The fate of fair ladies was always harsh.
Weary and silent, she faced the east wind.

Walking up to her and bowing, Pilgrim said, "Greetings!" "This insolent imp!" said the lady. "How brash could he be! During the time when I shared the glory with the Scarlet-Purple ruler, those grand preceptors and prime ministers would prostrate themselves before me and dared not even raise their heads. How could this wild fiend just address me with a 'Greetings'? Where did this rustic boor come from?"

Some of the maids went forward and said, "Madam, please do not be angry. He is a trusted junior officer of Father Great King, and his name is Going and Coming. He was the one sent to deliver the declaration of war this morning." On hearing this, the lady suppressed her anger and said, "When you delivered the declaration, did you reach the Scarlet-Purple Kingdom?" "I took the declaration," replied Pilgrim, "straight into the capital, reaching, in fact, the Hall of the Golden Chimes. After I saw the king in person, I took his reply back here."

"When you saw the king," said the lady, "what did he have to say?" Pilgrim said, "He claimed he was ready to fight, and just now, I have already told the great king about how the enemy forces were being disposed. That ruler, however, also expressed great longing for Madam. He wanted to convey a few words of special interest to you, but there are too many people around and I can't speak here."

On hearing this, the lady shouted for the two rows of vixen and deer to leave. After he closed the palace door, Pilgrim gave his own face a wipe and changed back into his original form. He said to the lady, "Don't be afraid of me. I am a priest sent by the Great T'ang in the Land of the East to go seek scriptures from Buddha in the Thunderclap Monastery of India in the Great Western Heaven. My master is Tripitaka T'ang, the bond-brother of the T'ang emperor, and I am Sun Wu-k'ung, his eldest disciple. When we passed through your kingdom and had to have our travel rescript certified, we saw a royal proclamation issued for the recruitment of physicians. I exercised my great ability in the therapeutic arts, and I cured the king of his illness of ardent longing. During the banquet he gave to thank me, he told me while we were drinking about how you were abducted by the fiend. Since I have the knowledge of subduing dragons and taming tigers, he asked me specially to come arrest the fiend and rescue you back to the kingdom. It was I who defeated the vanguard, and it was I, too, who slew the little fiend. When I saw, however, how powerful the fiend was outside the gate, I changed myself into the form of Going and Coming in order to take the risk of contacting you here."

On hearing what he said, the lady fell silent. Whereupon Pilgrim took out the treasure bracelets and presented them with both hands, saying, "If you don't believe me, take a good look at these objects."

The moment she saw them, the lady began to weep, as she left her seat to bow to Pilgrim, saying, "Elder, if you could indeed rescue me and take me back to the kingdom, I would never forget your great favor!"

"Let me ask you," said Pilgrim, "what sort of a treasure that is that releases fire, smoke, and sand?" "It's no treasure!" replied the lady. "They are actually three golden bells. When he gives the first bell one wave, he can release up to three thousand feet of fire to burn people. When he waves the second one, he can release three thousand feet of smoke to fumigate people. When he waves the third one, he can release three thousand feet of yellow sand to confound people. The smoke and the fire are not even as potent as the yellow sand, which is most poisonous. If it gets into someone's nostrils, the person will die." "Formidable! Formidable!" said Pilgrim. "I had the experience, all right, and even I had to sneeze a couple of times! Where, I wonder, does he put these bells?"

"You think he'd put them down!" said the lady. "He has them tied to his waist, and whether he is in or out of doors, whether he is up or lying down, they'll never leave his body." "If you still have some feelings for the Scarlet-Purple Kingdom," said Pilgrim, "if you want to see the king once more, you must banish for the moment all sorrow and melancholy. Put on your looks of pleasure and romance, and allow him to enjoy with you the sentiments of wedlock. Tell him to let you keep the bells for him. Then, when I have stolen them and brought this fiendish creature into submission, it will be simple to take you back to your dear mate so that both of you can enjoy peace and harmony once more." The lady agreed.

Our Pilgrim changed again into that trusted junior officer and opened the palace door to summon the various maids. Then the lady called out, "Going and Coming, go to the pavilion in front quickly and ask the great king to come here. I want to speak to him." Dear Pilgrim! He shouted his consent and dashed out to the Skinning Pavilion to say to the monster-spirit, "Great King, Lady Sage Palace desires your company." Delighted, the fiend king said, "Normally our lady has nothing but abuse for me. How is it that she desires my company today?" "Our lady," replied Pilgrim, "asked me about the ruler of the Scarlet-Purple Kingdom, and I told her, 'He doesn't want you anymore. He has chosen another queen from among his subjects.' When our lady heard this, she had to stop thinking about him, and that was why she asked for you." Exceedingly pleased, the fiend king said, "You are quite useful! When I have destroyed that kingdom, I'll appoint you a special court assistant."

Thanking him casually for his promised favor, Pilgrim walked quickly with the fiend king to the entrance of the rear palace, where the lady met them amiably and reached out with her hands to greet the monster. Backing off immediately and bowing, the fiend king said, "I'm honored! I'm honored! Thank you for your love, but I'm afraid of the pain in my hands, and I dare not touch you." "Please take a seat, Great King," said the lady, "for I want to speak to you." "Please do so without hesitation," replied the fiend king.

The lady said, "It has been three years since you first bestowed your love on me. Though we have not been able to share a bed together, it is still our foreordained affinity that we should become husband and wife. I think, however, that you must have some sentiments against me, and you are not treating me truly as your spouse. For I can recall the time when I was queen at the Scarlet-Purple Kingdom. Whenever the foreign nations presented their tributary treasures, the queen was asked to keep them after the king had inspected them. You have hardly any treasures here, of course; what you wear are furs, and what you eat are raw meats. I haven't seen any silks or damasks, any gold or pearls. All our coverings are only skins and furs. You may have some treasures, I suppose, but the distance you feel towards me prevents you from letting me see them or asking me to keep them for you. I have heard that you have some kind of bells or gongs—three of them, in fact—which, I suppose, must be treasures. Or else, why would you keep them with you when you are walking or when you are seated? You should let me keep them for you, and when you need them, I can take them out. After all, we *are* husband and wife, and you should at least show me some trust. If you don't, you must feel that I'm still an outsider!"

Breaking into loud guffaws as he bowed to her, the fiend king said, "Madam, your reprimands are just! Your reprimands are just! The treasures are right here. Today, I turn them over to you for safe-keeping." He at once hitched up his clothes to take out the treasures. With unblinking eyes on one side, Pilgrim saw that after the fiend had hitched up two or three layers of clothing, he had tied to his body three small bells. These he took down and, having stuffed some cotton into the mouths of the bells, had them wrapped up in a piece of

THE JOURNEY TO THE WEST

leopard skin before he handed them over to the lady. "Though these are lowly objects," he said, "you must guard them with care. Never shake or rattle them." Taking them over with her hands, the lady said, "I know. I'll put them right here on my dressing table. No one will shake them."

Then the lady said, "Little ones, prepare us some wine. I want to drink a few cups with the great king to celebrate our happiness and love." On hearing this, the servant girls at once spread out a table full of vegetables and fruits and laden with venison and rabbit meat. After they poured out some coconut wine, the lady put on her most seductive charms to deceive the monster-spirit.

On the side Pilgrim Sun also began his work; slipping slowly up to the dresser, he gently picked up those three golden bells before he inched his way out of the palace. When he arrived at an empty spot before the Skinning Pavilion, he opened up the leopard skin wrap to look at the contents. The middle bell was about the size of a tea mug, while the two on both ends were as big as fists. Not knowing how formidable these objects were, he yanked out the cotton. All he heard was a loud clang, and then the flame, the smoke, and the yellow sand poured out from the bells. He tried desperately to stuff the cotton back into the bells but to no avail. Instantly, flames leaped up and engulfed the pavilion.

Those monsters and fiends were so terrified that they rushed into the rear palace to report to the fiend king, who shouted, "Go put out the fire! Go put out the fire!" When he dashed out with the rest to the pavilion, he saw Going and Coming with the golden bells in his hands. "You wretched slave!" bellowed the fiend king, rushing up to him. "How dare you steal my treasure bells and mess with them here? Seize him! Seize him!" Those tiger warriors, bear commanders, leopard captains, striped-cat marshals, brown elephants, grey wolves, clever deer, sly hare, long serpents, huge pythons, and the chimpanzee all mobbed the pavilion.

Terribly flustered, our Pilgrim dropped the bells and changed back into his original form. Whipping out his golden-hooped compliant rod, he plunged into the crowd and fought furiously. After the fiend king had put away his treasures, he shouted the order: "Shut the front door!" On hearing this, some of the fiends went to shut the door while others surrounded Pilgrim to do battle. Suspecting that it would be difficult for him to flee, Pilgrim put away his rod and, with one shake of his body, changed himself into a tiny fly which alighted on one of the stone walls that was not burning. When the various fiends could not find him, they said, "Great King, the thief has escaped!"

"Did he walk out of the door?" asked the fiend king. "The front door is firmly bolted," they replied. "He hasn't left that way." "Then search carefully!" said the fiend king. Some of the fiends put out the fire with water, while others conducted a careful search all around, but there was not a trace of the thief.

'Who is the thief," said the fiend king angrily, "who is so audacious that he dared change into the shape of Going and Coming, come in here to speak to me, and stay by my side until he found the chance to steal my treasures? It's a good thing that he didn't take the bells out of the cave. If he had taken them up to the summit and had exposed them to natural wind, I wouldn't know what to do!"

"It's partly the profound luck of the Great King," said the tiger general, approaching him, "and partly the fact that we are not yet destined to perish. That's why we were able to discover him in time." "Great King," said the bear commander, "this thief is not just any other person. He must be that Sun Wu-k'ung who has defeated our vanguard. He probably ran into Going and Coming on the way and took our officer's life. After he robbed him of his yellow banner, brass gong, and name plate, he changed into his appearance to come here and deceive you." "Exactly! Exactly!" said the fiend king. "What you say is quite right! Little ones, continue the search, and be careful that you do not let him slip out the door." So, that was how things stood:

A clever move has turned to folly;

A playful act becomes something real.

We do not know how Pilgrim Sun managed to escape from the fiend's door, and you must listen to the explanation in the next chapter.

Seventy-one

In a false name Pilgrim subdues the fiendish wolf;
In epiphany Kuan-yin conquers the monster-king.

Form's emptiness, that's an ancient truth;
And emptiness is thus said to be form.
If one can grasp fully the mystery of emptiness and form,
Who needs to burn and refine cinnabar?
Cease not to cultivate the whole of virtue;
Strenuously you must toil and labor.
Only when work's accomplished will you face the Heavens
With godly features ever preserved.

We tell you now about that Jupiter's Rival, who ordered all the front and back doors tightly shut in order to search for Pilgrim. All the commotion lasted until dusk, but not a trace of the intruder could be found. Taking a seat in the Skinning Pavilion, the fiend king assembled the rest of the fiends and gave the order that guards were to be posted at all the doors, holding handbells and shouting passwords, beating drums and rattles. Every one of them was to put the arrow to the bow and go on patrol through the night with drawn swords. However, the Great Sage Sun, you see, had changed into a tiny fly and alighted on a door post. When he saw that the front was tightly guarded, he spread his wings and flew instead into the rear palace, where he found the Lady Golden Sage slumped on a table.

In clear drops the tears rolled down;
In low tones she voiced her grief.

Flying through the door, Pilgrim gently landed on her dishevelled black tresses to listen to how she was weeping. In a little while, the lady suddenly cried out, "O, my lord! You and I must have burned

The broken-head incense[1] in our former lives,
So that we meet in this one a fiend king.
Parted for three years, which day will we meet?
Stranded at two places—that is our grief.

340

The elder you sent has just conveyed the news;
Our union's thwarted when he lost his life.
Since it's hard to untie the bells of gold,
Our longings are keener than those of old."
When Pilgrim heard this, he moved up to the base of her ear and whispered: "Lady Sage Palace, I'm Elder Sun, the divine monk sent here by your country, and I haven't lost my life. What happened had to do with my impetuousness. When you were drinking with the fiend king, I approached the dresser and stole the golden bells. I managed to slip out to the pavilion in front, but I couldn't resist untying the wrap to take a look. Little did I realize that when I pulled out the cotton stuffed in the bells, smoke, fire, and yellow sand would pour out all at once with a clang. I was so flustered that I dropped the bells and changed back into my original form. I wielded my iron rod to wage a bitter battle, but when I couldn't break free, I feared that I might be harmed. That was why I changed into a tiny fly to fly up to a door post and hide until now. Now the fiend king is guarding the place more tightly than ever and refuses to open the doors. You must, therefore, trick him, in the name of conjugal duties, into coming in here to rest. Then I'll be able to escape and make another plan to rescue you."

The moment the lady heard these words,
    She shook all over
    As if gods were pulling her hair;
    Weak and fearful,
    She felt her heart thump and pound.
"Are you," she asked tearfully, "a ghost or a human being?" "I'm neither a human," replied Pilgrim, "nor am I a ghost. At the moment, I have changed into a tiny fly here. Don't be afraid. Go quickly and invite the fiend king to come." The lady refused to believe him. Shedding tears, she said softly, "You're not trying to bewitch me?" "Why would I want to bewitch you?" said Pilgrim. "If you don't believe me, spread open your palm and I'll land on it for you to see."

The lady indeed stretched forth her left palm, and Pilgrim gently alighted on her lovely hand. How he seemed like
    A black pea nailed to the lotus bud;
    A bee resting on peony flower;
    A grape having landed on silk brocade;
    A thick black dot by the lily branch!

Holding high her jadelike hand, the Golden Sage Palace uttered the cry, "Divine monk!" "I'm the transformation of the divine monk," answered Pilgrim with a buzz. Only then did the lady believe him. "When I manage to get that fiend king here," she whispered to him, "how will you proceed?" Pilgrim said, "As the ancients put the matter,

To ruin one's whole life there's only wine.[2]

And another said,

To break up all cares there's nothing like wine.

There are many uses for wine, and so the best thing you can do is still to make him drink. Summon now one of the maids closest to you and point her out to me. I'll change into her appearance and serve you by your side. When there's a chance, I'll act."

The lady indeed agreed, and she called out: "Spring Grace, where are you?" From behind a screen stepped forth a white-faced vixen, who knelt down and said, "Madam, what is your pleasure?" "Tell the rest of the maids," replied the lady, "to light up gauze lanterns, burn the musk-gland, and accompany me to the front court to ask the king to retire." Spring Grace at once went out to summon seven or eight deer fiends and vixen spirits, who came in with a pair of lanterns and a pair of portable urns. They stood on both sides of the lady, who arose with hands folded while the Great Sage soared into the air.

Dear Pilgrim! Spreading his wings, he headed straight for the head of the white-faced vixen. There he pulled off one piece of hair and blew a mouthful of immortal breath on it, crying, "Change!" It changed at once into a sleep-inducing insect, which he gently placed on her face. The moment that this insect reaches a person's face, you see, it will crawl toward one's nostril, and when it gets inside, the person will fall asleep. Our Spring Grace, therefore, gradually felt so fatigued that she could hardly remain on her feet. Rocking from side to side and nodding her head, she ran back to her previous resting place, laid down her head, and snored away. Pilgrim flew down and with one shake of his body changed into the form of Spring Grace. He walked out from behind the screen to stand at attention with the rest of the maids, and we shall leave them there for the moment.

We tell you now about that Lady Golden Sage Palace, who was walking out to the front. When the little fiends saw her, they immediately reported to Jupiter's Rival: "Great King, Madam has arrived." The fiend hurried out of the Skinning Pavilion to meet her. "Great King," said the lady, "the smoke and the fire have subsided, and the thief, too, has vanished. The night is deep, and I have come especially to ask you to retire."

Highly pleased, the fiend said, "Madam, please take care of yourself. Just now that thief was actually Sun Wu-k'ung, who, having defeated my vanguard and slain my trusted junior officer, came in here by means of transformation in order to deceive us. We have conducted a most careful search, but there's not a trace of him. This is why I feel quite uneasy about the matter." "That fellow must have escaped," said the lady. "You should not worry any more, Great King. Let's retire and rest."

When the monster-spirit saw the lady standing there with this earnest invitation, he dared not refuse. After he had given the order to the rest of the fiends to be careful with the torches and candles and to look out for thieves and robbers, he went back to the rear palace with the lady. Pilgrim, who had changed into the form of Spring Grace, was led inside also along with the two rows of maids. "Prepare us some wine," cried the lady, "so that we may relieve the great king of his weariness." "Exactly! Exactly!" said the fiend king, laughing. "Bring us wine quickly. I will help the dear lady to calm her fears."

The specious Spring Grace and the other fiends thereupon brought out some bowls of fruit and several dishes of game as they set up the tables and chairs. The lady picked up a goblet, and the fiend king also presented her with a goblet. After the two of them had exchanged their cups, the specious Spring Grace picked up the wine pot on the side and said, "Since the great king and madam did not exchange their cups until this very night, you should drain the cups so that I can pour you a Double Happiness round." They did so; again their cups were filled, and they drank that, too.

The specious Spring Grace spoke up once more: "This is such a happy meeting between the great king and madam! Let those maids who can sing, and those who can dance dance!" Hardly had he finished speaking when the entire hall was filled with the sound of songs and harmonious melodies; those who could dance did dance, and those who could sing did sing, as the two of them drank a good deal of wine. Then the lady stopped the song and dance, and all the maids were again divided into two choirs to leave and stand beyond the screen. Only the specious Spring Grace stayed behind to pour the wine, back and forth. The lady did nothing but engage in conjugal talk with the fiend king. Look at her! She displayed such sultry looks and amorous charms that the fiend king went limp with desire. But he simply had no luck in touching her. What a pity! Truly, he felt like "a cat biting on a urine bubble—empty delight!"

After they flirted for a while and laughed for a while, the lady asked, "Great King, were the treasures damaged?" "These treasures," replied the fiend king, "had been forged by the elemental powers of nature. How could they be damaged? When the thief pulled out the cotton, however, the leopard-skin wrap was burned." "How did you pack them up again?" asked the lady. The fiend king said, "No need to do that, for I've tied them again to my waist."

On hearing this, the specious Spring Grace pulled off a handful of hair which he chewed to pieces. He quietly approached the fiend king and placed these pieces of hair on his body. Blowing three mouthfuls of immortal breath on them, he whispered "Change!" and at once they became three kinds of vicious thing: lice, fleas, and bedbugs. They penetrated the fiend king's garments and began to bite him madly. Ridden by unbearable itch, that fiend king put his hands inside his bosom to rub and scratch himself. When his fingers caught hold of several of the lice, he took them up to the lamps to have a closer look. When she saw the insects, the lady said wistfully, "Great King, your under garments must have been soiled, I suppose. They haven't been washed for a long time, and that's why these things are growing on you."

Terribly embarrassed, the fiend king said, "I have never had these things grow on me before. Why does it have to be this very night that I disgrace myself?" Laughing, the lady said, "There's no disgrace! As the proverb says, 'Even an emperor's body may have three lice!' Take off your clothes, and I'll try to catch some of them for you." The fiend king indeed began to loosen his belt and his clothes.

On one side the specious Spring Grace stared at the fiend king's body: on every layer of his clothing fleas were hopping about, and every garment had rows of big bedbugs. Those lice, big and small, were so thick that they resembled ants pouring out of their hills! By the time the third layer of clothing was hitched up, one could see countless insects swarming all over the golden bells. The specious Spring Grace said, "Great King, give me the bells, so that I, too, can catch some lice for you."

The fiend king was both so embarrassed and frightened that he could not tell the true from the false. He handed over the bells, and the specious Spring Grace took them over and played with them for a long time in his hands. When he saw the fiend king lower his head to shake his clothing, he immediately hid the bells. Pulling off three strands of hair, he changed them into three exact copies of the golden bells, which he deliberately turned over and examined before the lamps. Then, as he swayed and wriggled here and there, he shook his body slightly and at once retrieved all those lice, fleas, and bedbugs. The specious golden bells were returned to the fiend, who, when he took them in his hands, was more unperceiving than ever. Unable to tell the difference at all, he held up the bells with both hands and presented them to the lady, saying, "This time you put them away most carefully, so that nothing like last time will happen again."

The lady gently opened her garment trunk, put the specious bells inside, and bolted the trunk with a lock of yellow gold. After she drank a few more cups of wine with the fiend king, she gave this order to her maids: "Brush clean our ivory bed and roll down the silk coverlets. I'll sleep with the great king." "I don't have the luck! I don't have the luck!" said the fiend king repeatedly. "I dare not join you. Let me take a palace maiden and go to the west palace instead. Madam, please rest by yourself." They all retired, and we shall leave them for the moment.

We tell you now about the specious Spring Grace, who succeeded in stealing the treasures. These he tied to his own waist before he changed into his original form. With a shake of his body he retrieved also the sleep-inducing insect. As he walked along, he heard the sound of rattle and gong announcing the hour of the third watch. Dear Pilgrim! Making the magic sign with his fingers, he recited a spell and exercised the Magic of Body Concealment to reach the front door. When he saw, however, that it was tightly bolted, he took out his golden-hooped rod and pointed it at the door; this Lock-Opening Magic immediately flung wide the door and he strode out quickly. "Jupiter's Rival," he cried with a loud voice as he stood before the door, "return my Lady Golden Sage!"

He yelled for two or three times, and all the fiends, old and young, were aroused. They dashed out to look around and found the front door ajar. As some of them brought the lamps over to have the door locked up once more, a few of the fiends ran inside to report, "Great

King, someone outside our main door is addressing you by name and demanding the return of Lady Golden Sage!" The maids inside slipped out of the palace door and whispered, "Don't shout! The great king has just fallen asleep." Meanwhile, Pilgrim yelled some more in front of the main door, but those little fiends dared not go disturb the fiend king. Three or four times it went on like this, but they did not report the disturbance. Outside the cave-dwelling, the Great Sage brawled until dawn, and he was unable to control himself any longer. Wielding the iron rod with both hands, he went forward and smote the door. Those various fiends were terrified; while some of them pushed against the door, others ran inside to report. Having just awakened, the fiend king heard a raucous tumult. He dressed hurriedly and emerged from the silk curtains to ask, "What's all this noise?" The maids knelt down and said, "Father, we don't know who it was who shouted abuses at us for half the night outside. Now he is even striking at the door."

As the fiend king walked out of the palace door, he ran into several little fiends, who kowtowed rather timidly and said, "Someone outside is shouting abuses and demanding the Lady Golden Sage Palace! When we said 'No' to him, he spewed out countless insults, simply awful stuff. When he saw that the great king did not go out even at daybreak, he began to strike at our door." "Don't open it yet," said the fiend. "Go and ask for his name and where he came from. Hurry back to report to me."

One of the little fiends ran out and asked through the door, "Who is here striking at our door?" Pilgrim replied, "I'm External Grandpa [Wai-kung][3] sent here by the Scarlet-Purple Kingdom to take Lady Sage Palace back to her own country!" When the little fiend heard this, he returned with these words as his report and the fiend king set out for the rear palace to make further investigation of his intruder. The lady, you see, had just risen, and she had not yet washed or had her hair combed when her maid said, "Father is here." Tidying her clothes hurriedly but leaving her hair unpinned, the lady met him outside the palace. After they took their seats and before she could even ask why the fiend king had come in, another little fiend dashed in to report: "That External Grandpa has smashed our door!"

With a laugh, the fiend said, "Madam, how many generals and commanders do you have at court?" The lady said, "We have forty-eight Brigades[4] and a thousand fine generals. At the various borders, there are countless marshals and commanders." "Is there someone with the surname of External?" asked the fiend king.

"Inside the palace," replied the lady, "all I knew was how to assist the ruler by giving admonitions and supervision to the palace ladies night and day. The external affairs are endless. How could I remember any name or surname?"

The fiend king said, "Our visitor calls himself External Grandpa, but no such surname, I'm sure, appears in the *Hundred Family Names*. Since you have come from an aristocratic family and you are so intelligent by nature, you must have read all kinds of books and chronicles when you were at the royal palace. Do you remember whether this surname has appeared in any text at all?" "Only in the *Thousand-Character Composition*,"[5] replied the lady, "there is the phrase, 'Externally one learns from the tutor's instruction [*wai-shou fu-hsün*].'[6] I suppose that must be it."

Delighted, the fiend king said, "Indeed, it is! Indeed, it is!" He rose and took leave of the lady to go to the Skinning Pavilion. After he had suited up his armor properly, he summoned his fiendish troops and went straight out the front door, his hands holding a spreading-flower ax.[7] "Who is the External Grandpa who comes from the Scarlet-Purple Kingdom?" he cried in a loud voice.

Gripping the golden-hooped rod with his right hand, Pilgrim pointed with his left hand at the fiend king and said, "Worthy nephew, why are you addressing me?" When the fiend king saw him, he was filled with anger. "Look at you!" he bellowed,

Your features are an ape's;
Your looks are a monkey's.
Seven percent a ghost,
And yet you dare mock me?

"Lawless fiend," replied Pilgrim with a laugh, "you are the one lying to Heaven and making a mockery of the ruler! And you have no eyes either! When I caused great disturbance in the Celestial Palace five hundred years ago, all those divine warriors of the Ninefold Heaven wouldn't have dared address me without the word 'Venerable' when they saw me. Now you call me your grandpa. Is that too much of a loss for you?"

"Tell me quickly your name and surname," snapped the fiend king, "and what sort of martial art you have learned that you dare act with such insolence around here." Pilgrim said, "You'd have been better off if you hadn't asked about that. For when I announce my name and surname, I fear that you wouldn't know where to stand! Step closer, stand firmly, and listen to my recital:

My parents who begot me were Heav'n and Earth;
The sun and moon's essence had me conceived
And carried in a stone for countless years.
A spirit root formed and nursed me. O, how strange!
As spring quickened nature, I was born that year.
Today I'm an immortal for all times.
Once a captain of many gathered fiends,
I made monsters bow before the red cliffs.
A summons issued the Great Emperor Jade;
The Gold Star Venus with a decree came
To ask me to hold an office in Heav'n,
But I was not pleased with pi-ma, the rank.
I plotted at first rebellion at my cave;
Then I disturbed with arms the royal court.
Deva Pagoda-Bearer and his prince
Both shrank back in terror after our fight.
Gold Star addressed the Cosmic King again
Who sent a pacifying decree next
To make me Equal to Heav'n, true Great Sage—
A proper name for fine talent of the state.
Because I disturbed, too, the Peaches Feast,
Wrath I incurred when I stole pills, half-drunk,
Lao Tzu himself before the Throne appeared;
The West Queen Mother at Jade Terrace bowed.
Learning that I had mocked the laws of kings,
Soldiers they called up and dispatches sent—
A hundred thousand savage planetoids,
And dense rows of halberds, lances, and swords.
As cosmic nets were spread throughout the mount,
We raised up our arms for a mighty meet.
The fight was fierce but neither side could win,
And Erh-lang arrived on Kuan-yin's advice.
To find out who was stronger we two fought,
Though he had the Plum Mountain Brothers' aid.
As we transformed ourselves to show our strength,
Three sages in Heaven pushed the clouds aside:

Lao Tzu at once threw his diamond snare down,
The gods caught and brought me to the steps of gold.
A lengthy confession I need not make;
I should be hacked to pieces for my crimes.
Axes and mallets could not take my life,
Nor was I harmed by scimitars and swords.
Fire and thunder could only do so much—
Longevity's offspring they could not hurt.
Then to Tushita the captive they sent
To be refined in all manners as they wished.
Not till the right time was the tripod opened,
But I from the center at once leaped out;
My hands holding high the compliant rod,
To Jade Dragon Terrace my way I fought.
Into hiding went each planet and star;
I was free to havoc through Heaven's halls.
Lord Inspector quickly sought the Buddha's help;
With me Śākyamuni a contest waged.
I, somersaulting from within his palm,
Did tour all Heavens before turning back.
The Buddha deceived me, foreknowing this;
I was pinned down by him at Heaven's edge
Till now afterwards some five hundred years.
My lowly self freed, I frolic once more.
To guard the T'ang monk going to the West—
This, Wu-k'ung the Pilgrim well understands.
He must on the western path the fiends subdue.
Which monster would dare not hold him in awe?"

When the fiend king heard the announcement of Wu-k'ung, the Pilgrim, he said "So you're that fellow who caused great disturbance at the Celestial Palace! If you have been released to accompany the T'ang monk to the West, you should simply stay on your journey. Why must you mind someone's business? Why must you serve the Scarlet-Purple Kingdom as a slave and come here to look for death?"

"You thief! You lawless fiend!" shouted Pilgrim. "You mouth such words of ignorance! I receive the most reverent invitation from the Scarlet-Purple Kingdom, and I am beholden to the king's most gracious hospitality. Old Monkey is regarded there as being a thousand times more exalted than the Throne, who honors me as his parents and reveres me as a god. How dare you mention the word, slave? You are but a fiend who lies to Heaven and makes a mockery of the ruler! Don't run away! Have a taste of your grandpa's rod!" A little flustered, the fiend jumped aside to dodge the blow before wielding the spreading-flower ax to strike at his opponent's face. This was a marvelous battle! Take a look!

The golden-hooped compliant rod,
The sharp spreading-flower ax.
One clenched his teeth as he turned violent;
One gritted them as he showed his strength.
This one was the Great Sage, Equal to Heaven, descending to
    Earth;
That one was a mischievous fiend king coming to the world.
The two of them belched out cloud and fog to darken Heaven;
They kicked up rocks and sand to hide the dipper halls.
Back and forth they went through many styles;
Up and down they emitted golden lights.
Together they used their power,
Each testing his magic might.
This one wanted to take the lady to the capital;
That one enjoyed staying with the queen at the mount.
This whole battle truly had no other cause:
For a king each had life and death forgot!

The two of them battled for fifty rounds, but no decision could be reached. When the fiend king saw how powerful Pilgrim was, he knew that he could not prevail against him. Using the ax to stop the iron rod, he said, "Pilgrim Sun, let's pause for a moment. I haven't had my breakfast today. Let me take my meal first, and then I'll come to fight to the finish with you." Pilgrim realized that he wanted to get the bells, but he put away his iron rod and said, "'A good hunter doesn't run down a tired hare!' Go! Go! Eat heartily, and return to receive your death!"

Turning around, the fiend dashed inside and said to the lady, "Take out the treasures quickly." "What for?" she asked. "The person who was shouting to provoke battle this morning," replied the fiend king, "happened to be the disciple of a priest on his way to acquire scriptures. His name is Sun Wu-k'ung, the Pilgrim, and 'External Grandpa' is only a false name. I fought with him for a long time but I could not prevail against him. Let me take my treasures out there so I can start a fire to burn this ape."

The lady was quite dismayed by what she heard. She did not want to take out the bells, but she was afraid to offend him; if she took them out, however, she feared that Pilgrim might lose his life. As she hesitated, the fiend king again urged her, saying, "Take them out quickly!" The lady had no alternative but to open the lock and hand the three bells over to the fiend king, who grabbed them and ran outside the cave. As tears poured down her face, the lady sat down in the palace, wondering whether Pilgrim could escape with his life. Neither she nor the fiend king, you see, knew that these were specious bells.

As soon as he got outside, the fiend king placed himself upwind of his opponent. "Pilgrim Sun," he cried out, "don't run away! Watch me shake my bells a little!"

With a laugh, Pilgrim replied, "If you have bells, you think I have none? If you can shake them, you think I can't shake them?" "What sort of bells do you have?" said the fiend king. "Take them out for me to see." Pilgrim gave his iron rod a pinch to reduce it to the size of an embroidery needle, which he stored in his ear. Then he untied from his waist those three true treasures and said to the fiend king, "Aren't these my purple-gold bells?"

Greatly startled by what he saw, the fiend king said to himself, "Odd! Very odd! How could his bells be exactly like mine? Even if they were cast in the same mold, there ought to be some mark here or a blemish there. How could they be exactly alike?" He therefore asked: "Where did your bells come from?" "Worthy nephew," said Pilgrim, "where did yours come from?"

An honest person, the fiend king said right away, "My bells belonged originally to

Lord Grand Purity, most steeped in the Way.

With gold in eight-trigram brazier long refined,

These bells called perfect treasures had been made

And left behind by Lao Tzu till this day."

Laughing, Pilgrim said, "Well, the bells of old Monkey also come from that time." "Where did they come from?" asked the fiend king. Pilgrim said,

The Father of Tao who elixir made

Had these gold bells in his brazier refined.

Two threes are six—cyclic treasures are they:

My bells are female while your bells are male.

"These bells," said the fiend king, "are treasures forged in the same process as that of the golden elixir. They are not fowl or beasts. How could you use sex to distinguish them? If you can shake something valuable out of them, then they are good treasures." "It's useless to talk," replied Pilgrim, "when only action's the proof. I'll let you shake yours first."

Indeed the fiend king shook the first bell three times, but no fire came out; he shook the second bell three times but no smoke came out; and he shook the third bell three times but no sand came out. Terribly flustered, the fiend king said, "How strange! How strange! The ways of the world have changed! These must be hen-pecked bells! The male sees the female, and that's why nothing comes out!"

"Stop shaking, worthy nephew!" said Pilgrim. "Let me shake mine for you to see." Marvelous monkey! He grasped the three bells in his hand and shook them all together. Just look at the red fire, green smoke, and yellow sand! They poured out together and began at once to engulf the mountain and trees. The Great Sage also recited a spell and, facing the ground toward the southwest, shouted: "Come, wind!" Indeed, a strong gust whipped up the fire, and the fire exploited the power of the wind.

In flaming red
And massive black,
The sky was full of fire and smoke,
And the earth full of yellow sand.

Scared out of his wits, that Jupiter's Rival wanted to flee but could not find a way out. For in the midst of that kind of fire, how could he possibly escape with his life?

Suddenly a loud voice came from midair: "Sun Wu-k'ung, I've arrived!" As he turned his head upward quickly, Pilgrim saw that it was the Bodhisattva Kuan-yin; her left hand was supporting the immaculate vase, while her right hand was sprinkling sweet dew with her willow twig to put out the fire. Pilgrim was so startled that he quickly tucked the bells in his waist, folded his hands before his chest, and bowed low. After the Bodhisattva had sprinkled a few drops of the sweet dew, the smoke and fire all vanished in an instant and there was not a trace of the yellow sand. Kowtowing, Pilgrim said, "I did not know the Great Compassion had descended to Earth, and I have caused offense by not avoiding your sacred presence. May I ask where the Bodhisattva is going?" "I have come," replied the Bodhisattva, "especially to bring this fiend to submission."

"What was this fiend's origin," said Pilgrim, "that it should necessi-

tate your golden form revealing itself in order to bring him to submission?" The Bodhisattva said, "He is actually the golden-haired
wolf that I ride on. Because the lad who looks after him fell asleep, this
cursed beast managed to bite through the iron chains and come here
to dispel calamity for the king of the Scarlet-Purple Kingdom."

On hearing this, Pilgrim quickly bowed and said, "The Bodhisattva
is twisting the truth! The fiend has mocked the ruler and cheated him
of his queen here; he has corrupted the customs and violated the
mores. He has, in fact, brought calamity to the ruler. How could you
say that he has helped the king to dispel calamity?"

The Bodhisattva replied, "You have no idea that when the deceased
king of the Scarlet-Purple Kingdom was still on the throne, the
present king, then the crown-prince, was exceedingly fond of hunting
when he was a youth. Leading men and horses, mounting hawks
and hounds, he once came before the Phoenix-Down Slope, where
two young birds, one male and another female, were perching. These
happened to be the offspring of the Bodhisattva Great King Peacock.[8]
When the young prince stretched his bow, he wounded the male
peacock, and the female one, too, returned to the West with an arrow
stuck in her body. After the Buddha Mother had pardoned him, she
decreed that he should be punished by being separated from his mate
for three years and that his body should be inflicted with the illness of
yearning. At the time, I was riding this wolf when I heard the sentence pronounced. Little did I realize that this cursed beast would
remember it and come here to abduct the queen and dispel calamity
for the king. It has been three years now, and his preordained chastisement has been fulfilled. You are to be thanked for arriving to heal
the king, and I've come especially to bring the fiend to submission."

"Bodhisattva," said Pilgrim, "the story may go like this, but he has
also defiled the queen, corrupted the customs, upset the relations, and
perverted the law. He is worthy of death. Now that you have arrived
in person, I shall spare his life but not his living punishment. Let me
give him twenty strokes of my rod, and then you may take him away."
"Wu-k'ung," said the Bodhisattva, "if you appreciate my epiphany,
then you must, for my sake, grant him a plenary pardon. This will be
considered entirely your merit, that of bringing the fiend to submission. If you raise your rod, he will be dead!" As he dared not
disobey, Pilgrim had no choice but to bow and say, "After the Bodhisattva has taken him back to South Sea, he must not be permitted to

return in secret to the human world again, for he can cause a lot of harm."

Only then did the Bodhisattva cry out: "Cursed beast! If you don't return to your origin now, when will you do so?" Rolling once on the ground, the fiend immediately appeared in his original form. As he shook out his furry coat, the Bodhisattva mounted his back, only to discover with one look that the three bells beneath his collar were nowhere to be seen. "Wu-k'ung," said the Bodhisattva, "return my bells." "Old Monkey doesn't know anything about bells!" replied Pilgrim.

"You thievish ape!" snapped the Bodhisattva. "If you hadn't succeeded in stealing the bells, even ten of you would not have been able to approach him. Bring them out quickly!" "But really, I haven't seen them!" chuckled Pilgrim. "In that case," said the Bodhisattva, "allow me to recite the Tight-Fillet Spell a little."

At once alarmed, Pilgrim could only mutter, "Don't recite! Don't recite! The bells are here!" Thus it is that

From the wolf's collar who'll untie the bells?

The one untying asks the one who ties.

After the Bodhisattva had slipped the bells back onto the collar of the wolf, she mounted his back again. Look at him!

Beneath his four legs lotus blossoms grow;

O'er all his body thick golden threads glow.

The Great Compassion went back to South Sea, where we shall leave her.

We tell you instead about the Great Sage Sun, who, having tightened his skirt, wielded the iron rod to fight his way into the Cave of the Mythic Beast and slew all the rest of the fiends. Then he went into the palace to beckon the Lady Sage Palace to return to her country. The lady could not have been more grateful after Pilgrim gave her a thorough account of how the Bodhisattva had brought the fiend to submission and why she had to be separated from her mate. Then Pilgrim found some grass which he tied together to make a straw dragon. "Madam," he said, "climb on this and close your eyes. Don't be afraid. I'm taking you back to court to see your lord." The lady followed his instruction as Pilgrim began to exercise his magic power: all she heard was the sound of the wind.

In the period of half an hour they arrived at the capital. As they

dropped from the clouds, he said, "Madam, please open your eyes."
The queen opened her eyes and at once those dragon towers and
phoenix bowers which she readily recognized gave her immense
delight. She abandoned the straw dragon to ascend the treasure hall
with Pilgrim. When the king saw her, he hurried down from the
dragon couch. Taking the hand of the lady, he wanted to tell her
how much he had missed her when all of a sudden, he fell to the ground
crying, "Oh my hand! It hurts! It hurts!"

Pa-chieh broke out in loud guffaws, saying, "O dear! You just don't
have the luck to enjoy her. The moment you see her you are smitten
to death!" "Idiot," said Pilgrim, "you dare give her a tug?" "What'll
happen if I do?" asked Pa-chieh.

Pilgrim said, "The lady's body is covered with poisonous prickles,
and her hands are full of vicious stings. Since she reached the Unicorn
Mountain these three years, that fiend Jupiter's Rival has never
claimed her body. For the moment he touched her, his body or his
hands would be pained. On hearing this, the various officials exclaimed, "What shall we do?" So the officials outside the court
became vexed, and the ladies of the palace, too, were alarmed. Meanwhile, Jade Sage and Silver Sage, the two other consorts, helped the
ruler to his feet.

As they stood there in confusion, they heard someone calling out
in midair: "Great Sage, I've arrived!" Pilgrim raised his head to look,
and he heard

Majestic crane cries in the sky,
As someone drifted down to court.
Auspicious radiance encircling;
Creative auras tremulous.
A coir and grass coat wrapped in cloud and mist,
He trod straw sandals rarely seen.
He held a fly-swat of rushes;
A silk sash wound around his waist.
Throughout the world he had formed human ties;
Footloose, he roamed all the great earth.
This was the Great Heaven's Immortal Purple Cloud,
Bringing salvation this day to earth.

Going forward to meet him, Pilgrim said, "Chang Tzu-yang,⁹ where
are you going?" The Realized Immortal Tzu-yang went before the

court and bowed, saying, "Great Sage, this humble immortal Chang
Po-tuan raises my hand to salute you." Returning his bow, Pilgrim
said, "Where have you come from?"

The realized immortal said, "Three years ago, I was on my way to
a Buddha festival when I passed through this region. When I saw
that the king was destined to be separated from his mate, I feared that
the fiend might defile the queen and upset the human relation, so that
afterwards it would be difficult for the king and queen to be reunited.
I therefore changed an old coir coat of mine into a new shining robe,
radiant in five colors, to present to the fiend king as an addition to the
queen's wardrobe. The moment when she put it on, poisonous
prickles sprouted on her body, but actually those prickles were the
transformation of the coir coat. Now that I have learned of the Great
Sage's success, I have come to bring deliverance."

"In that case," said Pilgrim, "we are indebted to you for coming
from such a great distance. Please deliver her, quickly." The realized
immortal walked forward and pointed at the lady with his finger;
immediately, the coir coat came off and the lady's entire body was
smooth as before. Shaking out the coat, the realized immortal draped
it over himself and said to Pilgrim, "I beg your pardon, Great Sage,
for this humble immortal must take leave of you." "Please wait for a
moment," replied Pilgrim, "and allow the ruler to thank you." "No
need, no need," said the immortal, laughing. He gave a long bow and
rose into the air. The king, the queen, and all the officials were so
astonished that they all bowed toward the sky.

Thereafter, the king gave the order for the Eastern Hall to be opened
in order that the four priests might be thanked with a huge banquet.
After the king led his subjects to kowtow to the pilgrims, he was reunited with his wife. As they drank merrily, Pilgrim said, "Master,
take out that declaration of war." The elder took it out from his sleeve
to hand over to Pilgrim, who passed it to the king and said, "This
document was to be sent here by a junior officer of the fiend. The
officer had been beaten to death by me at first, and I took him here
to announce my merit. When I went back to the mountain afterwards,
I changed into the form of the officer to get inside the cave. That was
how I got to see the lady. After I succeeded in stealing the golden bells,
I was almost caught by the fiend. Then I had to undergo transformation to steal the bells again. When he fought with me, it was my
fortune that the Bodhisattva Kuan-yin arrived and brought him to

submission. She also told me of the reason why you and your queen had to be separated." After he gave a thorough account of what had taken place, the king and all his subjects were full of gratitude and praise.

"It was the great good fortune of a worthy ruler in the first place," said the T'ang monk, "and it was also the merit of our humble disciple. This lavish banquet you have given us is perfection indeed! We must bow to take leave of you now. Do not delay this humble cleric's journey to the West." Having failed to persuade the priests to stay longer even with earnest pleading, the king had the rescript certified. Then he asked the T'ang monk to take a seat in the imperial chariot, while he and his consorts pushed it with their own hands to send the pilgrim out of the capital before they parted. Truly,

With affinity, your anxious ailment's purged;
With no thoughts or desires your mind's at peace.

As they go forth, we do not know what sort of good or evil will befall them, and you must listen to the explanation in the next chapter.

Seventy-two

At Cobweb Cave the seven passions delude the Origin;
At Purgation Spring Pa-chieh loses all his manners.

We were telling you about Tripitaka, who took leave of the king of the Scarlet-Purple Kingdom and proceeded westward on his horse. He passed over numerous mountains and forded countless waterways. Soon, autumn departed and even winter faded, and it was again the bright, attractive season of spring. As master and disciples stepped on the green and enjoyed the scenery, they came upon some houses shaded by trees. Rolling over on his saddle, Tripitaka dismounted and stood by the main road. "Master," asked Pilgrim, "why are you not moving on when this road is so level and smooth?"

"Elder Brother," said Pa-chieh, "you are quite insensitive! Master must be rather tired of sitting on the horse. You can let him get down to catch his breath a little." "I'm not trying to catch my breath," said Tripitaka, "but I see that there's a household over there. I would like to go and beg some maigre for us to eat."

"Look at the way Master speaks!" said Pilgrim smiling. "If you want to eat, I'll go and do the begging. As the proverb says, 'Once a teacher, always a father.' How could the disciples remain seated while the master goes to beg for food?" "It's not like that," replied Tripitaka. "Usually we look out into the endless horizon, and regardless of how far you have to travel, you go to beg for food. Today, there's a household nearby, close enough for me to call you if I need help. You should therefore let me go and do the begging."

"But Master," said Pa-chieh, "you're not thinking properly. As the proverb says, 'When three persons go out, the youngest child suffers.' You belong to the paternal generation, and all of us are your disciples. As an ancient text says, 'When there's any hard work to be undertaken, the young must do it.'[1] Let old Hog go." "O disciples," said Tripitaka, "today the weather's fair and bright, unlike the times of wind and rain. In those days, you will, of course, do it, even if you have to cover great distances. Let me go now to this household; when I find out whether there's food or not, we'll leave."

"Elder Brothers," said Sha Monk, smiling on one side, "no need to talk further. Master's temperament is like that, and you need not contradict him. If you offend him, he won't eat the food even if you succeed in begging it." Pa-chieh agreed and took out the almsbowl for him. After Tripitaka changed his hat and cloak, he strode up to the village to look around. It was quite a nice dwelling. You see

A stone bridge arching up;
Aged trees thick and neat.
Where the stone bridge arches up,
Gurgling water flows to meet a long stream;
Where aged trees are thick and neat,
The songs of hidden birds reach distant hills.
On the bridge's other side are a few thatched huts,
Quaint and elegant like an immortal shrine;
There's also a window o'erlaid with reeds
That make it seem clearly a Taoist home.
Before the window four lovelies appear,
All stitching phoenixes and doing needlework.

When the elder saw that there was no man but only four young women in the house, he dared not enter. He stood still beneath the trees and found that each one of them seemed to have

A womanly mind firm as stone,
An orchid nature fine like spring.
Pink hues adorned her lovely face;
Her lips were smoothly dabbed by rouge.
Her moth brows were slanted crescents;
Her hair piled up gossamer buns.
If she stood among the flowers,
The bees would mistake her for one.

He waited there for at least half an hour, but the whole place was quiet, without even a sound from chickens or dogs. He thought to himself, "If I truly don't have the ability to beg a meal, I'll make my disciples laugh at me. They'll dare say, if the master could not even succeed in begging food, how could the disciples go and worship Buddha?"

The elder could not think of a better alternative; though he knew perhaps he should not proceed, he nonetheless walked up the bridge. After he had taken several steps, he could see that there was within the courtyard of the thatched hut a small pavilion made of sandalwood. Inside the pavilion, there were three other young women kicking a ball filled with air.[2] Look at these three girls, who were quite different from the other four. You see

Halcyon blue sleeves fluttering;
Light yellow skirts swaying.
Halcyon blue sleeves fluttering,
They enshroud dainty, jade-white fingers.
Light yellow skirts swaying,
They half reveal shoes slender and shapely.
Their postures and styles are perfection all;
In motion or rest their heels go through many forms.
To pass overhead they must gauge the height;
The long pass must be accurate and true.
A turning kick is "Flower Beyond the Wall";
Backing up becomes "Traversing the Sea."
Trapping gently a lump of dirt;
Charging alone with limbs parallel.
When "A Pearl Ascends Buddha's Head,"[3]
They seize and separate with the toe.
They can catch a slender brick;
They kick almost lying down.
They squat with a straight torso;
They twist and kick with their heels.
They pull and stamp quite noisily,[4]
Their capes seem most elegant.
Through the legs the ball freely goes
Or it loops around the neck.
They kick like the Yellow River flowing backward,
Or like gold fishes sold on the beach.
That one mistakes it as the head;
This one turns round and strikes at once.
Firmly the ball's held by the calf;
Squarely they slam with their toes.
Heels lifted, straw sandals fall;
Scissor kicks send the ball backward.
Stepping back throws shoulder pads off;
The hairpin only once goes awry.
As the hamperlike net hangs low,
They will then kick toward the gate.[5]

When the ball hits squarely the goal,
All the fair ladies shout, "Bravo!"
So, each one of the silk gowns is sweat-soaked and the make-
     up's greasy;
Only when interest slackens will they cry enough.

We cannot end the description, and we offer therefore also another testimonial poem. The poem says:[6]

Third month's the time they kick ball in a field,
These fair ones blown down by immortal wind.
Their faces perspire like flowers bedewed;
Their dusty mothbrows are willows in mist.
Shrouding their fingers, the blue sleeves hang low;
Light yellow skirts awhirl, they show their feet.
They finish their kicking all faint and fair
With jewels askew and dishevelled hair.

Tripitaka watched them until he could no longer tarry. He had to walk up to the arch of the bridge and call out in a loud voice, "Lady Bodhisattvas, this humble cleric has come here to beg for whatever amount of food you care to give me." When they heard his voice, all the girls abandoned their needlework and their ball. Smiling broadly, they came out of the door to say, "Elder, pardon us for not coming to meet you first when you arrived at our rustic village. Since we dare not feed a priest by the wayside, please take a seat inside."

On hearing this, Tripitaka thought to himself, "My goodness! My goodness! The West is truly the land of the Buddha. If women are concerned to feed the priests, how could men not revere the Buddha?" The elder walked forward and bowed before he followed the girls into the thatched hut. After they passed the pavilion made of sandalwood, he looked around. Ah! There were actually neither rooms nor corridors, only

Towering summits,
Extensive ranges.
Towering summits that touch the cloud and mist;
Extensive ranges that reach sea and isle.
The door's near a stone bridge,
Borne by flowing water of nine twists and turns;
The yard's planted with plums and peaches,
Vying for splendor with a thousand stalks and fruits.

Vines and creepers dangle from several trees;
Orchid spreads its scent through ten thousand flowers.
From afar the cave seems better than Isle P'êng;
Up close the mountain and woods surpass Mount Hua's.
It's the bogus immortals' reclusive place;
No other household takes its neighboring space.

One of the girls walked forward, pushed open two stone doors, and asked the T'ang monk to take a seat inside. The elder had little alternative but to walk inside, where he discovered no other furniture but stone tables and benches. It was dark, and the air seemed to have turned very chilly all of a sudden. Becoming alarmed, the elder thought to himself, "This place betokens more evil than good. It's not a nice place at all."

Still all smiles, the girls said, "Please be seated, elder." The elder had no choice but to sit down, and after a while, he was so cold that he began to shiver. "From which monastery did you come, elder?" asked one of the girls. "What sort of alms are you seeking? To repair bridges and roads, to build a monastery or a pagoda, or to fund a festival and print scriptures? Please take out your alms book for us to see." "I'm not a priest begging for alms," replied the elder. "If you are not," said the girl, "why have you come here?"

The elder said, "I'm someone sent by the Great T'ang in the Land of the East to go to the Great Thunderclap in the Western Heaven to acquire scriptures. Passing through your honored region, I became hungry, and that was the reason for my approaching your lovely mansion. After I have begged a meal from you, I shall leave." "Fine! Fine! Fine!" said the girls. "As the proverb says, 'Monks coming from afar can read sūtras better.' Sisters, we must not slight our guest. Let us prepare a vegetarian meal quickly."

At that time, three of the girls kept the elder company by speaking with him, rather animatedly, on the subject of karma. Four of the girls, however, rolled up their sleeves and dashed into the kitchen, where they added fire and scrubbed the pans. What did they prepare, you ask. Human flesh sauteed and fried in human lard until black enough that it could pass for pieces of fried wheat gluten. They also pan-fried some freshly gouged human brains which they then cut up to look like pieces of bean curd. Two dishes of these they took out to set on the stone table and said to the elder, "Please eat. In such a hurry, we haven't been able to prepare a good vegetarian meal for you. But do eat some food to relieve your hunger; there's more of it in the back."

Taking a whiff of the dishes, the elder clamped his mouth shut when he found the food to be so stinky and putrid. He rose and bowed with hands folded, saying, "Lady Bodhisattvas, this humble cleric has kept a vegetarian diet since his birth." "Elder," replied one of the girls, laughing, "these *are* vegetarian dishes."

"Amitābha!" cried the elder. "If I, a priest, partake of such vegetarian dishes, I won't ever get to see the World-Honored One or acquire the scriptures."

"Elder," said the girl, "you are someone who has left the home. You should never be choosy with your patrons!" "Would I dare? Would I dare?" said the elder. "Since this priest received the decree of the Great T'ang to go West, he has not destroyed even the tiniest creature and he has tried to relieve suffering wherever he sees it.

I feed myself, picking up grain by grain;
I clothe myself, knitting threads one by one.
How could I dare be choosy with my patrons?"

"Though you may not be choosy with your patrons, elder," said another girl, laughing, "you are not afraid to put the blame on people after walking in the door. Don't despise the coarse and the unseasoned. Eat a little, please!"

"Indeed, I dare not," replied the elder, "for I fear I may break the commandment. To nourish a life is not as good as delivering a life, lady Bodhisattvas. Please let me go."

The elder tried to struggle out of the door, but the girls barred the way, refusing, of course, to let him go. "A business right at our door," they cried, "and you expect us not to do it? 'You want to cover up a fart with your hand?' Where do you think you are going?" All of them, you see, knew a little martial art, and they were also quite dexterous with their hands and feet. Grabbing the elder, they yanked him forward like a sheep and flung him to the ground. He was pinned down by all of them, trussed up with ropes, and pulled over a crossbeam to be hung high up. The way in which he was hung, in fact, had a name to it: it was called "Immortal Pointing the Way." One of his arms, you see, was stretched forward and suspended by a rope; the other arm was tied up alongside the body, and the rope was then used to hang up the midsection. His two legs were bound together and hung up by a third rope. The elder thus dangled face down from the crossbeam, held by three ropes. Racked by pain, his eyes brimming with tears, the elder thought morosely to himself: "How bitter is the fate of this priest! I thought that I could beg a meal from a good family, but I landed in a fiery pit instead! O disciples, come quickly to save me, and we'll be able still to see each other again. Two more hours and my life will be finished!"

Though the elder was sorely distressed, he nonetheless was also observing the girls carefully. After they had tied and hung him up properly, they began to take off their clothes. Greatly alarmed, the elder thought to himself: "They are disrobing because they want to beat me, or they may want to devour me." But the girls were only taking off their upper garments. After they had their bellies exposed, they began to exercise their magic power. Out from their navels poured coils of thread, with the thickness of a duck egg; like bursting jade and flying silver, the threads had the entire village gate covered up in a moment.

We tell you now instead about Pilgrim, Pa-chieh, and Sha Monk, all waiting by the wayside. Two of them were watching the luggage and grazing the horse, but Pilgrim, always the mischievous one, was leaping from branch to branch as he picked the leaves and searched for fruits. He chanced to turn his head toward the direction his master had gone and saw all at once a mass of light. So alarmed was he that he leaped down from the tree, shouting, "It's bad! It's bad! Master's luck is turning rotten!" Then he pointed with his fingers and said to his companions, "Look what happened to that village!" Pa-chieh and Sha Monk stared at the place and saw the mass of light bright as snow and shiny as silver. "Finished! Finished!" cried Pa-chieh. "Master must have run into monster-spirits! Let's go rescue him, quickly!" "Don't shout, Worthy Brother," said Pilgrim, "for you haven't seen the truth of the matter. Let old Monkey go up there." "Be careful, Elder Brother," said Sha Monk, and Pilgrim replied, "I know what to do."

Dear Great Sage! Tightening up his tiger-skin skirt and whipping out his golden-hooped rod, he bounded up there in two or three leaps. There he discovered a dense mass of cords that had to be a thousand layers thick, weaving up and down in a weblike pattern. He touched the cords with his hand, and they felt soft and sticky. Not knowing quite what it was, Pilgrim lifted his iron rod and said to himself, "One blow of my rod can surely snap ten thousand layers of this thing, let alone a thousand layers!" He was about to strike when he stopped and thought to himself some more: "I can snap something hard, but this is quite soft. All I can do probably is to flatten it a little. But if I disturb whatever it is, it may have old Monkey all tangled up, and that won't be good. Let me ask a few questions first before I strike."

Whom would he question, you ask. He made the magic sign, you see, and recited a spell, which had the immediate effect of causing an old local spirit to go round and round in his shrine as if he were turning a millstone. His wife said to him, "Oldie, why are you turning round and round? Is your epilepsy acting up?" "You don't know about this! You don't know about this!" cried the local spirit. "There's a Great Sage, Equal to Heaven, here. I haven't gone to meet him, and now he's summoning me."

"Go and see him then," said his wife. "What are you spinning around here for?" "If I go see him," replied the local spirit, "I'll have to see his heavy rod also. Without regard for good or ill, he'll strike at me." His wife said, "When he sees how old you are, he won't strike you." The local spirit said, "All his life,

He loves to drink free wine,

He likes to beat old men!"

The two of them thus chatted for a while, but he could find no other alternative than to walk out of the shrine. Trembling all over, he went to his knees by the road and called out, "Great Sage, the local spirit of this region kowtows to you."

"Get up," said Pilgrim, "and don't look so harried without a reason. I'm not going to beat you, I'll just leave it on your account. Let me ask you, what is this place?" "Where did the Great Sage come from?" asked the local spirit. "We were going to the West from the Land of the East," replied Pilgrim.

The local spirit said, "Did the Great Sage pass through a mountain ridge?" "We are still up there," said Pilgrim. "Can't you see our horse and luggage over there?" "That," said the local spirit, "is the Cobweb Ridge, beneath which is a Cobweb Cave. There are seven monster-spirits inside the cave." "Are they male or female fiends?" asked Pilgrim, and the local spirit said, "Female." "What sort of magic powers do they possess?" asked Pilgrim again.

The local spirit said, "This humble deity has little strength or authority, and he can't determine what sort of abilities they may have. I only know that three miles due south of here, there's a Purgation

Spring, which is a natural hot spring. Originally, it was the bathing place for the Seven Immortal Dames of the Region Above. Since the monster-spirits arrived, they took over the Purgation Spring, and the Immortal Dames did not even bother to contend with them. They simply let the monster-spirits have the place. If, then, even

Heaven's immortals did not provoke these fiends,

Such spirits had to have great magic might."

"Why did the monster-spirits want the spring?" asked Pilgrim. The local spirit said, "After these fiends took it over, they bathed in it three times a day. They did once already today during the Hour of the Serpent,[7] and they would come back again by noon." On hearing this, Pilgrim said, "Local spirit, you may go back. Let me catch them by myself." After kowtowing one more time, the local spirit, still trembling, went back to his own shrine.

Our Great Sage all alone now exercised his magic power; with a shake of his body he changed into a tiny fly, alighted on a blade of grass by the road, and waited. In a moment, all he heard was loud breathing noises,

Like silkworms devouring leaves,

Like tide rising from the sea.

In approximately the time it took to drink half a glass of tea, all the threads disappeared and the village came into sight once more as before. Then he heard the wooden gates opened with a creak, and loud, laughing chatter brought out seven young women. As Pilgrim stared at them secretly, he saw that all of them walked side by side and hand in hand. Laughing and joking, they proceeded to cross the bridge. Some beauties indeed! They appeared to be

Jadelike but far more fragrant;

Flowerlike but their words were real.

Willow brows stretched like distant hills;

Scented mouths framed by cherry lips.

Kingfisher plumes rose on hair pins;

Small feet gleamed beneath crimson skirts.

They seemed like Ch'ang-o coasting to the world below,

And immortals going down to earth.

"No wonder my master wanted to beg a meal at this place!" chuckled Pilgrim to himself. "So there are such lovely creatures around here. If my master is kept by these seven beauties, he won't even make one meal for them, nor will he be able to last for two days if they use him.

If they take turns to handle him, he'll die on the spot. Let me eaves-drop on them and see what they plan to do."

Dear Great Sage! With a buzz, he flew off and alighted on one of the hair buns. After they crossed the bridge, one of the girls walking behind called out to those up front: "Elder Sisters, after we take our bath, let's go back and have that fat monk steamed for food." "This fiendish creature," chuckled Pilgrim to himself, "is so headless! Boiling will save them some firewood. Why does she want him steamed?"

Picking flowers and fencing with blades of grass as they headed south, those girls soon arrived at the bathing pool, which was en-closed by a magnificent wall.

Wild flowers lushly fragrant covered the ground;
On all sides were orchids both fresh and dense.
The girl in the back walked forward and pushed open two doors with a loud crack; inside there was indeed a large pool of hot water.

At the time of creation,
The original number of suns was set at ten.[8]
Later, Hou I, the archer, stretched his bow
And shot down nine of these suns,
Leaving only one sun behind,
The true fire of supreme yang.
There are nine hot springs in the world,
All transformations of the former suns.
These magic springs of yang are:
Fragrant-Cold Spring,
Mountain-Mate Spring,
Hot Spring,
Eastern-Fusion Spring,
Mountain-Flooding Spring,
Filial Spring,
Wide-Whirling Spring,
And Torrid Spring.
This is the Purgation Spring.
We have also a testimonial poem, which says:
One climate without heat or cold,
E'en in autumn it's ever spring.
Hot ripples like a boiling cauldron's;
Snowy waves like newly made soup.
Spilling out it warms the crops;

Its still body washes our dust.
Its bubbles seem like swelling tears;
It churns like jade liquified.
Such moisture was never brewed;
Self-heated, it's clear and smooth.
A good sign of auspicious land,
Truly it's Heaven's creation,
Where the beauties wash their smooth, ice-white skins,
All dirt removed, their jadelike frames renewed.

This bathing pool was about fifty feet wide and over one hundred feet long. Inside, it was about four feet deep, the water being so clear that one could see to the bottom. A jet of water, like rolling pearls and swelling jade, continued to bubble up from the base, and there were on all four sides some six or seven outlets for the water to drain. By the time it reached some rice paddies two or three miles away, the water would still be warm. Adjacent to the pool were three small pavilions; behind the middle one was placed an eight-legged bench, on both ends of which there were also colored lacquer garment racks. Secretly delighted by what he saw, Pilgrim spread his wings and landed with a buzz on one of those racks.

Seeing how warm and clear the water was, the girls immediately wanted to bathe in it. They took off their clothes, put them on the racks, and leaped into the pool together. Pilgrim saw them

Undoing their buttons and clasps,
Untying their sashes of silk.
Their bosoms were white like silver;
Their bodies all resembled snow.
Their limbs appeared gilded in ice;
Their shoulders seemed kneaded with dough.
Their bellies looked soft and yielding;
Their backs were both shiny and smooth.
Their knees and wrists were round and small;
Their feet, no wider than three inches.
Desire ringed their mid-sections:
They showed their apertures of love.

After jumping into the water, the girls began to leap and bounce on the water as they swam and frolicked. "If I want to hit them," thought Pilgrim to himself, "all I have to do is to stick my rod in the pool and give it a stir. That's called:

Pouring hot water on the rats,

You wipe out the entire nest.

Pity! Pity! I can kill them all right, but old Monkey's fame will diminish somewhat. As the proverb says, 'A man does not fight with a woman.' A fellow like me would look rather feckless if I beat to death a few of these scullions. No, I won't strike at them. I'll devise a plan that'll make them unable to move. That ought to do some good."

Dear Great Sage! Making the magic sign and reciting a spell, he changed with one shake of his body into an old, hungry hawk. You see

Feathers like snow and frost,

And eyes bright as the stars.

Seeing him, the fiendish fox loses its wits;

Meeting him, the wily hare's terrified.

Steel-like claws gleaming and quick;

His looks both fierce and heroic.

He uses his old fists to serve his mouth,

Ready to chase himself all things that fly.

He soars through vast stretches of frigid air,

Boring clouds, grasping things, without a care.

With a flap of his wings, the hawk flew up to the pavilion, stretched out his sharp claws, and picked the racks clean of the seven suits of clothing left draping there before darting back to the ridge, where he changed into his original form to meet Pa-chieh and Sha Monk.

Look at our Idiot now! He met Pilgrim and said, "So Master has been imprisoned in a pawn shop!" "How do you know?" asked Sha Monk. "Don't you see," said Pa-chieh, "that Elder Brother has robbed it of all its clothing?" Putting them down, Pilgrim said, "These are things worn by monster-spirits." "How could there be so many?" asked Pa-chieh.

Pilgrim said, "There are seven suits altogether." "How could you strip them so easily," asked Pa-chieh, "and so well?" "I didn't need to," replied Pilgrim. "This place, you see, is called the Cobweb Ridge, and that village actually bears the name of Cobweb Cave. Inside the cave are seven girls who, having captured our master and hung him up, went to take a bath in the Purgation Spring. That spring is actually a hot spring formed by Heaven and Earth. After they took their baths, the monster-spirits were planning to steam Master for food. I followed them there, and when I saw them disrobing and getting into the water, I wanted to strike at them. But I feared that I might soil my rod and lower my reputation, and that was why I didn't move my rod. Instead, I changed into a hungry, old hawk and grabbed all of their clothing. Too embarrassed to leave the pool, they just squatted in the water. Let us go quickly to untie Master and we can be on our way."

"Elder Brother," said Pa-chieh with a chuckle, "whenever you do anything, you always leave something behind. If you have seen monster-spirits, how could you not kill them and want instead to go untie Master? Though they are too embarrassed to leave the pool now, they'll come out once it is night. They must have some old clothes at home, which they can put on and then chase us down. Even if they don't chase us, they can remain here, and after we have acquired the scriptures, we will have to take this road back. As the proverb says,

Rather give up your travel expenses;
Never lack what your fist dispenses.

If they bar our way and give us trouble by the time we return from the West, we will meet up with enemies, won't we?"

"What do you want to do then?" asked Pilgrim. "As I see it," said Pa-chieh, "we must first slay the monster-spirits before we go untie Master. This is the plan of 'Mowing the Grass by Rooting It Out.'" "I don't want to strike at them," said Pilgrim. "If you do, you go ahead."

Elated and delighted, Pa-chieh held high his muckrake and ran up to the pool with big strides. As he pushed open the doors to look, he found those seven girls all squatting in the water and casting abuses at the hawk, crying, "That flattened-hair beast! That wretched outcast! May a big cat gnaw on his head! He seized our clothes! How could we move?"

"Lady Bodhisattvas," said Pa-chieh, hardly able to contain his giggles, "so you are taking a bath here. How about asking a priest like me to join you?" When they saw him, the fiends became angry. "You are a very rude priest!" they cried. "We are women in a home, and you are a man who has left the home. The ancient book said, 'By the seventh year, a man and a woman are not to sit on the same mat.' How could you bathe in the same pool with us?"

"It's so hot now," said Pa-chieh, "that there's no alternative. Don't be so fussy and let me wash with you. Stop throwing the book at me! What's all this about sitting and not sitting on the same mat!" Refusing to permit any further discussion, our Idiot abandoned his rake, took off his black silk shirt, and leaped into the water with a splash. More incensed than ever, the fiends rushed forward and wanted to hit him. Little did they know that Pa-chieh could be extremely agile once he landed in water. With a shake of his body he changed at once into a sheat fish spirit. All the fiends reached for him with their hands and tried to catch the fish; but as they dove toward him in the east, he darted to the west with a swoosh, and when they plunged their hands down in the west, he spurted to the east once more. All slimy and slippery, he darted madly between their legs. The water, you see, was about chest deep; after Pa-chieh swam around on top of the water for a while, he dove straight for the bottom, so tiring the fiends that they all collapsed, panting, in the pool.

Only then did Pa-chieh leap out of the pool, change back into his original form, put on his shirt, and take up his muckrake once more. "Who do you think I am?" he bellowed. "Just a sheat fish spirit?" When they saw him, the fiends were terrified. "You are the priest who came in just now," said one of them. "You changed into a sheat fish when you leaped into the water, and we couldn't catch hold of you. Now you look like this again. Where, in fact, did you come from? You must give us your name."

"So, you bunch of lawless fiends really don't recognize me!" said Pa-chieh. "I'm the disciple of the T'ang elder, someone from the Great T'ang in the Land of the East who is on his way to acquire scriptures. I am Chu Wu-nêng, Pa-chieh, the Marshal of Heavenly Reeds. You have my master hung up in a cave, and you are planning to have him steamed for food. *My* master! Steamed for food? Stretch out your heads at once, and receive a blow, each of you. I want to finish you off!"

When they heard these words, the fiends were frightened out of their wits. Going to their knees in the water, they cried, "We beg the Venerable Father to forgive us. We have eyes but no pupils and we caught your master by mistake. Though he is hanging there now, he has not been tortured. Please spare our lives in your mercy. We are willing to give you some travel money instead to send your master to the Western Heaven."

Waving his hand, Pa-chieh replied, "Don't talk like that! The proverb has put the matter very well:

Once I was by the candy man deceived,
I could never the sweet talker believe.

No matter what, I'm going to give you a blow of my rake. Then each of us can be on our way!"

As he had always been rather crude and rough, more intent on displaying his power than on showing pity and tenderness to women, our Idiot lifted up his rake and, without further regard for good or ill, rushed forward to attack them. Terribly flustered, the fiends were no longer concerned with embarrassment, but with the far more important matter of preserving their lives. Shielding their private parts with their hands, they leaped out of the water and stood by the pavilions to exercise their magic. All at once the threads began to pour out of their navels, and in no time at all, Pa-chieh was enclosed inside what appeared to be a huge silk tent. Discovering, when he raised his head, that the sky and the sun had suddenly disappeared, our Idiot wanted to run away, but alas, he could hardly even take a step! All over the ground ropes and cords were strewn to trip him up. The moment he moved his legs, he began to stumble: he headed to the left and his face hugged the ground; he went to the right and he fell head over heels; he turned around and his snout kissed the earth; he scrambled up only to do a handstand. He tumbled over countless times until his body turned numb and his legs flaccid, until his head swam and his eyes could not see straight. Unable even to crawl, all he could do was lie on the ground and moan. After the fiends had him trapped like that, they did not beat him or harm him in any way. Leaping out of the door of the pool, they ran back to the cave instead, using the cobweb as a shelter.

Having passed the stone bridge, they stood still and recited the magic spell again to retrieve the web. Then they darted into the caves, all naked, and ran past the T'ang monk, giggling and still covering their private parts with their hands. After they took out some old clothes to put on from one of the stone chambers, they went to the rear door and cried, "Children, where are you?" Each of the monster-spirits, you see, had an adopted son, their names being Bee, Hornet, Cockroach, Cantharis, Grasshopper, Maggot, and Dragonfly. Those monster-spirits, you see, once set up a huge web to have these seven insects captured and were about to devour them. But as the ancients said, "Fowl have fowl talk, and beasts have beast language." The insects pleaded for their lives, declaring their willingness to honor their captors as mothers. From that time since,

They picked a hundred spring flowers to serve the fiends;
They searched out summer plants to feed monster-spirits.

When the insects now heard the summons, they immediately gathered before the monster-spirits to say, "Mothers, why did you send for us?" "Sons," replied the fiends, "earlier this morning we provoked by mistake a priest who came from the T'ang court. His disciple just now had us trapped in the pool; not only were we put to dreadful shame, but we almost lost our lives also. You must exert your strength and go out to make him turn back. If you prevail, you may then go to your uncle's house to meet us." And so, having escaped with their lives, the fiends went to their elder brother's house, where their damnable mouths would stir up greater calamity, and where we shall leave them for the moment. Look at those insects! Rubbing their hands and fists eagerly, they all went forth to battle their enemy.

We tell you now about that Pa-chieh, who grew faint and dizzy from all those falls. After a while, however, he managed to raise his head a little and found that all the cords and threads had disappeared. He scrambled up rather cautiously; taking a step at a time and nursing his pain, he found his way back. When he saw Pilgrim, he tugged at him and said, "Elder Brother, is my face swollen and bruised?" "What happened to you?" asked Pilgrim.

Pa-chieh replied, "I was completely covered up by cords and threads that those fiends let out. They even had tripping tethers set up on the ground. I don't know how many times I fell, but my torso went limp and my back was about to break, unable to move even a single step. I got my life back and returned here only because the ropes and cords disappeared after a while." When he heard that, Sha Monk cried, "Finished! Finished! You have caused a disaster! Those fiends must have gone to the cave to harm Master. Let's go quickly to rescue him!"

On hearing this, Pilgrim began to run toward the village, followed by Pa-chieh pulling the horse. When they arrived at the stone bridge, their way was barred by seven little fiends, who cried, "Slow down! Slow down! We are here!" Taking a look at them, Pilgrim said to himself, "How laughable! They're all so tiny! Even the tallest is no more than two and a half feet, and the heaviest can't be more than ten pounds." He then bellowed at them, "Who are you?" The fiends replied, "We are the sons of the seven immortal dames. You have insulted our mothers, and now you dare even fight up to our door. Don't run away! Look out for yourself!" Dear fiendish creatures! They rushed forward and mounted a wild attack. Our Pa-chieh was already sorely annoyed by his falls; when he saw how tiny those insects were, he grew vicious and began to strike out with his rake.

When those fiends saw how savage Pa-chieh was, each of them changed back into his original form and flew up into the air, crying, "Change!" Instantly, one changed into ten, ten into a hundred, a hundred into a thousand, and a thousand into ten thousand—there were in no time at all countless insects. You see

The sky full of flying maggots,
The ground covered by dragonflies;
Bees, hornets, diving at your heads;
Cockroaches going for your eyes.
Cantharides bite your front and back,
And grasshoppers, your crown and feet.
A huge, black mass striking your face,
Its chirr would gods and spirits faze.

Alarmed, Pa-chieh said, "O Elder Brother, they may say that scriptures are easy to get, but on the road to the West, even insects bully people!" "Brother," said Pilgrim, "don't be afraid. Go and attack them quickly!" "My face, my head," cried Pa-chieh, "all over my body, there must be over ten layers of them! How am I going to attack them?" "It's nothing! It's nothing!" cried Pilgrim. "I have my abilities!" "O Elder Brother," cried Sha Monk, "whatever ability you have, bring it out! My bald head's swollen from their bites!"

Dear Great Sage! He pulled off a bunch of hairs and chewed them to pieces before spitting them out, crying, "Change! Yellow, spar . . ." "Elder Brother," interrupted Pa-chieh, "what sort of street talk are you using again? Yellow? Spar?" "You don't realize," replied Pilgrim, "that yellow means yellow hawk and spar is the sparrowhawk. We have also the kite, the gerfalcon, the eagle, the fishhawk, and the harrier. Those sons of the monster-spirits are seven kinds of insect, and my hairs have changed into seven kinds of hawk." The hawks, of course, were most able to peck at insects; one peck of their bills and a whole insect was devoured. They attacked also with their claws, and they knocked the insects down with their wings. Soon the insects were eliminated; not a trace of them could be found in the air, but there was over a foot of their corpses on the ground.

The three brothers then raced past the bridge to go into the cave, where they found their old master suspended from the beam and weeping. "Master," said Pa-chieh, walking up to him, "because you wanted to be hung for fun in here, you have made me fall who knows how many times!" Sha Monk said, "Let's untie Master first before we say anything more." Pilgrim at once had the rope cut and lowered his master. "Where did the monster-spirits go?" he asked. The T'ang monk said, "They ran to the back, all naked, to call for their sons." "Brothers," said Pilgrim, "come with me to go look for them."

Holding their weapons, the three of them searched in vain for the fiends in the rear garden, even after they had climbed some of the peach and pear trees. "They are gone! They are gone!" said Pa-chieh. Sha Monk said, "No need to look for them anymore. We should go and wait on Master." The brothers returned to the front to ask the T'ang monk to mount up. "You two take Master out first," said Pa-chieh. "Let old Hog use my rake on their residence so that they'll have no place to live if they return." "Using your rake is a waste of strength," chuckled Pilgrim. "Why don't you find some firewood, and you'll finish everything off for them."

Dear Idiot! He indeed located some rotted pine, broken bamboo, dried willow, and dead creepers; he started a fire and soon the entire cave-dwelling was burned to the ground. Master and disciples then felt more at ease to proceed. Aha! After their departure, we do not know what will happen to the fiends, and you must listen to the explanation in the next chapter.

Seventy-three

Feelings, because of old enmity, beget calamity;
Trapped by a demon, the Mind Lord luckily breaks the light.

We were telling you about the Great Sage Sun who supported the
T'ang monk to proceed on the main road to the West with Pa-chieh
and Sha Monk. In a little while, however, they came upon some
towered buildings with palatial features and ornaments. Reining in his
horse, the T'ang monk said, "Disciple, can you tell what sort of a place
that is?" Raising his head to look, Pilgrim saw
Mountains ringing the buildings;
A brook rounding the arbors;
A dense variety of trees before the door;
Most fragrant wild flowers outside the house.
An egret resting in the willows
Seemed like jade immaculate in the mist;
An oriole singing amidst the peach
Appeared as brilliant gold within the flames.
Wild deer in pairs
Trod on green grass without a thought or care;
Mountain fowl by twos
Flew and chattered high above the redwood tips.
Truly it seemed like Liu and Juan's T'ien-t'ai cave,[1]
A fairy haunt, an immortal's house no less.
"Master," said Pilgrim, "that is neither the residence of kings or dukes
nor a house of the noble or the rich. It looks rather like a Taoist temple
or a Buddhist monastery, and we'll know for sure when we get there."
On hearing this, Tripitaka whipped his horse forward. As they arrived
before the door, master and disciples discovered a stone plaque
mounted on the door, which had on it the inscription, Yellow Flower
Temple. Tripitaka dismounted.

Pa-chieh said, "A Yellow Flower Temple has to be the home of a
Taoist. It might be good for us to go in and meet him. Our attire may
be different, but we follow the same practices of austerity." "You are

right," said Sha Monk, "we can go in and enjoy the scenery a bit in the first place, and we can also graze and feed the horse in the second. If it's convenient, we can ask them to prepare some food for Master to eat."

The elder agreed and the four of them went inside. On both sides of the second-level door was mounted the following new year couplet:

Yellow sprout, white snow[2]—an immortal's house;

Jasper grass, jade flowers—a feathered one's[3] home.

"This," said Pilgrim, chuckling, "is a can-carrying Taoist, who burns rushes, refines herbs, and works the fire in the reaction vessels."

Giving him a pinch, Tripitaka said, "Be careful with your words! Be careful with your words! We are not acquaintances or relatives of his, and we're staying here temporarily. Why should we mind what he's doing?" He had not quite finished the sentence when they went through the second-level door. The main hall was entirely closed up, but in the east corridor they saw a Taoist sitting there and making drugs and pills. How was he attired, you ask.

He wore a lacquered gold cap of scintillating red
And a dark, long robe of luminous black.
He trod on cloud-patterned shoes of spreading green;
He knotted a Master Lü sash of swaying yellow.
His face seemed like an iron gourd;
His eyes shone like bright stars.
His nose loomed up like a Mohammedan's;
His lips curled outward like a Tartar's.
Thunderbolts lay hidden in his Taoist mind,
Taming tigers and dragons, a true feathered one.

Seeing him, Tripitaka said in a loud voice, "Old immortal, this humble cleric bows to you." Jerking up his head and startled by the sight, the Taoist abandoned the drugs in his hands, pressed down his hair pin hurriedly, tidied his clothes, and walked down the steps to say, "Old master, forgive me for not coming to meet you. Please be seated inside."

Delighted, the elder went up to the main hall; pushing open the door, he saw the sacred images of the Three Pure Ones, before which were urns and incense laid out on a long sacrificial table. The elder took up several sticks of incense and stuck them into the urns. Only after he had bowed three times to the images did he greet the Taoist once more and took the guest seats with his disciples. The Taoist called for tea to be served at once, whereupon two young lads rushed inside to look for the tea tray, to wash out the tea cups, to scrub the tea spoons, and to prepare tea fruits. All their scurrying about soon disturbed those several fated enemies.

The seven female fiends of the Cobweb Cave, you see, were once schoolmates of this Taoist when they studied the magic arts together. After they had put on the old clothes and given instruction to their adopted sons, they came to this place. At this moment, they were cutting up cloth for clothes when they saw the lads busily preparing tea. "Lads," they asked, "who are the guests who have arrived that send you into such a frenzy?" "Four monks walked in just now," replied the lads, "and Master asked for tea to be served at once." "Was there a white, stoutish priest?" asked one of the female fiends. "Yes," they replied. "Another one with long snout and huge ears?" she asked again. "Yes," they replied. "Go take the tea outside quickly," said the female fiend, "and wink to your master as you do so. Ask him to come in, for I have something important to tell him."

The divine lads indeed took five cups of tea out to the main hall; smoothing out his clothes, the Taoist picked up a cup and presented it with both hands to Tripitaka. Then he served Pa-chieh, Sha Monk, and Pilgrim. After tea, the cups were collected, and as they did so, one of the lads winked at the Taoist. At once he arose and said, "Please be seated all of you. Lads, put away the trays and keep our guests company. I'll be back soon." The master and his disciples went outside of the hall with one lad to enjoy the scenery, and we shall leave them for the moment.

We tell you now about that Taoist, who went back to the abbot chamber, where he found those seven girls all going to their knees and saying, "Elder Brother! Elder Brother! Listen to what your sisters have to say." Raising them with his hands, the Taoist said, "When you first came, you told me already that you wanted to speak to me. It just so happened that the drugs I was preparing today had to avoid being exposed to females, and that was why I did not respond. Now there are guests outside. Can we talk later?"

The fiends said, "What we have to tell you, Elder Brother, can be told only with the arrival of your guests. When they leave, there'll be no need for us to tell you anymore." "Look at the way my worthy sisters speak!" said the Taoist with a chuckle. "What do you mean that it can be told only when the guests are here? Are you mad? Let's not say that I am one of those who cultivates the art of immortality in purity and quiescence. Even if I were a profane person burdened with the care of wife, children, and other domestic affairs, I would still have to wait for the guests to leave before I took care of my own business. How could you be so ill-behaved and cause me such embarrassment? Let me go out." All tugging at him, the fiends said, "Elder Brother, please don't be angry. Let us ask you, where did those guests come from?" Red in the face, the Taoist did not answer them.

One of the fiends said, "Just now the lads came in to fetch tea, and I heard that they were four monks." "So what if they are monks?" said the Taoist angrily. "Among these four monks," said the fiend, "there is a rather plump one with a white face, and there is also one who has a long snout and huge ears. Have you asked them where they came from?" "There are indeed two monks like that," replied the Taoist, "but how did you know? Have you seen these two somewhere before?"

"Elder Brother," said one of the girls, "you really don't know all the intricacies behind the matter. That monk with the white face happens to be someone sent by the T'ang court to seek scriptures in the Western Heaven. This morning he came to our cave to beg for food. Since your sisters have long heard of the reputation of the T'ang monk, we seized him." "Why did you want to do that?" asked the Taoist.

The girl said, "We have long heard people say that the T'ang monk possesses a true body that has practiced self-cultivation for ten incarnations. Anyone who eats a piece of his flesh will attain longevity. That's why we seized him. Later, we were trapped in the Purgation Stream by that priest with a long snout and huge ears. First he robbed us of our clothing; then he grew even bolder and wanted to bathe with us in the same pool. We couldn't stop him, of course. After he jumped into the water, he changed into a sheat fish spirit and darted back and forth between our legs. He was such a rogue that we thought he would surely assault us. Then he leaped out of the water and changed back into his original appearance. When he saw that we would not yield to him, he took up a nine-pronged muckrake and tried to kill us all. If we hadn't used a little of our intelligence, we would have been slain by him. We managed to flee, though terror-stricken, with our lives, and then we told your nephews to go fight with the monk. We didn't tarry, however, to learn whether they remained dead or alive, for we came straight here to find refuge. We beg you, for the sake of our friendship as schoolmates once, to exact vengeance this day for us."

When he heard these words, the Taoist became so angry that his color changed and his voice quivered. "So, these monks are so insolent, so villainous!" he said. "Relax, all of you. Let me take care of them!" Thanking him, the girls said, "If Elder Brother wants to fight, we'll help you." "No need to fight! No need to fight!" said the Taoist. "As the proverb says, 'You suffer three percent loss already once you fight!' Follow me instead, all of you."

The girls followed him into his room; placing a ladder behind his bed, he climbed up to the crossbeam and took down a small leather case, approximately eight inches high, a foot long, four inches wide, and bolted by a small copper lock. From his sleeve the Taoist also took out a goose-yellow handkerchief, tied to the fringes of which was a tiny key. He opened the lock and took out a small package of medicine, which was, you see,

The dung of all mountain birds
Collected to a thousand pounds.
When cooked in a copper pot,
The time and heat were both even.
A thousand pounds made just one cup,
Which was reduced to three pinches.
Three pinches were then pan-fried,
Cooked, and refined still some more.
This poison was produced at last,
Rare as fine jewels and gems.
Anyone who took one taste
Would see King Yama in haste!

"Sisters," said the Taoist to the girls, "if I want to feed this treasure of mine to an ordinary mortal, all I need is a thousandth part of a tael and the person will die when it reaches his stomach. Even an immortal will perish if he ingests three thousandth parts of a tael. These monks, I suppose, might be fairly accomplished in the Way, and they'll need the larger dosage. Bring me a scale quickly."

One of the girls quickly took up a small scale and weighed in twelve thousandth parts of a tael of this poison, which she then divided into four portions. The Taoist then took twelve red dates, into each of which he added about a thousandth part of the drug after he had crushed slightly the date with his fingers. The twelve dates were then placed inside four tea mugs, while two black dates were placed in another tea mug. After the mugs were filled with tea and put on a tray, he said to the girls, "Let me go question them. We'll let them go if they are not from the T'ang court. But if they indeed came from the court, I will ask for a change of tea, and you will send the lads out with this tea. The moment they drink this, every one of them will perish. You will be avenged, and your anguish will be relieved." The girls could not have been more grateful.

Putting on a new robe to affect a show of courtesy, the Taoist walked out and asked the T'ang monk and his disciples to take the guest seats once more. "Please forgive me for my absence, old master," he said. "Just now I had to go inside to give instruction for my young students to pick green vegetables and white turnips, so that they could prepare a meal for you." "This humble cleric," replied Tripitaka "came to see you with empty hands. How could I dare accept a meal from you?"

Chuckling, the Taoist said, "You and I are both persons who have left the home. The moment we see a temple's gate, we can count on receiving a little emolument. How could you mention empty hands? May I ask the old master, which monastery do you belong to? Why are you here?" "This humble cleric" said Tripitaka, "has been sent by the Throne of the Great T'ang in the Land of the East to go acquire scriptures from the Great Thunderclap Monastery in the Western Heaven. We were just passing through your immortal residence and we came in to see you in all sincerity."

On hearing this, the Taoist beamed and said, "The master is a Buddha of great virtue and great piety. This humble Taoist was ignorant of this, and he was remiss in not going the proper distance to wait for you. Pardon me! Pardon me!" He then called out: "Lad, go and change the tea quickly, and tell them to hurry up with the food." The little lad ran inside, and he was met by the girls who said to him, "There's fine tea here, all prepared. Take it out." The lad indeed took out the five tea mugs.

Immediately the Taoist presented with both hands one of the mugs containing the red dates to the T'ang monk. When he saw how huge a person Pa-chieh was, he took him for the senior disciple, while Sha Monk he regarded as the second disciple. Pilgrim, being the smallest, was taken to be the youngest disciple, and only the fourth mug was given to him.

Pilgrim was exceedingly perceptive. The moment he accepted the tea mug, he saw that the one left on the tray had two black dates in it. "Sir," he said at once, "let me exchange my mug with yours." "To tell you the truth, elder," said the Taoist, smiling, "a poor Taoist in the mountains does not always have on hand the proper tea condiments. Just now I personally searched in the back for fruits and found only these twelve red dates, with which I made four mugs of tea to serve to you. Your humble Taoist did not want to fail to bear you company, and that was why I made a fifth cup of tea with dates of less desirable color. It's an expression of respect from this poor Taoist."

"How could you say that?" replied Pilgrim with a chuckle. "As the ancients said,

He who is at home is never poor;
It's real poverty when he's on tour.

You live here. How could you claim to be poor? Only mendicants like us are really poor! Let me exchange with you. Let me exchange with you." On hearing this, Tripitaka said, "Wu-k'ung, this is truly the hospitality of our immortal. Drink it. Why do you want to exchange it?" Pilgrim had no choice but to hold the mug in his left hand; he covered it with his right and stared at the rest of his companions.

We tell you now about that Pa-chieh, who was both hungry and thirsty, and he had always had a huge appetite. When he saw that there were three red dates in the tea, he picked them up and swallowed them in two gulps. His master ate them, and Sha Monk, too, ate them. In a moment, however, Pa-chieh's face turned pale, tears rolled down from Sha Monk's eyes, and the T'ang monk foamed at the mouth. Unable to remain in their seats, all three of them fainted and fell to the ground.

Realizing that they had been poisoned, our Great Sage hurled the tea mug in his hand at the face of the Taoist. The Taoist shielded himself with upraised hand, his sleeve stopping the mug and sending it crashing to the floor. "How boorish can you be, priest!" snapped the Taoist angrily. "How dare you smash my tea mug?"

"You beast!" scolded Pilgrim. "What do you have to say about those three persons of mine? What have we done to you that you should want to use poisoned tea on us?" "Yokel," said the Taoist, "you've caused great calamity! Don't you know?" "We've just entered your door," replied Pilgrim, "and we've barely announced where we came from. We haven't even engaged in any lofty debate. How could we cause any calamity?"

"Didn't you beg for food at the Cobweb Cave? Didn't you bathe at the Purgation Spring?" asked the Taoist. Pilgrim said, "Those bathing in the Purgation Spring were seven female fiends. If you mention them, you must know them, and that means you, too, have to be a monster-spirit. Don't run away! Have a taste of my rod!" Dear Great Sage! He pulled out the golden-hooped rod from his ear and gave it a wave; immediately it grew to have the thickness of a rice bowl. He struck at the face of the Taoist, who stepped aside quickly to dodge the blow before meeting his opponent with a treasure sword.

As the two of them brawled and fought, the noise aroused the female fiends inside, who surged out, crying, "Spare your efforts, Elder Brother. Let your sisters capture him." When Pilgrim saw them, he became angrier than ever. Wielding the iron rod with both hands, he hurled himself into their midst and attacked them wildly. All seven of the fiends at once loosened their clothes and exposed their snow-white bellies to exercise their magic. From their navels threads and cords poured out, which became, in no time at all, a huge awning that had Pilgrim entirely covered down below.

Sensing that the tide was turning against him, Pilgrim at once recited a spell and somersaulted right through the top of the awning to escape. He suppressed his anger to stand still in midair to look at those bright shiny cords produced by the fiends: weaving back and forth, up and down, as if guided by a shuttle, they formed a huge web which in an instant had the entire Yellow Flower Temple enshrouded and removed it clean out of sight. "Formidable! Formidable!" said Pilgrim to himself. "It was a good thing that I didn't fall into their hands! No wonder Chu Pa-chieh fell so many times! But what shall I do now? My master and my brothers have been poisoned, and I have no idea even of the background of these fiends who have banded themselves together. I'd better go and question that local spirit once more."

Dear Great Sage! He lowered his cloud, made the magic sign with his fingers, and recited a spell beginning with the letter Ừ*m* to summon once more the local spirit. Trembling all over, the aged god knelt by the road and kowtowed, saying, "Great Sage, you were going to rescue your master. Why did you turn back here?"

"We did manage to rescue my master earlier," said Pilgrim, "but we ran into a Yellow Flower Temple not far from where we left you. We went inside with our master to have a look, and we were met by the temple master. As we visited with him, my master and my brothers were poisoned by his poisoned tea. Luckily, I didn't drink it and I attacked him with my rod. He began to talk about begging food at the Cobweb Cave and bathing in the Purgation Spring, and I knew that that fellow was also a fiend. Just as we were fighting, the seven girls came out and emitted their silk cords, but old Monkey was smart enough to escape. Since you have been a god here for some time, I thought you must know their background. What kind of monster-spirits are they? Tell me the truth, and I'll spare you a beating."

Kowtowing, the local spirit said, "The monster-spirits haven't quite lived here for a decade. This humble deity made some investigation three years ago and uncovered their original form: they are seven spider spirits. Those silk cords they produce happen to be cobwebs." Delighted by what he heard, Pilgrim said, "If what you say is true, it's nothing unmanageable. You go back, and let me exercise my magic to bring them to submission." After one more kowtow the local spirit left.

Pilgrim went up to the Yellow Flower Temple and pulled off from his tail seventy pieces of hair. Blowing a mouthful of immortal breath on them, he cried, "Change!" and they changed into seventy small Pilgrims. Then he blew also on the golden-hooped rod, crying, "Change!" and it changed into seventy rods forked at one end. To each of the small Pilgrims he gave one of these rods, while he himself took up one also. They stood by the mass of silk cords and plunged the rods into the web; at a given signal, they all snapped the cords and then rolled them up with their rods. After each of them had rolled up over ten pounds of the cords, they dragged out from inside seven huge spiders, each about the size of a barrel. With arms and legs flailing, with their heads bobbing up and down, the spiders cried, "Spare our lives! Spare our lives!" But those seventy small Pilgrims had them completely pinned down and refused to let go.

"Let's not hit them yet," said Pilgrim. "Let's tell them to return our master and our brothers." "Elder Brother," screamed the fiends, "return the T'ang monk to him and save our lives!" Dashing out, the Taoist said, "Sisters, I wanted to eat the T'ang monk. I can't save you." Infuriated by what he heard, Pilgrim cried, "If you don't return my master, take a good look at what your sisters will become!" Dear Great Sage! One wave of the forked staff and it changed back into his original iron rod, which he raised with both hands to smash to pulp those seven spider spirits. After he had retrieved all his hairs with two shakes of his tail, he wielded the iron rod and sped inside all by himself to search for the Taoist.

When the Taoist saw his sisters being beaten to death, he was struck by remorse and immediately met his opponent with upraised sword. In this battle each of them was full of hate as he unleashed his magic powers. What a marvelous fight!

The fiend wielded his treasure sword;
The Great Sage raised his golden-hooped rod.
Because of the T'ang court's Tripitaka,
All seven girls were first sent to their deaths.
Now the hands of rectitude showed their might
To work with magic the golden-tipped rod.
The Great Sage was strong in spirit,
The bogus immortal, audacious.
Their bodies went through the most florid moves;
Their two hands like a windlass spun and turned.
The sword and the rod banged aloud;
Low-hung and grey were the clouds.
With cutting words
And clever schemes,
As in a picture they charged back and forth.
They fought till the wind howled and sand flew to scare tigers and
      wolves;
Till Heav'n and Earth darkened, and the stars themselves removed.

That Taoist withstood the Great Sage for some fifty rounds when he gradually felt his hands weakening. All at once he seemed to have been completely drained of his strength. He therefore quickly untied his sash and took off his black robe with a loud flap. "My son!" said Pilgrim with a chuckle. "If you're no match for someone, stripping isn't going to help you!" But after the Taoist took off his clothes, you see, he raised up both of his hands and exposed a thousand eyes grown on both ribs. Emitting golden beams, they were terrifying indeed!

Dense yellow fog,
Bright golden beams.
Dense yellow fog
Spurted out from his two armpits like clouds;
Bright golden beams
Jetted from these thousand eyes like flames—
Like barrels of gold left and right,
Like copper bells both east and west.
This was a bogus immortal's magic,

The divine might of a Taoist.
Blinding the eyes, the sky, and the sun and moon
This dried hot air descended like a coop
And had the Great Sage Sun, Equal to Heaven,
Confined in golden beams and yellow fog.

Terribly flustered, Pilgrim spun around and around in the golden beams, unable even to take a step forward or backward. It was as if he had been imprisoned inside a barrel. As the blast of heat was becoming unbearable, he got desperate and leaped straight up into the air to try to pierce the golden beams. The beams were too strong, however, and he was sent hurtling back to the ground head over heels. Then he felt pain, and when he touched quickly that part of his head where it had rammed the golden beams, he could feel that the skin had softened somewhat. Sorely annoyed, he thought to himself, "What rotten luck! What rotten luck! Even this head of mine today has become useless! In former times, the blows of scimitars and axes could not harm it one whit. How could slamming into the golden beams now soften the skin? It may fester afterwards, and I may end up with a permanent sore even if it heals." After a while, the blast of heat was again becoming unbearable, and he thought to himself further, "I can't go forward or backward, I can't move left or right. I can't even crash out of here by going upward. What shall I do? All right, I'd better take the low road and get the mother out of here!"

Dear Great Sage! Reciting a spell, he changed with one shake of his body into a pangolin, also named scaly anteater. Truly

His four iron claws
Could bore through hills and rocks like sifting flour;
His scaly frame
Could pierce cliffs and ridges like cutting scallions.
Two luminous eyes
Seemed like a pair of refulgent stars;
A sharp, pointed beak,
Stronger than any steel chisel or diamond drill.
This was pangolin of medical fame;
Scaly anteater was his vulgar name.

Look at him! Hardening his head, he burrowed right into the ground and did not emerge again until he was some twenty miles away. The golden beams, you see, had managed to cover a distance of only some ten or twelve miles. After he changed back to his original form, he was overcome by fatigue and his whole body ached. Bursting into tears, he wailed:

O Master!
Since I left by faith the mountain that year,
We came West together in unceasing toil.
We had no fear for billows of the sea.
How could we capsize in a small gully?

As the Handsome Monkey King vented his grief, he suddenly heard someone weeping also behind the mountain. He rose, wiped away his tears, and turned to look; a woman in garb of heavy mourning, with a bowl of cold rice soup in her left hand and a few pieces of yellow paper money in her right, came toward him, sobbing every step of the way. Nodding his head, Pilgrim sighed to himself, "Truly as they say,

The person shedding tears meets the tearful one;
He whose heart's broken sees the broken heart.

I wonder why this woman is crying. Let me question her a bit."

In a short while, the woman came up to where he was standing, and Pilgrim bowed to say, "Lady Bodhisattva, for whom are you weeping?" "My husband," said the woman, blinking back her tears, "had a dispute with the master of the Yellow Flower Temple when he tried to buy some bamboos from him, and he was poisoned to death by that master with poisoned tea. I am taking some money to his grave to be burned, in order to repay his kindness as a spouse." When Pilgrim heard these words, tears rolled down his cheeks. On seeing that, the woman said to him angrily, "You are so senseless! I grieve on account of my husband. How dare you mock me with your tears and your sorrowful countenance?"

Bending low, Pilgrim said, "Lady Bodhisattva, please don't be angry. I am Pilgrim Sun Wu-k'ung, the senior disciple of Tripitaka T'ang, the bond-brother and royal envoy of the Great T'ang in the Land of the East. We were journeying to the Western Heaven when we had to rest the horse in the Yellow Flower Temple. We ran into a Taoist in that temple, some kind of a monster-spirit, who had made a fraternal alliance with seven spider spirits. Those spider spirits wanted to harm my master in the Cobweb Cave, but Pa-chieh, Sha Monk, my two brothers, and I succeeded in having him rescued. The spider spirits, however, went to the temple to tattle on us, claiming instead that we intended to assault them. My master and my brothers were poisoned by the tea offered by the Taoist, and all three of them including our horse are now trapped in the temple. Only I didn't drink his tea. When I smashed his tea mug, he fought with me, and those seven spider spirits also came out to let loose their silk cords to try to ensnare me. When I escaped through my magic power, I questioned the local spirit and learned of their original form. Then I used my Magic of Body-Division and pulled out the fiends by rolling up their webs. After I beat them all to death with my rod, the Taoist wanted to avenge them and fought once more with me. When he was about to be defeated after some sixty rounds, he took off his clothes to expose a thousand eyes on his two ribs. They emitted countless golden beams to have me completely enclosed, and I found it practically impossible to move at all. That was when I had to change into a scaly anteater to escape by boring through the ground. I was grieving just now when I heard you weeping, and that was why I questioned you. When I saw that you had at least paper money to repay your husband but I had nothing at all to thank my late master, I grieved even more. How could I dare mock you?"

Putting down her rice soup and paper money, the woman bowed to Pilgrim and said, "Don't be offended. I had no idea that you, too, are a victim. According to what you've told me, I can tell that you don't recognize that Taoist. He is actually the Demon Lord of a Hundred Eyes, and he is also called the Many-Eyed Fiend. But if you are capable of such a transformation that you could do battle with him for so long and still escape his golden beams, you must have great magic powers. Nevertheless, you still can't get near that fellow. Let me recommend a sage to you; with her assistance, you will surely be able to overcome those golden beams and bring the Taoist to submission."

On hearing this, Pilgrim bowed hurriedly and said, "Lady Bodhisattva, if you have such information, please instruct me. Tell me who is the sage so that I can go and solicit her assistance. If I succeed in getting her here, I shall be able to rescue my master and avenge your husband's death." "Even if I tell you, however," said the woman, "and even if you manage to get her here to subdue the Taoist, I fear that you will be able only to exact vengeance. You won't be able to rescue your master." "Why not?" asked Pilgrim.

The woman said, "That fellow's poison is most potent. After a person has been poisoned by the drug, even his bones and marrow will deteriorate after three days. Your journey to find the sage may prevent you from saving your master in time." "I know how to move fast on the road," replied Pilgrim. "No matter how great the distance is, half a day is all I need."

The woman said, "In that case, listen to me. About a thousand miles from here there is a mountain by the name of the Purple Cloud Mountain. At the Thousand Flowers Cave in the mountain, there is a sage by the name of Pralambā.[4] She is able to subdue this fiend." "Where is this mountain?" asked Pilgrim. "Which direction should I take?" Pointing with her finger, the woman answered, "Due south of here." When Pilgrim turned to look, the woman immediately vanished.

Pilgrim was so startled that he bowed hurriedly, saying, "Which one of the Bodhisattvas are you? Your disciple has been somewhat dazed from all that burrowing in the ground and he can't recognize you. I beg you to leave me your name so that I can thank you properly." From midair came the announcement: "Great Sage, it's I." Pilgrim looked up quickly and found that it was the Old Dame of Li Mountain.[5] He rushed up to midair to thank her, saying, "Old Dame, where did you come from to enlighten me?" The Old Dame said, "I was just going home from the Festival of the Dragon-Flower Tree. When I learned of your master's ordeal, I revealed myself under the guise of a mourning wife in order to deliver him from death. You must go to Pralambā quickly, but you must not reveal that it was I who gave you the instruction. That sage tends to put blame on people."

After Pilgrim thanked her, they parted. Mounting his cloud-somersault, Pilgrim at once arrived at the Purple Cloud Mountain. As he stopped his cloud, he saw the Thousand Flowers Cave, outside of which

Fresh pines enshroud the lovely scene;
Jade cedars surround a home divine;
Green willows fill the mountain paths;
Strange blossoms clog the brook and rill;
Fragrant orchids ring a stone house;
Scented grass on the ridges glistens.
The flowing stream's jade-green throughout;
The clouds hollow old trees seal up.
Wild fowl sing melodiously;
Quiet deer walk leisurely.
Each bamboo's refined, stalk by stalk;
Each red plum unfurls, leaf by leaf.

A cold crow rests on an old tree;
A spring bird squeals on a tall bough.
Summer wheat grows wide as the fields;
Autumn grain aplenty on the ground.
No leaf would fall in four seasons;
All flowers bloom in eight periods.
Auspicious air will rise often to the sky
And hallowed clouds will reach the great grand void.

In great delight, our Great Sage walked inside, level by level, and there was no end to the sight of this gorgeous scenery. But there was not a person in view; the place was completely silent, with not even the sound of a chicken or a dog. "Could it be," he thought to himself, "that the sage is not home?" He walked further in for another few miles when he came upon a Taoist nun sitting on a couch. How did she look, you ask.

She wore a five-flower patterned silk cap;
She had on a robe of knitted gold threads.
She trod on cloud-patterned phoenix-beak shoes;
A double-tassel silk sash wrapped her waist.
Her face had age like autumn after frost;
Her voice cooed like spring swallows before the shrine.
She had long known the Three Vehicles Law,[6]
Her mind often fixed on the Four Great Truths.[7]
The void intuited bore true right fruit;
Intelligence formed gave freedom complete.
This was the Buddha of Thousand Flowers Cave,
Who was called Pralambā, a noble name.

Without stopping, Pilgrim walked right up to her and called out: "Bodhisattva Pralambā, I salute you." Descending from her couch, the Bodhisattva folded her hands to return his greeting and said, "Great Sage, sorry for not coming to meet you. Where did you come from?" "How could you recognize me as the Great Sage all at once?" asked Pilgrim.

Pralambā said, "When you brought great disturbance to the Celestial Palace that year, your image was spread throughout the universe. Which person would not know and recognize you?" "Indeed," replied Pilgrim, "as the proverb says,

The good thing will not leave the door;
The evil deed will go a thousand miles.

I bet you didn't know that I have repented and entered the Buddhist gate." "When did you do that?" said Pralambā. "Congratulations! Congratulations!"

"I escaped with my life recently," said Pilgrim, "in order to give protection to the T'ang monk, who had been commissioned to go seek scriptures in the Western Heaven. My master ran into the Taoist of the Yellow Flower Temple and was poisoned by his poisoned tea. When I fought with that fellow, he had me enclosed in his golden beams, though I escaped through my magic power. When I heard that the Bodhisattva could extinguish his golden beams, I came here especially to solicit your assistance."

"Who told you that?" said the Bodhisattva. "Since attending the Feast of Ullambana Bowl, I haven't left my door. With my name completely hidden, no one knows me. How did you know?" "I'm a devil in the earth!" replied Pilgrim. "No matter where you are, I can find you." "All right! All right!" said the Bodhisattva. "I shouldn't leave, but if the Great Sage comes here in person, I will not destroy the good deed of scripture seeking. I'll go with you."

After he thanked her, Pilgrim said, "Pardon my ignorance and my urging. But what sort of weapon do you need to take along?" The Bodhisattva said, "I have a little embroidery needle which can undo that fellow." Pilgrim could not resist saying, "Old Dame has misled me! If I had known that only an embroidery needle was needed, I wouldn't have troubled you. Old Monkey himself can supply a whole load of such needles!" Pralambā said, "That needle of yours is only made of steel or metal, and it can't be used. This treasure of mine is not made of steel, iron, or gold. It is rather a product cultivated in the eyes of my son."

"Who is your son?" asked Pilgrim. "The Star Lord Orionis," replied Pralambā. Pilgrim was quite astonished. Soon, they saw the bright, golden beams, and Pilgrim said to her, "That's where the Yellow Flower Temple is." Whereupon Pralambā took out from underneath her collar an embroidery needle, not more than half an inch long and as slim as a piece of eyebrow hair. Holding it in her hand, she threw it into the air, and after a little while, a loud crack at once dissipated the golden beams.

"Bodhisattva," cried Pilgrim, exceedingly pleased, "it's marvelous! Just marvelous! Let's find the needle! Let's find the needle!" "Isn't this it?" asked Pralambā as she held out her palm. Pilgrim dropped down from the clouds with her and walked inside the temple, where they found that Taoist sitting there with tightly shut eyes and unable to move. "You brazen fiend!" scolded Pilgrim. "You're pretending to be blind!" He whipped out the rod from his ear and wanted to strike, but Pralambā tugged at him, saying, "Don't hit him, Great Sage. Let's go see your master first."

Pilgrim went directly back to the guest chambers, where the three pilgrims were still lying on the ground and foaming at their mouths. "What'll I do? What'll I do?" cried Pilgrim, shedding tears.

"Please don't grieve, Great Sage," said Pralambā. "Since I came out the door today, I might as well accumulate some secret merit. I'm going to give you three tablets which will serve as an antidote to the poison." As Pilgrim bowed quickly to receive them, the Bodhisattva took out from her sleeve a small, punctured paper wrap. Inside were three red pills which she handed over to Pilgrim, telling him to put one in each of the pilgrim's mouth. Prying open their teeth, Pilgrim stuffed the pills into their mouths; in a little while, as the medicine reached their stomachs, they began to retch. After the poisonous substance had been thrown up, they regained consciousness. Our Pa-chieh was the first to scramble up, crying, "This nausea's killing me!" Tripitaka and Sha Monk also woke up, both crying, "I'm so dizzy!" "You've all been poisoned by the tea," said Pilgrim, "and you should now thank the Bodhisattva Pralambā for rescuing you." Tripitaka arose and tidied his clothes to thank her.

Pa-chieh said, "Elder Brother, where is that Taoist? Let me question him why he wants to harm us in this manner." Pilgrim at once gave a thorough account of what the spider spirits had done. More and more incensed, Pa-chieh said, "If this fellow has formed a fraternal alliance with spider spirits, he, too, must be a monster-spirit." "There he is now," said Pilgrim, pointing with his finger, "standing outside the temple and pretending to be blind." Pa-chieh took up his rake and tried to rush out, but he was stopped by Pralambā, who said to him, "Heavenly Reeds, please calm yourself. The Great Sage knows that there's no other person at my cave. I would like to take the Taoist back and make him guard my door."

Pilgrim said, "We are all indebted to your great kindness. How could we not comply? But please make him change back into his original form for us to see." "That's easy," replied Pralambā, who went forward and pointed at the Taoist. Immediately, he fell to the dust and appeared in his true form: a huge centipede some seven feet long. Lifting him up with her small finger, Pralambā at once mounted the auspicious clouds to head for the Thousand Flowers Cave. Raising his head to stare after her, Pa-chieh said, "This Mama is quite formidable! How could she overpower such a vicious creature just like that?" Smiling, Pilgrim said, "I asked her whether she needed any weapon to break up the golden beams, and she told me that she had a tiny embroidery needle, a product cultivated in the eyes of her son. When I asked for his identity, she said that it was Star Lord Orionis. Now, the Star Lord is a rooster; so this Mama, I suppose, must be a hen. Chickens are the deadliest foes of centipedes, and that's why she could bring him to submission."

On hearing this, Tripitaka kowtowed some more before saying, "Disciples, let's pack up and leave." Sha Monk found some rice and grain inside, with which he prepared a meal. After master and disciples ate their fill, they led the horse and poled the luggage out. Once his master walked out the door, Pilgrim started a fire in the kitchen, which reduced the entire temple to ashes in no time at all. Truly

Thanks to Pralambā, the T'ang monk came to life;
Intelligent nature destroyed the Many-Eyed Fiend.

We do not know what will happen to them as they proceed, and you must listen to the explanation in the next chapter.

Long Life reports how vicious the demons are;
Pilgrim displays his transformation power.

Desires and feelings come from the same cause;
It's natural to have feelings and desires.
For all those who took the poverty vow,
Zen is desires and feelings all severed.
You must take care
To persevere,
Like the bright moon, spotless, high in the sky.
Make no mistake as work and merit advance;
Perfection yields a great enlightened god.

We were telling you about Tripitaka and his disciples, who broke through the web of desires and leaped clear of the stronghold of feelings. Urging the horse, they journeyed to the West, and soon it was the end of summer and the beginning of autumn, when the fresh cool permeated their bodies. You see

The rains the waning heat assail
As one wu-t'ung leaf turns pale.
Fireflies dot the sedged path at night;
Crickets chirp in the moon's bright light.
The mallows unfurl in the dew;
Red smartweeds the sandbars endue.
Rushes are first to decline
When cicadas sadly repine.

As they walked along, Tripitaka suddenly saw a tall mountain whose summit pierced the green void, truly touching the stars and blocking the sun. Alarmed, the elder called out to Wu-k'ung, "Look at the mountain ahead of us! It's so tall, I wonder if there's a road to take us through it." "What are you talking about, Master?" said Pilgrim, chuckling. "As the proverb says,

The tall mountains will have their passageways;
The deep waters will have their ferryboats.

How could there be no road to take us through! You may proceed without worry." On hearing this, the elder smiled in delight and urged his horse to go straight up the tall ridge.

They had not traveled more than a few miles when they came upon an old man with flowing white hair all tousled and sparse whiskers like swaying silver threads. He had a string of beads around his neck and held a dragon-headed staff. Standing far up the mountain slope, he cried out in a loud voice: "The elder going to the West, you must stop your horse and pull back the reins. There is a group of fiendish demons in this mountain who have devoured all the mortals in the world. You can't proceed!"

On hearing these words, Tripitaka paled with fright. The road was already none too level, and the announcement made him even more insecure on the saddle, so much so that he fell down at once from the horse with a thud and lay moaning in the grass, hardly able to move. Pilgrim went over to raise him up, saying, "Don't be afraid! Don't be afraid! I'm here." "Just listen to that old man on the tall cliff," said the elder. "He said that there is a group of fiendish demons in this mountain who have devoured all the mortals of the world. Who is courageous enough to go question him and learn the truth of the matter?"

"You sit on the ground first," said Pilgrim, "and let me go question him." Tripitaka said, "But your looks are hideous and your words, vulgar. If you offend him, I fear that you'll not be able to get to the truth." Laughing, Pilgrim said, "I'll change into someone more attractive to go question him." "You change first for me to see," said Tripitaka.

Dear Great Sage! Making the magic sign with his fingers, he shook his body and changed at once into a neat young priest, truly with

Lovely eyes and clear brow,
A round head and a square face.
When he moved, he acted like a gentleman;
When he spoke, he used no vulgar language.

Shaking loose his silk shirt, he ran up to the T'ang monk and said, "Master, is this a good transformation?" "It is, indeed!" said Tripitaka, exceedingly pleased. "How could it not be!" remarked Pa-chieh. "But he has put all of us down! Even if old Hog rolled around for two, three years, he couldn't change into someone this attractive!"

Dear Great Sage! Slipping away from them, he walked right up to the old man and bowed, saying, "Dear *Kung-kung*, this humble cleric salutes you." When the old man saw how young the priest was, though most attractive in looks, he hesitated a little before returning his salute half-heartedly. Patting the head of Pilgrim with his hand, the old man giggled and said, "Little priest, where did you come from?" "We came from the Great T'ang in the Land of the East," replied Pilgrim, "on our way specially to the Western Heaven to seek scriptures from Buddha. When we arrived here, we heard your announcement about the fiends. My master was quite frightened, and he asked me to come question you to learn exactly who these monster-spirits are who dare cut short our way. May I trouble you to tell me in detail, so that I can send them into exile."

With a laugh, the old man said, "You are so young a priest that you don't know any better. That's why you mouth these inappropriate words. The magic powers of those demons are enormous. How dare you say that you would send them into exile?" "The way you put the matter," said Pilgrim, laughing also, "seems to indicate that you feel rather protective toward them. You must be a relative of theirs, or at least an intimate neighbor. Otherwise, why would you exalt their intelligence, magnify their virtues, and refuse to disclose thoroughly their background?" Nodding his head, the old man smiled and said, "You *are* a priest who knows how to wag your tongue! You must have followed your master as a mendicant into the world and picked up a little magic here and there. You can summon a ghost or bind a spirit, I suppose, and exorcise a few houses for someone. But you haven't run into those truly vicious fiends!"

"How vicious?" asked Pilgrim. The old man said, "One letter of those monster-spirits to the Spirit Mountain, and all five hundred of those arhats will come to meet them. One tiny card sent to the Celestial Palace, and each of the Eleven Great Luminaries will honor it. The dragons of the Four Oceans have been their friends, and the immortals of the Eight Caves have met with them frequently. The Ten Kings of Hell address them as brothers, and all the deities of major shrines and cities regard them as friends."

When he heard this, the Great Sage could not restrain his loud guffaws. Tugging at the old man with his hand, he said, "Stop talking! Stop talking! If those monster-spirits were the servants and houseboys, the brothers and friends of mine, then what they are about to do would not be so significant. Let me tell you this: when they see this young priest coming, they'll move to some place else this very night. They won't even wait for the morning!"

"Little priest, you're babbling!" said the old man. "That's blasphemy! Which gods or sages are your servants and houseboys?" Laughing, Pilgrim said, "To tell you the truth, the ancestral home of this young priest used to be the Water-Curtain Cave of the Flower-Fruit Mountain, located in the Ao-lai Country. My surname is Sun, and my name is Wu-k'ung. Some years ago, I was also a monster-spirit who performed great deeds. During a party with some other demons, I drank a few cups of wine too many and fell asleep. In my dream two men took me to the Region of Darkness with a summons, and I was so riled that I used my golden-hooped rod to beat up the spirit judge and terrify King Yama. I almost overturned, in fact, the entire Hall of Darkness. Those presiding judges were so frightened that they brought out papers, on which the Ten Kings of Hell affixed their signatures, declaring that if I spared them a beating, they would serve me as my servants and houseboys."

"Amitābha!" cried the old man, on hearing this. "This monk has told such a tall tale that he will never grow any taller!" "Sir," replied Pilgrim, "I'm tall enough now!" "How old are you?" asked the old man. "Give it a guess," said Pilgrim. The old man said, "Seven or eight perhaps." With a chuckle, Pilgrim said, "I am about ten thousand times seven or eight years old! Let me bring out my old features for you to see. But you must not be offended." "How could you have some other features?" said the old man. "This young priest," said Pilgrim, "has in truth seventy-two features."

As that old man was somewhat dim-witted, he kept urging the Great Sage, who gave his own face a wipe and changed back into his original form. With protruding fangs and a gaping mouth, with two bright red buttocks half-covered by a tiger skin skirt, and with a golden-hooped rod in his hands, he stood verily like a living thunder god below the ledge. When the old man saw him, he paled with fright as his legs turned numb. Unable to stand up, he fell down with a thud, and when he scrambled up, he stumbled once more. "Venerable Sir," said the Great Sage, approaching him, "there's nothing to be afraid of. I'm ugly but kindly disposed. Don't be afraid! Don't be afraid! I am grateful to you for informing us of the demons. Just how many are there, tell me the whole truth, so that I can thank you properly."

Trembling all over, the old man could not utter a word; pretending also to be deaf, he refused to reply.

When Pilgrim saw that he would not talk, he turned and went back down the slope. "Wu-k'ung," said the elder, "have you returned? Did you find out anything?" "It's nothing! It's nothing!" answered Pilgrim, laughing. "There is, to be sure, a handful of monster-spirits near the Western Heaven. The people here, however, are quite timid, and they worry about them. It's nothing! It's nothing. I am here!" "Have you asked him," said the elder, "what mountain this is, what kind of a cave there is in it, how many fiends there are, and which road can take us to Thunderclap?"

Pa-chieh spoke up, saying, "Master, don't be offended by what I have to say. If we are interested in waging a contest in transformations, in playing hide-and-seek, and in pulling pranks on people, even five of us are no match for Elder Brother. But if you consider honesty, then even a column of him cannot rival me." "Exactly! Exactly!" said the T'ang monk. "You are more honest." "I don't know," said Pa-chieh, "why it is that he always takes care of the head but disregards the tail. He has only asked a couple of questions, and then he runs back lamely. Let old Hog go now and find out the truth." "Wu-nêng," said the T'ang monk, "do be careful."

Dear Idiot! He stuffed the muckrake into his belt and tidied his shirt before swaggering up the mountain slope and calling out to the old man, "*Kung-kung*, I'm bowing to you." After the old man had seen Pilgrim walking off, he managed to struggle up with the help of his staff and, still trembling all over, was about to leave. When he caught sight of Pa-chieh, however, he became more terrified than ever. "Holy Father!" he cried. "What sort of nightmare is this, that I have to meet up with this bunch of nasty people? That monk who left just now was hideous all right, but he had at least three percent human looks. But just look at the pestle mouth, the rush-leaf fan ears, the sheet iron face, and the bristled neck of this monk! He doesn't even look one percent human!"

"This old *Kung-kung*," said Pa-chieh, chuckling, "is not too pleasant, for he loves to criticize people. How do you regard me, really? I may be ugly, but I can stand scrutiny. Just wait a moment, and I'll look more attractive." When the old man heard him speaking at least in a human fashion, he had no choice but to ask him, "Where did you come from?"

Pa-chieh said, "I'm the second disciple of the T'ang monk, and my religious name is Wu-nêng Pa-chieh. Just now the priest who questioned you was called Wu-k'ung Pilgrim, my Elder Brother. Because my master blamed him for offending you and for not being able to obtain the truth, he sent me specially to question you again. We would like to know what mountain this is, what's the name of the cave in the mountain, how many fiends there are in the cave, and which is the main road to the West. May we trouble you to point these out to us." "Are you being truthful with me?" asked the old man. Pa-chieh said, "There has never been the teeniest fakery in my whole life." "You are not," said the old man, "putting on a high-falutin show like the priest before." "No, I'm not like him," said Pa-chieh.

Leaning on his staff, the old man said to Pa-chieh, "The mountain is called the Lion-Camel Ridge of eight hundred miles, and in it there is a Lion-Camel Cave where you will find three archdemons." "Pshaw!" cried Pa-chieh. "You're too fussy an old man! Only three demons, and you have to take all that trouble to announce them to us!" "Aren't you afraid?" asked the old man. "To tell you the truth," replied Pa-chieh, "one blow of my Elder Brother's rod will kill one of them, and one blow of my rake will kill another; I have a younger brother, too, and one blow of his fiend-routing staff will kill the third one. When all three of the demons are slain, my master will cross this ridge. What's so difficult about that?"

Smiling, the old man said, "This monk is completely ignorant! The magic powers of those three archdemons are vast indeed! Moreover, those small fiends under their command number five thousand on the south summit, and five thousand also on the north summit. Those stationed to guard the road leading east number ten thousand, and another ten thousand are guarding the road leading west. There must be five thousand on the patrol teams, and those guarding the cave entrance must run to another ten thousand. There are countless fiends tending the fires and gathering firewood. All in all, they must have some forty-seven or -eight thousand troops, each equipped with a name plate. They devote themselves to devouring humans in this place."

When our Idiot heard these words, he ran back, trembling all over. As he approached the T'ang monk, he dropped his rake and, instead of giving his report, began to evacuate his bowels. "Why aren't you giving us a report?" snapped Pilgrim. "Why are you squatting there?"

"I'm so scared," replied Pa-chieh, "that even my shit has come out! There's no further need for me to talk. Let's scatter while there's still time to save our lives!"

"This root of idiocy!" said Pilgrim. "I never was frightened when I asked the questions. How is it that when you go, you lose your mind?"

"What is in fact the matter?" asked the elder also.

Pa-chieh said, "The old man told me that this mountain is named the Lion-Camel Mountain. In it there is a Lion-Camel Cave, where three old fiends and forty-eight thousand little fiends reside and devote themselves to devouring humans. The moment we put one step on the side of their mountain, we'll become food in their mouths. We can't ever proceed!" On hearing this, Tripitaka began to shake all over as his hairs stood on end, saying, "Wu-k'ung, what shall we do?"

"Master, relax," said Pilgrim, laughing, "it's no big thing! There may be a few monster-spirits here, I suppose, but the people of this region are very timid. They frighten themselves with all this rumor about how many fiends there are and how big they are. Look, you have *me*!" "Elder Brother," said Pa-chieh, "you shouldn't talk that way! I'm not like you, and what I learn is the truth. It's not a rumor. The whole mountain and the whole valley are filled with fiendish demons. How could we go forward?"

"The mouth and face of an idiot!" said Pilgrim, chuckling, "Allow nothing to scare you! If the whole mountain and the whole valley are full of fiendish demons, old Monkey will use his rod. Half a night and they'll all be exterminated!" "Shame on you! Shame on you!" said Pa-chieh. "Stop the big talk! It'll take seven or eight days for those monster-spirits just to take their roll call. How could you exterminate them so readily?" "How do you think I'm going to slay them?" asked Pilgrim. "Suppose they let you grab them," replied Pa-chieh, "bind them, or stop them dead with the Magic of Immobilization. Even then, you can't kill all of them so quickly."

With a laugh, Pilgrim said, "No need for grabbing or binding. I give this rod of mine a yank on both ends, crying, 'Grow!' and it'll be four hundred feet long. Next, I wave it once, crying, 'Thicken!' and it'll have an eighty foot circumference. I roll it toward the south of the mountain once, and five thousand fiends will be crushed to death; I roll it toward the north of the mountain once, and another five thousand will be crushed to death. Then I roll it once from east to west, and forty or fifty thousand, who cares how many, will be reduced to meat patties."

"Elder Brother," said Pa-chieh, "if you roll them down like you roll out dough for noodles, you might finish them off by the second watch." "Master," said Sha Monk, laughing on one side, "what are you afraid of when Big Brother has such vast magic powers! Mount up and get going!" When the T'ang monk heard them debating about their abilities, he had no choice but to calm himself and climb up on the horse.

As they proceeded, they discovered that the old man who came to inform them had vanished. "*He* must be a fiend," said Sha Monk, "who exploited deliberately the reputation and power of the demons to come and frighten us." "Don't jump to any conclusion," said Pilgrim. "Let me go have a look."

Dear Great Sage! Leaping up to the peak, he looked all around without spotting anyone. As he turned his face, however, he saw colored mists flickering in the air. He immediately leaped up on the clouds to give chase and soon he caught sight of the Gold Star Venus. Rushing up to the god, Pilgrim tugged at him with his hands and used his vernacular name to address him, saying, "Long Life Li! Long Life Li! You're such a rogue! If you have anything to say, you should have said it to my face. Why did you assume the appearance of an old country bumpkin to beguile me?"

The Gold Star saluted him hurriedly and said, "Great Sage, I'm sorry for not informing you sooner. Please forgive me! Please forgive me! These archdemons, possessive of vast magic powers, indeed make for a rugged hurdle. If you exercise all your powers in transformation and all your cleverness, you may pass through. If you but slacken a little, it'll be difficult for you to proceed." Thanking him, Pilgrim said, "I'm grateful! If this is such a difficult place to traverse, please go to the Region Above and request from the Jade Emperor some celestial soldiers to assist old Monkey." "We have plenty of those for you," replied the Gold Star. "Once I bring your message up there, we can round up even one hundred thousand celestial soldiers if you need them."

Pilgrim took leave of the Gold Star and dropped from the clouds to face Tripitaka. "That old man," he said, "who came to bring us the information happened to be the Star Venus." Folding his hands before him, the elder said, "Disciple, catch up with him quickly, and ask him whether there is another road we can take." "There's no detour," said Pilgrim, "for this mountain as it is is eight hundred miles across. I don't even know how wide it is on both sides. How could we take a detour?"

On hearing this, Tripitaka could not restrain the tears flowing from his eyes. "Disciple," he said, "if it's so difficult, how could I ever hope to worship Buddha?" "Stop crying! Stop crying!" Pilgrim said, "Once you cry, you become worthless. This information of his can't be all true, for his main purpose is to arouse our vigilance. As the saying goes, 'To tell is to exaggerate.' Please dismount and sit here for the moment." "What sort of discussion are we having now?" said Pa-chieh.

"No discussion," replied Pilgrim. "You just stand here and guard Master with all diligence, while Sha Monk can watch the horse and the luggage. Let old Monkey go up the ridge to do a little detection to see just how many fiends there are. I'll catch one of them and question him thoroughly; if need be, I'll even make him write up a confession and list in detail the names of all their old and young. Then I'll order them to close up their cave and forbid them from barring our way, so that Master will be able to go through this place peacefully and quietly. Only then will you perceive the ability of old Monkey!" All Sha Monk could say to him, however, was, "Be careful! Be careful!"

"No need for all your instructions!" said Pilgrim with a laugh. "Once I get up there,

I'll open a pathway even if it's the Great Eastern Sea;
I'll punch an opening if its an ironclad mountain."

Dear Great Sage! Whistling, he mounted the cloud-somersault to leap up to the tall summit, where he pushed aside the creepers and vines to look all around. There was, however, not a sound or a trace of human beings. He spoke aloud to himself, "I've made a mistake! I've made a mistake! I should never have let the oldie Gold Star go. He was actually trying to frighten me. If there's any monster-spirit around here, he would have jumped out and played in the wind, or he would fool with his lance or rod to practice his martial art. How is it that there is no one . . ." As he was thus talking to himself, he heard the loud bangs of a rattle behind the mountain. Turning hurriedly to look, he discovered a little fiend, hauling a banner on his shoulder which had on it the inscribed word, command. He had a bell tied to his waist, and he was beating a rattle with his hand as he walked from north to south. Pilgrim stared at him and thought that he was about twelve feet in height. Smiling to himself, Pilgrim said, "He must be a postal soldier on his way to deliver a document. Let me eavesdrop on him to see what he has to say."

Dear Great Sage! Making the magic sign with his fingers, he recited a spell and changed, with one shake of his body, into a fly. He flew up to his cap and alighted gently on it to eavesdrop on the fiend. After he had turned onto the main road, the little fiend kept beating his rattle and shaking his bell, while he mumbled to himself, "Those of us patrolling the mountain should all be on guard against that Pilgrim Sun. He knows how to change into a fly." Astounded by what he heard, Pilgrim said to himself, "He must have seen me! How could he know my name and how could he know I might change into a fly, if he hadn't?"

But that little fiend, you see, had not seen him. It was actually those archdemons who somehow managed to give this instruction to the little fiends, and this one was just repeating what he heard. Pilgrim, of course, did not know this; suspecting that he had been seen, he was about to slay the fiend with the rod when he thought to himself, "I recall that the Gold Star told Pa-chieh that there were three old fiends and some forty-seven or -eight thousand little fiends. If those little fiends are like this one, another forty thousand won't make a bit of difference. But I wonder how powerful are those three old demons. Let me go question him, then I can raise my hands."

Dear Great Sage! How is he going to question him, you ask. He leaped down from his cap and alighted instead on a tree to allow the little fiend to walk a few steps ahead. Quickly he changed into another little fiend, having, in fact, the same clothes and like him, beating the rattle, shaking the bell, hauling the banner, and mumbling the same words. The only difference was that he was several inches taller than the other fiend. He ran up to the other little fiend and called out, "You on the road, wait for me."

Turning around, the little fiend said, "Where did you come from?" "My good man!" said Pilgrim with a giggle. "Can't you recognize someone from the same family?" "You're not in our family," said the little fiend. "What do you mean?" said Pilgrim. "Take a good look."

"But you look unfamiliar," said the little fiend. "I don't recognize you! I don't recognize you!" "I know I look unfamiliar," replied

Pilgrim. "I'm one of those who tend the fires, and you've seldom met me."

Shaking his head, the little fiend said, "Never! Never! Even among those brothers in our cave who tend the fires, there's no one with a pointed mouth like yours." Pilgrim thought to himself, "I've made my mouth a little too pointed." He lowered his head at once and gave his mouth a rub, saying, "My mouth's not pointed!" Immediately, his mouth was not pointed anymore.

"Just now," said the little fiend, "your mouth *was* pointed. How could it change like that after you gave it a rub? How baffling! You can't very well belong to our family! I have never seen you before! It's too suspicious! Moreover, the domestic laws of our great kings are very strict: those who tend the fires always tend the fires, and those who patrol the mountain will patrol the mountain. They couldn't have asked you to tend the fires, and then asked you also to patrol the mountain, could they?" Exceedingly clever with his mouth, Pilgrim at once replied, "You have no idea that our great kings had promoted me, when they saw how good I was at tending the fires, and asked me to patrol the mountain."

The little fiend said, "All right. There are forty of us who patrol the mountain to one platoon, and we have altogether ten platoons. Each of us is different in age, and each has a different name. To prevent confusion among the ranks and to facilitate taking the roll, our great kings gave us each a name plate. Do you have one?"

Now Pilgrim had changed into a semblance of only what he could see of the little fiend; namely, how he was dressed and what he was doing. Since he had not seen the plate, he, of course, did not have it on him. Dear Great Sage! Refusing to admit that he had none, he followed the drift of the question instead and said, "How could I not have a plate? I just received a brand new one. But you take out yours first for me to have a look."

Completely unaware that this was a trick, that little fiend hitched up his clothes and pulled out for Pilgrim to see a gold-lacquered plate, which was tied to his body with a small cotton thread. On the back of the plate Pilgrim saw the inscription, In Command of All Demons. In front there were three printed words: Little Wind Cutter. He thought to himself, "It goes without saying that those who patrol the mountain will be named some sort of Wind Cutters." He therefore said to the little fiend, "Lower your clothes now, and let me show you my plate." Turning to one side, Pilgrim yanked off a small piece of hair from the tip of his tail and gave it a pinch, whispering, "Change!" It changed at once into another gold-lacquered plate which had attached to it also a small cotton thread. On it were the three printed words: Chief Wind Cutter. When he took it out and showed it to him, the little fiend was greatly taken aback. "We are all named Little Wind Cutters," he cried, "but how could you have the name of Chief Wind Cutter?"

As he had always acted with the greatest calculation and spoken with the utmost shrewdness, Pilgrim immediately said, "You really have no idea that our great kings promoted me to be a patrol commander when they saw how well I tended the fires. They also gave me a new plate with the name, Chief Wind Cutter, and the charge that I would lead the forty of you in this platoon." On hearing this, the fiend bowed hurriedly, saying, "Captain, Captain, you've just been commissioned, and that's why you look unfamiliar. Please forgive me for offending you with my words."

"I won't blame you," chuckled Pilgrim as he returned his bow. "But I do have a request: an introductory gift of five ounces of silver per person." "Don't be too impatient, Captain," said the little fiend. "Let me join up with my platoon at the south of the ridge, and we'll all chip in." "In that case," said Pilgrim, "I'll go with you." Indeed, the little fiend walked ahead, while the Great Sage followed him.

In less than a few miles, they came upon a pen peak. Why was it called a pen peak, you ask. On that mountain the peak rose straight up for some forty or fifty feet, as a pen sticking up from its rack. Hence the name. After Pilgrim went up there, he gave his tail a wag and leaped to the tallest point to sit down. "Wind Cutters," he cried, "gather around!" All those Little Wind Cutters bowed to him down below, saying, "Captain, we wait on you." "Do you know," asked Pilgrim, "why the great kings sent me out here?" "No, we don't" replied the little fiends.

Pilgrim said, "The great kings want to devour the T'ang monk, but their only fear is that Pilgrim Sun has vast magic powers. He is capable of many transformations, they claim, and they are afraid that he may change into a Little Wind Cutter to walk on this road to spy on us. They therefore have promoted me to Chief Wind Cutter and asked me to make an investigation, to see whether there is any specious one among your platoon." "Captain," all those Little Wind Cutters said in unison, "we are all genuine." "If you are," said Pilgrim, "do you happen to know what sort of abilities our great kings possess?"

One of the Little Wind Cutters said, "I do." "If you do," said Pilgrim, "tell me quickly. If I agree with you, you are genuine, but if you make the slightest error, you are a specious one. I'll certainly arrest you and take you to see the great kings." When that Little Wind Cutter saw him sitting loftily on the peak and wielding his authority left and right, he had little choice but to speak the truth, saying, "Our great great king has vast magic powers and enormous abilities. With one gulp, he once swallowed one hundred thousand celestial warriors."

On hearing this, Pilgrim bellowed, "You're false!" Horrified, the Little Wind Cutter said, "Father Captain, I'm real. How could you say that I'm false?" "If you are," said Pilgrim, "why did you babble? How big is the great great king that he can swallow with one gulp one hundred thousand celestial warriors."

The Little Wind Cutter said, "Perhaps the captain does not know that our great great king is capable of such transformation that he can be big enough to reach the celestial hall when he wants to, or he can become as small as a vegetable seed. When the Lady Queen Mother convened the Festival of Immortal Peaches in a former year and did not send an invitation to our great great king, he wanted to strive with Heaven. The Jade Emperor sent one hundred thousand celestial warriors to bring him to submission, but our great king exercised his magic body of transformation and opened his mouth big and wide as a city gate. He charged at the celestial warriors, so terrifying them that they dared not do battle and closed up the South Heavenly Gate instead. That's what I meant when I said that he once swallowed one hundred thousand celestial warriors with one gulp."

On hearing this, Pilgrim smiled silently to himself, saying, "If it's this kind of ability, old Monkey is quite capable of it." He spoke out loud again, saying, "What sort of abilities does second great king possess?"

Another Little Wind Cutter replied, "Our second great king is about thirty feet tall; he has silkwormlike eyebrows, phoenix eyes, a lovely lady's voice, and teeth like long flat poles. His nose, moreover, resembles a dragon. When he fights with someone, all he needs to do is to wrap his nose around his enemy. Though that person may have an iron back and a bronze body, his spirit will expire and his soul will perish!" "A monster-spirit," said Pilgrim to himself, "with a trunk like that is not difficult to catch."

He spoke out loud once more, saying, "What sort of abilities does the third great king possess?" Another Little Wind Cutter said, "Our third great king is no fiendish creature of the mortal world, for he has the name of the Roc of Ten Thousand Cloudy Miles. When he moves, he whips up the wind and transports the seas; he reaches the north and rules the south. On his person he also carries a treasure, called the yin-yang double-force vase. If a person is placed inside it, he will turn to liquid within one and three-quarter hours."

When he heard this, Pilgrim became alarmed, saying to himself, "I'm not scared of the demon, but I'd better be careful about his vase." He spoke out loud again, saying, "You have all spoken quite accurately about the abilities of our three great kings, as accurately as I have known them to be. But do you know which of the great kings would like to devour the T'ang monk?" "Captain," said another Little Wind Cutter, "do you mean that you don't know?" "Don't I know more than you?" snapped Pilgrim. "You are the ones who may not know the truth of the matter, and that's why I was sent to give you a thorough interrogation."

The Little Wind Cutter said, "Our great great king and the second great king have long resided in the Lion-Camel Cave of the Lion-Camel Ridge. Our third great king, however, did not live here, for his original residence was located about four hundred miles west of here, in a city by the name of the Lion-Camel State. Five hundred years ago, he devoured the entire city—the king, the civil and military officials, the populace, male and female, old and young—and took over the kingdom. All the inhabitants of that city now are fiends. I don't know which year it was that he learned that the T'ang court in the Land of the East had commissioned a monk to go seek scriptures in the Western Heaven. That T'ang monk, so the saying goes, is a good man who has practiced austerities for ten incarnations. If anyone eats a single piece of his flesh, he will gain longevity and never grow old. But fearing his disciple, Pilgrim Sun, who is said to be exceedingly formidable, our third great king was afraid that he couldn't quite handle the situation all by himself. He came, therefore, to become a bond-brother with the two great kings at this place. The three of them are thus united in their determination and efforts to catch that T'ang monk."

When Pilgrim heard this, he was filled with anger. "These brazen fiends are so audacious! *I* am protecting the T'ang monk so that he may attain the right fruit. How could they plan to devour my man?" He was so mad that he clenched his teeth, whipped out his iron rod, and leaped down from the tall peak. All he had to do was to slam the rod down on the heads of the little fiends, and they were immediately reduced to meat patties! When he saw them like that, however, he was moved somewhat to pity. "Alas," he said to himself, "they were kind enough after all to have spilled everything about their family to me. How could I finish them off just like that? All right! All right! What's done is done!"

Dear Great Sage! Because of the impediment in his master's way, he had no choice but to do something like this. He took down one of the name plates and tied it to his own waist. The banner with the word, command, he hauled on his shoulder, the bell he hung on his belt, and he took up the rattle. Facing the wind, he made the magic sign and recited a spell to change with one shake of his body into the appearance of that Little Wind Cutter whom he first met on the road. In big strides, he followed the road back to search for the cave and to do some more detection on those three old fiendish demons. Truly, these were

The thousand kinds of transformation of Handsome Monkey King,
Ten thousand permutations, what real abilities!

He dashed deeply into the mountain, following the path on which he came. As he ran along, he suddenly heard people shouting and horses neighing. When he raised his eyes to look, he saw that the noise was coming from a huge mob of little fiends in front of the Lion-Camel Cave, all equipped with columns of scimitars, lances, spears, and halberds, with flags and banners. Delighted, our Great Sage said to himself, "Long Life Li's words are not far off the mark!" The way that those little fiends were arrayed, you see, had an order to it: two hundred and fifty of them made up one huge column, to which was assigned a tall colored flag. When he spotted some forty such flags, he knew that there had to be at least ten thousand troops right there before the cave.

Thereupon he thought further to himself, "Old Monkey has already changed into a Little Wind Cutter. Once I step inside, I would have to give some answers should those old demons question me on patrolling the mountain. If I am recognized because of some slip-up in my words, how am I going to get away? Even if I want to run out the door, how could I get out with so many of them barring the door? If I want to seize the fiendish kings inside the cave, I must get rid of these fiends before the door first."

How could he get rid of the fiends, you ask. Marvelous Great Sage! He thought some more to himself: "Though those old demons have never met my face, they have already known the reputation of old Monkey. Let me rely on that reputation, then, and exploit its power; let me give some big talk to frighten them a bit, and see whether those creatures of middle land[1] indeed have sufficient affinity to be rewarded by our taking the scriptures back to them. If they do, a few heroic sentences of mine will frighten the fiends enough to scatter them. If those creatures, however, do not have sufficient affinity so that we cannot acquire the true scriptures, then

Even if I preach till the lotus flowers appear,
I shall not dispel the spirits before the cave."

His mind thus questioning his mouth, and his mouth thus questioning the mind, he beat his rattle and shook his bell as he marched up to the entrance of the Lion-Camel Cave. He was immediately met by the little fiends of the forward camp who said, "Little Wind Cutter, have you returned?" Instead of answering them, Pilgrim lowered his head and walked on.

At the second-level camp, he was stopped again by some more little fiends who said, "Little Wind Cutter, have you returned?" "I have," replied Pilgrim. "When you went on patrol this morning," said the fiends, "did you run into Pilgrim Sun?" "I have," replied Pilgrim, "he's polishing his pole at the moment."

A little frightened, those little fiends said, "What does he look like? What sort of a pole is he polishing?" Pilgrim said, "He was squatting there by the side of a brook, and he still seemed like a trail-blazing deity. If he stood up, he would have to be over a hundred feet tall! He had in his hands an iron rod that resembled a huge pole, so thick it was that it had to have the thickness of a rice bowl. As he sprinkled some water on the stone ledge, he rubbed his rod on it while he mumbled to himself, 'O dear pole! I haven't taken you out for a while to show your magic powers. Now that you have been taken out, may you beat to death for me all those monster-spirits, even if there are one hundred thousand of them! Then, let me slay also those three archdemons and offer them as sacrifices to you!' Once he has polished his rod so that it shines, he will no doubt slaughter first those ten thousand of you before the door."

When those little fiends heard these words, every one of their hearts quivered and their galls shook, as their souls melted and their spirits dispersed. "Think on this, all of you," said Pilgrim again. "The flesh of that T'ang monk doesn't amount to many pounds, you know, and I doubt if we'll ever get to receive our portions even if he were divided up. Why should we withstand that pole for them? Why don't we ourselves just scatter?" "You are right," said the various fiends. "Let's look after our own lives and leave." All of these fiends, you see, were no more than wolves, tigers, leopards, and the like. With a roar, all these beasts and fowl simply dispersed in every direction. And so, those few subversive sentences of the Great Sage Sun worked like the songs of Ch'u² when they scattered some eight thousand troops.

Secretly delighted, Pilgrim said to himself, "Marvelous! Those old fiends are as good as dead! If words will make them run, how would they dare meet me face to face? When I get inside, however, I'd better repeat what I said. For if I miss saying something, a couple of those little fiends who have run inside just now may reveal my secret." Look at him!

He was set to approach the ancient cave;
With boldness he walked deep inside the door.
We do not know whether good or evil would befall him when he saw the old demons, and you must listen to the explanation in the next chapter.

The Mind Monkey drills through the yin-yang body;
The demon lords return to the true great Way.

We were telling you about that Great Sage Sun, who walked inside the cave to look left and right. He saw

A mound of skeletons,
A forest of dead bones;
Human hair packed together as blankets,
And human flesh trodden as dirt and dust;
Human tendons knotted on the trees
Were dried, parched, and shiny like silver.
In truth there were mountains of corpses and seas of blood;
Indeed the putrid stench was terrible!
The little fiends on the east
Gouged out flesh from living persons;
The brazen demons on the west
Boiled and cooked fresh human meat.
Only the Handsome Monkey King had such heroic gall;
No other mortal would dare enter this door.

After a little while, he walked through the second-level door to look around inside. Ah! What he saw in here was quite different from the outside; it was a place both quiet and elegant, both handsome and spacious. On the left and right were exotic grass and rare flowers; there were old pines and aged bamboos front and back. He had to walk, however, for another seven or eight miles before he reached the third-level door, through which he stole a glance. Inside the door and sitting loftily on three high seats were three old fiends, who appeared most savage and hideous. The middle one had

Teeth like files and saws,
A round head and a square face.
He had a voice like thunder
And flashing eyes like lightning.
His nose curled skyward;

His brows sprouted flames.
When he moved,
All other beasts trembled;
When he sat,
All demons shook and quivered.
This was the king of beasts,
The green-haired lion fiend.
The one to his left had
Phoenix eyes and golden pupils,
Yellow tusks and stubby legs,
Long nose and silver hair,
A head that seemed taillike;
Knotted brows beneath his round forehead
And a huge, rugged torso.
He had a soft voice like a lissome beauty,
But his white face was a bull-head demon's.
A brute of prolonged self-cultivation,
This was the yellow-tusked old elephant.
The one to his right had
Golden wings and leviathan head,[1]
Starlike pupils and leopard eyes.
He ruled the north, governed the south—
Fierce, strong, and courageous.
Coming alive he could fly and soar
While quails quaked and dragons dreaded.
When he shook his feathers,
All the birds went into hiding;
When he stretched his sharp claws,
All the fowl cowered in terror.
Able to reach a cloudy distance of ninety-thousand miles,
This was the great eagle-roc.

Below them stood some one hundred captains, all in complete armor and military regalia, and looking most truculent and fierce. When Pilgrim saw them, however, he was filled with delight. Not the least bit frightened, he marched through the door in big strides, and after he dropped his rattle, he lifted his head and said, "Great Kings." Smiling broadly, the three old demons said, "Little Wind Cutter, have you returned?" "I have indeed," replied Pilgrim in a ringing voice.

"Have you found out anything about Pilgrim Sun when you were on patrol in the mountain?"

"In the presence of the great kings," replied Pilgrim, "I dare not speak."

"Why not?" asked the first old demon.

"By the command of the great kings," said Pilgrim, "I went forward, beating my rattle and shaking my bell. As I walked along, I suddenly caught sight of a person squatting by a brook. Even then he looked like a trail-blazing deity, and if he had stood up, he would have been undoubtedly over a hundred feet tall. Bailing some water from the brook, he was polishing with it a huge pole on a rock. As he did so, he kept mumbling to himself that up till now, he hadn't been able to show off the magic power of his pole. Once he had polished the pole enough to make it glow, he said he would come and use it on the great kings. I knew he had to be that Pilgrim Sun, and that's why I have returned to make my report."

When that old demon heard these words, he perspired profusely. Shaking all over, he said, "Brothers, I told you not to bother the T'ang monk. His disciple has such vast magic powers that he has already made plans for us. Now he is polishing his rod to beat us up. What shall we do?" Then he gave this order: "Little ones, summon all the soldiers outside the cave to come in. Shut the door, find let those priests pass."

One of the captains who knew what had happened said immediately, "Great King, the little fiends guarding the door outside have all scattered." "How could they have all scattered?" said the old demon. "They must have heard the bad news, too. Shut the door quickly! Shut the door quickly!" The various fiends hurriedly banged the front and back doors shut and bolted them.

Becoming somewhat alarmed, Pilgrim thought to himself, "After they close the doors, they might question me on some other business in their house. If I can't answer them, I will give myself away. Won't I be caught then? Let me scare them a little bit more, so that they'll open the doors again for me to flee if I need to." He therefore went forward again and said, "Great Kings, that Pilgrim Sun said something that's even more dreadful." "What else did he say?" asked the old demon.

Pilgrim said, "He said that when he had caught hold of the three of you, he would skin the great great king, he would debone the second great king, and he would pull out the tendons of the third great king. If you shut your doors and refuse to go out, he is capable of transformations, you know. He may well change into a tiny fly, come in through a crack in the door, and seize all of us. What shall we do then?"

"Brothers," said the old demon, "be careful. There is hardly a fly in our cave. If you see a fly coming in here, it has to be that Pilgrim Sun." Smiling to himself, Pilgrim thought, "I'll give him a fly to scare him a bit. Then he'll open the doors."

The Great Sage stepped to one side and pulled off a piece of hair behind his head. Blowing a mouthful of immortal breath on it, he whispered, "Change!" and it at once changed into a gold-headed fly, which darted up and flew smack into the face of the old demon. "Brothers, this is awful!" cried a horrified old demon. "That little something has entered our door!" Those fiends, young and old, were so terrified that they took up pitchforks and brooms to swat madly at the fly.

Unable to contain himself, our Great Sage broke into loud giggles, which, alas, he should have never permitted himself to do. For once he laughed, his original features also appeared. When the third old demon saw him, he leaped forward and grabbed him, crying, "Elder Brothers, we were almost fooled by him!" "Who is fooling whom?" asked the first old demon.

"The one who was speaking to us just now," replied the third fiend, "was no Little Wind Cutter. He is Pilgrim Sun. He must have run into Little Wind Cutter, slain him somehow, and changed into his appearance to deceive us here." Greatly shaken, Pilgrim said to himself, "He has recognized me!" Rubbing his face hurriedly with his hand to correct his features, he said to those fiends, "How could I be Pilgrim Sun! I am the Little Wind Cutter. The great king has made a mistake."

"Brother," said the old demon, smiling, "he *is* Little Wind Cutter. For three times every day he answers my roll call. I know him." Then he asked Pilgrim, "Do you have your name plate?" "I do," replied Pilgrim, and he took it out at once from inside his clothes. More convinced than ever, the old fiend said, "Brother, don't falsely accuse him."

"Elder Brother," said the third fiend, "didn't you see him? He was giggling just now with his face half turned, and I saw for a moment a thunder god beak on him. When I grabbed him, he changed back immediately into his present looks." He then called out: "Little ones, bring me some ropes." The captains took out ropes immediately. Wrestling Pilgrim to the ground, the third fiend had him hog-tied before they hitched up his clothes to examine him. It became apparent at once that he was *the* pi-ma-wên all right! Pilgrim, you see, was capable of seventy-two kinds of transformation. If it was a matter of changing into a fowl, a beast, a plant, a utensil, or an insect, his entire body could be transformed. But when he had to change into another person, only his face but not his body could be transformed. When they lifted up his clothes, therefore, they saw a body full of brown hair, two red buttocks, and a tail.

When he saw this, the first old fiend said, "Though he may have the face of Little Wind Cutter, it's the body of Pilgrim Sun. It's he. Little ones, bring us some wine first, so that I may present to the third great king a cup of merit. Since we have caught Pilgrim Sun, there is no doubt that the T'ang monk will be the food of our mouths."

"Let's not drink wine just yet," said the third fiend. "Pilgrim Sun is an exceedingly slippery character, for he knows many ways of escape. I fear we may lose him. Tell the little ones to haul out our vase and put Pilgrim Sun inside it. Then we can drink." "Exactly! Exactly!" said the old demon, laughing loudly. He at once summoned thirty-six little fiends to go to their weapons chamber and haul out the vase.

How big was the vase, you ask. Why would it need thirty-six persons to carry it? Though it was no more than twenty-four inches tall, that vase was a treasure governed by the double primal forces of yin and yang. Its magic reactions inside were activated by the seven jewels, the eight trigrams, and the twenty-four solar terms. Only thirty-six persons, a number which corresponded to the number of constellations in the Heavenly Ladle group, would have sufficient strength to lift it up. In a little while, the little fiends had the treasure vase hauled out and set before the third-level door. After they had unpacked it from its wrappings and removed the stopper, they untied Pilgrim and stripped him naked. Then they carried him up to the mouth of the vase, and immediately he was sucked inside with a loud whoosh by the immortal breath of the vase. It was then covered again with its stopper, on top of which they added a tape to seal it. Beckoning his companions to join him to drink, the old fiend said, "Now that this little ape has entered my treasure vase, he'd better not think of the road to the West anymore. If he ever wanted to worship Buddha and acquire scriptures, he might as well turn his back, take up the wheel,[2] and seek Buddhist treasure in the next incarnation!"

We tell you now about that Great Sage, who found the vase to be quite small for his body once he reached the inside. He decided, therefore, to transform himself into someone smaller and squat in the middle of the vase. Finding it to be quite cool after some time, he could not refrain from chuckling to himself and saying out loud, "These monster-spirits are banking on their false reputation! How could they tell people that once someone was placed inside the vase, he would change into pus and blood after one and three-quarter hours. If it's cool like this, I can live here for seven or eight years with no trouble!"

Alas! The Great Sage, you see, had no idea of how that treasure worked: if someone who had been placed within it remained silent for a whole year, then it would remain cool for all that time. But the moment that person spoke, fire would appear to burn him. Hardly had the Great Sage spoken, therefore, when he saw that the entire vase was engulfed in flames. Fortunately, he was not without abilities; sitting in the middle, he made the fire-repellent magic sign with his fingers and faced the flames calmly. After about half an hour, some forty snakes crawled out from every side and began to bite him. Pilgrim stretched forth his hands, picked up the snakes, and with a violent wrench tore them into eighty pieces. In a little while, however, three fire dragons emerged and had him encircled top and bottom.

As the situation was fast becoming unbearable, Pilgrim was rather flustered, saying to himself, "I can take care of other things, but these fire dragons are hard to deal with. If I don't get out of here, the fire and the heat may overwhelm me after a while. What then? I think I'd better push my way out by making my body bigger." Dear Great Sage! Making the magic sign with his fingers and reciting a spell, he cried, "Grow!" At once his body reached the height of over a hundred feet, but the vase also grew in size with him. Reversing his magic, he reduced the size of his body, but the vase, too, grew smaller with him.

Greatly alarmed, Pilgrim said, "Hard! Hard! Hard! How could it grow big or small with me like that? What shall I do?" He had hardly finished speaking when he felt some pain on his shanks. Rubbing them hurriedly with his hand, he found his shanks were turning flaccid because of the fire. More and more anxious, he thought to himself, "What's to become of me? Even my shanks are weakened by the fire. I'll be reduced to a cripple!" He was hardly able to hold back his tears. Thus it was that

He thought of Tripitaka, having met demons and woes;

He missed the sage monk, when beset by fatal ordeals.

"O Master!" he cried. "Since that year when I embraced the truth because of the Bodhisattva Kuan-yin's persuasion and was delivered from my Heaven-sent calamity, I suffered with you the trek through various mountains and subdued many fiends, including the bringing to submission of Pa-chieh and Sha Monk. All my labor, all my bitter toil were done with the hope that we would reach the West together and attain the right fruit. Little did I realize that I would meet such vicious demons today! Having been thrown in here by my mistake, old Monkey will lose his life, and you will be stranded halfway up the mountain, unable to proceed. Could it be that my past misdeeds were what brought on my present ordeal?"

As he grieved like that, he suddenly thought to himself, "On the Serpent Coil Mountain[3] that year, the Bodhisattva gave me as a gift three life-saving hairs. I wonder if I still have them. Let me look." He touched his whole body with his hands and found three hairs on the back of his neck to be especially stiff. Delighted, he said to himself, "All my hairs on me are quite soft, and only these three happen to be stiff. They must be my life-savers!"

Clenching his teeth to endure the pain, he pulled off the hairs and blew on them a mouthful of immortal breath, crying, "Change!" One of the hairs changed into a diamond drill, the second one into a strip of bamboo, and the third into a piece of cotton rope. Bending the strip into the shape of a bow, he tied the rope to both ends and used it to guide the drill to drill away at the bottom of the vase. After a while, light filtered in through a small hole. "Lucky! Lucky!" he said, highly pleased. "I can get out now!" As he was about to use transformation to escape, the vase suddenly turned cool once more. Why, you ask. Once he drilled through the vase's bottom, you see, the two forces of yin and yang leaked out.

Dear Great Sage! He retrieved his hairs and, shrinking the size of his body, changed into a mole-cricket, so delicate that it was no thicker than a strand of whisker and no longer than a piece of eyebrow hair. He crawled out of the hole, but instead of leaving, he flew directly up to the old demon's head and alighted on it. The old demon was drinking merrily when all of a sudden, he put down his cup and said, "Third Younger Brother, has Pilgrim Sun melted?" "It's about time, isn't it?" said the third demon, smiling.

The old demon gave the order for the vase to be brought up to the table, and those thirty-six little fiends immediately went to haul it. When they discovered, however, that the vase had become very light, the terrified fiends cried, "Great Kings, the vase has turned light." "Nonsense!" snapped the old demon. "Our treasure is the perfect product of the double forces of yin and yang. How could it have turned light?" One of the more courageous little fiends picked up the vase all by himself and brought it near the table, saying, "See for yourself whether it's lighter or not."

Removing the stopper, the old demon peered inside and, when he saw a speck of light coming from the bottom, he burst out, "The vase is empty!" Unable to contain himself, the Great Sage shouted on his head, "My dear child! I'm gone!" "He's gone! He's gone!" cried the other fiends. "Close the doors! Close the doors!"

With one shake of his body, Pilgrim retrieved the clothes they took from him, and, changing back into his original form, bounded out of the cave. "Monster-spirits, don't you dare be unruly!" he shouted back at them as he left. "The vase has been punctured, and it can't be used on humans anymore. It's only good for a night pot!" Merrily and noisily, he trod the clouds and went back to the place where he had left the T'ang monk. The elder at the time was just saying a prayer toward the sky, using pinches of dirt as incense. Pilgrim stopped his cloud to hear what he was saying. With his hands folded before his chest, the elder bowed to the sky and said,

I pray to all immortals of cloud and mist,
All devas, and Gods of Darkness and Light:
May they my good pupil, Pilgrim, assist
And grant him vast and boundless magic might.

When the Great Sage heard such words, he was moved to even greater diligence. Causing the cloudy luminosity to subside, he drew near and said, "Master, I've returned." The elder took him by the hand and said, "Wu-k'ung, you've worked very hard! When you didn't come back after having gone deep into the mountain, I was very worried. Tell me truly what sort of good or evil may we expect in this mountain."

With a smile, Pilgrim replied, "My trip was a successful one this time only because the creatures of the Land in the East are blessed with goodly affinity; and secondly, because the merit and virtue of my master are boundless and limitless; and thirdly, because your disciple has some magic powers." Whereupon he gave a thorough account of how he disguised himself as the Little Wind Cutter, how he was trapped inside the vase, and how he escaped. "Now that I can behold the countenance of my master once more," he said, "I feel like I have gone through another incarnation."

Thanking him profusely, the elder said, "You didn't fight with the monster-spirits this time?" "No, I didn't," said Pilgrim. "You can't therefore, escort me across the mountain, can you?" said the elder.

As he had always been a person who loved to win, Pilgrim began to shout: "What do you mean that I can't escort you across this mountain?" "You haven't quite proven that you can prevail against them," said the elder. "Everything seems so muddled at the moment. How could I dare proceed."

"Master," replied Pilgrim with a laugh, "you are not very perceptive! As the proverb says,

A little yarn is no thread;

A single hand cannot clap.

There are three old demons, thousands and thousands of little fiends, and only one old Monkey. How could I possibly fight with them?"

"The few cannot withstand the many," replied the elder. "I quite understand that you can't cope with them all by yourself. But Pa-chieh and Sha Monk both have abilities. I'll tell them to go with you, so that your united efforts will sweep clean the mountain path and escort me through it." "What you say is quite right," said Pilgrim, turning somewhat pensive. "Sha Monk, however, should stay here to guard you. Let Pa-chieh go with me."

Terribly alarmed, our Idiot said, "Elder Brother, you're the one who is imperceptive! I'm rather crude, and I don't have much ability. Even when I walk along, I resist the wind. Of what use am I to you?" "Brother," said Pilgrim, "even though you may not have great abilities, you are still another person. As the common folks say, 'Even a fart is additional air!' You can at the very least build up my courage." "All right! All right!" said Pa-chieh. "I hope you'll look after me a bit. When things become tight, don't play tricks on me." "Do be careful, Pa-chieh," said the elder. "Sha Monk and I will remain here."

Arousing his spirit, our Idiot mounted a gust of violent wind with

Pilgrim and rode on the fog and the cloud to go up the tall mountain. When they arrived before the door of the cave, they found the door tightly shut and no one in sight. Pilgrim walked forward and, holding his iron rod, cried out in a loud voice: "Fiends, open your door! Come out quickly to fight with old Monkey!" When the little fiends in the cave reported this, the old demon was deeply shaken. "The rumor spreading for years about how powerful that ape is," he said, "has been proven true today!"

"Elder Brother, what do you mean?" asked the second fiend on one side. The old demon replied, "When that Pilgrim changed into Little Wind Cutter earlier this morning to sneak in here, we couldn't recognize him. It was fortunate that our Third Worthy Brother spotted him at last and we managed to put him inside the vase. But he had the ability to drill through the vase and he escaped after he retrieved his clothes. Now he's provoking battle outside. Who has enough courage to face him in the first fight?" To this question of his, however, no one made a reply. He asked again, but still there was no answer, for everyone inside the cave was playing deaf and dumb.

His anger rising, the old demon said, "We're earning ourselves a lousy reputation on the main road to the West. When Pilgrim Sun today can mock us like this and we do not go out to face him in battle, our fame will surely diminish. Let me risk this old life of mine to go have three rounds with him. If I can withstand him for three rounds, the T'ang monk will be the food of our mouths. If I can't, let's close up our door and let them pass." He put on his armor and opened the door to walk out. Pilgrim and Pa-chieh stood by the door to stare at him, and he was some fiendish creature indeed!

A jeweled helmet topped his iron-hard head,
With dangling tassels colorful and bright.
Like flashing lightning his two eyes did glow;
Like shining mist hair on both temples flowed.
His claws were like silver, both quick and sharp;
His sawlike teeth were even and thickset.
The armor he wore was one solid gold piece;
A smart dragon-head sash wrapped round his waist.
His hands held a shiny scimitar of steel:
The world rarely saw such heroic might.
With one bellow loud as a thunderclap
He asked, "Who is he that knocks on our door?"

Turning around, the Great Sage said, "It's your Venerable Father Sun, the Great Sage, Equal to Heaven." "Are you Pilgrim Sun?" asked the old demon with a laugh. "You audacious ape! I'm not bothering you. Why are you provoking battle here?" Pilgrim replied, "As the proverb says,

The waves will only rise with the wind;
Water will subside without the tide.

If you didn't bother me, you think I would come looking for you? It's because you bunch of thugs and hoodlums have banded together to plot against my master, planning to devour him. That's why I've come to do this." "You show up at our door in such a menacing manner," said the old demon. "Does that mean that you want to fight?" "Exactly," replied Pilgrim.

"Stop acting with such insolence!" said the old demon. "If I ordered out my fiend troops, placed them in formation, raised the flags, and beat the drums to fight with you, all I would be doing is to show simply that I'm the local tiger trying to take advantage of you. I'll face you alone, one to one, and no other helper will be permitted." On hearing this, Pilgrim said, "Chu Pa-chieh, step aside. Let's see what he'll do with old Monkey." Idiot indeed walked away to one side.

"You come over here," said the old demon, "and act as my chopping block first. If your bald head can withstand three blows of my scimitar, I'll let you and your T'ang monk go past. But if you can't, you'd better turn him over quickly to me as a meal."

When he heard this, Pilgrim smiled and said, "Fiend! If you have brush and paper in your cave, take them out and I'll sign a contract with you. You can start delivering your blows from today until next year, and I won't regard you seriously!" Arousing his spirit, the old demon stood firmly with one foot placed in front of the other. He lifted up his scimitar with both hands and brought it down hard on the head of the Great Sage. Our Great Sage, however, jerked his head upward to meet the blow. All they heard was a loud crack, but the skin on the head did not even redden. Greatly astonished, the old demon said, "What a hard head this monkey has!" Chuckling, the Great Sage said, "You don't realize that old Monkey was

Born with a bronze head and a crown of steel
That no one possessed in Heav'n or on Earth.
Unbreakable by the mallet or the ax,
It has gone in my youth into Lao Tzu's forge.

Its making Four Dipper Stars had overseen
And Twenty-Eight Lodges applied their work.
It could not be wrecked though drowned a few times,
For tough sinews had it all encircled.
Fearing still that it was not strong enough,
The T'ang monk added a fillet of gold!"
"Stop bragging, ape!" said the old demon. "Watch the second blow of
my scimitar! It'll not spare your life!" "Why talk like that?" replied
Pilgrim. "Isn't it enough that you hack away?"

"Monkey," said the old demon, "you have no idea that my
scimitar is

Metal in the furnace forged,
Wrought by lengthy work divine.
The fine blade and its mighty pow'r
Conform to military science.
It looks like the tail of a fly
And also a white serpent's waist.
In the mountain clouds would gather;
In the ocean waves would pile high.
Pounded and polished countless times,
It has been a hundred ways refined.
Though it's kept in an ancient cave,
It'll win once in battle it's placed.
I'll grab that nice, bald, priestly head of yours
And make two gourd halves with one mighty whack!"

"This monster-spirit is so blind!" chuckled the Great Sage. "So, you
think that old Monkey's head is a gourd! All right. I won't delay you.
You can give me another blow."

The old demon lifted his blade to hack away once more, and again
the Great Sage met it with his head. With a loud crack, the head was
split in two, but the Great Sage also rolled on the ground immediately
and changed into two bodies. Terrified by what he saw, the fiend
lowered his scimitar. From a distance, Pa-chieh saw everything and
said, laughing, "The old demon should strike again, and there'll be
four persons!"

Pointing at Pilgrim, the old demon said, "I have heard that you are
capable of the Magic of Body-Division. But why are you exercising it
in my presence?" "What do you mean by the Magic of Body-Division?"
asked the Great Sage.

"Why didn't you move when I gave you the first blow?" said the old demon. "Why did you become two persons after the second one?" "Fiend, don't be afraid," said the Great Sage laughing. "If you cut me ten thousand times, I'll give you twenty thousand persons!"

"Monkey," said the old demon, "you may be able to divide your body, but I doubt whether you can retrieve your bodies. If you have the ability to become one again, you may give me a blow with your rod." "No lying, now," said the Great Sage. "You said you wanted to hack me three times with your scimitar, and you have only done it twice. Now you want me to give you a blow with my rod. If I strike you even half a blow more, I'll give up my surname Sun!" "Well said," replied the old demon.

Dear Great Sage! He embraced the other half of himself and, with a roll, became one person again. Picking up his rod, he slammed it down on the old demon, who parried the blow with his scimitar and said, "Brazen ape, don't you dare be unruly! What sort of a funeral staff is that that you dare use it to hit someone right before his door?" "If you ask me about this rod of mine," snapped the Great Sage, "you should know that it has a reputation both in Heaven and on Earth." "What kind of reputation?" asked the old demon. The Great Sage said,

The rod was made of steel nine times refined,[4]
Forged in the brazier by Lao Tzu himself.
King Yü got it, named it "Treasure Divine"
To fix the Eight Rivers and Four Seas' depth.
In it were spread out tracks of planets and stars,
Its two ends were clamped in pieces of gold.
Its dense patterns would frighten gods and ghosts;
On it dragon and phoenix scripts were drawn.
Its name was one Rod of Numinous Yang,
Stored deep in the sea, hardly seen by men.
Well formed and transformed it wanted to fly,
Emitting bright strands of five-colored mist.
Enlightened Monkey took it back to the mount
To experience its pow'r for boundless change.
At times I would make it thick as a drum
Or small and tiny as an iron wire.
Huge like South Mountain or fine as a pin,
It lengthened or shortened after my desire.
Move it gently and colored clouds would rise.

Like flashing lightning it would soar and fly.
Its cold air, far-reaching, would bring you chills;
Its deadly aura could imbue the sky.
To tame tigers and dragons it I kept;
With me it toured all four corners of earth.
I once disturbed with this rod the Hall of Heav'n;
Its might broke up the Festival of Peach.
Against it the devarāja had no chance;
Hard task it was for Naṭa to oppose it.
Struck by the rod, the gods had no place to hide;
One hundred thousand soldiers ran and fled.
With thunder gods guarding Divine Mists Hall
I leaped and fought to Hall of Perfect Light.
All flustered were the ministers at court,
And all divine officers were most confused.
I raised my rod to topple the Dipper Hall
And, turning, smashed the South Pole Palace.
When Emperor Jade saw how fierce was my rod,
Tathāgata was asked to face my wrath.
'Twas natural for a fighter to win or lose,
But harsh confinement was my certain lot,
Which lasted for a full five hundred years;
Then came kind counsels from South Sea's Kuan-yin.
There was, she told me, a priest of Great T'ang
Who offered to Heaven a stupendous vow:
To save the souls from the City of Death,
He would seek scriptures from the Spirit Mount.
But demons infested the westward way;
The journey thus was no convenient trek.
Knowing the rod had in the world no match,
She begged me to be his guardian on the way.
Perverts, touched by it, would go to Hades,
Their bones turning to noodles, their flesh to dust.
Everywhere fiends had died beneath the rod,
In hundreds and thousands and countless scores.
Above, it busted the Dipper Palace;
Below, it smashed up the Hall of Darkness.
In Heaven it chased the Nine Planetoids
And wounded in Earth the summoner-judge.

It dropped from midair to rule mountains and streams,
Much stronger than Jupiter's new year sword.
To guard the T'ang monk I bank on this rod,
Having struck in this world all monster-gods!

When he heard these words, the demon shook violently, though he risked his life and raised the scimitar to strike. Beaming broadly, the Monkey King met him with the iron rod. At first the two of them fought before the cave; after a while, they leaped up to do battle in midair. What a marvelous battle it was!

A treasure that fixed Heaven River's depth
Was the rod, named Compliant, this world's prize.
Such vaunting talents the demon displeased,
Who raised his scimitar with magic might.
A conflict before the door might one resolve.
How could any be spared in a midair fight?
After his own feelings one changed his looks;
One's torso grew taller without delay.
They fought till clouds thickened in the sky
And fog drifted up from the ground.
That one made plans a few times to devour Tripitaka;
That one exercised his vast pow'r to guard the T'ang monk.
Because the Buddha wished the scriptures to impart,
Evil and good became clear, locked in bitter strife.

The old demon and the Great Sage fought for over twenty rounds, but no decision could be reached. When Pa-chieh down below saw, however, how intense a battle the two of them were waging, he could no longer stand idly by. Mounting the wind, he leaped into the air and delivered a terrific blow with his rake, aiming it at the monster's face. The demon was horrified, for he did not know that Pa-chieh was a blunderer, someone without any real stamina. When he saw that long snout and those huge ears, the demon thought that the hands would also be heavy and the rake vicious. Abandoning his scimitar therefore, he turned and fled in defeat. "Chase him! Chase him!" shouted the Great Sage.

Relying on his companion's authority, our Idiot raised high the muckrake and went after the fiend. When the old demon saw him approaching, he stood still before the mountain slope and, facing the wind, changed back into his original form. Opening wide his huge mouth, he wanted to swallow Pa-chieh, who was so terrified by the sight that he dove quickly into the bushes by the wayside. He crawled in there, without regard for thorns or prickles and with no thought of the pain of the scratches on his head; trembling all over, he stayed in the bushes to see what would develop.

In a moment, Pilgrim arrived, and the old fiend also opened wide his mouth to try to devour him, little knowing that this was exactly what Pilgrim desired. Putting away his iron rod, Pilgrim ran up to the fiend, who swallowed him in one gulp. Our Idiot in the bushes was so shaken that he muttered to himself: "How stupid is this pi-ma-wên! When you saw the fiend coming to devour you, why didn't you run away? Why did you go up to him instead? You might still be a priest today inside his stomach, but tomorrow you'd be a big pile of droppings!" Only after the demon left in triumph did our Idiot crawl out from the bushes and slip away on the road he came.

We tell you now about Tripitaka, who waited with Sha Monk beneath the mountain slope. All of a sudden they saw Pa-chieh running back and panting heavily. Horrified, Tripitaka said, "Pa-chieh, how is it that you look so desperate? Where is Wu-k'ung?" "Elder Brother," sobbed our Idiot, "has been swallowed by the monster-spirit in one gulp." When he heard this, Tripitaka collapsed on the ground, and only after a long time could he stamp his feet and pound his chest. "O disciple!" he cried. "I thought that you were so adept in subduing the fiends that you could lead me to see Buddha in the Western Heaven. How could I know that you would perish in the hands of this fiend? Alas! Alas! The merit of this disciple and others have all turned to dust now!"

The master was beside himself with grief. But look at our Idiot! Instead of trying to comfort his master he called out: "Sha Monk, bring me the luggage. The two of us will divide it up." "Second Elder Brother," said Sha Monk, "why do you want to divide it?" "When we have divided it," replied Pa-chieh, "each of us can go our own way: you can return to Flowing Sand River to be a cannibal, and I'll go back to the Old Kao Village to see my wife. We'll sell the white horse, and that should enable us to buy a coffin for our master in his old age!" The elder was already heaving in anguish. When he heard these words, he began to wail, calling on Heaven to help him all the time and we shall leave him there for the moment.

We tell you about that old demon, who thought it a smart thing to have swallowed Pilgrim. When he reached his own cave, the various fiends came to greet him and asked him about the battle. "I caught one," said the old demon. Delighted, the second demon said, "Which one did you catch, Big Brother?" "It's Pilgrim Sun," replied the old demon. "Where have you caught him?" asked the second demon. The old demon said, "He has been swallowed into my stomach in one gulp."

Horrified, the third demon said, "O Big Brother, I'm sorry I haven't told you, but Pilgrim Sun is inedible!" "I'm very edible!" said the Great Sage in the belly. "Moreover, I satisfy! You'll never be hungry again!" The little fiends were so frightened that one of them said, "Great King, it's terrible! Pilgrim Sun is talking inside your stomach!"

"I'm not afraid of his talking!" said the old demon. "If I have the ability to devour him, you think I have no ability to handle him? Go and boil me some salt water quickly. Let me pour it down my stomach and throw him up. Then we can have him slowly fried and eaten with wine."

The little fiends indeed went and brought back half a pan of hot salt water, which the old demon immediately drained. Opening wide his mouth, he retched in earnest, but our Great Sage seemed to have taken root in the stomach. He did not even budge. The old demon pressed his own throat and retched again and again until he became dizzy and dim of sight. Even his gall seemed to have been busted! But Pilgrim remained unmoveable as ever. After he panted for a while, the old demon cried, "Pilgrim Sun, aren't you coming out?"

"It's too early!" replied Pilgrim. "I don't feel like coming out!" "Why not?" asked the old demon. "You're not a very smart monster-spirit!" said Pilgrim. "Since I became a monk, I have led a rather penurious life. It's the cool autumn now, and all I have on is an unlined shirt. This belly of yours is quite warm, and it has no draft. This is exactly where I should spend my winter."

On hearing this, all the fiends said, "Great King, Pilgrim Sun wants to spend the winter in your belly." "If he wants to do that," said the old demon, "I'll practice meditation. With my magic of hibernation, I'll not eat for a whole winter and starve that pi-ma-wên."

"My son," said the Great Sage, "you are so dumb! On this journey in which old Monkey is accompanying the T'ang monk to go seek scriptures, we passed through Canton and I picked up a portable frying pan, excellent for cooking chop suey.[5] If I take time to enjoy your liver, chittlings, stomach, and lungs, I think I can last easily till spring!"

"O Elder Brother," cried a horrified second demon, "this ape is capable of doing this!" "O Elder Brother," said the third demon, "it's all right to let him eat the chop suey, but I wonder where he is going to set up the frying pan." "On the fork of his chest bone, of course!" replied Pilgrim. "That's bad!" cried the third demon. "If he sets up the pan there and starts a fire, you'll sneeze if the smoke rises to your nostrils, won't you?" "Don't worry," said Pilgrim, chuckling. "Let old Monkey punch a hole through his head with my golden-hooped rod. That will serve both as a skylight and a chimney."

On hearing this, the old demon became quite frightened, even though he pretended to be brave and said, "Brothers, don't be afraid. Bring me our medicinal wine. I'll drink a few goblets and kill that ape with the drug." Smiling to himself, Pilgrim said, "When old Monkey caused great disturbance in Heaven five hundred years ago, he devoured the elixir of Lao Tzu, the wine of the Jade Emperor, the peaches of the Lady Queen Mother, and all kinds of dainties like phoenix marrow and dragon liver. What, in fact, have I not tasted before? What kind of medicinal wine is this that he dares use to drug me?"

After the little fiends went and bailed two pots of the medicinal wine, they filled a large goblet and handed it to the old demon. The moment he took it in his hands, however, our Great Sage could smell the wine's fragrance even inside the belly of the demon. "I won't allow him to drink it!" he said to himself. Dear Great Sage! With a twist of his head, he turned his mouth into the shape of a trumpet which he placed immediately below the throat of the old demon. When the old demon drank in one gulp the goblet of wine, it was immediately swallowed by Pilgrim. When he drank the second goblet, it, too, was swallowed by Pilgrim, and in this way seven or eight goblets went down the throat of the demon. Putting down the goblet, the old demon said, "I'm not drinking anymore. It used to be that two goblets of this wine would make my stomach feel like fire. I drank seven or eight goblets just now, and my face hasn't even reddened!"

But our Great Sage, you see, could not take too much wine. After he had swallowed seven or eight gobletfuls from the old demon, he became so delirious that he began to do calisthenics without pause inside the demon's belly. He did jumping jacks and cartwheels; he let loose high kicks; grabbing the liver he used it for a swing, and he went through handstands and somersaults, prancing madly here and there. So unbearable was the pain that the fiend slumped to the ground. We do not know whether he died or not, and you must listen to the explanation in the next chapter.

Abbreviations

Bodde	Derk Bodde, *Festivals in Classical China* (Princeton and Hong Kong, 1975).
Chou	Chou Wei 周緯, *Chung-kuo ping-ch'i-shih kao* 中國兵器史稿 (Peking, 1957).
CTS	*Ch'üan T'ang Shih* 全唐詩, 12 vols. (Ts'ui-wên t'ang 粹文堂 edition; repr. Tainan, Taiwan, 1974).
CYC	*Chung-yao chih* 中藥誌, 4 vols. (Peking, 1959–61).
de Bary	Wm. Theodore de Bary, ed., *Sources of Chinese Tradition*, 2 vols. (New York and London, 1960).
Dudbridge	Glen Dudbridge, *The Hsi-yu Chi: A Study of Antecedents to the Sixteenth-Century Chinese Novel* (Cambridge, England, 1970).
Herrmann	Albert Herrmann, *An Historical Atlas of China*, new ed. (Chicago, 1966).
Hucker	Charles O. Hucker, "Governmental Organization of the Ming Dynasty," *Harvard Journal of Asiatic Studies* 21 (1958): 1–151.
HYC	*Hsi-yu chi* 西游記 (Peking, 1954). Abbreviation refers only to this edition.
JW	*The Journey to the West.*
Legge	James Legge, trans., *The Chinese Classics* (Taipei reprint of original Oxford University Press edition).
Needham	Joseph Needham, *Science and Civilisation in China*, vol. 1–5/3 (Cambridge, England, 1954–76).
Porkert	Manfred Porkert, *The Theoretical Foundations of Chinese Medicine: Systems of Correspondence*, M.I.T. East Asian Science Series, Nathan Sivin, general editor (Cambridge, Mass., and London, 1974).

Schafer   Edward H. Schafer, *Pacing the Void: T'ang*
                   Approaches to the Stars (Berkeley, Los Angeles,
                   and London, 1977).
SPPY   *Szu-pu pei-yao* 四部備要.
SPTK   *Szu-pu ts'ung-k'an* 四部叢刋.
T.   Taishō Tripiṭaka.
Tai   Tai Yüan-ch'ang 戴源長, *Hsien-hsüeh tz'ŭ-tien*
                   仙學辭典 (Taipei, 1962).
TPKC   *T'ai-p'ing kuang-chi* 太平廣記, 10 vols. (Peking,
                   1961).
TT   *Tao Tsang.*
Veith   Ilza Veith, trans., *The Yellow Emperor's Classic of*
                   Internal Medicine, new ed. (Berkeley, Los Angeles,
                   and London, 1972).
Wilhelm/Baynes   *The I Ching, or Book of Changes,* The Richard
                   Wilhelm Translation rendered into English by
                   Cary F. Baynes, Bollingen Series XIX, 3d ed.
                   (Princeton, 1967).

References to all Standard Histories, unless otherwise indicated, are
to the SPTK *Po-na* 百衲 edition.

Notes

CHAPTER FIFTY-ONE

1. Staff of my will: the author of *JW* is punning on the phrase *chu-chang* (first tone) 主張, which means to manage, to control, or to hold one's own opinion, and the phrase *chu-chang* (fourth tone) 主杖, which means, literally, the staff of a master or the staff of one's will. At the end of chapter 50 (see *JW*, 2: 417), the second line of the parallel couplet, "But Pilgrim, in a daze, knew not what to do 行者朦朧失主張," is a similar pun, since the chapter closes on Pilgrim losing his rod to the demon king. At the end of the present chapter, when Pilgrim regains his rod, the terminal couplet again plays on the same idea. And finally, in the paragraph immediately following the poem, the pun in fact leads directly to the narrator's allegorical interpretation of the incident: "Thus it was that Pilgrim, using the mind to question the mind, regained control of himself 以心問心自張自主."

2. A monkey who has no rod to play with: possibly an allusion to vaudeville shows in which monkeys perform. For this and similar practices, see *JW*, 2: 36.

3. K'o-han Bureau: 可韓司. I have been unable to determine the identity of this bureau in the celestial pantheon.

4. Three Forbidden Enclosures: the *san-yüan* 三垣 are three star groups consisting of the Purple Forbidden Enclosure (*Tzu-wei yüan* 紫微垣, so named because of analogy with the imperial court), the Supreme Forbidden Enclosure (*T'ai-wei yüan* 太微垣), and the Celestial Market Enclosure (*T'ien-shih yüan* 天市垣). For discussions of these three star groups, see Ho Peng Yoke, *The Astronomical Chapters of the Chin Shu* (Paris, 1966), pp. 67, 76, and 84; Needham, 3: 259–61; Schafer, pp. 44–53.

5. Bāhu: in the text of the *HYC*, there is a slight mistake; the author has the constellation Bāhu or Shên 參, when he should have Rohiṇī or Hsin 心 . I have not corrected the error.

6. The seven mansions of the West: another authorial error, for the following constellations belong to the northern group.

7. Three Charities: *san-t'an* 三檀, the three kinds of *dāna* or forms of giving. They are (1) the giving of one's goods; (2) the giving of the Law or *dharma*; and (3) the giving of courage, or *abhaya*.

432

8. Ning Ch'i: 宵戚, a talented person in the Spring and Autumn period, who sought to serve Duke Huan of the state Ch'i (齊桓公). When the duke met his guests at night on the meadow with torches blazing, Ning attracted his attention by singing loudly and beating the horns of his ox. See the *Lü-shih ch'un-ch'iu* 呂氏春秋, *chüan* 19, 17b (SPPY edition).

9. Mr. Chou at Red Cliff: the famous campaign at Red Cliff when Chou Yü defeated Ts'ao Ts'ao by attacking with fire boats. See the *San-kuo chih yen-i* (*Romance of the Three Kingdoms*), chaps. 48–49.

10. One . . . depths: the first two lines of this poem parody the passage in *The Doctrine of the Mean*, 26, 9, where it says: "Now, as for the water before us, it appears but a ladleful; but when we reach its unfathomable depths, we'll see that turtles, iguanas, iguanodons, dragons, fishes, and tortoises all live in them. . . ."

11. Spilled jade does not ordinarily gurgle, but this line is an allusion to two lines of a poem by Lu Chi 陸機:山溜何冷冷 飛泉漱鳴玉, (How the mountain spring gurgles;/The flying stream spills sounding jade). See the second poem entitled "Chao yin 招隱." in *Lu Shih-hêng chi* 陸士衡集, *chüan* 5, 3a (SPPY edition).

12. This and other quotations are presumably descriptive names of the styles the fighters assumed in the boxing match.

CHAPTER FIFTY-TWO

1. Bhikṣuṇī: this means, literally, a nun or an almswoman. But in the narrative context, it is most likely Mahāprajāpatī, the aunt of the Buddha who was also the first woman to be ordained.

2. The Eight Great Diamond Guardians: *pa-ta chin-kang* 八大金剛 is another name for the *pa-ta ming-wang* 八大明王, the eight diamond-kings who are usually represented as fierce guardians of Vairocana. They are 馬頭明王 (Kuan-yin), 大輪明王 (Maitreya), 大笑明王 (Vajrahāsa), 步擲明王 (Samantabhadra), 降三世明王 (Vajrapāṇi), 大威德明王 (Mañjuśrī), 不動明王 (Āryācalanātha), and 無能勝明王 (Kṣitigarbha).

3. See *JW*, 1: 163–64.

4. *Pin-lang*: the text here has 賓郎, which can be another form of the betel-nut 檳榔. I have not determined the meaning of the phrase so used.

CHAPTER FIFTY-THREE

1. Primal vow: *pên-yüan* 本願, *pūrvapraṇidhāna*, the original vow of a buddha or bodhisattva.

2. Wisdom: *chêng-chüeh* 正覺, *saṁbodhi*, a buddha's wisdom or omniscience.

3. *P'o-p'o*: the word, *p'o*, in Chinese can mean an old woman in general or the maternal grandmother. Since neither "old lady" nor "old woman" has quite the same flavor, I have kept the original.

4. Nation of Women: in the writings of the historical Hsüan-tsang, there is the reference to a Kingdom of Western Women (hsi-nü kuo 西女國), located on an island to the southwest of the land Fu-lin (拂懍). Since there are no males at all in this land, the King of Fu-lin sends men over annually to be the women's mates. See the Ta-T'ang hsi-yü chi 大唐西域記, chüan 11; cf. also the Fa-shih Chuan, chüan 4. For other Chinese sources of the Kingdom of Women, see the Shan-hai ching 山海經, chüan 7 (Hai-wai hsi ching 海外西經), 3a (SPPY edition); Liang-shu 梁書, chüan 54; Nan-shih 南史, chüan 79. Cf. also Dudbridge, pp. 13–14.

5. Marshal Wên: one of the four grand marshals of Heaven. See, e.g., chap. 51.

6. Aiming down there: i.e., at the genitals.

CHAPTER FIFTY-FOUR

1. Red leaves: in the reign of Hsi-tsung (874–89) of the T'ang period, a palace maid by the name of Han 韓夫人 wrote a poem on a red leaf, which floated in the imperial moat out of the palace. It was picked up by a scholar named Yü Yu 于祐, who also wrote a poem on another leaf and dropped it in the upper reach of the moat. The leaf was then picked up by Han inside the palace and kept. Years later when the emperor released some three thousand palace concubines, Han by chance married Yü, and when they discovered the red leaves in each other's belongings, they gave a banquet to thank the marriage go-between. On that occasion Han wrote another poem which had the lines:

Today we've become two happy mates;

今日却成鸞鳳友

We know now the red leaf's our fine go-between.

方知紅葉是良媒

See Chang Shih 張實, "Liu-hung chi 流紅記," in Liu Fu 劉斧, Ch'ing-so kao-i 青瑣高議 (Shanghai, 1958), pp. 46–49. Some accounts have Han married to another man by the name of Li Yin 李茵. Cf. the "Hung-yeh t'i shih 紅葉題詩," in Lang-yeh tai-tsui pien 瑯琊代醉篇, chüan 21, 14a–15b, ed. and annotated by Nagasawa Kikuya 長澤規矩也, vol. 7 of the Wahokubon Kanseki zuihitsushū 和刻本漢籍隨筆集 (Tokyo, 1973).

2. Scarlet threads: see JW, 2: 426, note 5 of chap. 30.

3. Live-in husband: a man who is asked to live with the wife's family after marriage.

4. The man set apart: a traditional form of self-address by a Chinese ruler, ku-chia 孤家 literally means the lonely one.

5. Estrade Numina: ling-t'ai 靈臺, an astronomical observatory. According to Schafer, p. 13, "Tradition puts an establishment with this title back in the reign of the founder of the Chou dynasty. Another observatory

with this name, as always closely affiliated with the divinity of the Son of Heaven [i.e., emperor], was erected in Han times. Then and later its function was to provide the divine king with an accurate statement of changes in the upper air and what they portended. Its formal charge was 'to calculate the verified evidence of stellar measures, the auspicious responses of the Six Pneumas, the permutations and transformations of the divine illuminates,' all with the purpose of foreseeing the sources of good and evil fortune, and ultimately of promoting the welfare of the country."

6. Chao-chün: another name of Wang Ch'iang, the legendary beauty of the Han period, who was sent off to marry a Hsiung-nu chieftain because she refused to bribe the palace portrait painter.

7. Hsi Shih: another famous beauty of the Spring and Autumn period, who was offered to the King of Wu by the defeated King of Yüeh. When the state of Wu subsequently declined as a result of the king's infatuation with the girl, he was in turn defeated by the King of Yüeh.

8. East Hall: tung-ko 東閣; I follow here the translation in Hucker, p. 29. In Han times, the East Hall was erected by the prime minister Kung-sun Hung 公孫弘 as a hostel for worthy counselors. See the Han Shu 漢書, chüan 58. By the Ming period, however, it had become one of the six Grand Secretariats nominally subordinate to the Hanlin Academy.

9. Heaven reveals the Yellow Road: the Yellow Road (huang-tao 黃道) is the ecliptic. The phrase is a traditional metaphor for a lucky or auspicious day.

CHAPTER FIFTY-FIVE

1. Water pudding: the fiend is punning on the phrase shui-kao 水高, which means high tide or high water level, and shui-kao 水糕, water pudding. The last two characters in Têng = Tou-sha-hsien 鄧＝豆沙餡, red bean paste, are homophonous to sha-hsien 沙陷, sand traps. Hence, the reply of the T'ang monk below.

2. Liu Ts'ui-ts'ui: 柳翠翠—the name of a famous courtesan in Hangchow at the time of the Southern Sung. See the Hsi-hu yu-lan chih 西湖游覽志, chüan 13.

3. Star Lord Orionis: this is mao 昴, one of the twenty-eight constellations or lodges (hsiu). Many scholars give Pleiades as the corresponding constellation, but I follow Schafer (pp. 76–77), who gives the constellation λ, φ¹, φ², Orionis.

CHAPTER FIFTY-SIX

1. Six Robbers: see JW, chap. 14 and note 1.

2. Three Vehicles: san-ch'êng 三乘 or triyāna, the three types of vehicles (classified as big, medium, or small 大, 中, 小) or conveyances which take living beings across the realm of saṁsāra (cycles of birth and death) to

nirvāṇa. The types of vehicle have different identities according to various schools of Buddhism.

3. Rice-cakes: literally, the *chiao-shu* 角黍 or *tsung-tzŭ* 粽子, the pyramid-shaped rice-cake wrapped in bamboo or lotus leaf and associated with the *Tuan-wu* 端午 or Double-Fifth Festival (the fifth day of the fifth lunar month). This is the traditional date for commemorating the suicide of Ch'ü Yüan 屈原 (343?–278 B.C.), the poet, in the Mi-lo River 汨羅江. On this occasion, there are dragon-boat races and the rice-cakes are thrown as sacrificial offerings into the water.

4. Five Grand Deities: five gods of folk beliefs, all having to do with wealth. They are *Chao Hsüan-t'an* 趙玄壇, *Chao-ts'ai* 招財, *Chao-pao* 招宝, *Li-shih* 利市, and *Na-chên* 納珍.

5. Ministers of the Five Phases: literally *san-chieh wu-ssŭ* 三界五司, or the Five Ministers of the Three Realms (i.e., the entire universe). The ministers, also called *Wu-chêng* 五正, are metal (蓐收), wood (句芒), water (玄冥), fire (祝融), and earth (后土). See the *Tso Chuan* 左傳, Duke Chao 昭公, 29th year (Legge, V:729).

6. Ten Quarters: i.e., the world of ten quarters 十方世界, they being: east, south, west, north, southeast, southwest, northeast, northwest, above (上), and below (下).

CHAPTER FIFTY-SEVEN

1. Caught the T'ang monk: for this episode, see *JW*, 2, chaps. 40–42.

2. Three Flowers: see *JW*, 1: 525, note 17.

3. Four Greats: *ssŭ-ta* 四大. In philosophic Taoism, this refers to the way, heaven, earth, and the king (道 天 地 王), according to the *Tao-te Ching*, 25. In a more sociopolitical context, the *ssŭ-ta* can also refer to great merit, great reputation, great virtue, and great power (大功 大名 大德 大權). See the *Tsin Shu* 晉書, *chüan* 89, "Wang Pao Chuan 王豹傳." In Buddhism, however, the *ssŭ-ta* usually refers to the four *tanmātra* or elements of earth, water, fire, and air (wind) 地,水,火,風, which join to form the human body (cf. the *Avataṁsaka sūtra*). Hence the expression, *ssŭ-ta pu-t'iao* 四大不調, which has the idea that when these four elements are improperly balanced, all kinds of sicknesses will arise (cf. the *Chin-kuang-ming tsui-shêng-wang ching* 金光明最勝王經 [the *Suvarṇaprabhāsauttama-rāja sūtra*], *chüan* 5).

4. Pass: *Kuan* 關, though this word has the literal meaning of a frontier gate or a pass (often fortified), it is also frequently used as a metaphor for certain vital narrows or passageways of the human body. Thus in the *Huai-nan Tzu* 淮南子, *chüan* 9 ("chu-shu hsün 主術訓"), the eyes, the ears, and the mouth are called the *san-kuan* (three passes), which are to be guarded with care against vain sights, sounds, and speech.

5. For this episode, see *JW*, 1, chaps. 10–12.

6. The change of voice here is intentional, since this section has been added presumably by the queen of the Nation of Women. See chap. 54 above.

7. The big fishes change: an allusion to the opening words of the *Chuang Tzu* 莊子, *chüan* 1: "In the northern ocean there is a fish, called the leviathan [*kun* 鯤], which is no one knows how many thousand *li* in size. The fish changes into a bird, called the roc. . . ." See de Bary, 1: 63.

CHAPTER FIFTY-EIGHT

1. Composite Prime: I follow Schafer, p. 28, in the translation of *hun-yüan* 混元.

2. For this episode, see *JW*, 2, chaps. 30 and 31.

3. For the names of these ten kings, I follow Waley. See *JW*, 1: 507, note 4 of chap. 3.

4. For this episode, see *JW*, 1, chap. 3.

5. Three Dukes: *san-kung* 三公, the three chief ministers of state. See *JW*, 1: 517, note 14.

6. Holy babe: in alchemical lore, realized immortality is often referred to as the baby (*ying-êrh* 嬰兒) or the holy embryo (*shêng-t'ai* 聖胎).

7. Six-eared macaque: *liu-êrh mi-hou* 六耳獼猴, the meaning of this animal's name is puzzling, though it may have something to do with the story, recorded in Hui-ming 慧明, comp., *Wu-têng hui-yüan* 五燈會元 (*Amalgamation of the Sources of the Five Lamps*, first published in 1253). When the Ch'an patriarch, Ma-tsu (Kiangsi Tao-i 江西道一), was asked by the Master Fa-hui 法會 about the meaning of Bodhidharma coming from the West, he struck that disciple on the ear, saying, "The sixth ear [i.e., the third person] does not share the same aims with us 六耳不同謀. Go away, and come again tomorrow." See *chüan* 3, 28a (1906 edition). From this story may have arisen the common Buddhist saying that "the dharma is not to be transmitted to the third person 法不傳六耳." I owe this suggested explanation to Mr. Stephen Soong of the Chinese University of Hong Kong.

CHAPTER FIFTY-NINE

1. Presumably this refers to the process of physiological alchemy.

2. Sūrya Kingdom: the Chinese here reads *ssū-ha-li* kingdom 斯哈哩國, which seems to be meaningless. Since Sūrya means the sun, I feel that the minor emendation is justified in this context.

3. *Kung-kung*: 公公 in Chinese can mean the grandfather (in most major dialects, but not all, the maternal one) or any aged male addressed in a deferential manner. I have decided to keep the original, as with *p'o-p'o*.

4. Rākṣasī: 羅剎女, literally means female demons. The *HYC* author may be punning with the term intentionally, or he may not quite understand its proper significance.

5. See *JW*, 2, chaps. 40–42.

6. See above, chap. 53.

7. See *JW*, 1, chap. 3.

8. See *JW*, 1, chaps. 19–20.

9. Snack: Pilgrim is punning here on the Chinese term for snack or pastry (*tien-hsin* 點心), which means, literally, a touch of the heart.

CHAPTER SIXTY

1. See *JW*, 1, chaps. 7 and 8 for these incidents.

2. Wang Ch'iang: the name of Wang Chao-chün, the legendary court beauty of Han, who was sent to marry a Hsiung-nu chieftain.

3. Wên-chün: this is Cho Wên-chün 卓文君, a beautiful widow who was moved to elope with her lover, Szu-ma Hsiang-ju 司馬相如, because of his fine music-making on a stringed instrument. See the *Shih Chi* 史記, *chüan* 117.

4. Hsüeh T'ao: 薛濤 (768–833), a famous courtesan of the T'ang period, who was reputed to be a gifted poet and an intimate friend of such men as Yüan Chên, Po Chü-i, and Tu Mu (all late eighth- and early ninth-century poets). For a sample of her poems, see *Sunflower Splendor: Three Thousand Years of Chinese Poetry*, ed. Wu-chi Liu and Irving Yucheng Lo (New York, 1975), pp. 190–91.

5. T'ien-t'ai: a famous mountain of southeastern China (in the modern province of Che-chiang), it is associated with several stories of immortals.

6. P'êng-Ying: i.e., P'êng-lai and Ying-chou, two of the three famous islands of immortals supposedly located in the East China Sea. For the narrative's description of these islands, see *JW*, 2, chap. 26.

7. Lion-king belt: *shih-man tai*. See *JW*, 1: 521, note 8 of chap. 13.

8. Three Lights: i.e., the sun, the moon, and the stars.

9. Eight instruments: literally *pa-yin* 八音, eight kinds of sound produced by silk, bamboo, metal, stone, wood, earth, leather, and the gourd or calabash.

10. Young boys: *ma-lang* 馬郎, generally understood as the unmarried young men of the Miao (苗) tribe. According to their custom, they would serenade young girls in the time of spring by playing reed pipes and singing erotic songs. It is apparent that the previous line of the poem (*lu-chi* 鱸妓, perch-courtesan or perch-cocotte) and this line both contain sexual imageries, since playing the flute (品簫) is the classic Chinese term for fellatio. As this section of the poem deals with aquatic creatures, *ma-lang* may well refer to some kind of fish or marine life, but I have not been able to determine what it is.

11. Eight treasure dainties: see *JW*, 1: 509, note 11 of chap. 5.

12. Purple mansion: another term for Heaven.

13. "Hook . . . broom": an allusion to a poem by Su Tung-p'o (1037–1101), who calls wine "the hook for fishing poems and the broom that sweeps away sorrow (應呼釣詩鉤亦號掃愁箒)."

14. These characters may have no apparent significance other than sound. On the other hand, all of the characters, with the exception of the fourth word (*hsi* 吸, to breathe in), have to do with the action of expelling breath from one's body, such as blowing or snorting. As such, these six words are all associated with the respiratory exercises of the alchemist. See "Fu-ch'i tsa-fa mi-yao k'ou-chüeh 服氣雜法祕要口訣," in *Yün-chi ch'i-ch'ien* 雲笈七籤 , *chüan* 61, 23b–24a (1929 edition, based on the SPTK edition):

天師云內氣者一吐氣有六氣道成乃可為之吐氣
六者吹呼嘻呵噓呬　呬　皆出氣也時寒可吹以
去寒時溫可呼以去熱嘻以去風呵以去煩又以去
下氣噓以散滯呬以解熱凡人者則多呼呬道家行
氣不欲噓呬長息之忌也悉能六氣位為天仙

CHAPTER SIXTY-ONE

1. Determination's staff: *chu-chang*, or staff of the will. See note 1 of chap. 51.

2. The hour of *shên*: about 3:00–5:00 P.M.

3. A bean-curd boat: bean-curds, then and now, are usually kept in containers filled with water so that they may remain fresh and soft.

4. "For Bull . . . changed": there is no episode in the narrative that warrants a literal understanding of this statement. The *HYC* author may be working with the same sort of dialectic expressed in *JW* 1, chap. 17 (p. 363), where the Bodhisattva Kuan-yin says: "Wu-k'ung, the Bodhisattva, and the monster—they exist in a single thought, for originally they are nothing." It is also apparent from this and other poems in the chapter (see below) that Pilgrim, Pa-chieh, and the Bull King are all correlated with the action of the Five Phases in physiological alchemy. Hence the continuous allegory structured in the verse.

5. *Hai*: 亥, one of the Twelve Branches, to which there are corresponding hours of the day, symbolical animals, points of the compass, and the Phases. The symbolical animal of *hai* is a hog or boar, and the corresponding phase is wood, just as the symbolical animal of the Branch *shên* is monkey or ape and the corresponding phase is metal. See also *JW*, 1: 50–51.

6. Completion's attained: *Chi-chi* 既濟, after or upon completion. This is the famous sixty-third hexagram (*Kua*) of the *I Ching*, with the symbol of *K'an* (water) above and *li* (water) below ☲☵ . According to Wilhelm/

Baynes, p. 244, "this hexagram is the evolution of T'ai, Peace [hexagram 11]. The transition from confusion to order is completed, and everything is in its proper place even in particulars. The strong lines are in the strong places, the weak lines in the weak places." Thus the phrase, *shui-huo chi-chi* (water and fire upon completion), usually means the state of perfect equilibrium in alchemical lore.

7. Ullambana Feast: a sort of All Souls Festival in Buddhism, when sacrifices are made for the deliverance of the hungry ghosts. For a description of modern practices of this rite, wee Welch, pp. 179–85.

8. Three passes: see chap. 57, note 4.

CHAPTER SIXTY-TWO

1. Twelve hours: the Chinese day traditionally is divided into twelve two-hour periods, and they are designated by the names of the Twelve Branches (e.g., the hour of *Tzŭ* 子 refers to the hours corresponding to 11:00 P.M.–1:00 A.M.).

2. Night and day: literally *po-k'o* 百刻, one hundred markings. This refers to the markings carved on the ancient clepsydra to indicate a twenty-four-hour period. The most well-known allusions to this instrument and the Official in Charge of Raising the Vessel (Ch'ieh-hu Shih 挈壺氏) are to be found in the *Chou-li* 周禮, *chüan* 28, 30. See Needham, pp. 3, 190–91, 319 ff., for discussions. For later descriptions of *po-k'o*, see the *Chiu-T'ang Shu* 舊唐書, *chüan* 35; *Liao Shih* 遼史, *chüan* 44.

3. One hundred and eight thousand rounds: the figure here should read, actually, one hundred and eighty thousand rounds. The *chou* 周 (round) refers to the period of one day or one hundred markings. In one year, there would be thirty-six thousand rounds (100 × 360), and in five years, one hundred and eighty thousand.

4. Cloudy tower: *yün-lou* or *yün-fang* (雲樓.雲房), names for the abode of religious Taoists.

5. Yüan-ming: 元 = 玄溟 or 元溟, is actually the attending spirit (*shên* 神) of the first month of winter, according to the *Li Chi* 禮記, *chüan* 4, "Yüeh-ling 月令." The use of the term, ruler (*ti* 帝), may be carelessness on the part of the *HYC* author or the constraint of tonal metrics.

6. Wei-yang Palace: a palace built by Hsiao Ho of the Han period, it is located northwest of the modern Sian.

7. Qoco Kingdom: this is the Kao-ch'ang kuo 高昌國, translated as Tibet in previous volumes of the *JW*. According to Fêng Ch'êng-chün 馮承鈞, *Hsi-yü ti-ming* 西域地名 (Peking, 1955), p. 60, it should be Qoco or Khoco. I owe this correction to Professor Y. W. Ma.

8. *Shên*, the period of 3:00–5:00 P.M.

9. See *JW*, 1: 283.

10. Finger-guessing games: a game usually associated with drinking, in which two players simultaneously call out numbers and stick out certain fingers in one of their two hands. If the number called by one party matches the total number of fingers put forth by both players, that party wins.

11. Śarīra Buddhist treasure: the relic or ashes of a Buddha or a saint after the person is cremated, it is usually depicted in Chinese fiction as an egg or pearl-like object; cf. *JW*, 2, chap. 31.

12. Chien-chang Palace: another palace, west of the modern Sian, built in the Han period.

CHAPTER SIXTY-THREE

1. Crescent-tooth spade: 月牙鏟, a spade or shovel-like weapon, with a crescent-shaped blade at the upper end. See Chou, plate 80, fig. 3.

2. First stroke of yang: i.e., the new moon. For the theory of the moon's appearance as correlated with *I Ching* lore, see *JW*, 2: 176–77.

3. Erh-lang and the sages of Plum Mountain: see *JW*, 1, chap. 6.

4. Stiff Bristles Hog: Chu Kang-lieh 豬剛鬣, this is another name of Pa-chieh, by his own account in *JW*, 1, chap. 19 (p. 382).

5. The nine-headed bird, according to tradition, is usually identified with the *ts'ang-kêng* 鶬鶊 or 蒼鶊, possibly the mango-bird or oriole. The source for this particular episode, which attributes its blood-dripping to the fact that a dog has bitten off one of its heads, may be traced perhaps to the " 鶬鶊目疸明 ," in *TPKC*, chüan 462, 5, 3799.

CHAPTER SIXTY-FOUR

1. Squire Eight-and-Ten: as we shall learn at the end of the chapter, Tripitaka has encountered a number of different tree spirits. The old man now speaking is the spirit of the pine tree, and his name is made of the ideographic elements contained in the Chinese word for pine, *sung* 松: ten (*shih* 十), eight (*pa* 八), and squire (*kung* 公).

2. Seven Worthies: see *JW*, 2: 437–38, note 10.

3. Six Hermits: *lui-i* 六逸. These are the five drinking friends of the T'ang poet Li Po 李白, who called themselves the Six Hermits of the Bamboo Brook 竹溪六逸. See the *T'ang Shu* 唐書, chüan 190.

4. Four White-Haired Ones: *ssǔ-hao* 四皓, four famous recluses at the time of Han Kao-tsu (r. 206–194 B.C.), all said to have flowing white hair and beards. See the *Han Shu* 漢書, chüan 72.

5. Middle land: *chung-t'u* 中土, another name for China.

6. Primal Origin: *yüan-shih* 元始, a reference to *Yüan-shih t'ien-tsun* (the Celestial-Honored One of Primal Origin). One member of the Taoist Trinity. Mallet and tongs, 鉗鎚, are metaphors for the religious laws or

prohibitions. Truth, *chên* 真, in the context of this line means literally the realized art of immortality.

7. "Make known . . . mindlessness": an allusion to *Chuang Tzu* 莊子, book 12, "Heaven and Earth."

8. Now, the Tao: the rest of Cloud-Brushing Dean's declaration consists of a series of quotations from a "Shêng-t'ang wên 昇堂文," by Fêng Tsun-shih 馮尊師, in *Ming-ho yü-yin* 鳴鶴餘音, *chüan* 9, 15a-b, in *TT*, 84/744. The original text reads as follows:

達磨羅什未生已有南華擊冠奈何
學者忘本逐末棄主憐賓不叩冲虛
執持梵語本安中國求證西方空費
草鞋尋簡甚麼石獅子剜了心肝野
狐涎灌徹骨髓在欲行禪望成佛果
葛藤謎語取把人瞞此般若子怎生
接引 . . . 無底籃兜汲水無根鐵
樹開花此箇規模如何印綬渾淪邦
畔不許商量靈寶峯前執能善腳

For the identity of Fêng, see the Preface to *Ming-ho yü-yin*, *chüan* 1:

會稽馮尊師本燕趙書生游沐過異人
得仙學所賦歌曲高潔雄暢最傳者蘇
武慢二十篇道遺世之樂後十篇論修
仙之事會稽費無隱獨善歌之聞者有
凌雲之思無復流連光景者矣

Cf. Ch'ên Chiao-yu 陳教友, "Ch'ang-ch'un Tao-chiao yüan-liu 長春道教源流," in *Tao-chiao yen-chiu chih-liao ti-êrh-chi* 道教研究資料第二輯, ed. Yen I-p'ing 嚴一萍 (Taipei, 1974), p. 304. For the *HYC* quotation of one of these famous *tz'ŭ* poems (the fifth) written to the tune of *Su-wu-man*, see the prefatory poem in chap. 8.

9. Six Periods: the epoch of the Six Dynasties 六朝 of Wu, Eastern Tsin, Sung, Ch'i, Liang, and Ch'ên during the third to the sixth century A.D., when the literary style was generally dominated by elaborate and florid constructions.

10. "The *Book of Odes* . . . compiler": Confucius was traditionally regarded as the chief compiler and editor of this classic anthology.

11. "Pushing the Needle": or the style of the thimble 頂針. This is the Chinese term for *anadiplosis*, repetition of the last word of one line to begin the next.

12. King's estrade: this is the Estrade Numina, *ling-t'ai* 靈臺, the royal astronomical observatory.

13. Reply in kind: *ho* 和; in the practice of writing a regulated verse (*lü-shih*) or a *tz'ü* poem, this means the composition of another poem using the same end rhymes as the first.

14. "Thrice-blooming . . . scent": this parallel couplet is actually a near verbatim quotation of two lines by the Chin poet Yüan Hao-wên 元好問 (1190–1257). The original, which I follow in the translation, reads: 金芝三秀詩壇端實樹千花佛界香 . See " 贈答普安師 ," in *I-shan hsien-shêng wên-chi* 遺山先生文集, *chüan* 10, 15b–16a (SPTK edition).

15. Long-lived thing: *ling-ch'un* 靈椿, an allusion to the trees mentioned in *Chuang Tzu* 莊子, book 1, where it is said that "in the south of Ch'u, there is the tree named Ming-ling, whose spring is 500 years and whose autumn is also 500 years. There was in high antiquity the tree named Great Ch'un, whose spring was 8,000 years and whose autumn was also 8,000 years." Cf. *Lieh Tzu* 列子, book 5.

16. Hall of Four Great Things: *Ssü-chüeh t'ang* 四絕堂. The term *ssü-chüeh* in the literary tradition often refers to four exceptional kinds of talent, such as poetry, calligraphy, painting, and seal-making or seal-script writing. However, it may also refer to an hour before the four dates of Spring Begins, Summer Begins, Autumn Begins, and Winter Begins (立春, 立夏, 立秋, 立冬). The context of the poem would make the second be the more appropriate reference.

17. Grand Pure Palace: *t'ai-ch'ing kung* 太清宮, one of the three Taoist Heavens, the other two being the Superior Pure Palace and the Jade Pure Palace.

18. Ch'i-Yü 淇澳, the names of two rivers, according to most traditional Chinese commentators, mentioned in the "Wei-fêng" section of the *Book of Odes* (book 5). Most modern scholars, however, take *yü* to mean a little bay or recess. Whatever the meaning, the main point here is that this region is noted for its fresh, luxuriant bamboo.

19. Wei: the name of a river in the modern province of Shensi. Tradition has it that its course is flanked by rows of lush bamboos on both banks.

20. "Mottled sheaths . . . contained": an allusion to the early Chinese practice of writing on bamboo strips. See T. H. Tsien, *Written on Bamboo and Silk* (Chicago, 1962).

21. Tzu-yu: 王子猷, who is one of the sons of Wang Hsi-chih of the Tsin period. Tzu-yu was so fond of bamboos that he once said that he could not live one day without their company. See the *Tsin Shu* 晉書, *chüan* 80.

22. Scholars' praise: the bamboo's particular association with scholars is attributable to the fact that brushes for both calligraphy and painting have bamboo stems.

23. T'ien-t'ai girl: the T'ien-t'ai Mountain is associated with many stories of divine beings or immortals; hence, a fairy girl.

24. Ta-chi: favorite concubine of the infamous tyrant, King Chou of the Shang Dynasty.

25. I have not been able to discover the source of this allusion to Han Wu-ti's association with *hsing* 杏 or apricot.

26. Confucius was said to have stood on a platform made of apricot wood to lecture his pupils. See *Chuang Tzu*, book 31.

27. Tung Hsien: this is Tung Fêng 董奉, a legendary physician of the Three Kingdoms period. Instead of asking for the usual fees, Tung requested that his patients pay him with apricot trees. Those with grave illnesses were to plant five trees, while those with minor ailments would plant only one. After a few years, Tung had a large apricot forest.

28. Sun Ch'u: 孫楚 was a Tsin official with considerable literary reputation. See *Tsin Shu*, *chüan* 56, for his biography. To my knowledge, however, there is no historical or documentary justification for his association with the apricot at the time of the Feast of Cold Food (*Han-shih* 寒食) which, according to Derk Bodde (p. 296), "came in spring immediately before the 'node' in the solar calendar known as Ch'ing Ming or 'Clear Brightness' (about April 6). During the three days, fires were extinguished and only cold food was eaten." The practice may have something to do with the story of Chieh T'ui 介推 or 介子推, who was said to have accompanied Duke Wên of Tsin 晉文公 for 19 years. When the Duke returned to his state to rule. Chieh insisted on remaining as a recluse on a mountain. When the Duke set fire to the mountain to force his subject to come out to serve, Chieh was burned to death as he hugged a tree and refused to let go. As I have noted, however, there is no basis for relating these stories to the theme of apricot. The only plausible explanation for this may be that the Feast of Cold Food and Sun Ch'u's elegiac essay for Chieh are mentioned side by side in the same column in the *T'ai-p'ing yü-lan* 太平御覽, *chüan* 30, 6a (facsimile of the Sung edition). In the entry on Feast of Cold Food, there is a reference to grinding almonds to make a broth or cream. The text thus reads: 今日適為大麥粥研杏仁為酪餳沐沃之. Immediately following, the text reads, 又孫楚祭子推文 . . . . The *HYC* author may have mistakenly lumped these two unrelated events together in his poem.

CHAPTER SIXTY-FIVE

1. Ghee: According to T'ien-t'ai Buddhism, the perfect truth of Buddha is likened to ghee or clarified butter, 醍醐. See, e.g., the *Nirvāṇa* and the *Lotus Sūtras*.

2. Three Passes: *san-kuan*. See note 4 of chapter 57 above.

3. "Dipper's . . . *yin*": *tou-ping hui-yin* 斗柄回寅, a traditional saying, based on *I Ching* lore, that when the Dipper points to the east (the position of *yin*), it is spring again.

4. Wang Wei's painting: Wang is the T'ang poet (701-61) famous for both his "pastoral" lyrics and his landscape paintings. For Wang's specific observations on painting mountains, see his "Shan-shui lun 山水論" in Chung-kuo hua-lun lei-pien 中國畫論類篇, ed. Yü Chien-hua 俞劍華 (Hong Kong repr., 1973), pp. 596-97.

5. Chi-tzu: 季子, the style of Su Ch'in 蘇秦, master strategist and rhetor in the period of the Warring States.

6. Side Door: a metaphor for heterodoxy or heresy.

7. "Ch'ien . . . Firmness": Ch'ien is the first Hexagram in the I Ching, and yüan 元, hêng 亨, li 利, and chên 貞 represent the first four words of the T'uan-tz-ŭ 彖辭 or "Judgments" section of the text traditionally ascribed to King Wên of the Chou dynasty. In my translation of these four words, I follow Wei Tat, An Exposition of the I-Ching or Book of Changes, rev. ed. (Hong Kong, 1977), p. 123.

8. Gullet the Gold Dragon: 亢金龍, one of the Twenty-Eight Constellations or Lunar Lodges (hsiu 宿). In translating this and other names of the starry chronograms (see below), I follow Schafer, pp. 76-77.

9. Wolf-teeth club: a club with spikes on one end and a long handle on the other. For an illustration of this Sung weapon, see Chou, plate 65.

10. Chên-wu: for the story of this god and his epiphany, first as a white turtle and a huge serpent, then as a gigantic foot, and finally as a very tall being with flowing hair and garbed in black, see the Lang-yeh tai-tsui pien, chüan 29, 9b-10a.

11. Wu-tang Mountain: a famous sacred mountain of Taoism, located in the modern province of Hopei. It was venerated by the Ming emperor Ch'êng-tsu (r. 1402-24) as Mount T'ai because Chên-wu, the patriarch, was said to have practiced austerities here.

CHAPTER SIXTY-SIX

1. Nine Streams: chiu-chiang 九江. There are several places in China by this name, which is also the designation for different rivers and their tributaries. In this context, however, it is likely that the term refers to nine rivers in the South: i.e., 浙江, 揚子江, 楚江, 湘江, 荊江, 漢江, 南江, 吳江, 松江.

2. Ching and Yang: probably a reference to Ching-chou 荊州 and Yang-chou 揚州, prefectures in Southeast China.

3. Chu and Lu: probably a reference to Chu Hsi (1130-1200) and Lu Chiu-yüan (1139-1192), two famous Neo-Confucian thinkers of the Sung period.

4. King Shun and King Yü: legendary sage kings of antiquity, King Shun was noted for his filial piety and King Yü was the Conqueror of the Flood.

5. Snake and turtle: the legend of Chên-wu had it that he defeated two spirits of turtle and serpent, who then became his disciples. Paintings of Chên-wu usually depict the god standing on top of the snake and the turtle.

6. T'ai . . . Hua: these are four of the nine sacred mountains in China.

7. Three lights: see chap. 60, n. 8.

8. Three Vehicles: 三乘 or Triyāna, the three vehicles which ferry living beings across saṃsāra into nirvāṇa. In the original, the first two characters of this line, to-shih 多時, are impossible—both in terms of meaning and tonal metrics. I have emended them to to-shih 多是, all because of or on account of.

CHAPTER SIXTY-SEVEN

1. The ancients: this is a quotation of the *Yu-yang tsa-tsu* 酉陽雜俎, *chüan* 18, 3b (SPTK edition).

2. Respond/respondant: *hsiang-ying* 相應, the author is making fun of the Buddhist doctrine of mutual union, the correspondence of mind with mental data dependent on five kinds of correspondences common to both; viz. the senses, reason, process, object, and time. This is called *hsiang-ying-fa* 相應法, which provides the pun on *fa*, the hair 髮 of the second line.

3. Triple peaks: Mount Hua 華山 of Shensi Province is famous for its three peaks named Lotus Flowers, Bright Star, and Jade Girl (蓮花, 明星, 玉女). Cf. the lines, "岧嶤太華俯咸京 ,天外三峯削不成," in " 行經 華陰," by Ts'ui Hao 崔顥, in *CTS, chüan* 130, 2:1329.

4. The ancients said: this is a quotation from the *Li Chi* 禮記, *chüan* 12, 4a (SPPY edition).

5. His claws: normally a python has no claws. But the *mang* 蟒 here is sometimes called a *mang-lung* 蟒龍, a python-dragon, in which case the creature, whatever it is, may have claws.

6. Great Yü: The legendary sage king who conquered the Flood in China.

CHAPTER SIXTY-EIGHT

1. One . . . places: this metaphor for an able physician is based on the *Tso-chuan* 左傳, "Duke Ting 定公," 13th year, where Kao Chiang 高疆 of Ch'i 齊 said, "I know he is an able physician [who can heal] an arm broken in three places."

2. College of Interpreters: *Hui-t'ung kuan* 會同館. According to Hucker, p. 35, "directly subordinate to The Ministry [of war] was a College of Interpreters . . . , which was actually a state hostelry for envoys from tributary nations."

3. Yü and T'ang: references to the Great Yü 大禹 (traditional date of accession 2205 B.C.), the founder of the Hsia Dynasty, and Ch'êng T'ang 成湯 (traditional date of accession 1766 B.C.), the founder of the Shang Dynasty.

4. Ch'êng and Chou: references to King Ch'êng 成王 (r. 1115–1079 B.C.) and his uncle, Duke of Chou of the Chou Dynasty.

5. P'ei of Lu: 魯沛: the District of P'ei 沛縣 of the modern Kiangsu Province was part of the state of Lu in antiquity. It was also the birthplace of Liu Pang 劉邦, the man who successfully challenged the rule of Ch'in and became the founder of the Han Dynasty.

6. Ssŭ-ma: 司馬, the surname of the family that founded the Tsin Dynasty in A.D. 265.

7. Conduits: ching-luo 經絡, usually translated as "meridians," but I follow Porkert (passim) in rendering it as conduits or "sinarteries."

8. Submerged or floating: ch'ên 沉 or fu 浮. In the literature of traditional Chinese medicine, various terms are used to describe the character or feeling of the pulse, which in turn will give indication of the state of the body's health. Thus ch'ên-mo, translated by Porkert (pp. 172–73) as pulsus mersus, is "a firm palpation" felt deep within, while fu-mo, pulsus superficialis, is "a delicate palpation" felt "close to the surface."

9. In and out: piao 表 and li 裏; according to Porkert (p. 25), "these common technical terms designate the structive and the active halves of a pair of energetic orbs [i.e., visceral systems of function]. . . . These aspects have a close affinity to the (primary) correspondences nei (inner side, inward things) and wai (outside, outward things)."

10. These several titles are all well-known texts of traditional Chinese medicine. The Candid Questions is the Huang-ti nei-ching su-wên 黃帝內經素問 (Candid Questions in the Inner Classic of the Yellow Sovereign), a text of the Han period. For a translation of the first 34 chapters, see Veith. The Classic of Medical Problems is the Nan Ching 難經, whose putative author is Pien Ch'iao 扁鵲 (fl. 255 B.C.). The term for pharmacopoeias is pên-ts'ao 本草, which in modern usage usually refers to the Pên-ts'ao kang-mu 本草綱目, the Great Pharmacopoeia compiled by the Ming author Li Shih-chên 李時珍 (d. 1593) and published in 1596. Since the earliest known hundred-chapter version of the HYC that we have now dates from 1592, I have refrained from identifying the term with Li's text. The Formulas of the Pulse is the Mo Chüeh 脈訣, probably a Sung document, and to be distinguished from the Mo Ching 脈經 (Classic of the Pulse), compiled by Wang Shu-ho 王叔和 in the fourth century.

CHAPTER SIXTY-NINE

1. Inch: In traditional Chinese medicine, the human pulse is divided into three sections on the wrist: the one closest to the hand was called ts'un 寸 or inch; the one further up the arm was called ch'ih 尺 or foot; and the one between these two pulses was called kuan 關 or pass. These three pulses are translated by Porkert, pp. 128–57, as pulsus pollicaris, pulsus clusalis, and pulsas pedalis, respectively. For the translation of the following

passage on Sun Wu-k'ung taking the pulse of the king, I am indebted to the kind assistance of Professor Nathan Sivin.

2. Made his own breathing regular: According to Veith, p. 45, "the physician was instructed to take as norm of the pulse beats one expiration and one inspiration of his own, during which time the normal pulse should pulsate four times." Cf. The *San-yin chi-i ping-chêng fang-lun* 三因極一病證方論 (Ssǔ-k'u ch'üan-shu 四庫全書 edition), *chüan* 1, 2a: "Those who want to examine the pulse must first make regular their own breathings so that they can take, by means of pressure, the pulse of the patient to determine the energetic levels 凡欲診脈先調自氣壓取病人脈息.."

3. Four Heteropathic *Ch'is*: *ssu-ch'i* 四氣. These are wind (*fêng* 風), moisture (*shih* 濕), cold (*han* 寒), and heat (*shu* 暑), the four possibly harmful effects of the four seasons. See the *San-yin, chüan* 2, 13 a–b.

4. Five Stases: *wu-yü* 五鬱; these are stases or blockages of normal (i.e., orthopathic) *ch'i* circulation as correlated with the Five Phases and located in the Five Yin (陰) visceral systems of function (i.e., "orbs"). See the *Su-wên, chüan* 21, esp. 26b–36a (SPTK edition).

5. Seven External Images and Eight Internal Images of the Pulse: Chao Shu-t'ang 趙書堂, in *Chung-i chên-tuan-hsüeh ch'ien-shih* 中醫診斷學淺釋 (Taichung, Taiwan, 1975), pp. 8–9, cites the *Nan Ching* 難經 (Classic of Medical Problems) to the effect that *ch'i-piao* 七表 and *pa-li* 八裏 are standard pulse images (叔和書載, 七表八裏九道, 為二十四道脈之標本). Though I have not been able to locate this passage in the *Nan Ching*, Chao's remark is confirmed by the *San-yin, chüan* 1, 25a–27b. According to these sources, the seven external images are *fu* 浮, *k'ou* 芤, *hua* 滑, *shih* 實, *hsien* 弦, *chin* 緊, and *hung* 洪. These terms are translated by Porkert, p. 30, as *pulsus superficialis, cepacaulicus, lubricus, repletus, chordalis, intentus,* and *redundans,* respectively. Each of these images is applicable to each section of the pulse (i.e., inch, pass, foot). The eight internal images are *ch'ên* 沉, *wei* 微, *ch'ih* 遲, *huan* 緩, *ju* 濡, *fu* 伏, *jo* 弱, and *sê* 濇, translated by Porkert as *pulsus mersus, evanescens, tardus, languidus, lenis, subreptus,* and *invalidus,* respectively. Porkert has no term for *sê,* the rough or uneven pulse.

6. The Nine Pulse Indications: *chiu-hou* 九候. There seem to be two different, albeit not unrelated, explanations for the meaning of this term. In the *Su-wên, chüan* 6, 9b–11a, the *chiu-hou* refers to different sections of the entire human body, beginning from the arteries of the forehead and moving all the way down to the feet. Specifically, the term points to the readings of the pulse at these various points of the body. See Veith, pp. 187–89. This is also the understanding of a modern text on traditional Chinese medicine. See *Mo-chên hsüan-yao* 脈診選要 (Shanghai, 1965), pp. 2–3. On the other hand, a text like the *Nan Ching, chüan* 2, 35b (SPTK edition), has the following statement: "As for the Three Sections and the

Nine Indications, what do they regulate? The Three Sections are the inch, pass, and foot, while the Nine Indications are the phenomena of floating, middle, and sunken [in each of the pulse sections]. 脉有三部九候各何所主 之然三部者寸關尺也九候者浮中沉也." Here the primary significance of the terms seems to point to the characteristic of the *ch'i* circulation as indicated by the pulse. See also the *Mo-chüeh* 脉訣 in Li Yen-shih 李延昰, *Mo-chüeh hui-pien* 脉訣彙辨 (Shanghai, 1963), pp. 34-35.

7. Light to medium to heavy: *fu-chung-ch'ên* 浮中沉 . From the second explanation of *chiu-hou* may have arisen the concept and the practice of reading with three different finger pressures the three sections of the radial pulse. These three types of readings that vary with pressure are called floating, middle, and sunken readings.

8. Cessation of menses: as it is impossible for a king to have menses, this is an obvious slip on the part of the *HYC* author in his incorporation of medical materials for this episode of the narrative.

9. Wên-hua Pavilion: one of the four within the imperial palace, with designated buildings and duties, staffed by Grand Secretaries subordinate to the Hanlin Academy. See Hucker, p. 29.

10. *Ta-huang*: 大黃, *Rheum palmatum*. For a description with illustration, see the *CYC*, 1: 43-49.

11. *Pa-tou*: 巴豆, *Semen crotonis*. For a description with illustration, see *CYC*, 2: 59-60.

12. Medical supplement: *yao-yin-tzu* 藥引子, this is a drug or drink added to compound prescriptions and used as a vehicle or conductor to convey the medicine to that part of the body where it is to take effect.

13. Horse-Saddle-Bell: *ma-tou-ling* 馬兜鈴 or *Aristolochia debilis*.

14. Double Fifth: for a brief description of this festival, which also bears the name of Correct Middle or Correct Yang (端午, 端陽), see Bodde, pp. 312-16. The most thorough discussion of the customs and activities associated with the festival will be found in Wên I-to 聞一多, "Tuan-wu k'ao 端午考," in *Wên I-to ch'üan-chi* 聞一多全集, 4 vols, (Shanghai, 1948), 1A: 221-38.

15. Realgar: on this substance used for alchemy or as an aphrodisiac, see Needham, 5/2: 284-86.

16. Mythic Beast: this is the *hsieh-chih* 獬豸, a fabulous animal said to possess a single horn like a unicorn.

17. Hour of Monkey and that of the Boar: between 3 and 11 P.M.

CHAPTER SEVENTY

1. Trained: literally, practiced self-cultivation.

2. Hare and crow: emblematic of the sun and the moon, which in turn are symbolic of the heart and the kidney.

3. The stars' transportive power: for the Taoist belief and practice in touring space with the help of the stars, see Schafer, pp. 234-69.

4. Four Images: ssŭ-hsiang 四象. According to the Ta Chuan 大傳 or the Great Commentary of the I Ching (also known as the Hsi-tz'u chuan 繫辭傳), "there is in the Changes the Great Primal Beginning. This generates the two primary forces. The two primary forces generate the four images. The four images generate the eight trigrams 易有大極， 是生兩儀， 兩儀生四象 ， 四象生八卦" (translation by Wilhelm/Baynes, p. 318). Four images here correspond to the four seasons of the year. In alchemical literature, however, the four seasons are further related to the configurative energies (i.e., ch'i) circulating in the body.

5. Two breaths: êrh-ch'i 二氣. This term usually refers to yin and yang, the two primary forces. But in alchemical lore, it may also refer to the primal breath (yüan-ch'i 元氣 or embryonic breath, hsien-t'ien ch'i 先天氣) and ordinary breath (hou-t'ien ch'i 後天氣 or hu-hsi ch'i 呼吸氣). Yellow Way (huang-tao 黃道), according to Tai, p. 142, is a spot below the heart and above the kidneys. The line here seems to refer to a form of respiratory exercise, whose great aim, as Needham says in 2:144, is "to try to return to the manner of respiration in the womb."

6. Three Houses: san-chia 三家, the term in spagyrical literature for spermal essence (ching 精), breath or configurative energy (ch'i 氣), and spirit (shên 神). For the importance of these three elements in physiological alchemy, see the oral formula given to Sun Wu-k'ung by his teacher in JW, 1: 88.

7. Mount T'ai-hang: 太行山, a mountain range straddling the modern provinces of Honan and Hopei. See Herrmann, C-2.

8. Cloud-Transcending Stream: Ling-yün tu 凌雲渡, a body of water said to be at the foot of the Spirit Mountain, the abode of Buddha. See JW, chap. 98.

9. Wayside stands: in ancient times, there were small pavilions built every ten miles (li) along main roads for travelers to rest in.

Chapter Seventy-one

1. Broken-head incense: tuan-t'ou hsiang 斷頭香, a metaphor (common in dramatic literature) for separation. See the Hsi-hsiang chi 西廂記, 張君瑞鬧道場.

2. "To ruin . . . wine": a quotation from the T'ang poet Han Yü 韓愈 (768-824). See "Ch'ien-hsing 遣興," in Han Ch'ang-li Ch'üan-chi 韓昌黎 全集, chüan 9, 17a (SPPY edition): 斷送一生惟有酒尋思百計不如閒.

3. External Grandpa: Wai-kung 外公, the maternal grandfather. The author is punning on the word wai, external or outward. See the passage below.

4. Brigades: *wei* 衛, translated by Hucker, p. 59, as "Guards." According to the *Ming Shih* 明史, each unit after 1374 had 5,600 soldiers, divided equally among five battalions.

5. *Thousand-Character Composition: ch'ien-tzu-wên* 千字文, a four-syllabic rhymed composition of 250 sentences, attributed to Chou Hsing-ssŭ 周興嗣 of the Liang Dynasty.

6. *Wai-shou fu-hsün*: 外受傅訓. As it is clear from the sentence itself, this has nothing to do with surnames. The queen is quoting a passage dealing with ideal deportment expected of a woman: 上下和睦,夫唱婦隨,外受傅訓,入奉母儀. The fiend, of course, is seen to be ignorant.

7. Spreading-flower ax: see *JW*, 1: 125 and note 11 on p. 508.

8. Great King Peacock: 孔雀大明王, said to be a previous incarnation of Śākyamuni.

9. Chang Tzu-yang: Tzu-yang 紫陽 is the *hao* of Chang Po-tuan 張伯端, a famous Taoist of the eleventh century and putative author of the *Wu-chên p'ien* 悟真篇, an important alchemical text of the Northern Sung.

CHAPTER SEVENTY-TWO

1. "When there's work . . . do it": a quotation from *Analects*, 2. 8.

2. A ball filled with air: though it cannot be dated with absolute certainty, it seems likely that the practice of kicking balls filled with air was already known in the latter part of the seventh century (cf. Hsü Chien 徐堅 , *Ch'u-hsüeh chi* 初學記). For the translation of the following poem, which makes use of some technical terms in traditional Chinese "soccer" exceedingly difficult to understand, I have consulted the *Tung-ching mêng-hua lu chu* 東京夢華錄注, annotated by Têng Chih-ch'êng 鄧之誠 (Shanghai, 1959), pp. 141–44; pertinent sections on "*ts'u-chü* 蹴踘 " in the *Ku-chin t'u shu chi-ch'êng* 古今圖書集成, *chüan* 802, vol. 59, 1062–71; and articles in *Chung-kuo t'i-yü-shih ts'an-k'ao tzu-liao* 中國体育史參考資料, 5 vols. (Peking, 1957–58).

3. "A pearl ascends Buddha's head": *fo-ting-chu* 佛頂珠, one of the many terms descriptive of the game's movements. See *Ku-chin t'u-shu*, 1071.

4. "They kick and stamp": I have translated this line, 扳凳能暗泛 , quite literally, but I am not at all certain that I have correctly deciphered its meaning.

5. Kick toward the gate: unlike the earlier practice in T'ang China, when the game resembles much more modern Western soccer in that two goals are used at opposite ends of a field, the practice in the time of the Yüan-Ming periods is to have a single "goal" in the middle of the field, separating the two opposing teams. The goal consists of a tall net on top of which is a hole; the team scores when the ball is kicked through the hole. See Fan Shêng

范生 , "Wo-kuo ku-tai tsu-ch'iu kai-shu   我国古代足球概述 " in *Chung-kuo t'i-yü-shih*, 1: 54–58, for discussion and illustration.

6. Poem: With only minor variations and a different last line, this poem is also attributed to the early Ch'ing novelist, Li Yü 李漁. Li's poem reads:

蹴鞠當場二月天
香風吹下兩嬋娟
汗沾粉面花含露
塵拂蛾眉柳帶烟
翠袖低垂籠玉筍
紅裙曳起露金蓮
幾回踢罷嬌無語
恨殺長安美少年

and it supposedly appears on p. 21a of the " 美人千态詩 ." See Chêng Shu-jung 郑树荣 , "Wo-kuo ku-tai ti nü-tzu tsu-ch'iu yün-tung 我国古代的女子足球运动 ," in *Chung-kuo t'i-yü shih*, 4: 40.

7. Hour of the Serpent: i.e., 9:00–11:00 A.M.

8. Ten suns: for the myth of Hou I, the Great Archer, shooting down the ten suns with his arrows, see the *Huai-nan Tzŭ* 淮南子 , *chüan* 8; the "T'ien Wen" section in David Hawkes, *Ch'u Tz'ŭ: The Songs of the South* (Oxford, 1959), p. 49.

CHAPTER SEVENTY-THREE

1. T'ien-t'ai cave: an allusion to the story of Liu Ch'ên 劉晨 and Juan Chao 阮肇 , who went into Mount T'ien-t'ai and nearly died of starvation. They were met later by beautiful immortal girls. For the story, see *TPYL*, *chüan* 41. 2b–3a.

2. Yellow sprout, white snow: *huang-ya* 黄芽 and *pai-hsüeh* 白雪 are stock metaphors for the materials of the alchemist. Most commentators of a classic text like the *Ts'an-t'ung Ch'i* 參同契 , according to Needham, 5/3: 67, agree "that the 'yellow sprout' (*huang-ya*) refers to metallic lead smelted from its ore, but Wu and Davis [Wu Lu-Chhiang & T. L. Davis, trans. "An Ancient Chinese Treatise on Alchemy entitled *Tshan Thung Chhi*, written by Wei Po-Yang about +142 . . ." *ISIS*, vol. 18 (1932)], on the basis of the words *Yin huo pai huang ya chhien* 陰火白黄芽鉛 , take it to be litharge." White snow is usually taken to be mercuric powder.

3. Feathered one: for early Chinese texts referring to a country of deathless, feathered people (*yü-shih* 羽士 or *yü-k'o* 羽客), see the *Shan-hai Ching* 山海經 , *chüan* 15, 2a (SPPY edition); *Huai-nan Tzu* 淮南子 , *chüan* 4; and *Ch'u-tz'ŭ pu-chu* 楚辭補注 , *chüan* 5, 5a.

4. Pralambā: Actually the name of a demon or asura killed by Kṛṣṇa, according to the *Mahābhārata*. For a brief account of the story, see John Dowson, *A Classical Dictionary of Hindu Mythology and Religion, Geography, History, and Literature*, 11th ed. (London, 1968), p. 240; Sukumari Bhattacharji, *The Indian Theogony: A Comparative Study of Indian Mythology from the "Vedas" to the "Purāṇas"* (Cambridge, England, 1970), p. 302.

5. Old Dame of Li Mountain: Li Shan Lao-mu 黎山老姆. For previous appearance of this figure in the narrative, see *JW*, 1: 459, and note 6 of chap. 23 on p. 529.

6. Three Vehicles: for the meaning of *san-ch'êng* 三乘 (*triyāna*), see *JW*, 1: 506, note 2; 3: chap. 56, note 2.

7. Four Great Truths: *ssǔ-ti* 四諦. For the meaning, see *JW*, 2: 420, note 11.

CHAPTER SEVENTY-FOUR

1. Creatures of middle land: i.e., the people of China, for which middle land (*chung-t'u* 中土) is another name.

2. The songs of Ch'u: 楚歌. When the forces of Hsiang Yü 項羽 were surrounded by the armies of Liu Pang during the final stage of their struggle, the latter sang the songs of Ch'u, the native region of Hsiang Yü's men. The songs moved them so deeply that many gave up fighting and left. See the *Shih Chi* 史記, *chüan* 7.

CHAPTER SEVENTY-FIVE

1. Leviathan: this is the *kun* 鯤, which according to the *Chuang Tzu* 莊子, book 1, is capable of changing into the roc.

2. The wheel: i.e., the wheel of transmigration.

3. Serpent Coil Mountain: see *JW*, 1, chap. 15.

4. Nine times refined: *chiu-chuan* 九轉, literally, nine cycles of refinement.

5. Chop suey: the term in Chinese is *tsa-sui* 雜碎, meaning, literally, miscellaneous things chopped up. In Cantonese cuisine, the dish is often prepared with slices of liver and gizzard (chicken or duck) stir-fried, quite different from the fare served in modern restaurants in America. Popular tradition also ascribes the invention of the dish to Li Hung-chang 李鴻章 (1823–1901), a prime minister in the late Ch'ing period, but, as this text has made clear, the dish is much older.